Politics & Patriotism:
The Fisk Conspiracy

Justin Oldham

POLITICS & PATRIOTISM: THE FISK CONSPIRACY
PUBLISHED BY TURNKEY PRESS
2100 Kramer Lane, Suite 300
Austin, Texas 78758

For more information about our books, please write to us, call
512.478.2028, or visit our website at www.bookpros.com.

Library of Congress Control Number: 2005937322

ISBN-10: 1-933538-32-5
ISBN-13: 978-1-933538-32-7

For my mother, who knew I would,
Nikki, because I said I would,
and my wife, who saw me through the whole thing.

Foreword

I am flattered to be portrayed in these pages. That doesn't change the fact that this is still just a story. Mr. Oldham has clearly done his homework. It is unfortunate that his research and background materials were destroyed in an unexplained fire. I would have liked to see for myself how he constructed this fast-paced plot. His very fertile imagination has conjured up the sort of tale that could only spring from today's headlines.

We live in a world where civic-minded politicians are called upon to wield increasingly larger amounts of power in service to the people who elected them. The rise of militant terror groups has made much of this growth in government necessary. As the threat to our nation continues to escalate, so too will the need of our public protectors to take ever greater degrees of action. It was only a matter of time before somebody put a new spin on this trend.

As entertaining as this conspiracy is, I did have a hard time reading about the deaths of people that I had known. To see their lives reinterpreted and spun into the fabric of this story took some getting used to. I forgive the author for his inaccurate depiction of my home life. Readers can look forward to many healthy debates about the motives of this fictional conspiracy, and the people who allegedly made it possible.

Larry Hodgekiss
White House Chief of Staff
2012-2016

"For our struggle is not against flesh and blood, but against the rulers,
against the authorities, against the powers of this dark world..."
-- Eph. 6:12, *Holy Bible,* New International Version

The funeral was over. The mourners had gone. Low-hanging clouds promised rain. Standing next to his wife's grave, Jason Cutter held his daughter's hand in silence while she cried. Nearby, a dark blue pavilion flapped in the breeze. Observant bodyguards were stationed at each corner of the tent. His "unofficial" guests waited for him patiently.

Approaching from the road, Harry Oswald returned from seeing off the last of the "official" mourners. Dressed in somber grey, he peeled off the clerical collar with some relief.

Jason stepped away from his daughter and went to speak with his friend. "Thanks again, Harry. Great job. You'd make a good priest."

"Sure. I'm just sorry I'm not a real one. Might be nice to get a little absolution for some of the things we've done over the years. You know?"

He gripped his friend's hand. "I'm going to send a check to the archdiocese. Sophie would be rolling if she knew this funeral wasn't legit." The fake priest bit had been necessary.

"I'm sure the nuns back at the academy would have my hide," Harry quipped as the wind whipped his thinning hair into a brown-grey frenzy.

Cutter snorted as they started to walk.

Harry nodded to unseen protectors as he received a message through the comm tucked inside his right ear. Touching Jason's elbow, he looked his old friend in the eye. "Time to round up the kid and hit the road." He cast a concerned look at his watch.

"Screw them," the widower retorted bitterly. His lean, aggressive face was framed by salt-and-pepper hair. Grey-green eyes flashed with the heat of his internal conflict as he began to walk away. This funeral wasn't just for his wife, and he knew it.

"Come on. We shouldn't be here when they arrive. Too much to explain." He laid a consoling hand on his friend's shoulder. "Say your goodbyes and let's get out of here."

Cutter's anguish was real. Anyone could see that. Grief had a way of slowing down even the most hardened and worldly professionals. Ignoring Harry, he took a half-step toward the pavilion.

"What's the matter with you, Jason? Say goodbye to whoever those people are, and--"

"Yeah, yeah." He struggled to control his emotions. The need to unburden his soul was very strong. Looking sidelong at his friend, he knew that would never happen. Both men had secrets they couldn't share with each other despite their long association. Harry worked for Central Intelligence, while Jason worked for National Security.

"Harry, I'm sorry. I've just got a lot on my mind. Tell Doris to collapse the perimeter, will you? Give Angel another five minutes. I've got to have a quick word with these people. Then we're out of here."

Harry didn't know the people in the tent, but he had his suspicions about who and what they were. "Right. Are we still on for dinner?" Jason would never talk about it. He knew that. He had his secrets, too. It was in the nature of what they did.

"Usual place?" Jason started walking toward the tent.

"Right. See you at 8." Harry waved before trotting off to find Doris.

Years before, the two men had been colleagues. Personality conflicts had caused Jason to leave the CIA for the NSA. Their friendship had survived everything from Watergate to the present.

The men and women observing the funeral from the guarded shelter watched Cutter approach. They appreciated Harry's participation in today's funeral, but they had no further interest in him. As the godfather to Jason's only child, they accorded him the respect he was due.

"He's cursed good, he is. I wonder if he'd be willing to speak at my wake." The Irishman's remark drew a few chuckles and one polite cough.

One of the East Coasters summed up the thoughts of many. "I've seen his file. He's got a real future with the CIA if he can get past his involvement with Jason. That, and he's not your type." The joke was greeted with silent nods. The diverse group had an intimate knowledge of each other's private lives.

Cutter wasn't just a grieving widower. He was their friend and savior. They owed him their lives.

Watching him approach the gravesite through the cold rain was particularly hard for the French operative who sat near the front of the group. "If there had been a more effective cancer treatment, I would have stolen it," she declared with a mild curse.

Some in the group understood better than others did. A handful of them were cancer survivors. Sophie Cutter's short, brutal war with the illness had been fought with all the Cold War skill that these old spies could muster. State secrets had been pilfered, wonder drugs had been stolen from high-tech corporate labs, and a whole host of other misdemeanors--and felonies--had been committed in an attempt to pay back the man who had brought them in from the cold.

"Looks like death warmed over," somebody else remarked in a Midwestern accent. "Reminds me of that night in Belgrade. I can still see the Chinese embassy in flames. Geez, but that was a mess."

NSA evaluators attributed Cutter's obsolescence to a deep-seated sense of patriotic loyalty and political guilt that was, at times, incompatible with Agency objectives. In an increasingly unstable world, he and the very few like him were classified as "inflexible."

Approaching the pavilion, Jason watched the group chat among themselves. Clamping down on his emotions, he was embarrassed by the sudden silence as he entered the pavilion. He folded his chilled hands over the front of his coat and looked back at them.

These men and women had been recruited to fight on the Cold War's shadow fronts. Some had been sacrificed to America's foes for the sake of their missions. Others had simply been forgotten as the decades had passed and national security needs changed. Most, if not all, were in their eighties.

While he had never been sacrificed, Jason knew that he had long since outlived his usefulness. His disaffection could be traced back to the failed 1961 Cuban revolution. The fallout from that aborted mission changed the way he looked at his work. This, in turn, changed him. In the decades that followed, he kept quiet about his patriotic beliefs while working to reclaim a handful of the Cold War casualties for which he himself had been responsible.

The NSA had, at first, put up with his covert repatriations. His superiors were no longer so tolerant. It was only a matter of time before they fired him for insubordination. NSA capture teams now worked harder than ever to reach disavowed assets before people like him got to them. These "deactivations" were, of course, made in the interest of national security.

"Sophie would be glad you were here. I know she'd be grateful for everything you've done." He turned to look back at his daughter, who knelt by the graveside, speaking her final goodbyes. "Harry said they're coming."

"They *were* coming," a tall, alabaster-skinned woman quipped with some delight. Her distinctive red hair made her stand out from the rest. Like the others, she knew true safety would only come in the grave. They knew too much. Modern politicians felt vulnerable.

"Were coming, Enola?" Jason grinned at her customary "old school" brass.

The woman smiled wickedly, raising a cell phone with her free hand. "They're good, but they're not that good. It'll be a few more years before the federal government has a truly centralized intelligence agency. Until then, they'll have to go on with their secret envy of the old Stasi," she sneered, referring to the defunct East German Secret Police. Some nodded, while others laughed mirthfully.

The break in tension caused Cutter to relax further. "I'm not sure who is protecting who just now. However, it really is time to go. I just have one thing to say. I've read your proposal, and I accept." His directness took them all by surprise.

"That's marvelous news, darling." Enola smiled as she stood to hug him.

"Don't thank me just yet." He raised a hand as he looked back at his daughter. "My career is over. My wife is dead, and I'm on borrowed time. The new NSA leadership won't tolerate me anymore. Honestly, I'm fed up with their use-'em-and-lose-'em attitude. I'm all for national security, but I draw the line at the betrayals we've been inflicting on our patriots for the last 50 years." Talking about it in such bold and open terms made him feel better. Harry didn't need to hear it. He had his own problems.

"My daughter doesn't need to know about this. She's been through enough. I could never explain to her that we're going to accelerate the decay of our government by helping more corrupt politicians get into office. She's only 13, for crying out loud. No. It's better for her to think that I'm dead."

"It may come to that," Enola said, speaking for all of them.

"I know. I'm prepared for that. Harry will take good care of Angel. There is one thing. I'm going to need some of my own people. If Dr. Hathaway's analysis is correct, the personality programming will last longer if I have Griff and Doris looking out for me."

"Oui. You will be très invincible."

Jason gave an embarrassed nod to the French woman.

The conspiracy they proposed required the leadership of a person who didn't exist. Cutter's unflagging conscience, courage, and conviction were simply not enough. They would have to be augmented. The plan called for Jason to undergo an intense mental and physical transformation. The personality programming they intended to embed in his psyche would make him into the leader they needed him to be.

Cold War psychiatric experts had taken the art of mental programming to new levels. Despite their successes, the field remained limited. Morality and ethics could be trained out of a subject, but they couldn't be instilled. Subjects could be taught virtually any skill for which they had a natural aptitude. False memories could be imposed, so long as they didn't conflict with the subject's sense of right and wrong. Jason's alter-ego would be able to deceive, betray, or manipulate at will because he would know that the lies were for a purpose.

"Are you certain that your cohorts will cooperate?"

Enola's question had been troubling Jason for some time. Griff and Doris were ten years younger than he was. They both had promising careers to look forward to, assuming they could get past the stigma of being associated with him.

"Doris will come over. I don't know about Griff."

Jason was aware that Doris held him in high regard. However, her admiration was covert. He wasn't sure if her feelings were personal or professional. The only certainty was her absolute loyalty. Griff, on the other hand, was more complicated. He routinely argued with Jason over Agency policy, departmental process, and bureaucratic procedure. Most of the time, he was right--a fact that Jason now worried over.

"I was under the impression that they don't get along well," somebody spoke up from inside the group.

Jason shrugged. "Yin and yang. They balance each other out. Doris can be a little too impulsive, but Griff keeps her in check." Laughter fluttered through the tent at the understatement.

Alone in the committee room, Doris stared up at the monitors. Nine large projection screens flickered with news feed from around the world. The recent presidential election was still generating fallout. George W. Bush had beaten his rival, Al Gore, by winning a hotly contested recount in the state of Florida, despite all projections to the contrary. Doris paid careful attention to the screen showing the feed from WNN.

Griff's familiar face popped up on the largest monitor. "Hey. How was your first treatment?"

Doris gave no hint that she resented the intrusion. "I'm not looking forward to the full body treatment." She looked up at the monitor. She raised her hands to let Griff see for himself.

"Can you tell the difference?" Griff squinted. In her early forties, Doris was exceptionally fit. She could have passed for 35.

"It hurts. A lot. Hathaway said the pain would go away over the next few hours."

"I think you're nuts for doing it. I wouldn't feel right with that kind of superscience in my veins. No, thanks. I'll grow old and die just like I'm supposed to."

Doris wiggled her fingers at eye level and looked back to Griff. "From what I hear, every member of the committee has had some form of this treatment. If it works as advertised, I should have no problem keeping up with the job."

Griff snorted. "The job" was giving him fits. He didn't understand how she could be so accepting. "Haven't you heard? They've got a new name. Some of the old fossils are so pumped for this project that they insisted on it. They're calling themselves 'the Founders.'"

15

Doris shrugged. "I don't care what they call themselves, so long as they don't meddle. Jason's put a lot of himself into this thing, and I'd like to see it succeed."

Griff hesitated. In her eyes, Jason could do no wrong. Arguing with Doris had always been futile. "Speaking of Jason, he wants to see you in the personal effects room. He's only got another hour or so before they put him under."

"Right." She nodded without looking up at the monitor. This might be the last time she spoke with Jason. Once programmed and physically altered, he would be inaccessible to her. Being clear on the concepts didn't make the reality any easier to cope with. The very idea of "making" somebody who had all the necessary attributes to lead them successfully struck her as being desperate.

Heading for the door, she passed row upon row of empty seating. She did her best to ignore the padded chairs and wide tabletops. Jason trusted the Founders for reasons that she couldn't comprehend. Only time would tell if her apprehension was justified. Over her head, Griff ran tense fingers through thick hair and sighed as he cut the connection.

Leaving the room, Doris nodded to the plainclothes guard who sat casually nearby. As she walked away, he stood up to close the door to the meeting room. A small light over the door changed from red to green.

Striding purposefully, Doris made her way into the medical wing. She stopped at two separate checkpoints to show her mag-card ID. *This is it. We're really going to do this.*

Pausing in an empty stretch of corridor, she looked down at her hands. Dr. Hathaway's regeneration process had truly turned back the clock. The fingers that she wiggled experimentally were those of a woman ten years younger. Rubbing her index finger and thumb together, she nodded with approval. As each minute passed, the pain lessened. *Strange, but I just can't see him being that young.*

"I know what you mean." Jason's deep voice stopped her cold.

"What?" She started when she realized he was actually standing directly in front of her. Deep blue eyes framed by silver temples matched well with his broad smile. It was altogether too easy to overlook the fact that she was a full inch taller.

"It's impressive, isn't it?" He pointed at his eyes. His craggy features contrasted starkly with the tight skin that now covered her fingers. Lowering her hand, Doris flashed a tiny smile of embarrassment that was gone in an instant.

"From green to blue. Very good. That's going to be very popular when it becomes commercially available."

"Can you believe it? They did this before breakfast." Jason rubbed at his eyes experimentally, as if he expected the new color to come off in his hand. "Adkins told me that this shade of blue is calibrated to be emotively appealing. I don't pretend to understand it all. Griff kept going on about the--"

"I don't care what Griff thinks. They look good on you. All you need now is some blonde hair and you're in business."

He gave Doris an appraising look. Her own long blonde hair framed very serious blue eyes. Shaking his head, he motioned for her to follow him down the hall. "They're working off a profile matrix. Everything about this guy will be made to order. All the best features. Add the mental to the physical and we've got ourselves a fearless package that won't stop. No matter what."

Doris nodded as a pair of medical technicians passed by. "Do they have a name for him, yet?"

"Preston Duquesne Fisk. You can read the background profile on the secured network. Griff's best work, and I mean that. He's got agents in the field now, seeding documents and hacking relevant databases. Give it two years, and Mr. Fisk'll be as real as anyone else."

"Parents? Relatives?" she asked as they turned a corner.

"The Founders are dredging up some of their old contacts to act as people from his past. Naturally, his parents died in accident of some kind. I'm thinking a car crash, but Griff leaning towards a house fire. Fewer loose ends."

Talking about the personality profile as if it were an actual person was hard for Doris. "Dr. Adkins assured me that the deprogramming would only be hard if you stayed under for more than--"

"It's okay. Really. I know the risks. Trust me. This guy's going to be so slick that Phase One will go down smooth as silk. It'll be like taking a ten-year nap. And it's not like I don't get anything out of the deal. A new face and a new body." Patting the slight paunch that rode up over his belt, Jason grinned broadly.

"I'm glad you're so confident. It's already too late to back out."

"Yeah. That's what I wanted to talk to you about." He led the way deeper into the medical unit. Doris followed. They passed a trio of lab technicians busy with a stack of computers. "I understand that Harry's still not buying in to my disappearance. What happened to the body that he was supposed to find?"

"The NSA got to it before he did. They had more than enough time to test the DNA and cremate. They're going along with the 'Cutter is dead' line only because they want to. As long as you stay gone, they could care less. That's more than we can say for Harry." They waited for three men in white lab coats to pass.

"Harry's not on profile. Again. I begin to see what Montague meant about him. It's a good thing we didn't try to bring him in. Geez, but I wish we had some kind of bone to throw him. We only need to slow him down for a few weeks. After that, my trail will be so cold that not even he will stick with it." Jason had known that his old friend wouldn't let his alleged disappearance go without a full accounting.

"There's another problem. Your daughter. She's being a real handful." Doris couldn't help but admire the teenager's pluck. Angel Cutter was taking her father's "mission-related loss" as a personal challenge.

"Yeah," Jason snorted, flashing his ID to get them past a checkpoint. "I can just imagine how that's playing out. She's a lot like her mother. Every time they told her that I was gone, Sophie made a joke out of it because I always came back. Angel once told me that I was way cooler than that spy guy they make all those movies about."

"No arguments here," Doris kidded.

"Watch her for me, will you, Doris? She's egging him on. Harry wants to find me and so does she. They're their own support group. I regret having to lie to her, but it had to be done. If I hadn't gone out like this, there's no telling what my old bosses would've arranged for me. This way, it's clean. You know?"

She did know. Her own introduction into the world of espionage had been messy. Parents and friends alike had to be convinced that she was dead. It was the only way to shield them from her very dangerous line of work.

"I can't afford to be seen with her. None of us can. The break was clean, and it needs to stay that way." He paused. "Have we made contacts in Social Services yet?"

"No. We can't do that kind of recruiting until we get the Fisk persona in place. What have you got in mind?"

Cutter paused to tap a six-digit security code into a secured door. "Try this. Get somebody to hack their system. Send a letter to the house addressed to me. Angel's bound to intercept it. The federal government is pushing adoption a lot harder these days."

"Ah," Doris nodded with a gleam in her eye as she followed him into the room. "The letter implies that Angel will be sent to a foster home. She goes to Harry, who she knows and trusts." She found herself watching Jason's every move with considerable interest. He shut the door behind her.

"Exactly. My will makes Harry the executor, and it authorizes him, as godfather to Angel, to adopt her. He'll feel threatened by the state. I know Harry. He'll be sidetracked for at least a week dealing with this."

"Is that going to be enough time?" She felt at ease admitting her concern to him. "He's got Keats and Pickering in his back pocket, you know. Those two have followed colder trails than yours. I'd feel better if we weren't relying on a 15-year-old--"

"She's 16 now," Cutter interrupted with fatherly pride.

"You get my point."

"Pickering's a computer nozzle. Keats worked with us twice, and as much as Harry talks him up, I'm not impressed. No, scratch that. He's good, but sometimes he doesn't know what he's looking for. Harry is the brains of their operation. Fool Harry and you fool them. Eventually, he'll figure that the NSA buried me. Then he'll go back to his regularly scheduled life. Angel gains a new father figure, and we get the week we need."

"Do I handle this personally?" Doris couldn't help the impulse to cut Griff out of the loop.

"Work it out with Griff. Let him handle the letter and any other records that have to be manipulated. He's got the touch for that sort of thing. No reason you should bother with it."

"Where does that leave me?"

"Whether he knows it or not, Harry might need some backup.

The NSA is patient. They'll keep looking for my personal files until they're certain there are none. When they don't find them, they might come looking for Angel."

Doris understood. Jason and many of his confederates didn't trust computers. Keeping sensitive information in offsite caches was common. The practice was as old as the profession itself.

"We'll handle it." Cooperating with Griff had always been hard. She was amazed that, even now, Cutter could still find ways to make them work together.

"You, I trust. I'm just a little thrown over this election. How did we miss that?" he said with a meaningful glance. He reached for a remote to turn on a nearby television set. The screen came alive with WNN coverage.

"Let it go. We're good, but we're not that good. We've only been recruiting for three months. The 6-2 sims gave George W. a one-percent chance to win in Florida, and he did. Come on, now. Why did you ask to see me?"

Cutter leaned against a nearby bookshelf. "Right. You know, Fisk's not going to have the luxury of making a mistake like that. Everything he does will have to be near-perfect. If Griff and his boys are right, we've got no more than 20 years before the government promotes some sort of homeland security initiative. Once that happens, it'll only take the political parties two or three years to co-opt it. The Fisk persona will be so thoroughly investigated and watched--if we get our president in--that, if they decide to use it against us, we could be found out in short order."

Doris straightened and spoke sharply. "Stop it. You're scared, and so am I. It's only natural to be second-guessing everything at this point. It's all going to work out."

"I know." He turned, stepping away from the shelf. Even he couldn't help talking about Fisk as if he were an "it." "We've covered all our bases. He's going to have a small army backing him up. He can't lose. I just wish that I..." He stopped. Admitting his fear was harder than he'd imagined. Even now, Doris seemed like the most logical person to confide in. Adkins and Hathaway had been quite specific about the need for him to unburden himself before the transformation.

"I promise. As long as I live, nobody will hurt you or your daughter. I've never known anyone else like you. I know you can do this." The depth of his convictions and the strength of his loyalties had been both scary and attractive, allowing her to enjoy his company. His very presence was empowering to her. His marriage, when it came, had allowed her to avoid revealing her feelings to anyone.

"Thanks. That means a lot to me." He felt the lump rise in his throat.

Hearing the catch in his voice, Doris was hard-pressed to stay composed. In all their years of association, Jason had never been so open with her. The implications made her uneasy. Even if he intended to let the mission consume him in one last act of foolish, macho bravado, she wouldn't allow it.

"It should." She hesitated, her mind racing to find a way to change the subject.

Jason reached for a long, black leather trenchcoat that hung on a nearby peg. "Do me a favor. As long as you're going to make the trip to the Fountain of Youth with me, you might as well hold onto this until I get back." Holding up the coat, he turned slowly, offering to let her try it on.

"What's that?" Doris pointed at the label inside the collar, in an effort to break free of the moment. In red thread, the initials *J.C.* had been sewn sloppily onto the label.

"Angel gave this to me before we went to Yemen." He regarded the coat fondly as he stepped closer to wrap it around Doris, who accepted it hesitantly. "She sewed my initials on the label so that I wouldn't lose it. All the cool spies wear black leather, or didn't you know?"

She found herself accepting the garment with nervous hands. "Yes, I think I recall hearing that somewhere." The mention of Yemen made her stiffen. Cutter couldn't help but notice. "We could have stopped the attack on that destroyer. We should have--"

"I know." He resisted the urge to take Doris by the shoulders. "We got the stand-down order straight from the White House. That's a fact that I'm not going to forget any time soon. The Middle Eastern thing is only going to get worse. The people in power know more about it than you or I ever will. If the Founders are right, our political elites are just waiting for the threat to grow large enough to help them achieve even greater power. From where I sit, it's just one more reason for us to do this."

Cutter was a very self-contained man. As generous as he was known to be, Doris couldn't recall seeing this side of him before. The realization made her grow bold. She looked down at the floor. "I had them. I would have taken then down if you had just given the order."

"From all the way across the harbor? You sure you could've made a shot like that?" He preyed on her secret vanity in an effort to bring her out of her depression.

"Depending on what I have to go through to keep you out of trouble, you might not get this back." His change of tack had been clumsy and obvious, for which she was grateful.

He gave her the once-over. "I'm just going to have to take your word for that. Dr. Adkins says that I won't remember any of it. Besides, they're supposed to jack me up by about four inches. That coat might end up too short for me."

"It's better that way. These coats...when they're too long, they drag on the ground and get all ratted out." Doris put an exploratory hand into a coat pocket.

"Mm." Cutter pulled a chair over and sat.

"Yes?" She hid her disappointment as her fingers told her that the pocket was empty.

"I met with the..." He licked his lips, suddenly speechless.

"I'm listening." Doris eased herself onto the edge of a nearby table.

"If I'm compromised, I could be killed."

She shook her head sharply. "I won't let that happen."

"The Founders have convinced me that it might be necessary for them to pull the plug on me if I lose control of the situation, or..."

"I--" Doris leapt to her feet, nostrils flaring with outrage.

"Or if it looks like my programming's going to fail. No matter how it turns out, I want you to be the one to do it, if--and only if--it has to be done."

"But..." She felt her heart sinking.

"No." He could see how she was reading him. "It's not like that. You said you'd protect me. That's exactly what I want. I want your promise that you won't let them--"

"I won't," she interjected bitterly.

"The Founders mean well. I see their point. If I need to be taken out for the sake of the mission, then so be it. I'm calling the shots, and what I say goes. However, I'm afraid that I might be sacrificed prematurely. Kind of like they were. They are getting on in years, and most of them won't live to see this thing through, even with a little help from their doctor friends. Their age may affect their judgment. These people are old school, and that means they won't--"

"I understand. That's why you want me to go through with the full treatment." She blushed with obvious relief. He really did intend to come back.

"I knew you'd get it." He favored her with what could have been an admiring glance.

"I--" Doris began.

"No. Don't. Just let me have this, will you?" He got to his feet.

"Yes," she finally managed to say after a long moment.

Jason reached out to pick up an old photo from the table near her. "Remember this?" The crisp black-and-white image depicted Cutter and a handful of men and women dressed in mottled camouflage. In the background, Doris was cradling a long black sniper rifle. Behind the group, on a backdrop of weeds and bushes, a pair of bulky instruments sat on black metal tripods. Doris craned her neck for a better look.

"Belgrade. Just before the Chinese embassy thing. You're not supposed to have this in here, you know?" She speared him with accusing eyes.

"Any regrets?" he asked, offering her the photograph.

"No comment. Get rid of that." She stepped back, her hands raised.

"All right." He picked up a convenient pair of scissors. "See?" He made a show of cutting up the photo. "All gone." Tossing the fragments into a garbage can, he was careful to pander just enough to be irritating.

Doris began to look around. "The only things that are supposed to be in this room--"

"Are things that will belong to him. Well, you know. I saw the photo..."

"Is there anything else?" She slowly turned.

"Just the coat." He pointed at Doris to get her mind off the photo.

She gripped the coat's lapels and pursed her lips. Glancing around the room, she took in the bookshelves that flanked a large armoire. Several tables held an assortment of personal possessions that had been selected to reflect the tastes and background of the man they were about to create.

Looking down at her hands, she raised one of them to the blonde hair on her forehead. The image of her own face suddenly flashed into her mind's eye. In a sudden whirl of emotion, she found herself conflicted. The strangeness of having younger hands had finally caught up with her. The stubborn hand that refused to let go of the coat lapel finally got her attention.

"Right. I..." she managed to say.

"You'd better go." He tapped at his wristwatch. "I've got to have one last look around this place to make sure that all this stuff is imprinted. Wouldn't do to have him mistrustful of his own stuff, would it?"

"Right." She turned to leave.

"Doris?" Jason put down the scissors and took a step towards her.

"Yes?" She found herself slowing.

"I don't know how well you're going to get along with Fisk. I'm not sure I'd like him if I met him. If you're around when they deprogram me, I'd like to get together. We could talk."

She nodded at this positive sign. "I'd like that." She was careful not to look over her shoulder as she closed the door.

Jason waited for three heartbeats, and then reached into the garbage can. He picked up a single piece of the ruined photo. It was a small fragment, just as he had planned. He squared off the image with the scissors and held it in the palm of his hand. Reaching for the wallet that lay close by, he wasn't sure of his motives. Hiding the photo fragment seemed both necessary and irresponsible. The impulse to save even a small piece of himself felt like the right thing to do.

Opening the wallet, he peeled back an inside layer of fabric. Working carefully, he slid the image into the hiding place. Feelings of guilt overwhelmed him as he closed the wallet and laid it down.

The moment he had just shared with Doris loomed large in his mind. Looking down at the garbage can, he stared at the remaining pieces of the photo until the lab technicians came for him.

Sitting alone in the observation lounge, Griff rubbed his stubbled chin. Accepting what he saw through the large bay window was still difficult. In the lab, Dr. Hathaway supervised the medical technicians. They worked in near-silence at a variety of computer terminals and monitoring stations. In the center of the room, shrouded in deliberate darkness, the patient remained sedated. Pacing around a separate workstation, Dr. Adkins busied himself with several readouts.

A knock at the lounge door made Griff turned his head. Doris entered the room dressed in athletic gear.

"You wanted to see me?" she asked with apparent disinterest. She used the towel wrapped around her neck to wipe sweat from her glistening forehead. Griff motioned for her to take a seat.

"I have news," he said as Doris flopped into a chair. Hathaway's process had worked as advertised. Griff looked back at the laboratory with a sigh.

"Give." She finished wiping her face. Being ten years younger was a biological fact now, but it took some getting used to.

"Harry signed the adoption papers this morning. He's even got Angel enrolled in that boarding school over by Quantico."

She nodded as she wrapped the towel around her neck. "Yeah. Our people have confirmed that he's going to be tapped for Homeland Security."

Griff straightened.

Doris shrugged. "Don't sweat it. Keeping him out was the right thing to do."

"How can you sit there and say that? He almost found us!" Griff threw up his hands.

Doris plucked at a small piece of fuzz on her sweatshirt. Harry really had come close to finding Jason and the other members of the conspiracy. Still, that wasn't the only thing bothering him, and she knew it.

"You're still freaked over the Trade Center thing. We're out of the business now. Deal with it. Stay on task. Nobody is more upset about the situation than I am. It never had to come to this. Jason was right. Anyone with half a brain and better than B12 clearance could have put a stop to the rise of these terror groups. It's not our fault that things have gone down this way. It's what the people in power wanted."

The conspirators suffered from the same frustration that was running through the American intelligence community. Time and again, they and their colleagues had been prevented from unmasking or otherwise defeating the terrorist network that had succeeded in using its operatives to fly hijacked passenger planes into the World Trade Center and the Pentagon.

"Okay. You're right. I give. I just--"

Doris sympathized. She had privately agonized the same way herself. "We all 'just'. You know what he would say. He'd tell us that we shouldn't be distracted, that the 'war on terror', in part, is just something used by the politicos to feather their own nests. It changes nothing. If I could, I'd go all the way back to Yemen and just say 'screw it' and pull the trigger, but I can't. It wouldn't change anything, even if I could."

Sunday
March 2, 2003
Secured Site 1
Undisclosed Location
11:45 A.M. Local Time

"Here he comes." Griff stepped back into the conference room. "What do you think?" Dr. Adkins asked Doris.

"Amazing." She couldn't take her eyes off the closed-circuit TV. The man now known as Fisk strode through the halls as if he owned the place.

Griff took his seat at the long table. "More than amazing. He's the real deal. Everybody remember that. Jason Cutter does not exist. He never did. You got me?" The assembled group stayed silent. The enormity of what they had done was still overwhelming.

Dr. Hathaway broke the tension of the moment with his customary self-promotion. "I am very pleased with the bone and skin grafts. Generating new bone to add height was really the hardest part. As you can see, the new facial structure is flawless. It's a good thing that the programming regimen kept him unconscious for the worst of it. I, for one, couldn't imagine submitting to that kind of pain."

Doris leaned over toward Dr. Adkins. "How much did he suffer?" If her own experience was any indication, Jason would be glad to not remember any of the experience.

Adkins gave her an appraising look. "You, and a few others, only had ten years taken off your biological age. No other modifications were made. He, on the other hand, was rebuilt from the ground up."

Hathaway continued, "As good as it is, he must never be closely examined. A routine physical might turn up any number of the modifications. His packaging is flawless, but a first year medical student would take just one look--"

"Will you keep it down? Here he comes." Griff glared at the bellicose doctor.

28

As part of laying the groundwork for the conspiracy, Adkins and Hathaway had been given enough money to start their own private clinic. It would ensure proper medical support for the Fisk persona and the other members of the conspiracy.

Griff took a last look around the room. "Everyone knows the drill. Think of this meeting as a shakedown cruise. Your questions and reactions are scripted to gauge his reactions. He thinks we're his old and trusted friends. He runs the show. Do not--" Griff stopped as Preston Duquesne Fisk entered the room.

Checking his tie, the tall, handsome man radiated confidence. "Sorry to keep you waiting. The finance committee went long." Sitting at the head of the table, he passed a stack of papers to Doris. She took a copy and passed the rest on. Everyone watched Fisk with too much interest--a fact that even he seemed to notice and ignore.

"We got the land. Construction will start as soon as the permits are in. When it's up and running, the telecom company will be the perfect front. In addition to being a legitimate business that might turn a profit, we will have a fully secure installation from which to run all of our primary comms and data." Holding up a one-page document, he seemed genuinely pleased with himself.

Adkins gave Hathaway a smug nod. The Fisk persona had been built on Cutter's moral and ethical foundations. It also borrowed heavily from his persistence and ambition.

Hathaway ignored Adkins. From his point of view, Fisk's mental programming would be useless without superior physical attributes. Anyone could see that.

"That was fast," one of the advisors said on cue.

Fisk reacted in what would become his customary way, blunt but honest. "We've had a few setbacks. The Founders have been vetoing a lot of my recommendations lately. Sometimes I get the feeling they know something I don't. Still, this telecom thing puts us one step closer to implementation. Can we move on to the next item?" Papers shuffled as the advisors consulted agendas and crib notes.

"I've got a question about your choice of presidential candidate," one of the advisors obviously read from an index card.

Adkins and Hathaway glared at the man. Doris and Griff looked at each other. They silently agreed--the offender would be transferred to other duties.

Fisk reacted as anticipated. "Take another look at her profile. This isn't a snap decision. Nobody else has those numbers. Her ambition index pegs the meter. If you look at the summary panel, she's a shoo-in for the Senate. If we can keep her out of trouble for ten years, her ambition and our background work will get us the White House. We spin things a little during her first term, and she does the rest for us."

Fisk's confidence and magnetism enveloped the room, focusing everyone's attention on him as if he were more important than he really was. The strength of his will came through in each word and gesture. Even Doris had to admit that he was everything they had hoped he would be.

"I think we're all on board with you. It's only natural for us to have misgivings at this point. Let's just stick to the agenda, and see if we can be finished by dinner. Okay?"

Snug in her seat, Doris nodded as Fisk spoke. Around them, the executive jet's soft lighting cast a surreal twilight as nearby staffers attended to their affairs. The soft glow from holographic computer monitors lent a sense of purpose to the relaxed atmosphere.

"When Argentina defaulted on its debts in 2008, the World Bank and the International Monetary Fund merged out of necessity. It was the only way to contain the damage. Antonio Ramirez and his people have been rebuilding economies as they fail. Along the way, he's managed to strengthen the UN's position and write his name in the history books in very large letters."

"I understand." She had gotten used to his tendency to lecture. Over the years, she had come to rely on it as a means of access. She hoped that by paying attention to Fisk, Jason might know, on some level, that she was paying attention to him, too.

Fisk smiled, his affable grin setting off his big blue eyes. "I wish I could have told you more before we left for Spain. Now that we're headed home, I didn't see any reason to hold back."

Doris nodded again. He wasn't aware that she was fully plugged into his world. She played her part without bitterness or complaint. Acting out her supposed lack of knowledge was the price she paid for full access. "I gather that Ramirez was pleased with the advanced package you had to offer him."

"That, and the extra briefcase." Fisk grinned wolfishly.

"So, what comes next?" She was careful to radiate only casual interest.

"The national debt crisis will boil over in roughly a year. Maybe less. The deal we cut with Ramirez will give the impression that

President Hill struggled for, and got, decent terms to settle the various debts with our overseas creditors."

"Amazing what a briefcase full of money will buy these days," she quipped. Only her knowledge of the truth allowed her to project confidence and be able to joke about what Fisk and his fellow conspirators had been doing for the previous 14 years.

"We're not in the clear yet. The World Bank isn't that easy to buy. The negotiating teams still have to meet. All we bought was a promise to go easy on us. The media will need a spectacle to report on, and the politicians will need something controversial to comment on."

"What was it they used to say about bread and circuses?" Doris asked rhetorically.

Fisk smiled again, appreciating the comparison. "When the General Assembly voted to merge the IMF with the World Bank, they created a whole new kind of greed--politics and economics taken to a whole new level. It's one step closer to that one-world government everyone keeps expecting."

"As long as it gets us what we want, I don't mind greasing a few palms. Is there anything else we can do to stack the deck in our favor?" Doris swept long blonde hair from her piercing blue eyes--eyes that, not accidentally, closely resembled Fisk's.

"No, not really. It's taken us more than 14 years to put it together. We have our president, and she's got her Congress. The only thing left to do is play the hand we built."

Doris drew strength from Fisk's pragmatism--Jason's pragmatism. The urge to press him about other matters helped her change the subject. "I've heard that the Treasury Secretary isn't fully on board with the plan."

He nodded and looked away. "An oversight. I've seen it before. Secretary Brown was just what we wanted him to be--an aggressive banker with a taste for money. The job changed him. Once he saw just how bad the situation was, he got religion, so to speak. We just have to accept that and go on. With luck, the second phase of our plan will never have to be put into motion."

The mention of Phase Two reminded Doris that Fisk thrived on challenge. It was part of the glue that held him together. "I'm still not sure that Mr. Garrison is the correct choice to lead Phase Two."

"Our president has workable majorities in both the House and the Senate, and she's got good popularity numbers. She can't help but stick to the script we've written for her. As for Mr. Garrison, I picked him myself. He doesn't know it yet, but he is definitely our man. Speaking of Garrison--"

Doris pointed at the overhead chronometer. "Roughly two hours. After he makes his speech, he'll download our eraser program into their database. When we receive confirmation, our Phase Two candidates will be in the clear." That Fisk approved of the operation she had personally arranged meant more to her than she admitted to herself. She adored both parts of him.

Continuing to play the pessimistic bodyguard, she reminded herself that they were being watched for any hint that Fisk was off profile. Jason had consented to become Fisk, but he could never truly *be* Fisk. Trapped below the surface, he would eventually reassert himself. Fisk's programming would unravel under the weight of an unclean conscience. The Founders knew this, and they waited for him to exhibit enough dangerous behavior to warrant his termination. She refused to accept the inevitability of it. Jason had all but promised her that he would come back. He always came back. This time would be no different.

Political parties now vied for power using extreme tactics that would have been unthinkable in the previous century. Fisk and his conspirators had been capitalizing on this trend. The political pendulum had never before swung so extremely in one direction. Would forcing the issue result in a restoration of the democratic balance of power, or was it too late?

The previous ten years had involved tumultuous relationships with some of the country's leading public figures. Fisk's carefully groomed background positioned him to be a top-notch policy and election strategist. Working through his network of unseen advisors, he had influenced the careers of more than two dozen corrupt senators and representatives, assisting them in attaining office.

In 2012, Fisk had succeeded in getting 'his' president into office. That's when the trouble started. His programming had started to fail some time after the inauguration. The burden on Jason's underlying conscience grew with each deception. Doris had begun noticing small changes in Fisk's behavior that could only be attributed to Jason. She was thankful that he wasn't acting out now. The Spanish mission and the flight home were proceeding as they should.

"Well?" Fisk jarred her out of her reverie.

"I'm sorry. Could you repeat the question?"

"I asked you to call him at some point during his window of action. Don't harass him. Just be supportive. Can you do that?"

Before she could respond, a feminine laugh intruded from the aisle. "Sorry to interrupt."

Looking up, Fisk and Doris saw the slender figure of Jasmine, Fisk's senior administrative assistant. Smiling easily, Jasmine handed him a manila folder and a fountain pen.

"What's this?" He raised an eyebrow as he reached past Doris for the folder.

"More of the usual. There's a letter to your new driver, who starts tomorrow, and a few other run-of-the-mill things. And my pay raise." Jasmine's Polynesian features remained half-hidden in shadow as she joked.

"I see." He unscrewed the cap on the fountain pen thoughtfully.

His legitimate consulting business employed many of the conspirators. It wasn't unusual for the paperwork of one to mingle with the administration of the other.

"You're cheap at twice the price, Jaz." He grinned. Flipping through the folder, he slashed out his trademark moniker on each page with a signature tab.

Doris allowed herself to feel a surge of possessive pride. *He looks like he's just signing without reading. I know better.* The only spoiler was that she couldn't guarantee his success or his safety.

Handing the folder back to Jasmine, Fisk capped the pen and passed it over. "I expect Madeline to be calling any time now."

"The line is already routed to your station. Enjoy." Jasmine smiled and waved.

Fisk turned back to Doris. "Enough about me and my diabolical plans. Tell me about this new driver."

Doris ran her hands over the trenchcoat folded in her lap. "His credentials are good. He has no federal connections, and he's not political. He's not even registered to vote. After six years on the job, he has only had trouble with one employer, and that wasn't his fault."

"What happened?" Fisk sipped from a drink that had been resting in a nearby cup holder.

"Hostile takeover." She shrugged as if that were all there was. *Christopher's boss wouldn't sell his share of the company, so his fellow shareholders cashed him out by having him killed. Nothing like the time-honored technique of a fake suicide.*

"So what makes this new guy such the valuable commodity?" Small talk came effortlessly when he allowed himself to be carried along by it. His deep and abiding trust of Doris helped him to relax even further.

"He demonstrates the kind of loyalty and ethics we're screening for," she replied, choosing her words carefully. Fisk was on the verge of uncharacteristic interest in an underling. Jason's inclusive personality made him care about anyone who worked for him, or with him. Fisk had been trained to be more distant, as befitted the stereotype on which he was based.

"Does Griff know that you hired this paragon of virtue?" He cocked his head to one side with a gleam in his eye. He preferred to regard her as something more than just his personal bodyguard. There was something about her that had nothing to do with trust. There were moments when he could talk to her about almost anything.

Doris grinned wolfishly. "As if it matters. You just signed Christopher's confirmation letter, so now I don't care what Griff thinks."

"Don't drag me into this. Someday, you two are going to be forced to make nice."

"Nothing's changed on that score. Doesn't matter. We're almost done. I have never compromised your safety, and I won't start now just for the sake of offering that bureaucrat the olive branch. People like Christopher are hard to find. He's good for the mission. If his holiness doesn't like that, he can take a hike."

"Can we bring him in?"

"Why should we? If your estimate holds true, we can close down some time in July. With Phase One of the plan complete, you and I are out to pasture. There won't be any need to bother him with the details of our agenda."

Fisk liked the sound of that. "What he doesn't know won't hurt him." As much as he believed in the plan, he knew he was being dragged down by the weight of his burdened conscience. Chances to tell the truth came along so infrequently that he relished moments where only minor deception was called for.

"I'll handle him personally. He won't know any more than he has to. The next two months will be a piece of cake." Fisk didn't think to question his trust in Doris, or that he seemed to know what she was thinking. He never did.

Leaning back, Doris tried hard to avoid scanning the interior of the aircraft for hidden surveillance equipment. He had been too casual. Too relaxed and easy-going. Too much like Jason. *They know. They have to know. If it were me, I'd know.*

Monday
April 21, 2014
Cosmopolitan Systems, Inc.
Potomac Heights, Maryland
3:56 P.M. EDT

"What is this? How do you lose a whole SWAT team?" Griff stared at the report in his hand as he marched down the fourth floor hallway with a group of advisors. Running nervous fingers through salt-and-pepper hair that had gone thin from stress, he shook his head in disgust.

"The plane is two hours out, and we've got Garrison one floor down giving the new Tier Five contacts a pep talk. Something about this feels wrong. Put the helicopter up and hustle Garrison out of here just as soon as he's done. I don't want Fisk traveling overland until we find out where these jokers are." He came to a sudden halt. "Is there any chance that this is a Homeland Security thing?" When nobody responded, he moved on.

Formed by Executive Order in the aftermath of terrorist attacks in 2001, the Department of Homeland Security had initially been tasked with coordinating antiterrorist programs run by the nation's law enforcement and intelligence gathering agencies. The Cabinet-level agency had since become a power unto itself.

The previous 14 years of Griff's life had been governed by the dictates of the Fisk conspiracy. He no longer believed in coincidences. Now that she had the presidency, Fisk's chief employer didn't need him anymore. That, too, was part of the plan. He easily suppressed his turmoil. His faith in the man behind the mask remained intact.

If she knew what his real agenda was, she'd be embarrassed about trying to kill him. I suppose I should be grateful. Stopping at the end of the hallway, he ignored the man on guard while punching his ten-digit access code into a wall terminal. *Hard to believe I've followed that woman through her state legislature and the Senate. Seems like forever.*

"The civilian helicopter is down for repairs. You signed off on that five days ago." The speaker was clearly reluctant to bring this up.

Griff huffed as they entered the secured room. "Yeah, I remember. It was a 72-hour down time for upgrades. What's--"

"The parts didn't arrive on time, and the maintenance was necessary."

Griff stopped next to a chair. "If this is a coincidence, I'll eat my hat."

"You want to send up the military bird?" somebody asked hesitantly.

"Not just yet." Griff waited for the door to close behind them. "Sit. Let's be sure that we act positively." His ulcer muttered. He nodded at its dire premonition as the man next to him shuffled a large stack of paper.

"I have the sim on that. Here it is--Aegis 1-1. This one's just five hours old. Looks like we have a 50/50 chance of mission success, assuming that we're dealing with a SWAT team. If the threat is mercenary, we lose ten percent. Intercept is going to be a problem, I can tell you that right now."

"Let's not get ahead of ourselves. Do we have confirmation?"

"We've got solid confirmation that the tactical van and the alert crew for the city's number two SWAT are not at their assigned station," a Hispanic man said as he passed a handheld computer around. Each member of the committee glanced at it and passed it on until it reached Griff. "A source in the Metro Detective's unit noticed it. He called us, and I sent someone in to have a look. Pictures and everything."

"This is Kinsey's work," another man said, admiring the images. "He's patient and thorough. If he says that SWAT team is gone, then that means he looked for it before making the report."

The observation underscored the limitations of Fisk's protective infrastructure. Fisk's rise to prominence as the country's most successful political strategist had brought with it a whole host of disadvantages. The need for discretion and camouflage had forced Griff to develop a small but flexible team that would canvas all of Fisk's security needs without coming to the attention of those with whom he associated. In the previous year, several intelligence agencies had probed Fisk's organization. The intrusions were expected and planned for.

"Clue me in. How is this a problem?" a red-haired man seated across from Griff asked.

Pausing to rub the bridge of his nose, Griff summoned his inner calm. *Lord, save me from the dragons of ignorance, or just let them eat me and get it over with.* "As the senior advisor and chief political strategist to this country's first female president, Fisk isn't your usual contract protection. This wouldn't the first time somebody tried to take him out. If I have to explain it to you, then somebody screwed up when they let you in here."

"Oh. Yeah. Right. Sorry, didn't think." The man blushed and shrank back in his chair. It had been a genuine mistake, most likely brought on by fatigue.

Nobody spoke for a long moment.

Now that she had the presidency, Madeline Hill felt she didn't need Fisk any more. During her rise to power, she and other American politicians had been strongly influenced by world events. Terrorism, both at home and abroad, was more common than ever despite the actions of federal officials to monitor, contain, and control. Under these circumstances, President Hill felt compelled to be rid of the only person whom she couldn't effectively control.

Fisk was returning from a three-day trip to Spain. The expected attempt on his life hadn't come. Advanced projections had predicted a high probability that his enemies would try to masquerade as Basque separatists. President Hill was ruthless to a fault. Everyone in the secured room had been briefed. They knew she wanted to be rid of Fisk.

Griff sighed. "We're all dead on our feet. She didn't have her people try for him in Spain. We have to assume that they'll try for him as soon as he comes back into the country. Once he's back on the ground and inside our safe zone, we can all get some sleep. Until then, we assume that anything and everything is a threat."

The red-faced man raised both hands in submission. "Please. I got it. My specialty is visual identification. I crunch numbers with digital enhancements. I'm sorry. I've been up for the last two days. I'll shut up now."

"Apology accepted. We were all hoping for some downtime once the plane landed. Our sims tell us otherwise. Let's be pros and work through this new wrinkle, okay? Next question."

A serious man on Griff's right asked, "How do we know that SWAT isn't off at some Homeland Security roundup or something like that? Nothing we have so far indicates the D.C.P.D. is after our man."

Griff nodded sharply. More than once, Fisk's protectors had prepared contingencies to threats that had never materialized. Tonight's perceived threat could turn out to be just as false. "You know the drill. It's our job to be paranoid so the man doesn't have to."

A blonde woman added, "The report I have here says that a search of all known law enforcement functions in a 700-mile radius came up negative. There are no police emergencies going on just now that require SWAT intervention."

A solemn-faced man on Griff's right piped in. "Looks like Doris was right. This fits right in with her post-mission profile. Contingency files, you know? Did you want to--"

Griff raised a finger to stall further comment. "I was just getting to that. The President has someone new running her under-the-table stuff. Everybody here should have seen the new sims by now. In the last hour, we've gotten new plots. Since we can't get a lock on who the mystery brain is, we could be in trouble."

He suddenly realized he had forgotten about the real reason he had called this meeting. Cursing his own fatigue, he reached clumsily for the remote. "In the last four months, somebody has been shadowing our assets. We have partial sightings and some extrapolated data from comm intercepts."

The image on the wall monitor showed an aerial view of the District of Columbia. "I've been working on this with a handful of part-timers and Ivan here. Each red marker indicates where we think we've seen our shadows." He touched a stud on the remote to add a seemingly-random pattern of red dots onto the image. "We've simmed it with all three primary threat filters, and the probability is that Madeline's new operator is working out Fisk's travel boundaries and in-house ground route plan. Add in the fact that our good president likes to make a try for Fisk every six months, and hey, she's about due."

The red-haired man clasped his hands in his lap. "I don't have any new faces in my database that would tell us who her new coordinator is."

Another advisor checked his watch. "Our plane is two hours out. We have people at Reagan and Dulles. If there's any real threat value to this, we need to act now. Can we cover him if we switch airports at the last minute?"

The solemn-faced man rifled his papers again. "It'll take us two hours to move our own tactical. We can option Baltimore-Washington International if we move in the next five to ten, but that's only an option. Overland will also be a problem if we're being watched. We move, they move."

Another stern voice rumbled from across the table. "We're heavily invested at Reagan. If we're being watched, that means our units are under surveillance. He's right; we move, they move. Frankly, I don't see any point in risking a change in airports."

"Until we get a lock on the situation, we've got to be one step ahead. Anyone care to brainstorm?" Spreading his hands apart, Griff looked around the table.

"Check it," a slender black man replied. "When I was in the Navy, we used to process some of the intell from JSTARS. The plots you have here are patterned like a recon job. If this is me, I'm looking for something specific. With coverage like that, I'm probably going be ready to jump on it when I find it."

Griff cleared his dry throat. "The new guy is on the ball. He, she, or they are looking for our hidden assets. They want to know if we have tactical capability and if so, how much."

The red-haired man dipped his head. "Yeah, and you know what that means."

"You think the President's got Homeland in her back pocket?" somebody asked.

The red-haired man shook his head. "No way. It's taken everything she's got to co-opt the Secret Service. Homeland Security is out of her league for at least another year."

Griff put down the remote and reached for a telephone handset. Keying in his access code, he waited for the line to connect. *I don't believe it. She was right again.*

Doris blinked as the wireless phone in her coat pocket beeped.

"I was wondering when we were going to get to that." Fisk sat up, reaching for his drink. A small voice in the back of his mind insisted that the call was from Griff. Fisk turned away from her as he tried deliberately to snatch the rest of the fleeting thought.

"That's not funny." She graced him with a stern look.

He turned back toward her. "Every time your phone rings, it means that something bad is about to happen." Rolling his eyes in mock terror, he settled back with a laugh.

Doris got up and walked to the rear of the jet as the phone continued to beep. Shrugging into the supple trenchcoat, she maneuvered past shadowy figures that ignored her. Fisk's display was out of character. *I saw it. They saw it.*

Coming to a stop in the galley, she turned her back on the flight attendant who was busy preparing drinks. Flipping the halves of the slim black phone open, she grinned wickedly. *I never could hide anything from Griff. How bad it is this time?*

She didn't consult with Griff if she could help it, and he wouldn't coordinate with her until things had reached crisis proportions. Fisk was right. When Griff did call, it was bad news.

Doris eyed the tiny green light on the lower lip of the phone. "Shadow. The line is secure. Talk to me."

"It's me. We've got a situation." Griff sounded tired.

"Outline it." She cradled the phone between her neck and shoulder as she put her hands into the deep pockets of her coat. She had seen Fisk do it a hundred times, and took comfort in knowing that he was mimicking of her own behavior.

"A D.C. Metro SWAT unit is missing. We can't account for it."

"Wasn't there a sim that dealt with that?"

"It's part of the Gemini series. You wrote it."

"Which permutation are you following?" She closed her eyes, trying to recall the details.

Like so many protective specialists in the modern world, Fisk's guardians used computer models to play out possible scenarios. The simulations not only helped them to develop solutions to a whole host of problems, they also pinpointed potential weaknesses in their organization. As valuable as the results were, though, each sim was still limited by the intellect and creativity of its programmer.

"You can look the numbers up later. It looks like we have a hunter scenario, and we're the target." He sounded irritated.

"We, meaning Overwatch?" Doris felt her blood surge. Fisk had made many enemies over the previous decade. A play this big suggested that President Hill's minions might be getting too smart for their own good.

"I'm looking at shadow plots right now. The sightings are marginal, but everything is in synch with an observation and surveillance profile. Somebody's watching us protect our man."

"What is the projected accuracy rating?" She had always dreaded this possibility.

"Thirty percent and change. That's not all. I've just been told that the civilian helicopter is down for maintenance, and we only have about three minutes to option a new airport."

"Which would show our hand if they're on the ground waiting for us," she replied, following Griff's line of reasoning to its grim conclusion.

"How do you want to play it? If we do like normal, we land him, limo him, and take him home. If they want to take him at the airport, they'll probably have some kind of trumped up warrant to search the plane so that they can get to him without making a scene."

The Methamphetamine Reduction Act of 2001 had suspended the requirement that police provide notification of search and seizure when they thought illegal drugs were involved. This legislation, combined with increased airport security in response to terrorist attacks in the previous decade, had perverted the good intentions of Congress. The media had given wide coverage to a number of unfortunate incidents in which TSA employees had unjustly shot and killed panicked travelers alleged to be resisting arrest. Modern conspiracy theorists were still speculating about those deaths.

Doris remained silent for a moment. In her mind's eye, she could see the deadly scenario played out. *Griff may be a bureaucrat, but he does know his business.* "They meet us at the plane. We react to them..."

"They call it a drug bust gone bad and whack everybody. All they'd have to do is make sure that a few kilos of dope turned up in the luggage or something."

"I told you--"

Griff bristled. "Don't. Just don't. Let's divert to BWI. This could be nothing, but I'm going to need time to work out the details."

"Oh, come on. There's only one way this situation could have cropped up. Madeline's new operator has been watching you and he's finally got your number."

"You don't know that. We don't even know who he or she is. Besides, we may be looking at Agency involvement." The admission caused Griff's ulcer to roar in agony.

"Haven't we got a Keyhole window coming up?" Doris checked her watch. For various reasons, the conspirators had tapped into the secured system of U.S.-owned spy satellites about five years previously.

Griff looked over at one of his aides, who made hand signals. "Keyhole? Looks like 18 minutes, and then we have to wait for two and a half."

"What's the current coverage?" She heard Griff swear as he fumbled with the remote.

"Two of the Mark-14s doing blanket coverage right now."

"One for business, one for pleasure."

"One for the regular work, and one for us. Great. Okay. We go with BWI, and see what happens. If we're too clever and there's nothing to this, we all go to bed late. If things get sticky, we shoot and scoot. I'll handle the tactical teams; you deal with Fisk as you see fit."

Doris snapped the phone closed, breaking the connection, and crammed it back into her coat pocket. The possibility of a firefight with a trained and experienced force sent a surge of adrenaline through her body.

She quickly reviewed what she knew about the three most recent attempts on Fisk's life. *Two car bombs and one close range shooter. Not very creative.* The encounters had been easily dealt with. Later investigation had uncovered circumstantial proof that somebody important had paid the would-be assassins to kill him and make it look like an accident.

Pausing to focus her thoughts, Doris closed the front of her coat and knotted the belt. Slipping her hands back into the warm pockets, she closed her eyes. The move was habit; she always felt better when fully wrapped in the black leather. The coat showed its age only in that it was out of style and cut for a man. It was both shelter and keepsake--a reminder of better days and a talisman of luck for the future.

Walking back to the middle of the plane, she found an unused workstation and sat down. Reaching for an interface jack, she grimaced as it slid in behind her right ear. Using the neural interface was uncomfortable, but necessary. The technology was still just a fad, but it was catching on. Doris began to assess her options as the jet changed course for Baltimore.

Monday
April 21, 2014
Cosmopolitan Systems, Inc.
Potomac Heights, Maryland
4:00 P.M. EDT

"I'd like to thank you all for coming. Please take a seat and we'll get started." Adjusting his tie, Bill Garrison looked down at the small control panel on the conference table. Touching a key, he adjusted the room's lighting.

A small red light on the phone flashed. He raised the slim receiver. "Garrison."

"Make it short," Griff said.

"Right." He hung up. Looking up, he saw the last attendee enter the room. She closed the door and walked to her seat.

"O-okay, before we get started, is there anyone who doesn't know why we're here?" The rhetorical question raised a few chuckles, breaking the ice. Garrison pulled back his chair and sat, glancing at the phone one last time.

"Mr. Fisk is still in the air, which is why I'm here. I know that everyone was expecting to hear from him, but hey, you know how it is." Smiling, he felt his confidence rising.

"It has been said that all nations rise and fall. The Cold War has been over for 25 years. New threats have emerged which should have united us. Instead, we find ourselves at the mercy of elected leaders who have divided and segregated us. They preyed on our fears in order to gain more power for themselves. It's been going on for so long that we, as a nation, have gotten used to it. It might already be too late to do anything about it, but we're obliged to try. What we started ten years ago, you are about to help us finish in the next 12 months."

He paused, scanning the room. The 16-person group was equally split between men and women, blacks, whites, and Asians. In the middle of the group, a Native American man appeared inscrutable as he took it all in. On the wall behind him, a voice-activated holographic projector lit up, showing a photo of Madeline Hill that had been taken at her inauguration just two years earlier. She beamed with pride.

"I know that Fisk would have liked to be here tonight," Garrison continued. "He would have congratulated you all on making it this far. He'd thank you for your time and effort. I can't hold a candle to the man, but I hope you will accept my own thanks. I don't think any of us ever expected to get involved in something like this.

"You all know the story. After the Argentine crash of 2008, it was only a matter of time before things caught up with us." On cue, the projector flashed a new picture showing a newspaper headline: "U.S. Debt Crisis Threatens World Economy."

Garrison rose from his chair and moved to stand behind it. "When she pulls this off, it will alter the course of our destiny, but it won't change all of the dark predictions. Settling with our foreign creditors is not going to be enough for us to clear the slate. If we really want our country to survive through the rest of this century and on into the next, we need to change the way our leaders look at the people who elected them. We need to change the way people look at politicians, too." Silently, the image behind him morphed into a magazine cover that asked, "What Are the Politics of Patriotism?"

"We could wait for these changes, but they might never come. That's why we're giving the whole mess a nudge in the right direction."

Around the room, several heads nodded. Some held more radical opinions about what needed to be done. Others felt that Fisk's plan went too far. All had their doubts about the outcome of the conspiracy.

Garrison began ticking off a series of well-known events as corresponding images flashed behind him. "In the last 40 years, we have seen Congress move to impeach two presidents. We have seen government troops used against our citizens. We have seen fraud and tampering at all levels of the federal election process. We have also seen the accumulation of the world's largest and most irresponsible government debt. This says nothing about the various antiterrorist wars we've been fighting in the last ten years. We could just wait. Our leaders might wake up in time to save us, but they might not. As I look around this room, I don't see anyone here who really thinks that this will happen."

Nobody spoke. Most of them had been members of Fisk's organization for at least five years.

Garrison steadied himself. "This president and her Congress have been a long time in coming. For the last decade, our organization has given a boost to every corrupt federal official that we've been able to reach. Without a doubt, the current administration is the most corrupt and self-serving that anyone has ever seen. All that remains is for them to play out the hand that we dealt them. They can't resist the forces that will compel them to resolve the national debt or to make their grab for ultimate power--a grab which we sincerely hope will fail."

Ten years of behind-the-scenes manipulation had resulted in the nation's first female president sweeping into office with solid congressional majorities in her favor. The House and Senate had been carefully groomed to be open to the issue of debt reduction so that she could achieve the public relations coup necessary to ensure her second term.

"If we're right, the President will be unable to resist the temptation to stay in power after her constitutionally allowed terms are up. When this happens, we will be faced with a new era of reforms or revolution."

Garrison licked his lips after making the prediction. Overhead, images of the previous three wars flashed by, mingled with newspaper headlines that told the tale of terrorism and conflict that had done so much damage to the world economy.

"Okay. Let's review committee assignments. We need to be done and out of here in five minutes." Touching a control on the tabletop, he looked to his left as a series of graphics lit up the wall.

Monday
April 21, 2014
21,000 Feet Over the Atlantic
4:13 P.M. EDT

Doris looked at the display once more. The model changed every three seconds as the program compiled and calculated each variable programmed into it. Mentally commanding the program to increase the simulation's variable range, she watched with relief as the numbers at the bottom of the screen flashed green.

"Phone: call Griff, now," she commanded.

Griff responded instantly. "Yeah?"

"Do you see it?" She closed her eyes as she waited for him to review her solution. It was quick and dirty, but she felt she could pull it off.

"We're looking at it now." He paused to speak to somebody out of range.

"Well?"

Griff choked on his anger as he saw the background plot from her sim.

"If you've got a better idea--" she prodded.

"I--" he began.

"Didn't think so. Check the margins. You've got my timetable. Better hurry." Stabbing the disconnect key, she cut all the datalinks to her workstation.

"Computer: reboot, and then dial this number. Unsecured line." Tapping Christopher's home phone number onto the workstation's keypad, she felt her adrenaline surge. Long-dormant job skills fed her intuition. In her mind's eye, the unseen enemy began to take shape. *It's a "he," and he works directly for her. This has nothing to do with Homeland Security. She's a control freak and she's not fond of men in general.*

She got to her feet as the workstation complied. *I have to give Griff*

49

credit. He's a jerk, but he isn't wrong very often. He was right about that missing SWAT team. He's right about a possible attempt on Fisk's life, too. I can feel it. He's wrong about Agency involvement. I can feel that, too. Two out of three.

Standing on the patio, Christopher admired the thickly forested hills. The sky was clear except for a few high wisps of clouds.

Turning, he looked at the fax in his hand. It had just come off the machine in his den. The letter signed by Preston Fisk meant more than just an end to his unemployment. It meant a fresh start.

The tall black man walked back into his apartment. Closing the sliding screen door behind him, he went into the living room to sit down. Collapsing on the long leather couch, he carefully put the fax on a nearby table.

"Oh, yeah." He was pleased to be going back to work.

Brushing crumbs from an earlier sandwich off his grey t-shirt, he checked his watch. The phone rang. Rising from the couch, he went to the kitchen. His running shoes squeaked on the gleaming linoleum. Scooping up the phone on the third ring, he leaned back against a cluttered counter.

"Hello."

"Mr. Christopher. Have you received our fax?" Doris' voice came through with a slight hiss.

"Yes, about five minutes ago." He straightened. Wiping his free hand on his shorts, he walked back to pick up the letter.

"Good. There's been a change. I need you to start work immediately."

He shrugged. "I don't see why not. Can you be more specific?"

"This isn't a secure line. I'm going to give you an address, and I want you to go there and pick up the limo that will be waiting."

Christopher jogged down the short hallway to his den. "Let me get something to write with."

51

"I'll give you 40 minutes to pick up the car."

Christopher raised a pen over a note pad. "Give it to me."

She rattled off an address, followed by a bay number and a six-digit code that would open a secured garage door. Christopher read it back. She hung up.

Leaning back in his chair, Christopher memorized the instructions and slid the page into a nearby shredder. Confident that he could make the deadline, he went to his bedroom to get dressed.

Monday
April 21, 2014
East Potomac Heliport
Washington, D.C.
4:22 P.M. EDT

"Got it. Give me a minute to clean it up." The radio operator glanced at his team leader.

"Play it for us now." SWAT Commander Lucas hooked his thumbs into the pockets of his urban camouflage pants.

The rear of the tactical van was crammed with state-of-the-art electronics. The team's coordinators could monitor anything from satellite and wireless phones to fax machines. It all could be handled by the single technician who now turned back to tap commands into a small keyboard. Behind Lucas, a shadowy figure checked his tie and straightened his cuffs. The recording came out through tiny speakers positioned around the van's interior.

"Hello."

"Mr. Christopher. Have you received our fax?"

"Yes, about five minutes ago."

"Good. There's been a change. I need you to start work immediately."

"I don't see why not. Can you be more specific?"

"This isn't a secure line. I'm going to give you an address, and I want you to go there and pick up the limo that will be waiting."

"Let me get something to write with."

"I'll give you 40 minutes to pick up the car."

"Give it to me."

"Run the address and see if we can't get somebody to head him off." Lucas turned to face his employer. A helicopter passed overhead, forcing everyone into momentary silence. "Whoever she is, she's on the ball. Using an unsecured line was a mistake, though. She's going to pay for that."

Stepping out of the shadows, Carl Metz ruffled his mustache with a crooked finger. "Bull. That's not a mistake that Fisk's people would make. She was trying to introduce a new variable into the situation."

"You think she's yanking our chain?" Lucas raised a dubious eyebrow.

Metz grimaced as he pulled out a cigarette case and lighter. "Fisk has presidential-grade protection. Check it out if you really want to. You might get lucky and pick up the driver. That unsecured call was no accident."

"Do you think--"

"Not unless she works for the people who compiled our sim. She's just doing her job."

"We don't have anyone in that area," the technician pronounced.

Lucas replied, "Run the address. Let's see what's there."

"It's a restaurant. A Greek joint called The Olive Leaf. I've been there before. Not bad," the tech commented, his hands staying busy.

Metz snorted as he lit his cigarette. "Told you. Still, you'd better get it staked out. I'd bet money that, whoever he is, he's new to their team. She probably sent him off just to screw with our sim."

Lucas turned to face Metz. "Don't tell me how to do my job. This isn't the Secret Service. Just shut up and watch. You'll get your money's worth. Now, put out that cigarette. The smoke is bad for the equipment." He fumed as he turned back to face the monitors.

The technician spoke quietly into a microphone, dispatching a single officer to the restaurant. Setting down the microphone, he began to update the simulation for the upcoming action.

Lucas ignored Metz as he confidently watched the graphics unfold on two screens. The simulation projected high odds that Fisk would be dead within three hours.

After half a century of struggling against the criminal influences that flourished in the District of Columbia, many of the D.C.P.D.'s precincts and units had been swallowed up by an unstoppable wave of corruption. Weak laws combined with an increasingly impotent court system forced many law enforcement professionals to choose between compromised ethics or certain death in the line of duty.

Lucas knew that he and his accomplices were operating as paid mercenaries. Still, he felt justified in defending the professional skill of his people. Their good standing with the press had vanished a decade ago, despite their own best efforts to remain true to an honored profession. The people taking part in this evening's operation no longer cared who they worked for.

Monday
April 21, 2014
Christopher's Apartment
Herndon, Virginia
4:23 P.M. EDT

Christopher had just gotten behind the wheel of his sportscar when the dashboard phone beeped. Looking at it, he hesitated. Checking his mirrors, he glanced around the underground parking area before picking up the receiver. He was alone.

"Hello?"

"It's Doris. There's a change in plans."

He wasn't surprised that she had his number. "I'm listening."

"I had to wait until you got to your car before we could talk on a secure line. I have a new address for you. The other one was a deception."

"No warehouse?" he guessed.

"It's a warehouse this time," she promised after giving him the new address.

"Security code?"

"Gloves. Break the back door window. Make it look like a B-and-E."

"Limo?"

"Yes. Key's are in the visor. Drive to the private ramp at Baltimore-Washington International. We should be on the ground ten minutes after you get there."

Christopher reached into the car's glove box for a pad and pen. "Say, if this is important, I know this guy who keeps his own heavy-duty limo. Full diplomat package. I can get it and still make your arrival if I go now."

"No more complications. We're pushing the envelope as it is. Bringing you in like this before you're fully briefed is an off-the-cuff move. I hope you're ready for a long night."

Christopher looked at the dashboard clock. "I've got to go if I'm going to make it there by the time you land."

"One last thing. Do you have your weapons permit on you?"

"Never leave home without it." He rolled his shoulders, feeling the bulge of the nine-millimeter pistol in his shoulder holster.

"Bring your submachine gun. Go back upstairs and get it now."

"How do you know I have a submachine gun?"

"The same way I know you don't fold your socks before you put them away," she quipped and hung up.

He shook his head.

Monday
April 21, 2014
East Potomac Heliport
Washington, D.C.
5:00 P.M. EDT

"Our people have confirmed it. They diverted to Baltimore," the technician announced.

Lucas turned to face his employer. "There you have it, Mr. Metz. All roads lead to the District of Columbia. Fisk's people will deplane him in Baltimore and drive him back to D.C., just as we thought."

"You're sure Fisk's helicopter is still down for maintenance?" Metz asked, putting out his cigarette in a cold cup of coffee.

"Look across the ramp. That's it over there, the one with the rotors off and belly hatch open. Trust me. It was all too easy to delay that mechanic. It's amazing what gets lost in the world of overnight shipping."

"There's no chance that he's going to call in a rental?"

"Nope. They're just as paranoid as you are."

Metz was satisfied. "I'll arrange for the first half of your payment to be brought in. The rest is up to you."

He reached into his coat pocket for a wireless phone. Flicking it open, he stroked the autodial key. When the phone connected, he turned his back on Lucas, speaking in hushed tones. "The package is in the pipe. Tell Pike to bring it." He cut the connection and put the phone away.

He could find no fault with the actions taken so far. After 22 years in the Secret Service, Metz had to admit that the D.C.P.D. was just as capable as it had ever been. *Not that easy to co-opt, either. It's taken me a year to get to this moment. Win or lose, the President will see that I can deliver the goods.*

He turned back to face Lucas. "The first half of your money is on its way. I'll be going just as soon as you've counted it."

"Our unit is at The Olive Leaf. No sign of a limo," the tech said.

Lucas stepped close to the console. "Run the address that the call went to. Let's see who she was talking to. They probably slipped an encrypted transmission past us to divert him."

"Gated community apartment. Herndon. My brother-in-law wanted to get into that place. They turned him down. Christopher, Apartment 12."

"Run him. Tickets, warrants, and priors."

Metz nodded when he saw that the tech was one step ahead of his boss.

"Class Two protection license. Concealed carry permits for three states. Automatic weapons cert and a chauffeur's license."

"What kind?" Metz asked.

"Diplomatic. That means he's on file with Homeland. You want it?"

"Check his registry. Let's see who he's working for."" Lucas bent over to scan the data stream. Metz waited silently.

"His last registered employment ended six months ago." The tech enlarged his display and shunted the feed to a pair of overhead monitors. "See this? The FBI gave him a clean slate after some court action."

"You think that's relevant?" Lucas challenged Metz.

"Not after six months. Let's step outside and let the man do his job." Carl wanted another cigarette, and he knew that he'd pushed his luck by lighting up in the van once. Stepping through the rear door, he walked down the folding stairs into the hangar that shielded the van from prying eyes. "Even if they pull him in to drive from Baltimore, it won't matter, as long as they stick to their usual pattern." He reached for his lighter. Fisk's people had been watched closely for the previous three months. Nothing had been left to chance.

Lucas tugged at his web gear as he came down the stairs behind Metz. "You're probably right. Besides, this isn't the first executive takedown we've done. Did you ever read about the Madison thing in the paper?"

"That was yours?" Metz dredged his memory for details.

"I was on the attack team. Didn't help him one bit to know we were coming." Lucas shook his head in grim recollection.

Metz took a deep drag on his cigarette, standing back to exhale.

"Yeah, well, that was four years ago. Times have changed. Fisk is better protected than your average congressman is, too. You're up against the A-list with him. How closely did you examine his profile?"

"Close enough to know that he's mortal. His protection is good under static conditions. The sims you provided showed us just how vulnerable he is when he's forced to be mobile over long distances, though. Your client has nothing to worry about. We always make our hits look like accidents or else gang-related. No police involvement, as advertised."

"Your pitch is good. My client will be glad to hear that you're so confident and detail oriented. Win or lose, I think you can expect to hear from us again."

Lucas shrugged. "Nothing in this life is certain. I thought I had a career in the military. I was wrong. You know what the difference is between what I do now versus what I did in the Army?"

Metz shrugged ambivalently.

"The Army expects you to keep the peace without hurting anyone."

"We should be landing at 5:45 or so. I've made arrangements to have a car pick us up at the private ramp." Standing in the aisle, Doris shouldered back into her coat. Fisk nodded, turning in his seat to face her.

"I just got off the phone with Griff. He explained the problem. He's not happy with the situation as regards Mr. Christopher, but I think he's just too angry to admit that he likes the unpredict--"

Doris brushed hair from her eyes. "Unpredictability is what we need right now. I can't escape the feeling that somebody is about to out-class us." She steeled herself to avoid any outward show of emotion. The admission was more than she would have made to anyone else. *'Out-classed' isn't the right word. It's a question of manpower. They have more people working on this than we do.*

"Griff says it could be one of the intelligence agencies. He didn't say the 'H' word, but if that's true, it gives us ten points up on our long-range assessment of Madeline. If she can make this work, she's got more than enough ambition to break all the rules when the time comes."

Doris put both hands into the pockets of her coat, favoring Fisk with a look of concern. *You talk about this as if it's not really your neck on the line. I sure would like to know what the 'real' you would do about all this.*

"President Hill will perform as you predicted. What bothers me is the here-and-now. The same woman you selected to execute our plan is now executing one of her own that may very well see you dead by the time she sits down to dinner."

"I hope she had an afternoon snack," Fisk said dryly.

"So do I." She turned to leave. The moment was hard for her, since she knew Fisk's flippancy wasn't real. There was a reason for his fearlessness.

Returning to her workstation, she thought, *You would have found a way to turn this around and use it against them. That's my job right now, and I know how much you hate it when I lose my focus.* She tried to put that thought out of her mind as she reached for the neural interface jack.

Grimly, she plugged herself back into the secured data net. Taking off her coat, she glanced at it, and draped it over the chair. Sliding into her chair, she wanted very much to believe in luck. *You'd also tell me it's foolish to treat this old thing like it's a good luck charm. Then again, you did ask me to keep it safe and give it back to you...*

Metz waited patiently for Lucas to finish scan-counting the money. Standing off to one side, he turned slowly to take in the dreary interior of the helicopter hangar. Chemical odors contrasted with the low lighting, reminding him of the wharves he had prowled in his youth. Roaming up and down the New Jersey shore, he had peered into the cargo holds of ships from all over the world. The sour tang of solvents and evaporated aviation fuel reminded Metz of his life that might have been. *Hard to believe that a college scholarship kept me from being a sailor.*

A folding table had been set up next to the tactical van. On the ground, an empty briefcase sat, lid open. Two of the team leader's trusted men used hand-held scanners to read the serial numbers and denominations off the stacked bills. The data was encoded on tiny strips of polymer alloy woven into the multi-colored cloth paper of each bill. The counting process took only a handful of minutes.

Metz walked over to the dark green sedan idling nearby. Tapping on the driver's side window, he glanced over his shoulder to see that the counting was still in progress. The car's window came down.

"You're done for tonight," he told the driver without making eye contact. Reaching into his coat pocket, he took out a manila envelope and handed it to the man. "Get out of here, and make sure to go some place public within the next half hour. Very public."

Without speaking, the slightly-built man took it and rolled up the window. Metz went back to the table as the courier drove off.

"Five hundred thousand dollars," one of the men announced.

"The machine doesn't lie. We'll send the other half out in the morning, as agreed."

Lucas appeared from the back of the van, tugging at his combat webbing. "We have FAA confirmation that Fisk's plane rerouted to Baltimore at the last minute. I'd love to be a fly on the wall when their security sweep comes up empty."

Metz wagged a finger in disapproval. "Sometimes we can be too clever for our own good."

Lucas wasn't impressed. "Clever is one thing, but this guy moves like he's keeping a secret. It's almost like he expects to be hit, you know."

Metz cocked his head to one side and shrugged. "It doesn't matter."

"It doesn't make you even a little curious?" asked one of the money counters.

His partner agreed. "Guys like him only hire that kind of protection when--"

"When they're afraid of guys like me," Metz cut in as he stared the man down.

Monday
April 21, 2014
General Aviation Ramp
Baltimore-Washington International Airport
Baltimore, Maryland
5:37 P.M. EDT

Christopher waited inside the limo on the edge of the turnway. The halogen lights on the ramp cast a stark white light over the concourse and taxiways. Christopher's vehicle was the only one in the pickup zone.

Rebuilt in 2009, this highly active portion of the airport had been altered to conform to new guidelines that established the General Aviation Division of the Federal Aviation Administration. The new office regulated the increasing numbers of private jet aircraft that crowded American skies.

Inside, a security guard looked up every few minutes, noting the lone car. From his kiosk, he had a commanding view of all entry and exit points. Jet engines roared as private and commercial flights took turns hurtling down the runways to blast into the night sky with a sudden roar and flash of running lights. The rhythm of take-offs and landings was of no interest to Christopher as he waited for his new employer to arrive.

I wonder if I'll get to meet the President? Getting the interview for this job had been surprisingly easy, although the session had been grueling in ways that had surprised him. Thinking of that made him think of Doris. *Probably not.*

Tapping his fingers on the steering wheel, he considered what he knew about Fisk. Checking his tie in the rearview mirror, he forced himself to remain relaxed. *The man's a high roller, to be sure. If he travels with this kind of security, he must be in pretty deep. Nope. Definitely no meeting the President for me.*

Six years as a professional bodyguard had sharpened his cynicism and paranoia, leaving him unimpressed with the rich and famous. The trappings of wealth and fame might attract others to follow or serve, but they did nothing for him beyond increasing his appreciation for the simple things in life.

The phone chirped for attention. He checked to make sure that the secured line indicator was lit, and then answered. "I'm here,"

"Take the car around to the diplomatic pickup," Doris ordered. She hung up.

Putting the phone down, Christopher checked to make sure his grey satchel was secured under his seat. It contained a compact automatic weapon. The permit was displayed on the dashboard next to a laminated copy of his chauffeur license and bodyguard certification. He started the engine and put the car in gear. *It's going to be a long night.*

Monday
April 21, 2014
General Aviation Ramp
Baltimore-Washington International Airport
Baltimore, Maryland
5:50 P.M. EDT

"We did what they wanted us to," Doris observed grimly.

"That's what it looks like," Griff replied.

She inspected the interior of the executive jet. Images from the holographic display she had been jacked into still burned in her mind. Behind her right ear, the concealed hookup tingled from prolonged use. Frustration over what she had seen made her even more tense.

Standing on the retracting staircase, she looked back into the aircraft. It was customary for her to be the first one out of the plane whenever she traveled with Fisk. Silence blanketed the cabin as the staffers began to realize that something was wrong. She held her phone up to one ear and loosened the belt on her coat with her free hand.

"It gets worse," Griff continued. "The primary tactical team has been taken out of play by what we think is a fake traffic jam."

"Secondary?"

Griff paused, double-checking. "Onsite. You can reach them on D channel. They're inside the concourse, roughly 200 meters from your position. Team leader confirms that the concourse is clean. It looks like the bad guys didn't think we had a backup team."

Doris nodded with cold certainty. "They planned for it. When we move Fisk, our tactical units will be out of synch. They know how we operate. They know our route system. We're in trouble."

She silently considered the situation. Whoever was coordinating the action was clearly operating on a level of complexity that Doris and her fellow protectors had not experienced before. In the course of his political life, Fisk had been the target of political opponents and other power brokers. The occasional threat to his life was taken in stride, as it would have been for any other member of the Washington elite.

"Hold." Griff paused to listen to one of his subordinates. "That's just great. We've got police cruisers coming up to our front door and the loading dock. Looks like a raid."

"Is Garrison out of the building?"

"Long since. He's on his way to that special function."

"I'll handle things on this end."

"Good. Be sure to phone him at the prearranged time. I think he'll need moral support. I'm taking Cosmo offline."

Both operatives hung up at the same time.

Monday
April 21, 2014
Diplomatic Terminal
Baltimore-Washington International Airport
Baltimore, Maryland
5:55 P.M. EDT

Christopher approached the entrance to the secured terminal. The guard at the gate waved him through.

Built in 2010, the terminal was located between the private and commercial parts of the busy airport. It was one of six such facilities on the East Coast. Diplomats and other foreign dignitaries shared the enclosed space with U.S. government officials and other important people. Passengers and their cargos were screened for hazards and kept safe inside the 500,000-square-foot facility, which could handle both large and small jets. Concerns about terrorism over the preceding decade had resulted in similar modifications being made to many of the nation's airports.

Christopher felt like a bug under a microscope as he drove across the vast expanse of indoor pavement. Overhead, dozens of closed-circuit cameras watched his every move as he approached Fisk's jet.

The aircraft was parked inside a large yellow rectangle. Its engines were shut down. Orange lines on the harshly lit pavement indicated where vehicles were permitted. Christopher moved forward slowly, heading for the pickup zone that was clearly marked near the doors to a VIP lounge.

Doris approached him as the car came to a stop. Each determined stride she took toward the car was deliberate and filled with urgency. *Very unhappy. That woman could hurt somebody.*

She met him just as he swung the door open. Despite his advantage in height, he was compelled to defer to her intensity.

Doris halted three paces away. "I don't have time for a long explanation. We have reason to believe that somebody is making a play for Mr. Fisk. This could be a kidnapping, or worse." When she saw that he was waiting for her to continue, she nodded approvingly.

"You will take Mr. Fisk to his home in Maryland. Choose your own route. Give yourself plenty of room to maneuver at all times. The car is equipped with an encrypted homing beacon. We change it every time we transport. It's got a four kilometer range, so we'll be able to track your movements to some degree."

"What--"

"Somebody has intimate knowledge of our methods. I need you to act as a nonvariable catalyst."

Christopher nodded. "Sim." He'd seen the computer models at a trade show last year.

"Glad to see that you've done your homework. Just take Mr. Fisk to his house. You'll find the address in the navigator. Our tactical teams will catch up to you as fast as they can. Here's the authorization code for the navigator." Doris reached into a coat pocket and handed him a small slip of paper.

He scanned it. The limo's onboard computer held up-to-date road maps and travel directions that he could access as he drove. Satisfied that he had committed the details to memory, Christopher handed the paper back to her.

Doris took it without saying a word. *Smart. Very smart.* She made a hand signal. There was movement inside the lounge. Two men casually walked out ahead of Fisk. Christopher watched the men as they walked three paces ahead of their employer. Their measured strides and serious expressions told him they were bodyguards. Each man carried a conspicuous black satchel slung over one arm. *Geez, is that what I look like?*

His trained eye made out the chunky outlines of body armor underneath each guard's sport coat. Neither man wore sunglasses or a tie. *Nothing to restrain movement or obstruct vision. These guys are the real deal.*

Fisk wore an expensive full-length grey wool trenchcoat. He carried his briefcase loosely. Christopher recognized him from years of media exposure. He took note of the man's long stride and outward confidence. *Suppose I should take that as a good sign.* His protectors orbited as Fisk approached the limousine.

"You would be Mr. Christopher." Fisk stopped alongside the vehicle, offering his hand to the taller man. Christopher shook it out of reflex, surprised by the swift, confident grip.

"Yes, sir. I'm sorry we couldn't meet under better circumstances."

"Don't worry about it. My guardian angel has everything under control." Turning, he gave Doris a wink and a nod.

"I wouldn't doubt it." Christopher stepped back. Reaching into the open driver's side door, he triggered the passenger door locks. "We should get moving." From what he had seen on television, Fisk wasn't the kind of man who stood around chatting. *It's better to make an all-business first impression.*

"Very good." Fisk moved toward the passenger door as Christopher went to open it for him. "That's all right. I've been opening my own car doors for a few years now."

"Sorry." Christopher pulled back.

"We'll cover the etiquette protocols later," Doris said so that everyone could hear. *If that's the worst thing you do tonight, you'll do all right.*

Fisk slid into the big car.

Christopher looked at Doris, an unspoken question furrowing his brow.

She favored him with an appraising look. *Let's see what you've got. I need to know just how useful you're going to be.*

Choosing to accept the look as a challenge, he closed the door. Glancing at the two protectors as he swung into the driver's seat, he asked, "You guys sure you don't want to come along?" *If something is going on...*

"The fastest way to attract the media is to make an open show of protection," Doris explained. *You're taking this seriously. I like that.*

A portion of Fisk's protection came from his well-planned media image. People like Fisk didn't see anyone without an appointment. This lack of public contact, combined with the seldom-seen envelope of protectors that surrounded such people of privilege, served to keep most threats at bay. The media would quickly notice anyone in such a powerful position who showed off their bodyguards in public. This gave the impression that nothing less than a truly premeditated effort stood a chance of threatening such people. Fisk's protectors relied on that.

"Can't blame a guy for trying," Christopher muttered as he closed the door.

Putting his worries out of his mind, he fastened his seatbelt. Turning, he looked into the back of the limo. Fisk nodded as he finished dialing his access code into a raised handset. Christopher backed the car away from the private jet. Reflexively, he raised the privacy shield that separated driver and passenger compartments. Within seconds, he was away from the secured hangar.

Satisfied, Doris followed the bodyguards back into the lounge. "Contact?" she asked a woman who sat nearby with a pair of open laptop computers.

"Two sweepers on the General Aviation ramp. Four more inside the terminal. Six waiting in baggage control."

"They would have had us," one of the guards said, giving Doris an appreciative nod.

"Primary tactical?" Doris sat down next to the woman.

"Here. Secondary is moving to link up with the car on the Interstate. Have a look." Turning one of the laptops so that Doris could read the display, the specialist stayed busy with her work.

Pursing her lips, Doris stroked a key on the laptop to divide the display. The location plot on Fisk's limo and the site map of the General Aviation terminal ran side by side. The phone in her pocket beeped for her attention. She flipped it open and perched it on her shoulder. "Yes?"

"You blew their sim. They've got to be mad." Griff and his ulcer were both relieved.

"Mm." She continued working the keyboard.

"You just make sure that the secondary tactical merges with Fisk in traffic. I'm going to clean the mess up on this end."

"Let them go. They probably have the air marshals waiting in the wings. This is their turf. As long as they don't get in our way--" She shook her head.

The General Aviation Division had been created in the aftermath of several failed terrorist actions. As concerns over the use of private aircraft as tools of terror or subversion grew, the FAA had been granted expanded authority through the Department of Homeland Security.

"No. They'll backtrack on us. We need to stop them cold."

The other woman nudged Doris. "Contact. Perimeter reports two sweepers coming our way."

Doris leaned over to look at the other computer display. "They're coming. Two. I'm going to take them out," she told Griff.

"Don't. The last thing we need is a firefight. I know you want to punish--"

Folding her phone, she looked up at the two bodyguards. "Merge with perimeter, take out the sweepers, and then meet me at the van."

Monday
April 21, 2014
Greenspan Lounge
Treasury Building
Washington, D.C.
7:29 P.M. EDT

Nestled in the warm softness of a high-backed leather chair, President Hill tried to avoid looking directly at her aides and advisors. They had long since learned to be silent when she was in a bad mood. Across the room, images on the television changed.

"Television, volume six." Recognizing her voice, the holographic television's computer raised the volume.

The cheerful blonde correspondent spoke straight at the camera. "While tonight's final meeting of the board of directors for the National Rifleman's Association won't come as a surprise to anyone in the national media, many of its supporters across the nation are taking it hard. Dissolution of the NRA was not expected until after the May 15th vote in the House of Representatives to try, once again, to repeal the law restoring the rights of convicted felons to vote in state and national elections."

The image on the screen became more panoramic, revealing an ivy-covered brick building with lighted windows. "It's official, though. After nearly two years of fighting scandal and financial mismanagement by a succession of leaders, the National Rifleman's Association is dead."

The reporter's teeth flashed white in what Madeline Hill felt was justifiable satisfaction. *One more stumbling block gone. If I thought I could get away with it...How many of you would support me if I told you I wanted to...*

The reporter continued with a jerk of her thumb. "Inside their headquarters, behind me, the board and a select gathering of high-paying contributors are wrapping up their closing ceremonies. The media has been barred from these final moments 'for a variety of reasons', according to Association spokespersons."

Moving her eyes around the room, Madeline pressed her lips together so that she would not betray any hint of emotion to the assembled people. *Waiting for my reaction. Good.*

"While many Americans are saddened by the loss of this once-powerful pro-gun lobby, other comments are streaming into news rooms all over the country, spelling out in no uncertain terms their satisfaction with the NRA's departure from the political scene. Many of those responding to this news, made public only a few hours ago, have been ordinary citizens. We have not heard anything yet from--"

"Off," Madeline commanded in a barely audible voice.

The entourage began to stir, awaiting the reaction of their president.

Madeline turned as a Secret Service woman offered her a wireless phone. "It's time," the agent said politely.

Taking the phone, Madeline adjusted her short blonde curls with her other hand. Striking the autodial key, she waited for the secured connection to ring.

Fisk spoke after the second ring. "Hello, Madeline. How are you?"

"I'm doing very well. I trust the flight wasn't too tedious?" she purred. It was all she could do to hide her anticipation.

"Madrid is nice this time of year," Fisk replied, as if he had no worries.

"I was told there were car bombings. The Basques are at it again." After nearly a decade of silence, the Basque separatist movement in Spain had recently come back to life.

"Ramirez mentioned that they were responding to more police crackdowns. By the way, we hit a home run. Your proposal has been accepted. I'll have a full briefing for you in the morning." His voice was momentarily blocked by static.

Madeline took a deep breath as she plunged into the scripted part of her conversation. "I'm glad to hear that. I need to see you now. Can you come to Treasury?"

"My report isn't ready. I need some time to go over it with my people."

Madeline closed her eyes, sighing theatrically. Luring him into the trap demanded her best acting. Traffic noises bled through as Fisk failed to respond.

"This isn't about your report. It's Mr. Brown. Again. He's made me quite upset. Somehow, he found out about my presentation."

"Has he seen it, or does he just know about it?" He sounded thoughtful.

"I don't know how he found out. He feels undermined. I went over to talk with him directly, but he's gone home," she lied, audibly distressed. Pausing to look around the room, Madeline was pleased to see everyone making a show of being interested in other things.

"He hasn't actually seen the presentation?"

"No, but he knows about it."

"Is it really that important to you? Now that we have a deal with Ramirez, we can afford to be lenient--"

Madeline resisted the urge to make it a command. "Please. I'll be down on the secured level. It's been a long day and--"

"As you wish," Fisk acceded graciously.

"Thank you." Her smile was genuine as she handed the phone back to the agent. *He knows. I can feel it.*

Monday
April 21, 2014
Capitol Hill
Washington, D.C.
7:31 P.M. EDT

Relaxing in the back seat of his limo as it rolled down Massachusetts Avenue, Fisk took a moment to look out at the darkening sky. Streetlights and brightly lit signs accentuated the city's nocturnal ambience. *Interesting how her call came after I left the airport.*

"I appreciate the call, Mr. Speaker. I know that the President likes your attention to detail. As a matter of fact, I'm on my way to see her now. I'll be sure to mention that we spoke."

"She called you at this time of night?" Speaker of the House Roger Langsford asked.

He nodded. "Yes. I'm just a consultant, you know. I don't get paid if I don't consult."

Fisk's protectors agreed that Madeline's request was a ploy to keep him from reaching the safety of his home in Maryland. *They have something planned.*

"The way I hear it, she's kept you busy with Treasury issues. My people are speculating that your legal team is developing a debt resolution package."

Fisk silently nodded again. Speaker Langsford wasn't known for mincing words. "That's not something I can talk about. If the President's office comes up with anything like that, you can bet the media will be all over it."

"I've seen the Secretary's report. Mr. Brown expects that we'll be forced into negotiations within a year. I don't have to tell you that there are a lot of people in both houses who would want a piece of that action."

Fisk thought, *Of course. If she pulls it off, she'd better share the credit.*

Through a series of carefully coordinated leaks, Fisk had let it be known that President Hill was working on a plan to appease the government's creditors. After 50 years of increased leveraging against a constantly growing economy, the mounting national debt was about to become unmanageable. Each succeeding president had submitted budgets to Congress that relied on unending future growth. Four decades of increasing prosperity had been eroded by more than ten years of terrorist attacks and a series of costly, though successful, wars.

Using his position as the country's best known political strategist, the conspirators had succeeded in maneuvering Congress into a decade-long spending spree, despite the obvious need for debt management. The goal had been to entice both Congress and each president to accelerate the accrual of debt, forcing them to settle the issue much sooner than most would have liked. The combination was finally creating a political climate that was amenable to dealing with the problem.

Sensing that the era of unimpeded tax revenues was about to pass, both houses of Congress now embraced the cause of debt reduction. Taking advantage of heightened public concern, Fisk had convinced many of the country's long-time political leaders that the issue would improve their standing with the electorate.

"I understand. When we pull this off, there will be more than enough credit to go around. Everyone in your party who sits in Congress when the ink hits the paper won't have to worry about re-election ever again."

Langsford sighed. "When you say it, it sounds so real. I'm just hoping that she doesn't blow it. That maverick she has running Treasury--"

"Brown won't be a problem, Every time he gets up in front of the press to crusade for debt reduction, the President's approval numbers go up. I'm covering all the bases."

The lie was trivial. Secretary Andrew Brown had come into office compliant. *The job's changed him. We should have recruited him when we had the chance.*

Langsford seemed satisfied. "Can you give me a sense of how things stand with the Senate in regards to the national ID card bill?"

The Speaker only believed in what he controlled. Senate activities, being out of his control, bothered him a lot.

National identification cards were still controversial. Enacted under the previous administration, they had been hailed by many as the answer to terrorism and subversion. Federal law enforcement leaders had become increasingly convinced that there was only one way to stem the growing capability of modern criminals. Long-term efforts by established political parties and lobby groups were finally beginning to pay off. Public opinion was being swayed in their favor. Legislation now before the Senate would take the program one step further. It was only a matter of time before the National Citizens' Registry was put into effect.

Fisk rummaged in his briefcase with one hand, and then pulled out a small notebook and turned on an overhead light. "Opposition is weak, but determined. They're in the minority. The one to watch out for is Theo Crantz. He's walked all over us before, and I think he'd like to do it again, if you know what I mean." *Good thing we can buy him. This time.*

"Crantz. He's the one who pulled the Commerce Coalition together at the last minute, isn't he?"

Conservative opposition in Congress had been eroding over the last decade, and it showed no signs of turning around. Despite their loss of power, a small number of the staunchest conservatives in both the House and Senate still had a few tricks up their sleeves.

"That's him." Fisk had been briefed on the Speaker's strategy two hours before he landed. *It's a good play, and it might have worked, even without my insurance.*

Langsford shifted the phone to his other hand. "I hope you have something good in your hip pocket to roll him with. I don't think you'll be disappointed, though I can't take credit for this one."

"Really?" Fisk asked, feigning ignorance. He was impressed that Langsford was willing to give credit where it was due. *Sometimes you actually make me want to believe in you.* In the distance, the Capitol dome was just dropping out of sight.

"Crantz also works for the Wilderness Group. It looks like he's fishing for cleanup dollars to keep his lobby's interests in the East going."

Fisk reached up to switch off the light. He was familiar with the popular movement to clean up industrially poisoned lands on the East Coast. *Be interesting to see if they can do it.*

The Speaker continued, "If we give him a two year tap on something like a billion dollars, and he gives us the right concessions, we can get the votes we need from the minority," the Speaker muttered with mild distaste. Conservative interest in environmental issues had grown since the start of the new century. If the trend continued, they would dominate the issue during the next presidential election.

Fisk put his notepad away. "Let me get my people to fax you some numbers. Madeline wants to be able to sign the Citizen Registry bill within the next four months. I think she'll give us both a little extra leeway if we can make her happy."

"You still think we might face real competition in November?" Though not up for re-election, the Speaker was sensitive to the need to keep his party's clear majority as strong as possible. "We've got the largest majority in history. In both houses. I can't think of a better reason to push for more. Madeline could be the only president in history to ever sit two terms with a veto-proof Congress. I kind of like the idea of retiring on a high note like that."

Fisk smiled. *Two more months, and I'm done. Wonder if they'll ever pick up on the real reason I've spent all these years--* "It would be quite a feat, if it can be managed."

"Amen to that. Okay, I'll get your fax in the morning?"

"Absolutely. Just don't get wound up. The most our good will is going to get us is the chance to set one or two targets for the new year."

As the President's chief political advisor, Fisk was very familiar with the give-and-take relationship that existed between himself, her party leaders, and the woman herself. He smiled as he recalled the last fight that Madeline had instigated with her party-faithful over what legislation would or wouldn't be championed in the media spotlight. *I need you to be afraid of her for just a few more years Mr. Speaker. Just in case things go wrong, and I'm somehow cut out of the picture.*

"We have a problem," a tiny voice said in Fisk's ear. The comm implant linking him to his unseen organization broadcast the voice flawlessly into his ear.

Fisk looked up as a red indicator light winked on just above his head. He leaned forward to see Christopher eyeing the rearview mirror. "Excuse me, Mr. Speaker. I've got an urgent incoming call."

"Quite all right. No peace for the wicked, eh?"

"Not for this wicked one," Fisk chuckled as Langsford hung up.

"What have we got?" The comm implant had been with him for so long that he'd gotten used to it. It didn't occur to him that his new driver would find his "thinking out loud" unusual.

Christopher lowered the privacy shield. "Accident ahead." Slowing the limo, he carefully scanned the traffic around him. Taking one hand off the wheel, he queried the navigator. The tiny screen projected details of the accident.

"How far are we from Treasury?" Something in Fisk's memory stirred, clamoring for recognition. Something about the situation was familiar, although his rational mind wasn't sure why. *It's happening again. What am I trying to remember?*

"I'd say about two miles," Christopher replied.

"You are currently two and a quarter miles from Treasury. Overwatch reports primary and secondary tactical are still five minutes out. We have a helicopter inbound. It's our military bird. You should be seeing a searchlight any second now."

Fisk nodded at the unseen advisor's comment. "That's a Phase Two asset. What's wrong with the civilian helo?"

"Huh?" asked Christopher, confused.

"Maintenance foul-up. Doris thinks it may have been a deliberate act of sabotage."

"What do you think?"

The tiny voice hesitated. "Me? I don't know. Cosmo is off-line so I can't update my sim. Cops are crawling all over the place. My gut tells me that it wasn't an accident."

"About what? The accident? I can't tell for sure yet. It's got to be something pretty nasty to tie traffic up like this," Christopher responded.

Fisk stroked his chin, turning away from the window. He visualized the police cruisers parked near both the front and rear doors to Cosmopolitan Systems. *I'm still amazed that we could keep our communications hub in the same location for more than ten years. Probably going to have to sell the company now. Too bad.*

"Anything else?"

"Yeah. Wait one."

Christopher shrugged. "No. Why? What do you see?"

The voice in Fisk's ear came back. "We're showing a lot of radio traffic on unofficial bands. Our eyes in the sky are making out possible IR tracks on snipers. Tell your driver to slow down so that we can take a closer look. Primary tactical is now three minutes out."

"Christopher, slow us down. My people need time to check this out."

He eyed Fisk through the rearview mirror, suspicion on his face. "Have you been talking to someone else? How? I saw you hang up the phone." *Have you got a radio back there that I don't know about?*

"Let's just concentrate on dodging this accident thing. I'll tell you everything you want to know after we get done with Treasury." Rubbing his jaw, he considered the implant. *Too late to explain. I'll have to recruit him tonight. That's all there is to it.*

The conspiracy relied on the discretion of its members. "Hiding in plain sight" was only possible through cautious recruitment of like-minded persons. Few of the conspirators had been recruited hastily. People from a wide variety of backgrounds participated in the overall plan Fisk orchestrated, mostly through the many legitimate businesses that the conspirators ran to finance their machinations. Usually, recruitment would only result after weeks of investigation, interaction, and observation.

"Sounds fine by me. We're going to be late, though. I can tell you that right now." Christopher slowed the big car to a crawl. Up ahead, flashing lights could be seen. Flares on the road backlit passing vehicles in garish red.

Fisk considered fastening his seatbelt.

"Our helo is on site," the unseen protector told Fisk.

A matte-black helicopter ghosted through the darkness, rotors throbbing in the night air as the insectoid shape circled overhead. Fisk leaned over to a side window, craning his neck as the faraway advisor briefed him. "Doris wants us to tell you that the helo has a full IR and thermal package. Give him a minute, and the pilot will scan the area. We should know if there's going to be any trouble in just a few seconds."

"How many snipers?" Fisk asked without thinking. *I've got two tactical units following me, so whoever you are, you'll need two layers to your envelope to catch me.* As alien as the circumstance was to him, something in the back of his mind grasped the reality of his situation.

"Six," the implant told him.

"What?" Christopher asked as he squinted over his steering wheel, following the chopper's movements. *Where did that thing come from?* Traffic crawled forward, closer to the accident site.

"Somebody bought the local SWAT, and now they're getting ready to ambush me," Fisk said.

Madeline Hill's ambition, coupled with her unflinching nerve, had been just what Fisk and his backers were looking for. Her ardent desire to be rid of Fisk and what she believed was his overshadowing influence gave her all the reason she needed to pursue his destruction.

"Overwatch reports that secondary tactical is two minutes out. Primary has just been stuck in traffic." The tiny voice sighed.

"We're already moving as slow as we can," Fisk assured him.

Christopher eyed Fisk in the rearview mirror.

The voice in Fisk's ear skipped a beat. "Sir, I don't think we're going to--"

"I know," Fisk said softly, switching his gaze to the accident scene ahead. "It'll be okay. You guys are the best in the business. You can handle it." *They must really think they're going to drop the ball.*

Overhead, the circling chopper played its belly-mounted search light over the ground below. The glare from the flashing lights of the emergency vehicles washed over the body of the helicopter.

Fisk noted with some satisfaction that the craft had no markings of any kind. *If that thing shows up on the late news, the conspiracy buffs will have a field day with it.* Reflecting on the irony of the moment, he smirked. *That's why they call it a conspiracy. Because nobody else knows about it.*

"Six positions confirmed," a new voice drawled through background static.

That would be the pilot. "Definitely shooters?" The car lurched as Christopher came to a stop. Ahead, police officers gathered around an older-model car, arguing with the driver.

"Affirmative. They're not very well protected, though. Tactical can take them out." The pilot sounded confident.

Fisk nodded. *Not going to make it in time.* "How long?" he asked, careful to keep his voice crisp and stoic.

"Ninety seconds. I can see them from here."

"We can't wait that long." He scanned the scene for more details. *Let's see what we've got here.*

A tanker truck lay on its side just ahead, closing two lanes of traffic. The hull of the tank was wrinkled where the rig had jackknifed into the pavement. The truck's cab lay crushed and smoldering amidst the remains of a luxury sedan that had been knocked over the guard rail and centerline greenery. Police cars formed the borders of an obvious funnel. *Nice gauntlet.*

Traffic inched forward, one car at a time, guided through the debris by police and fire officials waving flashlights.

Fisk said, thinking aloud, "We've got enough armor to stop rifle bullets, don't we?"

Christopher nodded as he continued to watch. *Any good sniper would know that. Something's wrong here.* "Hey, check out the bread van up on the left. Something about it seems out of place."

Fisk looked through the windshield. A van was high-centered on the median. The police and fire vehicles were parked well away from it. He flinched visibly as another memory fragment surfaced. *Something about this seems familiar.*

"Air unit, check out the bakery van to my left."

Christopher watched Fisk intently, turning back around as the chopper overflew the van. *He's got to have a hidden comm unit.*

The helicopter hovered over the van, playing its bright search light over the vehicle. "Four thermals. Oh, man. I'm scanning antitank."

Fisk raised his eyebrows. On the ground, the police were just finishing with the sedan and its difficult driver. Several of them turned their attention to the prowling helicopter.

"Antitank?" His heart sank. Even as he despaired, something inside him woke up. He marveled at how his understanding of life-threatening activities improved in moments of great stress. It was as if he were drawing on knowledge that he didn't know he had.

"If I was armed, we could ruin their day," the pilot said apologetically.

"You're not?" He arched an eyebrow in wonder. The surge of terror he felt was replaced by a hot flash, followed by a very out of place thought. *Madeline, my dear, if it was anybody else but me in this car, you'd be doing very well.* The boast felt both right and wrong.

"Sorry. We took delivery on this bird three days ago, and we're still bringing her up to speed. I was warming her up when the call came in. I'll bet you the police are wondering--"

"Overwatch? Tell me you've got something in your back pocket."

A breathless female voice came on channel. "We're building the sim right now. We've enhanced the thermal from the chopper. It really is an antitank missile. An old Russian job by the looks of it. You'll be in their arc of fire once you move another 16 feet."

This reliance on computer-based problem solving has got to go. He had repeatedly voiced his disapproval of the practice. While he understood that sims allowed his small detachment of protectors to respond efficiently, he didn't like the idea that his life was being so coldly broken down and analyzed.

Do it now. Take away their initiative. Fisk licked his lips and leaned forward to make himself heard. He didn't know what the "it" was. Following his instincts, he said, "Christopher, there's some kind of antitank weapon in the bakery van. The helicopter can see it with its thermal imager. If we move forward, we'll be in its line of fire."

He waited for the driver to make the connection. *Definitely going to have some explaining to do later on.* The next car in line rolled slowly forward.

"Somebody needs to talk to you about your choice of enemies," Christopher snapped, putting the car in neutral. With some effort, he reached under his seat, pulling out his satchel. *Might have to talk about a few other things, too.*

"Let's just get past this, and I'll answer all your questions."

"We can run it. They might not be able to hit a moving target."

"Wait a second." Fisk shook off a mild wave of dizziness.

The voice in his ear broke his concentration. "Secondary is now 60 seconds. Just stay where you are. We're coming."

Fisk tapped on the retracted privacy shield.

Christopher turned his head. "Yeah? What is it?"

Fisk pointed at the tanker. "I think the idea is to set off the tanker.

The signature of the explosives in the warhead will be lost in the petroleum residue. They won't even have to fudge to the investigators or doctor any reports. It'll look like the tanker cooked off on its own." *How did I figure that out?*

Christopher traced a mental line between the van and the tanker truck. *Use a missile to hedge your bets. Miss the limo, hit the tanker.*

The next car in line pulled ahead, slowing to allow the officers to talk with its driver. Fisk watched as a beefy cop with sergeant's stripes gestured at the tanker with his flashlight, his face tilted down to the driver's window. Behind him, two junior officers were watching the limo, whispering to each other.

Following the sarge's lead, he guessed. The observation made him go cold. "Christopher. How do you feel about shooting policemen?"

Several officers could be seen moving to their cruisers, each keeping a careful watch on the helicopter. A wind-blown patrolwoman plucked a microphone from the dashboard of her car. As she spoke into it, her gaze followed the circling aircraft.

They're wondering if it belongs to them, Fisk speculated.

"Shooting a cop? Are you kidding? No way." Squirming in his seat, Christopher began to wonder. *What have you gotten yourself into?*

The tiny voice in Fisk's ear was grim but determined. "Stay in the car. Tactical is onsite. They should be in your field of view any second."

Ahead of them, the sergeant straightened. All eyes now turned to focus on the limo, idling just a few feet away.

Fisk fidgeted with his seatbelt. "Suppose I tell you that these are dirty cops. They've been paid by a very powerful person to kill me." As he struggled to explain, his mind raged in turmoil. *What am I trying to remember? This isn't a familiar situation, but somehow, I feel... in control.* Memory fragments danced just out of reach in the back of his mind.

Christopher put his hands on the steering wheel, bracing himself. "Explain it to me."

Fisk watched the rearview mirror as emotions played across the driver's face. Coming up from behind, a group of dark-clad men jogged through the stalled traffic. Fisk's subconscious mind acknowledged the arrival of his bodyguards. Satisfied, his emotional torment decreased.

No longer so bold and confident, he began to accept the possibility of his own death. *We're so close to having everything in place,* he fretted. *I just hope it's enough.*

The sergeant played his flashlight over the limo's license plate, and impatiently waved the vehicle forward. The two junior officers stepped away, ready to flank either side of the big car.

Fisk opened his mouth to speak.

Christopher placed the car in gear and nudged the accelerator, coaxing the limo forward. His free hand fell to the clasp on the grey satchel. Fisk's mouth went dry.

"Tactical commander reports he is under fire," the tiny voice in his ear breathed.

Fisk turned to look behind the car. Three bodyguards lay on the ground just two car lengths short of the limo. "They're down," he said dumbly. Nearby motorists were gawking at the dead men. Someone honked. *Somebody has definitely done their homework.*

Christopher triggered the electric window controls. The driver's side window slid down into the door. Fisk turned to watch the bakery van.

His voice warped by static, the pilot exclaimed, "They had shooters hidden under IR suppression camo tarps. Tactical is down."

The police sergeant approached the limo casually, shining his flashlight deliberately into Christopher's eyes. "Pull forward, please. Stay in the center lane." His free hand reached for his gun.

Fisk watched, accepting, as the rear doors of the bread van swung open. In his ear, the Overwatch advisor had new instructions.

"Look around. Their shooters are busy with our people now. Get ready to open the car door. I'm going talk you through the escape and evasion plan."

Fisk easily made out the two-man firing team and their tripod mounted missile. Time slowed. He recognized the growing brightness around the van. *Backwash from the missile launch,* he decided. The van lit up in the glow of the helicopter's searchlight.

"It's okay," he said softly.

"Get out of the car! Do it, now!" The sergeant looked up, shielding his eyes against the intense glare. High winds rocked the limo, throwing up dust and road grit.

"What's going on?" the voice on the comm asked.

Fisk closed his eyes. *I'm dead.*

The missile team had realized that their prey wasn't going to cooperate. The trap had been laid with just such an eventuality in mind. Ignoring the placement of their own people, they fired the missile at the truck. The missile would have just enough time to arm before striking the aluminum skin of the tank.

Christopher drew his weapon from the satchel. Time slowed further. A fast-moving shape came down from above, obscuring his view of the van.

"They're going to set off the tanker," the pilot declared. Acting out of loyalty and instinct, the former military pilot shoved both control sticks forward. Falling out of the night sky, he put his sleek antiballistic-composite chopper directly in the path of the oncoming rocket. The missile slammed into the rear body panels, punching straight through the lightweight airframe as it strained to reach its minimum flight distance.

The missile cleared the helicopter's ruptured hull, veering off course and slamming into the pavement.

Christopher pointed his compact submachine gun at the police sergeant, charging it in one smooth motion. As the chopper exploded, he fired a three-round burst into the sergeant's face. High-velocity nine-millimeter rounds tore the man's head off. The decapitated corpse staggered, wreathed in a bloody mist. The body fell over Christopher's door, shielding him from the shower of hot metal and composites that ricocheted off the limo's armored exterior. The dead man flopped to the ground, leaving a wide crimson smear on the side of the car.

Without thinking, Christopher stomped on the accelerator. The limo lunged forward as he dropped the smoking weapon to the seat.

Shouts of anger and screams of pain pierced the night. The explosion had thrown the bread van over the centerline barrier and into the path of six lanes of on-rushing traffic. Crumpling metal and breaking glass, underscored by the squealing tires and backlit with fiery wreckage, gave the scene a feeling of unreality.

Barreling through a staggered line of police officers, the unwieldy vehicle sideswiped an ambulance as Christopher struggled to control it.

Amazed, Fisk remained silent as the car rocked through a series of high-speed turns. Pressed back into the seat, his gaze followed the streamers of gore as they left thin red tracks along the length of the limo's passenger windows. *That could have been me.* He imagined the scene--the charred interior of the limousine, silent, except for the slow, steady drip of his own viscera as it gathered slowly on the car's floor.

The tiny voice in his ear strained to keep from shouting. "Mr. Fisk?"

Still enthralled by the grizzly rain sleeting off the window, he didn't answer.

"Mr. Fisk? Do we have him on another channel? I'm not getting anything here."

"I'm okay." Without thinking, he clenched his jaw to turn off the comm implant.

Christopher slewed the car hard around slower traffic. The phone bleated for attention six times before he was able to answer it.

"He's okay. I think he's just in shock." Stuffing the phone into the crook of his neck, he put both hands back on the wheel.

"What's your situation?" Doris demanded.

Christopher looked at the rearview mirrors. "No tails. Oops. Scratch that. Two police cruisers, gaining fast." In the small slice of mirror, flashing red and blue lights closed in from behind.

"Take the next off-ramp."

"Potomac Heights, coming up on my right." He tapped the brakes, skidding around a bus. The bus driver laid on his horn as the big car snaked into the turn lane. Sparks flew from the limo's undercarriage as it bottomed out on the pavement.

"You'll see a red sportscar coming up on your left as you merge."

Hauling the limo through the off-ramp's curve, Christopher let the phone fall into his lap as he wrestled with the steering wheel. Tires squealed as the car listed, straining to meet the guard rail. Coming out of the turn, the car launched onto a wide boulevard, tires burning off long blue clouds of smoke as he kept to the center lane.

A red sportscar flashed past. Christopher risked a glance at his speedometer. *We're doing 65. I don't even want to think about how fast she's going.*

The sportscar moved directly in front of the limo. Brake lights flashed three times. Christopher triggered the headlights twice in response and began to slow. Flashing its brake lights once more, the sportscar fish-tailed into a nearby parking lot. Heeling over into a slow, choppy skid, he forced the limo to follow.

Coming to a stop in front of a brightly lit supermarket, Doris was intercepted by a slow-moving police cruiser. Rolling up behind, Christopher watched to see how things would play out.

The cruiser stopped in front of the sportscar. A single male officer got out, shouting.

Christopher watched Doris get out of the car in one fluid motion. She was instantly recognizable in her long black leather trenchcoat.

Moving quickly, she pulled a large silenced pistol from the inner door of her car and shot the cop through the head.

She'll want to have a look at him. Christopher cut the engine and turned to look at Fisk. Slumped in his seat, the consultant held a wadded handkerchief over his nose. It was clear that there was a lot going on in the man's life. *Dirty cops, my eye. This was a hit.*

"Should have worn my seatbelt," Fisk muttered.

The men watched Doris approach. Her coat ruffled in the night breeze. Christopher got out to meet her.

"You did well," she told him, reaching over the doorframe to trigger the autolocks. She opened the rear passenger door, ignoring the gore on the handle. Flicking blood off her fingertips, she knelt to attend to Fisk's injury.

Christopher watched her lay the gun down on the pavement. *Still within easy reach.*

Fisk seemed to be having trouble getting his nose to stop bleeding. "Here, let me help you," Doris said, reaching for the cloth. Her gentle tone surprised Christopher. Taking the handkerchief in both hands, she smiled at Fisk.

That's no ordinary smile, he observed. *Who are they to each other?* Feeling as if he were intruding, Christopher turned away, standing near the duo as the city continued to pulse around them.

Out on the street, another pair of police cars blasted by, lights and sirens shredding the night. Christopher flinched as he watched them pass. Turning back, he saw the looks between Fisk and Doris. He seemed to be taking the woman's ministrations calmly, as if he were following her lead. *I get the feeling that he trusts her implicitly.* She, on the other hand, had fire in her eyes and a smile that would have been happy under other circumstances. *She must care for him. Wonder if he knows?*

She guided Fisk's hand, folding the handkerchief neatly in his grasp. "Put it like this. Hold the bridge of your nose, and it'll stop the bleeding." He smiled as he followed her instructions.

Christopher couldn't help but notice the way she tilted her head--as if she were trying to say something.

Just as quickly as they had come to life, her eyes went dead and she became serious again. Picking up her gun, she stood, slipping it into a shoulder holster with practiced ease. "Let's get him to my car. The limo's too conspicuous."

Christopher reached into the front seat to pick up his satchel and weapon. Fisk pulled his briefcase after him as he exited the car. Christopher hastily stuffed his submachine gun into his satchel as a station wagon rolled by. Inside, a family of four seemed busy with their own discussion.

Fisk went with Doris, speaking softly as they walked to her car. Christopher quickly got into the limo and moved it to a parking space. He got out and locked it. After setting the alarm, he glanced at the dead cop. Sprawled over the front of his idling cruiser, the dead man drew no attention at all from the people inside the market.

The sportscar growled up beside him, as if prowling. Fisk was in the back seat, fumbling with a seatbelt. Christopher hefted his satchel and got into the front passenger seat.

"My name's Doris."

"I remember you from the interview. What now, Doris?" The sportscar peeled out as Christopher stuffed the satchel between his legs and the dashboard.

"We go to a safehouse," she said, downshifting. Pivoting around a corner and though a red light, she tapped the brakes with expert timing. Car horns blared around them as she ripped through the gears in a well-practiced brake-and-shift ballet.

In the back seat, Fisk clamped hard at his nose. The numbness that had gripped him earlier was gone. His mental clarity was returning.

Christopher watched silently as Doris hammered through the gears, sending the little red sportscar up through 75 miles per hour. Taking a circuitous route, she took them back into Maryland. In the back seat, Fisk said nothing as he held onto his bleeding nose.

Slowing to the local speed limits, Doris drove sedately into a residential area. Fisk and Christopher watched the homes roll by, each bordered by hedges and tiny lawns. Stopping at an intersection, she picked up the car's phone and thumbed in a number. "This is Shadow. I have the package. I'm one block out from your location. Are you secure?" She nodded at Christopher, casting a watchful eye over Fisk through the rearview mirror.

"Secured and protected."

"Expect me in one minute." She hung up.

The sportscar growled quietly down the dimly lit street. Christopher noted appreciatively, *No one house stands out from the others. Nothing to call attention to--*

Up ahead, a large black SUV was pulling out of a driveway. Its taillights flashed red as it drove away. Doris pulled into the same driveway, ignoring Christopher's arched eyebrows. He flinched, seeing movement in the shadows along the side of the house.

Doris switched off the car's engine. Pulling the key, she gestured at the house. "He's one of ours. We do our best to have a tactical team nearby at all times. There's one man with night vision on each corner of the house." Putting the keys in her pocket, she got out.

"Of course," Christopher mumbled, grabbing his satchel and exiting the car.

Fisk waited for Christopher before getting out. Hefting his

94

briefcase, he took one last swipe at his swollen nose before putting the blood-smeared handkerchief casually in his pocket.

Christopher noticed the gesture. *On some level, he's not afraid of blood. Wonder what his real story is.*

Christopher was used to being an outsider. Knowing the intimate details of his employers' business had never been a job requirement. It was something he hadn't questioned in a long time. *I think I'm going to regret not asking this time.*

"Let's go inside." They moved single file down a manicured stone walkway, approaching the front door of the split-level home.

Christopher flinched again as a man in black BDUs met them at the door. *That's some tactical support they've got.* Holding the door open, the guard said nothing. In the previous five years, it had become common for high-powered executives to hire trained weapons experts to enhance their security.

Christopher took in the doorman's body armor and weapon with an almost casual glance. He had limited experience with this kind of extreme personal security. The gas mask hanging casually around the man's neck was hard to ignore. *I'm in over my head.*

Closing the door behind them, the guard stepped aside as two men in dark clothing moved a heavy metal barrier to block the entire doorframe. A balding man came forward, his wrinkled polo shirt and cotton slacks contrasting with all the black uniforms around him.

"Mr. Fisk. I'm glad you're all right. I've sent my daughter away, and my wife's in the kitchen getting you a cold compress for your nose."

Christopher flashed on the black SUV that had pulled out of the driveway. *That must be some kind of standing arrangement.* "Daughter?" he whispered at Doris. She nodded as Fisk shook hands with the man.

"Standard operating procedure in situations like this. We didn't want them to worry about her. This way, they don't stress."

Christopher pulled the strap of his satchel over his shoulder and rubbed his nose. *She makes it sound like they do this all the time.*

An aide materialized, her slim hands cradling a wireless phone. "What's the cover story?" Fisk asked, smiling his thanks to the woman for acting so quickly to put the tale in place.

"We've just left a message with the President's office, telling them that you're running late," the aide replied, bobbing her head.

Fisk had good reason to suspect that it made Madeline furious when he didn't acknowledge his narrow escapes. The conspirators had no doubt that her summons was somehow connected to the plan to kill him. *Wonder what kind of mood she'll be in tonight?* The possibilities made him smile again.

"I'm sorry it had to come to this, Jerry. I really appreciate your hospitality." They exchanged hearty handshakes.

"We're here for you," the homeowner affirmed congenially.

Seeing Christopher's curious glance as it swept the foyer, Fisk asked, "Can I borrow your den? I have some things I need to discuss with Mr. Christopher."

Licking his lips, Jerry glanced at the driver. "I know that look. He doesn't know?"

"Not yet," Fisk admitted.

Jerry nodded abruptly. "Certainly. Let me show you the way. I'll have Gladys bring that compress in with some drinks. Is iced tea okay?"

Fisk touched his tender nose self-consciously. "I'm okay now, but some iced tea would be great."

As Christopher followed, he was struck by how normal the interior of the house looked. Family pictures filling the walls spoke of a son in college and a daughter in high school. *There must be at least half a dozen guys roaming around here in full battledress.*

Rich wood paneling covered the walls of the small den. Earth-toned carpet peeked out from under oak furniture. A colonial-style desk dominated one whole wall. Two more guards stood in separate corners. Clad in black BDUs and body armor, both were armed with silenced SMGs similar to the model Christopher carried. Their presence made the room seem even smaller than it actually was.

Jerry pointed at the big desk. "Gladys should be by soon with the drinks. The secured phone is in that bottom drawer. Here's the key."

Christopher couldn't hide his amazement as Jerry took a thin silver chain from around his neck. Handing it to Fisk, a tiny golden key sparkled in the light. *Mister Normal, carrying on like he's got a big secret.*

"Thanks," Fisk said, taking the key.

Doris stepped close to Christopher in one fluid move. "Give me the satchel, please." Her tone and the way she looked at him left no doubt in his mind that she was prepared to disarm him. Turning his head slowly, Christopher eyed one of the armored guards. The man looked straight at him, the unspoken promise of pain in his eyes. *The way she says "please" isn't really "please,"* he realized.

Fisk walked over to the big desk, taking a seat in the contoured wooden chair beside it. Running his hands over the polished arms, he waited for the tense moment to pass.

Christopher handed her the satchel. "What the hey."

"Check him," the guard by the door told Doris.

The shakedown went quickly. "No holster. No hold-outs."

"Okay," the guard said, satisfied.

Doris, carrying the satchel, followed Jerry out of the room. Stepping over to the door, the second guard closed it and stood off to one side.

Christopher looked at the guards again, as if to make sure they were real. The man nearest the door hefted his weapon as if reading his mind. A large clock seated on the desk ticked away the seconds, its gears and pendulum sounding loud in the otherwise silent room.

"Have a seat. Let's talk." Fisk gestured to an easy chair.

Christopher unbuttoned his coat and slid into the chair. *What have I gotten myself into?*

"You're probably wondering what you've gotten yourself into." Fisk put the key and chain into his vest pocket. *It's been a while since I've done this.*

"Yeah, it's crossed my mind."

Fisk steepled his fingers, trying to think of the best way to begin. "Do you know who I am and what I do?"

"Sure. Preston Fisk, advisor to the President. What? You're going to tell me you work for the mob or something?" The driver smirked.

Fisk shook his head, spreading his hands. "No. I do advise the President. But, as you can see, I also have other hobbies."

Christopher shrugged to keep from showing his rising fear. "Hey, why don't you just get to it? If you're a spy or something, just tell me and get it over with. All I do is drive. If people are trying to kill you, that's not my problem until they get too close to the car."

Fisk's chair squeaked as it swiveled. "Okay. My name is Preston Duquesne Fisk, and I am, in fact, the point man for what you'd call a conspiracy. For the last ten years, we've been helping every unscrupulous politician we can find. We make sure they have the backing they need to get into office. The plan is to choke the federal bureaucracy to death with it's own greed and corruption."

When Christopher didn't speak, he continued. "I've made it possible for more than 200 unprincipled men and women to get elected. Even as we speak, the federal government is more corrupt than at any other point in our history."

Christopher's fear was replaced by confusion and something else he couldn't put his finger on. "Do you know what that sounds like?"

"What?" Fisk threw back, his tone edgy but inquisitive.

"Like you said, conspiracy."

"Indeed it is." He rested a hand on the desk blotter. *This has to be hard for him.*

"Why?"

Fisk straightened. "There's a lot to that answer. For now, you have to take my word for it. We need to ease into this. I've found that most people that we recruit...need some time to think about it. I can tell you what I know, but there's a catch."

"Which is?" He noticed the guards and the way they became more alert. *How many times have you guys heard this speech?*

"We're too close to finishing what we started. That means I can't give you a lot of time to think it over. If I tell you what this is all about, I'll need to know where you stand before you leave this room."

Christopher licked his drying lips. "You mean, join or die?"

Fisk nodded, letting his hands relax. "Exactly, Now that we're revealing ourselves to you, we can't risk your betrayal. If you're not with us once you've heard more of the details, then..."

"You'd kill me?" He scrutinized Fisk closely.

"Yes."

The driver sat back, trying to relieve the stress in his neck.

"We're taking a big chance on you. When outsiders discover us, we generally observe them before we make our pitch. It takes time decide who is an asset and who isn't."

"Which makes me expendable? Why? Because this is a hasty introduction?" Christopher asked, the hair on the back of his neck rising at the implications.

"Well put. I'm glad you catch on so quickly."

"I don't like the idea of being expendable."

Fisk looked down at the blotter. "When it comes right down to it, I'm the expendable one. I can live with that. It's the rest of my organization that's vulnerable. I can't allow you to harm them. Even with what little you know, you could cause trouble for us if you're not sympathetic to our cause."

"Join or die." *I think I've seen this movie,* his mind rebelled. *I thought this lame conspiracy stuff went out with the last century.*

"Yes." Fisk nodded. *This is happening too fast.*

"Some choice," Christopher groaned. *You can't just drop this on me and expect--*

"If I had the leeway, I'd give it to you." He looked up at Christopher.

A polite knock at the door interrupted the conversation. The chauffeur watched incredulously as the guard near the door opened it. Nodding to the woman in the hallway, he stepped aside.

Must be Gladys. He took in the laugh lines around her eyes and the simple way she dressed. Carrying a bright orange tray, she glided across the room to offer Fisk the first of two large glasses of iced tea. Each glass sported a wedge of lemon and a red plastic straw.

She whispered to Fisk, "It's so good to see you. Is everything all right?"

The conspirator gave her his full attention. Smiling as if he were a judge at a carnival awarding her the blue ribbon for the iced tea contest, he relaxed took the drink. "It is now. I'm just sorry that we had to drop in on you this late." Droplets of condensation were already streaming down the sides of the large floral-printed glass.

"Oh. It's no trouble, really," she beamed.

Watching the exchange, Christopher looked skeptical. *No trouble? The man tells me that he's involved in some off-the-wall conspiracy, and she thinks all these big fellows with guns are 'no trouble'?* He cast a speculative glance at the door.

Fisk sipped approvingly at his tea. "What did you tell Cleo?"

Never make it, Christopher decided.

Gladys cast an uncertain glance over her shoulder at the driver. He smiled weakly back.

Fisk put a reassuring hand on her shoulder. "Mr. Christopher and I are just planning our next moves," he confided as if he were letting her in on a secret.

She stood up with a quick nod, her auburn curls bouncing. "I understand. I'll be back with the compress in a minute."

"That's quite all right. You don't have to bother. I'm fine now. We shouldn't be at this too much longer." He watched his driver's facial expression with interest.

Gladys moved to where Christopher sat. Offering him the second glass at arm's length, her eyes moved to where the nearest guard stood. That told Christopher that she was nervous about being so close to him.

Why are you afraid of me? Taking the cold glass in one hand, he looked her over once more. He nodded when he caught her eye. *I get it. I don't take hostages, lady. Besides, as weird this is, suppose it's for real. I could have walked into something worse, eh?*

Folding the serving tray under her left arm, Gladys paused just long enough to smile at the guard near the door before she disappeared into the hallway.

"Good decision. You would've been dead before you got to your feet," Fisk said.

"Was she armed?" Christopher looked at the guards. Neither guard spoke. The one nearest the door reached out a large hand to close it. Looking down at the chauffeur, he smiled wolfishly. *Wrong question. Be cool.*

"Probably." Fisk shrugged. *Gladys dislikes guns, but you don't need to know that.*

"Some kind of crowd you hang with. It's no wonder people are trying to kill you." He took the straw out of his glass, setting it on a side table.

Fisk placed his glass on the blotter. "We're at war. In a war, there are casualties. We're all at risk."

Christopher gulped at his tea, grateful for the relief it provided. "Why not start from the beginning? You've got nothing to lose if you really intend to kill me." *Might as well find out what it's all about.*

Fisk sat back. "Like I said, I'm the point man for a planned effort. As we sit here, that plan is only a few months from completion. You've stepped in at a rather ticklish moment."

Christopher drained the glass, plucking off the lemon wedge to suck on. "You think this is really what people want?"

"It's what a lot of people want. You watch the news. You've seen what people are saying in those on-the-street interviews. They're concerned about the way things are headed. We're just giving events a nudge in the right direction."

"According to you." The anger in Christopher's voice was matched by the fury that played over his face. *I know things are bad, but who put you in charge?*

"According to a lot of people, yes."

"Which you happen to represent?"

"Quite right. I'm a contractor, like you. People pay me to make sure that certain things happen; that things occur successfully. In this case, it's an agenda that has taken just over a decade to fulfill."

Christopher looked up at the ceiling. "An agenda. Do you know what you sound like?"

Fisk smirked. "Yeah. A bad novel. The Washington insider, bent on dominating the nation so that one day he can rule the world, all the while, being pursued by do-good government agents who will stop him at any cost." *If only this were just a half-baked novel.*

"Hole in one."

Fisk tapped the side of his glass. "I don't have time to debate the finer points. I'm here to give you those answers I promised. It's a lot to take in, but I get the feeling you're not the kind of guy who has to be led around. Here it is, pure and simple."

"Okay."

"We don't have a name or a secret hand shake. I'm not honestly sure when it started, precisely. When I ran into it 14 years ago, things were already cooking. The Founders lacked perspective. They recruited me and I gave them that perspective."

"The Founders?" He leaned on one elbow, sensing an important detail.

"As far as I know, the organization, if you can call it that, wasn't much more than an association of old friends. You know, the kind of group that looks out for each other. Some people think of it as nepotism, but these people took it to a whole new level. Their network is small, but they make up for it in ways that would surprise you."

Christopher gave a small nod. "I've seen that kind of thing. Some of the heavy hitters I used to guard for, give them a phone, and they could make or break you."

"Exactly. In our case, we influence government."

"Which is where you come in."

"Yes. I built the network we use. It has its limitations, though, which is also where I come in. I *am* that influence."

"Doesn't sound so limited to me. I've seen the things they write about you in the papers."

"In a story, I could have all the power I wanted. My organization could have its way. But this is the real world. All we can do is pull strings and get people elected. As an influence broker, I can steer the people we put into office. Not much more. The media makes more out of me than I really am."

"I don't understand."

Fisk swiveled in his chair. "Politicians bring their own networks and organizations when they get elected. These are connected people. Money helps to win elections because it buys goods, services, and ultimately, people. All we've done is look for the worst of the bunch and make sure that they fulfill their political ambitions. You won't see it talked about in the papers. And yes, I know the media's having a change of heart. I've seen it coming for the last few years. Still, there's more to it than meets the eye."

Christopher frowned. "Great. You packed the government with all the grifters, con artists, and unethical deal makers it'll hold. How's that supposed to be good for America?"

Raising a finger, Fisk replied, "Put enough of those people in power, and what happens?"

"The mother of all scandals. Just what we need."

"Not just a scandal--an 'event'. Scandal has become so common that people are numb to it. In my position, I know about things that will never reach the media, things that make me sick whenever I think about them."

"Okay. Bad people do bad things. Put enough of them in one

place, they screw it up for everybody. In this case, what? They grab for total power?"

"Exactly. We believe they'll fail. But first they have to try."

Christopher looked down, frowning. "Nice idea if it works. When you stop to think about it, it's not something you can guarantee, is it?" *Nobody cares any more.* He found himself slowly warming up to the older man. *Do I like him, or his plan?*

Fisk nodded, acknowledging the point.

"Which makes you no better than them. You're out to get something and you're not afraid of what you have to do to get it." *It takes a thief to catch a thief, is that it?* He smirked.

Fisk could feel Christopher building up to his point.

"Except for one thing. There are people who care about what's going on. The future of this country matters to them. There may not be many of them, but it means something to them that their elected leaders do the right thing. Those leaders don't have to be perfect, just mindful of who they serve." He could see that he'd reached the right conclusion as Fisk's smile revealed his perfectly white teeth for a moment. "These are the kind of people you work with?"

"Those are the people we hope to reach." Fisk nodded with open approval.

Christopher shifted in his chair. "Why not keep your secret and work with any-old-body that can do what you want?"

"Because it matters to me, too. What's the point in working to achieve something if you're not being backed up by the right kind of people?"

"Why all the cloak and dagger stuff? Why not come out in the open?"

"Like I said, we're at war. It benefits us to play by the rules."

"Whose rules are you playing by?"

Fisk watched comprehension spread over Christopher's features. "Theirs, of course. The very forces we've helped put into power."

"I've seen plenty of corruption. Greed, pay-offs, and good old-fashioned blackmail. Our little adventure tonight doesn't seem any different."

"What happened tonight was the result of a planned ambush."

"Planned by who?" While Christopher's former employers had

wielded considerable power, none of them had meddled with law enforcement.

"President Madeline Hill."

Christopher flinched, almost dropping his glass. "What?"

Neutrally, Fisk replied, "You heard me. The President of the United States."

The driver looked up at the nearest guard, who nodded imperceptibly. "Why?"

"It's personal. At least, it is for her." He tilted his head.

Christopher nodded. "Because of all the stuff you know. That I get. No, wait. You made her career. She owes you for everything she's got. Ambitious people don't like owing debts they can't repay, or people they can't manipulate." Recalling a corporate exec he'd once worked for, he understood. *The competition ruined him because he had too much dirt on them. They never did prove that it wasn't suicide, even with my testimony.*

"You're right. She doesn't need me any more. Which, ironically, is just what we were aiming for." *The understatement of my career.*

"She's the one you're betting all your chips on. Where she goes, Congress'll follow."

"That's right. She's a handful. This little game we're playing with her will end when she makes her bid to stay in office after her second term is up."

Christopher's mind buzzed with the possibilities. "What makes you so sure things will break the way you want them? Suppose she doesn't turn tyrant like you want? What if she just walks away?"

"She's been profiled down to the smallest detail. She honestly believes she deserves it."

"You could just be making things worse."

"A risk we're willing to take. We've been watching Congress for a long time. Where she leads, they'll follow."

"The last few presidents have thumbed their nose at Congress. Voter turnout is so low now that it might not matter if the President decided to stay in office. Might just make some people happy that they don't have to take the time to vote." Despite the weirdness of the moment, he found himself beginning to understand the "why" of Fisk's covert mission. *If we could clean house, what kind of America would we live in?*

"You're thinking too small. The fallout from this will be bigger than anything this country has seen since the Civil War."

"How so?"

"A scandal usually only takes down a few people with it--here today, gone tomorrow. An event like the one we're working towards will discredit hundreds of politicians. The entire federal government will be viewed with suspicion. It'll force people to take a hard look at the motives of their leaders."

Christopher's face soured. "Shotgun approach. That's going to hurt a lot of innocent people. What does your master plan have in store for them?"

Fisk toyed with his straw. "The event we have in mind has been carefully evaluated. The average person on the street will know exactly what's happening. It'll be crystal clear to everyone just who the bad guys are. As for the pain, I wish I had a fix for that, but I don't."

"What's the event that you're planning?" He felt his pulse quicken.

"That's need-to-know. For now, you don't need to know."

"And if you're wrong?"

"If I'm wrong, then all we've done is to bring a lot of the wrong people into power. In time, the voters will either get fed up and vote them out or grow old and die without knowing that things could have been better."

Christopher's expression hardened with disapproval. "And if you're right?"

Fisk closed his eyes. "If I'm right, then we'll get our event. The people we've brought to power will overstep their constitutional authority and fight like crazy to keep the new status quo."

"Is that what you really want?" *You want to start a civil war?*

"So much for need-to-know. Yes. Revolt. Possibly civil war. My organization is preparing to support whichever comes along. I'm breaking the rules by telling you this, but an uprising is our Phase Two option. Right now, we don't really see it happening." He gave a small wave with his free hand.

The driver swore. "What's the difference? You're going to bait Americans into killing Americans. Where's the good in that?" He rolled his wide shoulders, trying to work off some of his nervous energy.

"The national debt. That, and the whole Middle East thing. We didn't have to raise a finger, or make any moves at all, to affect that situation. When Argentina defaulted on its debts, it lit the fuse on the bomb that American politicians have been building for the last 50 years."

Christopher shrugged. "So you've got your limits. That doesn't answer my question."

Fisk paused for a breath and a fresh choice of words. "The 'good' you're looking for kicks in when people make up their minds."

"And if they don't get fed up? You're really just going to walk away? Simple as that?" He scrutinized Fisk closely.

"Yes." He laid both hands in his lap.

"Hmm. Somehow, I don't believe you."

Fisk was all too familiar with the accusation. "The plan calls for our organization to dry up and go away after a certain point."

"Which would be?" *To do all this, and not take advantage of it?* The implications forced a shiver out of the veteran bodyguard.

"Once we know where we stand." Fisk was careful to avoid revealing any more details.

Christopher mulled it over. "Nobody knows you're doing this, so I guess you could get away with it. If you trigger a revolt, don't you think you have some responsibility to see it through?"

Fisk arched an eyebrow. "Remember that Phase Two that I mentioned? I don't suppose it's occurred to you that the people already have put their favorites in office?"

Christopher felt his stomach crawl. In that instant, he understood that he himself had become numb to the corruption. He wasn't even registered to vote.

"It's a very real possibility, which is why we've entertained the prospect of being wrong from the very beginning."

"Nothing ventured, nothing gained." Christopher leaned back in his chair. His perception of Fisk had shifted during the conversation. *This is really big.*

"If I had never run into this organization, none of this would have occurred to me. I probably would have continued on in my former life, unaware and unconcerned. Like you, I wasn't even registered to vote. Now that you know about it, you've got to make some hard choices."

"Former life?"

"Not open for discussion," Fisk said, giving the driver a hard look.

"I understand." The younger man chewed on his lower lip for a moment.

Fisk let out a long breath, shaking his head. "If nothing changes, then at least we'll know that we tried."

"What convinced you to get involved with this? What do you get out of it?"

"I've asked myself that question many times." Fisk smiled. *There are times when I feel like I just walked into this by accident. Like I'm not who I think I am.*

"What pulls you through?" he prodded.

"Now that I know about it, I have to know how it turns out. I have to know that I gave it my best shot. Even when Madeline drives me nuts, or does something I don't plan on, I still find myself going back to that. I can't *not* do this." *Sometimes I think it's my reason for living.*

"Okay," Christopher exhaled.

The clock on the desk ticked loudly as the tense moment passed, reminding Fisk that he didn't have much longer to continue this discussion. He nodded to the guard nearest the door. "Ask Jerry to come in here, will you?"

The guard nodded, slinging his weapon. Leaving the room, he shut the door behind him.

Christopher took a long look at the other guard. "How'd you get involved in this?"

The guard's eyes flickered as he scanned the room.

"Go ahead and tell him. I'll be back. Nature calls." Fisk stood and left the room.

Monday
April 21, 2014
Safehouse
Maryland
8:44 P.M. EDT

Through the open door, Christopher heard the muted chatter of a police frequency scanner in the hall. Fisk's authoritative voice cut through the noise as he excused himself and moved around somebody. Christopher looked back at the guard.

"My dad was in the Army. He went to Somalia back in '93 as part of the peacekeeping mission. Supposed to bring food and medicine to starving people."

Christopher was aware that the guard was looking him over. *I'd be shot at least four times before I ever got out of this chair. He's really waiting for me to try. Wow.*

"He was part of the group that went out to rescue those guys who got shot down. The mission went okay, but they were left behind when the relief column pulled out. When they were found, the mobs cut them to pieces."

Christopher watched as the guard's silenced weapon slowly tracked onto him. *Those must be some hard memories.*

"There was a cover-up. I was in college ROTC at the time, so I wasn't able to find out the whole truth. That's when I ran into... them."

Christopher waited for further explanation. When it didn't come, he nodded. "These are pretty strange times we live in. I'll take your word about the cover-up. Are you saying the government fed you a line about how your dad died? Is that why you're here?" He himself felt no connection to events he could barely remember.

The guard shrugged. "There was more to it than that. I took my commission and figured I'd continue the family tradition, you know?"

Several heartbeats passed. Christopher nodded.

The guard shook his head. "I didn't want to believe it. Once the truth sank in, I started noticing other things."

"Like what?"

"You had to be there. Peacekeeping was still new. It wasn't like what you see on TV these days. President Clinton wasn't real friendly to the military, and we were getting all kinds of mixed signals from Washington. By the time they sent me to Kosovo, I started seeing similarities to Somalia. That's when I realized the truth about my dad."

"That's tough."

The guard frowned. "It opened my eyes. All the stuff on the news that people like you ignore because it doesn't affect you started making too much sense to me. After a while, I couldn't ignore it any more."

Christopher waited for more. His only clue that the guard wasn't going to say anything else came with the slow drop of the SMG's barrel.

Footsteps padded down the hall. Scratching his chest, Jerry stopped in the doorway. "Hi."

"Rambo was just telling me how he got involved with you guys," Christopher said.

Jerry moved to sit in his desk chair. He was obviously tense. "It's a lot to take in all at once." He scratched the back of his head, trying to find the right words.

"Tonight has been a lot to live through all at once," Christopher replied sarcastically.

"That bad?"

"Chased, shot at, and nearly blown up," Christopher summarized.

"Doris said you did well. That's high praise, coming from her," Jerry offered graciously.

"I killed a cop, if that's what you mean." He looked away.

Jerry licked his lips. "I can't begin to guess what that was like. I don't own any guns. I'm just glad you both got out alive."

Christopher could sense the man's growing confidence. *I'd feel pretty safe with a guy in armor and SMG just over my shoulder, too.* "Fisk means that much to you?"

"I think he's got a lot of responsibility to bear for what he does. I know I couldn't do it, even with all the help he gets."

"How's a guy like you wind up in a thing like this?"

"Some of us got involved because of things that were done to us."

"So I gather," Christopher nodded, watching the guard from the corner of his eye.

"Some of us just ran into it by accident." He smoothed the front of his polo shirt.

"That what happened to you?" *This isn't a very secret organization if anyone can stumble onto it and join.*

"I'm an engineer. I worked for a private company when it happened. We were building bridges for highways and railroads. Ten years ago, one of our crews found an undocumented power line. It turned out to belong to Fisk's people."

"What did they say that convinced you to join them?" *What could they possibly offer you? Were you threatened?*

Jerry grimaced. "It wasn't what they said, it's what they showed me. That power line? It was attached to an underground facility someplace in Vermont."

Christopher closed his eyes. "Let me guess. Secret government facility?"

"They were keeping copies of classified documents in long-term storage," Jerry replied.

"Scary stuff?"

"More than I can say. All the way back to World War II."

Fisk suddenly materialized in the doorway. "We wanted to show him that the government had been keeping secrets for a very long time. More than just national security--a long paper trail that more than proved our point that powerful people in this country have a thirst for ultimate power."

Stepping aside, he allowed the second guard to come back into the room. Shouldering past Fisk, the man took his place along the wall near the door.

Jerry was unsure about how much more he should say. "If I hadn't seen it, I wouldn't have believed it."

"More of that 'event' you're looking for?" Christopher quipped.

Fisk nodded.

As he tried to relax, Christopher's eyes roamed from Jerry to Fisk.

You'd never expect these two to have a meeting of the minds.

Jerry stood up to leave.

"One more question," Christopher stalled, searching for the right words.

"Er?" Jerry looked hesitantly at Fisk, who nodded his approval.

"What makes you think this is really what people want? You're not a politician. None of you are elected. You could lose everything if you were discovered. Your wife, your daughter, your career. Is it really worth all that?"

Jerry stopped, rubbing his hands lightly on his pants. "My father went to Vietnam in 1966. Part of his reason for going was patriotism, but the other part was to see it for himself. I never knew what he actually thought about the 'right' or 'wrong' of that war, but I do know that he never regretted going."

Christopher's brow furrowed. "A lot of old guys I've run into don't talk about that war. One guy I used to work with admitted to being in Desert Storm, but he never talked about it."

"Sorry. I'm not good at this. What I meant was, I got involved with this so that I could see it for myself."

"You're involved with Fisk because you want to see if he's doing the right thing?" Christopher asked in disbelief.

Jerry nodded silently. He wiped a line of sweat off his upper lip. "I'm all for cleaning up the political system. Even my wife thinks that things have gone too far. It's just that..." Hesitating, he looked over at Fisk with veiled eyes.

"What?" Christopher turned to look at Fisk. *Are you afraid to talk with him here?*

"It's just that I think he's wrong."

"You do?" The young man shot a surprised look at Fisk.

"I support what he's doing, in principle, but I think his methods are a little extreme. Gladys and I both do. There are some things going on that bother us, but we don't believe that our government has ever been actively moving against us. Fisk's plan to fight conspiracy with conspiracy isn't going to do anything more than call attention to some of the things that are hurting us."

"Would you listen to what you just said?" Christopher was on the verge of standing up.

"I know what I said. It can't be as bad as he claims, even with whatever he's done to speed things up. Exposing the corruption isn't wrong. I support that. But the idea that you can knock it all down at once, like a string of dominoes, is just not real."

Stepping forward, Fisk put a hand on the balding man's shoulder.

"Why don't you let us take it from here?"

Jerry nodded and left the room.

"You've got all kinds, haven't you?" Christopher breathed.

"He's being honest." Fisk sauntered back to the chair next to the desk.

"What's he afraid of?" *He seems a little timid.*

"The truth. He plays it down, so that he and his wife can feel better about what they're doing. Like so many people these days, they like the concept of a better tomorrow. They're just not sure they want to get their hands dirty with the details."

"Are you threatening him with anything?" He flashed back to the black SUV that had departed just as he arrived.

"Not at all. That's not the way we do things. Jerry's just hoping to be on the winning side. His heart's in the right place, but he's got commitment issues."

"Suppose he decides to turn you in some day?"

Fisk grinned. "We live in the shadow of betrayal every day. Any one of us can go to the authorities. Some of us believe more than others. There have been days when I've thought about doing it, myself."

"I find that hard to believe. Everybody hates his job from time to time. As wild as this is, I can't see you doing that. You've already said you're too committed."

The older man bowed his head. "Quite so. I'll see this through to the end because of one thing."

"Which would be?" He thought he already knew the answer.

"The alternative. If we just walked away now, we'd be wondering for the rest of our lives if we did the right thing. As things got worse, we'd always wonder if we threw away our only chance to make the difference," Fisk elaborated with a sweep of his arm.

As Christopher listened, he could feel a chord of sympathy being struck in his own mind. *Doing what you have to do is a matter of survival. Doing something because you don't like the alternative is a matter of principle.* Lost in thought, he didn't see Fisk leave the room. *How could the government miss a thing like this?*

Pacing seemed out of the question in the small room. He settled for standing and putting his hands in his pockets. Turning in place, he stopped as Doris silently appeared in the doorway. Her attitude was casual, as if she were waiting for something.

"What do *you* think?" he asked.

Doris rested both hands on her hips. "You need some time alone."

He pulled his hands out of his pockets to swing his arms in frustration. "I suppose they gave you time to think it over, too?"

"What happened to me is not your concern," she said coldly.

"Tell me." He took a step forward, ignoring the reaction of the guards.

"If you're not up for this, I'm going to shoot you. As for what happened to me, that was a long time ago. There were different circumstances involved. You wouldn't understand."

Christopher rolled his eyes. "Well, aren't you special. If I can get past this, I think I could understand a lot."

"I'll be back in five minutes," she told the guard by the door as she left the room.

Christopher watched as the man's thumb worked the safety on his weapon. *Yeah, right. Five minutes to live.*

Monday
April 21, 2014
Safehouse
Maryland
8:51 P.M. EDT

Fisk met Doris in the hallway. "What do you think?" he asked.

"I think it appeals to him, but he's hung up on the 'what ifs.'"

He looked speculatively at the light shining from the den. "How long did you give him?"

"Five minutes." She reached into her coat, adjusting the fit of her holster.

"I don't want you to do this. Let them take care of it."

She understood his concern. "This might be the last time we have to put somebody through this. I can handle it."

"What makes you say that? We never know when we'll be discovered. It's not as if we're really hiding. We're just not advertising ourselves."

"I know how much it bothers you when we have to eliminate people."

Fisk pursed his lips. "Do you ever think about the people we've had to kill? I do. If I just had more time, I know we could show him what he needs to see."

Even knowing him as she did, Doris wasn't sure which part of him had just spoken.

"Sir?" a voice called from up the hall.

"Yes?" He turned to see one of his assistants.

"Sir, we have a call from the Cascades. The medic's ready to doctor your nose, too."

Doris gave Fisk a stern look. "That's a Phase Two asset. Why are they calling you?"

"It's all right. Special arrangements for Garrison. We're spending a lot of money to train people for a fight that might never come, and

I want to make sure that they have their act together before they get their hands on him."

She knew better than to trust Fisk's stated motives. "William Garrison works out three times a week. He does his own taxes. Unless he shoots himself in the foot, he'll do just fine. Which reminds me. Do you still think I should call him to make sure it's done?"

Fisk started to walk away. "Yes. He'll need the reassurance. I'll finish up with Christopher. I'd like to hear for myself what he decides."

She watched him go to answer the phone call. The secret training camp had never sat well with her. The idea of training guerrillas for a civil war that might never come smacked of latent hypocrisy. The conspirators had labored long and hard to work within the political system. It didn't look to her like the contingency would never be needed.

Fisk's phone conversation didn't take long. When he and Doris walked into the den five minutes later, Christopher was still seated in the easy chair, rubbing his chin. Fisk waited for him to speak.

The big man glanced at the pair as he got to his feet. "It's not as simple as you make it out to be. I guess there's only so much you can tell me at this point. The rest, I think I have to see for myself."

Doris looked at Fisk, the unspoken question in her eyes.

Fisk stepped forward. "Cheer up. You're not losing your freedom."
I might be making a mistake here, but I'm tired of the lies and the killing.

"Only the chance to lose it." Christopher nodded solemnly at Doris, who said nothing.

"We'd better be going. I'm still expected at Treasury, and we've got to make sure that our cover story is believable." Working silently next to him, the medic finished applying an anti-inflammatory agent to Fisk's abused nose.

"Cover? You're just going to say traffic was bad, right?"

Doris replied. "Right. We pretend that these things don't happen."

The driver considered the effort that went into such deceptions. "That's got to make her mad," he speculated as they entered the foyer.

"And how. Too bad you won't be there to see it. I'll bet she's positively *cranked* when she sees me." Fisk smiled wolfishly as he admired his unblemished nose with a handheld mirror.

"You'll need a change of clothes," Doris observed, giving Fisk an appraising look.

Looking down at his shoes, he saw tiny dots of dried blood on the expensive fabric of his slacks.

"All this running around. You sweated in your shirt, too."

Behind her, a nondescript man produced a garment bag. Holding it up to get Fisk's attention, he smiled. "Perfect match to what you have on, down to the underwear."

Looking sidelong at the garment bag, Christopher stepped aside as Doris reached for it. "Does this happen all the time?" he asked, scratching an ear to hide his uncertainty.

Doris turned her back on the driver as she held the bag up for Fisk's consideration.

"The country's most well-known political consultant does not sweat or bleed." Taking the bag, Fisk unzipped it and peeked inside.

Christopher tried to keep his expression neutral. "I see. You'd better shower before you put those on," he observed with a hint of mirth.

"Sponge bath. No time to blow dry the hair. Besides, he's supposedly been tied up in bad traffic. Wouldn't do to have somebody notice that he's somehow freshly bathed," Doris said as she stepped out of Fisk's way.

"No point in making them suspicious, eh?" Christopher winked at his boss.

"All right, you two. Don't make me have you separated." Fisk swung the garment bag over his shoulder. Stepping around a nearby pedestal with a house plant perched on it, he shook a finger at the driver as he headed for the hallway. He reached up to tug at the collar of his shirt, revealing a tiny smear of blood. "You've got a lot to learn."

Shuddering inside, Christopher felt vulnerable and alone. He turned back to face Doris. "What now?"

"This is a lot to take in all at once. I'll see that you're taken home. You need time to think, and I need time to go over your dossier one more time." Pausing to swipe a lock of hair from her eyes, she swiveled her head to make sure they were alone in the foyer.

"You don't trust me?" He linked his hands behind his back.

Doris slipped her hands into the pockets of her trenchcoat. "I don't trust *anybody*. Not where he's concerned."

Monday
April 21, 2014
Winchester Suite
Headquarters
National Rifleman's Association
Washington, D.C.
9:15 P.M. EDT

Garrison stared silently at the nearest wall. The items adorning his half of the large office brought back a lot of memories. Watery brown eyes took it all in as he swiveled in his chair. Glancing at his reflection in the small oval of an engraved brass plaque, he ignored his thinning hair. *These things are nice to look at, but not much to show for five years of hard work.*

The pale orange glow of the lights from the news crews gathering outside glared through the window made Garrison think of Dante's *Inferno. Must be what the fires of Hell look like when you see them for the first time.*

Turning slowly in his chair, he watched a gaggle of technicians two stories below as they moved behind bright lights. Reporters from all across the country had gathered to bear witness to the organization's demise. He shivered with anticipation over what he was about to do. From where he sat, he couldn't see the reporters. *What can they be saying? Are they proud of what's happening here tonight?* Shaking his head slowly, he decided that he would rather not know.

While the American news media had undergone something of a renaissance in the previous five years, not even their new-found sense of integrity could dampen their journalistic fervor to pull back the veil of decency for a grisly peek at a dying organization. At 45, Garrison couldn't remember the media ever gloating so much over the demise of any special interest group. He had been just a boy during the years of ever-increasing membership, but he couldn't pinpoint just when things had started falling apart for the NRA.

Despite what it's cost me, I'd do it again. Turning back from the window, he heard a wave of applause well up through the floor from the large gathering hall below.

He understood the need to ensure that corrupt government officials would eventually overstep their constitutional authority, but it was hard to live with at times. *When the pro-gun lobby dies--which it would have done in a few more decades anyway--those in government who are most corrupt won't be able to resist the temptation to disarm the population once and for all. If they can justify that, they can justify doing away with the whole electoral system. When that happens...*

In as much as he believed that something had to be done to restore the United States to its former glory, he was skeptical about the conspiracy's ability to bring back the "good old days." *Understanding the mechanics of the plan is one thing. Following through with it has been a lot harder than I thought it would be.*

Though it had eventually cost him his marriage, Garrison had changed course in the middle of his rise to corporate stardom for the sake of the plan. He'd given the firearms lobby his devoted attention so that it wouldn't collapse before Fisk's plotters were prepared to take advantage of it. With each passing year, his involvement in the conspiracy had grown. So had his involvement with the gun lobby. Championing the cause of firearms ownership had proven to be enlightening for him. *I could spend my whole life without owning a single weapon, but I don't think I could stomach living in a society that stripped its citizens of the privilege to own guns. We're so close to losing all of our civil rights that people haven't thought much about the consequences of giving up just one of them. I only wish that I could've gotten Ellen to understand that.*

Before she had left him, his wife had lectured him about the stupidity of his idealism. *She must be feeling very sanctimonious right about now.* He looked back at the news crews. *Has it been worth it? I feel like a failure. It's so hard to reconcile the plan with what we're giving up here tonight. I wouldn't trade these last six years for anything except another shot at my marriage. I wonder if she knows that I still love her?*

Another round of applause ghosted up through the floorboards. The farewell banquet for the Association's staff and contributors had been planned two weeks in advance. Garrison, along with a handful of board members and generous contributors, had declined to attend.

The telephone warbled. Reaching over a pile of unsigned bankruptcy papers, he picked up the slim receiver. "Yes?" he answered tiredly. *This is it.*

"Bill. Do you know who this is?" The feminine voice was confident.

He checked to make sure that the phone scrambler was on. "Yes."

"Are you ready to do it?" Doris asked.

He felt a knot begin to grow in his stomach. "Yes. I was expecting this call afterward, that's all." The idea of saying something for the history books crossed his mind. *Nah. It's not like anybody will ever know what I'm about to do.*

"I know. You didn't expect it to be me, either. He's busy. I just wanted you to know that I was looking out for you."

"Looking out for me? I assume you heard about Cosmo."

"I heard you had to clear out pretty fast. If it helps, think of it as a warm-up for tonight."

"Ha-ha, very funny. I've already checked it out. We're good to go."

"Take care of yourself then. I'm running late. Got to go. Just remember--"

"Yeah. I know. Remember why I'm doing this. I'm just not liking it."

"Cheer up. This might be the worst thing you ever have to do. Which reminds me, Fisk will need to meet with you in a few days to discuss the next step."

"What next step? As of midnight tonight, I'm out of a job."

Doris was silent for a long moment.

As he waited, Garrison thought, *Do I want them to have another job for me?*

"We both have work to do just now, and you don't need any more distractions." The line went dead.

Garrison hung up and prepared himself for action. He was angry at being put off. His fear was gone, but it did little to inspire him. He walked slowly over to the window. Standing completely still, he surveyed the distant lights of Capitol Hill. Overhead, the few stars that he could see through the smog gave him hope. *Please, God, don't let all this be for nothing.*

Moving back to his work area, he took a small key from his coat pocket. Kneeling, he used it to open the bottom drawer of his desk. Removing stacks of papers and office supplies, he lifted the false bottom and hesitated. Nestled in the hidden space, a compact metal case gleamed next to a pair of surgical gloves. Gathering his thoughts, he scanned the empty office one more time. *Like the lady said, we have work to do.*

Picking up the case and gloves, Garrison slipped them into his coat pocket. Replacing the false bottom, he paused to look closely at its seams. Satisfied that the panel was securely in place, he sat. His fingers trembled as he put the papers and office supplies back inside the drawer.

Stay focused. Nobody will catch me. People hide all kinds of things in false drawer bottoms. He allowed himself a moment to relax before locking the drawer.

Getting to his feet, Garrison switched off his desk lamp and moved quietly towards the door. Through the floor, he felt the vibrations of another wave of applause, signaling the end of yet another speech. Opening the door as quietly as he could, he slipped out into the brightly lit hallway. Casting a furtive glance toward the stairwell, he grimaced. *I can do this.*

Walking casually down the hallway, he stopped in front of a polished wooden door marked *Servers and Hub. Ivan Gallagher, Administrator.* Garrison's worried look reflected back at him from the polished brass plate. This room held the organization's most complex computers. They, in turn, controlled access to the most important records.

Testing the knob, he satisfied himself that the door was still locked. *Means there'll be nobody in there.* Taking out his wallet, he removed the plastic copy of a key he'd been given some time previously. Inserting it into the lock, he turned it quickly. The lock clicked as the door swung open.

Going inside, he paused just long enough to put away the key and use a handkerchief to wipe fingerprints from inner and outer knobs. *Shouldn't do that until I leave.*

Eyes closed, he mentally mapped the room's layout and contents. He removed the latex gloves from his pocket. They squeaked loudly as

121

he struggled into them. Once they were firmly situated, he felt more confident. Opening his eyes, he took in the four workstations.

Computers, clocks, and disk drives all showed their red, green, and blue indicator lights with total indifference to his presence. The monitors at the workstations lit up in reaction to his presence. Each displayed the status of the Association's globe-spanning network. He did his best to ignore the red "offline" indicators on each screen.

Padding over to the nearest workstation, Garrison casually grasped the articulated chair in front of the desk. As he sat, the cool chair soundlessly conformed to his posture as he sat. Working from memory, he carefully entered the required passwords. His fingers moved deliberately over the keyboard. Menus flashed by as each security barrier received the correct response.

Though the pro-gun lobby had fallen prey to both internal dissent and external efforts to undermine its effectiveness, its computer security had never suffered. No attempt to hack the system had succeeded during his time in office. *Fat lot of good it did us.*

He eyed the master menu and considered what he was about to do. *Switch the real records of certain people for fakes. No problem.* The computer signaled its readiness.

He took the compact case from his pocket and looked hard at it one last time. Opening it, he took out a small device that was no larger than his thumb. Holding it up in the surreal lighting, he examined it, mumbling, "Virtual memory archive."

Reaching out with his free hand, he probed the front of the workstation's hardware case with his fingers. He flipped open a small clear plastic cover. Placing the rounded top of the archive between his lips, he pulled the cap off as if it were a fountain pen. Plugging the memory archive into the port, he took the lid from his mouth and put it into his coat pocket.

Sitting quietly in the electronic twilight, he watched as the computer accepted the archive's program. *Self-executing. How appropriate.*

A menu popped up on the screen, instructing him to remove the archive from the machine. Moving slowly, he did so, and then capped it and returned it to its case.

Breathing a sigh of relief, he shut down the computer. Taking his time, he carefully closed every menu that he'd opened. *Probably won't matter, but why take chances?*

Putting the case back in his pocket, he stood. Sliding the chair back into the workspace, he stopped to remove the gloves. Placing them in his pocket, he cautiously moved to the door. Opening it slowly, he risked a quick peek. The hallway was empty. He slipped out of the room, closing the door behind him.

Walking back to his office, he began to relax. He closed the door and sat down behind his desk.

Time passed slowly. Checking his watch, he licked his lips and tried not to fidget. Then the phone rang. He deliberately picked it up on the third ring. "Yes?"

"Status?" The voice was electronically masked, rendering it gender-neutral.

"It's done." Garrison sat back, running a calloused hand over his nearly bald head.

"Go back and wipe your fingerprints off the knob."

Monday
April 21, 2014
Outside Headquarters
National Rifleman's Association
Washington, D.C.
9:18 P.M. EDT

Handing the microphone to a technician, reporter Anne Carroll moved out of the bright spotlights. She made her way through the crowd of support staff to the large van holding the field editing unit. She shrugged into her overcoat with the confidence that came with her ten years in the business.

Overhead, a few stars peeked through the smog layer. Stepping up the ramp into the rear of the van, she noted with satisfaction that the lights and cameras from her shoot were already coming down.

Lou Ross smiled at her with his eyes as she took a seat next to him in the semidarkness. "Cue line optics. Let's take the wash out of the background." Above their heads, monitors glowed with images of her taped presentation as her report was cleaned up and prepped for the regular 11 o'clock broadcast.

"How long?" she asked in a whisper. Lou wasn't the best in his field, but he *did* know how to keep to a schedule.

"Ten to spare. Nice fudge on that 'reports coming in,'" he murmured, cupping a hand over his ear-mounted microphone.

"It'll be true by morning." Anne smiled.

"Lennie's got something for you. Go check it out," Lou grumbled, tapping out commands on his control board.

She moved quickly to the front of the van, taking care to avoid disturbing the other satellite coordinators. One was monitoring the competition's feeds. The close-up shot of a well-known talking head filled one screen as she passed.

"Truth or dare. Has President Hill been straight with us? We're in recession and our economy shows no signs of bottoming out. The last two presidents have failed to restart it. Ever since the Argentine crash, our overseas creditors have been skittish about our debt load. Tell me, can this president achieve what the last two have failed to?"

Anne smiled. "Len. What have you got?"

Lenora Casey looked up from her laptop computer with a start. The 23-year-old graduate student was still reacting to her environment, though her improved composure reaffirmed Anne's choice to hire her as an intern.

Lenora casually disconnected the wireless data link from behind her right ear. Anne's distaste for latest in human-computer interfaces was well known. Lenora had been careful to have the device installed with a synthetic flesh overlay to hide it from those who disapproved. *What she doesn't know won't hurt me.*

"Your source in Treasury confirms that the President is there. Your favorite person is supposed to be there, too." With a slight hesitation, her thin fingers moved over the tiny keyboard, and a color picture began forming on the pop-up plasma screen. The President and her entourage were shown into a lounge inside the new Treasury Annex.

Anne's curiosity was immediately piqued. "Really. When did this come in?"

"While you were taping. Six minutes ago."

"And his service says he's supposed to be where, exactly?" Anne asked, leaning over to study the digital image. *What are you up to now, Mr. Fisk?*

"Abroad. No details. Just out of the country. *Talk TV* says he's been seen with a certain actress from that show you hate so much." Lenora carefully avoided naming the program, which was her personal favorite.

"What about that entourage?" Anne was tempted to pull out her glasses.

"Staff. No Cabinet members, though. Just the usual Secret Service, gophers, and the guy with the keys to the nukes."

"Nothing special. What's the connection to Fisk?"

Though talented, Anne had made more than her fair share of career-altering mistakes. A ten-year veteran of the East Coast televised news markets, she'd been unable to break out of the local arena.

"Any idea why she's there? I thought she had a country to run." In the previous six months, Anne had begun to suspect that the President's most notable advisor and political consultant was more than what he appeared to be. After several months of following his every move, she found herself beginning to tire of the chase. *I can't put my finger on it, but something's just not right about you.*

Lenora pursed her lips thoughtfully. "Your source said he overheard one of the staffers. She called Fisk and asked him to come to Treasury for some reason."

"Fisk, who's supposedly out of the country?" she snorted.

"That would be him. He does that, you know. He's good at being in two places at once. There's just no telling what he's up to."

"Such as?"

"I don't know. President Hill doesn't make a move that Fisk isn't connected with. That guy gets more tabloid time than the Incredible Frog Boy does. Maybe she's got him doing something hush-hush."

Anne sighed. "I wish. For all we know, he was on vacation."

Lenora smiled with a clever gleam in her eye. "You know, there is a way..."

"A way for what?"

"SATS. It's the database for the FAA's General Aviation Division." She reached for her laptop and began tapping keys.

Anne nodded with interest. "They use it to keep track of all the private planes. Small airplane something-or-other."

"It's on Gov-net. 'Small Aircraft Tracking System'." She pulled up the web site.

Gov-net had been developed in the previous decade to serve as the federal government's own version of the internet. Self-contained, it was originally built to stand off cyberterrorist threats. Linking all federal agencies, the compact and highly secured network had sprouted a new bureaucracy entirely dedicated to its maintenance and expansion. With so much information at its disposal, this same bureaucracy was now lobbying Congress for the creation of a National Citizen Registry to justify expanding Gov-net's scope and influence.

Anne eyed the laptop suspiciously. "I'm not even going to ask. Just tell me what you're leading up to."

"Relax. This is the public version. Anyone can look at this if they go through the approved portal. What we need is here--flight plans."

"Flight plans?" Anne asked, incredulous.

Lenora snorted. "Yeah. We can get their flight plan if we know the registry number of the plane."

Anne swung into a tiny seat next to Lenora. "Pull up his file. It might be in there."

"Not here. Not in your notes," Lenora said as her fingers flew over the keyboard.

Anne wrinkled her nose in thought. "Airplane registry. Tail number. Look for photos of him anywhere near his jet."

"Got it. Now, we just put that number in..." Lenora sat back to let Anne watch the flight plan materialize on the little screen.

"Madrid to D.C. Spain?" Her heart sank.

Lenora began ticking off possibilities. "Some really cool vacation resorts. One of the many homes belonging to that certain actress..."

Anne sniffed. "Very funny. Somehow, I don't think Fisk went all the way to Spain for the food, the entertainment, or the company. People like him can afford to order out, if you know what I mean."

"Well, what about this?" she said, indicating the results a search engine had found.

"World Bank?" Anne asked skeptically.

Lenora pointed to an item at the bottom of the screen. "It's either that, or the Euro Union's offices for the Ministry of--"

"I get it. No, I don't."

"World Bank. You know."

"You win. I owe you lunch. Now be nice and tell your doddering old granny why this is important." The statement came out more calmly than she was feeling.

"The debt thing is all over the news right now." She switched screens with a keystroke to show the headlines posted by the country's largest financial think tanks.

Anne nodded. "Okay. That's not news, though. The President has the Treasury Secretary to do all that numbers and money stuff. She's got no reason to send her highly paid brain trust off to Madrid for that kind of thing."

"So we think."

"What's going on in the devious mind of yours?"

"Nah, it's probably nothing. It's getting late and I'm hungry."

Anne pointed a commanding finger. "Talk now. Eat later." Her own fatigue and empty stomach were causing her temper to flare.

"Okay. You're going to think I'm nuts, but look at this. See? 'Ramirez Insider Discounts U.S. Currency Recall Theory.' That got me thinking."

Anne had to squint to see the tiny logo. "That's a *Talk TV* source. It's bull. They make up that stuff. Everybody knows that."

"Yeah. I've heard that."

"What's a currency recall, anyway?"

"My friends in school have been talking about a currency control system. Conspiracy theory. I don't remember all the details, but they said that some kind of electronic recall would be necessary if the federal government had to pay up on its debts all of a sudden."

Anne began to see how Fisk might be interested in such a thing. "How does the theory go, anyway? I mean, just for the sake of argument."

The intern struggled to remember details from several late-night conversations over coffee and politics. "Most of the money we use today is electronic. It makes sense that the government might want all of its electronic money back in a hurry, particularly if it had to pay its bills all at once."

"I see, though I can't imagine what could cause our own government to want to rob us. That's the conspiracy part, isn't it?" Anne sighed.

"Yeah. There's supposed to be something in there about closing the banks and then reopening them with new money. The new money would have a new exchange rate that trades better for the countries that we owe our debts to."

"The national debt may be huge, but don't you think this is asking a little much?" She blinked, afraid that Lenora might be making sense.

"Depending on who you ask, our government has been robbing us for years." As she said it, the intern knew she'd just gone too far. Journalists just did not criticize the federal government without proof in hand. Such speculation, especially regarding the current administration, had ended more than a few very promising careers in the previous ten years.

Legislation designed to combat terrorism had paved the way for a series of laws providing penalties for treason, sedition, and a host of other offenses. Congress and the courts had been confronted with these infractions and their attendant disruption during the many wars fought to stamp out global terrorism.

"I know that look. Take a fresh look at this, and get back to you." Lenora's disappointment was obvious.

Anne spoke with an enthusiasm she didn't feel. "Yes, I think so. But let's do it a little differently." Working over the germ of an idea, she hesitated, giving herself time to think. *I lost my spot in front of the camera because I didn't look before I leaped. How do I teach her that lesson?* "Find out why they'd even need a currency recall, and we'll see what comes of it."

"Really? You want me to develop a story?" Lenora asked, flattered.

"Sure." *Chasing a dead-end might teach you a thing or two about being objective.*

"Cool."

"Wrap and go home." She gave the intern a pat on the shoulder as she turned to leave.

Monday
April 21, 2014
Outside Headquarters
National Rifleman's Association
Washington, D.C.
9:25 P.M. EDT

The night sky was clearing as Garrison reached for his keys. Alone in the parking lot behind the NRA's headquarters building, he walked slowly to his car. He had left the case and gloves in the false bottom of his desk drawer. According to his briefing, somebody would collect them later. *More cloak and dagger.*

Hard to believe that tonight is the result of the last five years. He came to an abrupt stop as he bumped into someone.

"I am so sorry!" Anne exclaimed as she dropped her keys.

"It's been a long day." He stepped back.

Anne stooped to pick up her keys. "Tell me about it. I only parked back here because the front lot was full." Straightening, she looked at him. He was about six feet tall and had a jacket slung over one arm. Broad shoulders. His well-tanned forehead highlighted a fully receded hairline. Approving, she took note of the way he filled out his clothes. *Well now, who are you?*

"I..." He stopped and stared at her.

Anne followed his gaze to the left lapel of her coat, where the laminated square of her press badge gleamed in the reflected glow of the nearby streetlights. Snatching it from her lapel, she stuffed it into her coat pocket. "This isn't what it looks like. I was just on my way home. Honest." Staring at him, she felt her face flush. *Do I like him, or do I just want to know his name?*

Garrison wasn't sure how to respond. He knew he shouldn't talk to a reporter.

"Anne Carroll. I, uh...I'm with Channel 6." She nodded at the NRA building. The way he nodded back intrigued her. *It's like he*

130

knows something that he's not telling.

He offered her his hand. "Bill. William Garrison, actually." *Fisk's people told me to watch out for a media ambush. I don't think this is what they had in mind.*

Anne shook the offered appendage. "I'm really sorry about running into you. I just wanted to find my car and go home. I'm starving and--" She closed her mouth abruptly. *Don't babble. It makes you look stupid.*

"It's no trouble. I'm sure you have had a busy day. This is one for the history books."

"Say, what do you do?"

"I'm between jobs." Smiling at his own joke, he started to walk around her.

"Were you with the NRA?" *You don't look familiar.*

"Yeah." He nodded, his insecurity growing.

"You want to talk about it?" she asked with a softness that surprised both of them.

"I'm not up for an interview."

"I didn't mean on the record. I was just thinking that it's got to be pretty hard to walk away from something that you've put a lot of time into." She had stared down the prospect of quitting more than once herself. *You stuck it out until the end. That says a lot about your character.*

Garrison kept his back to building. *Very insightful.* "You're right, the Rifleman's Association did mean a lot to me. It's going to feel strange tomorrow, knowing that it's really gone." *I suppose I had to say that to somebody.*

"Come on. Truce."

"And?" he asked, shuffling in place.

"I know this little Greek place not too far from here. You look like you have a lot on your mind. Let's go there and talk. Nothing more." Anne could sense that he was struggling to accept her as a person, not a reporter.

"The Olive Leaf?" he asked with raised eyebrows.

"You know it?" She felt herself relaxing as her fear of rejection faded.

"I do. My car's at the end of the row. I'll drive."

Monday
April 21, 2014
Treasury Annex
Washington, D.C.
9:30 P.M. EDT

Fisk blew into the lounge, nodding as he came to a stop. He smiled in Madeline's direction with just a hint of embarrassment. "Sorry to keep you waiting. I was unavoidably detained. Can somebody bring me up to speed?"

Turning in her chair, Madeline inclined her head imperiously toward a woman sitting nearby. Taking her cue, the lean brunette spoke up. "We're previewing the President's opening presentation for the World Bank's negotiating team. When the talks begin, we want them to see us in our best light."

"Really? I wasn't aware it was that far along. By the way, my people will have a full report on the meeting with Ramirez in the morning." He looked directly at Madeline, playing the ambushed flunky.

"How was your flight?"

Fisk shrugged and thought of his camouflaged nose. "I stayed busy. Beltway traffic was a real mess. Somebody rolled a tanker. Bad stuff."

"You had no problems with Ramirez?" The conversational subtext went unnoticed by the others in the room. Accepting her defeat, she waited. *You weren't supposed to make this meeting. We both know it. Let's get this charade over with.*

"He's agreed to play nice, if that's what you mean. That, and he accepted all four of our briefcases. He's bought and paid for, as long as you make good on the next two deposits to his Swiss account." Fisk casually stepped over to an empty chair. *Never mind that he wants to see our proposal six weeks before talks begin.*

"That leaves only two loose ends." The President nodded approvingly. *Congress and that idiot you talked me into appointing to Treasury.*

"All good things come to those who wait. Bide your time and keep your perspective," Fisk replied, grinning playfully as he sat down. The grin made his nose hurt.

"Very well. We'll go have a look at what I've prepared. I want your comments." Madeline rose to her feet in a single fluid motion. Her mood was clearly shifting as she took a harsh step toward him. *I'm going to be rid of you one way or another. I don't care how indispensable you are. You make me feel like...*

"Let's see what you've got."

Monday
April 21, 2014
Treasury Annex
Washington, D.C.
9:35 P.M. EDT

A brief ride on a secured elevator took the group deep under-ground. Nestled deep in the D.C. bedrock, the Treasury's newly constructed Currency Command Center was expected to be online within six months.

Protected by sophisticated electronics and a contingent of officially nonexistent troops, the C3, as it was nicknamed, reminded Madeline of the North American Aerospace Defense Command facilities located in Colorado's Cheyenne Mountain. *I've only visited NORAD once, but it made quite an impression.*

"Were you able to get any sleep on the plane? I'm sorry if I've upset your schedule," she said as the elevator continued on its downward journey.

At just over 6'3", Fisk towered over Madeline's petite 5'7". He met her gaze, smiling warmly as the usual gambit opened with the usual questions designed to fish for a hint of emotional distress.

"It was a working flight. My people had me pinned down with some kind of long-winded explanation about a problem in your C3 system," he lied with his usual facility. He was attempting to deflect the questioning by encouraging her to discuss a subject that made her both excited and anxious.

"Security?" Madeline guessed.

She had stood close to Fisk so that the rest of the entourage had room to cram into the elevator. He could easily read her reaction. *You want to pull this off almost as much as you want to be rid of me.* He nodded, waiting for her temper to boil over.

"What is it this time?" she fumed, almost ready to believe that he had actually been locked away in a meeting rather than narrowly escaping death on the Beltway.

Fisk carefully started with something that she already knew, to keep her anger smoldering. "Backups and primary safeties are being tested now. There may still be a flaw in the file transfer protocol, but it's proving impossible to find. I know you don't like it when my people double-check the work you're people are doing here, but they're also having some problems with the download time. They tell me that your systems should be 20 seconds faster." Acknowledging her familiarity with the more complex aspects of computing, he didn't hold anything back.

They got off the elevator. The President barely acknowledged the agent at the guard post as they passed down the brushed metal corridor. "What about uplink? I told the designers that the buffer-to-bus ratio was off by a factor of ten." *If it's not one thing, it's another.* Madeline's paranoia and stubborn pride combined with her computer competency to cause her to take the problem personally. *How hard can this be? It's not as if I'm asking for something that's never been done before.*

Once the facility was operational, President Hill would have total control over the nation's electronic money supply. While the currency exchange plan was being achieved in secret, she was looking forward to openly taking credit for successfully negotiating the America debt settlement. *There's no way I'm letting Congress rob me of this once-in-a-life-time opportunity.*

Inside his armored kiosk, the security specialist nodded toward the President. Closely examining each person as the group passed, he signaled the all-clear by pressing a button on a nearby instrument panel.

"Uplink it is. The moment you enter your command code, the data links will kick in and the currency transfer begins. My people tell me that the 20 second increase is necessary to prevent intruders from using capture programs."

"I've seen the software. Nobody's capture code is that good. They'd have to use a neural interface and write their snake on the fly."

"Which my people say they can do. They've simmed it, and--"

Madeline sneered. "According to your people, they can do anything."

135

"That's why I pay them." He was careful to add a touch of smugness to his tone.

"You must be so proud."

"It takes 42 hours, from start to finish. Once complete, you'll have pulled in something like 99 percent of the country's electronic money supply." He moved ahead of the crowd to swipe a grey key card through an electronic reader. The dominant physical move was intended to aggravate Madeline's insecurities.

A pair of roving Secret Service agents orbited the group as it moved through a thick Plexiglas door onto an observation deck. They filed in and took their prearranged seats. The armored gallery overlooked a computer complex that was still under construction. Minimally lit, it was cool, and just as luxurious as it was impersonal.

"Don't get bogged down in technical details. Have you succeeded in winning over Secretary Brown? All of this won't mean a thing if he doesn't get with the program."

Fisk rubbed his chin. "Andrew has become an idealist. We both knew that could happen with any of your Cabinet appointments. The job has changed him. We have to accept that."

The conspirators had gone out of their way to ensure that the Hill administration's Cabinet appointments were popular with the media, as well as compliant with the desires of their employer. Since becoming the Secretary of the Treasury, Andrew Brown had become surprisingly uncooperative. After just 15 months on the job, he had developed an incredibly strong sense of integrity and ethics. His desire to rid his country of its crippling debt was beyond question.

"His insistence on such outmoded thinking won't make my job any easier. If he weren't so popular with the media, I'd can him and appoint Alexander Kirsov. He, at least, would understand the politics behind this and support me."

Fisk nodded without speaking.

In her drive to claim all the glory, the President was pursuing the national debt restructuring with considerable energy and resources. The fact that the negotiations were tentatively slated to begin at the end of the current calendar year only fuelled her desire to succeed. *The president that pulls this off can have anything she wants*, she told herself as she turned to face Fisk. *And I want it all. If people have any real appreciation for what I've done, they'll--*

"The simulations all pan out. The Trojan horse will fool everyone long enough for the account transfers to be completed. All you have to do now is crack this 20-second thing. If not, it'll still be okay. At most, we lose some pocket change to a few overly resourceful hackers."

"That, at least, is under control. FBI and Homeland told me they're still working the bugs out of their integrated chain of command. When the time comes, we can count on having enough law enforcement in the field to make some major arrests. That reminds me, have you spoken to Langsford about the NCR? Arresting a handful of hackers will only be icing on the cake, but it'll add legitimacy to the NCR that we might want later."

Fisk glanced out at the still-dormant computer bay. "Actually, I have. He's got a lobby to pay off, but it's nothing that I need to be bothered with. I fed him the usual line about playing ball with you so that he could get his way on a few bills next year. Just make it look good when he thinks he's talking you into it. If you play your cards right, you might be able to schmooze him into being nicer to the boys in the Senate."

Madeline forced herself to relax as she thought ahead to the next year. "Has he...Has Andrew ever told you why he's opposed to padding the federal asset inventory? Now that the UN has merged the World Bank and the IMF--"

Fisk reached out to touch the arm of her chair lightly. "Old news. Remember me? I'm on your side. Nobody has ever negotiated a debt settlement this large. They're going to expect us to fudge our numbers to get the most out of what we have for collateral. If Andy won't play along, we'll just work around him. That's all there is to it."

"I assume that you'll know just how to 'work around' him." She looked away. *I'll never understand why it hurts so much whenever I have to ask you for something.*

In ten years, she had been utterly unsuccessful in subverting him. Her inability to find his weaknesses had hardened her determination to be rid of him so that she could feel secure in her role as president and leader of the most powerful nation on the planet.

"She just spiked the stress meter," a tiny voice in Fisk's right ear said.

He allowed himself to smile. "When the time comes, we will rock Andy Brown's world."

"Good. I'll look into that 20-second parameter. It's been a few years since I got my hands dirty with computers, but if I have to, I'll fix it myself," she said firmly.

Fisk raised an eyebrow, carefully playing his part to the hilt. "Everybody knows that you were into computers at one point, but--"

"You just keep things moving forward. I don't want those transactions hacked, diverted, or even probed. I want to give the World Bank my utmost assurances that, when the time comes, we can pull this off."

The voice whispered at Fisk again. "Research wants to index her stress variable. You need to make her mad so that we can get a fresh recording."

Fisk slouched, a look of concern spreading across his face. "You still haven't told me what should be done if all this goes wrong. Suppose you don't get the terms you want? Andy Brown is one thing, but these World Bankers are heavy hitters who can directly influence world opinion--"

"Everything will work out, and when it does, you'll see for yourself what comes next. Why must you always dwell on the down side of things?"

Madeline's angry look told Fisk that he'd hit the intended nerve. The fire in her eyes burned with the heat of her conviction.

A phone buzzed somewhere in the gallery. An aide looked at the President.

"How long?" she demanded.

"Thirty seconds."

Fisk sat back, grateful for the break in conversation. *You're not going to come out and say it, are you? You won't actually tell me that you plan to stay in office after your terms are up. We chose well.* He closed his eyes for a moment. *Maybe a little too well.*

President Hill had seen this presentation ten times during its initial development. Each time it grew just a little bit longer due to changes that she ordered. The main body of it was short and to the point. An outsider would never notice the embellishments.

The sound system in the gallery came to life with a muted

instrumental rendition of the American national anthem.

If this works, the future of this nation will be greatly improved, thanks to me. Once the world sees that I can handle this problem...

She asked Fisk, "You haven't seen this yet, have you?"

"No, I haven't."

Though she found his invulnerability maddening, she drew strength and comfort from his perpetual confidence. *So why don't I try some less roundabout means of bringing you into the fold? I just can't put my finger on what holds me back. You are, after all, just a man.*

The lights dimmed in the gallery. Down in the computer bay, the lights went out altogether. A massive hologram began to coalesce at eye level. The spectators had a perfect viewing position.

The sheer size of the image took her breath away each time she saw it. She hoped that it would have the same effect on the World Bank reps. *Magnificent. Art and propaganda in the same visual package.*

Images began forming on a vast expanse of blue sky. Even Fisk had to admit that the presentation would be a real show-stopper. *The negotiators won't expect this. It's confident and bold without being commercial. Just what the doctor ordered,* he decided as his wireless phone chimed.

He rose to leave the gallery. He touched the President lightly on the shoulder to signal his departure. Nodding, Madeline's deep blue eyes remained locked onto the presentation. She knew that, as her party's most favored advisor, Fisk could be called away at any moment to respond to the needs of her administration and senior party leaders.

"Security. Garrison has broken protocol," he heard through the comm implant

Closing the gallery door softly behind him, Fisk looked both ways to be sure that he was alone in the corridor. Knowing that concealed video cameras were watching him, he took out his wireless phone. Flipping it open, he checked to make sure that the secured line telltale was lit before activating it.

"Tell me about it," he said calmly, putting his free hand in his pants pocket.

"Overwatch checked in five minutes ago. Garrison appears to have run into a reporter as he was leaving the NRA. She got into his car, and they're en route." The voice belonged to the same man who had spoken through his comm implant.

"What's the probability?" Fisk knew that somebody would have started a sim just as soon as the "event" happened.

"Eighty-six percent random. Overwatch has instructions to notify you before taking any action. Garrison was told to avoid the press for the rest of the day. Looks like he didn't make it."

Fisk turned, head down. "Hold on. He isn't going to give us up now. Not after all he's been through. You said this was most likely a random encounter? I'm inclined to believe that. He was probably shuffling along with his head in the clouds. Did he make physical contact? Bump into her?"

"Yes."

"There you go. Dial him on wireless for me." Fisk glanced over his shoulder at the closed door to the observation deck.

"He's not carrying. He left it at home."

He paused to think. "Call me when he gets to a phone. I'll check this myself."

"Sir, the rules--"

"I know the rules, and I know him. He's only started dating again in the last two years, and sporadically at that. He's still not quite over his ex. I'm going to clear him, and that'll be that."

"Sir, he's a Phase Two candidate--"

"I don't have to be reminded of who he is. Cut him some slack. He's only human. Call me when you can reach him, and I'll talk to him."

"I'll have to report this."

"You do that. They know where to find me." Flipping the phone closed, he cut the connection. *Worrying about what the Founders think is the least of my problems.*

Satisfied that there was nothing more that he could do, Fisk slid silently back into the gallery, taking his seat just as the lights came up. *If Garrison won't work with me, all of our Phase Two planning won't amount to anything. I need to give him some room so that he'll go the extra mile for us.*

"I missed it?" He looked apologetic.

"You missed it. I'll have a copy sent to your office." Looking up at him from where she sat, Madeline's eyebrows arched questioningly.

Shifting in his chair, he arched an eyebrow in return and nodded toward the entourage to indicate that he had something sensitive to talk about.

"Go ahead. As much as I would like to tell them to go away, I've learned that there are limitations to my freedom. Please, continue."

"It was my office. The final report on the meeting with Ramirez is finished. You can have it now if you want it."

"That was fast." She nodded, envious.

"We aim to please."

Monday
April 21, 2014
Secured Site 3
The Olive Leaf
Washington, D.C.
10:05 P.M. EDT

"I find that hard to believe. You don't strike me as the kind of person to make a mistake like that." Garrison smiled.

Across the table, Anne nodded vigorously, dipping her head in an exaggerated shame. "Oh, yes, I did. The 'big three' networks didn't have the kind of competition they have today. *Talk TV* was just a twinkle in somebody's eye at that point. There were so many of us that were willing to go to the war zones. Anything to get in front of the camera. I had no idea that things would work out that way. It's one of the reasons why so many journalists try to stay close to the truth these days. We got burned for toeing the official line. You know?"

Anne felt at ease with Garrison. Something about the combination of the soft lighting, the way he looked at her, and his relaxed posture, brought down her guard. *You aren't judging me.*

"Sounds like the first three Gulf wars, or at least what I've read about the way the press was handled. As long as you had a real reason for doing it, I don't suppose it was truly a mistake. Truth is truth. It's hard to keep your convictions off the auction block, especially if you really like what you do." Out of the corner of his eye, he saw the waiter approaching.

The waiter was a small man with olive skin. He was gracious as he took Anne's order, than asked, "Is the wine to your liking?"

"Very," she nodded, raising the glass so that he could fill it.

"Mr. Garrison has excellent taste," he told her with a wink and a nod as he left.

"You must come here often."

"I own a share in the place. It's one of the few things that Ellen didn't want when we divorced." Garrison actually owned 20 percent of the restaurant, and his ex-wife really had taken no interest in it at the time of their settlement.

I'm not so sure it was a good idea to come here. Hidden underground, below the obvious basement, three additional levels housed equipment and personnel that were part of the conspiracy's infrastructure.

"Sorry if I touched a nerve. It must be habit for you to come here. This place is close to the Rifleman's..." She leaned back.

"It's okay. It's been six and a half years. I can talk about it now. Really. I hope you didn't think I was trying to set you up for something by bringing you here." *Haven't done this in a long time. I'm glad she's so easy to talk to.*

"No, not at all." She blushed, fighting self-recrimination. *I'm thinking like a news hound when I should be thinking like a woman.*

"So, tell me, how did we do tonight?" Changing the subject was a skill he'd learned during the last year of his marriage.

Anne raised an eyebrow. "It's been a long time coming, you know. A lot of people have gotten sick and tired of the NRA's rants about the 'true' meaning of the Second Amendment."

Her hard assessment made Garrison cringe. "Is that just the media's perception, or is it what people really think?" Even now, the urge to do combat was hard to suppress. *I'm tired and it's been a long day. Stop it.*

"I don't think you're going to like my answer. Especially since, as of tonight, you're out of a job." She was pleasantly surprised when he nodded for her to continue. His relaxed pose still hadn't changed. *You really want to know, don't you?*

Heartened by his interest, she chose her words carefully. "It's not just what the voters want anymore that counts. Things have changed in the last ten years. Governments and multinational corporations have a lot more in common than they used to. Call it what you like. They both have come to realize that the people who pay their taxes or buy their stuff are their most important assets. The NRA got in their way, so..."

There's more truth to that than you may know.

Anne noted that he was unfazed by her assessment. *Interesting that you're not asking me where I stand.*

The dapper waiter leaned toward Garrison as he placed a small salad in front of him. "Sir, there is a phone call for you in the office."

He flinched as the man withdrew.

Anne reached for her napkin. "I promise I won't run away. I can relate. I'm surprised that my wireless hasn't interrupted." They shared a knowing look over the frustrations of modern life.

"It's probably something to do with the restaurant. I won't be long."

Making his way slowly through the softly lit dining room, Garrison went to the manager's office in the back. *They're going to have my guts for garters because I talked to her. I just know it.*

The cluttered office was unoccupied when he opened the door. On the disorganized desk, a phone telltale blinked at him. Closing the door, he reached for a stack of cloth napkins. Using one to wipe his sweating palms, he sat down on the chair. Looking at the telephone, he tossed the napkin aside. Picking up the receiver, he punched the blinking line button.

"This is Bill Garrison. What can I do for you?"

Fisk's voice came through the line. "Bill, you rascal. I thought I told you to avoid the press?"

"It's not what it looks like."

"I figured as much. You should've kept walking. You know that, don't you?"

"I'm sorry. I ran into her in the parking lot as I was leaving. It just happened, you know?"

"I'm going to catch it for this, and so are you," Fisk replied, dispensing the mandatory criticism.

"We have an understanding, see?" Garrison felt the hairs on the back of his neck rise.

"You're 'off-duty,' is that it?"

"We called a truce. Look, I know I was supposed to steer clear, but this just sort of happened. You know?" He couldn't help repeating himself. *You've never been quick to judge me. Please don't start now.*

The other man's nod was almost audible through the phone line. "I understand. It happens. I'll back you up this time. We've had our eye on Ms. Carroll for some time. I don't expect you to have any problems with her as long as you stay focused. She respects ground rules, so make that work for you."

"Are you telling me this is okay?"

"It's okay now. I'll make the necessary calls. Nobody should give you a hard time about it. Just be careful. She's been doing some investigative pieces on me, and I don't want her to make the connection between us. Got it?"

"She can't..." *What have I done?*

"She can, if she makes the right moves. Come on, you know better."

"This is just dinner. I don't have to see her again," he said, flushing.

"Don't sweat it. I'm satisfied that you're not going to do anything stupid. Besides, as I said, we've had our eye on her for a while now. She's on our Phase Two list."

Garrison shot a quick glance at the door. "Really? I'm not on your Phase Two list, am I?"

"All things in due time. I'll have my office call you by the end of the week. We can talk about it then. Now, get back to your date, and let her do most of the talking."

Doris walked into the den rubbing her tired eyes. She removed her trenchcoat and draped it over the back of a chair. This was her favorite of Fisk's three homes. Stopping to enjoy the view of the bay, she squinted. A ferry crept over the choppy grey-green water, plowing a trail of white froth. Framed by storm clouds, its lights were bright under the false dawn.

Near the large bay windows, a mahogany desk squatted on thick legs. Brass inlay glowed despite the lack of sunlight. She walked over and sat down in the large padded chair behind it. As the chair accommodated her body's contours, she allowed herself to relax and yawn. *I am so glad this is nearly over and done with.* On the desk next to her, the phone buzzed.

"We're about to wake him," a female voice said through the phone's speaker.

"Is there any way we can bump his schedule a few hours?" Doris rubbed the back of her neck. *He didn't get to bed until 1:30.*

"He has an advisory meeting today at the Vermont site. I know that he had a late night, but this really can't wait. Do you want me to call?"

"No. Let's stick to the schedule." *I wish I felt better about that.*

"Okay. Can we get you anything?"

"Is there any of that fresh fruit left?"

"Sure. Lots."

"Great. I'll be down in a little while to get some." Doris sighed, disconnecting the intercom with the push of a button.

Opening the left-side desk drawer, she flipped up the clear plastic cover over a number pad mounted next to a row of buttons. The

146

instrument panel controlled a whole host of security devices. Punching in her six-digit code, she waited for hidden computers to do their jobs. Indicators on the panel lit up, showing her that the room was fully secured.

Getting out of the chair, she walked over to a large walnut cabinet set into the wall. Each of Fisk's homes had the same high-tech computer station built into their respective dens. *I like this place,* Doris reminded herself. *It's the view that does it for me.*

Opening the well-oiled doors of the cabinet, she waited for the keyboard to slide out. She tapped the keys, flying through the commands needed to establish a secured comm link to the Founders. The shadowy group was located at Secured Site 1. Most were in their late nineties, if not older.

What am I going to say? She knew what she *wanted* to say, even as the computer began to make the connection. The monitor stayed dark. She sat down in a nearby recliner, making herself comfortable as the encryption programs ran final checks.

Enola's European sophistication flowed through hidden speakers. "So good of you to call. How are things going?"

"Yesterday was a raging success."

"That's good to hear. But you sound worried about something."

Doris looked straight at the tiny camera mounted on top of the monitor. *So, you're watching me.*

"Yes, dear, I'm watching. Unlike my fellow geriatrics, I'm not afraid of this technology."

Doris nodded. *You're the oldest of the bunch, if memory serves.* "I'm glad to hear it. I was worried that someday there wouldn't be anybody left to contact."

The older woman's voice fluttered with a kind laugh.

The conspiracy had been designed with an inherent mortality. The Founders had intended the whole thing to fall apart if it took too long to implement. The oldest among them called it a "vanishing conspiracy." It was meant to safeguard the lives of those involved, as well as their families.

"I promise to let you know if our numbers become so few that we risk extinction. Now tell me, what else do you have to report, and what is bothering you?"

Doris leaned back. *Formal, but to the point. Fine.* "He's been taking unnecessary risks lately. I expect him to start rebelling pretty soon."

"You're speaking of what happened last night?"

"If Christopher hadn't been there to moderate his actions, I'm afraid he might have turned on his pursuers. As it was, he noticed the trap."

"You think his programming is breaking down?"

Doris took another look out the window, hesitating. The ferry was making steady progress as rain began to fall. "I do. And I know what it means to say that, but we can't afford to ignore the facts. He wouldn't want me to."

"I'm so sorry, dear," Enola replied compassionately.

"I don't want your pity. I want consideration. I was there. I know what you saw, and I know what Griff's report will be."

"This is a lot to surmise, and, as you've pointed out, the implications are most dire."

"He won't break. But I know for a fact that the ambush pushed the limits of his stress tolerance. I know him better than anyone else, and--"

"I believe you. I understand how you feel. It wasn't easy to give him up. Lord knows I couldn't accept that kind of loss. It would probably have done to me what it's doing to you."

Doris said nothing as she watched the ferry crawl across the bay. "Can't we just leave him alone? He's only got to stay on top of this thing for another month." It was all she could do to remain physically calm.

"You have something in mind?" The Founder's tone was rich with interest.

Doris looked sharply at the computer and blinked. "One step ahead, as usual." She nodded at the camera, rubbing her palms over the arms of the chair and sighed.

"Indeed. I've always known that you would be the one to make this call. That's why he chose you; to be his guardian angel."

"You knew?"

"That night, in the personal effects room? Yes. Naturally, we got the whole thing on tape--which I seem to have lost."

"Excuse me?" Doris felt the hairs on the back of her neck rise.

"Do you still love him?"

The question stung Doris as much as it surprised her. Her answer was a silent nod.

"May I presume that you don't like the idea of--"

"No. I don't. That's why I'm here. To--"

"There is no need. I'm not like the rest. The plan is not written in stone, and I don't stay awake at night thinking about it. Besides, you're not the only one who has attachments to the man."

"All right. I'm sorry. I have so little contact with any of you that it's hard not to form certain judgments. After all this time, I didn't think that any of you would..." She paused.

"Indictment accepted. Apology accepted. Now, shall we get down to the task at hand?"

"Which would be?"

"Please, trust an old woman just this once. You and I have a lot in common."

"How do I know you and I are talking about the same thing?" *What are you up to?*

"We both know that Preston Fisk is more than the sum of his parts. We owe him a great deal. You have paid your debt to him with your protection. Perhaps it is time that I repaid mine as well." Enola paused to take a breath.

"You're with me?" A metallic taste invaded her mouth.

"Yes. Jason was right to fear us. We've never talked about it, but I've always known that the others might prefer to liquidate Fisk. Most of us have been 'non-persons' for more than 40 years. As far as they are concerned, Jason Cutter become one when he agreed to the Fisk programming. To them, he's already dead."

"Really?" She was chilled to hear her worst fears put to words.

"It has been 14 years. In that time, half of us have passed beyond the veil. The events of the last ten years have made all of us bitter. We've seen some of our best work perverted in ways that you can't imagine. It's almost as if our plan wasn't needed. I've wondered about that. We were wrong about so many things."

In the previous ten years, the federal government had assumed more power than it had held at any time during the twentieth century. A series of successful overseas military campaigns lent momentum to the crusade against terrorism, serving to justify presidential requests for even more comprehensive legislation. The trend towards greater authoritarianism showed no signs of slowing.

Doris nodded. "You must be on his wavelength. He made similar confessions to me."

"I know about those remarks. So do the others."

"He's not wrong. He's never been wrong about this. Our plan is still sound. If we didn't push this president, there is no telling how long it could take..." Fueled by her protectiveness and convictions, Doris worked hard to reign herself in.

"I envy you your beliefs. If he and I are truly on the same page, you will have to forgive us our fears. Chalk it up to being in the field for too long."

Doris nodded, surprised by the older woman's admission.

"Thank you. Naturally, I will follow your lead, if you think your years away from the trade haven't dulled your skills."

Doris gave the camera a meaningful look. "No interference. We do this my way. Is that clear? I'll be ready if things go wrong. I want him to succeed. Then I want him to be deprogrammed, just like the plan calls for. All I need from you is one thing." Standing, Doris took a step towards the computer, knowing that her image would be enlarged in the camera's view.

"A free hand," the sage voice extrapolated with casual ease.

"I assume they'll take him out at or near the Phase One termination point. Would they take his comm out, first?"

"It is always wise to defang the cobra. It will also allay any suspicions on his part. He will remain compliant as long as he thinks he will be released from his obligations."

Tuesday
April 22, 2014
Terrorism Section
Counter Insurgency Division
Department of Homeland Security
Langley, Virginia
5:08 A.M. EDT

Harry was a realist. True to his roots, he believed that whatever took place before normal business hours didn't actually happen. The dodge was an old one, used more frequently than ever these days to defy the courts.

Reclined in his chair, he cast a patient eye toward the clock as he leafed through the latest overseas projections. *It's not as if we can do anything about it,* he griped silently as he reached for a new report. *No budget means no capability.*

The intercom chirped. Reaching over to a small instrument panel set into desktop, he keyed the response mode.

"Jordan Pike has just signed in."

He nodded. "Get Pickering and Keats in here." He sat forward in his high-backed chair.

"Sir, Mr. Pickering is in the secured comms lab. I don't have authorization."

"It's okay. Pass the word to Keats, and tell him where Pickering is. He'll know what needs doing." Turning off the intercom, Oswald picked up his phone and dialed an in-house extension.

"Monitoring." The sleepy man's voice was tinged with unmistakable boredom.

Harry read from the security badge clipped to the lapel of his coat, "Oswald, 2-1-8. I need full monitoring." He paused again to allow the lethargic specialist to access the particulars through his workstation.

"For how long? And did you want the spectra?"

He chewed his lower lip for two full heartbeats. "Live monitor.

Give it the works. I have an appointment coming up to my office now. I want the whole session scanned and plotted. See that the Director gets it, afterwards."

The sleepy man came alive. "Now? Yes, sir. Full package. I'll get right on it."

Oswald listened to the brisk tap of suddenly nervous fingers on a keyboard. "Good enough." He hung up.

He looked at the stack of reports on his desk. *I know the Director told me to make any kind of deal that would get us in good with the President, but this is too sleazy, even for us.* The thought of sitting through another exchange with Pike made his ulcer twinge. The nausea was enough to make him regret having breakfast. A knock on the door saved him from having to initial everything he'd just read.

"Come!" he bellowed gruffly.

Thomas Keats poked his head into Harry's office. "Bill's on his way. There's some heavy stuff coming off the bird over the Philippines--"

"Come on in. How do you handle it without going nuts?" His smile was jovial, though his eyes glinted with a hateful spark as he recalled life in the secured communications lab.

Keats checked the knot of his tie and the cuffs of his white shirt as he sat down. His broad, dark face framed a mischievous smile. His short, curly hair gave only the merest hint of his Jamaican heritage.

"You need to get laid more often. Bill gets laid at least twice a week. He isn't any fun to be around when he's missed his appointments, either." He shook his head in mock consternation. Folding his hands over the arm rests of his chair, he relaxed.

"That your secret?" Oswald raised an eyebrow as he moved the reports.

"I'm not saying. You white men always start feeling sorry for yourselves when--"

Both men paused at the knock on the door. Bill Pickering entered without waiting for acknowledgement. "Here, boss. Doesn't that little prick ever sleep? It's five o'clock in the morning, for crying out loud!" The pasty-faced man scurried across the room with a sheaf of papers under one arm. Dressed in collared shirt and tie, Pickering's agitation hinted at his humorless nature.

"Cheer up. This is just a formality. Our president owes us a favor. That's what the Director wanted, and that's what he got." Homeland Security wasn't like the other agencies it had jurisdiction over. *Oversight, riiight.*

"How did it go last night?" Keats asked.

"The way I heard it, they nearly got him," Pickering replied, taking the cap off a red ballpoint pen. His assignment involved monitoring civilian datalinks for subversive content. That included anything electronic transmitted that might lead to the arrest of terrorists or seditionists.

"That was an A-6 sim. How'd they blow that?" Keats asked.

Pickering began rapidly marking up the hard copy he held. "Who cares? Pike's probably here to see if he can get us to do an after-action analysis."

"I hope they cancel him." Keats' expression fouled.

Pickering stopped marking pages to give his colleague a sharp look. "Like I said, who cares? I've never had a president owe me a favor before. Guys like Pike are a dime a dozen."

Keats pulled at his shirt cuffs. "The favors we can use. I'm just tired of having to get my shots updated after dealing with this guy. Say, I ran--"

Oswald pointed at Keats. "Can it. You know better than that. We do for them and they do for us. Especially with this president." He paused to punch up the intercom. "Pike?"

"Elevator," the staff assistant replied.

"Show him in when he gets here." He switched off the intercom and looked at Keats and Pickering. "Pike is a bag man with a big connection. Don't make him mad. Let's just hear him out and send him on his way. Got it?"

Pickering looked up from the stack of papers. One glance at Harry's stern glare forced a nod out of him.

Keats held out for a moment longer before signaling his cooperation.

Pickering held up the ruffled pages. "There you are. See? I told you I'd find that code variance before lunch." All three men started when the door swung open.

"Jordan Pike to see you." The staff assistant showed the tall, thin man into the office.

Oswald stood, determined to start the session off on his terms.

Pike took in the sparse furnishings of the office as the Section Chief shook his hand. As a behind-the-scenes fixer, he rubbed elbows with people from all walks of life and levels of power. Despite the lack of machismo suggested by the decor, Pike's estimation of Oswald was tempered by seven years of hard-won experience. *He doesn't like me. Neither do they.* He nodded at the other two men and moved to the chair in front of Oswald's desk.

Pickering quickly sat on the pages that he was holding.

Pike gave a sour look. "I was under the impression that your simulation was designed to take in all the variables?" *We shouldn't pay off for this,* his ego lamented. *We didn't get what we wanted.*

Pike had learned that the prestige of one's employer often rubbed off on the person making the deal. The fact that he was working for the President of the United States made him feel more than just a little ungrateful to the man he was now sitting in front of.

"The person you're interested in is a very exceptional individual," Pickering stated flatly. *They're lucky they got off as light as they did. If either one of Fisk's tactical teams had been in place, I'd bet my paycheck that the District of Columbia would have one less SWAT unit this morning.*

"So I'm told." Pike waited for further explanation.

Having seen the news reports of the "accident" on the Beltway, Harry had no doubt that Fisk's escape was a matter of purest luck. "The sim we ran on him suggested that the executive kidnapping scenario would be the most effective. It's not our fault that your people chose to get creative with our numbers."

"Point taken."

The agent put on his best self-effacing grin. "Come on. You must have read the brief."

Pike's finely tuned instincts caused him to put on his poker face.

Harry inclined his head in a knowing gesture. "You're a smart guy. You know how the game is played. We crunched nearly 4,000 gigabytes of data to develop your sim. When you get right down to it, we're working with data from other agencies. If we'd gathered it ourselves, things might have been different. As it is, your people went their own way."

"The fault lies in the execution, not the plan itself. Is that what you're telling me?"

"That's how we see it." Oswald folded his hands on the desk blotter.

"How do you propose that we regain control of the situation?" Pike asked, seizing upon the chance to return to his employer with something more than confirmation of failure. Knowing Madeline Hill's temper as he did, he was very certain that she would spare him the worst of her anger if--and only if--he brought her an option.

"We can't make any further recommendations unless we review the scenario data. Which we don't have." Harry nodded sympathetically, deliberately playing for the hidden cameras. He spread his hands, waiting for Pike to take the bait or back down.

Pike fingered the briefcase in his lap. "That's why I'm here. I've got the surveillance data, but I'd have to make sure that--"

Oswald leaned forward slightly, shamelessly exploiting Pike's ego. "We can keep this between us. You've got to understand one thing. We might not find anything that you can use. If that's the case, we won't be getting back to you."

Though his ability to charm had been lost years ago, Harry's skill at deception had grown considerably. *People like you resent the smallest hint that you don't know the inside scoop. Let's see just how thin your skin really is.* He grinned slyly.

"I understand. I'm glad you appreciate my position." Jordan licked his lips to give his brain a chance to catch up to his mouth. He glanced meaningfully at Oswald. *If you can find something for me to use, I'd be willing to return the favor later.*

Watching Pike finger the handle on his briefcase, Harry felt certain that he was taking the bait. *We find something you can use, and you're our 'buddy.' I've got enough on video to compromise you now. Buddy.*

Harry sat back in his chair with a sigh. "Well, there you go. If you don't hear from us, you'll know why." Even as he spoke, his mind was already beginning to wander.

Looking sidelong at the telephone on his desk, his attention drifted to the small photo of his goddaughter perched nearby. The picture was over 20 years old, and the golden-haired little girl in pigtails had gone on to bigger things than being snuggled by her godfather. The photo had faded with the passing of time, though the memories attached to it had not. Harry silently told the giggling little girl, *Your daddy would be proud of what you've done with your life. I know I am.*

"Your resources are extensive. I know it may take some time, but I have no doubts that you'll find something that I can use."

"Fair enough." Harry did his best to look disinterested as Pike opened the briefcase. He paused, guiltily. *Jason would have never made this deal.* The man he had once looked up to had vanished on a failed operation fifteen years earlier. Though he never talked about it, his feelings stemmed largely from his all-too-brief guardianship of Cutter's daughter. Having somebody to take care of had turned out to be more satisfying than he had ever imagined.

Pickering looked away. Beside him, Keats leaned on one elbow and said nothing as he studied the wall.

Pike removed a manila envelope from the briefcase. "Can I tell my employer that you'd be interested in another try?" Holding the envelope securely, he closed the briefcase and set it on the floor next to his chair.

Oswald grinned. The surveillance data on the disk that Pike was about to give him was worth a lot. It would allow Harry and his team to backtrack the manpower involved just far enough to provide an accurate picture of the events that had transpired the previous night. It would also tell them, in no uncertain terms, just how dangerous Madeline Hill really was.

Harry rubbed his chin to disguise the look of contempt spoiling to get out. *I'm guessing that your days were numbered. If there is another transaction, you won't be the one conducting it. I've seen three different presidents use guys like you to do their dirty work. None of those bag boys are alive today.*

Personal and political matters tended to overlap to such an extent that the contemporary U.S. presidency had become equally dangerous to those who worked for and against the current office holder.

The farmhouse nestled among the pines gave no indications that it was anything more than that: a farmer's home located just a little too close to the Interstate highway. Standing next to the fireplace, Fisk resisted the urge to take off his trenchcoat, settling for rubbing his tired eyes. Outside, the van that had delivered him here was pulling away. Enjoying the warmth of the fire, he spent several minutes watching the grey clouds in the sky. Raindrops were already rolling down the windows of the southern exposure.

The events of the previous night were already beginning to fade. He'd already turned off his comm implant in preparation for the meeting. The silence was beginning to get on his nerves. *It's as if I don't feel quite right unless I have somebody else's voice in my head.*

Turning toward an owlish man in threadbare clothes, Fisk motioned to get his attention. It took some effort to push the irritation and fatigue from his mind. *I wonder if I look as tired as I feel.* "What does the media have to say about last night's tanker accident?"

Joe Kinsey had been in jail when he'd been introduced to the Fisk Group. As a private detective, he'd gotten a little too close to the wrong people at the request of a wealthy client. Ruined and reduced to living on the street, he had chosen to make his situation work for himself and his new associates. Knowing what people wanted and why was stock in trade for an older man trying to make it on the mean streets of D.C.

Kinsey turned his attention from the papers on the table in front of him and looked up at Fisk. Running a hand through his tousled grey hair, he used a small remote to bring up the volume of the three tiny portable televisions that squatted on the table next to him.

"...been able to confirm the deaths of ten bystanders after a gasoline tanker exploded..."

"...are still investigating reports of a black helicopter at the scene of the accident..."

"...said in a press conference, and we're quoting, 'There is no terrorist connection'..."

"The networks are going on about the NRA, too. The gun control folks aren't being bashful, either. They really think they struck a blow for freedom." Kinsey lowered the volumes and laid the remote down. He smiled wanly, scratching the back of his head to signal his disapproval.

Fisk nodded.

"It's playing out like Griff thought it would. I'm not cleared for the really juicy details, but I'd sure like to think you could trust me to do the right thing, you know?"

Fisk held out his hands. "I'd like to help you. I'm not the only one who appreciates what you do, but you know that we're shutting down in the next few months, don't you?"

"Yeah. I know what I've been told, but I also know that pirates like you don't stay out of sight for long. I was kind of hoping..."

Fisk reached out to give him a pat on the shoulder. "I know. The thing is, we've done what we set out to do. The presidency and the Congress are hot-loaded. That's all we wanted. You know the rest."

"No, I don't know the rest. Look, I've seen a lot of things in my life. You've been good to me, and you've given me a chance to play a little part in this wild plan of yours, but I'm not stupid. I want in on what comes next."

"If there was a next--"

"Give me a break. You paid me with an offshore account. I'm probably one of the wealthiest homeless people on the street. You wouldn't be paying me five grand a month unless you had enough juice to go on to the next thing. You hear what I'm saying?"

Fisk turned sideways as if he were about to divulge a secret. "Tell you what I'll do. I'll pass your name on to some people I know. Is that good enough?" The lie came out flawlessly, despite the feeble protest of his battered conscience. *It's too bad we can't clear you for Phase Two. I think you would have liked it.*

"Yes, that'll do." Kinsey stuck out his hand.

"Okay, then." He accepted the handshake.

"They're waiting for you in the back," Kinsey said, checking his watch.

"Right. I'd better get going."

Moving to the back of the house, he was met by another advisor. They walked down into the basement as the man talked.

"The sneak-and-peek boys have finished their report on the Beltway barbecue," the man remarked, waving a fistful of paper.

"And?" Fisk prompted, holding the door to the basement open for him.

"It's grim. Somebody laid down a lot of bucks for this operation. Griff and his sim jocks are still up to their ears in the math. We won't hear from them until tomorrow morning." He moved down the stairs ahead of Fisk.

"What do you think?"

"Me? I figure it was a full SWAT unit. You'll have my report."

"Tell me the rest."

"All that simulation stuff creeps me out."

"What does your gut tell you?" Fisk prodded, recalling that the man was a veteran field investigator employed by a large, well-known private security firm.

"We're going to ID the SWAT. I've seen this before. A few years ago, our firm was contracted to protect this guy named Madison. You probably read about him in the paper."

"This is the same MO, is that what you're telling me?"

The man paused, looking Fisk in the eye. "They used a tactical unit to take down a tactical unit. They expected us to commit our resources, and we did. There's the Madison connection."

"They got the whole team, didn't they?" Instinctively, Fisk knew that the question and his obvious concern were somehow wrong--out of character.

"We lost the pilot and all eight men in the tactical squad. Our military chopper is toast. Your driver capped one of the cops at the road block, and the tanker blast sent four more to the morgue. Pretty spendy for both sides, all things considered."

Fisk nodded, unable to speak while his mind was preoccupied.

Unfamiliar vibrations were setting off his emotions.

Pausing at the landing, the advisor switched on a dusty, yellowed light. "Whoever put this together knew their stuff. I don't need a computer to tell me that."

"If there's a way to unmask their new operator, Griff will find it. Between your gut and Griff's computers, I know I'm safe." He stopped next to a stack of clutter and toed a tiny hidden switch near the floor. The jumble skidded noisily aside to reveal a dark and cold passage. *It's gone. I don't feel it anymore.*

The advisor shook a rolled up printout at Fisk. "You'd better stay on your toes. We can't afford any more casualties."

"And the beat goes on." He started to put on his gloves. *That feeling is like--*

"We're not geared to fight small armies. If you didn't know that before, you do now. Somebody on her payroll figured out how to get past us last night. If Her Highness gets any more creative, things are going to get very messy. You take care of yourself, you hear me?" the man said, turning to go back upstairs.

"I'll try to keep that in mind." Fisk waved as he entered the concealed passage. His rational mind found itself suddenly back on track. *He's right. The odds are not in my favor any more.*

The pile of clutter scraped back into place, hiding the secret entrance once more. Tiny domed lights came on to illuminate the length of the corridor.

Taking care to step around the small patches of ice on the floor, Fisk's breath began to vaporize in the chilly air. *I just hope we can hold out long enough to get the job done.*

Overhead, the constant throb and hum of interstate traffic filtered down through six feet of earth and steel-reinforced concrete. Fisk continued to move purposefully down the dimly lit passage. *Wonder if anyone knows that this old bunker dates back to World War II?* With its original purpose lost to history, the bunker now served as a meeting place for the conspirators.

Coming to the end of the chilly corridor, he squinted at the heavy steel door in front of him. To his left, a glossy black panel was set into the wall. Bracing himself, he removed a glove and placed his hand on the cold, slick surface. The palm reader beeped its approval. The door slid open with a pneumatic hiss.

Stepping into the room, he was immediately struck by how chilly the place felt. *Is it me, or does it get colder each time I come here?* Even under his stylish trenchcoat, the icy air gnawed at his tanned flesh.

Deep shadows cut across the seated figures, cloaking them in near-total darkness. At ground level, a podium was starkly lit by overhead fixtures. Raised seating enveloped the speaker's platform to give the impression of an amphitheater.

As he approached, Fisk looked up at the bright lights. Each time he came here, he found himself looking up at those fixtures. Even now, the impulse seemed strange to him. *Something about the color of those lights. Irresistible.*

Stepping onto the raised platform, he paid attention to the sensation that came over him. For no discernable reason, the short hairs on the back of his neck went up and he was afraid. The nameless fear lasted only for an instant before it faded. *Why does that happen every time I stand under these lights?* Stopping in front of the podium, he glanced around the room.

The bitter cold and inky darkness were intended to ensure that he would never correctly guess the identities of his most powerful advisors. They had to know him so that they could support him without reservations. He, on the other hand, could never be allowed to know them.

Because he didn't know them by sight, Fisk allowed himself a momentary lapse in good behavior to improve his mood. *Every one of these jokers is sitting in a chair that's equipped with an integral heater. Jerks.* The icy cold of the underground room was, he knew, a precaution against detection by orbiting satellites.

He took some small degree of satisfaction from the knowledge that the same bright lights that hid their identities from him also served to make the cold room a little more bearable during meetings like this. *My own little secret.*

Without preamble, he took a single folded sheet of paper from his breast pocket of his coat. Unfolding the page, he could feel the spotlight's warmth penetrating his chilled fingers. *Hard to believe it's taken 14 years to get to this moment. Makes me wonder if we couldn't have done better.*

Taking a few moments to glance at the notes, he forced himself to concentrate. *Doesn't matter what I think anymore.* "I'd like to call this meeting to order. Let's have the committee reports." He couldn't help but glance up at the warm, bright lights one more time. Something about that tightly grouped pattern was inviting. It almost always...

It's back. Feels like a word that's on the tip of my tongue, but won't come. The elusive "feeling" that sometimes invaded his mind had first occurred five years before. Uncertain of its meaning, he had kept it to himself. *I sure hope nobody notices.*

Griff levered himself out of his seat in the front row. Dressed in a winter parka, he allowed his hood to fall back far enough to reveal his face. Keeping his hands in his pockets, he turned to face the audience. He spoke, his voice quivering slightly due to the cold that was already chapping his face.

"There's no easy way to say this, so I'm just going to come right out with it. We lost one of our tactical teams last night. We're still running final numbers; my report should go out tomorrow morning. We were not compromised by a federal agency. I want to make that clear right now. Somebody in the President's organization set up an independent operation. Homeland Security is not involved.

"As you know, the Overwatch model relies on two tactical teams and three contingency layers. We lost one of our tactical teams and the tertiary contingency layer. For those of you who are familiar with the base plots, this means that we have to assume a level two compromise. From now on, we can't guarantee containment, nor can we guarantee--"

A mittened hand went up in the back of the room. "Are we sure that it was a rogue SWAT unit that did this? There are at least 15 different antiterrorist detachments in the D.C. area. That doesn't say anything about the two dozen mercenary units that have offices near Capitol Hill."

Griff bristled at the interruption. "Give me some credit, will you? I don't have to remind any of you that the nine point intercept is a standard trap-and-zap pattern used in the field by any department, agency, or mercenary group you'd care to name." His assessment was greeted with nods from the assembled advisors.

The hand rose again. "Excuse me. This is hindsight. Why didn't you see it coming?"

The accusation was something that Griff had expected and prepared for. "Reaction planning doesn't work that way. We have limited assets, so we need to be--"

"Your sims should be--" the questioner tried to interrupt.

"Hey! I was up to my elbows in this kind of work when you were still in college. Our sims give us options, not firm answers. Scenario modeling and profiling are common these days. It's not our fault if somebody else ran their own numbers."

"I disagree. I saw the live feed. The introduction of the new driver reduced the coincidence curve. You made no effort to use or accelerate that option. Fisk saved himself. My report will reflect that."

Pausing to regain control of himself, Griff pushed his hands into the deep pockets of his coat. "That's your prerogative. But the rest of you had better get one thing straight. Our cover is only skin deep. It's always been that way. We've been far too successful for far too long. It's only natural that we're cocky. We stopped them last night by the skin of our teeth." Turning to look up at Fisk, he continued more calmly. "We did not screw up last night."

Fisk laid down his notes and raised his hands. "Hey. Let's stop this before it goes any further. I'm still here. I still have all my fingers and toes. It takes Madeline's people an average of four to six months to pull one of these parties together. We only need two more months at most; then we're all out of here."

His words were met with silence. Some heads lowered in quiet submission.

"I have nothing else to say," Griff rumbled, and then sat.

"Fair enough. I've got one request, though." Fisk watched as the shadowy figures looked at each other and then at Griff. He checked his watch. "I don't have a lot of time. Let's skip the rest of the committee reports and get down to new business. I want you to update my Omega sims. After last night, it is possible that somebody's going to take a closer look at us."

Griff straightened, giving Fisk a confused look.

"The plan calls for my termination if the Founders or this advisory group feel that I'm a security risk. After the close call last night, I want to make sure that my exit plans are still valid."

In the back of his mind, something fluttered in response to Griff's expression. *He's looking at me like I'm out of my mind. Why?*

"The Omega group is updated every 24 hours. Why? What are you thinking?" Griff was clearly bothered by something.

"She was angry last night. She went through her presentation charade like a trooper, but I could tell that she wasn't happy about doing it. When I break the news to her, she may see my resignation as a challenge."

"You walk away, and you win," somebody said.

"With all her dirty laundry." Fisk glanced around the cold, dark room. Heads nodded as a murmur of hushed conversation rippled through the assembly.

"Speaking of dirty laundry, Bill Garrison had dinner with Anne Carroll last night. If you check your program, you'll see that he is the primary leadership candidate for Phase Two. Ms. Carroll has been preliminarily rated as 'acceptable' for the Phase Two media component.

"I want you to cut him some slack. I investigated the incident personally. It was just dumb luck that they ran into each other. Some of you will have a problem with this, and you're certainly allowed to file your reports. Just bear in mind that these people don't know what we plan to do with them."

Fisk paused. "Garrison is my friend. He can't golf, but he's an uncomplicated, honest man. He hasn't dated much recently because he isn't quite over his ex-wife. He's only started again in the last two years. I've spent enough time with him to know that he's not a fast healer where emotional wounds are concerned. Nevertheless, he is everything we need him to be.

"Let's give him a break, just this once. We all have our fingers crossed, and we all hope that Phase Two will never be needed. When the time comes, I want him to cooperate with us because I'm his friend, not because I ordered it."

Overhead blowers kicked in, crushing the silence. Several heads converged in the shadows to exchange whispers.

A strong male voice with an Australian accent spoke up from the darkness. "A relationship would be undesirable just now. There's just too much to go wrong. I've seen her dossier. She's a real thinker. She could mess us up."

A sharp female voice cut through the cold. "Recruit him now. Send him to the camp in the Cascades. He won't finish for six weeks. When he comes back, you're gone and out of sight, and he's primed for Phase Two. She won't get close to him unless his handlers allow it."

Fisk nodded at the unseen woman to show his acceptance the compromise. "More than fair. Objections?"

A solid majority of heads shook.

"Somebody have my office call him and set up a meeting. Be vague. Don't spook him."

Across the room, another advisor spoke up. "We might as well introduce him to the Treasury team. They're going to handle his finances if Phase Two is activated."

"I like it. We'd better move to get Carroll approved or denied. Can somebody tell me what her profile looks like?"

A hand came up near the front. Fisk pointed at the cloaked person. "She scores 95 on the Brookings test. Her background has all six of the markers we were looking for, and she has no family on the East Coast. Her only attachment seems to be an intern that she's bonded with."

"Hasn't she done some investigative pieces on Fisk?" another man asked from the back, his voice thick with an East Coast drawl.

The other speaker replied with a shrug. "Speculative. She's working off a gut feeling that she doesn't have the resources to follow up on. Her instincts are at the top of the Addenwaller chart, but she's not going to blow our cover any time soon. She's just not looking in the right places."

Another advisor spoke. "She has the scores. I believe that her age and career setbacks will temper her judgment. She will be much harder to co-opt than the others on the list will. She could be easier to place if she's partial to Garrison. I do not oppose this move."

Fisk liked what he heard. "Their relationship is still developing. Are you sure that they can be kept apart until Phase One is complete?" Despite his bond with Garrison, he was compelled to ensure the success of his mission.

The room was nearly silent for several minutes as the advisors conferred. The advisor who had spoken before Fisk asked the question summed up their decision. "She will get the White House assignment and her intern will be directed elsewhere. They will both be so busy with their new jobs that they won't have any time to consider Mr. Garrison's past--or his future."

Tuesday
April 22, 2014
Presidential Quarters
The White House
Washington, D.C.
10:35 P.M. EDT

Pike reported within minutes of being summoned.

Madeline's voice was calm, almost cordial, though the venom in her eyes showed clearly. "Jordan. Consider yourself fired."

"I don't understand." He shuddered. *You can't do this to me!*

"It's very simple. Your services are no longer needed." Speaking firmly, the President laid her napkin aside. Standing up from the table, she signaled the attendant that the meal was over.

Pike also stood, and followed her into the nearby sitting room. *She's angry. Just let her rant, and then go home. Tomorrow is a new day.* "I only did as instructed, and Mr. Oswald has promised to--"

Madeline moved to her favorite chair by the fireplace. Standing next to it, she placed her hands on top of the chair, as if she were about to sink her manicured nails into the plush fabric. *Idiot. I can't risk using the same resource twice.*

From past experience, she knew that Fisk's security experts would backtrack the assets used in her latest attempt. As bold as she was, Madeline's ruthless nature took a back seat to her paranoia where Fisk's protectors were concerned. *Can't give them even the smallest shred of evidence to use against me.*

"I've done everything you asked." After a moment's hesitation, he decided, *You must have a reason from giving up so easily. Whatever your new plan is, I want to be a part of it.*

The President maintained eye contact as she moved around the chair. The short curls framing her face bounced slightly as she sat. "I want to rid myself of Preston Fisk, but I haven't forgotten what he's taught me."

You're afraid of him, so you don't want to use the same tool twice. That kernel of wisdom, so tried and true, fueled his interest. "With the insight that they now have, wouldn't it be wiser to allow Oswald and his people to develop a new simulation? Surely they can't fail twice." *If you fire me, it could ruin me,* he thought indignantly. Without the credential of presidential middleman, Pike would be just another fixer in a crowded field of covert go-betweens and deal makers.

Unimpressed, Madeline adjusted her skirt, pursing her lips.

Pike felt himself go cold inside. *Here it comes.*

"Go home. Break the news to your boyfriend and have your desk cleared out by 9 a.m. My office will prepare a letter of recommendation for you. It should be in the mail within a week." *Not that I can let you live that long. I can't let Fisk have you as proof of our secret war.*

"How will you--" *You have to bargain with me. I know too much.*

"I'll do what I've always done. I'll find a way. Without you." Looking up at him, her thoughts churned quickly through the process of evaluating his future.

"You'll still need somebody to handle this for you. I know too much as it is. Why not--"

Madeline cut him off with a knife-like gesture.

Mustering the last of his courage, Jordan locked eyes with her. He'd seen Fisk do it, and succeed. *That man has to have ice water for blood.* "I've been very useful to you, and I will not be tossed aside like some dirty rag. I will go home, and tomorrow I will find another solution to your problem. You have my word on that." *Strength and confidence. I have nothing to lose.*

"That, and two dollars, won't get you the cup of coffee it would take to keep me interested in what happens to you after tomorrow morning. Which is when I expect your resignation on my desk."

Defeated, Pike left without asking for his overcoat. *Resigning is better than being fired,* he mused morosely.

Sitting alone for the next several minutes, President Hill reflected on what it meant to be lonely at the top. Her bad mood was made worse by the realization that she had just committed herself to killing a man that she found useful. While she had made substantial progress in co-opting the Deputy Director of the White House Secret Service protective unit and several of his minions, she had doubts about the man's ability to have Pike dealt with in a way that wouldn't arouse suspicion.

She thought about Walter Carns. *Fisk? He's done it before. And I liked the way he handled it.* Killing the financial analyst had been an act of pure spite more than anything else. *He was just too smart for his own good. I'm sure Fisk would enjoy the irony of dealing with Pike, if he knew the details.* As much as the idea appealed to her, she found herself unwilling to pick up the phone.

With the dishes cleared, the attendant ventured out of the shadows to stand attentively in front her, waiting for her "official recognition." Madeline looked up, and studied the face of the Asian man in white livery. "Yes?" she asked after a long moment. White House serving and maintenance staff referred to the delay for "official recognition" as "Madeline's Way."

"Would you like something to drink?" he asked, careful to keep his eyes centered on her nose, avoiding full eye contact. Nothing more than the intent of the question came through in his voice.

I could get to like this man if I got to know him.

"Yes. I would like some brandy." *It feels good to be honest about something after dealing with that weasel.*

"Yes, ma'am." Jeffrey nodded and withdrew.

As she waited, Madeline closed her eyes and let her mind wander. *Men like Pike are a necessary evil.* Fisk had taught her that. *"People like that,"* his voice counseled her from the distant past, *"will do anything you want them to do, just to remain in your good graces. They thrive on it."* Shifting slightly in her chair, she admitted that he'd been right. *Pike, and those like him, are easily replaced.*

Secure in the knowledge that the attendant would do as she asked, she let the question of Pike's erasure creep through the back passages of her mind. When she heard Jeffrey's quiet footfalls on the carpet, she opened her eyes. *If I thought you would do it and get away with it...*

"How many presidents have you served?" she asked, taking the glass.

"You're my first," he said with pride.

She sipped at her brandy. "What did you do before you got this job?" *I picked you myself. Do you know that? Your résumé wasn't long on details, but you passed the background check.*

"Ocean liners. Mostly Pacific Rim cruises, but I liked it. Did it for 15 years."

Madeline smiled up at him as she caught the reflection of happy memories in his eyes.

"That seems like an awful lot to give up, just for this," she lied. *Why is it that the people least interested in politics are the most enjoyable to be around?* Jeffrey had a way of putting her at ease, just by doing his job.

The sparkle left his eyes. "It's not safe for me to go home. The Philippines are just too unstable. This is a much nicer place."

Her heart raced at having touched such a tender spot in the man's past. *I remember the briefing I got on that. It must have been horrible. At least we won.*

"I see," she said sympathetically.

Jeffrey looked at her expectantly, hoping for a change of subject.

"Close the kitchen and turn down my bed." She did her best to ask instead of order.

"Very good, ma'am." His smile bordered on friendliness.

Switching off the lamp next to her chair, Madeline sat alone in the darkness.

Tuesday
April 22, 2014
West Wing
The White House
Washington, D.C.
10:39 P.M. EDT

Pike fumed as he returned to his desk. He'd passed only one uniformed guard, who hadn't reacted as they passed in the silent hallway. That slight further angered him as he barreled into the large room filled with cramped cubicles. Lights snapped on as motion sensors reacted to his presence.

Each workspace held just enough room for a narrow table surface and small chair. Pike stomped through the maze until he came to his office. Glaring at the laptop computer that seemed too large for the table surface, he flopped into his chair with a deep exhalation.

"How did you manage to lose control?" he asked himself caustically, reaching under the desk to feel around for his briefcase. *I need time to think about this. She can't just throw me away like that. I can't put my finger on it, but that woman has changed.*

He hauled the briefcase into his lap and opened it. He began clearing the smaller items from his area. In his anger, both office supplies and personal effects went into the briefcase with equal force. *It's just as well. The assassination of a man like Fisk can't be done without public inquiry. Best to be as far away from it as possible when it happens.*

"She keeps giving me the dirtier jobs, anyway. I've got my pride," he told his computer as he picked it up roughly. *Not that anyone else would do them.*

"I'm glad to hear that," a soft voice said.

Pike jumped. "Who's there?" Stepping away from the cubicle, his briefcase fell to the floor.

"Just me," the woman said as she stepped into view. He immediately noticed her long blonde hair and blue eyes.

His heart sank. *Press Secretary. She doesn't like me.*

Straightening her blouse, the woman moved toward Pike in slow, sure steps.

"I thought I was alone." Pike whined, reaching for his briefcase.

"Why are you clearing out?" Angel Cutter cast an inquisitive look around the deserted room.

"My services are no longer needed. She's deigned to accept my resignation in the morning." Briefcase in hand, he stopped abruptly. *My God. I'm all packed. There's nothing left to show I was ever here. Didn't take long, either.*

"For what?" Angel leaned against a cubicle wall, hands clasped in front of her.

Pike looked straight at her, unfazed by her matter-of-fact demeanor. *If only you knew.*

"Did you blow the meeting with Oswald?" she asked, looking concerned.

"How would you know about that?"

"Lucky guess." She gave a sly smile.

"It's not something I can talk about." Pike shrugged. *I just need to go home and think about this.* Nervously, he straightened the lapels of his sport coat.

"Hey, I can help you. But you need to fill me in." *Play the part. Project sincerity.*

He reached back into his cubicle. His hand grasped the empty coat hook. He cursed under his breath. Reaching into his pants pocket, his fingers wrapped around a set of keys. A quick check revealed that his wallet was still snug in the pocket of his jacket. *Thank goodness.*

"Oh, man. I need time to sit and think about this. I'll call you when I've had a chance to sort it out." He shook his head in exasperation as he picked up his briefcase.

Angel put a hand on his shoulder. "Okay. Just let me know if you need anything."

"Like what?" He stopped, briefcase held to his chest. *And why?*

"Protection...or a new job?"

"How can you protect me?" His eyebrows rose in a mixture of fear and consideration.

"She can't hurt you if she thinks you're still useful, right?" Angel's gaze slowly shifted until she acquired direct eye contact with him.

He looked at her and hesitated. She was known to be an eye reader. The thought paralyzed him even further. *Spooky habit,* he mused. *I wonder if it works?*

"Tell me more about this job." He licked his lips and lowered his briefcase.

"It's not a stretch. All I need is you in a certain Senator's office."

"That's a rookie job."

"We leaked some things to a certain senator. It helped him. Now he owes us. Trouble is, he's dragging his feet on the payback. I need more than just a pair of ears. I need a pair of hands. You help me, and I help the President--"

"I don't do that sort of thing anymore. I've got my future to think about. You'll have to do better than that." Keeping his nervous gaze focused on her, Pike could feel her piercing blue eyes boring into him.

Angel sensed that he wasn't afraid of her. "I'm glad to see that you've still got your pride. If you do this, I'll know I can trust you with bigger things." Something about Pike suggested that he placed a premium on being trusted. *All I want from you is confirmation.*

"How big?" he asked as his fear diminished.

"I want to be Director of Communications next term. If I get what I want, I can get you a real job, one with your name on the letterhead." As she spoke, she could see a flash of understanding in his troubled eyes.

"What's the catch?" He could hardly believe she was sincere. *Everything in this town has a catch.*

"The catch is that you've got to be man enough for the job."

Pike sat down in his chair, still holding the briefcase. He had a reputation on Capitol Hill as a bag man, and he knew it. *This could be a chance to do something different.* The idea appealed to him. *The catch is that I have to be indispensable to two people at the same time.* "I can't. I'm smart enough to know that I can't divide my loyalties like that."

Angel stood back, shaking her head in an effort to make him feel guilty.

"You appointee types. You plot and scheme with some degree of protection. All I have is my credibility." Pike stepped around her.

Angel reached out an arm to bar his way.

He looked at her questioningly. *Just great. Now I've offended you.*

"You were working on Madeline's Fisk problem, weren't you?" *Let's test your reliability.*

"I don't know what you're talking about." Pike shouldered past her and moved off. The fear in his eyes seemed luminous as he swept past her.

Once Pike was gone, Angel sat quietly in his empty cubicle. *Reliable, but very expendable.* His behavior confirmed her suspicions. *She really hates the man, and she wants him dead.*

Angel was no stranger to political maneuvering. The disappearance of Carns had been a learning experience. There was no doubt in her mind Hill could, and would, have people killed to fulfill her personal and professional agendas. *She's just the person I need to get what I want.*

This certainty fueled her secret hate for the establishment that had caused her father to disappear without a trace. Unlike her godfather, Angel hadn't made peace with her loss. Despite Harry's advice, she guarded her hatred as it if were her most precious possession.

Going back to her office, she paused to speak with the roaming guard. "Thanks for letting me know about Mr. Pike."

His nameplate read *Crain.* "Not a problem," he replied with a relaxed smile, continuing on his rounds.

Angel hesitated before going back to her office. Knowing what she had in store for Mr. Crain gave her a momentary chill. *He's perfect for the job. Nobody would suspect him of being an obsessive personality. It's perfect. They betrayed a patriot. It's only fitting that a patriot betrays them.*

Running a finger over the etched letters in the brass plaque on the polished wood door of her office, she focused her thoughts before she went in. The politics of patriotism provoked conflicting emotions whenever she thought about them.

Looking around, Angel was glad to see that none of her assistants were working late. Going into her office, she carefully locked the door behind her. Sitting down behind her desk, she took a small silver key from the top drawer.

She'll decide to have Pike killed while she's having breakfast. If I can get to him first and put the evidence under wraps, it should prove to her that I could handle her Fisk problem.

For Angel, the elimination of Fisk was just one more thing to be done while rising through the ranks of the Hill administration. Her planned vengeance, as conceived, required that she overcome her personal inhibitions.

She recalled a bit of her father's wisdom: *"Sometimes it really does take a thief to catch a thief. Sometimes we have to become things that we would rather not be."*

Opening the bottom drawer with the key, she took out a compact wireless phone. Opening it, she hit the autodial. Green telltales lit, indicating that local area jamming and scrambler connect modes were enabled. The line rang several times, before a groggy voice picked up on the other end.

"Yeah." Harry let out a yawn.

"It's me," she said quietly.

"Yes?" He seemed to wake up a little more.

"I need you to take care of some wet work for me. I know it's out of the blue, but it'll be good for me." She was brief because she knew her godfather preferred things that way. *As long as you keep thinking that this is all about my career, everything will be fine.*

"Who?" He failed to hold back another yawn as he sat up on his bed.

"Jordan Pike. Madeline fired him a few minutes ago."

"I didn't think he was going to make the cut. You want the credit." Harry was well acquainted with Angel's no-nonsense approach to ladder climbing. *Not quite the chip off the old block that your father would have imagined.*

She stole a glance at the door. "Yes. She places a high premium on ambition, audacity, and action. Is there anything I should be aware of?"

Harry scratched the back of his neck and thought. "Carl Metz. She's been grooming him for jobs like this. He's going to be a problem."

"Was he the one who set up the action against Fisk?"

"Yeah. He's a real pit bull. If he catches your scent..."

"He won't."

"Go out to dinner. Be seen," he told her tactfully as he hung up.

Harry placed his feet on the carpet. *So much for getting to bed early.*

Liquidating low-level operators had become common practice. *How could burning Pike backfire?* He heaved himself up off the bed and went to the bathroom. Putting on a bathrobe, he walked into the kitchen. *Now that I think about it, I kind of like the idea.*

Peering into the nearly empty refrigerator, he muttered at the lack of sandwich fixings and poured a glass of milk. Shuffling into the living room, he sat in his favorite chair.

"Computer: on." The machine was perched on a cluttered table. He finished his milk as it completed its start-up sequence.

"Computer at your command," the machine's confident female voice told him.

"Telephone, scrambled, Keats." He set his glass on a nearby table.

A "waiting" pattern appeared on the monitor as the call was placed. A bleary-eyed face materialized after the second ring.

"Keats here. Oh, it's you. What can I do for you?"

"You shouldn't spend so much time in front of those monitors, Tommie. Those things'll fry your eyeballs." Harry wasn't surprised to see stacks of printouts surrounding his friend.

Keats waved a large hand. "I should be so lucky. But we have new stuff on the Director's favorite terrorist group. Naturally, he wants our threat set and probability matrixes on his desk yesterday." He picked up a stack of paper and riffled the pages.

Harry noticed that Keats wasn't in his office. *Probably in the tank.*

"The tank" was slang for the Agency's secured computer lab. Each federal law enforcement and intelligence-gathering agency had one, linked to all the others through the Department of Homeland Security. Tank facilities were shielded from even the most hard-core ground scans and satellite probes.

"Sorry to interrupt. We've got a request for wet work from our little friend." He was careful not to say names. *There's no such thing as a secured line.*

"That would be Pike, right?" Keats rubbed his eyes.

"Yes." He suppressed his irritation. *Just blab it all over the net, why don't you?*

"Okay. We have a team on standby for the al-Qaeda thing. I don't think they'll mind a quick diversion. When?" He took a drink from a plastic water bottle.

Harry smiled inwardly. Keats' father, a veteran Agency programmer had also done occasional troubleshooting. "Now."

Keats swore, throwing up his hands. "Why does it always have to be *now?*"

Oswald grinned. "No peace for the wicked, I guess. I won't be able to sleep. Let me come in and help you."

Keats sighed as he rubbed the bridge of his nose. "I'm drowning in image counts. I'll see you when you get here." Without looking at the controls, he cut the connection.

Taking his glass back to the kitchen, Harry reprogrammed his coffee maker and headed for the shower.

Thursday
April 24, 2014
Presidential Quarters
The White House
Washington, D.C.
8:20 A.M. EDT

Sitting on a small couch in the outer reception area, Madeline indulged in a few moments alone. She sipped languidly at a cup of black currant tea. The day's appointment schedule sat unread on the table next to her. Josephine Harper had brought the large leather-bound book in just before eight.

Eyes closed, Madeline drank in the silence. She could visualize the whole room. Sunlight filtered through the sheer curtains covering the bullet-resistant glass composite of the window and its sheer curtains. In her mind, the light danced across the polished glass and gold chain of the chandelier. Furniture and decorations slowly materialized as her vision of the room evolved.

The sheer size of the presidential quarters didn't bother her. If anything did, it was that she couldn't escape the feeling that she was just visiting. The previous two years had been more eventful than she could have imagined. Despite being in the thick of national and international happenings, the place had never acquired the feeling of home.

She placed the cup on the table without opening her eyes. *I feel like I'm a guest, because I know I'll be leaving just like I came in--at the whim of other people. With 15 years or more to work with, there would be no limit to what I could do.* It would take a miracle, she knew, to grant that most secret of wishes.

Shifting, she smoothed her skirt. The room vanished from her mind's eye, replaced by a glowing vision of what the country could be like under her long-term leadership. *Was this what Catherine the Great and Queen Elizabeth went through? They had enough time at their disposal to reshape the world, didn't they? Monarchs had that luxury.* There was little doubt in her mind that the world had been improved by their efforts.

As Madeline thought about making the world a better place, her thoughts turned briefly to Pike. She recalled how relieved she'd felt on hearing that he had vanished. The news had come as part of the official morning briefing, surprising her. *Not so much as a trace left of him. Much neater than that business with Carns. So nice of Carl to play it down like this.*

Carns had interfered with her in the presence of others, making him an "official" problem. *I hope the worms are choking on him.* He had openly disagreed with her decision to begin construction of the Currency Command Center. It had been his contention that to do so without congressional approval could be considered illegal enough to warrant her impeachment. *Nobody's afraid of impeachment anymore. The only bad part about it was the media prowling around the mess for a week before they found something better to do.*

Thoughts of her vulnerability forced her to reconsider Pike's disappearance. *Carl second-guessed me? I never got around to telling him to deal with Jordan.*

Thinking back to the briefing, Metz had reported Pike's vanishing as if it were completely irrelevant. *He's playing it cool. Maybe he's learned a few things from Fisk.* The thought was unsettling. *Thank God there aren't very many people like Fisk.*

Metz hadn't come under her influence until after Carns' disposal. She'd sized him up quickly enough. *He's a fast learner. Saw what happened to Carns and put it together for himself.* As fast as his star was rising, Metz showed no signs of being co-opted by the rigid hierarchy of the Secret Service.

Thinking about her own recent experiences, Madeline felt her lips form a mild smile. *Secret Service and Homeland Security. How's that for a few new tricks?*

"Excuse me," an unseen female voice said, breaking the spell.

Madeline opened her eyes, blinking.

"Miss Cutter is here for her 8:45 appointment."

Madeline glared at the ceiling as if she could blame all her problems on the intercom. "Send her up."

"Yes, ma'am."

Thursday
April 24, 2014
Presidential Quarters
The White House
Washington, D.C.
8:45 A.M. EDT

Angel took the stairs up to the presidential quarters. She paused at the landing just long enough for the Secret Service agent to inspect her belongings and give her a nod. She continued up, making each step deliberate.

Another Secret Service agent stopped her on the upper landing. The contents of her briefcase were examined again. As she waited, she stole a glance at a nearby mirror. Dressed in her favorite grey pantsuit, her black flats added to her understated appearance Her blonde curls, courtesy of an extremely early salon visit, were also subdued. She had found out the hard way that a low-key approach worked best with Madeline. The President didn't like to be shown up.

"Go right on in. You're expected."

"Thank you, Josh," she said with a smile. Though she had made this trip over a hundred times in the previous two years, it hadn't lost its appeal. She didn't get up here as often as she'd like. Her job was demanding. Sometimes it was downright nightmarish.

Madeline was waiting, as she preferred, alone. The media had picked up on this quirk and taken to it instantly. Calling her a "maternal" president, her tendency to keep her Cabinet officers separated was misinterpreted as a desire to be more personal. Settled on the antique couch that she liked so much, she smiled warmly while her eyes remained neutral. "Good morning, Angel. Have a seat."

"Thank you." She sat in a matching chair.

"I'm sorry if I seem a little too relaxed, but I can't remember for the life of me what we were supposed to be discussing this morning."

Angel nodded. Eyes level, she looked directly at Madeline. "I believe that I have the answer to your Fisk problem."

Madeline paused for another sip of her tea. Tension grew. "I'm sorry, I thought your specialty was press relations?" Her eyes telegraphed the challenge, giving the lie to the apology in her words. *You had better know what you are talking about.*

"Pike. I had him dealt with." *That ought to get your attention.*

"I see. Pike aside, what makes you so certain that I have a problem with Mr. Fisk?" *We're all fast learners today, aren't we?*

"Unless I miss my guess, you're finished with him. We both know that you don't just fire somebody like Preston Fisk. He knows too much. You've brought in outsiders to compromise, discredit, or kill."

Madeline couldn't help nodding. "Hmm. What else?"

"I also suspect that you're headed back to the drawing board, which is why I'm here. I have a new option for you."

"That's a very bold assessment. It tells me what you've been doing with your after-hours time. Why would I want to be disconnected from the most effective political advisor anyone's ever seen?"

"You pay me to know the difference between fact and fiction. I'm not your conscience, but I do have to look out for you. As in the case of the late Jordan Pike."

"And this is what you think I need?" *Today's young professionals really do come tightly packed, don't they?*

"Yes." Angel sat back and tried to look comfortable. She had practiced this conversation many times and had decided that being direct would give the best odds of success. Her eyes were drawn to a small Swiss clock as it chimed 9 o'clock.

"Have you talked to anyone else about this?" Madeline cocked her head to one side, her thoughts going instantly to Metz.

"No, I haven't talked to anyone else about this. As long as you pay me, I'm yours." *Confidence, have to project confidence.*

Madeline pursed her lips. The boldness of the approach reminded her of Fisk and the way he'd first introduced himself to her. The similarity in their methods of conversation piqued her interest. *Even if you were cut from the same cloth, you still can't hold a candle to the man himself.* "All right, then. Before we take this any further, why?" The challenge melted from her stern features as she smiled.

"Why not? It's not enough for you to be the first woman to hold this office. You need an edge. This might be the 21st century, but it's still a man's world. To win, you've got to play their game better than they do."

Madeline's eyes narrowed. "What's in it for you? What do you get out of solving my problem?"

Angel shrugged. "Your trust--and some advancement"

"To what?" *There's more to you than meets the eye, isn't there?*

"Something better in your next term. There's a lot that I can do for you, if I have the right tools." Angel's eyes lit up as she spoke.

"Draw me a picture. How do you become more valuable to me?"

Recognizing it as a test, Angel remained unruffled. "There are things that you want. Things that presidents always want. Look at what's going on right now. The media is your friend. Congress is in your back pocket. Every terrorist on the planet is afraid of what you're going to do next. As far as you're concerned, the sky is the limit."

The President chuckled. "That is a very optimistic assessment. Just tell me one thing."

"That seems fair," she nodded, pleased with the reaction. *Well within profile.*

"How do you come to be involved in this?"

"I gave Metz his 'in' with Homeland. They did the sim he used for his action against Fisk. I knew he wouldn't tell you, so I waited."

"Waited for what, exactly?" she asked coldly.

"I waited for him to fail, of course. He's useful, but only to a point." Angel's voice held just enough venom to play on Madeline's prejudices. *Through you, I can have my revenge.*

"We have not had this conversation. You will not mention it again unless I directly ask you to talk about it. Is that clear?" The President leaned back, using physical distance to emphasize the point. *So, the man to get Fisk is a woman? Interesting.*

"Yes." Angel's heart sang with the thrill of taking one step closer to her ultimate goal. *I hope a president is enough for you, Daddy.*

Alone in her condo on the Chesapeake, Angel had run through this part of her plan during many sleepless nights. American presidents had known about the misdeeds of their intelligence-gathering agencies for more than a century. She had long ago resolved that a president would pay the price for her father's disappearance. *Uncle Harry might not approve, but then again, he won't be able to stop me.*

As uncertain as she was about the nature of her father's disappearance, Angel firmly believed that powerful people in the government had been behind it. Though Harry never talked about it, Angel felt certain that he blamed himself for Jason Cutter's having vanished while on agency business.

Instead of accepting the loss of her father, she had kept the hate alive inside her like a torch, feeding it on grief and rage. Harry had known about her grudge against the government. He had tried off and on, both as her guardian and as her godfather, to persuade her to end her hatred. When she stopped talking about it, he assumed that she had finally dropped it. *Even if he wanted to help,* her conscience assuaged, *Harry doesn't have the pull that I need to get the job done.*

Madeline's commanding tones broke into her thoughts. "Satisfy my curiosity. Tell me about the 'late' Mr. Pike, and how he came to be that way."

"I'd rather not."

"I don't think I made myself clear. You must have thought I gave you a choice. Tell me. Now."

Angel could see the stubborn flame that lit the President's gaze.

"I have freelance connections that took care of it."

Madeline seemed impressed.

"I've worked long and hard to establish those connections. You'll understand if I don't feel comfortable revealing them." Angel took in the President's nod while noticing the guarded look that now hid her emotions. *She's thinking that, if I can arrange Pike's death, I might be able to arrange hers. She'll watch me closely.*

"All right, talk to me."

"The problem is two-fold--getting past his sphere of protection, and then taking away his credibility so that he can't hurt you from beyond the grave."

"Hmm." *Devious.*

"You're always going after him. In a sense, you're going *to* him. All you have to do is turn it around. Let him come to you. The rest writes itself."

Madeline nodded, reaching for her cup. It was empty. *Just as well.*

"He comes into this building all the time. Each time he does, he leaves his sphere of protection. If such a trusted advisor were to die while in your service, on your turf, nobody could touch you. Especially if the person who pulled the trigger were to be brought to justice while you openly grieved."

"Which I presume you can arrange?" Hill smiled thinly, but radiant. *I need to step up the surveillance on the people that work for me.*

"Yes. Afterwards, I can deflect any dirt that his people try to use against you."

"I don't like guns," Madeline said truthfully.

"Anything else is too hard to explain forensically. A gun gives us method, and, in this case, a very short trail. It also works for you in regards to future gun control legislation. Remember, the NRA just folded."

"Legislation that Congress will gladly give me as I grieve over a trusted friend."

"The tool will only see what we want him to see. He can't tell the police anything beyond what he knows, right?"

"If he lives that long." She glared.

"Doesn't matter. All the variables have been calculated."

"Who is he? Professionally, I mean. Does this person work here? No names." *So daring, and yet so simple. I've been going about this all wrong.*

"He's a new Secret Service guard, one of the uniforms. His psych profile says he won't last very long. He has a fixation on authority figures. The Service doesn't like that sort of thing."

"How did he get past the screeners?" *Not that I expect you to tell the truth.*

"It won't take his section leader very long to figure it out. His records have been fudged, but they'll reevaluate him and fire him soon enough."

"How does he get close enough to...do Fisk?" Even with the White House contingent in her back pocket, Madeline knew that the Service as a whole wasn't so easily trifled with. The hairs on the back of her neck prickled at the thought of failure.

"That will take some help from you. We can make him into a

hero, and you can show your gratitude by letting him near you for a day or so." She licked her lips.

"He'll have to be some kind of hero to make that leap. Nobody gets onto the presidential detail easily."

Angel nodded. As far as she understood, most Secret Service agents who got into the White House protection unit had been on the job for at least six, if not ten, years. "Metz will arrange it. During that time, he could do what you need him to do."

"I get the idea. It sounds like this option has a limited window. How long?" Something about the idea touched a nerve--a very pleasant nerve.

"The Service screens all its people every two months, like clockwork. That includes the people in uniform, not just the suits. You have seven weeks or so before the next round of evaluations."

"And you don't think he'll pass his evaluation?"

Angel shook her head. "Very unlikely. The uniformed guards are judged to the same standard as the folks who watch you. He might pass once, but never twice."

"Does anyone else know about this?"

"Yes," Angel replied as Madeline stood and walked over to a small desk. The lie was necessary to convince President Hill that she wasn't bluffing. *As long you think I can blackmail you...*

"I'm not used to working with such a short leash. Would I be able to pass on this opportunity if I wanted to?"

"You would."

Madeline picked up the phone and dialed an in-house extension. "Josephine? Where's Stanley? Oh, no matter. Please reschedule all of my morning appointments. Keep me free until at least 11."

Josephine hesitated. "I can move the social appointments, but I don't have access to the matters-of-state-and-policy calendar."

The President smiled at Angel, once more stymied by the limitations of her power. "Well, we'll just have to fix that sometime, won't we? Be a dear and handle it for me, will you? Find Stanley and let him know. He's probably trapped in a meeting someplace."

"I'll do my best."

Madeline hung up and moved back to the couch with a glint in her eye. "Tell me more."

Saturday
April 26, 2014
West Wing
The White House
Washington, D.C.
11:20 A.M. EDT

Fisk made his usual rounds as he moved through the corridor toward the presidential offices. A quick handshake and a shared word with each person he encountered gave him both the appearance of being everybody's friend and the opportunity to gauge the morale of Madeline's advisors and staff. He was impressed that these people could accomplish as much as they did, considering Madeline's need to micromanage the affairs of state.

Pausing at a mirror, he adjusted his tie and chose his smile before entering the office of the President's appointment secretary. *If only there were another way.*

"Good morning," he said cheerily as he strode into her small but neat office.

"Yes?" Josephine replied loudly, startled from her thoughts. Turning from her small computer terminal, she quickly moved a coffee cup from the edge of her equally small desk.

"I--" he began, but was cut off by the ringing of the telephone.

Scooping up the receiver, Josephine listened more than she spoke.

Fisk noted the model of the telephone, and marveled that someone in such an important position would be stuck with such an outdated device. *There's my opener.*

"Yes, I'll let him know." She hung up. Looking up at him, she paused to brush a strand of dishwater blonde hair out of her eyes. Making eye contact, she blushed.

"That was, no doubt, about me." He sat in the only other chair in the tiny office. *We've been through this song and dance at least a dozen times now. I feel like I know you well enough to just come right out and tell you that we'd like you to join us. But then again, there's no guarantee that you'll approve.*

A white flash on the edge of his peripheral vision signaled the death of the odd thought. His heart to skipped a beat. *What? What was I...?*

"Yes, you've been asked to wait." Her intelligent green eyes remained focused on him.

"Can I ask why?" The question was designed to appeal to her profile.

"They didn't tell me."

"That's all right, I don't blame you."

"Blame me for what?" She leaned forward, worry lines creasing her forehead.

"Hey, if I had to put up with a cramped office that had old equipment and no windows, I'd be a little stand-offish myself." He grinned. *Didn't see that coming, did you?*

"I don't know what you're talking about. It's not like I'm really important or anything." Josephine sat back in her chair, eyeing the telephone. Despite her awe of him, he was just too easy to talk to.

Fisk allowed her a moment to examine her windowless walls. "Baloney. Anybody who's anybody in this building has an office with at least *one* window." *People like you always wish for windows.*

Josephine was likeable enough, though unassuming. While he knew there was a higher purpose behind what he was about to do, in the back of his mind he wished that he could get to know her under different conditions. *There's so much about yourself that you haven't discovered yet.*

During the previous 14 years, he had found that moments like this were among the hardest. All of the lies, half-truths, and deceptions weighed heavily upon his conscience. He felt the fires of regret rise as he watched Josephine choke up.

"But I'm just--" she began. *Windows! I've never told anyone. How could he know?*

"You are the President's appointment secretary," he said, scooping her schedule book from the desk with a flourish.

Turning the leather-bound book around, he held it up to show her the presidential seal embossed on the cover. He glanced at the pages for the next week's appointments as they slid through his fingers. *Opportunities are never to be missed, no matter where they may be found.*

"I don't handle anything really important," she protested, reaching out to take the book from him. The warmth of his grip was quite appealing as she tried to pull the book from his grasp. *I like being invisible.* Being noticed by anyone usually resulted in demands, or worse, harsh criticism.

Fisk playfully withheld the scheduler. "Maybe so, but you have your professional image to think of."

I'm just a secretary. In spite of the way he rode roughshod over her personal insecurities, she had secretly come to like Fisk. The fact that his tone with her had never been demanding had gone a long way towards forming her opinion of him.

He got to his feet, intentionally breaking the moment of pseudo-intimacy. "Do you know why you need windows? You need windows not just because of who you work for, but to remind you that there is life after work." He looked down at her with a confidence that told her that he really did know about her secret desire for an office window.

"Oh, n-no, I don't. This was the office that the last secretary had. It's fine. And I do know that there is life after work." *Am I really having this conversation? Why would somebody like you take any interest in somebody like me?* The way he managed to intrude into her personal space so smoothly caused Josephine to consider the possibility that she had actually let him in.

Pausing dramatically, Fisk produced a stylish silver pen and wrote quickly into the book, just below the 3:15 appointment notation slating the Senate delegation from Alaska to meet with the President.

TALK TO C.O.S. ABOUT WINDOWS

Taking the book away from him with what she hoped was a professional yank, Josephine gasped when she read the entry. He had gone too far. Holding the open scheduler to her chest, she eyed him carefully.

Slipping the pen back into his coat, he gave her a challenging look. *Calm down, there's nothing to this. Is there?*

"You are not allowed to amend the presidential calendar." *So much for being invisible.*

"You'll spend the rest of your life being invisible unless you stand up for yourself. I'm sorry if I offended you, but Madeline pays me to get things done. Would you like me to talk to the Chief of Staff about that window? I won't do it if you insist on this." He spread his hands to take in the little office. "We both know you want it. Just one little window. What can it hurt?"

"I..."

Fisk pointed at the drab wall clock mounted behind her. "Would you look at the time? I'd better go. If I'm not orbiting close by when she summons me, the President gets a little cranky." He left the room before she could say a word.

Standing quietly with the scheduler still held close, she savored the moment. She imagined she could feel the warmth of his hands on the leather cover. *Windows...*

Saturday
April 26, 2014
Oval Office
The White House
Washington, D.C.
11:27 A.M. EDT

When Fisk arrived, an aide told him that the President was still on a conference call. Knowing that he might be waiting for most of the afternoon, he decided to play out the last of his scheme to win Josephine over. "I'll be right back. Too much coffee," he said with a wink.

"Yes, sir."

Not everybody suffers from the stain of corruption. I'm looking forward to the day when those untainted people get back to the business of just being themselves rather than hiding from people like me.

Fisk wanted his efforts to do more than instigate reform. He hoped that he might somehow achieve redemption for all the things he had done to bring this Congress and this president to power.

He walked down the hall to the Larry Hodgekiss' office. Getting in to see the White House Chief of Staff wasn't difficult for Preston Fisk.

Hodgekiss rose from his chair to shake hands. "What can I do for you, Mr. Fisk?"

Though the African-American man was large and balding, Fisk knew that looks were deceiving. *He jogs five to eight miles a day and doesn't eat anything not approved by his dietician.* "I've got just a few moments before I meet with the President, and I was hoping to do a favor for her appointment secretary."

"Stanley? What's he done now?" Hodgekiss shook his head woefully.

"Not Stan. I'm here about the young lady that handles domestic appointments."

"Hopper. Jane, isn't it?" Hodgekiss said as he planted himself into his chair. Backlit by a large picture window, his salt-and-pepper hair glinted like finely drawn wire.

"Josephine Harper," Fisk offered solicitously as he moved to stand next to a bookshelf. *Be casual. Larry thinks I'm an overpaid cream puff.*

Hodgekiss was a seasoned deal maker and fundraiser with a well-developed sense of self-interest. "*You're* doing a favor for *her?* Must be some favor. Shoot."

"She wants an office with a window. Something with a view that doesn't involve traffic." *We cream puffs do like a good view.*

"Is that all? With somebody like you asking for it, she can get the Rose Garden if she wants it." *Nobody says no to you if they can help it. Everyone in Washington knows that.* Larry set aside his fears in favor of what was good for him, recalling that he had been the one to relay the President's termination request empowering Fisk to make Carns disappear.

"She's been meaning to stop by and ask you herself, but she's been so busy that there hasn't been time." *I see that look in your eye. You want to say no so badly that you can taste it.*

"Really?" He put on his poker face, realizing that the consultant had him pegged. *Window space for a virtual nobody isn't a small thing.*

"I just thought I'd save her the leg work."

"Well, day after tomorrow, if we can. Rose Garden. She moves in at her leisure. How's that?" *At least the President will know that I'm the one responsible for this. If Preston Fisk is going to bat for a secretary that nobody knows or talks about, then she must be one of the President's newly favored.* He was well aware that Madeline liked her "preferred" staffers to be well cared-for.

"That's up to Ms. Harper. I'm just the messenger. I'm sure you'll see to it she's taken care of."

"Count on it." He rose to walk Fisk to the door.

"Say, how about that round of golf you've been talking about?" *Might as well pay off now, rather than later.*

"Next Wednesday?" Hodgekiss fired back, reaching to open the door. *That's Fisk, always ready to pay up and have done with it.*

"Early?" He knew Larry's penchant for rising at the crack of dawn. "5:30?" *You're important, but you're still soft.*

"Oh, no. Six o'clock is as early as I get. Make it 6:45, and I'll be grateful."

Hodgekiss hid his scorn for the delay. "Done. Got any preferences for company?" Fisk decided to work with the golfing commitment he had previously made for the same time. *No telling who you'll bring along.* He scratched the back of his head. "Well, I can't confirm it just yet, but I can try for Speaker Langsford." The look in Larry's eyes told Fisk that the Chief of Staff was going to be rehearsing his casual conversation with the Speaker of the House well in advance of the game.

"Sounds good. I hear he's got a handicap." Hodgekiss grinned with anticipation.

"Four strokes off par."

"Ouch. I'll have to leave my wallet at home."

```
Saturday
April 26, 2014
Oval Office
The White House
Washington, D.C.
11:35 A.M. EDT
```

Returning to the President's outer office, Fisk did his best to appear nonthreatening. At times like this, he appreciated Josephine's desire for invisibility. *If they didn't notice me, I couldn't influence them. That is, after all, the whole point.*

He found an empty alcove and made himself comfortable. As he waited, he found himself thinking back to the few conversations with the appointment's secretary. *I could get to like her.* Time passed quickly.

"Mr. Fisk?"

He started, straightening. "Yes?" One hand smoothed his tie as he levered himself out of the chair. *Daydreaming again.*

"The President will see you now," the woman replied courteously, looking over the rims of her half-moon reading glasses.

He smiled congenially. *I almost forgot. Time to nudge you in the right direction, too.* "Thank you, Lorraine. Say, can you do me a favor?" Standing, he glanced at the clock. Less than an hour had passed.

"Yes?" She produced a small note pad and half-sized pen from a sweater pocket, her eyes betraying her desire to be noticed.

"Please let Josephine know that Larry approved her request," he said casually, careful to make Josephine sound like a close personal friend.

Lorraine blinked. "Josephine. Josephine Harper?" Her trained hand kept on writing in a neat cursive. *What has that quiet little thing been up to?*

"One and the same. There's more to Ms. Harper than meets the eye." The remark was deliberately calculated to spark the rumor mill.

"Yes, sir," she acknowledged with an obsequious nod. As Fisk headed for the nearby security station, she began to speculate.

Don't disappoint me, Lorraine. I expect you to start gossiping within the hour. Pausing to flash his ID at the Secret Service agent, he entered the Oval Office. The usual feeling of awe washed over him.

Edging past a technician who was struggling to disconnect a mass of telephone scrambler cables, Fisk moved to stand behind the massive padded leather chair that Madeline liked so much. Legend had it that it had once belonged to J. Edgar Hoover. *A flawless duplicate, and very expensive, too.* Despite his intended mission, he allowed himself to relax and study the movements of his president. Without thinking about it, he laid both hands on the top of the chair's wide back.

Madeline was bent over her desk, carefully making notes on a pad of fine, white vellum stationery. Careful to avoid the presidential seal, she started writing as close to the top of the page as she could. Peripherally, she registered the slight vibration of Fisk's hands as he set them on the chair. The realization that his grasp was so close caused her to pause in midsentence.

Registering her hesitation, Fisk removed his hands. *You'd like me to keep going, wouldn't you?* The invasion had been unintentional, triggering a reflex in him to apologize. The impulse quickly subsided.

Profilers in his organization had projected a 63 percent probability that President Hill would have secret feelings for him. The longer he remained associated with her, the more likely it was that she would desire him. *That sexual tension blinds you to my true motives.*

Madeline's pen flowed across the page, gathering speed. Each stroke spelled out her thoughts in ruthless precision.

Unnoticed, the busy technician left with an armful of equipment. Silence prevailed, punctuated only by the *scritch* of the presidential pen.

I wonder if you have any idea how good it makes me feel to have you this close? The notion that Fisk stood close by for personal, not professional, reasons appealed to her. The warm feeling it gave her was tempered by the reality of their 14-year association.

Looking up, she glanced around the office. The furnishings were lit with a coppery fire cast by the midday sun streaming through the armored glass in the window panes. The damage-resistant material contained antireflective particles that amplified the sun's corona during certain times of the day.

The quasi-romantic notion of making love to Fisk in the Oval Office became less attractive each time she thought of it. *We're using each other. I know it. He knows it.* Casting a sidelong glance at the closed doors, she forced herself to continue writing. The teleconference had been long and complicated.

Fisk stayed motionless as he read over Madeline's shoulder from a distance that could not be construed as intimate. *It's the EU again,* he observed with a grin as the context of her notes became clear. *Their currency is flat. Their retirement systems are broke. They're in worse shape than we are.*

"Ten countries have settled their national debts in the last five years. You would think that would be enough for them. I'm just about fed up with the garbage everybody's dishing out," Madeline observed bitterly. She methodically screwed the cap back onto her pen and laid it down, careful to leave the emblem of her alma mater showing. "You would think that the EU would have more respect for us, after ten years of nonstop terrorist hunting. We can, and will, pay our debts. When we do, the world will be better off for it. I just wish those people--"

"This isn't like paying off the balance on your credit cards. The EU is in trouble. Their currency's in the toilet and they need the leverage our debt provides. Paying off is good for us and bad for them. When you factor in the war on terror, they're jealous. That's all it is. Relax. You won't have to take their flak much longer. The deal we cut with Ramirez will--"

"Spare me." Madeline put her notes away.

"Hey, this is me you're talking to. You knew before you took office that this process would involve taking some abuse. Besides, you know you're going to enjoy sticking it to them when the time comes." *They'll know that we cheated them, but they won't be able to prove it. If that doesn't feed your ego, nothing will.*

"Short-changing them is just part of the game. The French President just finished telling me, in no uncertain terms, that we'd be wrecking his economy if we paid off more than ten percent of what we owe them. How much sense does that make? I never thought it would be like this," she breathed.

Fisk nodded at the back of Madeline's head. "As I said, they're jealous. We're riding high on our war record. Our military success against al-Qaeda and the other groups like them have made us look a little too good. We have too much good PR going for us, and it's making our allies look bad. That's all."

"If this is what I feel like, I can only imagine what the debt negotiators from Treasury are going to have to put up with." Her jaw clenched.

"They'll take the bullying in stride. Bad-mouthing the United States will never go out of style. They'll hate us when we drop the ball, and they'll hate us when we slam-dunk. Just take it for what it is, okay?"

She looked up at him. "It's just getting me down. It feels like half the known world prays for our downfall."

Fisk moved around to perch on the edge of her desk. "Ramirez is bought and paid for. Besides, he's got the touch. Turning the Mexican situation around and stabilizing half the currencies in Latin America has given him a lot of practice in dealing with debtors. Factor in what he did with Afghanistan..."

She fidgeted, breaking eye contact. "I know all that. We've been over this before. I was just fishing for moral support." The light in her eyes was fierce, challenging him to take advantage of her honesty. *I wish I had your optimism.*

"Your memo said you wanted to discuss those upcoming Senate races." *Trust me. You can't lose.*

"The party's positioning in the polls is unbeatable. I don't care about that right now. I just wish there were some way that we could get a leg up on them." She indicated the entire world with an imperious wave. She relented, her smile becoming sincere. "I'm sorry. It's just been a long day. The EU has been talking down to me since I took office. It just rubs me the wrong way."

Fisk held up both hands in mock surrender. "Hey, I'm not your enemy. As far as you've come, you still have a long way to go before you reach your full potential." *Easy, let's not just blurt it out.*

"You have no idea how true that is. There are days..."

Fisk silently turned aside. *I've never said it to you, have I? Come on, pry it out of me. You know you want to.*

When he didn't respond, she hid her disappointment and settled for a drink of water from glass on the edge of her desk. *Fine. Be that way.*

"How long have you known me?" *Wounded pride*, he diagnosed. *After all, you're tired of feeling like you're my puppet.*

"Get off it. You got me here. I'm grateful." *It will be so very thrilling to be rid of you.*

"Then trust me now. I know what you're thinking. The future is very promising for both of us. You like what you see, and it makes you want more." He was careful to pause so that he could gauge her mood. "If there was a way to deal with somebody more sympathetic than Ramirez, I would have found it by now. You've given me enough resources."

"You haven't asked for more in two whole months. What am I supposed to think?" She seemed to be calming down. *You make me feel like you don't need me, and I hate you for it.*

"I'm not one of your federal agencies. I'm also not one of your other worker bees. I don't ask for more money just because I know I can get it. I have more respect for you than that."

During her rise to power, Fisk had been careful to nurture Madeline's belief that money could solve her problems. Encouraging her to bribe while at the same time refusing her party's money was a calculated risk. In-depth analysis suggested that she could be frustrated sexually and politically as long as she remained unable to manipulate Fisk. Her pent-up frustration would most likely result in a thirst for greater amounts of power and prestige.

"My people have looked at it from every possible angle. As far as I'm concerned, it's practically a done deal. You're about to go down in history as the woman who saved this nation from bankruptcy. Isn't that worth a little temporary heartache?"

"Point taken. Tell me more about my future. I like the sound of your optimism."

"Forget about the whole mess. My people have worked with yours, and the fix is in."

"Does that include our Treasury Secretary?" Madeline asked petulantly.

Brown was the country's youngest Secretary of the Treasury. He had been a hotshot accounting executive with a reputation for getting things done. Prior to his confirmation, he had made front page news by single-handedly prevented the third-largest American energy concern from going bankrupt due to poor management practices.

In his new capacity as Secretary of the Treasury, Brown routinely clashed with the chairman of the Federal Reserve Board. Despite their conflicts, the two had managed to restart the economy after the most recent recession. In 2013, he had been selected as the Man of the Year by the nation's leading financial groups.

The struggle to negotiate more than a dozen high-profile deals had caused changes that surprised even Brown himself. After his first year in office, he had become a crusader for financial reforms and had developed extremely moral behavior and higher professional standards. Fisk's unseen advisors were at a loss to explain it. In two years, Brown had gone from being a corporate gunslinger to a populist crusader. He was no longer easily led.

"This is the calm before the storm. Make the most of it and be ready to take advantage of what comes afterward. We'll deal with Mr. Brown as circumstances dictate."

"Storm? It's not going to be that bad, is it?" The President's eyebrows rose.

"Sure, both here at home and overseas."

"I haven't seen anything from Treasury."

"Of course you haven't. Andy doesn't know about the currency recall yet. As difficult as he's being now, you shouldn't tell him, either. Not until you've had a chance to get to his people. After that, it won't matter."

"Ah. You're talking about the panic when the banks close."

"Tip of the iceberg. You have to remember that half of the countries on the planet don't like us. They'll be doing everything they can to use their share of our debt to hurt us. That's the storm."

"Too bad for them. This has been coming for a long time. The people are ready for it. They've already gone through several currency changeovers. It won't be a stunner when they're told that we have to do it again."

Fisk was careful to make his warning sound trivial. "You're giving them too much credit. The conspiracy nuts will go crazy when the banks close. Even the media will be running old film clips from the 1930s."

"You're not telling me anything I haven't thought of."

"I'm not so sure about that. That's why you need to be ready to take full advantage of what comes when the storm has passed."

"What?"

"Once you've got the World Bank off your back, it'll be time to make some decisions about your own future."

Madeline's irritation melted away.

Fisk went on as if he hadn't noticed her silence. "So?" Her lack of ire told Fisk that he was on the right track. "Let the economy crash. Let the mobs take to the streets, if it comes to that. Then go to the UN. Be humble, and ask for peacekeepers." As many times as he'd practiced it, actually saying the words made his flesh crawl. *I feel like a traitor.*

His pause sparked Madeline's impatience. "Letting the economy fall apart would be easy enough. I'm not an economist but I think I could figure it out. Why can't I use the Army to restore order?"

"The Army is dangerous. They have ten years of successful campaigning behind them. Busting terrorist groups and the occasional rogue nation has given them a taste for righteous action. Their patriotism runs counter to your political interests."

"So how do we reconcile politics and patriotism?"

"National survival. Politicians govern. Patriots defend. The two are opposite sides of the same coin. All you have to do is set the stage for the patriots, and they'll defend your political interests."

"Do you realize what you're saying?" Madeline arched her eyebrows with interest. *If you're not the Devil's advocate, I'll bet you have his phone number.*

"Why be satisfied with solving the debt crisis when that same debt, no matter what the terms, can give you what you really want?" Bile rose in his throat. White flashes at the edge of his vision were followed by the stirring of something angry and nameless in the back of his mind. As quickly as it appeared, the elusive presence was gone. *God forgive me.*

Silence held for several tenuous moments. Fisk, in his agony, didn't notice the beginnings of Madeline's change in mood.

"What do I really want?" She could almost *feel* his next words.

"Total power."

She cut him off with a wicked expression. "You know me too well."

"That is what you pay me for," he stated, careful to match her mood.

"You've got my attention. Tell me more." She licked her drying lips.

"The New World Order," he breathed, sounding more dramatic than he'd intended. " The conspiracy buffs have been screaming about it for years. They claim that America will be looted and torn apart once we become too weak to fight for our national survival. It's the perfect cover. Granted, it'll take a lot of finesse on your part to make it look like you were forced--"

"I can do that." Madeline nibbled at her lower lip.

"Don't be so fast to suppose--"

"I can do it. The fools will be expecting to see a weak-willed woman. They'll be quick to excuse any mistakes I make as long as I don't over play my hand."

Cast in shadow by the afternoon sun, Fisk's face was unreadable. "This isn't something you can do half way. Once the peacekeepers arrive, you'll be committed. You'll have to be prepared for the public backlash. It'll take time to win back the trust that you had to abuse in order to make all this happen." His mouth went dry. The conflicting emotions playing across his face went unnoticed.

"How long?" Her mind churned with the possibilities.

"Debt negotiations will start any time now. They should take the next two years. Larry's already pointed in the right direction. Your reelection theme is the debt and all the preparations you've made to deal with it. If all goes well, you can expect action some time during your second term."

"Would I be wrong to assume that we could screw things up just enough to prevent national elections?"

"It's your Congress. I've done all I can to make sure of that. Any decisions you make about a national emergency declaration will benefit them, too."

"Mm."

Madeline's receptive attitude was affecting Fisk more than he would have admitted. *If we're right, you'll spark a revolution.*

"So, let me see if I can fill in the blanks. I've provoked social chaos to lure in the UN's peacekeepers. I assume that I'm supposed to rally the mob, mobilize the Army, and send the peacekeepers packing."

"Right." Fisk wiped at his parched lips.

"Dangerous. You're talking about achieving total power. Even if I can stir things up, how do I keep it?"

He ignored the lurch in his stomach. "Take the last step. You'll make a lot of enemies if this all works out. You'll have to put them down if you're going to have any real power."

"Do you know what you're saying?"

Fisk shrugged. "If I'm wrong, all you have to do is modify your tactics."

Madeline raised her head in admiration of his insight. *It's what I've wanted all my life. How can I make you understand that?* Madeline was suddenly uncomfortable with sharing her thoughts with Fisk. With a jolt, she realized, *He's far more ambitious than I am. No. Bolder,* she corrected. *More dangerous to me than I ever considered. It's only a matter of time before you replace me. If I let you live that long.*

Friday
May 2, 2014
Fisk Group Consultants
Washington, D.C.
9:00 A.M. EDT

Fisk Group Consultants, like so much of the new construction in the District of Columbia, gleamed with promise yet was humble in appearance. The current architectural trend in the nation's capitol was to reflect cleanliness rather than importance. It was meant to physically differentiate between the old and the new.

Driving into the heart of the city, Garrison felt a twinge of regret as he drove past his former office building. It, too, had been constructed to meet the new architectural guidelines. The logos and patriotic symbols had been removed, ensuring that it still looked clean and humble. *A fitting tomb for a dead idea.* He'd made his peace with the NRA's passing and resolved to move onto the next thing.

Turning into the driveway of the Fisk Group's parking lot, he waited as a gate guard checked the credentials of the driver ahead of him. He rolled slowly forward, stopping to flash his ID and building pass. *How much does he know about what really goes on here?*

Driving slowly, he found his assigned spot in the underground garage. He opened his briefcase at the security station near the elevators so the plain-clothed security specialist could inspect it. Once cleared, he took the elevator to the ground floor.

Like so many modern buildings, this one could only be accessed through the underground garage. Security concerns in the previous decade had turned much of D.C. into a highly compartmentalized bureaucratic honeycomb.

Garrison walked casually across the lobby. He understood that the impersonal feel of the decor was deliberate camouflage. *Just another consultant working out of a building that he may or may not own.*

The reception desk was staffed by two smartly dressed women, each tapping away at a keyboard while whispering into an ear-clipped microphone. One woman looked up and smiled.

"Conference Room Two, Mr. Garrison," she said before merging back into her work.

He nodded and walked on.

The building's four stories were reached by ramp rather than elevator. He had always been a physical man who didn't mind walking. The trip to the second floor was uneventful. As he passed several open doors, he tried not to stare at the people working in the offices. *Consultant, or "consultant,"* he observed cynically.

He paused at the door to the conference room just long enough to smooth his coat and straighten his tie. He made a deliberate effort to project confidence as he opened the heavy oak door and strolled in. *Conference rooms are battlegrounds. I might not know why I'm here, but they don't need to know that.*

He had met three of the five people seated at the table previously. The others were unfamiliar. *Ah. This would be the Treasury team.* He had been peripherally aware of the massive effort that the conspiracy had put into getting its people on the Treasury's currency management and debt monitoring boards within the previous year.

He sat down to wait. Silently, they took turns looking at each other. He acknowledged the others, smiling and nodding. Garrison recalled chatting with the three he knew over drinks at several different parties. The idea of being at a party made him think about Anne Carroll. *Wonder what she would think about all this?*

Eventually, the door opened and Fisk entered with his usual display of confidence, authority, and style. He greeted everyone with a smile, patting Garrison on the back as he passed. Taking his own seat at the head of the table, Fisk took one more look at everyone. He touched a spot on the table, causing a small holographic control pad to light up.

"All right, let's get to it. Some of you know Mr. Garrison. For those who don't, you might want to remember his face. I've asked him here today to brief him on the next phase of the project that will follow the debt negotiations. He doesn't know it yet, but he is the Phase Two candidate."

Everyone began to take a new interest in Garrison, making him uneasy. Fisk triggered the holographic projector, causing an image of a well-groomed Latino male to form in the center of the table.

"This is Antonio Ramirez, the chief administrator of the World Bank. He's held the position ever since the World Bank came more uniformly under UN control. He's known as the savior of more than a dozen economies. He may not like us as a country, but he's more than respectful of the power of our currency.

"Mr. Ramirez has studied our economic situation and is well aware of what we can and cannot pay when refinancing our national debt. Because his is not a political appointment, we can expect him to take a different view of the UN's policy regarding what is and isn't collateral. We can also expect him to factor in world opinion whenever he makes a decision. As the heads of your respective departments, each of you will control some aspect of the actual negotiations."

Garrison raised a hand. "Can I ask a question?"

"By all means."

Garrison paused to gauge everyone's reactions. "I think I might be missing something. I'm not familiar with this type of finance. What did you mean by Phase Two? If I didn't know better..."

Fisk shook his head. "I'm sorry to spring it on you like this. We've had to move up our timetable--"

"Why? What exactly is Phase Two?"

Fisk's expression tightened. "Well, now. This isn't going quite as I planned. Would you do me a favor?"

"Okay."

"Listen to what these people have to say. Introductions will come later. Just hear them out and give them your honest opinion."

"What do you mean? I thought you..." *What do you people know that I don't?*

"I have another job for you. Let's finish this, and then we'll talk about it in my office."

"All right." Garrison searched the faces around the table. *You don't want me to remember who they are so I can give you an unbiased opinion.*

Anita Crowell sat forward, restraining her urge to take a sheet of prepared notes from her briefcase. Her nervousness only showed in her eyes. She shot a withering look at Fisk. *No more games.*

"What Mr. Fisk is trying not to say is that you've been selected to oversee the next phase in our project. If you like, you can think of this as an icebreaker. If and when the next phase is implemented, we will be your financial advisors."

"Does this have anything to do with the NRA files?"

Fisk ignored Anita's dirty look. "It does. We can talk about that later. For now, it's important that you listen to what they have to say about the debt situation. Just hear them out and respond as you see fit."

"Why?" Garrison asked suspiciously.

"I need to show them that you're the right man for the job. Since I couldn't think of a better way to break it to you, your patience and perseverance will help me get out of this very embarrassing moment with all my fingers and toes." Fisk fixed Garrison with a meaningful gaze. *Work with me.*

That's the "work with me" look, Garrison told himself as he watched the other man fidget. Scratching the back of his hand, he nodded at Anita. *Okay. Let's see what you've got.*

"Mr. Ramirez is a lawyer-economist with an ego larger than most GDPs. He's never passed up a chance to curry favor with the world community when negotiating for national restructuring. It makes him look good, which he likes--a lot. In recent years, his terms have included harsh payment schedules for nations whose records on civil rights haven't been so good. He also has a passion for making deals that turn a profit for the World Bank."

"Which benefits the UN by allowing them to pay their bills with those profits," observed Garrison.

Fisk was careful to direct his remarks at Garrison. "Make no mistake. The Secretary General is developing a taste for paying the bills with what he regards as his own money. In the next two decades, the UN will be a force to be reckoned with."

"I take it that the United Nations will play a part in your...our... plans? Can I assume that Mr. Ramirez is a willing participant?" Garrison pointed at the hologram.

"Nope. He has no idea. We've profiled him and those around him to the most minute detail. All he has to do is be his image-conscious self, and everything should work out just fine."

"He sounds like he's been in training for the U.S. problem all his life. Okay, I'll play. What's the big deal with him and his kick on UN self-sufficiency?"

"Know your enemies. What exactly does self-sufficiency for the UN mean under these conditions?" Fisk asked, turning to the well-dressed man to his right.

Jarrett Lee smoothed his thinning brown hair and smiled. His book, *The New World Bank*, chronicled the rise of UN fiscal power, starting with the 1999 gold bullion transfers made by the IMF to shore up the debts of Third World nations. The scheme had been a precursor to the merging of the IMF and World Bank into the single financial powerhouse that now stood ready to refinance the faltering U.S. deficit. Lee's book also chronicled the crash of the Argentine peso and other debt issues which had since been tackled by the UN's financial arm.

"Once the UN had the purse strings of the IMF and World Bank firmly in its hands, the Secretary General directed that the World Bank should be able to take land, resources, and facilities as collateral against new loans or outstanding debts. The General Assembly eventually voted those rules into the charter, and the UN, as a whole, has benefited ever since."

He paused to glance at the nervous man next to him, appearing to wait for something before he forged ahead. "To date, Ramirez has been retained by two Secretaries General, and he shows no sign of being out of a job any time soon. As of last fiscal year, the UN was officially able to pay for its own administrative functions. Each time the UN settles a country's debt, they get a piece of that country's national infrastructure. Hence, they are nearly self-sufficient, short of military or humanitarian operations. That plum is still out of their reach." *For now.*

"Will they be capable of independent military action once they take whatever they get from us?" Garrison asked.

"Indeed they will. I can see that you've been doing your homework. The last four countries that settled have forked over some of their military bases to get what the World Bank calls 'peace credits.' I see no reason why the United States will be any different."

Garrison exhaled. "Debt forgiveness through technology transfer and logistical support. I think I read about that in some journal." Eyebrows went up approvingly.

"I told you he was our man," Fisk commented.

Crowell favored Garrison with a kind glance. "We can expect that Ramirez will direct his administrators to really sock it to us. As of noon yesterday, calculations showed that we could repay only a third of the debt with the fullest possible currency redemption. Add domestic precious metals and other transferable mineral and geologic wealth to that, and the percentage goes up to almost 50 percent. The federal government has been running budget surpluses off and on over the last decade on general domestic accounts. However, our management of the overall debt load hasn't been quite as diligent."

Garrison looked at Fisk. "Have you cut a deal of some kind?"

"Good guess. My mission was strictly under the table. No official channels. As far as the world knows, there has been no contact between the American President and the World Bank."

Anita pressed on. "He'll want concessions to round out the package. With such a large shortfall, he'll want, and get, more."

"Like us handing over a little technology and a few military bases, which his people will attach some very large numbers to, just so we'll go along with it," Garrison speculated.

Having been idle for several minutes, the projector shut off. Ramirez's image vanished.

Fisk turned in his chair to look benignly at a sour-faced little man, who was busy with his tie. "On the whole, a very difficult situation. The next 20 years should be interesting, to say the least." Looking expectantly at the little man, Fisk waited for him to speak.

Harvey Jewel stared back for a brief moment, hands still clasped around his tie. Realizing that he was on the spot, he looked frantically at the others. Salt-and-pepper hair receded atop a forehead that was permanently puckered with worry lines. Bobbing his head, he spoke as if he were afraid of offering bad news.

"T-this can mean liens against the banking system, or some other kind of currency kick-back. More than likely, it will also involve some kind of l-land deal. Factories or resource areas. Ramirez likes those kinds of things because they guarantee long term capital flow." Pausing, he looked around the room. "It'll take everything in our bag of tricks to p-put the President over the top. It's all in my report."

Fisk knew Harvey wasn't shy about his role in the conspiracy. He was just shy about people in general. *He writes a heck of a report, though.* He eyed the brunette at the end of the table. "Ms. Sandoval, put the cap on this for us."

Cordelia Sandoval's intense gaze made her look fearless. Capitalizing on it, she glanced over at Jewel, inwardly satisfied at his discomfiture. She spoke with just enough force to ensure that everyone around the table was looking at her.

"We've got an anti-American crusader to contend with. When he turns his people loose on us, he'll expect blood and accolades. If we do our jobs right, we can see to it that he has to fight for every point in the polls and every dollar that he gets. When I'm done with him, he won't know whether to smile or cry. Based on today's projections, I think we have good odds. President Hill will come out on top, and so will the country."

Fisk nodded. "Once our president takes the credit for settling the debt, she'll be so popular that she won't be able to resist the temptation to overstep her limits. That's exactly what we want her to do." Fisk turned to look at Garrison.

Clearing his throat self-consciously, he said, "That sounds like my cue to ask about Phase Two."

"Anita?" Fisk saw her sour expression and cocked an eyebrow at her.

She turned toward him, hands folded on the table. "Can I be honest? This was a sneak attack. If I'm going to advise him in the future, I'd rather not be part of anything that takes advantage of his trust. He's been very patient with us. Shouldn't we be telling--"

"We've already had this discussion. Bill? Would you please meet me in my office? I'd like to have some time alone with these people."

Garrison started to slide forward in his chair. "Look, I don't--"

Fisk nodded sharply. He paused to look at each member of the group. "No, I'm sure you don't. I apologize for the subterfuge. I just wanted these people to meet you without any preconceptions. That way, they could draw their own conclusions."

Garrison sensed a mix of emotions from the assembled financial experts. He rose to his feet. "You're holding back on me. What is it?"

"Be grateful," Harvey muttered.

Garrison left the room.

"Well?" Fisk looked around the room after the door closed.

"He's good," Cordelia said.

"He doubts his own abilities." Anita pursed her lips in consideration.

"He's afraid," Harvey quietly offered.

Jarrett said nothing.

"Sorry to keep you waiting, Bill," Fisk said as he shuffled into the office. He made sure that his comm implant was turned off.

Garrison was standing near a wall, looking at the awards, plaques, and diplomas spread across the walnut paneling. He turned towards Fisk. "I understand. It has to be difficult holding all this together. Just shoot straight with me. That's all I ask." *After everything I've lost, I can't stop now.*

"Okay. The whole truth, and nothing but the truth, so help me God." Fisk relaxed into the chair behind his desk.

"Phase Two sounds pretty big," Garrison prodded, taking a seat.

"The biggest. I'll tell you up front that even I don't have all the details. For security purposes, my involvement ends with the completion of Phase One. That little thing we had you do with the NRA records was the opener for Phase Two."

"I see. Phase Two has nothing to do with banking, eh?"

Fisk grinned. "No. Jarrett Lee insisted on seeing you for himself before he gave his blessing. The rest of his team backed him up, so here we are. Phase Two is military."

Garrison was silent for several heartbeats. "I...see. You're planning for a revolt?"

Fisk rewarded him with an informal salute. "There are two possible outcomes to Phase One. Either people will get fed up with the corruption that we've helped to grow or they'll come to accept it. You know the finer points."

"If the politicos resist, there could be trouble."

"That's where you come in. I want you to head up our Phase Two operations." He took a small key out of his vest pocket and unlocked a drawer.

"Say that again?" Garrison blinked.

Fisk took out a glossy blue folder. "The plan gives me very broad discretionary powers. My authority dries up when we complete Phase One. I'm using that authority now to choose the leader for Phase Two."

"And you want me?" Garrison was flattered.

Fisk handed over the folder. "I don't have the luxury of getting to know many people in my line of work. In the last five years, you and I have spent a lot of time on the NRA problem. I watched you do things that you hated. I watched you, and I learned from you. You and I are very much alike."

Garrison accepted the folder and sat back. "Hey, I appreciate the vote of confidence, but don't you want someone with a military background to do this?" He could feel his heart rate begin to climb.

Fisk chose his words carefully. "I'm the right person to lead Phase One. I understand the political landscape. My instinct for politics is better than average. I realize there are shades of grey in every situation. I know that the people in power have lost their desire to serve. They now prefer to be served." He pointed at Garrison. "You understand the difference between right and wrong. Your ethics are more finely tuned than most. You're also familiar with the attitudes of politicians and community leaders who put themselves ahead of the people they're supposed to serve. And like me, you know what has to be done. That makes you the right person for the job."

"Me? I don't know what has to be done." Unnerved, he began to fidget.

"Phase Two may never happen. If Phase One doesn't pan out the way we intend, you won't have anything to worry about. If it does, I want you to be there to capitalize on our success. I want you to be the one who helps the people of this country take back their freedom."

"That's a lot to ask from an ad hoc military."

Fisk pointed at the folder. "The network that's being constructed for your use will have nonmilitary assets. At your discretion, you'll be able to talk or tackle, as you see fit."

Garrison looked at the folder he clutched in his hands. "Say that again? I really do think I missed something." *Where did this idea come from?*

"You know about our political agenda. If our manipulation doesn't pan out, we're preparing a military option."

"You want me to be a militia commander?" Garrison asked, incredulous.

"I want you to be the commander of all our militias."

"Have you forgotten who you're talking to? I don't have any military experience. I wouldn't know where to begin." *What's wrong with me? That should have come out as no!*

"Our militias are not military. There's not a recently discharged military member among them. They're mostly civilians. Family-oriented, hard working people. These are people that you can identify with."

"Like you identify so closely with the politicos. Okay. But what's the point in avoiding people with recent military experience?" *That didn't come out right, either.*

"One reason. In the last 20 years, the regular Army has become a political machine. We couldn't risk the possibility of infiltration." He waited as Garrison opened the folder.

The other man looked up, surprised. *I did it. I opened the blasted folder. I am so screwed.* "This is a list of names and addresses. I don't think I know any of these people." He riffled through the pages a second time.

Fisk said sympathetically, "Arrangements have already been made. You don't know them, but they know you. They chose you." *He seems to be taking it well enough.*

"You think these people can fight a war?"

"No, not a war. They'll support any grassroots movement that crops up. It will be your job to determine whether to use them as political activists or guerilla fighters."

Garrison struggled to keep his emotions under control. "Which means what?" *Stop!*

"The people on that list will be your advisors. They know who you are and they think you're the best person for the job. You've got my blessing, and theirs."

Garrison looked down at the folder. *This could work.*

Fisk waited.

Garrison exhaled wearily. "Ballots or bullets, whichever the situation requires." *Am I buying in to this? Please, don't let me be hooked.*

"As you see fit, Bill. If there's no movement toward reform, you won't act. Your organization disappears, just like mine."

Closing the folder, Garrison looked at the consultant querulously. *It is sooo tempting to say yes.*

"I can't make you do this, and I won't. If you choose not to, I have an alternate that I can brief by the end of this week."

"What's the catch?" Garrison's mouth was dry.

Fisk cocked his head to one side. "Now that you know all this, I need your answer."

"Now?"

"Now." Fisk replied, grim.

Garrison stared blankly at the folder for a long moment. *Screwed. Definitely.* "I have total control?" he asked, still looking at the folder.

"So total that once you leave this office today you'll never see me again."

"Suppose I really do decide that this isn't necessary?"

"Pull the plug."

"If it comes to conflict, I suppose you could--"

Fisk shook his head. "Nope. If you're final answer is yes, you'll never see me again."

"Never?" Garrison was stunned and hurt.

"Never."

"I can't--" Garrison choked up as his face reddened. His mind raced through a maelstrom of details. "I can't make this work by being some shadowy controlling figure. I'll have to make compromises with those blasted advisors. I'd have to be, well..."

Fisk grinned. "Out in the open?" *You're in; you just don't know it yet.*

"Yes. Visible. People would have to know I really stood for what I said I did. I'm not sure what the right word for it would be."

"Publicly responsible?" Fisk offered.

"I'd have to be *you*." Garrison ran a taut hand through his thinning hair.

"Or, at the very least, *like* me." *Which you are.*

Garrison looked at the folder that was now rolled up in his hand. "I don't know if I can. I mean, I think I can do this, but I can't become you. I can't be anything like you."

"Why not?" Fisk asked earnestly. "The former Assistant Vice President of the NRA is a known man. Single, good-looking, and ready to speak his mind on the subject most dear to him. If you call them, the news hounds will come. Granted, you're not as well regarded as I am, but you're more like me than you know. You always have been. If the time should come, you'll do just fine."

"I have just one more question." Garrison laid the crumpled folder on the desk.

"If you're in, I'll answer as truthfully as I can."

Garrison fidgeted, trying to make up his mind.

"Are you in?" Fisk prompted. *I wish I could tell you the rest. I really do.* He was careful to remain physically neutral. "Yes or no. What's it going to be?"

Garrison stopped fidgeting and closed his eyes. Opening them, he looked around the room. "I'm in. Just tell me one thing. How do you live with it?"

"Live with what?"

"The public sees you as some kind of stylish super-fixer who can make a president. The advisors treat you like some kind of good luck charm while they go on about their business. How do you live with knowing that you might be killed for what you're doing?"

"How do I keep it all in perspective? It's like trying to be somebody else. I can't tell you why, but that's how I look at it. Some days, I feel like I'm trying too hard. Other days, I don't feel like I'm giving 100 percent." He took out his wallet and opened it.

"Tell me about it," Garrison exhaled loudly while shaking his head. "When I was with the NRA, as hard as it was for me to let it all go down, I knew that it had to be done. That's really all that got me through it."

Fisk took a small photo from his wallet. "We told you that what you were doing was necessary to alter the political landscape." Handing the image to Garrison, he sat back.

He examined the picture. "Right. The loss of the pro-gun lobby makes it more likely that she and her cronies in Congress will overstep." He could see that the image had once been part of a larger photo. A single face was visible on the cracked and fading portrait. The tanned visage was framed by greying hair and pale sideburns. The eyes and mouth seemed to project defiance from the fading black-and-white image.

"Who's this?"

"The reason that I've come this far." Fisk smiled.

Garrison squinted, absorbing every detail in the photo fragment. "He's the one who got you started?"

"Yes."

"What's his name?" Garrison asked, handing the photo back to Fisk.

"Don't know. I never actually met him." Bracing himself, he rode out the lightning shock that ripped through his mind. *Happens every time I look at that photo.*

Garrison gazed at the old picture, oblivious to the other man's silent introspection. *Grey hair. Serious eyes. As old as this thing appears to be, this guy is probably dead.* "That must have been some pitch he fed you."

"We communicated indirectly. And yes, it was. He was very persuasive. I owe him a lot," Fisk said softly before putting the photo back into his wallet.

Garrison pursed his lips. "You don't sound very grateful."

Fisk found himself nodding in agreement. "He gave me a lot to think about. He also gave me a lot to do. I've been thinking about what I'll say to him when this is all over and done with."

"He still around?"

"I don't know, but I intend to find out."

"How do you like it?" Larry asked, beaming at Josephine. *Just remember who did this for you.*

The secretary stood next to the mahogany desk, one hand on the back of the tall leather executive's chair. She split her stunned glance between the Chief of Staff and the small window overlooking the Rose Garden.

"Mr. Fisk was quite specific about the furnishings," he said, placing his own spin on the single furniture-related remark that had come up during their golf game. *I picked the room, though.*

"Really?" She blushed. Looking down at her pleated burgundy skirt, she thought, *This office is better dressed than I am. I'm going to have to fix that.*

"Nothing here is more than a month old, except for the desk. That little gem came from the East Wing. It dates from the Clinton administration."

"Oh, my." Josephine looked down at the dark wood. Its polished surface and tiny brass fittings gleamed. She vaguely remembered the Clinton presidency. She'd been just a little girl, not quite in grade school, when it had begun in 1992.

The telephone warbled. Josephine stiffened and looked down at the machine. The new six-line unit had a cordless handset, flash priority call screening, and voice recognition dialing. She remembered seeing one like it on one of the home shopping channels that she occasionally watched.

Hodgekiss smiled benevolently at her from the doorway. "I'd better let you get that." He turned to leave.

Sitting in her new chair, she luxuriated in its firm warmth as the line rang again. *How do I use this thing?* Raising a hesitant hand, she slipped into her business persona, picked up the receiver, and pressed the blinking button for line six.

"Presidential scheduling, this is Josephine. How can I help you?" As she listened, her eyes began roaming around the room, stopping on the window. *What more could I want?*

"Hello, Ms. Harper. Do you like it?" The silken tones of Fisk's voice seemed to gather in her ear before making their way to her brain.

"Like what?"

"Your new office. It's not too much?" He sounded like he was in traffic somewhere.

The note of concern in his words touched her in a way that she found unexpected. *It's just an office, but it matters to him what I think.* "It's perfect. Really. Everything's so coordinated."

"Glad to hear it. If you have problems with the computer system, you'll find the number for my tech support in your telephone file."

Computer? Turning around, she looked at the workstation behind her desk. It hadn't struck her as being anything special when she first saw it. The new holographic monitor sat snugly atop an adjustable viewing stand. The voice-activated keyboard winked a tiny blue light at her, letting her know that it was paying attention.

"That's not GSA approved," she said uncertainly. Decades of employee abuse and politics had caused the General Services Administration to become quite picky about who could buy what office equipment.

"It is now. You'll find it on the official Senior Executive Service buy list. Trust me."

Reaching out to touch the keyboard, Josephine watched the computer come to life. The screen lit up, showing her a series of menu options. "I can get in trouble for that."

"You work for *the* senior executive, don't you?"

Josephine's ears warmed at the shark-like tone in his voice. *This is a trick question.* "That's chief executive, and you know I can't accept special favors."

"Senior exec, chief exec. Depends on which GSA manager you talk to."

She struggled to hold back a tiny smile. *He knows I want to keep the thing. He's just having fun with me.*

"Right. I still can't accept favors. You'll have to let me--"

"I wouldn't have it any other way, Ms. Harper."

Her mouth dropped open as she considered what he was reading into her remark. "But--" Tongue-tied, her mind raced to find the right words.

"Good-bye, Josephine."

She looked at the receiver for a long moment after the connection went silent. Fisk was the only person she'd ever known who could part so smoothly.

I owe him a favor. What does that mean? Hanging up the phone, she turned back around to eye the new computer. A knock at the still-open door to her office startled her.

"Excuse me. I've got the correspondence files you asked for," Lorraine said, stepping into the room.

Josephine hid her amusement as she watched Lorraine surreptitiously examine the office. *I'm not invisible any more.*

"Come in, Lorraine." She waved to a chair across from her desk. *I'm not sure that I like all this attention.*

"A new office? That's the Rose Garden out there. You've moved up in the world." She pointed an accusing finger at the window. Sliding the stack of folders onto the desk, she planted herself primly in the offered chair. She made a great show of taking in the new surroundings. *Who are you involved with?*

"I didn't have anything to do with this," Josephine protested with a wave. As soon as she said it, she regretted her choice of words.

Lorraine moved forward in her chair. "Who is, I mean are, they?" Nobody was safe in assuming anything about anyone's preferences any more. Homosexuality on Capitol Hill had been out in the open for decades. Congress had recently confirmed a female appointee to the Supreme Court, fully aware that she was a lesbian.

"I can't say. It wouldn't be right." Josephine felt her palms begin to sweat.

Lorraine studied Josephine's face, leaning her head to one side. *I'll find out soon enough.* "Why are you so flustered? You're obviously getting a good deal for...whatever it is you're doing."

"I'm not doing anything with anybody. I promise." Realizing how silly she must sound, she watched in horror as Lorraine stood up and winked mischievously.

"Your secret is safe with me," she promised as she left. *Whoever it is, they'll stop by to pay you a visit. They always do.*

Though she was alone, Josephine could still feel the heat of her denial. In her mind's eye, she could imagine the gossip. *"You know that Harper woman? Well, I heard..."* All her life, she had been the classic wallflower. *My days of being seen and not heard are definitely over.*

Wednesday
May 7, 2014
Parking Level
New Treasury Annex
Washington, D.C.
3:15 P.M. EDT

"I told you." Fisk shook his head slowly.

Walking beside him, Hodgekiss shrugged into his overcoat. The underground garage was chilly, causing him some discomfort.

Fisk sauntered along with his briefcase in one hand, apparently unaffected by the cold. He belted his coat as he walked.

"The nerve of some people. If I hadn't seen it, I wouldn't have believed it. You really laid it all out for him, too." He shoved his hands into the pockets of his coat, not caring what Fisk thought about him now that he was warm. *You might not be as soft as you look.*

Stopping abruptly, Fisk turned to favor Larry with a hard glance. "There's only one thing left to do." Because he knew that he was supposed to, Fisk ignored the Secret Service protector escorting Hodgekiss.

"Let's talk in my car." *Let's not talk about this in the open.*

They walked over to the limousine pickup ramp in silence. Fisk suppressed a shiver. It was enough for him to silently cow Hodgekiss by appearing unconcerned about the chill. *Power manifests in many forms.*

Reflecting on his meeting with Andrew Brown, Fisk had no doubts about their course of action. He had boldly laid out Madeline's proposed negotiating strategy. He'd even hinted at the currency recall. After two hours of polite sparring under Larry's watchful eye, Fisk was now genuinely frustrated.

As they approached the ramp, he pointedly veered toward the limo waiting for Hodgekiss so that Christopher would know that he was not yet needed. Inside the warmth of the big car, Christopher waved his acknowledgement.

Larry's driver was waiting with the limo door open when they arrived. The Secret Service man piled in after them, perching on a jumpseat in the front of the passenger compartment. Picking up a telephone handset, he spoke quietly into it as the chauffeur got in.

"She'd have your head if she knew you told him so much. I'm with you, though. No worries. What have you got in mind?"

Fisk laid his briefcase aside and paused before responding. Checking to make sure that his comm implant was active, he relaxed. "Turn him, or get to his subordinates."

Larry shrugged. "Divide and conquer. Nothing new about that. What's your twist?"

"Turn him, or break him. Failing that, we give him the Carns treatment." He gleaned some inward satisfaction as he watched Larry flinch at the statement.

"Wouldn't know about that," Larry replied, his voice rising. *So, you're the one who did Carns. All this time, I thought it was Metz.* "I can set up the meeting. We'll bring in all the Department bigwigs for a closed-door confab. Wine them, dine them, and get their endorsements. If we had him there, it would take the wind out of his sails. You know?"

Fisk nodded, ignoring the joke. *Everybody knows that Andy likes to sail. Ha-ha.* "Set it up. I'll keep him occupied while you and Madeline run the bases. Just one thing."

"Yeah?"

"Make sure Kirsov steers clear. Based on what Andy said, he might be willing to work with us." Alexander Kirsov was the Undersecretary of the Treasury.

"If he gets the chance." Larry nodded sagely.

"Keep him clean. If we have to use him, he'll need to come up to speed pretty fast. If he's too busy fending off the media, he won't be any good to us."

Hodgekiss bobbed his head in acceptance. Political scapegoating was something that he understood all too well

Anne bustled into her editor's office. "He's expecting me," she explained to the anonymous staff assistant. She took a seat that let her see what was going on through the open door. *It's been a while since he called me to his office.*

Stan Leihman's door was always open. He had a telephone in one hand and papers in the other. His tone was quiet, yet firm. Unruffled, the assistant continued hammering away at the keyboard on his lap, eyes locked onto the computer screen in front of him. Still in coat and tie, the young man's intensity was attractive.

She whiled away the minutes by watching his every move. *He knows I'm watching him. Probably thinks I'm waiting for him to make a mistake. Reminds me of myself when I first started in this business.*

As she watched him, she spied the glint of metal under his ear. *Another one of...those.* The fact that he was typing manually instead of using the jack gave him a bump up in her estimation. Her prejudice quickly drowned her worries about why she had been summoned. *Once we stop working with our hands, what will we be?* She knew her bias was outmoded. More than once, she'd taken a certain amount of pride in being called obsolete. *Look at Stan. He doesn't jack in to answer his phone.*

As Leihman set the phone down, the assistant stopped typing just long enough to touch his left ear and speak softly into a hidden microphone. "Ms. Carroll to see you."

The gesture surprised her. *Twerp. Guys like you are getting just a little to common for my liking.*

The aide looked at her indifferently and nodded over his shoulder.

223

Rising from her chair, she glanced at the computer screen to see what he was typing. He was already back at work, writing copy to be read on the air. Details scrolled by too fast to read. *I wonder if Lennie has one of those.*

Stan's office was decorated in earthy tones. The chief editor of content for D.C.'s largest television station looked like he was on display.

Stan laid down the papers. When he looked at her, she knew he was holding his emotions in check.

"Hello, Annie. You know, it'd be nice if you managed to be on time, just once," he said with a smirk. The old-fashioned leather chair squeaked slightly as he relaxed.

"I didn't know you wanted to see me until just a few minutes ago. I sent Lennie to the satellite room and came straight here. What's going on?"

"I have some good news and some bad news."

"The bad news is?" *If you tell me to do another public interest piece, I'll scream.* As she recalled, her last fluff piece had received public recognition--even if it had been from the Capitol Hill Kennel Club.

"Right. Well, it's like this. Lenora applied for more than one internship. She came to work with us because we said yes before anyone else."

"She got a better offer?" Anne felt a knot forming in her stomach.

"*Talk TV* has an opening in their training program and they like her transcript. She is on the Dean's List, you know."

The news hit her hard. *This hurts because Lennie's getting the shot at the big time that I've always wanted.*

Talk TV was a media powerhouse. Called "*Trash TV*" by some, the multimedia group that owned it dominated the global market. Its line-up consisted of hugely popular talk shows, sit-coms, and reality-based programming that showcased sensational journalism and dysfunctional people in crisis. Several of the country's current top media personalities had come up through the ranks of *Talk TV*'s hierarchy before transitioning to other networks. Many in the field now saw trading the sensational for the legitimate as a rite of passage.

"When does she leave?" She felt her poise sliding into place.

"She graduates at the end of the month. I've already talked to the owners, and they've agreed to cut her loose. They don't want to hold her back. It's enough that she worked here. If she makes it big, we can put her picture up on our wall."

"We saw her potential before anyone else did, yada-yada-yada." Anne swallowed. *I remember when you said that about me.*

Stan waited for her to make eye contact with him. *I've seen that look on half the faces in this station. You feel left behind.*

"Good for her. What's the good news? I think I could use some right about now."

Stan nodded. "I just got off the phone with WNN." He rolled his eyes in mock disbelief. "They want you," he proclaimed with a genuine smile.

She gave him a skeptical look. As long as she'd known him, Stan had never successfully delivered a punch line.

"I'm not kidding, so wipe that look off your face. I've never seen anybody get a third chance at network. Believe me, I checked this thing out before calling you in. It's the real deal."

Anne knew she was past her prime and not very likely to succeed in the highly competitive world of global journalism. As she paused, Leihman's assistant silently darted into and out of the office, leaving behind a fresh stack of paperwork. She noted how skillfully he maneuvered. "World News Network really wants me?"

"Yes, I know. *The* WNN. Isn't that great?" Stan's smile deepened the laugh lines around his eyes. Unable to resist, he stole a quick peek at the new pile of paperwork on his desk.

With a sigh, Anne relaxed. "Well. You have to admit, that's some kind of good news."

"Absolutely. I don't know why they picked you, and frankly, I don't care. You're good at what you do, but you've been here too long."

"What's the assignment?"

"Interviewing the presidential staff," he replied, smiling again.

"Does that include Fisk?"

President Hill had been very particular about what media coverage she and her staff got. The times, places, and people doing the interviews had all been chosen by her or a member of her inner circle. Press Secretary Angel Cutter handled things so well that Hill had been dubbed the most media-savvy president of the 21st century. Rumor had it that Madeline herself controlled the media's access to Preston Fisk.

"Go easy on that, but yes, he's on their list. I checked. Just be a team player, will you? Your fascination with that man will get you in trouble if you're not careful."

"Oh." Shock gave way to a flood of enthusiasm and determination. Anne considered what this could mean to her career. *What it will mean, because I won't blow it.*

"Did they say why they wanted me?" she asked, suddenly eager to know.

"Don't go there. I didn't ask, and neither should you. It's another chance, and it's the White House press pool. Take it for what it is. You won't see a chance like this again. We both know that. Now go back to your desk. There's a packet waiting for you."

Anne stopped at a water cooler to get a drink and collect her thoughts. She walked back to her desk with as much self-control as she could muster.

The reporters' area was open, with not so much as a single cubicle. As she entered "the pit," she noticed that the atmosphere was tense. Everyone was at his or her desks, keyboards clacking. A few were sipping at coffee mugs while cradling telephones in mid-conversation.

Somebody blabbed. Slinging her purse over her arm, she moved through the organized clutter, aiming for her own desk.

Nobody wants to make eye contact with me. Fine. Let's play. Keeping her own face straight, she shouldered her way past dangerously stacked files and overfilled wastepaper baskets. From across the room she spied Lenora. She was reading something that looked like a press release. Her dusky features were creased in concentration.

When she saw it, Anne nearly stumbled. A royal blue folder sat conspicuously on the edge of her desk. *The packet.* Seeing it made her flinch at the implications. Media access to the While House had tightened considerably during the previous administration. President Hill had further increased the restrictions when she took office. Reporters from nonsyndicated news organizations, once common in

White House press pools, were now an endangered species.

Without realizing it, she stopped. Looking around, she noticed that everyone else was also silent and staring--at her. Somewhere in another department, a phone rang unanswered. She blinked and looked at Lenora.

The younger woman put down the press release, smiled, and began to clap. Like a wave gathering force, everyone else joined in.

Ruby Baker, the station's news anchor, appeared from nowhere. Navigating through the clutter like the pro that she was, she reached out to scoop up the packet from Anne's desk. She held it up over her head as the applause died down.

Dressed to go on the air, Baker's thin figure and dark brown complexion made her look every inch the fashion model that she had been. Her business attire seemed to magnify her presence. "Ladies and gentlemen, children of all ages, it is my pleasure to present for your viewing pleasure, WNN's newest rookie White House correspondent," she announced in her free-wheeling style.

Laughing at the overblown presentation, Anne stepped forward to accept the folder. Turning it over in her hands, the holographic presidential seal reflected a kaleidoscope of color as she showed it off to those around her. She turned to face Lenora. Her heart skipped a beat as she thought about the intern. Her smile faded slightly. *Things just aren't going to be the same for either one of us, are they?*

Lenora held up a bright red folder, careful to display the splashy *Talk TV* logo. The crowd gave another burst of applause just as Anne's desk phone buzzed.

"Come on, let the girl do her thing. Let's make some news," Ruby said authoritatively. The happy moment fell into chaos as the impromptu celebration ended.

Anne's phone buzzed twice more before she could bring herself to sit and answer it. "Channel 6." She traced the cool surface of the folder with an index finger.

"Anne Carroll, please. William Garrison calling."

Looking at the phone in her hand, Anne was surprised to find that she couldn't speak. *Calm down. This might not be what it looks like.*

"This is Anne." *Way to go. Great opener.*

"Hi. I was wondering..."

"Yeah?" Anne was suddenly aware that Lenora was watching her. *An audience. Great.*

"Well, are you busy tonight?"

To her trained ear, Garrison sounded embarrassed. She smiled. *We're both out of practice, aren't we?*

"Sure. I mean no, I'm not." She waved Lenora off with a stern flick of her wrist.

Lenora pointed to Anne's folder. Using her free hand, she made drinking motions, waggling her head back and forth with a reckless grin.

Anne pointed across the room with a scowl. Nodding vigorously, Lennie picked up a stack of video disks and left. Anne struggled to keep from laughing. *Is it that obvious?*

"What's so funny?" Garrison asked good-naturedly.

"Nothing. What did you have in mind?"

"How about more of the same?"

His oblique suggestion made her smile. She reached out to pick up the folder. She looked forward to sharing her news with him.

"Sure. I could use the company."

"How about 7 o'clock?"

"Could we make that 7:30? I'd like to avoid some of the traffic." *You don't need to hear about all the work I've got to do.*

Wednesday
May 7, 2014
Fisk Group Consultants
Washington, D.C.
4:59 P.M. EDT

Standing in the middle of Fisk's office with the door closed, Doris radiated frustration. Her trenchcoat was flung onto a nearby chair.

Fisk sat behind his desk with his jacket off, loosening the knot of his tie. Something about the way she moved as she paced, and the familiarity of it, struck him as funny. He struggled, and failed, to keep his grin to himself.

"Give me some credit. He's just doing what comes naturally to somebody in his situation. Don't you think he deserves to enjoy his last few days of relative freedom?" *You're taking this personally. Why?* When she didn't respond, he pulled his tie off.

Softening his tone, he continued. "I think he deserves to have some personal time. Do you really understand what he's being asked to do? He's been lied to and he doesn't even know it. Once he figures it out, he's never going to trust me again. Just this once, I'm not going to feed him a line or go back on my word. Besides, he'll be on our turf. What can go wrong?"

Doris paused to reign in her temper. "He's not like you. He may feel the need to tell somebody. He hasn't been through the program yet. His conscience might get the better of him." She was surprised at how good it felt to say the words. *It's the double meaning. I'm talking about him but I'm really talking about you.*

Fisk raised his head sharply to look her in the eye. "If Bill fails to live up to our expectations, then he'll be dealt with." As he spoke, he was keenly aware that he was pronouncing the same judgment that his own advisors would make against him if they felt the need. *The irony is that Bill's right. He really is becoming me.* He shuddered.

"How? What have you done?"

"Nothing more than what you would have done. I called Griff. He agreed. It's the only way to be sure."

"You put secondary tactical on his tail. If he says or does anything that's off profile or hazardous to the mission, they'll kill him." Stunned into silence, Doris felt her hands go limp at her sides. *I should be happy. You're behaving properly.*

Her reaction surprised him. "That's not even the good part. I had our people fix it. Anne Carroll is getting a new job that will keep her busy for the next six to ten weeks. She's been approved for Phase Two, and this new job will only help things along."

Doris couldn't hide her admiration. "That's good. That's very good. We only need--"

"There's more. Bill thinks he's going on a hunting trip. He leaves early Friday morning. Our people will take him to the camp."

"Which takes six weeks. Griff must have outdone himself." She beamed.

"He did. You would have enjoyed it." Fisk chuckled as he deactivated his comm implant.

Doris turned to look at him. "You know that this won't put an end to their relationship?"

"I've been thinking about that. I know what the last 14 years have been like for me. I keep thinking about what the next 20 will be like for him. If I did my job right, he won't have anything to do except collect a generous retirement. If, on the other hand, we missed something, he might be called in to do his thing."

"What are you talking about?"

"I don't want him to follow in my footsteps. There are days when I just don't feel like myself. All the schedules, briefings, and back-channel stuff make me feel like I'm a scripted character in somebody's book. I want...I want Bill to have a life while he's waiting to see how things pan out. I don't want him to be alone."

Wednesday
May 7, 2014
Secured Site 3
The Olive Leaf
Washington, D.C.
8:05 P.M. EDT

"So." Bill watched Anne intently from across the table.
"So." She smiled halfheartedly, hesitating to reach for her wine glass.

Their meager supply of small talk had run out, making them both feel embarrassed. Sitting at a secluded table in the back, they had nothing to look at except each other.

"Try it. It's an '89 vintage. I like it."

"Okay." She raised the glass to eye level. "Did you pick this one yourself?"

"Yeah. It's one of the perks of owning your own restaurant."

Sipping from the glass, Anne tried not to stare at the red wine suspended in the fine crystal. The moment was awkward only because she wasn't sure what to expect. Looking directly at Garrison over the rim, she could tell that he was suffering from the same uncertainty. His tan was just noticeable. His hair wasn't bleached, suggesting that he spent time in a tanning booth rather than outdoors. Despite the intimacy of the moment, he was relaxed. To the untrained eye, he was nothing less than confident and in control. She liked him. *Not bad for a guy who lost a very public job.*

The station's biographic index told her that he went to a health club at least three times a week. It also told her that he was divorced. *Need to update that file. It didn't mention anything about this restaurant.*

Silently watching her, Bill saw that she was making her mind up about him. The way she looked at him while tasting her wine suggested that his stock had gone up. The idea warmed him inside. Reaching for his own glass, he was pleased at the feel of the cool crystal in his hand. It told him that he was in full control.

"Does it pass?"

"It does. It's just the thing." Putting her glass down, Anne leaned back in her chair. "Can I tell you something?"

"Sure." He sipped his wine.

There was no agenda for the evening. The understanding that passed between them was only possible due to their maturity and life experiences.

"I got another chance. I'm going to the White House."

"That sounds like a good thing. What are you getting another chance to do?" Their glasses met briefly over the single tapered candle in the middle of the table.

"The press pool. It turns out that WNN likes to hire reporters from regional markets to cover national stuff. All the big networks do it, actually. It's a way of scouting for new blood without taking too many risks."

"Sounds like you want it."

"Oh, yeah. I don't mean to bore you with my life story, but do you remember what I told you about my first run-in with a network?"

Garrison nodded.

"Well, that was ten years ago. I was unafraid. It was a dumb thing to do, and it cost me my anchor job and my shot at breaking out of the East Coast markets. To be honest, this will be my third chance at the brass ring."

"I can buy the fearless part, but I can't really believe that somebody like you would have made the wrong decision under those circumstances. It's a fact of life." He became wistful for just a moment. "Hindsight isn't always correct. If you made your best judgment call, then that's what happened."

"It might have been the right thing to do at the time, but ten years is a long time to be in the trenches. I blew it twice..."

"Are you sure?" His grin was small, but visible.

She returned an equally modest smile. "Thanks for the vote of confidence. There are two kinds of destiny. The kind that you make for yourself, and the kind that other people make for you."

Leaning forward on one elbow, Garrison shivered at the remark. "What you did then, and what you do now are two different things.

As long as you make the best decision that you can at the time, your future will be everything that it's supposed to be."

Anne relaxed. "That's very Zen. It also tells me that you've made a few of those decisions, yourself."

"I have, but that's a subject that we can save for another time. Let's order. After that, you can tell me more about this White House thing."

Anne raised her empty hands. "I haven't seen a menu. If this is a second date, I'm entitled by tradition to order something a little more expensive." She smiled teasingly. *I don't mind making a little destiny every now and again.*

"Traditions are good, but I like to chart my own course when I can. The menu is whatever you want it to be. They'll make it if I tell them to. Once we've ordered, you can tell me about this new future of yours. Then we can see if this is a second date."

Thursday
May 8, 2014
Fisk Residence
Georgetown
Washington, D.C.
7:05 A.M. EDT

Doris struggled to hold back a yawn as she left the dining room. She stopped just long enough to pour a cup of coffee from a percolator that had been set up in the hallway. Nodding at one of the day-shift bodyguards, she regarded herself in a mirror as she turned to go upstairs. *No outward signs of fatigue. Good.*

Clad in grey slacks and a white blouse, her attire was unremarkable enough to maintain the illusion that she was just another one of Fisk's retainers. The irony caused her to frown as she passed Griff.

"Hey, have you seen the report yet?" He focused his bloodshot eyes on her while he fumbled with his tie.

Doris nodded. "I'm really proud of them. They handled the Garrison surveillance without any screw-ups. How did the Harper thing go?" The backup security team had been split in half to both cover Garrison and assist Doris in entering and leaving the White House undetected. Both missions had been spur-of-the-moment affairs. As much as she hated to admit it, Griff and his by-the-book methods had stolen the show.

Griff fussed with the buttons on his light blue sweater. Sunlight from a nearby window reflected off the chrome coffee pot.

"Your people were on the ball. It's been a long time since I visited 1600."

Griff stopped to pour a cup of coffee, huffing as he took a sip of the very hot beverage. "Funny how some things don't change. Did you find any of our old gear while you were creeping around?"

She grinned with nostalgia. "Uh-huh. There was an old Mark Two optical rider in junction 40. It was disconnected, but it was still there."

Animosity put aside for a moment, they laughed. Their former lives were long gone, rendered inaccessible as part of the overall plan. Despite the deliberate separation, they relished their memories

Griff pulled his cup away from his quivering lips. "Mm. Wow, but that was a long time ago. Say, I don't suppose..."

"Here. Consider it a peace offering." Doris reached into her pocket and handed a small black box to him.

Griff tossed it in the palm of his hand. "Thanks. I've been riding you pretty hard."

It wasn't a complete apology, but Doris accepted it for what it was. She raised her cup in mock salute. "So noted. What's the word on Mr. Garrison? I understand that he didn't make it home last night?" Doris knew perfectly well where he was and what he was doing, but she was looking for a way to move away from the sort-of-apology.

"Yeah. You know, I'm beginning to think the man was right." He turned to look back into the dining room.

Flanked on two sides by his advisors and assistants, Fisk was dressed casually. He used both hands to pass a large platter of scrambled eggs. The massive oak dining table was cluttered with dishes and stacks of paper. Laptop computers cast their small holographic displays in limited focus as the group ate and spoke in the casual rhythm of a long established routine.

"He's usually right." Doris stepped to one side for the full view.

Griff lowered his voice. "I mean it. Think about it. Garrison agreed with what he's been told. There's a lot he doesn't know. We should cut him some slack. He didn't say anything at all last night that you could call suspect."

"This could have been handled differently. It's way off-profile. It makes me nervous. It's not Garrison that worries me, you know?"

Griff nodded. "They called you?"

Doris lied without hesitation. "Yeah. Every time he breaks profile, he gives them one more reason to cancel him."

"I've got to admit, I've never seen him act like this. If I didn't know better, I'd swear he had a conscience." He emptied his cup.

"Right. We're on the same page."

Griff set his cup down, motioning for Doris to follow him. They stopped next to a large closet.

"You want to mutiny?" he asked bluntly.

"I made a promise. I intend to keep it."

Recalling that night more than 14 years before, Griff and Doris briefly relived their final moments with Jason Cutter. The last-minute exchanges of private words and personal sentiments flashed through their minds.

"I didn't make that promise out loud, but I'm with you. It's one thing for the bad guys to get him. It's another thing for us to just stand by and let our own people whack him."

Doris looked hard at Griff. His unflinching commitment to protocol and procedure had earned her anger many times over. It was a trait he had always been known for. The flexibility that he now shared with her was heartening.

"That's how I see it. We've taken the Founders for granted. We forget that they can still reach out and touch us. He's not the man they knew, not any more. They're getting old and impatient for results. Taking him out of play is a convenience. It's the way they're used to doing business."

Griff looked at his hands. "What do you need from me? I can't make a move that they won't see. I'm going to have to sweep this house for bugs and recorders as it is, just to make sure that this stays between us."

"What makes you think I have any plans?" She couldn't help the defensive reaction. Accepting his help meant putting aside animosities that went back three full decades.

Griff shrugged. "You're the yin to my yang. That's why he pulled us in. That's why he asked us to put up with each other. That, and you haven't played by my rules yet. I can't think of any reason why that would change now."

She nodded, conceding the point. "So?"

"What do you need from me?" he asked again.

"Sorry. Just give me a free hand. I've got something in the works, but it's going to take time. You can be most use--helpful--if you don't question me about any requests I might make."

"That's kind of what I thought. I'll go along with it. There's just one more thing. I think I know how they intend to do it." Griff moved in closer. "The Alpha program gives you the responsibility for termination. The only sim we have on file is marked as a B-level contingency. As part of his planned retirement, he'll have his locator and comm implants removed before they decompile the personality program."

"Accidental death while undergoing routine surgery," Doris pronounced bitterly. The tactics of the retired Cold War spies who made up the ranks of the shadowy Founders might be out of date, but they could still be effective under the right conditions.

"It's not original, but it does let them take you out of the loop if they don't think you'll follow through."

"Old school. They'll call him in just after he resigns. They'll sacrifice the clinic to a wrongful death suit, and the cover-up will be complete. It's good, but not good enough."

Griff raised a finger. "Don't tell me anything. I've got to get something to eat and then get back to work. Garrison and his lady friend were having a little morning bump when I left. He's probably in the shower by now. You do what you have to." Retreating down the hall, he stopped to refill his coffee cup before going back into the dining room.

Alone in the corridor, Doris held her empty cup in both hands

Leaning against the headboard, Garrison surveyed the room. He looked at the closed bathroom door. Water hissed from a shower head, the sound coming through the door as white noise. Looking down, he checked the fold of the white towel covering his middle. He smiled. *I've driven past this place a hundred times. I never thought I'd be here under these circumstances.*

He looked at the pile of clothes on the dresser. His clothes. Anne had scooped up her own before heading off to the shower. The thought made him grin. *At least we didn't fold them and put them in the drawers.*

Their lovemaking had been punctuated by a few anxious moments, but that hadn't come until the early hours of the morning. *Hmm. I'm not very tired for someone who only got three hours of sleep.* He reached for his watch on the nightstand, checking the time. *Okay, two hours of sleep.*

His jacket hung on the back of a nearby chair, bathed in the sunlight that streamed through partially closed blinds. He avoided looking directly at it. The wireless phone that lurked in the inner pocket worried him. *They know where I am. What am I so afraid of?*

The sounds of running water stopped. The noise of the shower door sliding open jarred him from his ruminations. He got up and walked over to the dresser.

Moments later, Anne came out of the bathroom, wreathed in steam. Leaning out the door, she brushed her damp hair aside. "Can I have the other towel?"

"Yeah." He tossed it across the room.

"Thanks."

Looking down to make sure his belt was cinched, he enjoyed the moment. *We're comfortable with each other.* It was a feeling that had been absent in his life for many years.

Being a workaholic, he had passed up many chances to date after his divorce. The wounds from that had never completely healed. It was one of the personal truths he had shared with Anne during their hours of give and take. Her acceptance was therapeutic.

I don't like to commiserate, he admitted, stealing a glance at Anne's naked body. *All I wanted was a chance to tell somebody how I feel.*

Watching her from behind as she toweled off, he felt a brief pang of regret as memories of his marriage flashed through his mind. The moment was surprisingly brief, and it left him feeling unburdened.

"If you keep looking at me like that, one of us will go blind." Wrapping a wet towel around her torso, she winked at him.

"Speaking for myself, it would be worth it."

"You're just saying that because you're already dressed. That, and you used most of the hot water." She stepped back into the bathroom.

Garrison shrugged. He appreciated her easygoing manner. It wasn't something she allowed others to see. He understood the need to project power and confidence, as well as to be circumspect with others. *Who we are and what we are don't always match up. Being yourself isn't always good for your career.*

"Sorry. I'll be more careful next time."

"You think so?" She pushed the door open and bent to dry off her legs.

"Uh."

"It's okay, I didn't mean to be harsh."

"I know. Can I tell you something?"

"Sure." She leaned in the doorway, giving him her full attention.

"I think we might have something here. I know that we haven't made any promises or anything, but I'd like to see you again. I know you've probably got your hands full with the new job..."

"Give me a couple of weeks. It's going to be crazy. You know how it is. I'm not trying to put you off, but this really means a lot to me. Once I get my bearings, I'll be up for almost anything."

His unassuming behavior was very appealing. There was so much that didn't need to be said. *You're not possessive, but you do make your point.*

"That works for me. Besides, I have to take care of a few things of my own. Some friends have talked me into a guided hunting trip. When I get back, I've got a speaking engagement to gear up for." He sat down on the edge of the bed and reached for his shoes.

"When do you leave?" Anne asked, stepping behind the bathroom door to get dressed.

"Monday. It's a five-day outing."

"Mm. Where are you going?"

"Montana, I think." He sat up and stretched to get the kinks out of his back.

Sport hunting had been drastically curtailed in the previous five years. Local, state, and federal laws had become more restrictive in the wake of three well-publicized court cases. The nation's top firearm manufacturers had banded together to fight the many lawsuits filed against them, and lost.

The downfall of the NRA had come just two years after the final appeals had been exhausted. Pro-environment lobbyists had teamed up with supporters of gun control to back politicians who would promote their agendas. The resulting legislation ensured that sport hunting was all but forbidden on the Eastern seaboard. Ownership of firearms had been discouraged further through a series of successful ad campaigns.

"You'll have to tell me all about it when you get back. I've never been camping. We can have dinner at my place if you want. I'll cook." She emerged fully dressed. She pulled the towel off her head.

"I'd like that. I'll call if there are any delays. It's been a long time since I've been out in the wilderness. Who knows? I might get lost." He favored her with his best smile.

"I thought that's what the guide was for," she sneered gently.

"It'll be good for me. I'm not really sure what comes next." He turned to face her with the same concerns that he'd shared only hours before. "The speeches and guest lectures will run out in another couple of months. I know that something else will come along. I just don't know when."

Lorraine watched as Fisk strode into her field of view. Doing her best to look busy, she surreptitiously watched him make his usual round of greetings. In all her years as a civil servant, she had never met anyone who had seemed so magnetic. *There have been a few that came close, but this one has something extra.*

"Good morning, Lorraine."

Looking up at him disinterestedly, she nodded courteously while continuing to tap away on her keyboard. *I'll bet you could get my blood moving, if you wanted to.*

Sensing her standoffishness, he moved on. *Fine. Be that way. Let's see if this gets your attention.* Straightening his tie, he hid his amusement behind an outgoing smile.

Lorraine stopped in midstroke as Fisk stepped into Josephine's new office and closed the door. *So, the rumors are true, after all.* "Ah-hah," she muttered as she watched other eyes roam toward the door. *That solves that mystery.*

Turning back to her work, she felt the smallest twinge of jealousy. It had been a long time since she had been the topic of such juicy office gossip. *Oh, but they were such good times.* She lost herself in her work while she daydreamed of those long ago intimacies. *Enjoy it while it lasts.*

Monday
May 12, 2014
The White House
Washington, D.C.
11:58 A.M. EDT

Fisk winked at Josephine as he slipped into her office and closed the door.

Still on the phone, she waved him to a seat without looking.

Making sure he hadn't locked the door, he smiled and moved to the chair directly across from her. *That should give them something to talk about. I wouldn't have it any other way.*

Hanging up, Josephine glowered at him for an instant. Her frown melted into a hesitant smile when she made eye contact. The gleam in his eyes caught her attention. She surprised herself by enjoying the moment.

"Why on earth did you close the door?" She began to stand.

"To make the other women jealous," he admitted, folding his hands on his lap.

"No!" She blushed, images of Lorraine-the-gossip-mongerer flashing through her mind. Momentarily caught between pleasure and embarrassment, she melted back into her chair.

"You can hurt a guy's feelings like that, you know." He reached into his coat pocket. Unfolding a small piece of paper, he silently offered it to her. *Too bad I have to gain your trust this way. Still, once you think I saved...*

White light flashed on the edge of his peripheral vision as the all-too-well-known headache flared. *If I didn't know better, I'd say I've done this before.*

Still trying to find the right words, Josephine accepted the slip of paper. Their fingertips brushed. Fisk looked intently at her. Embarrassed, she unfolded the note and read it.

"Really?" She looked up, allowing her eyes to roam the room.

"How do you know?" *My office is bugged? Why? I'm not anybody important.* She looked back at him with raised eyebrows. *Am I?*

"Why don't you let me explain it to you over dinner." He half stood, his expression softening. Straightening, he took a step back from the desk

Fear filled Josephine's eyes. She looked at the note, and then back at the door. All thoughts of gossip vanished as she looked down at her phone. Out of the corner of her eye, she caught Fisk's warning look.

"I can't, really." Something about the look on his face made her blood run cold. His acknowledgment of her fears about the phone made her want to trust him that much more.

"I'm due to meet with the President tomorrow. It's in your scheduler. Treasury. It'll be a long day and I'm sure I'll want some fun company afterward. If I drop by, and you're still here..." He raised his eyebrows, leaving the question unfinished.

"I don't know." She reached for her day planner. *Make up something, anything...*

Her hand froze over the book when she saw Fisk shake his head in silent warning.

The original plan had called for White House security to discover the bug in the scheduler during a routine sweep of the administrative offices. Somehow, the detail had missed the device. *Being spied on makes you worth knowing.*

Using the skills learned in her former life, Doris had slipped in to plant the bug in the planner. The discovery of the bug was meant to bring Josephine to the attention of the President.

Uncertain, Josephine pointed at the planner. *Not the scheduler!*

He nodded. *Once you calm down and report this, you should be a lot more receptive. After all, I just saved you from this unexpected violation of your privacy.*

"We'll see how it works out, then. I'll look forward to seeing you." Standing in the doorway just long enough to straighten his tie, Fisk left the area with a spring in his step. *Madeline's going to have a fit when they play this back for her.*

He was well aware that the brief conversation would come to the attention of in-house security monitors. As much as he risked provoking Madeline's anger by playing out the gambit with Josephine, he enjoyed the idea of yanking her chain.

Alone in her office, Josephine looked around the place with new eyes. Images of tiny cameras and hidden microphones flitted across her mind. Looking back down at the scheduler, she seemed to see it for the first time. Grasping it, she turned it over in her hands. She squinted at the back. She had carried it with her every time she'd gone on official business. Larry Hodgekiss had given it to her the day that she started work in the White House. *I scraped this last year when I dropped it.* She shuddered inwardly when she saw that the leather was clean and unscuffed. She smoothed her hand over the spot where the scratch had been. *I remember feeling so bad about it. I've never told anyone.*

Looking back at the door, Josephine caught Lorraine's eye from across the large office. Lorraine shot her a crooked grin and went back to her typing.

How could Fisk know that my planner was bugged? Of course, he seems to know everything else. Why shouldn't he know about a bug in my office?

Josephine knew that all White House phone traffic was recorded, and that most common areas were equipped with video surveillance. The intrusion that Fisk had come to warn her about was something altogether different. *I have to tell somebody.*

Laying the scheduler back on the desk, she picked it up again and moved it further away. *How long has this been going on?*

Anger flashed across her face as she considered the implications. Somebody was listening in on her. That reflected directly on the President. *Not if I can help it.* Reaching out to pick up the phone receiver, she hesitated. *Why would he warn me? Unless he knows something I don't? I'd better be careful.*

Leaving the scheduler on her desk, she stood up. Stopping, she went back to pick up her coffee mug. Another veteran office accessory, the blue and white mug had been with her since she'd started working for the government. Lurching to a stop, she stared at the mug. *They wouldn't? Would they?* Turning it, she couldn't decide if the chip on the bottom had been there the day before. She set it down as if it were about to burn her fingers. Jerking her hand away, she growled in frustration and left the room.

She marched down the hallway toward the Secret Service kiosk where an agent sat reading a magazine. The dark-suited man put down his magazine as she approached.

"Can I help you, Ms. Harper?"

"I need to talk to somebody about security."

"Oh?" She had his undivided attention.

"Yes. I think my office is bugged."

The agent, still attentive, sat up straighter. His left hand moved to rest on a compact telephone receiver. "We have monitors in all the rooms, for everyone's--"

"Please. I know about that. I'm talking about something more." She realized that she was still carrying Fisk's note clenched in one hand. *Do I tell him?*

"What makes you so sure?" The way he asked the question indicated a request for information rather than disbelief.

"It's a gut feeling."

"Please, go on. I believe you." It had been almost 30 years since a Secret Service agent had ignored a White House staffer's claim of being bugged. The fate of that unfortunate agent was legendary.

"It's more than that. It's my scheduler. It's not mine. It's like somebody traded a newer one for the one I've always used, and..."

The agent gave her a comforting pat on the shoulder and smiled. Picking up his phone, he tapped in a number and spoke.

"Control, this is Post Five. I think we have a Code 15 up here. Ms. Harper's office. A leather-bound scheduler. Can I get somebody to come up here?"

Josephine stepped out of the way as another staffer passed by with a stack of notebooks.

"Right." The agent hung up his phone and turned back to Josephine. "Could I ask you to come with me, Ms. Harper?"

"Where are we going?" She hoped he didn't see the slip of paper in her hand.

"Downstairs. We may need you to answer some questions."

Walking ahead of him, she headed for the stairwell door. "I haven't been in that office for very long. I don't know why anybody would want to do this. But since this involves the President, I just didn't think it wouldn't be right to take any chances."

"I understand." They turned to watch as a trio of men entered her office. Passing through the doorway into the stairwell, she palmed the now-soggy slip of paper into a nearby trash can as she passed.

Alone in the rear of the plane, Garrison watched the lush green countryside flash by as the nimble turbo-prop made a smooth landing on a grassy meadow. He glanced up at the overcast sky. *Appropriate.*

The plane bounced twice before coming to a stop. The pilot expertly throttled the engines, turning the plane in a quick 180-degree arc. They taxied towards a collection of Quonset huts and olive drab tents.

If she only knew. Thinking back to the previous day, he smiled. His impulsive visit with his ex-wife during his St. Louis layover had been harder than he'd thought. *Still not sure why I did it.*

Garrison shook his head, remembering the lengthy speech he'd made. Standing next to an intercom in the vast lobby of a 30-story condominium, he'd had an audience as he poured out his thoughts. *If I can handle that, I can handle being trained to lead a guerrilla war that might never happen.*

He unbuckled his seatbelt and gathered his belongings. The long rifle case felt strange as he clutched its molded handles. *I wonder if Fisk knows that I never really got over her.* Hitting his head on the ceiling of the plane's cramped cabin, Garrison stifled a curse. *He probably does.*

The combination door-and-ramp at the rear of the plane folded down loudly, causing the whole airplane to shake. He heard voices in the distance as the engines wound down. The smell of wet grass invaded the plane's interior.

Moving clumsily, he heaved his duffle bag to the rear of the plane. Using both hands to guide the gun case, he wriggled toward the back of the cabin and his uncertain future. In the cockpit, he heard the pilot speaking into a microphone. Garrison stopped to rub his bruised head.

A burly man in a camouflage smock stuck the upper part of his body into the cramped interior of the plane. "Good morning."

Still rubbing his head, Garrison looked up just in time to see the big man grab the duffle and yank it out the door with practiced ease. "Good morning. I think." He flushed.

"Don't worry about it. A bump on the head is going to be the least of your problems." The big man waved a paw, grinning.

This man is going to enjoy hurting me, Garrison concluded grimly. Pushing the gun case over the back of a seat, he reached the open hatch.

Once he was out of the plane, the big man took the rifle case and quickly ushered Garrison to a tent. Pitched on the outskirts of the large encampment, it looked slightly larger than some of the others that he could see nearby.

"Welcome to Camp Killjoy. Your kit's already laid out. If you want to eat, just follow your nose to the mess tent. The Colonel's given you one hour to change and get your bearings." He handled the duffle and rifle case as if he could carry them in his back pocket. The man shouldered his way into the tent. A single LED lamp shone white light over the sparse interior. An old-fashioned canvas cot lurked in one corner. Its wooden frame showed scars from decades of abuse. In a neat pile in the center of the cot, a full set of BDUs sat next to a short stack of manila-bound manuals.

"Anything else I should know?" Garrison wedged himself in behind the large man. *With the two of us in here, it seems a lot smaller.*

"Yes. Aside from me, the Colonel is the only other person in this camp who knows who you are and why you're here. As far as everyone else is concerned, you're just another recruit."

I had no idea things would start out like this. "No special treatment."

"None," the large man assured him, the toss of his head emphasizing his bull neck.

"I see."

Bill gazed around the rest of the tent, noting the small chemical toilet and the folding table the lamp sat on. The floor was packed earth.

No rocks, weeds, or even lone blades of grass showed. He assumed that he was somehow supposed to keep it that way.

"Okay. Dress and mess. Just be glad you brought your own boots. The ones we supply around here are specifically designed to break ankles." He hammered Garrison's shoulder with a reassuring pat, and then turned and left.

Bill stepped over to the cot. Sitting on the end, he had to stand abruptly as it threatened to flip over. Catching his breath, he knelt next to it to thumb through the stack of manuals. *Basic Infantry Weapons.* *"Introduction to Unarmed Combat." "Principles of Military Leadership." Learn it, do it, and then advocate for it. Got it.*

Wasting no time, he stripped down to his underclothes. *Glad I put on the Army skivvies this morning.* Looking down at himself, he wrinkled his nose at his evenly tanned legs. *So much for three days a week at the health club.*

Clawing his way into his BDUs, he turned reflexively to look for a mirror. He saw that the uniform had no patches of any kind. Pulling his combat boots out of his duffle bag, he put them on. After two tries each, he got them laced and tied.

Leaving his tent, Garrison smoothed his hair and looked around. He heard the sounds of men and women being put through their paces. *I wonder what Anne would say about all this? Probably be mad at me since this isn't Montana.* In the distance, gunfire crackled with the rhythm of practiced routine. *Focus. Got to focus. Put her out of my mind.*

Recalling the big man's advice, he took a deep sniff of the air around him. His nose told him that he was downwind of the mess tent. *Smells like oatmeal on fire.* Walking slowly, he found it after only a moment of searching. A hand-painted sign over the entrance read "Mess." Garrison wondered if the sign painter might have had a sense of humor.

In the distance, he heard the loud whine of turbo-charged propellers. He looked up in time to see the plane pass overhead. *I'm here for the duration.*

Passing through the mosquito net draped over the entry, Garrison took his place in line. Six other men were ahead of him. Each took a metal serving tray from a small table as they passed. *Those two are probably in their late teens. The other four are well into their thirties. Interesting mix.* Each was also dressed in surplus camo. He noticed that they didn't have patches on their uniforms, either. The similarity was reassuring.

As he neared the front of the line, Garrison saw that the food was laid out on a self-serve buffet. Urns of steaming coffee squatted beside cauldrons of hot soup, all surrounded by plates of cold sandwiches. Dishes and cutlery were stationed at regular intervals along the front of the table. Behind the serving table, he watched as people clad in cafeteria whites prepared more food. Craning his neck, he looked towards the end of the long table. Stacks of paper cups flanked several fruit juice dispensers. He selected what looked like tuna on white and a small bowl of vegetable soup. Gathering cutlery, napkins, and two cups of juice, he looked for a place to sit. The tent was filling fast.

Garrison sat on an empty bench and began to eat. *Food's decent enough. Madeline Hill, goaded by unchecked greed, will lead the country down the wrong path. The resulting internal strife will give us the chance to clean the corrupt politicians from our government.*

Chewing slowly, he took a closer look at the people around him. He felt out of place. *What can I give them that they don't already have?*

"I think the word you're looking for is 'perspective'," a voice interrupted. Startled, Garrison looked up into steel grey eyes. The man was dressed in BDUs with a pair of shiny brass tabs glinting on his collar.

"The Colonel, I presume." Garrison offered the seat across from him.

"Right the first time." The Colonel hoisted a leg to sit down on the bench. His weathered face was craggy and scarred. His perfunctory manner made it clear to Garrison that he was used to being in charge.

"Bill Garrison." He offered his hand. The other man's grip was strong.

"Glad to see that you made it in without any problems. Weather this time of year sometimes keeps the plane grounded for a while."

"I was told to expect Montana," he replied, picking up his sandwich.

"There are several antigovernment militias active in Montana. We have nothing to do with them, but we're prepared to use them as a cover in the event that somebody finds out that our people have been playing soldier. It's a small but necessary deception."

"I was told this was a hunting trip. Fisk talked me into it. Said it would be good for me. I was under the impression that I wasn't supposed to--"

"That was a large and very necessary deception," the Colonel replied.

Garrison noticed that people avoiding his table. *The Colonel must not be too popular.*

"Don't mind them. The only time I don't want them to be afraid of me is when they leave."

"Better to rule by fear than to be loved?" Garrison put down his half-eaten sandwich.

"Machiavelli," the Colonel said, nodding his approval. "Right."

"Extreme." Garrison pushed his tray aside, preparing to listen.

"Considering the stakes, I don't think it's unreasonable at all. The American people have been intentionally pacified for the last 50 years. Told that they can't, and shouldn't, resist authority. Now that the NRA is dead, the next Congress is certain to repeal or amend the second amendment. Add several decades of legislation that have picked away at our civil liberties, and yes, the stakes are high enough to merit giving these people a hard time."

"Which toughens them up. Makes better fighters out of them."

"We're giving them a better idea of what they *can* stand up to. This isn't the kind of facility that can give you anything like full military training. We're teaching these people that it's possible to fight back."

"So you're providing on-the-job training,"

"We're showing them that they can strike back and *win*."

"How do I fit into all this? If I understand the situation correctly, this will be a highly decentralized conflict. I'm just not clear on the type of leadership that you expect from me." *What kind of "perspective" am I supposed to give to people that they don't already have?*

"What we want from you is your convictions. That, and your conscience."

"Why me? Why not you? You've been around. You've got experience. What can I do that you can't?"

The Colonel didn't answer for a long moment, and then shook his head. "If this happens, and I hope it doesn't, it's not going to be a battle that the professional soldier can win. People like myself can kill other people and break things, but we can't take back the soul of a nation."

"Why not? Tell me. I'm interested." *This could be what I'm missing.*

"I still wear these collar tabs because I feel naked without them. But that doesn't answer to your question. The soldiers of today aren't what they used to be. You might find some that will pay lip service to the idea of patriotism, but for most the concept of national pride has been bred out of them." He stopped to scratch his nose with a gnarled finger.

"That's quite a statement, considering our war record. We've kicked the stuffing out of every terror group in the known world. How is that not--"

"Our guys are loud and proud of their profession. They're proud of their war record, but they aren't proud to be Americans. Leastwise, not in the same way you and I think about being proud of our nationality."

"Nationalism isn't really the 'in' thing these days. At least, not for Americans," Garrison replied, quoting from something he'd read on the plane.

"That's the view from Washington. It's a twisted variant of the divide-and-conquer strategy. They don't want our people, or our military, to believe in the greatness of their own country. It's an inconvenience that they would prefer to do away with. It makes it easier for them to stay in power." He looked around the busy mess tent. "These people you see here, these men and women, are a different story. They're believers in the greatness of the nation, and they need one of their own to lead them." Pausing to realign his backside on the bench, he looked back at Garrison speculatively.

"So it's a grassroots guerilla movement, by the people and for the people."

"If that's what it comes to. We're not going to saddle these folks with a military mindset. We want them to know that it's okay to think well of both their country and themselves. We're not just teaching armed resistance here. We're teaching people to think for themselves. It'll be a lot harder for the pencil pushers in the Pentagon to stop what they don't understand."

"If it comes down to that. Don't take this the wrong way, but it sounds to me like you're trying to make me into something I'm not."

"Everything's in the works. By the time we get done with you, you'll be ready to get the job done. If it comes down to it. I know what you're thinking. Some leaders are forced into it. Others are created as the need arises."

"Sounds like wishful thinking."

"I hear you. This camp is the first stop on your way to a new life. It's a life that will be different from anything you've ever known. Try to think of it like a new job," the Colonel replied mischievously.

"Your knowledge and my core beliefs. I'm beginning to get the idea. I've seen the way Fisk is handled. Is that what I'm headed for?"

"You've got the right notion, but you won't be at the mercy of your handlers like he is. Don't get me wrong. We're going to kick your butt into shape. You're probably going to hate me for it. But you'll still be the same guy when you leave."

Garrison noted the cryptic references to Fisk but said nothing.

"Cheer up. It's only going to get worse."

"Worse?" he asked, visibly chilled.

"Your life, as you know it, is over."

"I thought you said--" Garrison felt his stomach knotting up.

"Oh, you'll still be the same person when you leave here. We're just going to take the next six weeks to teach you some new job skills." The older man chuckled at Garrison's obvious concern. "I know, I know. You told everyone who would listen that you were going on a guided hunting trip to Montana."

"What have you done?"

"Relax. Your trip was scheduled to last seven days. When you're supposed to be going home, your plane will crash. We'll fix everything. We can fake five weeks of hospital time." The Colonel's mirth began to subside.

"Was that really necessary? Why didn't you clue me in? I'm sure that we could have worked something out." He thought of his ex-wife and their brief encounter. *What about Anne?*

"You know better than that. Besides, whether you know it or not, you've already taken your first steps towards becoming the man you need to be."

Garrison eyed the Colonel fiercely, unable to speak. *I was right. I am becoming Fisk.*

"It's not all that bad. You learned how to be a spy when you doctored the NRA records. Now it's time to learn soldier stuff."

Garrison shot a fast glance around the tent. Most of the rebels-in-training were busy eating or talking. A few faces were obviously turned in his direction. He remembered tampering with the NRA computers. *I recruited an army and didn't know it.*

"I don't mean to sound uninformed. I just never knew that things would play out like this. For a man who has a lot of conviction, I feel a little bit lost just now."

"Understandable. However, I've seen your profile. I even had a hand in choosing you. When the time comes, you'll do just fine. Please believe me when I say that the deceptions were necessary. Relax." He made a dismissive gesture. "You're not the first person who had to give up his old life. If there was another way, we would have found it."

Tuesday
May 13, 2014
Presidential Quarters
The White House
Washington, D.C.
6:32 A.M. EDT

"Why on earth did you close the door?"

"To make the other women jealous."

"No!"

"You can hurt a guy's feelings like that, you know."

"Really? How do you know?"

"Why don't you let me explain it to you over dinner."

"I can't, really."

"I'm due to meet with the President tomorrow. It's in your scheduler. Treasury. It'll be a long day and I'm sure I'll want some fun company afterward. If I drop by, and you're still here…"

"I don't know."

"We'll see how it works out, then, I'll look forward to seeing you."

Madeline turned off the disk player. Her manicured nails clicked lightly on the machine's tiny buttons. Inside, she was numb. *Why does this bother me so much? He's turned his charms on more women than I can count.*

She paused to sip at her coffee. *Larry must really think that he can score points with this. Fisk was right. He doesn't care about the "why" of what I want.*

Fisk had specifically recommended Hodgekiss. Over the previous two years, he had proven to be more than capable of carrying out her orders. Though she'd made few mistakes, all of them had been attributed to her Chief of Staff. It was a burden that he'd willingly accepted, as the occasion required. *The media will call him inept today, and a genius tomorrow. He's the perfect man for the job. I can't imagine a competent woman putting up with that kind of abuse.*

Absently stroking her nails over the player that Hodgekiss had hand-delivered to her the day before, her predator's mind returned to the problem of Fisk. *You're finally throwing down the gauntlet, eh?*

Before bringing her the recording, Larry had done his homework. Metz had skillfully worked around his boss to make sure that no one filed a report about the bugged scheduler. Everyone knew that the man in charge of the White House Secret Service protective unit was unpopular with President Hill. *I won't give Conroy Horn the satisfaction--*

A phone rang, breaking into her thoughts. She rose from her seat and walked over to a small desk to pick up a wireless handset. The scrambled unit rang again as she activated it. Even as she flicked the handset cover open, the cold dread of failure gripped her.

"Yes," she said neutrally. Looking at the recorder on the side table, she mentally reassured herself. *I have the Secret Service in my back pocket. I am in control.*

"Metz. I'd come to see you personally, but Conroy is coming in early today. I don't--"

"He knows?" Madeline walked back to her chair. *Your turn is coming, Mr. Director. I promise.*

"No. He might suspect that we're holding out on him but he has nothing to go on. Trust me. He's no Preston Fisk."

The mention of the consultant caused her to stiffen. Thinking of today's appointment, she could already picture him coming into the Oval Office. As much as she looked forward to crushing Brown's resistance to her policies, she couldn't really enjoy it. Fisk's impregnable image of powerful confidence grew gigantic in her imagination. His shadow fell over her, leaving her cold and lonely.

In the kitchen, Jeffrey was still working on her breakfast. The noise he made was slight but detectable by her keen ears.

She drove the unpleasantness away with a shake of her head. Close blonde curls bounced as her eyes roved back to the disk player. "Do you have anything new to report?"

"That's why I called. I had to send the device we recovered from Ms. Harper's office to an outside source to keep it out of Agency hands. The cracker that I do business with decrypted the chipset. The code is being decompiled as we speak. I'll have a full report for you in a day."

"Is it possible that it belongs to Fisk?"

"Not a chance. I can think of easier ways to get close to Josephine Harper. If that's what he's trying to do, it's the most unusual thing I've ever seen. Can you think of any reasons why he'd want to manipulate her?"

In all the years that Fisk had managed her career, Madeline had never been able to get close to him. His invulnerability was attractive and maddening at the same time. *Not one lousy date.* Her love/hate fixation had matured into a hotbed of jealousy and envy. Famous or unknown, the women that he had spent time with all had one thing in common. They had all benefited from his attentions. Being seen in public with him was enough to bring media attention to bear on even the most unknown.

He's mine. He's paid for. I own him. Anger flashed through her mind as her heart went cold with the certainty of her mission. *I can't let him have this power over me any longer.* She looked up as Jeffrey wheeled a cart into the breakfast nook.

"Josephine is bright and capable. She gets things done. I don't care who is responsible for that bug. Find out who they are. After that, let's see what we can do about it. In the mean time, I'll re-evaluate Ms. Harper's place in my organization. If she's worth spying on, she could be useful to me." She stood and walked back over to the desk. Closing the cover on the phone, she deliberately hung up.

She walked over to the breakfast nook. Jeffrey accepted her smile as he waited to serve.

Madeline's eye caught the covered dishes on the serving cart. She remembered the omelet she'd ordered. *I always have omelets.* "I've changed my mind. I think I need something to cheer me up. How long would it take to whip up some blueberry pancakes?" she asked, spoiling for conflict.

"As you wish," Jeffrey nodded, unruffled. With a steady hand, he removed the silver cover from one of the three plates on the cart. A stack of six blueberry pancakes rested neatly in the center of the fine white china. Steam rose in thin wisps, filling the alcove with their cheerful aroma.

She caught sight of the tiny porcelain bowl of whipped butter on the table. A small decanter of maple syrup sat innocently next to it.

"How did you know?" she asked, beside herself with an odd mixture of gratitude and rage. Despite the inner conflict, her smile was bright, almost warm.

"A recommendation from Mr. Fisk. By fax, early this morning," Jeffrey explained as the laugh lines around his eyes tightened.

Madeline started. *He really has thrown down the gauntlet. Oh, that monster!* In her mind's eye, Fisk appeared. Surrounded by his protectors, they laughed at her attempts to kill him. One of these guardians nudged him, whispering the notion of blueberry pancakes in his ear.

"Cruelty through kindness," Fisk's image sneered as it warped into a mask of contempt.

Clutching a hand behind her back, Madeline's nails dug deep into her palm. The pain was exquisite. Her mind cleared. "How thoughtful. You're just full of surprises, aren't you?" She smiled with all of her teeth as she took her seat at the table.

Jeffrey appreciated the compliment, nodding sagely as he served the pancakes.

Glancing back at the serving cart, Madeline considered the other two covered dishes. What surprises lay hidden under those polished silver domes? Looking up at the server, she took her napkin and nodded. *Very soon,* she mused, *you'll have to come up with these little surprises on your own.*

Taking her time, she ate in silence. Her inner conflict mellowed as she enjoyed the pancakes. Ghostly memories of a long-gone childhood whispered in her ear as she applied syrup to each one. For a few brief minutes, she was at peace. *It'll just take a little house-cleaning before everything breaks my way.* Even Fisk had alluded to that during her last meeting with him.

As she finished, the clock over the fireplace chimed 7. Patting at her lips with the cloth napkin, the President rose from the table. Walking gracefully back into the sitting room, she picked up the disk player. Turning it over, she felt the raised lettering on the back.

So bold. He had to know I had her office bugged. Why is he doing this? She's nobody. Thoughts of Josephine Harper flashed like lightning through her mind. *Dull Josephine. Simple Josephine. Unless...*

Possibilities began to form. Probabilities began to emerge. Fisk's long-ago advice came, unbidden, from her own lips. "When you look at a problem, be certain that it really exists."

Putting down the player, she walked to the nearest phone. Picking up the receiver, she dialed. The Director of the White House Secret Service element was known for being an early riser. As much as she disliked dealing with him, she was not yet ready to have him dismissed in favor of his more compliant deputy.

He picked up on the second ring. "Madame President, what can I do for you?" The voice was pleasant, but neutral.

"What is the latest on Josephine Harper?"

"Excuse me? Madame President, you need to talk to the supervisor of the surveillance unit."

Madeline leaned against a nearby table. "Director Horn, I'm talking to you." *Yes, I'm forcing you to do things my way.*

"Yes, ma'am." Conroy Horn sat back in his chair. To be caught at something wrong in Washington, D.C. wasn't as damaging as it used to be. The previous three presidents had proven that.

"Now, about Ms. Harper?"

"She was right. Her scheduler was bugged. And no, it wasn't one of ours. I expect to know more by lunch today."

"Really?" Madeline feigned interest. *Kudos to you, Carl.*

"Yes. I'll have Carl deliver the lab report when it comes in." Horn's tone was chilly.

"Where is she right now?" *You really don't know what Carl is up to, do you?*

"I will have to get that information from the surveillance unit. I don't have anything to do with those things directly." *And I won't, no matter what you offer me. I just hope I'm here long enough to testify at your impeachment.*

"All right. I want her followed after work," Madeline replied, meeting Horn's obstinance head-on. *We'll see if there really is anything to this.*

"I will pass that request on to the surveillance unit," Horn responded uncomfortably.

"You do that." She hung up.

Her anger smoldered, and then ebbed. *What can Fisk want with Josephine Harper?* Walking back to the couch, she mulled it over. She knew that the appointment secretary was tireless in the pursuit of her duties. She was also certain that Larry didn't have the nerve to lie to her. His account of Josephine's grief over the bugging put Madeline in mind of a child's grief over knowing that the cookie jar was empty. *He's not trying to get to you. He's trying to get to me. He's pushing my buttons. I just don't know why. Yet.*

The majority of her political appointees wouldn't arrive for another half hour. Most would be trapped on the Beltway. Gridlock hit Washington by 5 a.m. these days. Some federal workers hit the road at 4 just to make it to work by 7:30. *Fisk will be here at 9 to facilitate the Treasury meeting. Wonder what he's having for breakfast?*

Going back to the phone, she dialed the White House operator. "Have Angel Cutter come to my quarters when she gets in," she ordered, and then hung up.

Before she had taken office, President Hill had requested that all of her senior Cabinet appointees have office space within the White House. This departure from tradition had required some remodeling. The move had been designed both to keep her top advisors on a short leash and with public opinion in mind. The polls indicated that they had reacted favorably to the "reformed" presidential chain of command.

Madeline considered what she knew about her press secretary. Angel exhibited quiet ruthlessness. Powered by an unseen fire that was only hinted at by the occasional gleam in her determined eyes, her ability to size up the President's needs was remarkable. Madeline remembered her understated appearance at their last meeting. *You dress to meet my expectations. Reminds me of Fisk.*

Tuesday
May 13, 2014
Christopher's Apartment
Herndon, Virginia
7:45 A.M. EDT

Alone in the kitchen, Christopher held back a yawn and rubbed his chin. Watching the movers clear out his apartment, he reached for a glass of orange juice. Sipping it, he looked around the room. *I've lived here for six years. I'm going to miss it.*

Doris slipped through the front door, dodging a black leather couch as two men struggled to raise it onto a trolley. She made her way to the kitchen.

Christopher turned as she entered, reaching for another glass. "I was wondering when you'd get here." He leaned into the refrigerator for the bottle of juice.

Doris returned his nod. Smoothing the folds of her trenchcoat, she waited for Christopher to finish what he was doing. "I like the couch."

"I'm not surprised. Black leather seems to be the in thing for people in our line of work." He turned, offering her a glass of juice.

"No, thanks."

"Think of it as a peace offering."

"Why?" *Too soon for you to make nice.*

"The other night, you knew how confused I was. You could have put a bullet through my brain but you didn't."

"Mr. Fisk is a generous man," she said, shrugging.

"This has to do with you and me. We're both in the same line of work. We protect people. Me, I'm just a driver with a concealed carry permit. You're like his guardian angel."

"And you want to make peace with the guardian angel." Doris smiled thinly.

"Yeah." He offered the glass again. "I thought about it last night.

Some drug addicts only quit because they have a bad trip. I guess you're trying for a bad trip on the government so it gives everybody the chance to wise up."

"I'm not sure I've heard that analogy used before, but I like it," she replied, taking the glass.

"Well, I'm still not okay with it. I wanted to tell you that because you need to know. I'm willing to play along, but I need to see more before I'll feel comfortable with this whole thing." He made a face as he picked up his glass. Doris swirled her juice, turning the glass from side to side. The memory flared, and then bloomed. *Twenty years ago, I stood in the kitchen of my own apartment and said something very similar. It was night and I was still in shock. If I hadn't actually seen it with my own eyes,*

I don't think I would have gone along with him.

"All right, then. Peace." She lifted her glass.

Tuesday
May 13, 2014
Presidential Quarters
The White House
Washington, D.C.
8:15 A.M. EDT

Angel dropped her coat and briefcase in her office. Leafing through a stack of overnight press releases and collected news clippings, she conferred quickly with her secretary before going up to the presidential quarters. After passing through the security checks, she stopped just long enough to smooth her hair and check her clothes. *This is it. This is really it.*

"You kept me waiting," Madeline chided from the comfort of her favorite couch.

"There was a lot of wire service activity last night. More good war news. Sorry." Angel paused when she saw Madeline's impatient look. Her apology had been cautious. Whatever else happened, she intended to do her job as well as possible.

"I asked you to come up just as soon as you got in. What part of that didn't you get?"

Angel lowered her head submissively. *Have to be more careful. Remember Carns and Pike.*

"I understand." she replied with all the humility she could muster.

"Come on in. It seems that events have caught up with me, and I'd like to take you up on your offer." Madeline smiled.

Angel's heart thundered in her chest. *It's really happening.* Taking small steps, she moved to sit near the President.

"I want it done by the end of next month. Can you handle that?"

"I...I don't see any problems."

"I'll convince him to take a vacation. That way, nobody on staff can tip him off." *What Fisk doesn't know won't hurt me.*

"Is there anyone on staff loyal to him?" Angel's brow furrowed. *He's good, but he can't be that good.*

The older woman chuckled as she thought of Josephine. "He's responsible for choosing most of my appointees. Half of them think he's in league with the Devil. The other half thinks he's God. Director Horn is the one you should be worried about." She steadied herself. *Another reason to get rid of him. I can't stand divided loyalties.*

"How so?"

"The White House Secret Service is mine, with the exception of Director Horn and a handful of his old school cronies." She gestured imperiously.

"I don't see him around much. I can't remember the last time I talked with him. He strikes me as being very guarded."

"He doesn't approve of my methods. He cooperates, but only as far as he must. He suffers from a true lack of vision."

"He's got to go, then." The young woman looked earnestly at Madeline.

The President nodded, pursing her lips. "I can arrange that in due time. Concentrate on Fisk."

Tuesday
May 13, 2014
East Portico
The White House
Washington, D.C.
8:54 A.M. EDT

Fisk checked his watch as his limo cleared the gate and rolled up the driveway.

"You ready for this?" Griff asked from behind the wheel.

"It's what I live for." He unbuckled his seatbelt.

"Area secure," the tiny voice in Fisk's ear told him.

"I was talking with Jarrett Lee. He says that Treasury is going to do a war game to get ready for the UN bank board," Griff said off-handedly, swinging the big black car into the shadow of the portico.

"That's right. Madeline thinks it's her idea." Fisk gathered his coat and briefcase.

"How'd you get that one past her?"

"I didn't. I'm just letting her take the credit for it," he smirked.

"Secretary Brown has already arrived," the comm whispered.

"Can you bring him around? From where he sits, he's just doing his job."

"That's why we're here today. Divide and conquer. If he won't cooperate, we'll end-run him and get to his unit supervisors to." Fisk opened the door and stepped out. He handed his briefcase and coat to a waiting security specialist and shut the car door.

Griff pulled away from the curb.

Walking to the open door, Fisk handed over his wallet, keys, and wireless phone. The lone agent also accepted his White House pass. Swiping the pass through a reader, the woman nodded for Fisk to proceed as the scanner beeped affirmatively, showing green lights.

This is an upgraded system, he thought, noting the new equipment.

A little bigger than the one they had here last time. Wonder if it's good enough to read the silicon lattice of my implants?

He headed for the first floor conference room. *She doesn't want this meeting held in the West Wing? Why?* As the thought occurred, Madeline and her entourage intercepted him. *Speak of the Devil, and she shall appear.*

Stanley, her elusive personal secretary, was in tow. The ubiquitous Secret Service agent trailed discretely behind them. This president's preference for being shadowed by only one agent had earned her a lot of good will from the overworked White House protective unit.

Fisk nodded at Stanley, acknowledging his presence. He smiled at Madeline. "Good morning." *How are we feeling after our morale-boosting breakfast?*

Madeline took in Fisk's neat appearance and well-muscled physique. As usual, his suit and tie seemed to accentuate his powerful aura. Madeline smiled appreciatively in spite of herself. "You look like you're ready to butt heads with the best of them. One thing before we go in. I need you to take care of somebody." She laid her palm flat on Fisk's broad chest.

Fisk stepped away from Stanley, careful to avoid drawing him into their discussion. He lowered his head, listening. "Yes?"

"Director Horn. I'm tired of him."

The consultant nodded. Conroy Horn had been watched by the conspiracy for some time. His distaste for Hill and her methods was well documented. *We screwed up when we didn't recruit him. Perhaps it's time to remedy that mistake.*

"You want him replaced?"

"Yes." She hesitated, choosing her words with care. "There is no 'right' time to do this. Just move him out. Get him another job somewhere. I don't care what you do."

Fisk's unseen helper said, "We'll get a workgroup together. He has a lot of time in system. That's going to be a problem."

"He's got seniority. He'll be hard to move, but I'll look into it."

"Can't you just give him a job? I want to be rid of him now," Madeline griped.

"Make her work for it. Profile says she's due for an ego spike. You know the drill. Make her push," the tiny voice in his ear prompted.

"Let me make a phone call. I'll get one of my people on it," Fisk said.

"A week. I want him gone in one week." Her features hardened.

"It's not that easy. You don't just dismiss the director of the White House protective unit."

"Let's make a trade." Madeline smiled as she reigned in her temper. "I'll handle the Treasury department heads all by myself and you go one-on-one with Mr. Brown. That should cut two hours off this meeting. That'll give you enough free time to make any arrangements you like in regard to Horn. Fair enough?"

Fisk gave a slow nod of approval.

Madeline's cheeks flushed with the thrill of command.

"Seven point two on the meter. Yikes!" The advisor snickered through the comm.

Angel approached the group from behind. Her secretary followed with an armload of freshly printed news releases. A uniformed guard strode confidently after the two women.

"Hello, Angel." Madeline leaned away from Fisk, giving a cordial wave.

"Madame President. This is the very helpful person I mentioned to you this morning." Angel reached back, pulling the guard forward. Checking his tie and hat, the man nodded. Making full eye contact, he regarded his president with considerable interest.

Fisk took note of the way the guard was deliberately ignoring him. The snub wasn't unexpected, but it made him uncomfortable. *Why is this bothering me? Why do I even care that it's bothering me?*

Madeline glanced at the man's name plate. "I understand you've been quite helpful. You have my thanks, Mr. Crain."

"Just doing my job." He looked back at Angel with a barely-smothered grin.

Madeline turned and stepped away from Fisk. "Well, why don't you keep right on doing your job, and escort us the rest of the way to the conference room?"

Crain's glance trailed back to the dark-suited agent. "Shouldn't he--"

Madeline motioned the plain-clothed agent forward. "Nonsense. Give Mr. Crain the key and let's get going."

The agent furrowed his brow. "This is against regulations," he calmly stated as he held up the small plastic card.

Taking the keycard, Madeline turned to face Crain. "All you have to do is lock the door after we go in, and then give the key back to him." She nodded peevishly at the other agent. She made eye contact with the uniformed guard and graciously wrapped his fingers around the electronic key.

Fisk admired the plain-clothed agent's willingness to be difficult. *Metz will take you off his Christmas card list for that.*

"Yes, ma'am. Right this way," Crain said enthusiastically.

"I'll see you later. We've got to get these releases sorted," Angel said.

Madeline waved her assent as she turned to follow the uniformed guard. "Very impressive. Just one secretary," she said to no one in particular. "Lead on, Mr. Crain."

She eyed Fisk as she stepped past him. *You don't even suspect, do you?* The realization that she was within easy reach of the consultant's assassin buoyed her spirit.

Fisk waited while the agent whispered into his lapel mike, informing the rest of his team that their routine had been compromised. "What have you got in mind?" he asked, keeping up with the President easily.

"Nothing more than what we've discussed. I have an idea that will help me deal with his department heads easily enough. Which reminds me, have you managed to get in cozy with anyone on the negotiating team?"

Fisk shook his head as they turned a corner.

"Larry tells me that he's not having any luck, either. I understand that a fellow named Jarrett Lee will lead the team. From what I've read, he's Mr. Brown's alter ego in these matters. Is there any chance that you might get to know him better?" she asked.

The conspirator hid his smile, recalling his last meeting with the banking pro. *Already got to him. About six years ago.* "Larry?" he said, feigning surprise.

"Directable, as always. He's not a creative thinker. He keeps coming at this problem as if it's just another election. In the meantime, watch him and learn. I might be able to show you a thing or two in the next few hours." She stopped when Crain indicated that she do so.

"I'll bet you will. You're everything I hoped you'd be."

Madeline stopped just short of the door. Fisk remained inscrutable as he allowed her to probe his features. *She's looking for that emotional connection again. Better be careful.*

The large antique clock on the wall chimed nine. At the conference table, Treasury Secretary Brown turned to see President Hill enter the room. Fisk followed at a respectful distance. A Secret Service agent slipped unobtrusively into the room behind them. He quickly moved to a chair in the corner and sat.

"All right, gentlemen. Let's get down to it." Flanked by analysts, Brown nodded.

Closing the door to the conference room, Crain locked the door. Handing the key back to the plain-clothed agent, he touched the brim of his hat. "There you go." He beamed.

"Thanks," the agent said with a sour smile as he accepted the key.

Crain walked away with a spring in stride.

Breathing hard, Bill pounded down the mountain trail. His booted feet kicked up small clods of soggy earth with each muscle-shaking stride. His vision was blurred with the mix of sweat and rain that rolled off his forehead. A light drizzle had started, making the trail dangerously slick. He was running it from memory. *Feels like I've slammed into every tree along this track.*

Rounding a steep bend, he used the energy of the turn to sling the load of bricks in his pack to a more comfortable position. The old Army surplus rucksack was too small. Every time he stumbled, the load-bearing harness dug deeper into the abused flesh of his shoulders.

Up ahead, the trail twisted to the left and plunged downhill. Bracing himself, he wiped feebly at his eyes before lunging into the final stretch of the confidence course. Skidding through the mud, he reached out and grabbed a sapling to steer himself down the incline. Branches tore at his olive drab t-shirt, raking sharply over the right side of his body. Mud splashed up to mid-thigh, darkening the folds of his camouflaged pants.

Blowing hard through his nose, Garrison relaxed his body movements as he prepared to hit the soft grass carpeting the flat clearing just ahead. *Mushy. Fell down last time.*

Standing off to the right of the trail, the bear-like sergeant stood silently. Wrapped in a forest green rain poncho, he watched as each runner came past his position. Holding a stopwatch in one huge hand, he kept the other braced on a nearby tree trunk as if he were enjoying the scenery.

Garrison loped past, the soles of his boots hammering through the clearing's squishy grass. "Hey," he wheezed as he ran past.

"Less talk, more run." Checking his digital stopwatch, the sergeant held up the tiny display so that his old eyes could see the little numbers. His wireless phone beeped as Garrison vanished into the trees. He pulled it out and thumbed it on. "Hunziger." He wiped a line of dripping water from the faded brim of his boonie hat.

"How's he doing?" the Colonel's voice cut through the static.

"Making good time. He won't make the Olympics, but he's pretty fast for a fellow his age."

"His profile says he goes to the gym three times a week. Looks like he actually worked out while he was there. Not like some of our other athletes."

"Yes, sir. He's everything they said he was. If he ain't dead when he gets to the bottom, I'd like permission to work him a little more. Nothing drastic. Just enough to keep him dragging for the rest of the day." Hunziger looked up the path, watching for the next runner.

"If he's too tired, the subliminals won't take hold."

The very latest in subliminal learning electronics had been concealed inside the frame of Garrison's cot. Each time he slept, he was exposed to the mild intrusion of an educational program that whispered facts, figures, and other useful information into his receptive subconscious mind. His transition wasn't meant to be as radical, or as invasive, as Fisk's had been.

"Is he still complaining about headaches?"

"Yeah. I told him that it's the altitude. Thinner air in the mountains, and all that. He's going to get suspicious in another couple of days. Once the headaches stop, he'll start to have those dreams, you know?"

"You've got the right idea. Ride him hard for as long as you can. I don't want to come clean with him until I have to."

"I don't think I can keep him distracted for more than a week." Hunziger paused to wipe water off the phone.

The Colonel sighed. "All right. Today is his first full day. Don't break any bones. We need him to be fully receptive for at least 72 hours so that the really good stuff can kick in. The specialists tell me that the first three sessions are critical."

"What do you want me--" Hunziger turned abruptly to be sure he was still alone.

"If he resists, we put him in the chair. You know that."

"Yes, sir." He shuddered at the thought.

"Let's count our blessings."

Hunziger squinted at movement in the trees. "Got to go. Next runner's coming."

"Out."

The next candidate came down the trail fast. The sergeant clicked the stopwatch when the runner passed a large white mark high up on the trunk of a tall conifer. Satisfied with the runner's time, he waited for her to jog past before he took out his notebook to recorded her time, as well as Garrison's.

"Heck of a way to make a living," he muttered.

Fisk rubbed his nose. Across the wide expanse of the conference table, Secretary Brown sat locked in whispered combat with his advisors. Giving Madeline a sidelong glance, Fisk nodded. *He's losing control of the situation.*

"Gentlemen. Perhaps you need time to think this through. Why don't we break for lunch?" President Hill's tone was mild and solicitous. Resting her hands on the table, she looked just as frustrated as the Treasury team.

Flanked by stacks of notebooks and three active laptop computers, Fisk knew that she was not nearly as frazzled as she looked. *She lives for the fight.*

"Madame President, what you're asking for is out of bounds. It's not legal, and it's extremely risky." Brown sat forward, his ebony features creased with concern. He paused to take off his reading glasses. "In proposing that we misrepresent any of our federal assets, you risk provoking all of our trading partners." He looked directly at Fisk as he spoke. *This is your fault. You're pulling her strings. Making her do this.*

Fisk met the challenging look with one of his own.

The moment of silent confrontation was broken as the President spoke. "None of our trading partners can agree on the value of our currency, much less our assets." She got to her feet, gesturing with both hands to take in the cluttered tabletop. "Mr. Secretary, as the leader of this nation I am responsible for these upcoming negotiations. I've been planning for this eventuality for quite some time. When I approved your appointment, you assured us that you were a team player."

"My loyalty isn't the issue here. This scheme will destroy my credibility."

Fisk was impressed with his ability to stay cool under Madeline's assault.

"Unless you want your credibility to become an issue, you will come to some accommodation here. Now." Madeline's face darkened with a calculated measure of rage. Rigid, she sat down.

Flawless performance. Temper channeled to a purpose. Playing his own part, Fisk looked away from his president in a show of veiled fear.

"This isn't like cooking the books for a private sector tax audit. This will be the messiest debt reconstruction in the history of the world. Tens of millions are going to suffer, no matter what we do. What you propose is only going to make things worse. This will leak, and when it does…" Brown was so choked up that he was unable to finish his sentence. *We have to be honest about what we're up against, and pay on honest terms.* The rest of his team sat back in nervous silence.

"When it leaks, we will handle it. There are mitigating factors you are not aware of." Lowering her voice, the President continued, "Make no mistake. I play to win, and right now, the only thing standing between me and what I want is you." She folded her hands primly on the polished conference table.

Brown was no fool. He knew his principles were getting him into trouble. Watching the movements of his team out of the corner of his eye, he considered his options. The other six men were trying very hard to not call attention to themselves. Some took notes in an effort to hide. Others simply watched the exchange with calculating eyes. There was no show of sympathy.

"What factors are you talking about? Is there something you're not telling me?"

Madeline said nothing as she sat back in her chair, making a show of being stubborn.

"Let's break for lunch," Fisk interjected with practiced ease. "Please. We're all uptight. This is new to all of us. It's groundbreaking stuff. Let's back off for a few minutes and get something to eat. When we come back, I'm sure that we'll all have a better perspective."

Secretary Brown looked meaningfully at his team. He was met by a round of nods and approving hand movements. "Lunch it is." He started to get up. *Just let me make a few phone calls, and--*

"One thing. We can't let this discussion leave the building. Not until we've reached an accommodation. When the time is right, you may all take as much of the credit for this initiative as you please. Until then, you play by my rules, or you get off my team. Is that understood?" Madeline stood slowly, sweeping the room with a deprecating smile.

Brown bristled at Madeline's ploy. "Is that an ultimatum?" *She can't get to me directly, so she'll do it through them.*

"Yes. It also means lunch in my quarters," she replied.

Brown couldn't miss the significance of that. His team reacted approvingly, aware of the boost to their prestige that would come from it. All he could do was say, "Thank you."

In Washington's inner circles, Madeline's lack of a husband had been the subject of much discussion and tawdry speculation. The presidential quarters had been nicknamed "The Nunnery." Tabloids speculated endlessly on secret liaisons with rich and famous bachelors ranging from movie stars to politicians. Fisk himself had figured prominently in those speculations during the first year of her presidency. Regardless of who they were, anyone who had actually been invited up to its well-decorated interior could claim a certain degree of celebrity from having dined or conferred in the presidential quarters.

Madeline stepped away to confer with the Secret Service agent in the back of the room.

Fisk shot a glance over his shoulder, as if he were afraid of being overheard. "Andy. When she takes this to Congress, they'll rip it to pieces if they think they can get away with it. She needs you."

Brown noticed the gesture. *Who are you really manipulating, me or her?*

Madeline stepped aside as the agent nodded.

"Let's talk," Brown said as he got to his feet.

Fisk nodded gravely, looking down at the papers in front of him. *Got you.*

Brown's team closed portfolios and shut down computers. Whatever game he was playing, none of the senior Treasury staff wanted to cross paths with the likes of Preston Fisk. The now-legendary disappearance of Walter Carns told them that they shouldn't even try.

Carns had been a big wheel in the private sector banking world. If *he'd* gambled and lost, what chance did they have? For that matter, rumors were already starting to circulate about the disappearance of Jordan Pike. Nobody had seen him in days. What did *that* mean?

"You can leave everything here. The agents can handle it," Madeline said as she came back to the table.

Secretary Brown nodded his understanding and continued packing. His team reluctantly followed his lead.

Madeline shrugged off the snub, though Fisk could see the lines around her mouth tighten with the effort of being polite.

Remember it, and take it out on him later, Fisk thought.

"Excuse me. I'd like to have my presentation materials locked up while we're not in session." Secretary Brown went around the table to speak with the Secret Service man.

The agent shut the door and turned to face the Treasury chief. "I can vouch for their safety. Somebody will be in this room at all times."

Fisk moved to stand next to the troubled man. "These guys are pros. If your laptops run for it, they won't make it out of this room."

Brown shook his head with a tight-lipped grin. The agent smiled thinly. Relenting, he turned to his team. "Appetites only. Leave the rest."

Madeline nodded in Brown's direction as she headed for the door.

Fisk waited for the advisory team to finish packing. Madeline came back to stand beside him.

"Mr. Secretary, I am aware that you have some heartburn over this. Just to show you that I have a sense of humor about it all, I've arranged a little fun for lunch."

Brown raised a questioning eyebrow. "What have you got in mind, Madame President?" *My career is on the line, and she wants to have fun with my lunch?*

Touching him lightly on the shoulder, her expression became mock-serious. "Baloney sandwiches," she said, smiling.

Fisk chucked Brown on the shoulder to reassure him. "Better than turkey surprise, eh?"

Tuesday
May 13, 2014
Presidential Quarters
The White House
Washington, D.C.
1:35 P.M. EDT

Fisk reached for another finger sandwich. The members of Secretary Brown's task group sat around the breakfast nook in various stages of false relaxation. The picnic-style lunch had included potato salad, pickles, and condiments for the sandwiches.

Brown sat quietly as the President made the rounds.

Fisk spoke softly next to him. "I like you, Andy. I really do. I don't enjoy being this blunt with people I like, but you haven't left me any choice. You can deal with me or you can deal with her."

"I'm not afraid of you. Or her."

Fisk nodded as he chewed. *If you could look me in the eye and say that...* "Meet me half way. Take the numbers we built and game with them. Let your people get used to them."

"No. If you push me, I will go to war with you over this." Brown moved closer.

"Let's talk in the other room." Fisk pointed towards the sitting room.

Realizing that he had just crossed into uncharted territory, Brown said nothing.

Fisk rose to his feet, getting Madeline's attention. "We'll be in the sitting room."

The President nodded, giving Brown a wolfish stare that lasted only an instant before she went back to chatting with his advisors.

Walking into the well-appointed sitting room, Fisk took a seat next to the fireplace. Brown followed reluctantly, sitting rigidly across from him.

"Did you see what's going on in there?" the consultant asked him.

"Couldn't miss it. She's undermining me with baloney."

Seeing how uneasy the Treasury Secretary was, Fisk thought, *Your altruism is something we should have looked into.* "Let me spell it out for you. When you leave here today, you're out of options. Don't even think about making that call to your buddies at the Federal Reserve. You'll just be wasting your time. The fix is in, and there's nothing you can do about it."

Brown scowled. Hill's ambition was well known, and her willingness to use up her political appointees was becoming legendary. *Is it really going to be that easy to take me down?*

Brown looked back at the alcove where President Hill was robbing him of his credibility. "I meant what I said. I won't let you jeopardize everything I've worked for. The World Bank eats multinational corporations and Third World economies for breakfast. They look for cooked books along with any other form of cheating that you can think of when they go into these debt settlements."

How'd we miss recruiting you? "Suppose I tell you--" Fisk began.

Brown interrupted, "I've spent my whole career preparing for this debt crisis. Antonio Ramirez heads up the World Bank. I went to school with him. You're good, but you're not that good. If there's even the smallest hint of misrepresentation on our part, he'll pick up on it.""

Fisk closed his eyes. *It's time to tell him.* "Andy, he's going to let her get away with it. I was hoping to protect you, but...here it is. The deal has been made. She's kept you out of the loop because you haven't been a team player. You've missed all the polite signals. Now the gloves are off. Call it what you like, but if you don't go along with this, you're done."

Stunned, Brown settled back in his chair with a sigh. *It can't be that easy. Can it?* A chorus of laughter came from the breakfast nook, underscoring his misery.

"Andy, there's something else I need to tell you. I think it'll give you some perspective on this. Over the last few years, you may have noticed--"

"I'll tell you what I've noticed." He got to his feet. "You! Always you. Wherever *she* is, you're not far behind."

"There's a reason for that." Fisk also stood.

"Save it. I should've seen this coming." He moved past Fisk.

"That wasn't part of the plan."

Brown turned abruptly. "I don't want to hear it! You're gambling with the future of our country, and I won't stand for it."

"Andy--" Fisk reached out, touching the other man's shoulder.

Brown snarled as he brushed off his grip. "Don't. I don't need to hear any more of your secrets or your lies. From now on, you steer clear of me. Understand?"

"There really is something you need to know--"

"That's what this is all about, isn't it? Whatever you want, need, or just got to have. From now on, you stay away from me. Period. If you don't, it'll be the last mistake you ever make."

Fisk smiled at Madeline as they waited for the newscast. *Feels so strange to be sitting here like this.*

The afternoon portion of the Treasury meeting had been cancelled. Brown had fought all of Fisk's attempts to console him. Despite his best efforts, the consultant hadn't succeeded in communicating his hidden agenda to the angry man. *Just as well. If he hadn't believed me, we'd still be in the same boat.*

Jeffrey opened the television cabinet. The polished cherry wood gleamed in the afternoon light streaming through the window

"He's not going to go through with it, is he?" Madeline asked.

After his stormy departure, Secretary Brown had begun making his phone calls. Within the hour, his worst fears had been confirmed.

Sitting across from her, Fisk watched his president closely. Lounging in the high-backed chair, she seemed in control of herself and her future, despite the sudden turn of events.

"Score one for Larry," he said, unable to quite hide his chagrin. Hodgekiss had gotten wind of Brown's next move through his own connections. Fisk's network hadn't. "There's no time for him to do anything else. He has the initiative. This press conference was a real stroke of genius."

"What do you think he's going to do?" President Hill asked, unconcerned. Her meeting with the senior Treasury staff had left no doubt in her mind that she would have the backing she needed. The Undersecretary's people had assured her of that.

Turning on the set, Jeffrey glanced over his shoulder, careful to position the screen so that it could be easily seen by the duo, and then stepped out of the way.

"This is an insurance policy. Andy's not stupid. He might not talk about it, but he has Carns on his mind. He knows he crossed you today, and he's only got one card left to play."

"I don't understand why you're being so cavalier about this. He's only got 15 minutes of air time, but he can still--"

"What's he going to say? He has no proof of what we talked about. The only thing that he knows for sure is that he's been outfoxed. The tapes have been erased and anything on paper was shredded and incinerated 20 minutes after he left."

"Okay, I get your point. I still want him taken care of. If he walks away from this, others might start to think that they can test my authority." Madeline ignored the commercials parading by on the big TV screen.

The WNN newscast came on with a flurry of condensed media images, underscored with a flamboyant soundtrack. They watched in silence.

"Our top story at this hour is a press conference being held by Treasury Secretary Andrew Brown, being held at the Treasury Annex Building in Washington, D.C. We will take you there, live, in just a moment. This briefing was announced just two hours ago, which is very unusual for this administration. The White House Communications Director could not be reached for comment on this unusual turn of events. WNN's own Rosco Hardy is covering the event."

The image on the screen shifted seamlessly to take in the vast interior of the Treasury's new multimedia press gallery. The main floor was jammed with reporters and financial correspondents representing most of the world's top news syndicates and investment consortia. Each of the assembled reporters was seated at his or her own tiny workstation.

"This is Rosco Hardy, reporting live for WNN. We're here at the new Treasury Annex, waiting to hear from U.S. Treasury Secretary Andrew Brown. We've been told that the Secretary intends to discuss his future plans to combat America's massive federal deficit." He stood next to a balcony rail overlooking the assembled press. A holographic image of Secretary Brown faded in over Hardy's shoulder.

"In just the last hour, intense rumors have begun to circulate about the U.S.'s posture in regard to its debts. These rumors also hint at a deliberate plan to negotiate with the UN's International Bank for Reconstruction and Development. This agency, also called the World Bank, is headed up by Antonio Ramirez." The hologram morphed to show Brown and Ramirez in separate frames. "Ramirez is famous the world over for his track record in deficit management. We understand that Secretary Brown is holding this conference to stem any false reports that might affect the stock markets when they open tomorrow."

The anchor interrupted. "Rosco, the stock markets have been closed for a few hours now with all indices up. We keep getting favorable war news from the administration regarding the ongoing campaign against global terror. Has there been any sort of justification for this quick-and-dirty briefing? They don't normally go in for this sort of thing."

"Right. Your guess is a good as mine. Let's go live to the podium and find out." Rosco nodded at his off-screen producer to shift focus.

Down on the main floor, digital cameras flashed as a group began to cross the large stage at the front of the hall. At the head of the procession, Secretary Brown looked worn out.

The smiling face of Rosco Hardy vanished, replaced by a close-up of the large black podium set into the center of the massive stage. Flash units pulsed as handheld digital cameras filled the air with multispectrum light to ensure the best possible images. Behind the podium, Secretary Brown's entourage sat down in one long row, each person resting in his or her own swivel chair.

Nodding to the group, the Secretary turned to face his audience. *Calm. Stay calm. Think first, and then speak.* A quick touch to the podium's control panel elevated the platform so he could look out over the microphone array and make eye contact with the assembled reporters.

"Good afternoon. I'd like to thank you all for coming on such short notice. Everywhere we look these days, it seems like something is going wrong. Over the last decade and half, this country has been through some rough times. I don't think anyone who can recall the events of September 11, 2001, would have guessed that we would be where we are today." He paused.

"For some time now, many of you have been speculating about this administration's policy in regards to our national debt. Today, I'd like to put an end to that speculation."

Obliquely, Fisk watched Madeline's expression harden.

"Our government's finances have become something of an embarrassment. Despite our success in stamping out worldwide terror, we continue to sink deeper in debt." He reached for the small glass of water on the podium and took a sip. Replacing it, he continued.

"Previous administrations have preferred to fight their wars abroad. Today, this administration has declared a new war. One that will be fought here at home. This conflict will be for the financial soul of the nation."

Madeline sputtered as she turned in her chair to spear Fisk with her angry gaze. *Insurance policy, my eye. He's turning against me.*

"He is," Fisk affirmed with a wry grin as the press gallery buzzed with activity. *If we can't recruit him now, we're just going to have to kill him.*

Brown paused again for proper soundbyte effect. "I met with the President today. She made her wishes abundantly clear. As soon as it can be arranged, we will begin formal negotiations through the United Nations World Bank to compensate our creditors. We are going to settle the issue of our national debt once and for all."

The buzz in the gallery had lowered as the assembly hung on every word. On the podium, telltales began to light up, showing him which reporters had questions. All of the indicators were lit.

Randomly, Brown activated one of the switches. In the back of the huge room, overhead lighting winked on to illuminate a reporter seated at a terminal. Startled, she looked around. Her short dark hair bobbed as she met the surprised and incredulous looks of the reporters around her. Straightening her skirt as she stood, she cleared her throat.

Tradition had long since cemented itself. Reporters from the larger news groups were always seated closer to the front of any big news conference. They also got first crack at the questioning. Brown's move had startled everyone.

"Cynthia March, *Polar News*. Are you telling us that this initiative comes straight from the President?"

"That is correct," Secretary Brown replied, nodding congenially.

"Where does Congress stand on this matter?"

"You'll have to ask them. President Hill was quite specific about what she wanted. I have no doubt that she will make any deal that is necessary to achieve her goals."

"Why we are no longer able to deal with our creditors individually? What can the World Bank do for us that we can't do for ourselves?"

"That's a very good question. The outstanding loans that make up our nation's debt have been acquired over a full century. There are simply too many of them to reconcile individually. If we tried, we'd never succeed." The admission was as bold and honest as he could make it. He took some solace in that as he waited for the assembly to calm down.

"Why is that?" March queried in an effort to keep the Secretary's attention as her recorders rolled. Her regional network had never gotten this much direct coverage of anyone in the Hill administration. She was determined to take all she could get.

Brown knew he was giving the reporter more time than was customary, but just went with it. "Negotiations take time. Between individuals and institutions, we have something like 4,000 creditors. Since it could take as much a year to finalize a deal with each and every single one, you can see that it just wouldn't be cost effective to spend the next 4,000 years reaching consensus and paying off."

A brief wave of laughter swept through the gallery.

Allowing himself a moment to indulge in the levity, Andrew had mixed feelings. To distance himself from President Hill, he was portraying himself as being less than capable of handling this high-level affair. Fearing the consequences of her misdeeds, he chose to compromise himself professionally so that he could remain close to the problem.

"The President has directed the Treasury Department to begin negotiating with the World Bank just as soon as possible. Actually, I won't have anything directly to do with that process." Brown looked abashed.

Madeline flinched at the barb that she knew she was meant to hear.

Knowing that speaking would only upset her, Fisk remained silent.

Keep your friends close, and your enemies closer.

"What makes the World Bank so important to refinancing our debt?" March asked in a more sympathetic tone, sensing a hidden meaning in the Secretary's words.

"As you know, that institution has grown in scope and capability in the last several years. By dealing directly with it, we can provide a kind of one-stop repayment program for our creditors. Before we can do that, though, we have to come to an agreement over what we're worth and what kind of payment schedule we can afford to maintain without damaging our own economy."

Sensing that she had reached the end of the line, she risked asking the question they all wanted to ask. "This is a rather sudden admission. Why is it we're finding out about the President's plan like this? Are you trying to distance yourself from this policy?"

"No. Next question," Andrew said with a slight tremor in his voice.

Sitting back down, March got ready to type. Thanks to her quick thinking, *Polar News* now had a two-minute head start on this story--a small eternity in the fast-paced world of internet news services. Her story would put the tiny news company on the map for a few precious hours. Depending on circulation, her career might even get a boost.

All the telltales were still lit. Secretary Brown laid the next plank in his gambit. "In the last 50 years, any president could have dealt with this issue. I won't fault President Hill for waiting this long to tackle it. The first two years of her administration have been full of activity."

"Oh, please," Madeline scoffed, waving a scornful hand.

"This briefing is just a sign that we're willing to stay on top of the issue." Brown paused to wet his lips. "As the Secretary of Treasury, the President holds me responsible for informing the public of measures that may impact our country's economic health. The steps she intends to take to handle the national debt are such measures. That's why I'm here now."

Again, the telltales on the podium winked for his attention. Knowing that the private sector was listening, he selected the representative of a midsize investment firm. The overhead lighting focused on a dark-haired man.

"Byron Shiffer, Rodger's Commercial. The market's up and the chair of the Federal Reserve hasn't made any fiscal statements in nearly a month. Our troops are coming home victorious from all corners of the globe. What prompted this turn of events?" Several reporters nodded.

"I have no comment. And as for the rapid nature of my response, hey, you know that I won't hold back from anybody if I don't have to." He slipped into his "official" mode as his trepidation turned to acceptance.

Fisk looked at Madeline, who chuckled.

"Sounds like cloak and dagger stuff to me."

Brown raised a hand, palm out. "Stop right there. These negotiations will be carried out under the eyes of the world. This isn't the kind of thing that you can keep secret. If I did know about any covert options in use by the administration, I would feel obligated to make them known. Congress confirmed my appointment with the understanding that I would not misuse my post. I intend to live up to that promise."

The press conference lasted another two minutes, during which President Hill sat quietly.

"Well, it's done. The rest will take care of itself." Standing up, she moved over to the TV cabinet and turned off the set. Hands on hips, she looked at Fisk.

"I want to thank you for your help today. I know that it's still not considered acceptable for me to lean on my Cabinet officers because I'm a woman." Her tone was cordial despite the irritation brought on by Secretary Brown's recalcitrance.

"How are you feeling?" *We screwed up when we didn't recruit him. He wouldn't join us now, would he?*

"I feel like I don't know my Cabinet at all. How is it that you come by all this insight? As long as I've known you, you've always been able to peek under everybody's skin."

Fisk smiled, taken by the irony. *This from the woman who wants me dead because I threaten her supremacy.* "It's what you pay me for. I'd hate to think what would happen to me if I were any less useful to you." His eyebrows went up in mock concern.

Displeasure migrated from her flushed cheeks to her eyes, where it burned fiercely. For a long moment, she continued to probe his expression for hidden meaning. *You won't say it, will you? You won't acknowledge that I've actually tried to have you killed. You won't even ask me why, because you know I'm right.*

He stood and put a reassuring hand on her shoulder. "I don't blame you for being paranoid, but you have to remember one thing."

"Which would be?" It was hard for her to resist the urge to lean into him. The warmth of his hand seemed to burn through the fabric of her blouse.

"That you are the President. It's a fact that people need help getting to this office, but once you're here, it's all yours. People give you advice, but it's there to take or to ignore. It's my job, for as long as I'm here, to provide you with some of that advice." Giving her shoulder a squeeze, he stepped away. *I could have chosen my words a lot better. She'll probably take that as a sign of weakness.*

"All right. A fair assessment. You can be so diplomatic in the way you tell people to stop complaining."

Hands at her sides, she watched him check his coat and tie. *As long as you're here? Hmm.* Though she would never admit it, she had always been prepared for Fisk to come to her with anger in his deep blue eyes, demanding to know why she was plotting his death. The reconciliation, as she imagined it, would open new vistas for both of them. As far as she knew, Fisk feared no man, nor any thing. Even now, it put her in awe of him. *You aren't even afraid of me and what I'll eventually do to you.* The way he acted with such confidence and lack of fear assured her once more that he was unlike any man she'd ever met. *Confront me!*

"'Remember that thou are mortal,'" Fisk quoted. "Also, never forget that your enemies can bleed. I've got some things to attend to, so if there's nothing else?" *You don't want me to leave. I can feel it.*

"Just the briefing on that new gun control law that my people want, but I can have that rescheduled for first thing tomorrow." Madeline's expression lightened.

"Better have a look at it tonight," Fisk told her with a shake of his head. "The minority whips are going to pull out all the stops to kill it in committee. Don't let your guard down. Just because the NRA is gone doesn't mean things will go your way."

"I know." Her shrug couldn't mask the spark of her temper.

"Besides, now that the cat's out of the bag, you'll want to start getting people used to the idea of debt negotiations." *Should be quite the thing to read about in the paper tomorrow.*

Madeline glanced at a nearby clock. *Now or never.* "How about dinner? It's the least I can do. Just to show my appreciation." Her tone was genuine, her eyes plaintive.

Fisk quivered inside. For the previous 14 years, he had put himself in harm's way to ensure the success of his conspiracy. Even as fear mingled with resolve, the short hairs on the back of his neck began to prickle. *This is about to get messy.*

"Actually, I have dinner plans. I owe your scheduling secretary, Josephine, a little attention. She's been very helpful to me, so I've made arrangements to take her to dinner and do a little schmoozing."

"I see. Can I ask what she's done to earn such favor?" Madeline shrugged to hide her disappointment.

"For the last two years, she's been ignored by a lot of people. Even so, she calls me to let me know when I'm rescheduled and doesn't ask questions about what I do."

Madeline nodded. Each time he lavished his attentions on somebody for the sake of her career, she became intensely jealous. No matter how many times it happened, the effect was always the same. "So send her some flowers. Order her something that she wants but can't afford. I'll let you use my phone," she offered. *Why does everybody have to be your close, personal friend? You don't treat me like that.*

Fisk nodded, thinking of the new computer his people had arranged for Josephine. *It'll take you months to notice that. Better stay quiet about it.* Knowing how close he was cutting it, the danger only fueled his ambition. Sidestepping Madeline's jealous wrath one more time made him feel energized in a way that he couldn't describe.

"Give Larry my regards. Tell him to keep a short leash on Mr. Brown for the next month, just in case. This is the most volatile issue of your presidency. Pull it off, and you can have that second term handed to you on a silver platter." *With any luck, you won't be satisfied with that, and we'll be ready for you.*

"Makes me wish I could come along. To celebrate." She pouted.

Stepping over to his briefcase, Fisk nodded apologetically. "Hmm.

Yes. We'll have to try and work something out." He pretended to give thought to the matter. *You're trying very hard to hang onto me. If I'm hurting your feelings, then so be it.*

"I can't remember. When was the last time you and I went out to dinner?" Madeline asked nostalgically. She shook her head in frustration. The pursuit of her ambitions had robbed her of many such recollections.

"The night before you were sworn in. Just you, me, and 16 of your closest friends from the Secret Service." *Really quite the evening, considering that we had the whole restaurant to ourselves.*

She looked away for a moment. *Even when I know what you're going to do, I can't seem to stop you from doing it. If you asked, I would do almost anything to know you the way everyone else does.*

Picking up his briefcase, Fisk glanced at his watch. *4:30. It'll be my luck, she's given up and gone home.* "I think we'll look back on today and both agree that it was a turning point. Inside of another week, you'll have your debt position fully accepted by Treasury, and the media will be eating out of your hand with gratitude over your handling of the crisis."

"You think so?" Madeline smiled.

"Everyone loves a good crisis. I'll hand-deliver your final package to Ramirez when it's ready. Who knows? You may get more generous terms than you imagined."

Clearing the security checkpoints, Fisk allowed himself a moment of reflection. Walking slowly down to the administrative level, he stopped at a restroom. The white-tiled interior was accented by marble and mahogany. Brass fixtures adorned the antique porcelain sinks. Laying his briefcase down on a marble counter, he listened for the sounds of anyone else in the room. Satisfied that he was alone, he relieved himself and washed his hands.

He turned on his comm implant with a flick of his tongue. "She still there?" he asked quietly to avoid the amplifying echo of the tile.

"We haven't seen her car. Now that we've compromised our own bugs, we don't have a real clear idea of her situation."

Fisk considered the news as he dried his hands. "I'll go and look for myself. Is the car on the way?" Knowing that Madeline was likely to be aware of his conversation with Josephine didn't change anything. *If she's jealous, it'll make Josephine more credible in the long run.*

"Ten minutes. The weather's starting to turn. Doris thought you might like your coat." Fisk tossed the wadded paper towel into a trash container. The machine hummed as it processed the waste. Smiling at the mirror, he brushed a few stray hairs back into place. Doris always seemed to be one step ahead of him. Picking up his briefcase, he left the restroom and walked casually to Josephine's office.

Tuesday
May 13, 2014
West Wing
The White House
Washington, D.C.
4:42 P.M. EDT

"It's almost 4:45. What are you still doing here?" Lorraine asked as she bustled in through the open door.

Josephine turned from her computer, one hand resting on the keyboard. "Now that I have this, I can update my files through the network."

"This is a bad thing? A lot of us would like to do that." Lorraine moved to sit in the plush chair across from Josephine's desk. Openly envious, she eyed the large holographic display with obvious desire.

"I'm just not that good with these things. If I have to check another index, I'm going to scream." She pointed to the open manual on her desk.

The big volume reminded Lorraine of the D.C. phone book. "Well, why not call tech support? I don't think they go home until five."

"I already tried that. They don't have anybody on staff who knows how to handle this kind of system. It's too *new*."

Recent developments in computer technology had so far outstripped government procurement schedules that the information technology specialists were hard pressed to cope with the average system, much less the very latest platforms. *I think I'm out of luck.*

"They actually told you that?" Lorraine asked, incredulous.

"Yes." She slumped. *I'm not ready to handle this kind of thing.*

"Well, as long as it looks good, dear. That's all that matters." Lorraine got up and moved around the desk to take a closer look at the machine.

Josephine nodded in silent understanding. The federal work

force had ballooned over the previous ten years. Specialists had much narrower fields than their predecessors. Three now did what had once been done by one. The White House administrative division was no exception.

"I don't care what it looks like, I just want to use it."

Behind them, Fisk stood unnoticed in the doorway.

"Fat chance. Only supervisors get that kind of training, and they don't share that with the rest of us." Lorraine stepped back. Modern federal managers relied heavily on technology to manage more workers. This required them to have a moderately higher degree of computer literacy than their employees.

"I know, but I can dream, can't I?" She reached over to turn off the computer.

"Careful what you wish for. You just might get it," Fisk said, startling the women. Walking into the room, he radiated charm.

Lorraine stepped away from Josephine. Both women blushed.

"I didn't mean to--" Josephine stammered as he sat in the chair across from her.

"It's okay, I should have been more considerate."

Picking up on the cue, the far-away advisor said, "Try showing her page 100 in the manual. The tutorial instructions start there and run to about page 250. The automated part shuts off by itself once the computer figures out that you've gotten the basics down."

Lorraine took another step back as if she were unsure of her balance. Josephine glanced back down at the huge manual.

Fisk got up and stepped around his briefcase. Using both hands, he turned the manual around so that he could read it. "All you have to do is run the tutorial programs. They shut off automatically after you've mastered the basics. I have one of these at home, and I still have to use the manual, even with the tutorial set up." Thumbing through the tome, he found page 100. Handing the book back to Josephine, he returned to his seat.

Lorraine and Josephine looked at each other for a moment, and then back at Fisk. Josephine blushed. "Thank you. I'm so embarrassed." *You have one of these at home? Wow.*

"Hush, now, before you dig yourself in any deeper," Lorraine chided. Looking up at Fisk, she smiled sweetly. "I'll just be going," she said primly, pulling at the edges of her sweater. She quickly left the room.

"Well, now that we have that settled, how about that dinner?"

Josephine's eyes went blank for an instant, and then lit up with terrified recollection. *Oh, no.*

"Is something wrong?" Fisk studied her face carefully.

"Oh, no, I just, well, I didn't expect you to actually--"

"You're right. You're quite right. What was I thinking?"

"I didn't mean I didn't want--" *This isn't going well at all.* All day long, she'd thought this through. Fisk wasn't easy to say no to, but then again, she had to admit that turning down his dinner invitation was the last thing she wanted to do.

"I know, but I do understand."

"You do?" Her heart sank. *He's going to call it off?*

"Yes. So, I'll tell you what. Give me your address and I'll send a car for you at six." He stood, carefully hiding his amusement at her distress.

"You will?" It was all she could do to keep her mouth from hanging open. *How you stay single, I don't know. With moves like that, you must never be lonely.* Finding out more about him, she decided, was going to be the best thing that had happened to her all day.

"Absolutely." He straightened.

"I'd appreciate that. Where are we going, anyway?" In her mind's eye, the contents of her closet unfolded in a simple but unimpressive, highly functional parade. *What will I wear?* Snatching up a note pad, she scribbled her address then handed him the page.

"I have a little place in mind. Nothing too formal."

"Really?" She gave him a questioning look. *I don't even want to think of what your idea of formal involves.*

"Really." He tucked the small square of paper away in his inner coat pocket.

She breathed a sigh of relief. "Thank you. And thanks for the help with this computer."

"That's quite all right. It took me a long time to get to be any good with them, myself." He picked up his briefcase. *It's a good thing that I'm surrounded by people who know them so well.*

Josephine watched him leave and sat again. The earlier frustration over the computer began to melt away. Glancing down at the manual, she felt a new sense of confidence. *At least he didn't patronize me by walking me through it in front of Lorraine.* The notion that he regarded her as competent made her feel good. *Being noticed might not be so bad, after all.*

Tuesday
May 13, 2014
West Wing
The White House
Washington, D.C.
4:51 P.M. EDT

Standing inside the entry, Fisk waited for his limousine. Behind him, Curtis Crain whispered quietly with another guard. Both men sat on high stools next to the security scanner.

Fisk watched them out of the corner of his eye. *I don't know what it is about you, Mr. Crain, but you bother me.*

Looking out through the armored glass doors, he noticed the low rain clouds. The big grey thunderheads were moving in fast. Headlights flared on the driveway as a large silver limo pulled up to the curb.

"Griff should be pulling up," the voice on his comm told him.

"I see him. Where's Mr. Christopher?" Fisk waited while a plain-clothed agent stepped out of a nearby kiosk to walk around to the driver's side. He lost sight of her as she spoke with the driver through a rolled down window.

"Still relocating to secured quarters."

The agent stepped away from the car, waving her hand to let Fisk know he was in the clear. Leaving the building, he smelled ozone. Looking up at the sky, he watched the dark clouds gather. *Going to be a real soaker.*

Moving to the passenger door, he thumbed the lock. It recognized his thumbprint and opened quietly. Sliding into the back seat, he noted the new car smell and the two-inch security glass. The driver's shield was down, giving him a full view of the car's interior. Watching him in the rearview mirror, Griff waved with one hand while keeping the other on the steering wheel.

The door hissed closed automatically. "I didn't think we had this in the budget," Fisk commented as he secured his briefcase and then himself. The seatbelts were large custom restraints that made him feel like he was belting up to go into space.

"Hey, they don't tell me everything, either," Griff rumbled as he put the car in gear.

Fisk nodded. Even if the conspiracy did have budgetary limits, exceptions had to be made. *Probably in response to that mess on the Beltway.* "I like it," he declared enthusiastically. *I understand that. I'm not sure it would have done us that much good at last week's barbecue, but it's nice to have the added protection.*

"Yep. This baby is heat shielded and mostly laser-proof." He tapped the accelerator and the limo began rolling forward.

"Mostly?"

"Relax. Think of it as just another upgrade."

"Well then, I approve." He stretched and looked around the interior.

"You should. It came out of your paycheck." Craning his neck over the steering wheel, Griff guided the car around the driveway loop.

"I see. Speaking of money, did you see Andy Brown's ad hoc press conference today?"

"I saw it. He sounded very much like a man who was buttering his bread on both sides." Griff slowed the car at the gate to let the guard see his credentials.

Fisk thought the comment over as the car bounced over the security ramp then merged into rush hour traffic. Fisk ignored the cars surrounding them. "She's aware of his feelings, and now he's got some notion of what she plans. I want to meet with the team. There has to be some way we can get to him. If not--"

"You turned your comm off during the press conference, but we did hear the row you had with him over lunch. He really doesn't like you."

"That's too bad. Andy's a good man, but he's in the way. We can't afford to co-opt him. We have to recruit him or take him out of play. He's just angry enough to start poking around in places that we don't want him to go." Fisk relaxed and took off his cuff links.

"Wally Carns all over again." Griff shook his head in disgust. Fisk had been built to go beyond the politics of patriotism--to do what had to be done. Griff, Doris, and the others had to fend for themselves during such moments as this.

Doris' voice came over the implant. "He'll have to be killed. His sense of duty is too well refined, and he won't accept anything less than by-the-book conformity." The hint of static in her transmission indicated that, as usual, she was somewhere nearby.

"Find me a way to get to him. Both of you. I want your best effort. If I can't convince him to cool out until she fulfills her mission, then you're right, he'll have to be killed."

Josephine watched the traffic from the picture window of her apartment. Smoothing the pleats in her favorite skirt, she had a clear view of the sidewalk below. Running a hand over her blouse, she worried. Looking down at her shoes, she worried even more. *Too much or too little?*

She was about to turn away from the window when she spotted the big black limo rolling up the drive. Down on the street, heads turned. The sight of the big luxury car made her smile. *Not something you'll see every day around here.* For a moment, she hesitated. *Is that limousine really here for me?* The notion that Preston Fisk would send a taxicab to pick her up just didn't sit right. *No, that's not his style.*

Watching the limo, she started when the car's headlights winked on and off. *The driver can see me? How embarrassing!* Blushing, she stepped back from the window and went for her coat and purse. She glanced at the small oriental clock on the neat little table, and then left the apartment. Stopping just long enough to tap the code into her front door's electronic lock and burglar alarm, she walked quickly down the hallway.

Stopping at the front door to the complex, she paused to catch her breath. *Walk, don't run. He might be in the car. I don't want him to see me out of control.* Stepping through the door, she closed it calmly behind her.

Walking down the steps, she approached the limo. The car's engine rumbled softly. Across the street, a group of neighborhood teens watched her every move. Dressed in the bright colors and flashy bangles that the sports pros and movie stars liked so much, they called attention to themselves just standing there.

Conscious of their curious stares, Josephine avoided looking right at them. Hefting her purse and coat over one arm, she approached the right rear passenger door. *I thought chauffeurs got out and opened the door?* The car's door lock popped with an audible click. The door slid halfway open.

She slid into the car. Hidden by the privacy glass, she vanished from the view of the teenaged gawkers. The door swung shut without a sound. She marveled at all the soft black leather.

The lock clicked back into place and the driver's shield dropped with a slight hiss. Turning to face her, the driver smiled. "Good evening, Ms. Harper. I'm sorry I didn't get out to open your door, but I can't risk being seen. It's just part of my job."

"Really?"

"Yes. People are watching you, and I can't let them get a good look at me. If I have to protect you, it'll throw them off if they don't know just what to look for."

Josephine maintained her calm expression despite her inner worry.

"Please, don't be alarmed. The people who are watching you won't know where you're going. Mr. Fisk is a very public person. There are people who take issue with him some times. It makes it very hard for him to go out and have a good time, if you know what I mean."

She nodded. *I can't even imagine what that must be like.*

Dressed in a white short-sleeved shirt and black tie, the man seemed ordinary except for his size. Turning his broad shoulders, he took a fast look around before picking up a wireless phone. Thumbing in a number, he spoke quietly.

Unable to hear what he said, Josephine sat back, sinking into the soft, warm folds of the car's massive rear seat. *What have I gotten myself into?* The idea that Fisk could have enemies that wanted to hurt him was scary. She couldn't imagine having an enemy. *To be the advisor to a president, especially these days, would certainly do the trick. It must be hard to keep friends in his line of work. Unless all his friends have enemies, too.*

"Would you please buckle your seatbelt?" the chauffeur asked as the frosted driver's shield began to rise back in place. The limo started forward slowly as she hunted for the restraints.

Setting her coat and purse aside, she reached into the deep folds of the seat. Buckling up, she adjusted them to fit her small frame. *I wonder if he was the last one to ride in this car.* The thought of sitting where powerful people had been only hours before was daunting.

Tuesday
May 13, 2014
Capitol Hill
Congressional Zone
Washington, D.C.
8:16 P.M. EDT

Josephine found it very easy to ride quietly in the back of the limo. Captivated by the sights of the city as they scrolled past tinted windows, she was seeing the District of Columbia from a completely new perspective. From behind the privacy glass, the streets looked a little less mean and gritty. *So, this is what it looks like when you're rich and powerful. Look at the way people watch or turn away as I go by. Like some are jealous, while the rest are angry.*

A small, flat television screen set into dark wood paneling caught her attention. The set's controls were visible just under the screen. *I didn't think they made TVs that small anymore. What does somebody like Preston Fisk watch while he rides in a car like this?* Curious, she turned it on with the push of a button.

The holographic emitters built into the set expanded the picture, making it easier for her to see. Sitting back in the soft seat, she imaged Fisk's weight and warmth filling out the space next to her.

"...update on the condition of William Tyler Garrison, the last Assistant Vice President for the National Rifleman's Association. An out-spoken booster of the NRA for more than eight years, Garrison was seriously injured when his plane crashed in the Montana wilderness while on a guided hunting expedition." The WNN logo rotated slowly in the bottom left corner of the screen as the female news anchor spoke.

Josephine blinked, trying to place the name.

High and to the right of the commentator, a file photo of Garrison showed off his gleaming smile. The woman paused to allow new graphics to materialize over her shoulder. "In other news, financial analysts around the country are still digesting the content of a spontaneous press briefing held earlier today by Treasury Secretary Andrew Brown. His remarks, delivered several hours after the markets closed, have sparked a heated debate over President Hill's stand on the national debt..."

Wriggling forward, Josephine fought the seatbelt to reach out and turn off the television. *News. I should have known better.* Settling back, she let her eyes roam back to the windows.

Rolling into the Congressional Zone, the big limo stopped at three separate checkpoints. Each time, Josephine saw the driver's muscular arm reach out through his window to hand a Congressional police officer a large plastic card. At each stop, the federal cop, dressed in a black rain slicker to keep the evening drizzle off, ran the card through a reader mounted on a big metal post. When the card reader signaled with a green light, the car was waved through. *So, this is the Congressional Zone. Wow.*

Created in 2008, this renovated section of Capitol Hill had been built in response to a series of terrorist attacks. It was meant to act as a social haven, a place representatives and senators could feel that they could safely and effectively do their jobs without being vulnerable to extremists during their non-working hours. High-level federal employees were also granted access. Fear of victimization and a long-smoldering sense of mistrust had caused the political elite to shield themselves from members of the general public, who were still subject to infrequent terror by agents from abroad.

```
Tuesday
May 13, 2014
The Green Room
Capitol Hill
Congressional Zone
Washington, D.C.
8:20 P.M. EDT
```

Nestled in the labyrinth of Capitol Hill's recently constructed Congressional Zone, The Green Room catered to the nation's most influential celebrities and statespersons. Hidden under a colonial brick facade, its ultra-modern facilities catered to a wide range of tastes. Never advertised, clientele learned of its world-class delights only through word of mouth and hard-to-get invitations or reservations.

Standing inside the restaurant's entry, Fisk peered out through the smoked glass. Rain splattered on the immaculately street beyond the elaborate portico. Despite his familiarity with the place, he was lost in thought about its origins.

The idea for the Congressional Zone came up around the time of the Oklahoma City bombing, didn't it? When was that? 1994? Daydreaming, he didn't notice that the limo had arrived.

Stepping out of the car, Josephine was met at the polished marble curb by a tall, handsome doorman in a tuxedo.

"Her car is pulling in."

The voice in his ear brought Fisk back to reality. He watched as Josephine spoke to the doorman, surrendering her coat and purse as if she weren't sure that she should. Escorting her inside with a bright smile, the doorman nodded at Fisk, leaning down to point him out to Josephine. Her uncertainty was refreshing. He checked his comm implant to make sure it was on, and then moved forward to greet her. "I was worried that you might change your mind," he said.

"I...This is a very nice place. I'm flattered." Watching the doorman go to the cloakroom with her things, she looked back at Fisk.

"Right this way." He gestured grandly toward the interior. Walking on tiles of green jade, they entered the club's sumptuous interior. Exotic plants presided over expensive carpets. Each tile was inlaid with a rendering of a golden leaf.

Approaching the front desk, Fisk raised a finger to get the attention of the maître d'.

"Mr. Fisk, I'm so glad you could join us tonight. Your usual table is ready." The man bowed.

Leaning over the polished sandstone counter, Fisk spoke quietly to the short bald man. Josephine strained to listen, but couldn't quite catch what he said.

"Yes, by all means. This way, please," the maître d' replied calmly.

Josephine watched interestedly as Fisk beckoned her to follow. "What did you say to him?" she asked as she matched his stride.

"I asked for a private room. I didn't think you wanted to be on display."

She nodded and walked on in silence. *I'm not sure I'd like all these people knowing who I am. Whoever they are.*

They soon arrived at a well-appointed room shut off from the rest of the establishment by a carved oak door. *Looks like an apartment,* she observed as the maître d' departed. *I wonder where the bathroom is.*

"It's in there," Fisk said, pointing to her left as he headed for the full service bar. A small dining table was set with service for two.

"What's over there?" She turned to look. A burnished wooden door with a shiny brass knob caught her attention.

"Sorry. I thought you were looking for the bathroom." He shrugged and started rummaging through the bottles.

"That's all right. It's just that this place reminds me of my apartment." Walking back over to the bar, she perched herself on one of the leather-topped stools. *That's right, you just had to look for the bathroom. That'll really impress him.*

"Well, if you think this is big, you really should see the bathroom." He held up a frosted bottle, squinting at its label. Josephine laughed as he set it down. He looked up.

"That's funny. You've got a different sense of humor than I thought you might." She tossed her hair back, still chuckling.

Hefting another bottle, Fisk waggled it in triumph. "What kind of person did you think I was?" He casually poured a tumbler of vodka.

"I don't know. You're always so serious. It's hard to tell when you mean to be funny. If you mean to be funny at all." She looked down at her feet and the plush brown carpet.

"Fair enough. What would you like to drink?"

"What are you having?" She looked down at his glass.

"Russian vodka. I developed a taste for it while writing my doctoral thesis in college."

"Let me guess. By the way you stand there, you were a bartender. You worked your way through school." *You look like you're just waiting to pour somebody a drink.*

"Hole in one," Fisk nodded. *You're more observant than your file indicated. Very good.* "Two years at a cozy little joint just off campus. It paid for everything that my scholarship didn't."

She peered over the bar at the rows of bottles. "I went to school at NYU. Scholarship and grants. I couldn't imagine having to work and go to school at the same time."

"Good for you. A lot of people these days don't seem to be able to get through college at all." He leaned against the bar and picked up a towel.

Josephine nodded, still scanning the bottles. "You still didn't mention which school you went to."

"Yale," he replied with just a hint of pride as he wiped at the bar.

"Well, I never would have guessed." She sat back, her face rounded in mock surprise.

"My grades weren't good enough for Harvard. You still haven't told me what you want to drink."

"I haven't made up my mind yet. I haven't seen most of this stuff before." She nibbled at her lower lip. Talking to him was surprisingly easy. *He has a way of just drawing me right on out.*

"Well. We'd better work this out right now, or we'll never get to order our meal." Selecting a bottle, he held it up. "Gin?"

She waved the bottle away. "No, thanks, I can't stand the taste. I usually have something with melon liqueur in it."

Fisk set the towel down and put the gin back. "That wasn't so hard," he said, holding up a pint-sized bottle.

"Bartender's touch," she replied, tapping the side of her nose.

Professionally pouring the drink into a finger glass, he presented it to her on a small paper napkin, complete with straw, cherry, and umbrella.

I wonder if he misses doing this kind of thing? "You must have made a killing in tips," she speculated as she accepted the drink.

"I worked behind a bar for two years. I paid off my car and a few debts," he admitted, sipping his vodka.

"I would have figured a guy like you to come from a rich family." She nibbled at the cherry.

"I did, but I had some bad habits that my father didn't approve of. It got me cut off during my third year." He put down his drink.

"Gambling?" She finished off the cherry in two small bites. *I suppose everybody does stupid or crazy things when they're young. Almost makes me wish I had been wild and crazy during my college days.* Daintily, she put the stem on the napkin.

"And speeding tickets." He moved around the bar to sit at the table, inviting her over with a gesture.

She sat down across from him, looking over the table setting. Silver and crystal gleamed in the low light. *Very nice. I think I understand why. Treat people this good and who knows what they'll be willing to do for you.* "This is nice. Do you treat everyone like this?"

"Whether they know it or not, people have power because others decide that they should give it to them. Those of us with influence should remember who allowed us to have it and repay that kindness every now and again." He surprised himself with the amount of honesty expressed in the statement. *It feels good to tell you what I really think.*

"Wow. I sure wish that was true. Most of the politicians that I've ever seen are, well..." She rolled her eyes. *Way to go. Wreck it with shop talk. I sound like Lorraine.*

"Most of them are what?" he teased.

"I shouldn't talk about them." She lowered her head for a moment.

Fisk put his hands on the table. "I'm not a politician, per se, and I get paid to keep secrets. So tell me, what about most of the politicians you've met?"

"It's not something I should talk about." Her composure slipped, letting Fisk see her worry.

He was tempted to give her the words but the thought of getting her to say them on her own had more appeal. *She really is the right one. We chose well.* "If you normally did, you wouldn't be here. I don't like people who walk all over their co-workers, myself. Goldbrickers who aren't there half the time, and won't work when they are, have no place in my organization."

Giggling softly, Josephine hid her smile behind a napkin. "Am I really that easy to read?" *Those would have been my words, exactly.*

"Easily read? I'm not sure I follow."

She accepted his statement without responding. "I don't see a menu."

"That's not how it works here. You just tell the waiter what you want." He stood and pushed a button on a wall-mounted telephone.

"Oh. But how do you know what they have, or what it costs?"

"Everything and anything is on the menu here. Please, indulge yourself. This is my treat." He leaned over the table as he sat again, his face hovering near hers for an instant.

"Really? That must be very convenient." She watched him sit down, attracted by his brief closeness.

The door to the room buzzed and opened. A tall, thin waiter came in, closing the door behind him. His black coat and tie accented his Mediterranean features. Approaching the table, he smiled at Fisk, and then at Josephine.

"Monsieur Fisk, it is a pleasure, as usual."

Josephine noticed that the man didn't seem to have an order pad.

"Armand, may I present Ms. Josephine Harper, scheduling secretary to the President."

Stepping adroitly around the table, Armand bowed to her. "Enchanté, mademoiselle. Welcome to our humble establishment. I am sure that you will find everything to your liking." He spoke with a hint of Italian accent in his French.

"I'm sure I will. It's all so beautiful," Josephine bubbled.

Armand took a step back, folding his hands at his waist. "How may I serve you?"

She narrowly escaped asking about the daily special. "I would like steak and lobster, please." *I've got to stop thinking of this place in terms that I can relate to.*

Armand waited patiently, as if expecting her to continue.

What else do you have with steak and lobster? The riddle was unsolvable. She cast a furtive glance at Fisk, who was apparently distracted with his salad fork. "I'd also like a salad," she added, catching the hint. *Thank you.*

"Would mademoiselle care for something to drink with her meal? I can suggest an excellent vintage, with Monsieur Fisk's approval, of course."

Fisk looked up, nodding at the waiter's choice.

"That will be very good," she replied, doing her best to follow Fisk's lead. *Oh, that sounds so lame.*

"Thank you very much, Mademoiselle Harper." Armand pivoted with fluid grace. "Monsieur Fisk, how may I serve you?"

"I'd like the trout with lemon and port sauce. The truffle soufflé, only if it has just been made, and could you tell me who is the chef tonight?"

"Jacques Renard is our chef for this evening. I seem to recall that he is your favorite. Shall I send him your regards?"

Fisk nodded his approval. Though unspoken, he understood that sending regards would also include a generous gratuity.

Armand bowed to them both and left the room.

Josephine watched him go, impressed with his manners and bearing. "He didn't ask me what I wanted on my salad." Looking at Fisk, she already suspected that he would take her query in stride. *Just like he does everything else.*

"They'll bring you a selection. That gives you a chance to taste them and rule out what you don't like."

"Oh."

"Can I get you another drink?" He pushed his chair back and stepped away from the table expectantly.

Nodding, she handed him her glass. It was all she could do to ignore the touch of his warm fingers on the fine crystal.

"I don't blame you for your views on politicians. It gets harder to trust them as each year passes, doesn't it?" Fisk moved behind the bar and poured without looking at her.

Josephine said nothing until he came back. Passing her the fresh drink, he watched her body tense at his nearness.

"What's it like to work with the President?" she asked, her eyes begging him to allow the change of subject.

"It's like nothing else I've ever done--groundbreaking, heart-stopping, and life-threatening, all at once. Some days have more excitement than others. Right now, at this moment in history, I wouldn't want to be anywhere else." He raised his glass, locking eyes with her as he took a drink.

The intensity of his gaze combined with the power of his voice kindled her desire to know more about him. The fires that raged in the chilly depths of his blue eyes spoke of passion, commitment, and unbreakable will. They also hinted at a personal torment that would have consumed a lesser man.

"She's not easy to work with, is she?"

Sitting back in his chair, Fisk's expression became more relaxed, with a hint of softness around the eyes. Josephine had seen the look before in others who held power. It was the predator's false calm. He was now on guard. Drawing on her experience with President Hill and members of Congress, she understood. *You nearly let your guard down, didn't you? You almost let me in.*

"She can be difficult to work with. Then again, so can I." He drained his glass and set it down. "She's got a lot on her plate. Being the first female president is hard. Everyone's watching her very closely. In certain respects, she's being judged to a higher standard than her male predecessors were. That's enough to make anyone tough to work with."

"Yeah." She relaxed.

"I'm not telling you anything you don't already know. You get around. You see things. You *know* she likes you. You make things happen."

"I don't--" she protested, blushing.

"Take it easy. She's still nervous," said the voice in his ear.

"You do. You're the right person, in the right place, at the right time." He straightened, emphasizing his authority.

Josephine recovered, shrugging. "I appreciate the compliment, and the new office. I really do. It's just that I'm not used to being noticed. Not like this." She swept a hand to take in the room.

"Well, I've got some bad news for you. You'd better get used to it. You've proven your worth, and now it's time to take it to the next level."

"Oh?" She felt words slip away as the enormity of the situation unfolded.

"Meter's pegged. She's freaked," the advisor informed Fisk.

"Is that why I'm here?" *Are you coming on to me?* The thought was overwhelming.

"Yes. This dinner is more than a reward. I want to talk to you about your future."

"If I didn't know better, I'd say that you have something in mind."

"I do."

"Be careful. She's reading you the wrong way," the voice counseled.

"What does a man like you really want? Even when you're being nice to me and showing me a good time, there's something else going on. I can feel it. What do you truly want?" She rested her hands on the table. The question had come out more confrontationally than she had intended. *If you want to sleep with me, I--*

"What do I want?" He raised an eyebrow, as the door buzzer rang. Turning in his chair, he watched Armand direct a junior waiter into the room.

Josephine was stunned at the unexpected arrival.

The man expertly wheeled in a linen-covered cart that held covered dishes and an assortment of condiments in polished silver bowls. Armand presided from a distance.

"Steak and lobster for mademoiselle, and the trout with soufflé for Monsieur Fisk."

The formality of serving interested Josephine despite her inner turmoil. She watched as Armand directed the placement of every item on the table. He completed the ceremony by he presenting Fisk with the bottle of wine he'd selected. Once approved, he extracted the cork with a small jewel-inlaid screw. The cork came out with barely a squeak in his expert hand.

Fisk deftly waved off the ritual of testing the cork's bouquet. Armand poured each glass with casual grace, and excused himself with equal skill.

She marveled at the array of dishes set before her. An exquisite six-ounce piece of prime rib rested on a plate, surrounded by a garnish of vegetables. The lobster, resting on a tray of polished wood, seemed massive. Surrounded by condiment bowls and a hand-painted white china dish that cradled her garden salad, the whole thing took up a little more than half of the table.

Josephine watched Fisk lay his napkin on his lap and reach for his dinner fork. The size of his one plate drove a shock of anxiety through her. The blued Irish porcelain platter that held Fisk's entire meal seemed tiny in comparison to the massive plank that held just her lobster. *Oh, no! He must think I'm such a pig.*

Eating her salad with measured bites, she watched him from the corner of her eye. Embarrassment was giving way to uncertainty. She noticed the way he kept his distance. *Does he know why I'm so uncomfortable?*

Tasting each item on his plate, Fisk watched her with outward calm. *I was afraid this might happen.*

"Wait for it. Let her speak first," the advisor urged him.

Fisk knew from her file that Josephine wasn't used to such formal dining. *Still, she's taking it all in rather well.*

"This is very good. I've never had a meal quite like this," she finally said halfway through her steak.

Fisk smiled in appreciation and put down his fork.

"Stay casual. Let her come down slowly," the advisor said.

"They normally bring each course to you, one at a time, but I asked them to bring it all at once."

"Why?" She was uncomfortable that he might think her unworthy of the full treatment.

"I wasn't sure if you'd be put off by all the interruptions. A meal like this normally arrives in six courses."

"That's very considerate. What do you know about being overwhelmed?"

"While I was growing up, this sort of dining was routine. When I went to college, I wasn't prepared for fast food or popcorn at the movies. Making the transition was challenging. It took some getting used to. I just didn't want you to be unnerved by all this," he said, gesturing to take in the lavish surroundings.

"I've been around. I've even been to state dinners." While the statement was technically true, she had never stayed long enough to eat with the guests. "I find it hard to believe that you didn't know how to deal with fast food and popcorn. Anybody who can advise the President must be able to tackle a hamburger and fries." *I almost wish that were what I'd ordered.*

He acceded the point with a small nod.

Hoping to get beyond the awkward moment, Josephine tried to work out the mechanics of the pliers and the lobster. *I've never had one of these before. I don't remember seeing any at the last White House social I attended.* She tapped at the bright red shell with a fork. *He's trying to be kind, and I'm making it hard for him.*

"So, how did you handle it?" she asked as she inspected the long, thin fork and tongs next to her plate. *There's something he wants to either tell me or ask me. I can feel it.* Hesitantly, she laid one hand on the silver and gold cracker.

"I didn't," he replied with a twinkle in his eye.

She looked at him intently for a moment. *Waiting for me to ask for help?*

"Well, I guess you could say that I did, but I had to have help," he finally admitted with a tight smirk, sliding his chair around the table to sit near her. Putting his napkin aside, he reached out gently to take up the cracker and fork.

"At first, I couldn't stand them. Too greasy." He laid into one of the lobster's huge claws with the cracker. "But eventually somebody finally showed me how to dress them up with cheese, ketchup, mustard, and whatever else." The shell gave way. He set the cracker down.

"Ah." She watched Fisk put the bright red shards aside. Inside the claw, succulent pink meat steamed, courtesy of the self-heating platter. *Lobster. Pliers. Makes sense now.*

"Who helped you figure it out?" she asked quietly as he separated the meat from the shell.

"You know, I don't remember." He hesitated as he finished dismantling the claw. "I wish I could." White light flashed at the edge of his vision as he spoke.

Bits of memory bolted through Fisk's mind, each faster than the last. Partial images of quasi-familiar faces and the smell of greasy food overlaid with the smell of beer. A crowded gathering place. Music. Just as quickly as each memory appeared, it vanished with a twinge that made the back of his head hurt. *I can't see their faces*, his conscious mind ranted.

Something in his voice told her that he was troubled about the recollection. "That's all right. I don't remember half the people I went to school with, either." She placed a consoling hand on his arm.

Spearing a small piece of lobster, Fisk held it up for her consideration. "It's the faces. I can recall their names, but for the life of me, I can't remember what they looked like." He raised the fork to her lips. His headache began to fade.

Watching his every move, she leaned over slowly. Parting her lips, she plucked the meat from the fork and sat back. Her fears about his motives evaporated amidst the flavor and aroma of the lobster.

"P3 is solidly in the green. She's all yours," the voice on the comm relayed with satisfaction.

"That *is* good," she said with an emphatic nod.

"My pleasure." He started to hand her the fork.

"I think I need some more help." She smiled warmly. *I could get to like this a lot.*

"It's what I live for." He speared another piece of lobster with a precise flick of his wrist. Offering it to her slowly, he allowed himself to linger in the moment. Somewhere, deep down inside, a long-neglected part of him was enjoying this.

"Always the servant, eh?" She gave him disbelieving glance.

"If that's what it takes to make things better."

"I think I see. You really are a complicated man. I've read about people like you. 'Make it better from the inside'. Is that really what you're doing?" She took the next bite with greater confidence.

"That's me." He offered her a sip from her glass.

Setting the glass down, she was fully at ease. "Working for the President, that's working from the inside, isn't it? What are you doing to make things better by working for her?" *A very complicated man.*

He began to crack the rest of the lobster. "Interesting that you should ask. I've been at it for a long time. The presidency is just the capstone. I really do feel like I've been working from the inside out to make things better." *I had no idea that you'd be so receptive. Then again, maybe I'm just reading too much into a good time.*

"Have you succeeded?"

"Not yet, but I will once I have enough help." He put down the cracker.

"President Hill must be very helpful to you, then. I'm curious. What's she really like? I've never seen her privately."

"I don't think any of my efforts would be possible without her." He guided the long fork in a delicate arc to her waiting mouth.

She took a moment to savor the latest bite. "Mm. She's harsh, but I think it really matters to her to be the president, you know?"

Fisk silently twirled the fork, and then replied, "Madeline has a real sense of her destiny."

Josephine had the distinct impression that he was laughing at a private joke. She watched him expectantly.

After a brief hesitation, he allowed his fork to hover over a piece of lobster tail before plucking it off the plate with an emphatic thrust. He slipped the succulent piece of meat between her lips. *I'm glad I'm the one doing this. Moments like this are worth living for,* he thought as he watched the pleasure dance in her eyes. They talked about inconsequential topics for the rest of the meal.

Once they finished eating, Armand took them to the building's top floor. Surrounded by exotic scents, the domed lounge framed the night sky in a vibrant lattice of vines and flowering creepers. Even as they were shown to a table, Fisk found it difficult to avoid looking up at the stars. Josephine had no qualms about doing so.

Guiding her carefully through the maze of leafy alcoves, Fisk kept her hand clasped in his, letting her take it all in. He remained quiet so that she could continue to be enthralled by the faraway jewels in the night sky. He turned off his comm implant with a flick of his tongue as she stargazed. She sat at their table a full minute before coming back down to earth.

"I didn't mean to be distracted, but it's just so beautiful. I suppose that the people who come here take it for granted." To avoid looking directly at him she dropped her gaze to the tabletop.

"Most of them do, which is why I come up here from time to time." He watched her scan the dark wood of the table and the small antique lamp at its center that bathed the area in soft candlelight. As he spoke, he ran his fingers under the table, searching for listening devices. *Come on, I know you're under here.*

"I don't understand. You want to ignore this, along with everyone else?" *Oh, that was dumb.*

"Most of the Congress comes here to get away from everybody else." Leaning closer to her as if to confide, his index finger finally found the tiny irregular bump on the otherwise smooth surface. "And I don't blame them, but I come here for other reasons," he said carefully as he crushed the life out of the high-tech eavesdropper. *Too bad they're going to put that on my bill. Those things are expensive.*

"I could come here just to think," Josephine said dreamily, watching the blinking lights of a passing jet liner as the dark shape blotted out individual stars in passing. "Please, don't mind me. I'm just so, well, so..."

Fisk nodded sympathetically as she looked back at him. "I couldn't have said that any better myself. I do come here because it makes me think. Being surrounded by all these people who want to forget the outside world helps me focus on what's important." He gave her hand a reassuring squeeze. In his own way, he was opening up. The feeling of relief that it engendered went beyond his ability to describe. *This is what I'm working for. So that people can live without concern for what their government is going to do to them. So that they can have more moments like these.*

"I know I'm repeating myself, but at the risk of sounding boring, what does a man like you really want?" She lightly touched his hand.

"I didn't mean to give you the wrong impression. This isn't about sex." He deftly lowered his voice in an effort to sound contrite.

"Oh, I know that," Josephine laughed at the now-absurd idea. "Well, I didn't earlier, but I do now. I wasn't really sure what to think about all this. I think I get it now."

"It's good to be my friend. You earned this. And I meant what I said about your future. Now that I've had a chance to meet the real you, I'm definitely convinced that you're the right person, in the right place...at the right time."

"I don't know what you're selling, but I'm tempted to buy it."

"Just working from the inside, trying to make a difference."

"That would take a long time. I'm no expert, but things are getting pretty bad. Even the media says that. I'm not sure if all of these little wars are bankrupting us, or what. Every time I turn on the news, the national debt comes up."

"The government's going broke. Social Security, Medicare, the federal retirement system, you name it. Never mind the fact that we've had one war or another going for the last decade. Fighting terrorism is expensive. Put it all together and something has to give. You saw the Treasury press conference today?"

She shook her head. "We're not supposed to have televisions or radios in the office. Mr. Hodgekiss says the President doesn't like it. She thinks we'll get distracted with soaps and game shows," she confided with obvious disdain.

"Well, if you had seen it, what would you have said?"

Josephine considered that, her hand still resting on his. *Okay, so he knows I saw it. It's not as if he'll turn me in.*

"Secretary Brown? Scared. I see him at least once a month, and he's normally very casual. This afternoon, he was definitely on the defense about something."

"Like what?" Fisk's eyebrows went up.

"I've seen people waiting for the President. Sometimes, when they come in to schedule, they talk about what they're doing. I try not to listen, but you know how it is?" *I can't believe I'm admitting this. Nobody's ever made me feel like that.*

Fisk nodded. His estimation of her value was on the rise.

"Lorraine calls it the 'bad dog' thing. Like when a dog knows it did something wrong."

"Something in the voice, or body language," he commented to show he understood.

Josephine squeezed his hand in approval. "Right. Can we get something to drink?"

"Make a wish, and touch the base of the lamp."

Taking her hand away from his, she touched the edge of the lamp. It chimed softly, revealing its true nature.

"Coffee, with cream and sugar. For two."

Wednesday
May 14, 2014
The Fisk Residence
Chesapeake Bay, Maryland
1:08 A.M. EDT

Fisk entered the den. He went to the bar and poured a drink. "I understand you wanted to see me?"

"You deliberately turned off your comm this evening. Can I ask why? That's very uncharacteristic of you," Doris scolded, hands on her hips. Folding her arms, she sat down in the chair across from him. *The last thing I need is for you to start acting out of character.*

"You're upset." He sat down. *You're not telling me something.*

"You're getting difficult about the comm. That sort of thing shows up in the reports to the Founders. You know that, don't you?"

He took a long drink. "Mm. Why is that important now?"

"This could be your last recruitment, and I don't want them getting the wrong idea about you."

"I see." He watched her over the rim of his glass. *Definitely not telling me something.*

"You're starting to get wild. You purposefully blacked us out. You even went so far as to kill the bug in the arboretum."

"That was one of our ours?" he asked, surprised.

"No, it wasn't, but we had the bit stream tapped."

"What's the big deal?" *I turn the thing off all the time. Why does it matter now?* He watched her carefully.

"You know we don't have a lot to work with. Harper wasn't part of the original package. She's only been under our surveillance for a year. That's not long enough to guarantee that--"

"She's a perfect candidate. I don't need a sim to tell me that. She's moral, ethical, and well on her way towards our way of thinking."

"And you deliberately kept us from monitoring your conversation. We needed to hear what she had to say. You knew that."

Fisk nodded and closed his eyes. *She's right. It was a planned operation and I deliberately blew it.* Admitting it to himself also meant admitting it to Doris. "Look, the plain truth of the matter is that I'm fed up. Nobody is more aware of our situation than I am. I know how close we are to putting everything in place. If I compromised operations tonight, it was only because I wanted to be able to live a little." *How can I make you understand? I've lived with bugs and tracking devices for 14 years. Sometimes, I feel like I'm somebody else, like this isn't really my life at all. I wouldn't be surprised if I had a bug up my butt that nobody told me about.*

"I understand. As each day passes, you're worn down just a little more. You're tired of the lies and the need for so much secrecy. Anyone else in your position would have cracked years ago. I know that, and so do the Founders." Doris rested her hands on the arms of her chair with a grave nod.

He nodded, his lips pursed with just a hint of a smirk. His tongue moved reflexively inside his mouth to make sure that his comm implant was still turned off. *So, they're worried about my performance, are they?* "Which means?"

"It means that you'd better consider this your wake-up call. I've interceded for you as much as I can, but you're the one who made the rules. If you don't straighten up just long enough to see this thing through, measures will be taken."

"Measures?" Fisk quivered inside over the implications.

"According to your own rules, if you deviate sufficiently from your profile, you are to be consider 'unsafe'." She folded her arms over her chest to emphasize her point.

"'Unsafe' warrants being taken out of play." He rubbed his hands together.

"Yes."

For a long moment they sat, lost in thought. The antique clock on the mantle ticked away the minutes.

Watching Doris from the corner of his eye, Fisk marveled at the image she presented. *The way she looks at me, it's like she knows something that I don't. Sometimes, I don't think I measure up to whatever yardstick she's using to judge me.* The notion disturbed him.

As long as he'd known her, Doris had been the one person that he could always trust. In many ways, she had been his guidepost. Always there. Always one step ahead of him, somehow. *I think the word I'm looking for is "faithful."* That struck him as being funny.

The concept of loyalty and the many forms that it took meant a lot to him despite the fact that he took advantage of those same ideals on a daily basis. People like Andrew Brown and Doris all seemed so interested in doing the right thing. *As far as I can tell, the right thing usually involves making sacrifices for the benefit of everyone else. Is it so wrong that I should want a little for myself? Politics and patriotism don't mix very well, do they?*

"I'm getting used up. I guess I don't want to admit it, but it's true. I've given away so much of myself that I'm starting to wonder if I'm still all here."

She looked up at him, her eyes bright. Furrows of concern creased her features. *That's exactly what I'm afraid of.*

With his eyes closed, he didn't see her reaction.

"I know." Her voice dropped an octave as she attempted to choke back her pain. *After tonight, you'll be watched a lot closer now. That's not something I can do anything about.*

"I'll try harder to be on my best behavior, but I may need some reminding. Between this and that thing on the Beltway, is there any chance that they might be thinking seriously about--" He sat up, blinking.

"Yes. They've already spoken to me about it." She couldn't hide her distress.

"And?"

"You know the answer as well as I do. This plan only comes with one retirement option."

"Well." His mind jumped at the possibilities. "Things are too far along. Phase One has less than a month to go. They can't possibly make all the arrangements in time. Hey, I asked the Advisors to rethink my 'unsafe' options at the last meeting. That by itself will slow them down."

"It slows them down, but it doesn't stop them from giving the order."

"Which they'll give to you?"

"Yes, but you know how they are. They'll have a backup. 'Old school' doesn't mean 'stupid'. Look, I've been trying to tell you about this for a while now."

"I know what I'm up against. They're getting old. They want to see results. When you stop and think about it, I was probably never supposed to make it this far. I wonder how many of them look at it that way."

"Most of them." She carefully avoided mentioning her conversation with Enola. "You're probably right. Back in their day, they sacrificed people for the sake of the mission all the time. It's kind of ironic that all of them were sacrificed by their agencies. That's why they went into hiding." She felt her nose wrinkle in disgust.

"Politics and patriotism. They feed on each other."

"I'm not so sure. Politics is one thing. Patriotism is something else." Doris brushed a long strand of hair out of her face.

"Sounds like a good topic for a book," Fisk observed dryly.

"Who knows? When this is all over, you can be the one to write it."

"Something to look forward to." He grinned to show his approval. "Might be kind of nice to tell our side of the story. For now, let's concentrate on completing Phase One."

She merely nodded as the Fisk persona asserted its directives. "I saw you talking to Jasmine when you came in. What was that all about?"

"They want to take the implants out next week. Turns out that I've had a short-range tracker inside me, too. Did you know that?" He wasn't surprised when she nodded.

"Yes. It helps us stay close without being too close. The plan calls for the removal of those implants so that you can merge back into polite society."

"I see. You think they ordered that removal now so that I'd be easier to contain?" Despite his outward calm, he was afraid.

"It fits. Only a few people know about them. The vast majority of us are very loyal to you. If you wanted to, you could fight them."

"Look, I'm no spy, and I don't pretend to know how they think. It seems to me that they're planning to get rid of me out of reflex. That's something that the politician in me can relate to. Whenever anyone acts on reflex, they run the risk of making mistakes. My best chance for survival is to find out which mistakes they've made so that

I can capitalize on them."

"Do you want to oppose them?"

"No." His answer surprised him with its suddenness and emphasis.

"It's not going to be enough to compromise their intentions. You need to understand that. You'll be making powerful enemies."

Fisk sat back. "You have something in mind?"

"I do. It's a long shot."

"They'll find me if I run." He allowed his nervous hands to fight with each other in his lap.

"Believe me, I know."

"What are you thinking of?" he asked as his hands rested in deadlock.

She gave him a sage wag of her head. "Can't tell you. You know better than that."

Wednesday
May 14, 2014
Terrorism Section
Counter Insurgency Division
Department of Homeland Security
Langley, Virginia
5:00 A.M. EDT

Harry showed his ID to the guard behind the counter. The armored door leading to the computer center slid open. A large green light winked on overhead. Shuffling past two empty workstations, he hesitated before maneuvering his bulk past cluttered shelves to reach the secluded work areas. Stopping next to a handcart loaded with boxed files, he watched Pickering. Fully engrossed in his work, the man hadn't noticed the arrival of his boss.

Harry marveled at the stark whiteness of Pickering's complexion. *He really hasn't seen the light of day in a heck of a long time, has he?*

Pickering leaned on one elbow with his shirtsleeves were rolled up and his tie undone. His wire-rimmed glasses were perched on the end of his nose, giving him an aggressive look as he hammered away at the keyboard. Harry watched lines of data flash by on the holographic screen. Menus popped up and went away in a rhythm that matched Pickering's heavy keystrokes. Looking up at the clock, Pickering pushed his glasses back up to the bridge of his nose and began to reach for the phone.

"I'm right here," Oswald said conversationally, looking for a safe place to sit or lean. The area was full of hard copy files, stacks of laser disks, and computer parts, all of which routinely migrated to other parts of the agency. *That's what I like about him. He gets the job done.*

"I didn't hear you come in." Pickering's chair squeaked as he moved.

Finding no safe place to put himself, Harry settled for sliding his hands in his pockets. "What have you got that's so interesting?" *Keats finds everything interesting. You're harder to impress. This ought to be good.*

"Metz. We, uh, we picked up another call." The analyst rooted through several stacks of paper on his cluttered desk. Peeling through handwritten notes, he yanked two pages from the middle of the stack.

"Who was he talking to?" Harry took his hands out of his pockets.

"His favorite people. And before you ask, yes, Angel's phone codes have been updated. I did it myself," Pickering replied as he scanned the lines of scribbled blue ink.

"Is Metz trying to set up a fresh hit?" Interested, Harry took a half step forward. Knowing that Madeline Hill wanted to kill Preston Fisk was one thing. Having the proof was something else. In addition to keeping track of more than two dozen threats to domestic security, Harry remained more than just a little interested in President Hill's gambit to rid herself of Fisk. *Put that in our back pocket and we won't have to put up with any more of her crap.*

"Here. I decoded it myself, just to be sure." Pickering handed him the wrinkled pages.

Holding one sheet in each hand, Harry eagerly scanned them. "What am I looking at?"

"This." Pickering attacked his keyboard one more time.

Harry took one long step to stand directly behind him. Reading over his shoulder, a text rendering of the recorded call stood out in white letters on a black background.

[begin]
"Yes."
"It's me. Have you reviewed the package I sent?"
"Yes."
"And?"
"What do you want me to tell you? There are never any guarantees. You know that."
"Have you figured out what you did wrong?"
"Yes."

"I want you to try again."

"We can't run the same op again, you know that."

"You can if the conditions are nearly the same."

"Hah. His people will be ready for any move we make."

"Wait. Hear me out. I've got the angle on this thing."

"Which is?"

"She's going to send him back to Spain in a few weeks."

"Really?"

"Yeah. The thing is, he doesn't know he's going. She hasn't told him. Yet."

"Why?"

"She wants him dead, remember?"

"Why is he going back to Spain?"

"I think she's got something going on under the table."

"So she's probably got a package for him to deliver."

"Don't think about trying to snatch that package. Just do him. Nothing more."

"There's a lot of talk about the national debt in the news..."

"Forget about it. Just do what I say."

"Are you sure there isn't something in that package we should know about?"

"What do you care? You stash your cash offshore, anyway. Ignore the package."

"A few weeks is kind of vague. That means a retainer, and a kill fee if we need to abort."

"How much damage did you take?"

"Six dead, four wounded. His people are good, but not that good."

"That's not as bad as I thought. Good."

"The retainer?"

"I know, I know. It'll be dropped off at the usual place. Same amount?"

"Same amount. That includes the pay-off. The kill fee will be doubled this time."

"I thought you said his people weren't that good?"

"We've got six deaths to cover up. That's not cheap."

"Nuts."

"Say, can't you feed this guy to some terrorist cell? Set him up and *let them do it. The Basque separatist movement is very active in Spain these days."*

"Can't. I don't have that kind of pull. Even if Homeland would allow it, we can't risk it."

"Okay. That changes things. Last time, we played by your rules. This time, we do it my way."

"Fine. Forget my plan. We do it your way. I can't give you any new intell, so you might as well run your own show."

"It's a pleasure doing business with you."

[end]

"Gold. Pure gold. Too bad he didn't say the name," Harry breathed. *All we've got to do is archive this and wait for the right time to use it.* He chucked Pickering on the shoulder. "Do we know who the caller is?" *Not that I care.*

"SWAT commander Deon Lucas. We have him in the audio bank. He's old news. You can have his dossier if you want it." Pickering shrugged.

"Anybody special?"

Pickering twirled a ballpoint pen through nervous fingers. "Not to us. His claim to fame is the Madison job. Poor fellow really thinks he did something extraordinary. If he knew that we let his rent-a-cops through on purpose, he'd be crushed." He smiled mirthlessly.

The Department of Homeland Security had accrued a number of black marks during the early years of its existence. Friction over jurisdiction had resulted in a lot of bad blood between federal, state, and local law enforcement.

Pickering was part of the new breed of Congressionally-monitored spy who held "lesser" law enforcement agencies in contempt. *Corrupt cops will not compromise this country's first line of defense.* The fate of the Soviet KGB and its gradual decomposition into the SVR was all the incentive that men like Pickering needed to follow Oswald's lead.

"How'd she get the Secret Service let her get away with this? If we snatched that call, so did they. Easily." Oswald's angry speculation was fuel by naked envy.

"Metz." Pickering pushed his glasses back up to his nose. "I'd have to say that Carl has a source in their main hub that runs interference for him. Besides, even if the Horn knew about this, what makes you think he'd move against her?" He swiveled in his chair to look at his old friend.

"Yeah. And yes, I know, it's not her on the line. It's that weasel, Metz. He's covered as long as his boss doesn't report him." Harry puffed out his cheeks and blew out a breath of frustration.

"Don't you know Conroy Horn?" The pen's circuit stopped in mid-arc to point at Harry.

"I did, back when I was with the Company."

"And?" Pickering's pen resumed its orbit.

"The man I knew didn't take any flak. Period. He was a real straight shooter. The only thing that makes any sense to me is that Fisk got to him."

"How did he do it?" The pen stopped to point at its pale owner.

"I don't know, and I don't care. As soon as Metz can arrange it, he's toast. That is all I need to know." Harry frowned.

"Fisk is the best manipulator I've ever seen."

Harry tried and failed to ignore the pain in his lower back from standing. "Doesn't matter. His days are numbered." *He does get the woman what she wants, that's for sure.*

"What's next?" Pickering's fingers felt cold as they brushed Oswald's grip on the papers. He turned, placing the pages back in the stack from which he'd taken them.

"After Fisk is gone, Angel steps in to fill the void. As soon as we make it clear that we own her, President Hill will give us what we want or she'll miss that second term that she wants so very much. As long as we can link her to the deaths of Carns, Pike, and Fisk, we have our shield. Who knows? It might be enough to get us all the budget we want."

"You don't see anything to be gained by tipping him off?"

"Fisk? Nah. We'll sit on this and use it when we need it."

Pickering sneered as he kept working. "You know, if he were here..."

"I'm not so sure. Jason Cutter was a patriot. He had no stomach for politics. He was too much of an idealist to ever think seriously about stopping something like this. He'd be all too happy to let these animals feed on each other."

Friday
May 30, 2014
Christopher's Apartment
Congressional Zone
Washington, D.C.
9:00 A.M. EDT

Christopher stood up from the padded workout bench. Putting down the pair of dumbbells, he flexed his tired arms. He was reaching for a towel to wipe the sweat off his forehead when the doorbell rang. Wrapping the towel around his neck, he walked with long strides to the door. *Nice to have a room for my exercise equipment.*

Stopping by a tall rubber tree in a huge clay pot, he plucked a compact pistol from its hiding place. Chambering a nine-millimeter round, he slipped the gun into the towel. Holding the towel in one hand, he activated the monitor that showed him who was standing down in the lobby.

"You have a visitor," the guard told him, his face large in the screen.

Stepping away from the camera, he poised his fingers over a row of buttons. Doris nodded at the camera from across the counter.

Christopher relaxed. "I know her. Send her up." Unwrapping the gun, he quickly popped the clip and ejected the loaded round. Sliding it back into the clip, he reactivated the safety and placed the gun back in its hiding place. As a veteran security specialist, he understood that there was no such thing as too much caution when it came to his personal safety. *You can't guard anybody when you're dead.*

A triple knock sounded at the door. *That's the right signal.* He checked the monitor one last time to be sure that it was indeed Doris waiting for him in the hall. He slid back each of four deadbolts.

Once he opened the door, Doris met his gaze with an uncharacteristically mild demeanor. *She wants something.*

"Good morning." She walked casually into the apartment.

"Good morning. Can I take your coat?" he asked, pointing to the nearby closet.

"No, I'll be fine." She put her hands in her pockets. *Coming here makes me feel more insecure than I already am.* It was rare for anybody to ask her about the coat. As a result, she almost never thought about who had once owned it. *I'd like to give it back to him when this is all over with.*

"Welcome to the new digs. I presume this isn't a social call." He closed the door and locked it. The idea that Doris would come by to shoot the breeze with him made no sense. *That'll be the day.*

"Not really. Is anyone else here?"

"Other than the people connected to your cameras and microphones?" He pointed to the dining room table where a handful of wires and little black boxes lay scattered.

"I guess I deserved that." *Nice try, but you didn't find everything.*

"*You* had that stuff put in?" He wiped his face with the towel again.

"I gave the order. I even did some of the work myself. That's one of the reasons why I'm here." She took her hands out of her pockets.

"I'm listening," Christopher said as he disappeared into the kitchen.

"You know I don't trust you." Doris wandered over to the dining room table where she could see into the kitchen.

He pulled some orange juice out of the refrigerator, closed the door with a swing of his hips, and poured two glasses of juice. "Can't say as I blame you. I keep thinking it over, and I still don't fully understand what's going on."

Pushing aside the gutted eavesdropping gear, they sat across the table from each other. Handing her a glass, Christopher dodged back into the kitchen for his sweaty towel.

"What is it you don't understand?" Doris sipped at the juice. *Fresh squeezed. Not the concentrate you served me last time.*

"Well, you say you're putting all these fat cats in power and giving them enough rope to hang themselves." Behind them, computer-controlled blinds silently adjusted the angle of the wooden slats in the windows.

"Right." Doris drained her glass, holding its empty coolness in both hands.

"That's a lot to swallow in one bite. If you put these people in power, that means you have the dirt on them. Why couldn't you just use that dirt to keep them out of power in the first place?" He downed half his juice in one gulp.

"Politics versus patriotism," she said cryptically, recalling Fisk's words.

"You seem to have a handle on it."

"That's because I've been doing this for a while." She smiled.

"Talk to me."

Recalling her late-night conversation with Fisk, Doris took a deep breath. "Some people see politics and patriotism as two sides of the same coin. I've heard it said that you can't have one without the other. What I know is that politicians can work for the greater good or they can work for themselves. Patriots, on the other hand, have only one mission--to do what's right for their people."

"That's pretty deep." Christopher gave an admiring nod.

"Yeah, I get around," Doris shrugged.

"Hmm. I've never read anything like that."

"Most people don't stop to think about it. I know that I didn't. I've been where you are," she recalled with a shudder.

"How did you handle it?"

"When this is behind us, I'll tell you."

"Come on. I thought we had a truce."

"We have an understanding. I'm here to further that understanding."

"Hey." He could see that she was uncomfortable.

"I know. I've come to ask for your help."

"Sure. What do you need?" He spread his large hands.

She found it hard to accept Christopher's laid-back attitude. "Fisk has enemies. Those enemies are planning to move against him in the near future. I need your help to protect him."

"Does Griff know about this?

The fact that he was taking it all in stride told Doris she had been in the field too long. *I've kept too many secrets. Just telling you this much is killing me inside.* "No," she fibbed.

"This doesn't have anything to do with the President, does it? Just tell me the truth. That's all I ask."

"It's not the President. This is something else. Something just as bad." She shook her head emphatically, aware that she was playing a dangerous game with Christopher's loyalty.

"Tell me what you can."

"The President wants him dead. That's old news. What you don't know is that there are people behind the scenes in our own organization that also want to get rid of Fisk, for different reasons."

"Circles within circles. You guys take the cake, you know?"

"I do." She shrugged.

"I don't suppose you can tell me who these shadows are."

"No. You wouldn't believe me, anyway."

"Try me. I'm into some freaky things these days."

"It's not that I don't want to tell you..." She sensed his growing frustration.

He threw up an angry hand. "Why did you bother coming to see me? After what I've been through in the last few weeks, you have no reason to question my loyalty. I've been straight-on with you all the way."

"It's not like that."

"No. You spill it right now or you leave."

"I can't. I need your help."

"I can't help you if you don't clue me in." He got to his feet with a sigh.

"It's a simple body threat. There are people in our own ranks that want to kill him. I can't tell you any more than that. Considering the terms of your contract, I don't owe you any more."

Christopher's nostrils flared with anger. "Don't you dare pull that contract mumbo-jumbo on me. I'm a professional, and I've cut you all the slack that I'm going to give. There's the door. Talk to me seriously or get out. My contract doesn't say anything about being jerked around."

"All right. You win. I've handled this badly." Lowering her head slightly, her face was hidden by a cascade of long blonde hair.

"That's cool. Let's try this again. From the beginning."

"Have you got any tea?" Doris pulled her hair back while regaining her composure.

"Yeah. You want some?"

"Yes. This is going to take a while." In her coat pocket, she could feel her wireless phone vibrate for her attention.

"Right. I'll be back in a flash." He headed for the kitchen.

Doris took out the phone and flipped it open.

"He is a good choice, my dear," Enola said in dulcet tones.

Doris eyed the phone with deep suspicion, despite the secure telltale.

"Have no fear. I'm still with you. Now, be a dear and hang up before he comes back with your tea. I just wanted to give you some moral support in your moment of need. The two of you have much to discuss."

Friday
May 30, 2014
Christopher's Apartment
Congressional Zone
Washington, D.C.
11:42 A.M. EDT

Doris sat back in her chair, teacup between her hands. She was finally at ease with Christopher. *I feel better.*

"You miss the point. We call them the Founders because they laid the groundwork for the whole thing." She could feel her burden lift further with each word, despite the occasional necessary lies and omissions.

"He knows who they are? Has he ever met them?"

"Yes, but that's not their only reason for wanting to kill him. More than anything else, it's because he's a loose end. Our organization is highly compartmentalized. He's the only one with access to all of those compartments. As long as he lives, there is the smallest chance that their plans can be discovered and stopped."

"Ruthless." He finished his tea and set the cup down.

"I'm taking a very big chance. Coming to you like this is very dangerous. Fisk has two adversaries to dodge. A long time ago..." She paused, considering how to inject a grain of truth into her story. "A long time ago, I promised that I'd keep him safe, no matter what. This new wrinkle has increased the threat level. It's more than I can handle on my own."

"You know what these Founder guys sound like to me?"

"What?"

Christopher nodded toward a nearby bookshelf. "Spies. I read a lot of Cold War spy fiction. It's full of that sort of thing. Governments sacrificing their agents for the sake of the mission. Have you ever considered that possibility?"

She pursed her lips in apparent disbelief. *Amazing. Right on the first try.* "That's a little hard to believe. I'm just a security specialist, like you. I don't know that much about espionage. I would think that anyone from that period, in that line of work, would have to be dead by now."

"I know. It's out there." Christopher shook his head,

"Well, whatever they started as, I won't let them hurt Fisk. I never realized that it might come to this, and that's my fault. I need your help to correct my mistake." She stood up to his probing gaze just long enough to be convincing.

"I'm not sure what you want me to do. They don't let me drive for him all the time. That has to mean that they don't trust me totally. Not that I blame them."

"Griff likes to get out of the office now and again. You're probably right. He might not trust you that much, but he doesn't trust me either."

"I thought he just didn't like you." Christopher's eyebrows rose.

"In this business, trust and affection are the same thing."

"I've worked with people I didn't like."

"Did you trust them?"

"Point taken."

"Well, then, you see the pickle I'm in." Doris put her cup aside.

He paused, thinking. "Right. What do you want me to do?"

"Be loyal and trustworthy. Don't give Griff any excuse to doubt you. When the time comes, I'll call you with instructions."

"I'm supposed to come running, just like that?" Christopher didn't like the idea.

Doris nodded, silently admiring his stubborn streak. "Mr. Fisk is your primary concern. You're already on the payroll for that. This isn't politics as usual. I'm here to appeal to your sense of patriotism."

"I get you. I'll help you. Just don't mess with me. If this is some game you're playing..."

"It isn't. I promise." *I don't make promises very often, but I keep them when I do.*

"You make me want to believe you, but I know better. There's something you're not telling me. Am I right?"

"Of course there is. You know I can't tell you everything. I've already told you a lot more than you really need to know. You're just going to have to accept that and wait for my call."

"How did you people ever make it this far?" Christopher asked in exasperation. *I sure wish I knew why I was going along with this.*

Sensing a chance to deflect his anger, Doris chose to answer him. "President Hill and the top leadership of her party think that they're responsible for their own rise to power. They view Fisk, and others like him, as tools. Pawns to be used and discarded as they see fit."

"Politics for the sake of patriotism. You fed their egos so that they wouldn't question their success." He'd seen corporate ladder-climbers do the same thing.

"Exactly. His 'masters' are allowed to take all the credit for his brilliance, which allows him to operate undetected. His camouflage is, and has always been, his best defense. That's how we managed to get this far."

Sucked in, Christopher filled in the missing points. *This is starting to make sense.* "So, he's been too good at his job. No wonder President Hill wants to get rid of him. I suppose...Well, I guess..."

"I know," she said quietly.

He paused, looking at Doris with new appreciation. "It makes more sense. This must be a living nightmare for you."

"It's been hard on all of us."

Christopher softened his tone. "I've seen the way you look at him. Everyone else follows him out of respect or fear. You don't really 'follow' him at all. You shadow him protectively. A month ago, you shot a man in cold blood, and then walked over to nurse Fisk like he was somebody very important to you. If I didn't know better, I'd say you were in love with him."

"That's not open for discussion," Doris bristled.

"It goes a long way toward explaining why you're here. This is more than loyalty for you, isn't it?" He brushed at his chin to hide his own discomfort.

"If there was more to it than that, the subject would still be off limits."

"Okay. I'll put that down as a yes and move on." He could tell that he had touched a nerve. The rising anger lighting her eyes told him that he crossed an unseen line.

"Choices. It's all comes down to choices--whether we want

something badly enough or not. I had to choose between the man and his mission."

"You don't have to talk about this," Christopher said softly.

"You and I are in the same boat. You have to make the same choice." She tugged at the folds of her coat.

"I got you. It's the nature of our business. Keep the client alive or let them do their own thing until they crash and burn."

"I can't believe I'm having this conversation with you. Then again, I should have known better." Doris felt lump rise in her throat.

"Why is that?" His thoughts went back to his previous client. *If I had chosen the man instead of the mission, he might still be alive today.*

"Your file. You and I have made the same mistake."

"You seem to have chosen both. Sorry, I didn't mean that. I get your point. We chose the mission instead of the man."

"I thought I could have both. The truth is that, up until recently, I couldn't separate the two from each other." She was surprised when the tears didn't come.

"You knew him before all this got started. You broke the first rule. He's more than a protection contract to you." He wasn't guessing.

"I made him a promise, too. One that I intend to keep." She continued to wonder at the lack of tears while her stomach roiled in agony.

Friday
May 30, 2014
Office of the Press Secretary
The White House
Washington, D.C.
5:10 P.M. EDT

Anne quietly admired the simplicity of the furnishings within Angel Cutter's office. The desk was probably decades old, though its black walnut finish gave no clues to its real age. Mementos of an eventful career occupied only one wall of the moderately sized office. Earth-toned furnishings rounded out the effect, causing her to reflect that this was definitely a working person's office. *No slacker's paradise here.*

"I want to congratulate you on completing so many interviews in such a short timeframe. It's not common to see somebody like you working so hard on this kind of assignment." Angel put her coffee cup down, brushing a stray hair from her face.

"Thank you, but all I do is ask the questions and turn in the video. The network does all the filtering and editing." Anne was well aware that the statement was a backhanded compliment. *Just because I come from a regional market doesn't mean I'm stupid.*

"Which reminds me--I've heard a rumble that, because your work is going so quickly, WNN wants to package your interviews and run them as a three-part series. Prime time slots, too." Angel leaned over, glad to play the part of benefactor.

"Sounds good. I'll let you know if they get back to me about that." *I'll believe it when I see it. The only time I hear from WNN is when their courier stops by to pick up my disks.*

"In the meantime, here is the remainder of your interview schedule." Angel nodded, handing Anne a single page from the pile on the desk. She waited as Anne scanned the list. She checked the hang of her blouse, covertly watching for any sign of irritation. *I suppose I*

337

shouldn't expect anything. You probably had to pull some very long strings to get this assignment. This is a last chance for you, isn't it?

"I see that the Secretary of the Treasury isn't on the list. Can I ask why?"

"Ah." Angel paused, giving herself time to think. "How do I put this? The President is in the middle of some very difficult financial matters. She and the Secretary don't exactly see eye-to-eye on certain things. We think it would be best if his schedule were kept clear so that he could have all the time he needs to work things out. Mind you, that's off the record," she said with a conspiratorial nod.

"You're shutting him out."

"You don't miss much, do you?" She gave the reporter an appraising look.

"That's why I'm so well-liked. Look, let's get one thing straight. I'm older and wiser than I once was. As long as I don't do anything stupid, this assignment might just put me back into the game. Whatever you have going on here, I don't want to know about it unless it walks right up to me."

"I'm glad to hear you say that." Angel folded her hands on the desk blotter.

Looking at the page in her hand, Anne knew she'd passed a test. *Great. I'm a sellout.* "Can I ask why you aren't on this list?" She smiled mischievously. *At least I'm a sellout with a conscience.*

"I prefer to stay out of the President's limelight." *It also makes me harder to sacrifice.* She reflected on her desire for revenge. *I don't know when, where, or how, but somebody will pay for what they did to you, Daddy. I promise.*

"Modesty is good. But can I ask you why? I've seen your press packet. It seems a little strange to me that the woman who speaks for the President should be unwilling to speak for herself."

"You're not the first person to ask me that, and you won't be the last. When I took this job, I had to make some hard choices. As the mouthpiece for the President, I need to keep the 'me' separated from the 'her.' President Hill needs to know that I won't make policy--that I won't obligate her to things that she doesn't want to be obligated to. I'm sure you can understand the tightrope that has to be walked in situations like this."

"I won't argue with that. It must be hard not to say anything that can be misquoted or twisted around to imply something else." *It's no cakewalk on my end either. I have to ask provocative questions in order to get something besides a yes or no answer.*

"Thanks for the sympathy. You do get the VP." Angel reached for her coffee cup.

Anne gave a perfunctory nod. The Vice President had been noticeably absent from the media scene during the previous two years. In that time, he had held only six carefully scripted--and very short--press conferences. Unhappy with the limited access, the media had been quick to turn its back on him.

Picking up the interview list, Anne scanned it again. "Really? There he is. The name slipped past me. What's he like?"

"Don't worry, he's a pussycat. A very nice man, really. Did you know he used to be in media relations?"

"I've read his books. And yours. You two have a lot in common."

"You'll love his wife if you get a chance to meet her. She comes from the President's home state. If you need an icebreaker, try asking her about..." Angel paused. "Try asking her about the time she spent working at one of the refugee camps in Macedonia, during the Yugoslavia thing. It's how she met him. She loves to tell that story."

"Why am I going to have to wait three weeks, though?" Folding the schedule in half, Anne slipped it in a pocket on the side of her leather carryall.

"Mr. Fisk suggested that you be given some more interviews, which explains some of the names on your list. Both he and the President like your work, but don't tell anybody I said that. Besides, it gets you the full six week tour that WNN is paying for."

"What will I do with the gaps in the schedule? I can't see them paying me to sit around doing nothing for two days at a shot." *It must be sooo obvious that I've never had a really big-time gig.*

"Relax. These are the major leagues. Just watch and wait. Keep your recorder handy, and don't be afraid to jump in."

"You mean jump somebody else's story?" Anne's asked, incredulous. *Ouch. That was smooth. No wonder I never made it this far. Me and my tender sensibilities.*

"Call it whatever you want. I've watched you work, and if you don't mind me saying…"

"I don't have the killer instinct. I know. My editor's been trying very hard for years not to tell me that."

Angel held up both hands, palms out flat. "I didn't say that. You did. However, let me say this, just so we understand each other. Most of the talent that comes through the press pool is either on its way up or on its way out. Everybody looks for that one big story that will get them out of here."

"What are you getting at?"

"Almost nobody stays in the White House press pool any more. I remember when reporters working for the major networks were assigned to the White House for years. The point is, we'd like you to stay here for a while. We can put in a good word for you. If you play your cards right, WNN will keep you right where we want you for the next two years."

"How exactly do we--"

"I know this president, and I know what the polls are telling us. She's quite sensitive to these things. We can use a consistent truth-seeker in the press pool, and you can use the change in employers."

"I appreciate the confidence, but you're asking me to be a conduit, somebody that you can arrange leaks through. I'm not sure if I can do that."

"In three weeks, you'll go back to Channel 6. Is that what you really want? Yes, you'd be our conduit, from time to time. It's a fair trade for what you'll be getting."

"Which is?"

Angel shot a skeptical look at her. "It may have escaped your eagle eye, but this administration isn't known for its news leaks. When we do avail ourselves of that tool, you can bet your career that it'll be worth your time to help us out."

"Mm." Anne pursed her lips.

"It's that simple. You've been noticed, and we're willing to make you our friend." Angel parted her hands magnanimously.

"Who noticed me?" Anne shifted in her chair.

"That's not important. This administration is like a family. We do what's good for each other. We look out for each other."

Politics & Patriotism

"Can I assume that you made this deal with other people in the press pool?"

"Divide and conquer. If you decide to work with us, you can be told more. A lot more." She smiled broadly, the implied bribe of insider information being all too obvious.

Anne stepped around the end of the desk, one eyebrow raised. "Will I get to interview the President?"

Madeline Hill had granted precious few interviews to the general press since taking office. Her media image was carefully cultivated, groomed, and maintained by Fisk's consulting group.

"All things in due time, Anne. The more you do, the more access you get."

"How are you doing?" Anne asked, holding the phone tightly.

"Better. It's hard to get used to...this," Garrison replied. He sounded tired.

"I couldn't help myself. I just had to call. Are you in a cast? It wasn't easy to find out where you were, by the way," she scolded, sitting on the couch and smoothing her sweatshirt. *It's as you dropped off the face of the earth.*

"I didn't know where I was for the first week or so. They've got some really good drugs here. Thanks for calling. I mean that." *I did drop off the face of the earth, but you still managed to find me.*

"Do you need anything? I was absolutely sick when I heard about your crash. When you didn't call, I...well, you know." She supposed that Garrison's fatigue was the result of his injuries. *It's been three weeks. What in the world was he thinking?*

"I'm sorry. The last ten days have been a blur. The doctors told me it could have been a lot worse. Some of the people on my flight are really messed up. I guess you could say that I was the lucky one." *Wow. Have I really been here three weeks?*

"Well, you'd better be. I don't go to all this trouble for just any-old-body, you know." Anne felt the tension slowly drain out of her body. *This is so bizarre. I can't believe I'm doing this.*

"I do know that, and I am sorry for the scare. When this is all over, I'd like to see you again." He remained upbeat despite the fatigue in his voice. *This is so bizarre. I can't believe that I'm really doing this.*

"I'd like that. When will they let you go?"

"Three more weeks. I have knee surgery and physical therapy

to look forward to. If it's okay with you, I'd like to save all the gory details for later."

"Was it bad?" It was hard for her to reign in her journalistic instincts.

"I never saw this coming. I mean, I knew that something was going to happen. I just never imagined it would be like this."

"I'm sorry, I should have known better."

"I'll tell you all about it when I get back. This trip has changed my life. I see things differently. We'll have a lot to talk about, I promise."

"That sounds pretty deep. Did you find religion, or are you going to dump me?" Her response surprised both of them.

"No, it's nothing like that. I already believe in God, and I believe in you, too. I've never faced my mortality like this. It's changed me. I'm not sure what my future holds anymore." He sounded almost irritated.

"I see."

"The weather in Montana is nice this time of year. I've got a great view. When they cut me loose, I'll come and look you up. I've got a few appointments right when I get back to D.C., but after that, I'm all yours."

```
Saturday
May 31, 2014
Training Camp
Cascade Mountains
Washington State
10:20 A.M. EDT
```

His chest aching, Garrison heaved a sigh, and then turned off the phone and set it down.

"Well done. Have you had lunch yet?" the Colonel asked with an approving nod.

"No. Do you really think she bought that?" He wiped a calloused hand over his moist forehead. The atmosphere inside the big tent was muggy and dark, despite the blowing fan and carefully placed LED lamps.

"Sure she did. She was so concerned about you that she didn't even stop to ask questions. Don't sweat it. We'll keep tabs on her." The Colonel's mustache twitched with his grin.

"Still, you're going to have to call her back in the next week or two, just to keep her from being antsy. Wouldn't want her trying to pull a surprise inspection now, would we?" Hunziger said from across the tent, hunching like a gargoyle in his chair.

"I hadn't thought of that," Garrison replied.

"Just part of the service. We'll watch your back while you're here. By the way, are you still having those headaches?" Away from prying eyes, the sergeant was downright congenial.

"Yeah. Some days are better than others."

"It's the altitude. Happens to a lot of the people we bring through here. Why don't you go get some chow, and let me talk to the sarge?"

"Go. I'll come get you in half an hour," Hunziger said.

Garrison got to his feet with a groan. "When does the hurting stop?"

"In your case? Four more weeks." The Colonel looked at him for a long moment.

"Gee, thanks." Garrison stepped over to peel back the tent flap.

"We don't treat everybody like this. You're special, remember?" the Colonel replied.

Hunziger snorted.

The closing tent flap muffled Garrison's curse. The Colonel sat quietly for a moment, waiting for him to be out of earshot.

"I told you so," Hunziger finally said.

"We'll just have to get somebody to monitor the gear while he's asleep. He's not going to buy that altitude sickness thing for very much longer."

"You want me to make the call?" the sergeant asked, less than enthusiastic.

"Nah." The Colonel sighed. "I've got to talk to Griff about our security situation, anyway. Now that Loverboy has a girlfriend, we need to be on our toes."

"You don't think she'll try to pay him a surprise visit, do you?" Hunziger leered.

"The word from Fisk is that she's up to her eyeballs in a new assignment. His people are supposed to make sure that she can't get out of town for the next month. That reminds me, how's our schedule?" He opened a notebook.

Hunziger stood up. "He's a fast learner. He reads everything we give him, and then some. He's still all thumbs when it comes to certain things, but he's made good progress. He's nearly a full sleep cycle ahead of schedule with the sublims. Oh, yeah. If we can't get the sublims to synchronize, we're going to have to rethink the last two weeks of his program. I can't keep running him ragged like this. He's going to get hurt sooner or later."

"He's in better shape than some men half his age. As clumsy as he is, I'm surprised he's still in one piece," the old soldier admitted with a shrug.

"He's got a lot of heart." Hunziger glanced in the direction of the mess tent.

"Keep him tired. Just don't break any bones. The equipment hidden in that cot is worth $20 million. That's a lot to invest so that one man can learn at six times the normal rate."

"I better go get some lunch. I need to check on the group from Alaska while I'm at it. Good luck with that phone call." The sergeant took a step toward the tent flap.

"They're just going to tell me to make do."

Saturday
May 31, 2014
Fisk Residence
Georgetown
Washington, D.C.
5:00 P.M. EDT

"Something's got to be done," Jarrett said.

Fisk set his drink down. "I hear you. Andy's been causing trouble. He's not talking to me. He hasn't returned my last few calls, and he's not going to any of the inner circle meetings."

"Griff gave me the rundown this morning. His people are gaming with Madeline's numbers. And here's the kicker. They've cut him out of the loop on their own."

Fisk nodded as he rose. Putting both hands in his pockets, he began to pace.

"The gossip hounds in the financial sector are running wild with this thing. I had the chairman of the Federal Reserve in my office on Friday." Lee's frown turned sourer.

"And?" Fisk leaned on the edge of a polished mahogany desk.

"He's been talking to Kirsov."

"They suspect?" Fisk raised an eyebrow.

"Oh, yeah. The Chairman told me in no uncertain terms that he thinks the President is making her move. He wants in. If *he* can put it together, you know Kirsov can't be far behind." The old banker was clearly agitated.

Fisk's mind raced. "If they want to play, let's deal them in."

"I was hoping you'd say that. My committee doesn't see it that way. Just so you know, I expect them to file a dissenting report." Lee's sighed as Fisk returned to his chair.

"We can't pull our punches. Not now. I'll talk to the right people when I get the chance. You need to stick to your guns. I wanted to spare Andy any more grief, but..."

"I hear you. It's Wally Carns all over again." Lee's tone was calm but supportive.

"All right. Here's what I want you to do. No phones. Go to each member of your committee. Tell them that we're going to take Andrew Brown out of play. If we can't recruit him, we'll have to find some other way to sideline him."

"How soon do I tell them to expect action?" Lee straightened, resignation in his eyes.

"Within 24 hours. I'll take care of this myself."

"Thank you."

"One more thing. I need you to leak Madeline's plans to Langsford. Nothing solid; just a few things he won't be able to confirm through his sources."

"Can't you get somebody else to do that? If my name comes up at all, Alex Kirsov will be down my throat in a hot minute. He'll want to know how I found out about it before he did," Lee asked, rising to his feet.

Fisk walked his friend to the door. "Langsford is old school. He won't give up his source. He will, however, come looking for me to get confirmation. That's exactly what I want."

Griff looked at his advisors in stern silence. "Well? Can we do it?" he demanded as the air conditioner hissed to life.

"It's iffy," one of them finally said. "We know that Mr. Brown likes to go sailing every Sunday, weather permitting. He and his wife are fixing up an old two-master. He calls it the *Almighty Dollar*. At sea, he's vulnerable. He only goes out with one protector. When he's on dry land, he's got the full package. If you really want to reach out and touch him, do it while's playing sailor."

Everyone at the table nodded. High-ranking government officials were now better protected than their private sector counterparts were. Various acts of terrorism, both at home and abroad, had added fuel to the paranoid flames, causing many federal agencies to spend large sums on the protection of their employees.

"This is where I come in," another advisor said as he reached for a remote. "Most of the time, it's this guy." The image of a tall, blond man in loud swim trunks appeared on the tabletop screen. The black utility belt around his well-tanned middle, complete with water-resistant holster, left no doubt that he was a protection specialist. The man's eyes left no doubt about his willingness to do his job.

"Secret Service or Homeland?" Griff asked, not to making any assumptions.

"Secret Service. Homeland watches the boat while it's tied up. They've got a secured marina for all the big shots."

"Do we have anything on him?" Griff studied the man's eyes.

"No. Not even a name. Brown was never on our list, so we haven't been watching him very closely. This photo is old. All I can tell you is that Brown sails with just one protector, plus his wife. They've been making repairs and improvements to that boat for the last four years. If they go down at sea, it'll be a surprise to the people who know him, but our sims project an 88 percent chance that the media will buy it completely." The advisor turned off the image.

Another concerned specialist spoke up. "Does Fisk really have to get close to this guy? I don't see the point in trying to recruit him. Not now. It'd be a whole lot easier to kill him and have done."

"It should be, but it's not. We got the updated sims last night." Griff responded, shaking his head. "The risk factors are the same either way. Recruit him or kill him, it doesn't matter. Politics over patriotism. If Fisk wants to look this guy in the eye one last time, that's his call. Who knows? He might pull it off."

Sunday
June 1, 2014
Aboard the *Golden Hinde*
Off The Maryland Coast
11:00 A.M. EDT

Fisk sat alone in the salon. Poring over the stacks of papers, he paused to take a drink of cool orange juice. Signing where needed, he went through the documents with his customary speed. On the desktop near by, a small television showed the news.

"WNN's financial analysts have been following the shake-up that resulted from the Treasury Secretary's impromptu press conference nearly three weeks ago. The sudden and unexpected mention of the U.S. national debt sent shockwaves through the financial world. President Hill's people have been on their toes ever since."

Fisk watched with interest as the image on the screen changed to show Angel Cutter striding toward a podium.

"Treasury Secretary Brown made his announcement with the full blessing of the President. Anyone who says otherwise is just trying to cause trouble. President Hill came into office knowing that she would be the one to tackle this issue.

"There is no easy way to introduce this subject to the American people. In her own way, she's grabbed the tiger by the tail. The president of the World Bank has been in contact with key members of the administration. We don't expect to have anything more to report for the next few months. When we do, we'll get right back to you."

"I'll bet you will." Fisk took another sip of juice. *She doesn't like what I represent--politics. She strikes me as being an idealist. She hides it well, but I can feel it.*

The news anchor came back into full view. "The stock markets finished mixed on Friday as investors tried to make up their minds about where to put their money. Bond traders have been squeamish all week, despite assurances from the chairman of the Federal Reserve

Board that he has no plans to change the federal lending rate any time soon."

A knock at the salon door broke Fisk's concentration. "Come!" He put down his pen and turned off the TV as Griff stuck his head in.

"We have him on radar. We're five minutes out. You'd better get ready."

Sunday
June 1, 2014
Aboard the _Golden Hinde_
Off The Maryland Coast
11:30 A.M. EDT

Fisk knocked and then shuffled into the communications room. Smoothing out the wrinkles in his short-sleeved shirt, he checked his watch. "Sorry if I kept you waiting. I had another call from the Colonel."

Griff waved him to an empty chair. "I know all about it. The subliminal transmitter array won't stay lined up. We've got to fly somebody out there."

"Bill's going to be mad when he finds out. What are you doing about it now?" Fisk asked as he sat down next to the yacht's radar control computer.

"We've had people on the horn with Dr. Adkins ever since they reported it. The Colonel says Garrison can't take much more of the headaches before he begins losing sleep. Adkins thinks he should go out there himself to manually operate the system."

Fisk thought for a moment. "Have George talk to his committee. We'll have to rely on their judgment. How is Garrison holding up, anyway?"

"By all accounts, doing better than expected. He has no idea that he's learning faster than he should. He's nearly two full sleep cycles ahead of schedule." Griff reached over to activate a small screen.

"They can stop the sublims a week before he leaves. I don't see why this had to be brought to my attention." He turned to look at the screen.

"The Colonel's under a lot of strain. He has to close that camp in another few months, and he's falling behind on all his quotas. He's worried that he might make a mistake with the Garrison project. Since this could impact security, I thought you should know about it."

"I can call him tonight. Show me what we've got lined up for Andy Brown."

"That's him." Griff pointed to the radar display. "He's the red dot."

Fisk leaned forward to study the screen.

Griff continued, "They're heading out to sea. The weather's good, and as it turns out, Brown filed a sailing plan with the Coast Guard."

"Is that going to be a problem?"

"My people have been up all night. We think we can jam their comms, but we've come up short on just how to take them out. As it is, we're going to have to rely on something that's just a little unconventional."

"Doris?"

"Right." The big man felt his ulcer twitch at the thought.

Sunday
June 1, 2014
Aboard the *Golden Hinde*
Off The Maryland Coast
11:50 A.M. EDT

"There he is." Griff handed Fisk a pair of digital binoculars.

Standing on the yacht's foredeck, Fisk scanned the horizon. The twin masts of Brown's sloop were visible on the horizon. The long, sleek hull was just coming in to view. Overhead, clouds continued to scatter as the wind picked up. "Any word from Doris?"

Griff looked back at the wheelhouse and the helm operator's hand signals. "Nope. The area's clear. It's just him and us. You'd better get ready. We'll be off his bow in ten minutes or so. I've got to go and prep the launch."

"You still think this is a waste of time?" Fisk handed the binoculars back.

"Yes, but I see your point."

"After everything we've been through, this feels so wrong. We should have--"

"Don't let it tear you up. I blame myself for this just as much as you do. A lot of us do. We read him wrong. We knew the risks, too. We haven't gone into it blind. Look, the advisors might not like your decision to come out here, but they understand it, and they respect it." Griff pulled his windbreaker close and gestured for Fisk to follow him.

"It's not going to matter, is it? I could see it in his eyes. The man hates me."

"Patriotism over politics. His instincts are dead on. He just doesn't know how right he is. In his own way, he's a patriot. He looks at you and sees a politician. For him, the debt is a problem to be solved honorably. For you, it's an 'opportunity.' That's how he sees it." He held the door open for Fisk.

The consultant shook his head as the door swing shut behind them. "And he's not wrong. We could never have come this far if there had been more people like him in government, you know?"

"Come on. You're preaching to the choir."

Sunday
June 1, 2014
Aboard the *Almighty Dollar*
Off The Maryland Coast
12:10 P.M. EDT

Andrew Brown enjoyed the sweat rolling down his back as he speared a lanyard hook through an aluminum-ringed eyelet on the sail's trailing edge. With his shirt off and the sun on his back, the national debt crisis was the last thing on his mind.

Releasing the sail, he took several steps backward around one of the many lockers on the scarred deck of the old sloop. He grabbed the pulley ratchet with both hands, taking up the slack in the lines. The sail billowed in the cool Atlantic breeze.

The sound of an air horn broke his concentration. Giving the ratchet one last hard crank, he made sure the safety was in place before turning around to see who was hailing. His wife, clad in a bikini and sun visor, sat at the tiller. She pointed at the gleaming bow of a big motor yacht coming up from astern, her voice drowned out by the ocean.

Taking a moment to admire his wife's sun-burnished curves, Brown pushed his sunglasses back up on his nose. Regarding the sleek lines of the approaching vessel, he tried to guess who it might be. *That's not Speaker Langsford's boat. Too big.*

A man in loud diving trunks and a utility belt gripped the deck expertly with his bare feet as he returned from his perch on the bowsprit. To the Browns, he was more of a friend than a bodyguard.

Andrew waved the man over, shouting, "I don't know who this is."

The Secret Service was spread thin, between protecting high officials and its other duties. Professional friction between the Service and the Department of Homeland Security ran deep. It had been there since the founding of the transjurisdictional agency in 2001. Each new director of Homeland Security found himself in stiff competition with the Secret Service for the privilege of protecting the nation's top-ranking officials. Standing hard on tradition, the Secret Service refused to give up its role as protector to the President and other high officials.

"*Golden Hinde*," Dillon Gibbons said clearly into Brown's ear. "Preston Fisk's boat. I've been aboard her. Do you want me to see what he wants?"

"Slayer of the gods, eh?" Brown snorted. "As much as I don't want to, I'd better see what he wants. Trust me, the man's a real shark. He belongs out here."

Nodding, Gibbons duck-walked aft, stopping to speak to Mrs. Brown. Gibbons took the tiller from her as she went forward to help her husband with the sails.

"What's going on? Who is that?"

"Fisk." Andrew looked up at the still full sails. "And wouldn't you know it? I think we just about got it." He glanced up at the nearly trim sail as it rippled slightly in the wind.

Corin Brown kissed him lightly to assuage his disappointment and reached into a locker for a pair of gloves. Working together, they pulled in the sails, careful to coddle them into perfect stowage.

As it slowed, the length of Fisk's yacht cast a long, cool shadow over the smaller sailboat. Riding calm in the light swell, both vessels were kept close by their steersmen.

"Nuts," Brown muttered as he watched the yacht's crew lower an inflatable boat. *Must be an emergency if they aren't bothering to use a loud-hailer.* Within seconds, his suspicions were confirmed as Fisk clambered down a retractable staircase to the rubber boat. Making his way back to the stern, Brown waited for his wife.

"We can have a chopper out here in 15 minutes if you want it," Gibbons said, patting the radio on his utility belt. He kept an eye on the approaching dinghy.

Brown shook his head. *It better not come to that.* The shame of rolling over on the national debt calculations made his guts roil. "Corin, would you please go into the cabin?" he said as the inflatable tied up alongside. Ignoring Gibbons, he sucked in a breath and stepped over to the rail. "You've got some kind of nerve coming all the way out here. This had better be good."

Riding in the front of the dinghy, Fisk confidently looked up at him. Behind him, the operator scanned the horizon, making a point of not paying direct attention to what was happening.

"I thought you should hear it from me. There's something you need to know." Fisk reached up to grip the sloop's gunwale while making sure that his comm was active.

"What are you talking about?" Brown stopped short of helping the consultant over the rail.

"There's something going on that you need to know about," Fisk replied, hoisting himself aboard.

"What?" Brown did a double-take.

"Please, just hear me out."

Sunday
June 1, 2014
Aboard the *Almighty Dollar*
Off The Maryland Coast
12:26 P.M. EDT

"I still don't see what this has to do with me," Brown protested, trying to remain civil.

"It has everything to do with you. You and the rest of the country weren't supposed to know about her plans until she was certain that you'd go along. Those plans include what's going on under the Treasury building."

"What's going on under the Treasury building?" Andrew asked, unable to believe how fast he was losing his temper. His outburst drew a concerned look from Gibbons.

"It's a computer network that, when activated, will recall the nation's currency back to the Federal Reserve. That includes both electronic and paper monies. It's an extension of the Federal Deposit Insurance Corporation."

"I know the FDIC like the back of my hand. The law is already on the books to do that. Why would we need to--"

"Because it would take Congressional approval, and that would take you bringing the matter to Congress. This project was put in place without your knowledge to prevent you, or Congress, from saying no."

The impact of Fisk's statement took a moment to register. Nodding slowly, Brown asked, "How could that happen without my knowing about it?"

"It was an ongoing effort, over about the last ten years. The Army Corps of Engineers actually built the levels now in use, along with a few National Security Agency contractors. Presidents have been passing it along quietly, hoping that it wouldn't be needed." *I'm pulling my punches. What's the matter with me?*

"Sounds like a lot of people know about this place. How did you find out? Through Madeline?" Brown asked, trying to reign in his hostility.

"This is Washington, land of secrets."

"The Army?" Brown hesitated. *I know they build things, but still...*

"Ever since that mess with Yugoslavia in '99, our military has been bending over backwards to make itself useful to each new president."

The conflict involving Yugoslavia and the member nations of the North American Treaty Organization had marked a turning point in U.S. foreign policy. With its prestige damaged, America's ability to rally NATO to its moral and humanitarian causes had been lost.

As mistrustful as he was of his country's very political military machine, Brown couldn't bring himself to believe that the Army could be party to such a huge deception. *Circles within circles,* he thought, recalling the writings of Machiavelli. *I'm sure the President will have a reasonable explanation.*

"Why are you telling me this? Are you here to help me or to bury me?" Andrew asked resignedly, sensing the trap closing around him. *You've already forced my hand once. I won't give in so easily this time.* He forgot his earlier misgivings about the President's reasons for inflating the value of the nation's negotiable assets in favor of defending himself against Fisk.

"I'm here to help you. What's going on is bigger than either of us. By helping you, I help myself. Together, we can make this work."

"How so?" Brown asked, cold tendrils of fear beginning to climb up his bare back. The chill shade created by the bulk of Fisk's yacht took on a metaphorical significance that he didn't want to think about. *This is my last chance, isn't it?*

He felt the bile rise in his throat as he thought about the way his department heads had turned on him at the meeting and subsequent luncheon with the President. In the week that followed, he had been virtually shut out of their dealings. He recalled being told once by an elderly Senator, *It's not the deals you make that come back to haunt you, it's the deals you don't make that ruin you. When I made that speech to the media, I cut my own throat, didn't I?*

"You have to know she's going to get what she wants. I came out here to tell you that there's more to all this than meets the eye." Fisk shivered in the cool breeze.

"Like what?" Brown reached under the tiller bench for a sweatshirt. "You're not making a whole lot of sense. I can't keep rolling over every time you want something. If I want the President to take me seriously in the future, I'll have to ride this thing out." He struggled to poke his head and sunglasses through the neck of the grey top. *Does the President even know you're here?*

"Look, I made her what she is today. She's in the White House because I put her there. You're in danger of becoming a casualty. She's been my project long enough for me to know that she will have you removed. By the time you sit down for dinner tonight you'll be drawn, quartered, and sold for bait." *This isn't going well at all.*

Brown got to his feet, wanting to pace, and then sat again. *You said she was your 'project?' You're the one I need to watch out for.* "Why are you doing this?" he asked, squirming. *So help me, I'll resign before I'll be your puppet.*

"Because I need you. I need you around so that you and your scruples can hang Madeline out to dry if and when she gets out of line."

"What line? Are you saying that you're pulling her strings?"

Fisk made hard eye contact with Secretary Brown. "Yes. But there's more. I didn't count on your professionalism, or your sense of patriotism. I misjudged you, and now I'm here to bring you in on the program. There's another agenda in play here and you--"

Brown threw up his hands. "What you want me to believe is impossible. The worst thing I've seen this president do is con me into inflating the value of our national assets. I don't like it, but I understand the reason behind it. What you're asking me to believe goes so far out of bounds that I can't even tell you how paranoid you sound." *You made a president. Now you want to use her and I'm in your way.*

Fisk could sense the other man's growing fear. "Presidents are never their own people. Madeline Hill isn't the first president to be manufactured."

"So, what happens now?" Brown felt his career melting away.

"Madeline's going to do what I need her to do, with or without you. I can explain, but you've got to want to hear it."

Brown slapped his fist into the palm of his other hand. "Do you understand what you're saying? You've admitted to having your own agenda--which, by the way, is not news. If I understand correctly, you're telling me that President Hill is on some sort of preprogrammed course, one that you put her on. Am I missing anything?" He leapt up, bouncing on the balls of his feet. *Somebody needs to cut you down to size.*

"Relax. You're making your friend nervous." *We've lost him.*

Gibbons got to his feet, one hand still on the tiller. "Sir, I'm afraid I'm going to have to ask you to leave. You're upsetting Mr. Brown."

Fisk looked up at the agent. He noticed that the man was cautiously unzipping a compartment on his utility belt. "Andrew, I have my reason for doing this. If you give me a chance, I'll explain."

It was all he could do to keep from screaming. "Get off my boat. I don't know what you're selling, but I don't want any part of it. If anybody's going to be fish food tonight, it's not going to be me!" *When the President hears about this, I hope she's in a bad mood. People like you have run this country into the ground with all your secret agendas.*

"Andy--" Fisk got to his feet, carefully keeping both hands in plain view.

Brown pointed at Fisk. "Get him off my boat. Then get that helicopter,"

"Sir." Gibbons flexed his muscles at Fisk. "I have to remind you that I'm a witness to this conversation, and that it will be reported."

Careful not to provoke the agent, Fisk edged his way back over the rail, down to the waiting dinghy.

Brown stormed into the cabin.

"Did you get all that?" Fisk asked the advisor through his comm implant.

"Loud and clear," the tiny voice affirmed.

"I'm ready," Doris said, cutting in on the channel.

"I should have tried harder," Fisk lamented quietly as the dinghy's operator steered a wide circle back towards the *Golden Hinde.*

"You did try," Doris replied with the barest hint of sympathy. "You're in the habit of believing that you can convert anybody. I've jammed his remote telephone connection, and we just used up our one asset to take the Secret Service comms in this area down for the next 15 minutes. Our lines aren't blocked, but they won't be able to get anything out."

"What about the agent's panic button?" Fisk asked.

"Also jammed. He can push it all day if he wants to. The satellite relay is in our back pocket for the next 35 minutes."

"Griff?" Fisk looked up at the yacht.

"Here," a rough voice acknowledged through the implant.

"Doris?"

"Yes?" Her serious tone cut through his numbness.

Fisk was choking on the order. "Do it." The words left a sharp, coppery taste in his mouth. "The Service guys are too good. Brown's agent will find a way out of this if we give him the chance."

"I have a speedboat in the water with the necessary equipment. I can be there in 20 minutes," she replied through the roar of background sea spray.

"You found one? All the boats we looked at were secured, or in use. Where did you 'jack it?" Griff sounded genuinely impressed.

"It's not meant for deep water. When I'm done with it, I'll sink it and you can pick me up."

"No evidence. I like it," Fisk muttered.

"It's the least I can do."

Down in the cabin, Andrew poured iced tea into a white plastic cup. Setting the self-cooling pitcher down on the counter, he made sure that its nonskid bottom had a solid grip on the polished oak.

"What was that about?" Corin asked as she slipped into a bright green jumpsuit.

Brown turned to face her. "I think we're in trouble. Remember when I said that this national debt thing would be the biggest thing in American history since the abolition of slavery?"

"Yes. And I remember how you wanted to be the man to fix it." She put her arms around him, snuggling in close.

Andrew gulped at his tea as he returned her hug. "Well. Mm. Yeah. I guess I did want to be the Treasury Secretary, didn't I? I'd give almost anything to be back in Manhattan just now." He recalled his life as a mere bank president nostalgically.

"You knew there would be some hard deals to make. Fisk is her right hand. He came out here because she told him to. Believe me, I know how you feel. When I made partner at the firm, I had no idea what I'd be letting myself in for."

Andrew shook is head at his wife's pragmatism. *That's the lawyer in you talking.*

"Did you hear what he said to me out there?"

"No. I don't like that man. He gives me the creeps."

"He told me that I was finished if I didn't back his president. He talked about her as if he owned her. I'm no stranger to politics, but this is all wrong. I know it was rude, but I just couldn't listen to him go on like that." He released Corin and stepped back.

"He had more to say?" Her brow furrowed as she considered his statement.

"Yeah, but after what he put me through a couple of weeks ago, I wasn't in the mood for it. You know what really gets to me? He comes off like he's got his own agenda, and the rest of us are just pawns."

"He does have an agenda. He gets people elected and he keeps them in office. He makes a lot of money doing it. He's used to thinking of people like that." She sat down to put on deck shoes. Though she was just a junior partner at a law firm that didn't yet bear her name in its title, Corin thought she understood politics a little better than her husband did. *I love your idealism, but the world doesn't always turn on honest numbers.*

Up on deck, Agent Gibbons fretted over the bursts of static coming from his radio. Opening the back panel, he kept an eye on the *Golden Hinde* as it crept away. He checked the connections and then reached for another small transmitter on his belt. *We're being jammed.* It could only mean one thing.

"Secretary Brown! Andy!" Padding across the rough planks, he knocked loudly on the door. "Andy, I need to speak with you *immediately*." Pushing the large red button on the small box in his hand, he growled when it didn't respond.

The accordion door swung into its recess. Corin frowned, clutching her husband's hand as she looked up at the agent.

"What is it, Dillon?" he asked as he untangled himself.

Gibbons shielded his eyes against the sun, following the progress of Fisk's yacht as it moved away. "My radio's being jammed. The panic button isn't working, either. I think we're in trouble. We'd better get under weigh."

"No helicopter?" Climbing back up to the deck, Andrew was glad that his wife couldn't see the expression on his face.

"No." The agent turned his head to scan the horizon.

"You really think we're in trouble?" Brown's mouth puckered with uncertainty.

Pointing after the retreating yacht and tossing the inactive handset from one palm to the other, Gibbons replied, "These radios are the most reliable on the planet. I don't know if their malfunctioning has anything to do with Mr. Fisk, but I'm not trained to take chances with your safety."

"Okay," Brown nodded, leaning back down into the cabin. "Come on up, honey. I need you to take the tiller while Dillon and I get the sails up."

"What's wrong?" Corin asked, reaching for the pitcher.

"Maybe nothing. It's just that we need to get back so that I can talk to the President about that situation I told you about." He gave Gibbons a meaningful look.

The agent nodded. *No need to panic the wife.*

"On my way!" Corin shouted.

Andrew frowned as he turned away. He was keenly aware that his wife was unhappy about losing the rest of their day together. He stood, watching the big yacht as it plowed relentlessly through the water, thinking about the man aboard it.

During her run for the presidency, rumors of secret assassinations had dogged Madeline Hill and her closest advisor. With her media image intact, Hill had ascended to the presidency untainted.

"Do you think he'll come back?" Brown asked over his shoulder.

"I don't know. We really should be going. The helicopter will come for us once we've been out of contact for a while, but there's no telling how long that could be. If he does come back, we won't be able to outrun him."

The implications were scary, causing Andrew to shiver. *What if the rumors about Wally Carns are true? Am I next?* There was only one thing to do. "You take the pulleys. When Corin has the tiller, I'll run the lines."

Agent Gibbons had been sailing with the Browns since the previous summer. He had drawn the assignment because he had his own boat and had sailed as a crewmember during a World Cup race while in college. The trio had become good friends. Gibbons' in-depth knowledge of sailing and hull design had been very helpful during the restoration of the *Almighty Dollar*. The old sloop wouldn't win many races, but she was well on her way to looking as she had when she was first built, nearly six decades earlier.

"Corin!" Andrew banged on the doorframe of the deckhouse.

Within moments, all three of them were straining to raise and trim the sails.

Sunday
June 1, 2014
Aboard the *Golden Hinde*
Off The Maryland Coast
12:50 P.M. EDT

"He's getting under weigh."

Griff stood on the fantail next to Fisk. Both men had put on dark blue windbreakers. He stepped away from the binoculars fixed to the aft rail to let Fisk look.

Fisk watched the trio aboard the sloop as their sails came up. "Do we know for certain that their comm is jammed?"

"Yeah. We got the Secret Service comm, too," Griff replied, referring to the panic button. "We have a blanket outage on wireless and shortwave for as long as it takes repair crews and technicians to trace and fix. Just remember, we can never do this again. It took us nearly ten years to get the assets in place. We used them; now they're gone."

"Impressive. I'll bet the conspiracy buffs are going to have a lot of fun with this."

"Ha! We've given them a lot to talk about in the last ten years, haven't we?"

"Doris thinks I should write a book about all this." He turned his back to the wind, walking toward the aft salon.

"What are you going to do? Set the record straight?" Griff wheeled to follow Fisk.

"I don't know. Maybe explain why we did it."

"The Founders aren't going to let you do that, as much as it might appeal to their egos. You know that." He trailed after the consultant.

Fisk entered the salon. He peeled off his windbreaker and tossed it aside, heading for the bar.

"I could sell it as fiction," he sneered while pouring orange juice, "or I could just write something for the universities about the nature of politics and patriotism." Pouring a second glass, he sat down next to Griff and offered it to him.

"Good luck. After you retire, I've still got work to do." He accepted the glass.

"Maybe, maybe not." Fisk took a drink.

"You still think we don't need Phase Two?" Griff drank deeply.

"We had to put it in place. It was the one compromise we had to make to get enough support from the others. When you think about it, we've done a lot with just a little. None of this would be possible if we had tried to do it any other way."

"Does that include Andy Brown?"

"Yes. It also includes everyone else that we suppressed, discredited, or killed. Even Walter Carns. As much as I disliked that, I'm just going to have to live with it. We've made our fair share of mistakes. Nobody's perfect. We've been making it up as we go along for the last few years, anyway. We've been lucky, too." He rose to his feet.

"Speaking of luck, where's Doris?" Griff stretched.

"On my way," Doris yelled to be heard over the roar of a large engine. The feedback through the comm system made Fisk's inner ear tingle. "I'm between him and the bay. Did you notice if he had more than one bodyguard?"

Listening in, Griff raised a finger to confirm a single bodyguard.

"Just the one. And his wife," Fisk said aloud, as if Doris were in the room.

"I'll start heading towards him. Put comms on the line and tell them to feed me his GPS numbers. This little boat doesn't like deep water and I'm low on gas."

"You think he's going to run?" Griff asked through his own link.

"His protector will tell him to. I've got a lot of respect for the Secret Service. He'll definitely tell Brown to run when he finds out that his panic button doesn't work."

"There's one way to settle this real fast. Just keep us into the wind. Let it take us out to sea. Dillon seems to think that they might be waiting for us back at the docks." Andrew moved closer to his wife.

"Who?"

Andrew stopped before naming his fears. *You wouldn't believe me. I don't believe me.* "Whoever jammed Dillon's radio." He wiped his forehead and stripped off his sweatshirt. "Which reminds me..." Wadding it up, he scampered down into the cabin, motioning for Gibbons to follow him.

"Yes?" the agent queried as he followed Andrew into the cabin.

The Treasury Secretary proudly opened a sideboard to reveal a compact black box with digital touchpad controls.

"Radio. We had it installed on Tuesday while the hull was being scraped. It automatically tunes to the Coast Guard distress frequency. Do you think you can use it to get us some more help? If it turns out we really need it, I mean." Running a hand through his bristly black hair, Andrew was surprised to find that he was actually calming down.

"There's one way to find out." Gibbons squatted in front of the radio. "Please just stay right here so that I can see you. Whatever Fisk was up to, it could very well involve making sure that you don't get back safely."

"You didn't buy it, either?" *Fisk must want a larger say in how it all turns out. Why else would he be working so hard to put his spin on this debt thing? That should be--oh, man! That should be my job!*

Gibbons turned the radio on, touching the controls lightly. "I'm not supposed to have an opinion, but after what I saw, and factoring in the jamming of my set, I'd say that whatever's going on might not

370

be so good for you. Or any of us."

"At least this radio still works." Brown smiled as the speakers came to life with the muted chaos of coastal traffic.

Gibbons tuned in the Coast Guard distress frequency. "I'm guessing, which means I can be wrong, but our radios can't be jammed from an outside source without causing a lot of trouble. Blocking my radio could mean--"

"You think the Secret Service wants me--" the older man choked out fearfully, looking up to see his wife through the slats in the door.

"Never. Don't even think that. Not now, not *ever*. The Service has been protecting people for more than a century. While we sometimes get sucked into politics, we never--and I mean *never*--kill the people we protect."

"Sorry. I'm just not clear on what to do...or who to trust."

Griff was standing by the binoculars when his wireless phone beeped. "Go." He didn't take his eyes off the sloop as it tacked into the wind.

"They're calling the Coast Guard. Their agent is trying to raise them now," Jasmine said from below decks.

"Where's comms? Why are you telling me this?" Griff felt his blood pressure spike.

"I just came from there. They're working on some sort of problem. I was asked to pass the message along, so here I am."

Nearby, Fisk had been just turning to leave. "Problems?" He cast a glance at the sailboat.

"We blew it. They have a civilian marine radio. They're trying to raise the Coast Guard." He directed a nod at the receding vessel. "Jaz, let me know when they get things back under control. Thanks."

"No problem." She left the line.

Folding the phone, Griff walked over to Fisk. "We weren't ready for this. Our intell said that they had no radio. I'm not sure that Doris will get to them in time. Even without witnesses, we're out of luck if Brown talks to a Coast Guard officer."

"Doris?" Fisk asked the air, unwilling to believe that his fiercest guardian would fail.

"I'm six minutes out," Doris bellowed over the roar of the speedboat.

Fisk held up the digits of one hand and the index finger of the other to tell Griff how far away she was.

Griff held his phone up to his ear, pressing a button with his large thumb. "What's the delay?"

"I told you, I couldn't get a bigger boat. The further out I get, the harder it is to make time."

Laying one palm flat, Fisk made wave motions. Griff nodded.

Hey, what was that? Looking down at his undulating hand, Fisk wondered at the signal. *Where did I pick that up?* Something about the hand motion and its context caused a memory flash that blinded him for a single heartbeat.

A sailboat. A woman at the tiller, laughing. A little girl in blonde pigtails, laughing. The woman's name is Sophia.

"What's wrong?" Griff asked, noticing Fisk's sudden fascination with his own hand.

"Nothing." He gazed at the hand a moment longer. The image was gone, but the name stayed on the tip of his tongue. *No, that's not right. It's Sophie. She likes to sail. Won't let me sell the boat.*

"Yeah, the waves." Griff watched Fisk clasp both hands over his chest. Something in the way he moved was wrong. *You never hold your hands like that.* Something in the way Fisk looked at him wasn't right. Both the look and the gesture belonged to somebody else. *It's you, isn't it? You finally found a way out.*

The two men looked at each other for a long moment. Unsettled, Griff gave Fisk a reassuring pat on the shoulder. "It's okay. We're almost done." *Can you hear me? Doris, why didn't you tell me things had gotten this bad? No wonder they want to cancel him. How many times has this happened?*

As the shock passed, his understanding deepened. Long dormant memories sparked and faded. The conclusion was appalling. *You weren't supposed to make it this far, were you?*

Squatting on the floor, Gibbons calmly spoke into the microphone. "Coast Guard, this is Secret Service Protective Agent Dillon Gibbons. I have an emergency." He let up on the transmit button.

"Roger." The woman's voice was nasal, thick with New England accent. "*Almighty Dollar*, we are receiving Agent Gibbons. Please state the nature of your emergency. Please also be sure to give us your position. Do you have GPS?"

Brown shook his head. The global positioning system had come back on line shortly after the millennium crisis failed to materialize. Better than ever, the new satellite-based navigation system was highly regarded. It was also the next thing the Browns had planned to buy for the sloop's renovation.

Dillon scowled as he transmitted his reply. "No GPS, just a tiller compass. Look, I've got a very important person out here with me, and I think we're being pursued by somebody who intends to board us." Making it up as he went, Agent Gibbons didn't waste time on the details of their situation.

"Too late," Griff guessed as his phone beeped.
"They're talking now. That agent's a fast thinker," Jasmine said.

"Put comms on the line."

"Comms here. I don't know what went wrong. Everything else is working. I can't tell you why we don't have shortwave jamming in that area."

"Anything from Cosmo?" He clamped down hard on his rising anger.

"All rooftop connections check out. All mainframes pass diagnostic. All assets have reported in. The problem is not our end. Wait. Cosmo says they're going to try for a satellite bump. They'll be ready in six minutes, give or take."

"Let me get back to you on that. Tell them to hold when ready." The big man scowled. "Stand by, I've got to talk to the boss."

Holding the phone down at his side, Griff waited for Fisk to step away from the binoculars. "Cosmo says they can screw up the shortwave repeater net, but it'll take a few minutes."

Fisk pointed landward, where a tiny white dot bounced up and down over the waves. "There. Prompt, as always." He allowed himself to breathe a sigh of relief that carried over the open channel of his comm implant. The sailboat had been just slipping over the horizon when he noticed the approaching speedboat.

"I'm glad you haven't lost faith," Doris quipped as the waves broke over her bow.

"Never. We just cleared the horizon. Won't see what comes next."

"Just as well. You'd better get back to dry land and see what it'll take to put the right spin on this." Doris hesitated as a chilly wave lashed her with salt water, partially flooding the 16-foot racer.

The invisible thing stirred in the back of Fisk's mind again. Closing his eyes, he let it come. "Just don't have too much fun," he said with a smirk. The words rolled off his lips effortlessly. *It's an inside joke,* he realized with a sudden shiver, *something that--*

"What?" Griff looked at him out of the corner of his eye.

"What? Why are you looking at me like that?" Fisk wavered at the protector's worried glance.

Griff couldn't speak. Bobbing his head, it was clear to Fisk that he was fighting back the urge to say something.

"Say nothing," Doris commanded over the roar of her engine. "We'll deal with it when I get back."

Fisk blanched when he realized the remark wasn't meant for him. "Doris? Talk to me. What's going on?"

Several seconds dragged by in silence. Doris had left the channel.

Sunday
June 1, 2014
Off The Maryland Coast
1:10 P.M. EDT

The speedboat's jet unit screamed as it propelled the vessel over the tops of the waves. Lifting up out of the water, the 16-foot white-and-chrome hull blasted through the sea spray on a collision course with the *Almighty Dollar*.

Doris swiped wet hair out of her face. *Heading out to sea. Not bad. If they get far enough out, I can't follow.* She closed to roughly one mile, and then eased the throttles back to allow the speedboat to ride the waves more evenly. Putting Fisk's "incident" out of her mind was proving to be impossible. *Stay on task*, she reprimanded herself, *one problem at a time.*

She wiped the spray off her sunglasses and raised a pair of compact fiber-optic binoculars to her face. Her trenchcoat insulated her from the chilly air. Clutching the wheel with one white-knuckled hand, she held the binoculars with the other. Touching the magnification control with the tip of her thumb, she brought the fleeing sloop into focus. *One problem at a time.*

Gibbons stood next to the tiller, watching the little speedboat approach through his own compact fiber-optic binoculars. The racer came into crisp focus the instant it crossed the visual horizon.

"Who is it?" Andrew shielded his eyes with a raised hand.

"Trouble," Gibbons pronounced. He gave the other vessel a professional look. "That's a 16-footer. It's not built for deep water. My guess is that somebody was waiting for you to head back. We didn't, so they came out here."

"Who? How many of them are there?" Brown realized with a chill that his decision to brush Fisk off was about to have consequences. *When I get back, I'm going to...*

"Ha! There's only one person. Female. Tall. Blonde. Sunglasses. Black leather," Gibbons verbalized as his training took over. *If we can get into some steeper swells, she'll swamp that speeder and that'll be that. Too bad we don't have an engine in this thing.*

"What?" Brown asked. Then he realized what the agent was doing and shut up.

Gibbons lowered his binoculars. "Whoever she is, she's very serious about coming after us. We better let out the rest of the sail. We've got twice the length of that speeder. That should be our best defense until the Coast Guard gets here."

Corin spoke up from her position at the tiller. "Suppose we head south? If we risk the shoals, we can get into some six-foot swells. Should be more than enough to stop that little thing."

Gibbons watched the speedboat close in. "I like it. We might lose the keel, but it's a risk worth taking. Let's do it. Coast Guard units will be all over these waters in less than an hour."

"We've got an emergency locator beacon," Corin offered.

"We can use that," the agent replied, nodding.

"I'll get it." Andrew smiled at his wife and scuttled quickly back into the cabin.

"You two are pretty calm, all things considered," Gibbons said as the speedboat began to slow down.

"It comes with our jobs. Andy and I used to work at the same law firm. Even then he was a real thinker." Corin glanced up to watch the sails, adjusting their course slightly.

"You'll have quite the story to tell when this is over." Gibbons shut off his binoculars and placed them in his fanny pack. With ten years of experience in Treasury investigation and two more in protective service, he knew enough to keep his doubts about their situation to himself.

"Yeah. One thing's for sure, I'm not going to argue with Andy the next time he wants to pay somebody to work on this old tub." She tugged hard on the tiller to bring the bow over a few more degrees.

Andrew came back up on deck. "Got it. It's the old kind, with a flotation collar." Holding up the dome-shaped buoy, he pulled a pin set into a yellow plastic collar. The collar expanded with a tiny hiss to form a bright yellow donut around the beacon's waterproof housing. He handed the beacon to Gibbons, pointing to a large red button in the center of the white plastic top. "Push this button, and it starts beeping, or something like that."

"Could I ask the two of you to put on your life jackets? We should be ready to swim away from the boat, just in case--to make it easier for the Coast Guard helicopter to pick us up."

Andrew nodded, reaching into the cabin to pull out three bright yellow life vests. "Here you go," he said, handing one to his wife and another to the agent. Shrugging into his own, he fastened the quick-release clip.

Out on the water, the speedboat leapt forward on a plume of white froth.

"Down! Get down! Here it comes!" Forcing Andrew down to the deck with one powerful hand, Gibbons pulled Corin off the tiller bench.

Sunday
June 1, 2014
Off The Maryland Coast
1:20 P.M. EDT

Doris rammed the throttles all the way forward. Bucking in her seat as the speedboat took off in a scream of jet-powered fury, she focused her attention on the old sailboat. Blasting over the wave tops, she steered in close to it. Majestically riding the swell, the sloop appeared to be standing still as her speedometer crossed 30 miles per hour and kept climbing.

Steering with one cold hand, Doris reached into the passenger's seat. Tangled in the safety belts, an old 37-millimeter grenade launcher rested with its dull plastic grips at the ready.

Taking up the single-shot weapon, she flicked off the safety. Raising the long black muzzle, she elevated it slightly and pointed it at the sloop. *Too bad I have to throw this thing overboard. It's a piece of history.* The lightweight launcher was identical to the one she'd used in Yugoslavia. *I wonder what Jason would say if he knew that I still had the same weapon he trained me on tucked away in a storage locker?*

The sound of the speedboat drowned out the natural roar of the ocean. Hugging the deck, Andrew reached for his wife's hand. She looked at him and smiled.

Gibbons reached for his pistol. Thumbing off the safety, he chambered a 9-millimeter round. "Stay down!" he yelled before slithering over to the gunwale.

At a distance of no more than 60 feet, the speedboat was boring through the water on a parallel course. Grasping the rail, Gibbons watched and waited. His training in antiterrorist tactics and his experience with domestic terror investigations, left little doubt in his mind about the danger he and his friends were in.

The grenade launcher that had appeared in the woman's hand seemed enormous. *She'll sink us!* Standing up slowly, he took his pistol in both hands and squeezed off eight shots.

Triggering the grenade launcher, Doris was punched back into her seat as two of the agent's armor-piercing bullets punctured the bullet-resistant liner of her coat.

The rocket-propelled grenade slammed into the old wooden hull of the sailboat. The explosive charge, built to penetrate lightly armored vehicles, ate into the aged planking. The explosion ripped the old vessel in half. An orange column of flame engulfed the stern.

Sunday
June 1, 2014
Off The Maryland Coast
1:21 P.M. EDT

Doris screamed, struggling to keep the speedboat from flipping. Slowing she made a wide, sloppy turn back to the burning sloop. The two halves of the old sailboat parted, canting over as smoke and flames reached for the sky.

Dropping the grenade launcher into the passenger seat, she brought the speedboat to a stop. Two hundred feet from the wreck, she kept an eye on it while assessing her wounds. She fingered the hole in her coat just where it covered her left shoulder. A tear in the old-fashioned antiballistic liner told her that she'd been hit by an armor-piercing bullet. Gritting her teeth, she turned to check the seat behind her. It was painted in the bright red common to blow-through exit wounds.

"Mm. Come on. Where are you?" She smothered a curse as she probed her chest with both hands, looking for the second strike. Inside her clothes, she felt a trickle start down the left side of her chest. The slow creep of the warm blood made her feel unclean. *Maybe I only got hit once.*

Disappointment came fast as her probing fingers found the truth. "Agh." Looking down, she drew comfort from the brightness of the blood staining her hands. *Flesh wound.*

Realizing that she was going into shock, she brought her attention back to the sloop. She picked up the grenade launcher. Then she reached into a side compartment and brought out a pair of high-explosive loads. The bulbous tips of the old-fashioned rocket-propelled grenades gleamed like polished copper.

Breaking open the rifle-style launcher, she plucked out the spent casing. Tossing it over the side, she pushed one of the fat little cylinders into the open maw of the barrel. She snapped the weapon closed and put the other grenade in her pocket. Standing up to her ankles in chilly water, she adjusted her sunglasses. She ignored the blood trickling down her chest.

The first grenade had done a good job of killing the old boat. Both halves had slipped below the waves in short order. What remained to be seen was whether there were any survivors.

It's not as if I snuck up on you. If your Secret Service man was any good, I'm sure he was ready for me. The pain of her wounds was proof of that. The agent had been more than ready for her.

Seconds ticked by. Doris began to get lightheaded. Wreckage started bobbing to the surface of the rolling ocean. *No engine. No oil slick. I'm glad to see that our intell was right about something. Not that it would have mattered.*

A bank of clouds moved to cast a dark, sinister shadow over the rolling waves. Doris couldn't afford to wait much longer. *Losing blood. Got to get a dressing on that shoulder and get back.*

Aiming the large bore just to the left of where she thought the old boat had gone down, she pulled the trigger. The launcher whumped. The grenade sped away on a flaming arc, disappearing beneath the waves without a ripple. The high-powered explosive round blew a column of water 70 feet into the air.

Doris ignored the sudden rain shower as the displaced water came crashing down. Loading the second grenade, she aimed it to the right of where the sloop had gone down and fired. She was showered with more water as the explosive detonated.

Settling back into the seat, Doris flinched. *When did I take off the seatbelt? I don't remember it. Shock must be getting worse.*

Tossing the launcher into the sea, she took a deep breath. Feeling around, she searched for a first aid kit. When she didn't find one, she sat back to catch her breath. *Just like old times.*

She nudged the throttles forward. Steering conservatively, she reached into her coat pocket for her phone. Flicking it to the open and "on" position, she held it up to her ear.

"I'm sorry, but you can't use me right now. I have been damaged. Please take me to an authorized factory technician so that I can be repaired."

Doris looked incredulously at the phone before throwing it overboard. "Just like old times."

Sunday
June 1, 2014
Off The Maryland Coast
1:25 P.M. EDT

Andrew exploded to the surface. Screaming with the effort to pull air into his starved lungs, he kicked desperately at the green-blue water. The shredded life jacket floated away from his thrashing body. Towing his wife behind him, he hoisted her head and shoulders out of the water. "Come on, wake up!" he shouted, scissoring his legs to keep some buoyancy.

He struggled to peel the remains of Corin's life jacket from the front of her body, gagging when a strip of her smooth ebony skin came away with a swatch of burnt plastic and the crusted remains of her jumpsuit. He moaned with horror as the water around him darkened with her blood.

"I'm sorry!" Bile rose in his throat as he struggled to keep her head above the undulating waves. The matted curls of her hair clung to his face, filling his nostrils with the stink of charred flesh and burned hair.

"No! Come on, wake up! I need you!" Andrew screamed, barely able to hear himself. Holding her up with all his strength, he couldn't think of anything else to do. When her face lolled towards him, he vomited at the sight of the ruined flesh. Her eyes conveyed total surprise through a milky film of death. He lost control of himself and sank beneath the waves.

Fear clutched at his guts when her limp body slid past him, gliding slowly toward the dark depths of the ocean. He flailed through the murky cloud of vomit, ignoring the tunnel vision that gripped him, straining to reach for the descending corpse of his wife. The last thing he saw as he blacked out from lack of oxygen was the upturned face of his wife, with whom he had shared everything for ten years. Her mouth hung open, accentuating the astonishment in her wide-open eyes.

Sunday
June 1, 2014
Aboard the *Golden Hinde*
Off The Maryland Coast
1:27 P.M. EDT

Fisk stood at the starboard rail watching the crew retrieve Doris. His windbreaker flapped in the breeze as he looked down at the tied speedboat. Two of the yacht's crew were helping her. The crimson streaks along the rear of the passenger compartment told a grim story.

In all the time he had known her, Doris had never been injured. *You never get hurt.* Something about the thought triggered a memory fragment. White light danced on the edge of his vision, causing him to grip the rail. A searing hot flash was followed by an image.

Rain. The inside of a burned-out building. Doris with her shirt peeled open. Camouflage fabric. Left shoulder. Stitches. Blood. The expected headache drove the memory away, causing him to take a sharp breath.

"How's it coming?" Griff asked, moving to stand beside him.

He pointed at the speedboat. "Blood. Looks messy."

"Don't sweat it. She's too mean to die."

"Has she been hurt like this before? Shot, I mean?" Fisk turned his back on the crew as they brought Doris up the gangway.

Griff walked around Fisk to lend a hand. "Yes, but that was a long time ago. She's gotten much better since then." He didn't have time for concern, though he now understood what drove Doris to such worry. *They warned us that the stress could break you.*

"Bite me," Doris growled when she realized that Griff was making fun of her.

385

Sunday
June 1, 2014
Aboard the *Golden Hinde*
Off The Maryland Coast
1:40 P.M. EDT

"It's done," Griff said as he entered the salon.

"Best $20,000 I ever spent," Doris drawled from the couch. Beside her, another of Fisk's many confederates finished pulling the last stitch through. The knobby little wound wept serum and bright blood as it was closed. An old scar from a similar bullet wound resided slightly higher on her bare shoulder.

Griff moved to a nearby chair. "Where's Fisk?"

"Been and gone. Are we done?" She sounded groggy from the drugs she'd been given.

"Straight up. Only took three ticks to close the exit wound. I'll be back in a while to check your pain," the paramedic said in an Aussie accent as he packed his things and left.

When he was gone, Doris worked her shoulder experimentally. "Just like old times." She grimaced, wiggling her fingers despite the pain.

Griff snorted. "Yeah, right. We didn't have Dr. Hathaway's miracle rejuvenator back then. Once he gets done, you'll be as good as new."

Doris pulled on a clean shirt. Buttoning it, she looked across the room where the leather trenchcoat lay in a bundle, soaked through with seawater. Tiny crimson beads fell from it to the floor.

"Tell me." She had to sit up straight to avoid pulling the sutures in her back.

"Looks like you got away clean. We're tracking the Coast Guard helo, and it's ten minutes out. More than enough time for us to be gone. Let's just hope there were no survivors."

"I used three grenades. One on the boat, two in the water. Just a little something I had laying around." She tittered.

"Sounds good to me. I've got my people working on a new contingency. When we get back to shore--"

"Tell me what happened. I need to know," she insisted as the painkillers robbed her of strength.

"I had no idea--"

"Get to the point before I pass out," Doris slurred.

"I don't know what to say. It had to be the stress. He just wasn't himself. It only lasted for a second, you know?"

"Did he say anything?" She wobbled as her motor control failed.

"No. I'm not sure if he was trying to speak. His eyes. It was him looking right at me. He nodded like he understood me."

"W-what did you say?" Doris leaned over on her good shoulder, fighting the drugs.

"I told him it was okay. I told him that we were almost done. What else was I supposed to say? It was him. Jason. I only hope..." He stopped as Doris passed out.

Sunday
June 1, 2014
The Fisk Residence
Chesapeake Bay, Maryland
4:50 P.M. EDT

Fisk stopped at the top of the landing to dismiss his guardian. "I'll be fine."

"Can I get you anything?" the other man asked, halfway up the stairs.

"Let me know when Doris comes around. I have to make a call. Then I'm going to change my clothes." The guard nodded, turning to go back down stairs.

Fisk entered the den and closed the door. Walking slowly across the thick carpet to the computer cabinet, he stopped. *Am I really going to do this? It's been so long since I talked to them.*

Opening the cabinet, he slid out the keyboard tray. *We have bigger fish to try, but I just have to know.* Touching the keys lightly, he initiated the secured comm link. Enola's European accent came through crisply.

"Fisk, darling. How are you?"

Walking back to his desk, he sat down. "I'm doing well, all things considered. I don't mean to cut the pleasantries, but..."

"Business. Always business. Very well. We've become quite worried about this turn of events with Andrew Brown. What can you tell me?"

"We can handle it. And before you say it, I do know just how much of a problem this is. First Walter Carns, and now this. Fortunately, Brown's number two has no scruples. Whatever Madeline wants, he'll give her."

"I presume that Mr. Brown is no longer with us?"

"That's right. You'll get the details on the 72-hour update."

"Ah. Tell me more." The older woman's tone was laced with skepticism and mischief.

"There are complications, which is why I called."

"Do tell." Her tone was soothing.

"Something went wrong on our end. Brown had a shortwave radio on his boat. For some reason, we failed to jam it. That's all I know. I just wanted you to hear it from me."

"Commendable. This will not sit well with the committee. You know what they may prescribe."

Fisk nodded. "That has crossed my mind."

"They'll want to speak to you in person. I have no doubt about that. Do you think you can satisfy their concerns?"

"I don't know. I always knew that Phase One would be harder to wrap up than it was to start. Give me one week and I can be much more specific."

"You'll have to give up your comm before they permit you to visit. If they decide against you, the matter will be settled then and there."

The cold undertones in her voice left no doubt in Fisk's mind about what she meant. "I understand." The skin on the back of his neck crawled with goose pimples.

"The committee knows that you intend to resign in two weeks. We've already set the date for the removal of your comms and short range tracker, haven't we?"

"Yes," Fisk replied with a sinking sensation. *What did I expect?*

"Have no fear. Things may yet work out."

"You know something that I don't?"

"Always, my dear. Always. You sound so very tired. Are you sure you're all right?"

"Nothing that a few weeks in Bermuda won't fix." He gave the computer a mocking salute to indicate his acceptance. *Not going to get anything out of you, am I?*

"Please don't be cross with me. You know how this works. If I could tell you more, I would," the old woman pleaded softly.

"Hey, what are you getting at?" He straightened in his chair. *I've missed something.*

"Doris is quite concerned for your safety, did you know?" Though phrased as a question, he could hear the iron in the statement.

"She is a remarkable woman. Worrying about me is just what she does. Are you trying to tell me something?"

"Yes, darling. She and I, we've kept it to ourselves. We're both quite worried about you."

"Which means?" He listened closely to the tone of her voice. *This can't be good.*

"There are only six of us left, out of an original dozen. Old age has thinned our ranks, as well as made some of us impatient to see our efforts bear fruit. Do you understand what that means?"

Fisk nodded. *Telling me without telling me. Warning me.* "The closer we get to completing the plan, the more likely it is that you'll all decide to have me killed because of the risk I represent." *I could have found a better way to say that.*

"When Congress investigates this administration, they won't hesitate to subpoena you, your records, and anybody that ever worked for or with you. The plan is quite specific about what happens in that event. Neither one of us wants that. Your only chance to avoid that fate is to stay out of trouble. I'll grant you that you might not have been able to handle Walter Carns any better, but the others just won't see the Andrew Brown situation that way."

"Let's not start composing my obituary just yet. Today's not over, and I still have a few tricks up my sleeve."

"Really? I should have known better. Nothing stops you, does it?"

"How do you cope?"

"Two things," the Founder admitted with a sigh. "First, a deep conviction that, so long as there is one good citizen left in this country, all is not lost. Second, I think of the man who came to us all those years ago. I think of his courage, and his vision. I think almost daily of his sacrifice and what he may ultimately have to lose in order to achieve our goals."

Fisk nodded. *You're talking about me, but I get the feeling you're also talking about somebody else.*

"As you know, there will be a vote. It will come while you are in the clinic, having your implants removed. Majority rule. If they judge you negatively, I expect they will rely on your good graces to bring the matter to a close."

"I'm supposed to go quietly?" He was surprised at the outrage he felt.

"Not if I have anything to say about it. Doris and I have an understanding. We are working together to ensure that you will be spared. It's just not right that a group of brooding old men should--"

"Suppose I come see them now? Out of the blue?" he asked, arching an eyebrow.

"They won't let you near them as long as you are capable of resisting. As much as it would please me to see you confront them, you'd better not. The comm implant gives you direct access to 60 percent of your network. Your followers would likely come to your aid if you called them."

Fisk went back to his room to change into a suit and tie. Stopping just long enough to use an automatic shoe buffer, he considered his options. *Simple. Evade Madeline's executioners, and sidestep the Founders. We don't dare try to recruit Brown's replacement. Or do we?*

The Fisk persona had been built around Jason Cutter's natural tenacity. He was, quite literally, incapable of giving up. Even now, his agile mind sought new options.

Checking to make sure his comm implant was on, Fisk cleared his throat. "Tell me about the number two man at Treasury."

Through the implant, the advisor quoted from memory. "Alexander Kirsov, Undersecretary of the Treasury. Madeline appointed him, over your objections. He's a party crossover. More?"

"No." He switched off the shoe buffer. In the current political climate, party crossovers were common. Republicans and Democrats switched labels and affiliations as necessity dictated. *Kirsov will have no loyalty to anyone. His version of the "right thing" means making the right policy decision for the right price.*

Charging down the wide staircase to the ground level, he was surprised when a trio of EMTs came in through the front door escorted by two plainclothed protectors.

"What happened?" he asked the closest guardian as he reached the bottom of the stairs.

"We're here for Doris," the man said. He was carrying one of the EMTs' bulky rescue cases.

Fisk followed the procession.

Jasmine appeared through the kitchen's side door. "There he is. Come on." Pulling Christopher through the door, she forced him between Fisk and the paramedics.

"What's going on?" Fisk demanded. Something about the situation was wrong. Jasmine was somehow troubled. He could feel it.

"They're going to move her to the Adkins-Hathaway clinic," Jasmine replied. *Calm. Be calm.*

"Hey, let's hit the road." Christopher smiled uneasily. *This is getting weird.*

"Out of my way, people," Fisk said as he began to force his way past Christopher. *What's going on here?* "Has anyone talked to Griff about this? Jaz, don't let them take her anywhere until I get confirmation from Griff." The sudden need to protect Doris caused him to hesitate in midstride. *She's in good hands. Why am I worried?*

"I already talked to Griff. He's the one who called them." Jasmine blocked the doorway leading to the kitchen. She held a small beeper unit in one hand. Her thumb mashed down on its buttons repeatedly. *Come on, where are you people? Hathaway said we can't let Fisk too close to Doris while she's wounded. The combination of stress and sympathy might undo him.* Seconds later, the hallway behind Fisk filled with armed guards.

Jasmine thrust out her chin as she confronted her boss. "Sir, I don't have to remind you what trauma does to a person's composure, do I? Your mind won't be on what you're doing, it'll be on what you saw. Trust me, if you want to pull off the rest of today's charade, you'll need all your focus."

"What?" Fisk looked over his shoulder. Remembering that his comm implant was still on, he pulled himself up short. *Patience and cooperation. Whatever is going on here will reveal itself soon enough.* "You're right. I just got carried away." He touched the knot of his tie. *Patience and cooperation. We're all keyed up. That must be it.*

"It'll be okay," Jasmine assured him, stunned at his sudden acquiescence. *What? It's not like you to give up so easily. Doris must be right.*

"It's okay, guys." Fisk waved off the guards. Jasmine smiled at them, nodding. Within seconds, they were gone. Fisk watched the last man holster a pistol as he left.

"Well, since we seem to be very involved in charades just now, call Ms. Harper. Tell her I want to take her out." *When in doubt, stir the pot and see what happens.*

"Is that wise?" Jasmine could feel her own composure slipping. *What are you up to now?*

"This thing with Brown is all wrong. Things are going to get harder from now on, I can feel it. If I don't slam-dunk her now, she might have second thoughts later on. Is that spare phone in my briefcase?"

"Right." She couldn't fault him for cracking the whip. *That's more like it. Punish me by tossing me a curve ball. I can take it. Keeping you on profile is going to be harder than I thought, though. I hope Doris knows what she's doing.*

"I'll make the call. Just remember, she's a Phase Two asset, and she's got a thing for you. It affects how she thinks. Don't do anything stupid."

"You've been talking to Griff, again," Fisk replied, shaking a finger at her as he turned.

Jasmine pointed sternly at the door.

"Going." He quietly followed Christopher out to the limo.

"I have instructions to take you to your office," the driver said as he got in.

"Fine." Fisk raised the privacy shield. *I need some time to think.*

The big limo rocked on its reinforced suspension as it accelerated into traffic. Riding in silence, Fisk took his time with the seatbelt. *I feel like somebody just walked on my grave.* Buckled in, he laid his head back and thought about everything that had happened. In his mind's eye, the face of a man materialized--a man that he knew. *It's the same face in that photo fragment in my wallet.*

"How's Doris?" he asked after five minutes.

The tiny voice that came over the implant was female. "She's going to be fine. They've got her in the ambulance now. She was shot twice. No real damage. That leather coat she always wears may have saved her life."

He nodded. The image of Doris that sprang up in his mind was clad in the black leather coat. *I don't think I've ever seen her without it.* Smiling, he closed his eyes.

"That coat. Where did she ever come up with something that dramatic?" Opening his mind to it, he thought about the leather and the way it smelled after it got wet.

"Don't know. I'll make a note of it and get back to you." The woman's voice was neutral, leading him to believe that she really didn't know.

"No, that's quite all right. It reminds me of one of those things you used to see in the old Cold War spy movies."

Sunday
June 1, 2014
The Fisk Residence
Chesapeake Bay, Maryland
5:10 P.M. EDT

Doris waited patiently while the house buzzed with activity.

Jasmine came into the kitchen. "He's gone. The tracker in the car says he's on the expressway now." Closing the door, she walked over to sit at the table with Doris.

"Thanks. I appreciate it." Doris sipped from a glass of juice.

"You know what you're doing?"

"Making it up as I go along," Doris replied through her pain. "I need to drop out of sight for a while. I have to assume that my movements will be reported, so I need *them* to think that I'm on my way to the clinic."

"I'm not the only one who files movement reports. The best you can hope for is a few hours." Jasmine swept a long strand of hair out of her face.

"I'll only need five or six hours, tops."

"What do I do now?"

"Wait for them to call. When they tell you they want his comm removed ahead of schedule, protest. Tell them whatever you want. Fight it before you give in. If we get lucky, they might become angry and make the appointment for you. Either way, I get what I want." Doris tried to find a more comfortable position to avoid pulling stitches.

"Okay."

Doris gritted her teeth as she stood. "One more thing. Talk to Griff before he leaves the house. Tell him that I want an extra man put on Fisk for the next 24 hours."

"He's in on it, then?" Jasmine cocked an eyebrow.

"Yes, he knows," the other woman replied as she tested the limits of her mobility.

"How far do I trust him?" Despite their long association, she had only recent gotten to know Doris. Griff was still an enigma to her.

"All the way."

"I thought you didn't get along with him." Jasmine glanced at the closed door.

"I don't," Doris muttered as she reached for her coat.

Sunday
June 1, 2014
The White House
Office of the President
Washington, D.C.
5:19 P.M. EDT

"You heard me. Find Stanley another job," Madeline told her Chief of Staff.

"Do you remember who his father is? He bankrolls half the races back home. We can't just boot him," Larry replied, clearly exasperated.

"We can, and we will. The man is positively helpless. He can't say no to anyone and he's always bogged down in other people's meetings. He's never around when I want him. You should see the backlog I have to deal with." Her favorite pen turned a slow, steady arc between her nervous fingers. On the small desk in front of her, a stack of papers sat unread while a clock ticked loudly.

Hodgekiss turned to make sure the door was closed. "We can get him an assistant, somebody to carry the load. You know, one of those eager beavers from the party office. Those kids are always looking to make a name for themselves." Larry hated taking calls from the "special" phone at home. They upset his wife, making him hate his job.

"I want Josephine Harper, and I want her to start tomorrow." Promoting Josephine would fulfill two goals. *She's capable, and I want to know what her connection to Fisk is.*

"Come on. She's a nobody. I think you're just trying to play her to find out why Fisk has taken an interest in her."

"Don't be ridiculous," Madeline replied scornfully.

"He was buttering her bread, making her feel important so that she would work harder. Even he knows that sometimes you've got to throw the little people a bone."

The logic, as convincing at it sounded, made the bile rise in her throat. *He went out to dinner with her and he didn't sleep with her. He pulled strings to get her an office and he didn't sleep with her. There must be something going on that I don't know about. There has to be.*

"Okay. Let me see what I can do. I have lunch tomorrow with some guys from the State Department. I just know they're going to hit me up for access. I'll see if I can work it in."

"I don't care if they make him the ambassador to France. Stanley follows orders better than he gives them. Just get him out of my hair." She stopped twirling her pen.

"Okay. Look, I have to go. The kids have a soccer match tonight, and we need to be there an hour early to get through security."

"Thank you. I'm sorry to bother you on your day off. I've just got a lot on my mind today. You've been a help. Have a good night."

As she put the receiver down, the phone beeped to announce an incoming call. She glanced at the caller ID. "What do you want, Metz?"

"It's Fisk. His people called Josephine Harper."

"When?" Madeline face suddenly flushed.

"Just a few minutes ago. She wasn't home. Her machine picked it up. Before you ask, our people said she's gone shopping."

"Did the message say what he wanted?" Her blood pressure began to settle.

"No." He paused to speak to somebody with his hand over the receiver. "Hey, we just got news. There's a guy on the line from Coast Guard. Says his post got a distress call from one of the people in the protective unit. Looks like Brown's boat went down."

"He did it." She drew in a long slow breath.

"Did what? You had Fisk kill Brown?" Metz nearly bit his tongue.

"Calm down. Listen carefully, we don't have a lot of time."

"You knew this was going to happen? Why didn't you tell me? I need at least 24 hours notice before--"

"Shut up and listen. I don't have to check in with you every time I want to do something. You know how our arrangement works. This was a spur-of-the-moment thing. You've got to think on your feet."

"I've got to go. I have to stop this from getting out. Horn doesn't like you. We're all screwed if he gets his teeth into this."

"Contain it. Call in all your favors. I don't want to hear a single word from the Director of Homeland Security for at least 24 hours. Whatever Fisk has done, we need time to assess and exploit. Do you understand me?"

"Yeah." Metz cupped his hand over the receiver to issue another order.

Madeline stopped, considering her options. "I have staff briefings for the rest of the day. Purge this conversation from the recorders and amend your logs. We never had this discussion."

"Just one thing. If he really did this, Fisk is just too dangerous. I can't let him--"

"I know. You have my blessing." Madeline chuckled.

"Really? That's great. Just so we understand each other, I'm going to do this my way. I'll need time to sniff out the facts--"

"I know. With any luck, he made a mistake that you can exploit. If not, we will just have to make the best of it. Losing Andrew Brown is a tragedy. If we play our cards right, we can generate enough sympathy to use as we see fit."

"If he's got the brass to do a Cabinet officer, he won't think twice about doing you or me. The first chance I get, he's going down."

Sunday
June 1, 2014
Concourse
Congressional Zone
Washington, D.C.
7:15 P.M. EDT

Fisk looked up at the dark sky, watching a jet liner pass over. Around him, the customers at the sidewalk cafe enjoyed each other's company. The nightlife was brisk, and vibrant.

Christopher and a second bodyguard sat at a nearby table. As the driver looked around, he was not surprised to see other protective professionals blending in. Checking his watch again, he read a paper and drank coffee.

A male voice spoke over Fisk's implant. "News. Our people have confirmed that somebody with a lot of juice is sitting on the call that Brown's bodyguard made to the Coast Guard. The word from Cosmo is that two of their sims have fingered Metz as the operator."

Fisk shivered. "More," he subvocalized, flipping the paper over to scan the next page.

"We've got new leads on the SWAT cops that tried to cook you," a female voice replied. "We've backtracked money from six different shell accounts to more than a dozen others. The bad news is it looks like the accounts belong to a sanctioned money transfer group. In all cases, the contact is Metz."

"Wow," Fisk muttered, careful to appear interested in his paper.

The woman continued. "That's the short version. We've got our best crackers working the trail now. These are really old accounts, too. The kind of thing that gets passed around, you know?"

"Mm." Fisk paused at the financial page.

Griff came on line. "The Coast Guard is having a brain cramp. They have Secret Service people running all over the place. We've got photo confirmation that Metz is involved. We got him live and direct, giving some guy from Homeland a real song and dance."

"What does that mean?" He squinted at the tiny print for effect.

"Metz is trolling. She sent him out to look for anything that could implicate you."

"Good for him." Fisk grimaced and turned to the next page.

"Just keep your eyes open, will you? Our stuff is nearly two hours old. If Metz is really on her team, you can bet that he's just itching to take another shot at you. Whatever she promised him, it must be one heck of a reward."

A new male voice broke into the conversation. "The E-3 group has completed its projection. We recommend a press leak as soon as possible. If Metz is left in control of the situation, he can fabricate enough grade-two evidentiaries to implicate you."

"What's the rasher on that?" Griff demanded.

"Forty-four percent, climbing by the hour."

"Tell the group that I'll come down as soon as I get off this line," Griff ordered.

"Roger." The man left the line.

"Don't sweat this," Griff told Fisk as he made some notes. "Doris is safe and snug at the clinic and we've got things under control. Ms. Harper has been picked up and should be at your location in the next 15 minutes. Recruit her and come home. Okay?"

"Mm." Fisk nodded at a passing waiter, who refilled his coffee cup.

Overwatch reported in as Fisk raised his drink. "We've got Speaker Langsford on video. He's in the Opera House, at a pay phone. Looks like they're having an intermission. He's checking with your service to see where you are. Estimate better than 60 percent that he will come to you."

Fisk looked sideways at Christopher and his companion, signaling "company." Both men continued to chat pleasantly as they began to look around.

"Lee must have gotten to him," Fisk speculated as he folded the paper.

Earlier that day, Fisk had instructed Jarrett Lee to approach Speaker Langsford with a leak as a hedge against fallout resulting from the news of Brown's death. Fisk's advisors were convinced that the stock markets and other financial sectors might suffer when the news got out.

The plan was simple. By tipping Langsford to the President's hidden agenda, he would set off an internal party struggle. In the end, she would have to share any adulation that came from a successful debt reconstruction. The short-term benefit, which had a more direct bearing on Fisk, was that Langsford and his political cronies would provide a great show of support for their president in her time of grief. Combined, they would ensure that the final elements of Fisk's own agenda were put into place and left undetected. The resulting flurry of activity might even work to his advantage as he tried to extricate himself from the tangled web that he'd made.

"I've got the call in. We can fudge Ms. Harper's arrival. You probably won't need very long with His Nibs," Griff said.

Overwatch came back on the line. "We have a visual on Lee. He's in the lounge at the Opera House with his wife. He must have run into Langsford."

"Yeah. Great. Lee probably told him you might be in the area."

Fisk nodded. Within minutes, Langsford ambled around the nearby corner, struggling to light his pipe. Fisk watched him out of the corner of his eye. The wily old politician strolled along as if he had no worries. Fisk knew the tactic well.

"Mr. Speaker. What brings you out at this hour?"

"The wife and the opera." He put away his lighter, jerking a thumb at the Opera House as he ambled over to sit with Fisk.

"Mrs. Langsford is enjoying her season tickets, eh?" Fisk asked good-naturedly.

"Yes. If you ever do that again, I'll have to rethink the nature of our relationship." Langsford grasped his pipe and shook it at Fisk.

"I think I owed you for sticking me with a certain somebody's campaign reorg. Ten weeks of misery and stupidity, all for nothing. If memory serves, the opera season is ten weeks long."

"Mm. Quite right." Langsford bowed his head in defeat. "That's not why I'm here."

"Talk to me." Fisk leaned back.

"I just had the most interesting conversation. After I calmed down,

I decided to go looking for you." The Speaker stroked the bowl of his pipe with a gnarled thumb.

"You found me." *Good work, Jarrett. I asked for a leak and I got one.*

"Oh, that's rich. Still, I suppose you've got your loyalties. All right, here it is. I know about her plans to recall the currency. I know it's part of a larger plan that she's developed to solve the national debt. I know that Secretary Brown is, shall we say, on the outs. Lastly, I know that she's had you running errands."

Fisk nodded.

"You're not denying it?"

Fisk put down his cup. "I know better than to try to outfox you. You've been at this since before I was born. It's true. All of it. Andy jumped the gun with his press conference, and it's really not going to help when she finds out that you're on to her." The silent offer of a deal was there, waiting for the Speaker to take, if he wanted it. *Which, of course, is why you're here.*

"Her secret seems pretty safe so far. My source is loyal to Brown, and feels like the man's getting a raw deal. I can't understand for the life of me why Brown spilled his guts like that."

Langsford reached for his lighter as Fisk let the remark pass. *Jarrett is going to laugh when he finds out that Langsford didn't name him.*

"He must have had a price. What did he want for his confession?"

Langsford successfully fired his pipe as he considered. "The usual." *Which he's not going to get.*

"Rats off a sinking ship. I don't know why he thought he could get something out of you for that. I assume you blew him off." Fisk assumed a more guarded posture.

"Told him I'd see what I could do." Langsford grimaced.

"Okay. Let's talk," Fisk replied, leaning in closer.

Langsford was legendary for being direct. "I want in before the Senate banking committee gets a whiff of this. If she can pull this off--I mean really do it--anyone close to her would be able to write their own ticket. The prestige alone would guarantee that our party held both houses for the next 20 years." Looking directly at Fisk through the smoke, he smiled thinly.

"It's big stuff, all right. I'd really like to help you. You've done a lot for me, and I'd like to return the favor. She's played this one very close. The currency recall thing was there when she took office. It's been quietly passed from one administration to the next. You know?"

"Heard the rumors," Langsford conceded.

"Believe me, this is the real deal. A lot of people have been turned into fertilizer to keep this thing quiet." Fisk licked his lips in a show of controlled fear.

"Carns?" Langsford speculated with a raised eyebrow.

Langsford had been a venture capitalist before entering politics. He had known Carns as a trendsetter in the world of high finance. His accidental death was still talked about in some circles. Langsford didn't believe in accidents that took the lives of wealthy and influential people.

Fisk lowered his voice. "Carns. You still want in?"

Langsford smoked for a full minute while he weighed his options. "She's got a plan? A real plan? Infrastructure, contingencies, the whole thing?" He could feel himself drawn to President Hill's conspiracy.

"The whole thing. I've seen it," Fisk confirmed.

"When can I get an introduction? More importantly, how do I avoid getting burned?" He tapped the ashes from his spent pipe into an ashtray.

"Let's trade insurance policies." Fisk felt his heart beat faster.

"Such as?" Langsford began to look around, nervous about such a public discussion.

"I want out. You want in. We trade places," Fisk replied, spreading his hands.

"That hardly seems fair. She's a very dangerous woman."

"You have no idea. Still, you want to play, you've got to pay."

"What's your share in all this?" Langsford asked as he silently marveled at Fisk's candor.

"I made my millions. I helped drag a political party back from the edge, and I even got to make a president. All I need to do now is live long enough to enjoy it."

"That's all you want?"

"That's all I want. I'll have my courier bring you a package."

"When?" Langsford considered having another smoke.

"In a few weeks." Fisk ran his finger around the rim of his coffee cup. "Once your inner circle has had a chance to look it over, your next move should be obvious--be ready to back her up or hang her out to dry, as circumstances dictate. If she fails, make sure that nobody calls me."

"I can arrange that. Our party owes you a lot. The only thing we can't account for will be the media. As long as you stay off the beaten path for a few years, you should be fine."

"That's exactly what I had in mind."

"One last thing. My source?" The Speaker began to stuff his pipe.

Fisk appeared to give it some thought. "Pull him in close. Butter him up and gain his trust. Use him as a conduit. Whatever he does, it might be worth your time to have an insider's perspective."

"Mm. You are one sneaky fellow," Langsford chuckled as the pipe caught.

Sunday
June 1, 2014
Arboretum
The Green Room
Congressional Zone
Washington, D.C.
9:26 P.M. EDT

Fisk sat with Josephine in one of the quiet little nooks of the Green Room's arboretum. Sipping from a tall fluted glass of champagne, he was looking up at the night sky when she interrupted his reverie.

"I don't know why I came. Believe me, I don't normally do this sort of thing." *I usually don't get a second date, either.*

Fisk looked back at her, taking a moment to admire the depths of her hazel eyes. "I, for one, am glad that you did. As it turns out, I have a lot to celebrate." He reached over to gently touch the rim of his glass to hers.

"Something to do with Speaker of the House Roger Langsford?" She had seen the Speaker walking away from Fisk when the car dropped her off.

"You know him?" he countered, cocking an eyebrow with interest.

"Kind of. He does his own scheduling. He calls me, I mean. He has a hard time keeping appointment secretaries. The rumor is that he yells at them until they get fed up and quit."

"I've heard that." He nodded sagely as Josephine put down her glass.

"What are you celebrating? Did you overthrow somebody's government or something?" Relaxed, she felt good about joking with him.

"What makes you say that?" He was hard pressed not to laugh at her choice of words. *Overthrow? You don't know the half of it. Yet.*

"You could be anywhere, with anybody. What made you choose

me?" Her tone and the way she had warmed up to him told Fisk all he needed to know about her attraction to him.

"Ever hear of harmonic convergence?" he asked, recalling that she had an interest in metaphysics.

"You know I have, which means now I've really got to know. Tell me, what happened today that put you in such a celebratory mood?"

"My day started with defeat. It's now ending in success. I can think of no better reason to celebrate."

"That would have to be some kind of defeat for a man like you."

"I'm not known for small defeats," Fisk replied, saluting the remark with his glass.

"Wise words, worthy of celebration." She brushed a hand over her blouse.

As Fisk spoke, the shadow of something very real to him moved over his consciousness. An overpowering urge made him turn off the comm implant in his mouth. "You're right. I didn't ask you out by accident. Getting a date is the last thing I have to worry about."

Josephine sat quietly for a single heartbeat, unsure of what he meant. *No wonder I never get a second date. I can't tell whether I'm being built up or put down.*

Sensing her fear, he reached out to take her hand. "I need your help. You're the right person at the right place and time. If you weren't, we wouldn't be having this conversation." The heat of his determination burned in his eyes.

Josephine appeared to wilt under the intensity of his gaze. "What can I possibly do for you?" *Something big is happening here.*

"I want you to help me save our country." He squeezed her hand.

**Sunday
June 1, 2014
Arboretum
The Green Room
Congressional Zone
Washington, D.C.
9:52 P.M. EDT**

"That's some story." Josephine looked at Fisk with a completely new understanding. Never one to question authority too closely, she was a product of her generation. Sitting there next to the very embodiment of what she considered to be real power, the world seemed to stop.

"I wish it were only a story. Somebody had to do something. Armed rebellion isn't the answer, so long as it can be avoided."

"Suppose the corrupt people you've put into office are smarter than all that?" she asked.

"A statistical possibility, but not one that's very likely. Especially not with this president." *Madeline doesn't know the meaning of conservative action.*

"Is that where I fit in?" Josephine nodded. *You make it sound so simple.*

"It sounds unbelievable--but we're only going to succeed if we put the right people in the right places. Sometimes we get lucky. Sometimes we have to bunt and hope for the best."

"Lucky?" She picked up her glass, rocking it playfully between her fingers.

"You're everything we need." He touched the gilt lamp at the center of the table. "More champagne." Looking at her, he smiled. *Her open-mindedness surprises me.* The fact that he could speak so openly and honestly with her about his plans thrilled him more than he would have admitted.

"I still don't understand. What can I do?" The question was

Justin Oldham

reflected in her eyes. *Sure, things are out of kilter these days, but I'm just one person. It's not as if any of us could really stop these people. They're too powerful.*

"Before I was a political strategist, I was somebody else. With help, I was able to become who I am today. I want to give you the same kind of help so that you can become a part of my organization." The words rolled off his tongue easily, letting him know that the specter in the back of his mind agreed.

"What exactly does all that mean?" *You make me want to trust you. Spell it out for me. Make me understand what it is you want from me.*

"All corrupt governments have one thing in common. It's only a matter of time before they overstep their legal authorities and reach for the only thing they don't have--total power."

"I understand all that. They're bad people doing bad things. If nobody's doing anything about it now, what makes you so sure anybody will care if they take over tomorrow, or ten years from now?"

"If you give somebody enough time, they'll get used to just about anything. Traffic noise outside their apartment, or bad food, it doesn't matter. Everybody adapts. Our greatest fear is that we're all going to wake up one morning and find out the hard way that we got used to living without our freedom."

"There are so few of you. What makes you think you can succeed?" Taking up her empty glass, she lightly touched it to his to dispel any hostility. *I know I'm starved for attention, but this is really pushing it. I've listened to Mom and Dad complain about this sort of thing for a long time--the loss of personal freedoms, the terrorist wars, the national debt. Is that what makes me want to do this? For them? Or am I just going along because I feel something for this man?*

Speechless, Fisk paused. *Ironic. You believe me, but you don't believe that I can succeed.* "Somebody's got to make the effort."

A waiter came with two fresh flutes of champagne. Quickly and silently, the man gathered the empty glasses and vanished.

"I can't spy on her. I don't even know her that well. Why would she trust me when she won't trust you?"

"The President *will* trust you. When we're done enhancing your position, she might even confide in you." He raised his glass to chin level. *Even a tyrant needs somebody to confide in.*

He continued, "Within another few years, our economy will be under direct attack. The debt negotiations will make us or break us in the eyes of the world. Nobody's afraid of the U.S. Army anymore. Ten years of hunting terror groups has changed the way our neighbors look at us. Last time I checked, Panama's ambassador to the UN was the only one who had anything good to say about us." *I'm not even going to mention China.* Even he had to admit that America's decade-long battle against global terror was giving the Chinese a free shot at the Asian subcontinent that they couldn't afford to pass up.

"Don't forget China," she replied, raising her glass. "It's weird to think that you're behind some of the failures in our government. How does that make you feel?" She took his hand.

Looking into her eyes, he got the impression that her heart going out to him. *She knows.* He pulled away gently. "It makes me feel responsible. Sometimes it makes me feel guilty. Before you ask, the answer is no, I don't think there's another way. Ambition can't be stopped, corrupt ambition least of all. The good men and women among us are simply outnumbered. We don't dare start a revolution because our side can't win. All we can do is feed their need for power and hope that it's enough to ruin them." *Our feeble attempts to start a guerilla cadre won't amount to much if things get that far.*

"You could be a very famous man some day. Just think, you could be the next George Washington."

"I'm already famous. Besides, this isn't something that any one person can take credit for, even if it works. There are thousands of us. People just like you. We're all trying to make this happen because we don't want the alternative."

"Reform, status quo, or revolution," she responded.

"I'm going to be gone for the next couple of days. We can talk some more about all this later. For now, let's just enjoy the stars." He tipped back his glass, draining the last of the champagne. Looking up through the clear dome of the arboretum, he was glad to change the subject.

"I like the way you think. Just tell me one thing." Josephine moved in a little closer.

"Like what?"

"What happens to you after you get out of this business?" Her tone suggested that she was looking for something more.

"What makes you think I'm on my way out?" he asked, noting how Josephine's eyes betrayed her thoughts. *Very perceptive.*

"The way you describe all this to me. The way you describe my part in it, it's as if you're putting the finishing touches on a house, you know? My feeling is that you're almost finished with all these behind-the-scenes things." The slight tilt of her head told him that she was searching for the right words.

Fisk closed his eyes, nodding slowly, grasping her hand. "Not a bad analogy. It does remind me of building a house of cards."

"I saw a performer do that once, in Las Vegas. Everybody thought it would fall down, but it didn't. You know why? Because the magician took his time and he was careful about what he did." Smiling, she squeezed his hand lightly.

"You know what? This isn't as hard as I thought it might be."

"Speak for yourself. I'm still freaked."

"It doesn't show."

"I get to see more than people think. I may be quiet, but I'm not slow." She tossed her long hair aside.

Fisk paused to take a phone from his coat pocket. "That's why I'm here. If you're really up for this, I have something for you." Sliding the tiny black phone across the table, he pulled his hand back and looked at her expectantly.

"What's this for?" Josephine picked it up.

"It's a phone," Fisk replied with a grin. "You use it to talk to people far away."

"What's so special about this one?" she asked, waggling the little device at him.

"It's your invitation to join my organization."

Sunday
June 1, 2014
Joint Operations Center
White House Protective Unit
Old Executive Office Building
Washington, D.C.
11:08 P.M. EDT

Metz closed the door to his office before picking up the phone. "What have you got?" he asked, reaching for the remote to opaque his office window.

"We just zeroed his backup. We got a lock on the locator in his limo." Lucas sounded pleased with himself.

Metz caught his breath, stunned at his good fortune. "When can you move?"

"He's in the Zone with some chick. We tapped the video. We'll know when they leave. Just one thing. We need to renegotiate the fee. He's got a full squad waiting in the wings, and I'm willing to bet you they aren't your run-of-the-mill bodyguards."

"How close are they?" Metz felt his enthusiasm cool.

"We're working on it. I have a call in. We'll know in half an hour, maybe less. Look, the fee. This guy's loaded for bear. If you want him, I've got to call in a lot of markers just to get the manpower."

Metz remained silent for a long moment.

"We want six times the usual."

"Are you nuts?" Metz struggled to avoid throwing the phone in the trash.

"I'm not the one who wants to cap this guy. He's got his bases covered. I told you," Lucas snorted.

"Maybe we should wait..." Metz began to pace.

"Maybe you should pull your head out of the sand. He's probably got that kind of protection 24/7. A lot of politicos have that much backup these days. We can get to him, but we won't be doing anything

413

until we have your money."

"Do you think he had this much back up last time?" Metz willed his feet to stop moving.

"We planned for it. What's the matter with you? It's only money. We got past his goons once before. We can do it again. You know how this works. Casualties on our end make it more expensive."

Metz pulled himself together. "Okay. Look, I can't meet your price. If we wait, can you manage something that's a little less expensive?" The bank accounts he was using didn't replenish very fast. The cash crunch hurt his ego.

"How high can you go?" Lucas was not ready to let go of Fisk so easily.

"Four. I can go four times the going rate."

Lucas paused, considering. "We'll take it. Get it here in 20 minutes. We're going to take him out on his way home. He'll never know what hit him."

```
Monday
June 2, 2014
Cosmopolitan Systems, Inc.
Potomac Heights, Maryland
12:14 A.M. EDT
```

"Overwatch to all stations. Set condition red." The overhead lighting in the situation room changed from multispectrum to crimson as Griff paced.

"We've lost contact with Primary. Things got wild after their last check-in," the night watch coordinator told him from her console.

On the large overhead display, Griff could see the images from the security cameras in the Congressional Zone. The volume had been muted because sound quality was poor. Despite the silence, the action on the screen was intense. He watched in frustration as the primary tactical team exchanged fire with people clad in black armor and protective headgear. Both sides employed silenced automatic weapons. The muzzle flashes lit the black-and-white scene with an eerie glow.

"Comms are being jammed," a large man said.

"Roll the backup?" The coordinator looked at Griff expectantly.

"Have we got a profile on this yet?" he asked, turning to a group of people near the far wall.

"Pulling it up now," replied another man as data flashed on his screen at impossible speed. "A-16 with a standard variable. Classic ambush." He caressed the fiber-optic cable jacked into a socket behind his right ear.

"They were looking for us," Griff rumbled as his ulcer began to announce its irritation.

The coordinator checked her display. "They found us. Better than a 50 percent chance they have security on their flanks. I concur, A-16."

Griff jogged around to look at her display. "Get him moving. His comm's off. Call Christopher and talk him through it. Get his backup on line and tell him to escort Ms. Harper home. All the way home. Stay there until we tell him differently. Make sure that Christopher knows to bring the car to the VIP exit."

Another woman raised a hand. "Send her home in a cab. Use the other limo to spoof."

"Do it," Griff responded. He pointed. "You, you, and you. Have secondary tactical move in on the decoy. Get satellite time and run the car's phone. Do everything it takes to look real. These guys have done their homework. Run the full reverse play. Make Fisk look like he's the decoy."

"We'll direct him to the Georgetown house. Can you get there ahead of him? We have to assume they'll try for him there."

"Are these guys the same cops who tried for him a few weeks ago?"

"Seventy-seven percent likely." The coordinator looked at her screen as new data came in. "The new variables are going into the system now. I expect that probability to reach 90 percent. You'd better take the lawyers. I wouldn't put it past the bad guys to try to serve a bogus warrant."

Monday
June 2, 2014
Georgetown Expressway
Washington, D.C.
12:25 A.M. EDT

The little green sportscar had been following the limo for several minutes. "Is he still with us?" Fisk wondered aloud. Alone in the back seat, he gave no indication of being worried.

"Yes," Christopher replied without taking his eyes off the road. A light rain was falling, leaving tiny streaks on the windows.

"Any idea who's following us?" Fisk asked quietly.

The tiny voice in his right ear replied, "Got to be one of those cops again. We lost satellite coverage six minutes ago. Homeland tasked the NSA bird we were piggybacking. The good news is that the bad guys are still tracking on the decoy."

Fisk waited while the unseen advisor spoke with someone off mike.

"The bird-dog following you thinks you're the decoy. He has a co-pilot, too. Before we lost our window, we got a partial face on the driver. Trust me, we'll let you know when we have more. Just stay cool."

Fisk nodded. Within the previous few years, his people had been lucky. Tapping into the government's satellite-run surveillance net was no small thing. Passive viewing of agency images improved their overall intelligence picture. The one drawback was that his protectors had no control over where the satellites went or what they saw.

"I'm two minutes from the house. Our people there report no activity. As soon as you hit the off-ramp, your tail is going to know where you're going." Griff's voice had an electronic echo.

Fisk scanned the interior of the limo, considering the warning. He continued to speak through his comm instead the encrypted car phone. "How are things with the decoy? How are they doing?"

"Primary was taken out. Secondary is still in play." Griff's voice betrayed no emotion.

Fisk decided to change the subject. "Josephine?"

"En route. No complications."

Christopher activated the hands-free feature of the car's secured phone. "Off-ramp's coming up. If they're scanning for comms, they'll be looking for a call from this car about now." He adjusted his mirrors to keep the sportscar in view.

"Good job," Griff said enthusiastically. "Take the ramp. Follow the route we're feeding to you now." The nav screen lit up, showing a street map with red tracing.

"You want me to shake this guy before I make the approach?" Christopher merged into traffic, keeping three car lengths clear in front and behind.

The coordinator replied, "Negative. You're going into residential. There are at least four police cruisers in the area. That's just what we know about. Let's not give them any excuse to pull you over."

"Sounds like you're in control," Fisk said, glad to be able to offer some encouragement.

"We'll handle it. Let us know if your situation changes."

"Griff, What's your take on this?"

"We just tapped the traffic cams at the off-ramp. There's a single cruiser. One cop. He's getting something out of the trunk. Wait one."

Fisk leaned forward instinctively as the limo rolled down the off-ramp.

"It's a spike strip. One guess who that's for."

"Christopher..." Fisk prompted.

"Going." The driver mashed down the accelerator while shifting gears.

Fisk touched a tiny button on the door control panel. The limo's rear passenger windows went dark as the big car gained speed. The vehicle slanted steeply through a tight right turn, causing him to slide across the broad leather seat.

"Buckle up. We'll be into the gridlock soon, and I need to be able to drive without worrying about you."

Fisk struggled into the seatbelt and shoulder harness as the limo shot down the off-ramp, slewing expertly between two slower cars.

"I'm going to drive past the house. The security team should be able to pick off whoever's following us," Christopher said loudly as he dug his fingers into the soft grip of the steering wheel.

"Roger that. Keep this line open." Griff's connection had improved.

Taking one hand off the wheel, Christopher adjusted the volume on the phone, and then fastened his own shoulder harness. His seatbelt was always fastened. He generally kept the shoulder harness undone because the webbing restricted his movement. He was surprised to realize that he was taking it all in stride. *After everything I've seen in the last few weeks, this makes sense.*

Fisk fastened down his briefcase. In the back of his mind, he could almost hear a tiny familiar-but-not voice speak. *Why does this happen to me only when I'm in danger?* Opening his mind to it, he rested both hands in his lap and closed his eyes in concentration as the limousine roared into traffic.

Christopher caught a brief glimpse of a uniformed officer as he passed. The rolled spike strip was still tucked under one arm.

Ignoring the commotion, Fisk struggled to hear the inner voice. Though he had never told anyone, he regarded moments like this as a strong attack of deja vu. High stress or life-threatening moments would be enough to bring on its presence. A mild headache began as the whispered words became audible.

"Stop the car at the next light," he said to Christopher. Ahead, the glare of dozens of brake- and taillights lit slowly moving cars as they moved toward the clogged intersection.

The memory fragment exploded into white-hot clarity. The intensity of the mental image made him go rigid. Despite his best efforts, it vanished as quickly as it had come. *I know what's happening...*

The traffic light went from yellow to red. The limo stopped as it reached the edge of the intersection. A large group of teenagers in flashy night gear hustled across the busy street. Traffic lights in this part of town were notoriously fast. The intersection was crowded with all manner of cars and trucks. D.C.'s late-night traffic had become just as bad as daytime gridlock.

Fisk craned his neck, scanning the cars and pedestrians nearest him. *What am I looking for?* The voice was silent, despite his best efforts to summon it. *Come on. What am I looking for?*

"Overwatch here," a male voice interrupted from the comm implant. "Your tail has gone to ground. Still got them on the traffic cam. They pulled to talk with the cop. He's putting away the spike strip. Times like this, I wish we had a lip reader on staff."

Fisk listened intently as the impression he'd been struggling to recall crystallized. Understanding sparked like lightning as floaters appeared in his vision. *They planned for us to spoof them.* He said, "I'm beginning to think the bad guys expected us to bait and switch. They may be planning to intercept both cars no matter what."

Out of the corner of his eye, he spotted a brightly colored sedan with its front passenger window open. A tiny circle of reflected light told him that the person sitting there was watching him with a high-definition zoom camera. *How did I know to look for that?*

Two men in casual athletic wear stood facing in opposite directions on the sidewalk, looking at everything but the limo.

Fisk leaned forward. "Christopher. Look left and tell Overwatch what you see."

"Intersection, left. Two men. Sweats. Holding in a regular surveillance pattern."

"Going to have to take your word for that. We don't have any taps in that area. You're just out of view." Griff paused to get input from his team. "We're moving. Just keep your transponder on and stay in the car."

"You want to split the difference and meet me half way?"

Fisk settled into the seat, straining to see into the night around him. "There's a bright yellow four-door parked just off to my left. Probably got comms to the spotters."

Christopher swiveled a side mirror to confirm that the car was there. *Why am I not surprised?*

"How well do you know the neighborhood?" the tiny voice in Fisk's ear asked.

"We need some place real public," Griff interjected.

"Roger. You know where that internet cafe is?"

"Sure. Near the campus." Fisk glanced at the stubborn red light.

"I've been in there a few times," Christopher said as the light finally changed. He allowed the big limo to surge forward.

"We have the address. Lose your tail and go there." Griff's voice was muffled as he gave orders to the people around him.

"Play it cool. We're in their groove. Let's see if we can bluff them," Fisk told Christopher.

"Cool's my middle name."

"This thing has an in-built vibration that'll probably screw up their long range mikes. Our biggest problem will be being hemmed in. If you want to bluff them, we've got to make it look like we're going to make a run for it while we're still in the commercial blocks."

A female voice interrupted. "Overwatch concurs. If you run their blockers, the odds are high that they'll jump the gun and try for an intercept. It'd be nice to have *them* out of position, for once."

"You heard the lady. Let's put them out of position." Fisk rechecked his seat harness. Without warning, a large white van shot out of traffic, skidding in front of the limo just as it cleared the intersection.

Christopher braked through a flashy S-turn, one hand on the autoshifter as he fought the G-force. The big car shuddered as tires squealed. Sidling past the van, Christopher got the car back into the regular traffic pattern as if he were making a run for the safety of Fisk's Georgetown residence.

"We just passed a white panel van. Tried to cut us off as we made the intersection," Fisk elaborated for the benefit of his unseen advisors.

"Contents?" the feminine voice in his ear asked.

Fisk closed his eyes, working to retrieve the memory. "Six. Street clothes. Mostly black and Asian. Could have been more, but we're moving fast."

"You're popular tonight," Christopher barked sarcastically as he fought the wheel.

Fisk touched the window controls and the rear window became transparent again. He was just able to make out the white van as it slewed onto the street to pursue.

"Won't matter. They had their chance. They're out of position now. It's about time we caught a break," Griff crackled back at him, the connection having gone bad again.

Christopher pulled heavily at the wheel. The steering column creaked slightly as the big car slid off the street and through an empty parking lot.

"What's the situation with the other car?" Fisk asked.

"Mopping up now," Overwatch replied.

Fisk watched another cluster of tough-looking teenagers gawk at the limo as it shot by. In the intersection to their right, a small green sportscar ran the red light.

"Three o'clock. Our tail is back," Fisk said. He watched Christopher do a double-take.

"Where did he come from? That green sport is back," he told the phone as he drove. "We're not outrunning him."

"That's good news, actually. If he's there by himself, that means they have no more blockers. Lose him and get to the pickup point." Griff's voice was choppy with static.

"Brace!" Christopher bellowed as the limo bounced over the median.

Slewing in to the expressway traffic, he was quick to match speed with the cars around him. Unable to jump the median because of low ground clearance, the green sportscar faded fast.

"We're five blocks out. Look for a light blue four-door with Florida plates. We'll flash our lights when we see you," Griff rumbled.

"We've got you. I'm driving past you now, in the opposite direction," Overwatch said with some relief.

Fisk glanced out of the passenger window to his left. Traffic flashed past, shiny colors illuminated by the harsh glare of the streetlights. "I didn't see you," he said with forced calm.

"It's okay, I see you. Oh! Look--"

Christopher swore as a white panel van shot up from a nearby on-ramp. As if on cue, traffic slowed to a crawl as the speeding van pulled up next to the limo.

Fisk watched as both side doors opened up. Six men in dark clothes got out. One beefy man held a wireless phone while the rest took out flashlights.

"Jump the traffic!" Griff and the Overwatch commander said at nearly the same time.

Sounds of breaking glass and tearing metal could be heard behind the limo. Fisk turned to see a sedan, hood crumpled, hung up on the meridian five car-lengths back. Car doors were swinging open as shadowy figures spilled out into the traffic.

"Get down," Christopher ordered as he revved the engine.

"Get us over the meridian. Overwatch says--" Fisk began, laying over in his seat.

"I know. Figured it'd be something like that."

The tires squealed again. The big front bumper protested with a loud grinding sound as the limo slammed into the low concrete barrier.

Bouncing upright, Fisk caught a glance of the men advancing on the limo, their flashlight beams tracking the car's movements. The man with the phone was starkly lit as he stood under a street lamp, cars jammed in around him.

Somebody honked in protest. The limo became high-centered on the meridian for a long, agonizing moment.

Fisk began to sweat as he watched Christopher's frustration. A glance to his left showed one of the attackers moving towards the passenger door of the limo with an autolock tool in his hand. Reflexively, he hit the door controls several times, convincing himself that the car's doors were truly locked.

Still working the steering wheel, Christopher reached out to the dashboard. A small panel opened under his touch. The car's passenger windows went completely black.

"Warning. Anti-hijacking package activated," the car's alarm system stated.

Christopher began to rock the limo back and forth to give the car's all-wheel drive a chance to find traction. Outside, two of the attackers spun away from the car, hit by bright blue streamers of electrostatic energy. Heavily stunned, both men fell to the street.

The limo's rear tires squealed as they found purchase on the pavement. Hopping off the median, the big car landed in the path of oncoming traffic with a heavy bounce. Back in his element, Christopher spun the heavy car neatly, missing a light pickup that swerved by with its horn blaring.

Fisk looked at the secured phone. Thumbing the reset button, he keyed in his code. Nothing happened.

"Don't worry about that phone. Once I activated the alarm unit, it went into auto mode. Right now, it's screaming to your people for help."

Fisk watched the back of the man's head. *Very little sweat. Good guy to have on my side.*

"Some kind of night, huh?" Christopher quipped as he turned down a side street.

"Keep moving. We still have your homing signal. We'll meet you at the pickup. Have a mocha for me. We'll see you when we get there," the tiny voice in Fisk's ear insisted.

"You drive. Leave the panicking to me." Fisk scowled.

Christopher grunted in reply as the car shot through a red light into near-darkness. *They have a lot of manpower tied up in this op. I wonder who they are.* "Residential. If I'm right, we're only a few blocks from that coffee joint," he said after several minutes of sedate driving.

Fisk sat up, thinking about the last few minutes. "Stop the car." *No more Mr. Nice Guy.*

Christopher slowed the limo to a stop away from the glow of the street lamps.

"No! Do not stop the car! Stay mobile!" the tiny voice in Fisk's ear bellowed.

"Something about that sportscar is bothering me," Fisk elaborated, raising a hand to his right ear. "How did he catch up to us so quickly?" He grimaced, waiting for the sharp ringing to stop.

Christopher mulled it over, keeping both hands on the wheel. "They assumed that we'd run for the house." As they spoke, a pair of headlights glowed through the limo's rear window. In the distance, a small car turned onto the dark and deserted street.

"One guess who that might be." Christopher gripped the steering wheel.

"This limo is swept for trackers and bugs just before I use it, right?"

"That's right," Overwatch quietly confirmed.

"What are you getting at?" Griff's staticky voice came back.

"Every time," Christopher muttered back, lightly tapping the gas pedal. The limo began gliding forward. Both men watched as the green two-door sportscar emerged into the halo of a street lamp.

"There's our little buddy," Fisk drawled, putting it together, "homing in on *our* tracker. Since his pals couldn't get close enough to plant one of their own, I'd say we're giving away our own location." He leaned over to get a glance at the driver's rear view mirror. *That's what I'd do,* he reassured himself with a nod.

Christopher opened the glove compartment and swore.

Fisk unbuckled his seatbelts and slid forward.

"It's the car," Christopher said, reaching into the glove box. He fingered the tiny blue light that shone in the darkness "These things are color coded. We change them every time we use this car. Somebody screwed up and didn't change this one out like they were supposed to."

"Is he sure?" Griff sounded beside himself with agony.

"Is he sure?" the tiny voice in Fisk's ear echoed.

"You're sure?" Fisk asked.

Christopher huffed, sitting up and gripping the steering wheel. "I'd swear to it. I saw this one yesterday."

Behind them, the little sportscar slowed.

Griff finally lost his temper. "You're kidding me. I'm going to have somebody's head." Overwatch was painfully silent.

"Somebody's been waiting for us to make this mistake."

"They've been recording our transponder freqs." Griff was beside himself with rage.

"Which means--" Fisk raised his voice.

"Which means they'll expect us to stay with the car," Christopher concluded.

"Do not leave the car," the tiny voice inside Fisk's ear insisted.

"Let me lose these guys. Then we can sort this out." Christopher slammed the car into reverse.

The limo raced backwards, tires smoking slightly on the pavement as he guided it on a collision course with the sportscar. The other driver reacted reflexively, standing on his brakes. The limo struck the sportscar squarely, its rear bumper meeting fiberglass and plastic with a bone-jarring crunch.

Fisk, caught without his seatbelts, was flung forward.

"Excuse me. A little parting gift for our friend back there."

Christopher reached past Fisk's head and shoulders to the glove compartment, tearing out the tracker. The little black box sparked and went dark as it was ripped from its power supply. Christopher threw the little box out the window. "It's probably got a battery backup in it," he sneered, putting the car into gear.

"Worth a few minutes of quiet time," Fisk replied, fastening his seatbelts. *I'm really starting to wonder if I actually have done this before.*

"Let's make the most of it." Christopher peered into the night around them.

The limo launched out of a side street. All around them, the nightlife of Georgetown was advertised in bright lights and neon. Christopher cut the headlights and bullied the car through a wild reverse turn. Tires squealed as the limo slid into a parking lot next to a dark, silent store. Christopher cut the engine and hit the control stud that opened the sunroof.

"I think we just went to ground," Fisk said quietly.

"Roger that. We have contained the blockers," Overwatch advised. The channel was suddenly clear of static.

Fisk sat quietly, letting the security specialists do their jobs. As the sunroof retracted, the two men waited. The sounds of traffic and pedestrians came flooding into the darkened interior of the limo.

Christopher shut his eyes, mentally counted to 20, took a breath, and opened his eyes. "Thank goodness," he breathed.

"No pursuit," Fisk agreed.

"Good job." Griff's distorted voice tickled the inside of Fisk's ear. "My flankers have a visual on that sportscar. He's not going anywhere. Looks like you're in the clear. You can't use the car, though. Tell Christopher--"

The driver interrupted, using the hands-free phone. "I can hear you. I know this area. We're just a few blocks from the cafe. I think we can walk it."

"Overwatch?" Griff asked, his voice nearly drowned out by static.

"Here. Ground clutter is blocking your signal. We concur. Fisk should walk."

"You heard the lady. Go." Griff's voice got softer as the connection began to fade.

"Give me your briefcase. I want to check it for bugs," Christopher breathed.

Fisk unfastened the securing straps and handed over the thin leather case.

"We're going." Christopher reached out to turn off the car phone as he unbuckled his restraints. Fisk watched intently as the man used a small flashlight to go over every inch of the briefcase. Huddled in the driver's compartment, the driver was careful not to let the tiny light shine in the direction of any of the car's windows.

The secured phone warbled for attention. They looked at each other. Fisk's eyebrows were knitted in thought as he started to reach for the phone.

"Your people won't call on this line now. They won't take the chance that somebody cracked the code."

Fisk looked at the handset and nodded.

"Nothing. Not even inside," the driver muttered.

Fisk began patting himself down. *Nobody's laid a hand on me that I haven't known about in the last 12 years.* The phone stopped warbling. Fisk breathed a sigh of relief.

"Shh. Car coming," Christopher hissed. They strained to hear the noises coming in through the sunroof. A searchlight probed the empty storefronts.

"Out." Christopher triggered the autolocks.

Fisk bolted from the limo, briefcase in hand, closing the door behind him.

"You'd better turn off your comm," Overwatch said, sounding unhappy.

Fisk clamped his teeth together, deactivating the implant.

Christopher hit the switch to close the sunroof, and then reached under his seat to remove his grey satchel. Leaving the vehicle quietly, he joined Fisk as the probing searchlight moved closer. The two scuttled between parked cars and garbage cans, watching from concealment as a police cruiser rolled by.

The cruiser slowed as it passed the limo. The searchlight played over the vehicle, settling on the rear license plate.

"This must be costing her a pretty penny," Fisk muttered to himself.

"What?" Christopher tried to remain quiet despite his irritation. *We're hiding from the cops, and you're laughing about how much this costs?*

Indicating the cruiser with a nod, Fisk quietly replied, "The D.C. police. These people have cleaned up their act a lot in the last ten years, but some of them are still dirty. If I didn't know I was on their menu, I'd be happy to see them."

As he spoke, a uniformed officer opened the passenger door and left the vehicle. Unlimbering his large flashlight, the police officer started to approach the darkened limo.

Christopher reached into his coat pocket and brought out a small black box. Aiming it at the limo, he pressed a button.

Fisk eyed him expectantly.

"Car alarm. Preston Fisk doesn't leave his ride all alone in this part of town without locking it up first, right?"

While Christopher was speaking, the officer walked up to the limo, shining his flashlight into the interior. He gingerly tested a door handle. The vehicle beeped three shrill tones at him. He stepped away from the car, cursing quietly.

"I see what you mean," Fisk smirked.

Walking briskly back to the cruiser, the cop leaned over to talk to his partner. Fisk and his driver both strained to hear what he was saying.

"He's not here. The car's locked up, too. Hood's still warm. He's probably in some hidey-hole by now, laughing at us. Better call it in and tell them better luck next time." Whatever his partner said was drowned out by traffic noise.

"If he's on the street, they'll find him. I don't think he'd be enjoying himself in this neighborhood, anyhow." Getting into the cruiser, the cop took off his hat and closed the door. The vehicle glided off into the night.

Fisk and Christopher stayed in hiding for several moments after the cruiser was gone.

"What is going on here?" Christopher demanded.

Fisk looked at the driver, trying to decide what he should say. "They're looking for me. Roaming patrols, and searchers on foot." He paused to ponder once more just what had clued him into the details of tonight's ambush. *Past life? If so, I must have been some kind of guy.*

"The President sent these guys?" Christopher asked, cradling the grey satchel in both hands.

"She's got the Deputy Director for the White House protective unit in her back pocket."

"She can't buy the Secret Service. Those guys are--"

"She did. Trust me. I made it possible." Fisk moved closer in the darkness.

"Was that part of your plan?" The driver felt his blood run cold.

"Calm down." Fisk put a hand on the nervous man's shoulder. "I bought her. She bought the Deputy Director, and he's buying the services of these cops. It's the cycle of political life."

"It's still treason. Don't give me any of that dog-eat-dog stuff, either. I understand what you're trying to do, but this is just too much."

He nodded, standing. "Agreed. It's a lot too much, but it's not treason. I put people like President Hill on the path, but I don't make them walk it. I did it, knowing full well that they would be true to their natures. She, and all the rest like her, doesn't need any encouragement from me. As a matter of fact, they don't need me at all any more."

"Which is why we're here," Christopher replied as he, too, rose to his feet.

"Dirty cops, being paid by dirty government officials. Isn't that worth fighting against?" Checking his tie, Fisk stepped out onto the sidewalk. As they moved out from behind the limo, each looked in a separate direction.

Christopher said nothing as he slung the satchel over his shoulder. Intermittent neon signs and sodium-vapor streetlights accentuated the sounds of Georgetown at night. Traffic bustled through a nearby intersection.

"Where to?" Fisk asked, stopping near the crosswalk.

"Two blocks down, on the right." Christopher turned to scan the area.

"I know somebody who lives not too far from here," Fisk commented as he pointed at a street sign.

"Reliable?"

"Totally." He started walking when the indicator lit.

"Care to tell me who that might be?"

"Just another one of my many friends," Fisk admitted, feeling good. *Something about all this feels right, in a dangerous way.* From his coat pocket, his phone beeped.

Christopher looked at him accusingly.

"I forgot I had it. Honest."

"Don't answer it. Give it to me." He held out his hand as they reached the other side of the street.

Fisk handed him the phone as if it were contraband.

Exasperated, Christopher hurled the offending object into traffic. He came up next to his employer as they moved on. "This is not a game! You think you're untouchable because of who you know, and what you get into. This is real beyond real! The bad guys are seriously interested in having you all to themselves for a while. In case you hadn't thought it through, that would be a *bad* thing."

"Point taken." Fisk kept walking. *Okay, calm down. He's right.*

They walked on in silence. The noise of the traffic seemed deafening as they reached the next intersection.

Fisk stood at the corner as Christopher pressed the button to activate the crosswalk signal. In the back of his mind, he thought about the personal locator beacon that was hidden somewhere inside his body. *Do I tell him?* He looked sideways at the driver.

Christopher came up beside him. "Don't turn around. Two walkers are coming up the street on your side. Long coats and all too serious for this part of town."

Fisk smiled, turning his head just enough to register the two men on the sidewalk only a hundred feet away. The pair walked side by side, matching their strides. They seemed to be looking at everything except the sidewalk in front of them.

"Don't look," Christopher growled, keeping an eye on traffic as they crossed. "One thing about this part of town, the lights are fast after dark."

Fisk turned to look back. The two trackers stood at the crosswalk, watching him. The lights had already changed, allowing the traffic to surge through the intersection, temporarily cutting off pursuit. Smiling triumphantly, he flashed his pursuers a mock salute and started walking.

"What was that?" Christopher demanded, catching up to him.

"Just part of the game. Now that they know we saw them, they'll fall back and try to come up on us from a different direction." They passed through a gaggle of rowdy teenagers, drawing stares and snickered remarks.

"Let me do my job. You're challenging them to come and get you. When you yank their chains, you only make them try harder," the driver spat.

Fisk continued walking. Somewhere in the back of his mind, a voice *dared* them to try harder. "Give me a break. These people aren't any different from the politicos I deal with. If you make them mad, they get stupid," he lectured as they moved through a crowded section of sidewalk. *I'm a well-dressed man in the wrong part of town. THAT is pretty stupid.*

"Turn." Some instinct tied to his former life made Fisk give the order. They veered into the doorway of a rundown tenement. The consultant pushed his way through the door to the foyer as if it were the natural thing to do.

"What's going on?" Christopher asked, taking in the ramshackle lobby.

Fisk thought of the crowd that would now gossip about having seen them. "If the guys following us aren't deaf, they'll hear that crowd talking about two guys who are overdressed for this part of town." Crossing the stained carpet, he approached the front counter. A cover story was already developing in the back of his mind. A pair of dirty yellow lights illuminated the area.

Christopher took a step to one side and waited near the battered front door, one hand over the clasp of his satchel. He split his attention between the door and his employer. "You've done this before."

"I know people. Our clothes stand out in this neighborhood, particularly at night." Fisk peered over the counter. A stained guest register sat on the front desk. He let his eyes track to the open door of the back room where a stocky older woman sat, fast asleep in a rickety office chair with a baseball bat in her lap.

"You called it. They're coming." Christopher peered through a dust-smeared window.

"Come on." Fisk walked boldly into the darkened corridor just off the lobby.

"Looks like the same guys, too," Christopher told him as he caught up.

"They keep the first floors of these places blacked out any more," Fisk observed. Common wisdom held that property owners could reduce the amount of property damage done to their buildings during random anti-terrorist sweeps by keeping the ground floor apartments locked and empty.

"Can't say I blame them. Crime sucks." Christopher followed him into the gloom.

"Yep," the consultant muttered, feeling his way along a rough, dirty wall.

They stopped moving as they heard the front door open. Two pairs of flat-bottomed leather shoes made their way across the old carpet.

"I told you he didn't come in here. He knows better."

"Do a walk-through. We're getting paid by the hour, so who cares if we find him?"

Christopher quietly swore, fondling the strap of his satchel.

Fisk plucked at the younger man's coat sleeve, indicating that he should follow. Inching his way along the dark hallway, he probed further into the interior of the old building. They moved quietly past a dozen silent apartments. Trash on the floor rustled as they went by. Working on a hunch, Fisk kept going until he came to the low-hanging swivel door of a laundry chute. Taking a moment to prop it open, he moved on.

"They're not that stupid, are they?" Christopher whispered.

"Just giving them a little something to work with." He grinned.

The elderly woman behind the counter had been roused and was now talking.

"She's pretty trusting, isn't she?"

"They *are* cops. These folks are used to random searches. What do you want?" Fisk muttered in reply. Coming to a stop, he felt around a metal doorframe.

Like so many poorer sections of most major cities, Georgetown had become accustomed to "security sweeps." One more wasn't going to faze the jaded residents of this building.

"Feel that heat?" Fisk murmured.

Christopher put his hand on the door. A slight vibration came through the warm metal.

"Boiler room. We'll go out through the old coal chute."

"The *what?*" Christopher responded, casting a glance behind them.

Fisk tested the doorknob. Locked. Thumbing at the inside of his coat lapel, he sighed. "I don't suppose you have a lockpick, do you?"

Christopher gave him a dirty look.

Though both men were nearly invisible to each other, Fisk didn't miss the gesture. "What?"

Christopher remained quiet, hands working through his own coat pockets. *I can't believe this. He's asking me, of all people, for a lockpick. Like I should have one.* "I suppose you left yours in your other suit?" He pressed two short lengths of stiff wire into Fisk's palm. *This I have to see.*

"Something like that," Fisk mumbled.

"Fifty bucks say you can't do it."

"How hard can it be?" He fumbled with the wires. His fingers came to life, working the lock with a finesse that was strangely comfortable.

"Less talk, more work," Christopher replied as he kept a mental time count.

Back in the lobby, one of the trackers was using his phone. "Aw, come on. Get off your can and do it, will you? It's easy money. If we catch him, there's an extra grand in it."

The lock made a soft click. Fisk opened the door and slipped into the room. Christopher followed.

"Make sure the door's locked," Fisk said.

"Done." Christopher flashed a relieved smile. *He's not fast, but he's quiet. Have to ask him if he really has done this before.*

They moved into the dimly lit room. The machinery was dusty and tarnished, coated with nearly a century's worth of soot and grime. Fisk was careful not to disturb anything as he passed a workbench. Its rusty tools looked just as ill-kept as the rest of the place. He stopped and pointed to a ramp barred by a rusty red locked gate.

"That's a coal chute. Back in the days when this place was heated by coal, they used to dump it by the ton down into this area so that it could be shoveled into the furnace." He looked around for the furnace, but found none.

"Hmm." Christopher eyed the locked gate.

"What?" Fisk looked at the gate and stepped towards it.

Watching quietly, Christopher marveled at how fast Fisk was able to tease the old lock open.

"You *have* done this before." He followed Fisk up the ramp.

"You're surprised?" *Sure wish I knew how I did that.* He tried not to slide on the concrete slope. Reaching the top of the chute, he hit the old wooden doors several times with his shoulder to force them open.

They emerged into a garbage-strewn alley. The stench made Fisk gag for a moment.

"I just drive the car," Christopher quipped dryly, taking short, shallow breaths.

"So I noticed," Fisk replied, trying to be cheerful as he picked his way through the garbage.

"I've driven for some tough customers before, and I've put the pedal to the metal for you twice now, but this is the first time I've ever had to leave my car and follow a client through a bad neighborhood while up to my knees in garbage," he griped. As he spoke, his feet slid through something that let out a foul odor.

Fisk stopped to look back at him.

Christopher was obviously angry. His voice had grown loud enough to echo all the way down the length of the alley. He tramped out onto the sidewalk, scraping something black and oily off the toes of his shoes.

Fisk waited for him, scanning the nearby storefronts. Nobody seemed to take notice of them. *Yet.*

"Hey, this might be a regular day at the office for you, but for me, this is some really twisted stuff."

"Trust me. This is a new development." Fisk paused to check his own shoes.

"She must want you real bad. Is it really worth all this? I know what you told me before, but tell me again. Is it really worth getting killed?" He pulled something off his coat sleeve and flicked it away.

They stopped to look in through the armored window of a pawn shop as a crowd passed. Large signs posted over the gun cases informed prospective buyers of the lengthy background checks required by the federal government.

Ten day wait. Fingerprints. Photos. All sales final on approval from the Department of Homeland Security. What will they want next? A urine sample? "Is it worth dying for? Yes. Look in there and tell me what you see." Ignoring the harsh glare, Fisk tapped lightly on the armored glass.

Christopher stared into the shop for several heartbeats. The tough-looking attendant looked down at his tiny portable television. Most of the merchandise was displayed in large, obviously locked, transparent cases. The store was empty. The clerk was just killing time.

"I don't know. I'll tell you one thing. See those gun cases? Now that the NRA is gone, shops like this will be out of business."

Fisk nodded sagely and turned away. He started walking. "Does that bother you?"

"Keep going. To the corner and turn," Christopher said as fell in beside him. "Yeah. I guess it does bother me. The thing is, most people won't care. They'll be happy to see places like that go out of business."

"But you won't?" Fisk carefully kept a slow pace.

"Pawn shops make a lot of money selling guns. Guns that people already bought once. Secondhand guns aren't any different from brand new guns. What the heck does this have to do with anything?"

"Think about it." Fisk turned up the collar of his coat against the night chill.

"Yeah, yeah, yeah. Second amendment and all that. If we lose one of them, we can lose all of them. Our freedom might be worth dying for, but this is something else. What you're doing here is, well..." Christopher shook his head in exasperation.

Fisk let Christopher ponder as the pair turned the corner. "It's not different. The means are unorthodox, but the desired result is--"

"Walk faster. I think we have a new tail," Christopher said quietly.

"Where?" Fisk continued to survey the storefronts as if he were looking for something.

"Behind us. The beat cop who isn't trying too hard to make his rounds."

As they passed by a piece of flashy molding, Fisk caught sight of the slow moving cop. "I hope what you've got in your bag there isn't just a water pistol." He slowed his ambling, briefly considering using his implant.

"It's real, all right. The same one I used last time we were in a jam."

"Okay. It's your call." He pretended to yawn as they reached the middle of the block.

"Yeah. Run!" Grabbing Fisk by the arm, Christopher pushed him forward.

From behind them came a single sharp command, "Halt!" The cop went for his gun.

"That'll be a real attention-getter." Christopher pounded down the pavement after Fisk.

They raced down the sidewalk, muscling their way through a crowd that was just exiting a movie theater. Overhead, the marquee flashed and pulsed in the latest styles of realistic holograms and dazzling neon.

"Coming through!" Fisk shouted.

"Gun!" Christopher yelled, causing the crowd to scatter in panic.

Ten long years of constant media hype had blown the threat of terrorism out of proportion. Working on adrenaline and the kind of reflexes that came from living in a bad neighborhood, some of the panicked people drew their own concealed weapons.

The beat cop charged into the crowd. Several in the throng who had drawn handguns had them raised as they took defensive stances. Realizing the mistake he was about to make, the cop came to a skidding stop.

The mass of people scattered. A few young men held their ground, unsure about the policeman.

The cop eyed the hideaway pistols and shivs pointed at him. "Rats!" He swore, bolting back the way he had come.

Monday
June 2, 2014
The Coffee Modem
Georgetown
Washington, D.C.
1:02 A.M. EDT

"In here." Christopher pointed to the entrance.

"Looks very...rustic," Fisk drawled.

"It's a coffee shop. What do you want?"

"Point taken." Fisk smiled, walking in as if he'd been going to the place for years.

The interior was dim. Many of the customers were preoccupied with glowing computer terminals, surfing the internet through neural interface connections. Out-of-date cathode ray monitors contrasted sharply with the few holographic systems clustered in the center of the shop. After a decade of decline, computer coffee bars like this one were starting to make a comeback.

"I always did like these kinds of places. They remind me of my college days." Fisk sat down with two steaming cups of Jamaican vanilla blend. Wistfully, he handed one to Christopher.

The driver sipped his coffee, looking between the front and kitchen doors. "They should have been here by now."

"Probably tied up in traffic." Fisk grinned rakishly as he slurped the foam off his cup.

"You are one cool fellow. And I know what I saw. You've done this before."

"You're trying to make something out of nothing." *I'd still like to know how I picked that lock,* he thought as he stirred some sugar into his coffee.

"Uh-huh. All the top guns I drive for have 'Overwatch,' and they all know how to pick locks while running from professional hitters. You're just another regular guy."

"Will you keep it down? It's only a matter of time until somebody recognizes me. That wouldn't be too convenient right now, if you take my meaning."

"Sorry. Like the contract says, no questions. You just surprised me, that's all."

"Apology accepted." He paused, his eyes settling on a trio of college students in the far corner. They were looking right at him. "On your right. Told you so. Happens every time," Fisk mumbled, pretending to take a sip.

"It really is hard to be you. I'm going to make a phone call."

"Right." Looking back at the three students, Fisk had a sudden flash of insight. *Oh, no.* He slid his chair back, getting ready to stand. "I'll go with you. We're about to have company."

Christopher drained the last of his coffee as he took stock of the situation. "For a man who's working without a net, you've done pretty good so far. They're just college kids. Talk to them." He set his cup on the table and picked up his satchel.

"Let's go," Fisk insisted.

"Why?" Christopher asked with a chilly smile as one of them approached.

"Hey, me and my friends were--"

"Yeah?" Christopher interjected as he stood, seeing Fisk's growing frustration.

"Are you Preston Fisk, the advisor to the President?"

"Yes, but--"

"Yes!" The young man turned to flash his friends an A-OK.

"Look, I've really go to be--"

"C-could we just ask you one question? I mean, just a short one?"

"Really, I have to be going," Fisk insisted. From the corner of his eye, he watched Christopher's head swivel towards the door. Turning to look out through the window, he saw his favorite pair of trackers walking by.

Christopher pointed at the men and squinted, placing a hand over his eyes.

Fisk nodded. *Lights are too dim. They can't see us.* "All right, today's your lucky day." He flashed the best smile he could manage and sat down. He motioned for the other two young men to join him to help with their camouflage.

"I'll go make that phone call," Christopher said as he slid his satchel under Fisk's chair.

Fisk nodded, moving it between his feet as the trio gathered around him.

"Thanks for talking to us," one of them said quietly, as if sharing a secret. "I'm Chuck. That's Pete and Harley."

"You guys are out kind of late, aren't you?" He tapped his watch disapprovingly.

"So are you," Harley observed, his beefy shoulders hunched over the table.

Fisk read the expectation on their faces. They were hoping to match wits with him. *Ah, the boldness of youth. Let's see what you've got, guys.*

"My limo broke down, and I needed a phone so that I could make contact with...my people."

"We're working on a class assignment. We're trying to show how an antigovernment conspiracy is no longer possible," Pete explained.

Okay. You're the group's optimist, Fisk thought.

"Yeah. A lot of political science theory these days says that government can be modeled as a series of math equations, or idea models, which means that we can show why it can't be done," Harley kicked in.

You'd be the pessimist, Fisk decided. "You don't sound convinced. You think somebody could successfully plot against the United States government?" He raised an eyebrow.

"Yeah, if they had to. I'm into chaos theory. I say that, even if you could predict the likelihood of a conspiracy, you couldn't stop it. The government would lose." He seemed pleased.

Pete shook his head pityingly. "But I say that, not only could you predict the likelihood of a conspiracy against the government, you could also model the means by which to stop it."

Geez, guys. You sure picked the wrong person to discuss this with. "Where do you stand on this, Chuck?" Fisk probed.

"I don't know. I can buy the idea of being able to stop a conspiracy once you know that one exists, but it sounds too much like fortune-telling to say that you can predict one." The youth sat forward, hands held to his chin.

Fisk nodded silently. *You'd be the undecided one. I could get myself into sooo much trouble here.* Taking a breath, he summoned his best "guru" voice.

"Harley is convinced that such a thing is impossible because he doubts that you could accurately gauge public sentiment. Fundamentally, this is true. It's not easy to know how people feel about their government."

"Exactly. And, no matter what, somebody's always going to be unhappy with it," Harley responded, brightening.

"But no matter which segment of society acts against a government, it only has so many options open to it, based on the level of control that a government holds over it," Pete replied.

The totalitarian supposition didn't surprise Fisk. "I see." He paused, draining his cup. "So, in theory, such a regime would allow its citizens fewer options for revolt and, as a result, cut down on the chances for conspiracy to overthrow it."

"Precisely." Pete swelled with pride.

Fisk looked at him for a long moment. *How did we miss recruiting you, kiddo?* "You imply that those governed should have no say in how they are led." He craned his neck to watch Christopher in the back of the cafe, head and shoulders bent low over the pay phone.

"That's the trend," Pete replied.

"The trend?" Fisk fidgeted with his empty cup. *Now that's hitting too close for comfort.*

"Modern democracy isn't so much equal representation as it is equal treatment. Look at what's happened since 9/11. Governmental power has risen dramatically with no real drop in equality. In most cases, you'll find that people think of equity and equality as being the same thing. So long as people are treated well, then hey, the level of power exercised by the government can be as much or as little as those in power are willing to accept."

Fisk shuddered inwardly. *You don't know how right you are. Somebody has to stop this long, slow, march towards total power. Liberals and conservatives alike seem bent on going that way, and I don't think it's a transition we can survive.* "Chuck?" He looked expectantly at the third student.

"It's all a matter of interpretation to me." He was clearly trying to pass on the topic.

"Do you mean of the Constitution?" Fisk probed. *Kids like you are another reason why I'm doing this. You don't want to get involved. You just sit tight, hoping it'll go away.*

"Yeah. I suppose it's all tied up in the way our leaders interpret the laws. If they choose to interpret them with a pro-government bias, then you get what Pete's talking about."

"I disagree," Harley said, folding his arms on the table as if that were the end of it.

Fisk pointed casually at him. "You disagree because you don't think that the impulse to act against a government can be predicted with any degree of certainty? From a mathematical perspective, that is." As he spoke, he thought of Griff and his reliance on computer models.

"Yes," Harley nodded, his eyes reflecting his conviction.

"Well, then, what do you want from me? Your points of view seem straightforward enough. You're for it, he's against it, and Chuck thinks there's more to it. Call him undecided."

"Can anybody actually overthrow today's government?" Chuck piped up.

The advisor leaned forward to make sure his voice didn't travel. "You need to separate your hypothetical government from any real government. Pete's referring to a hypothetical government. You and Harley are talking about the real world U.S. government. You guys need to settle on just one definition.

"If a hypothetical government falls victim to a hypothetical conspiracy, then you have to ask yourselves why. Governments either serve or they dictate. Men and women are free or they aren't." He pointed at Chuck, who nodded.

With any luck, they'll misquote me or decide not to tell anyone that they talked to me. "Chaos theory wasn't the 'in' thing when I was in school, but I can tell you this much. When I sit down with the President and she asks me about options, I can't just predict. I have to support my prediction with facts."

He looked earnestly at Harley. "Since you're so mathematical, why not ask yourself this question? What constitutes a 'real' conspiracy? If a government falls prey to a covert action taken by its citizens, at what point does that action become a conspiracy?"

"Any unlawful act which is undertaken by two or more people in secret is a conspiracy," Pete shot back.

"Says who?"

"The law," Pete insisted with an edge to his voice.

"That still doesn't..." Harley started, his mind churning with factoids and permutations.

When the awkward moment did not pass, Fisk pushed ahead. "Now you're starting to get into what is called 'assumption of authority'--the idea that a government is entitled to whatever power it has or can get. That's important. There's your chaos theory link."

Pete looked at Harley. "Both sides can't be right, or can they?"

Harley took out a small pad and pen as Chuck remained silent, apparently overwhelmed.

Fisk kept his face neutral. "Before anybody answers, let me pass on the benefit of my experience. As far as most world leaders are concerned, the only 'good' conspiracies are the ones they initiate. The average citizen would say the same. To someone having it done to them, a conspiracy's a bad thing."

Harley seemed impressed with what his pen was doing on the pad. "Whoa. Political and populist forces. Politics and the pursuit of power versus the concepts of patriotism and the pursuit of the greater good. Wow." He stopped to scribble out a line. "That says nothing about national or ethnic identities. Dude, I think you just gave me my Ph.D. thesis." He gaped at Fisk.

"That's heavy." Chuck gazed at Fisk with new appreciation.

Fisk smiled benignly.

Pete remained silent for a long moment, eyes closed.

Fisk could sense the anger pulsing through the young man's veins. *So much for the assumption of authority, eh?*

"I have to admit, I hadn't thought about it like that. The political perspective and the populist point of view are at odds with each other. Hypothetically, I would suppose that a balance should exist between the two. If there is equilibrium, there can be no conspiracy." Pete watched Fisk intently.

Harley stopped writing. "If there's no balance, one force or the other could push hard enough to achieve near total power, which might restore that missing equilibrium." He seemed genuinely excited by his conclusions.

Chuck finally found his voice. "The losing side would conspire. Wouldn't matter what kind of government or society it was. This is good." He bobbed his head with muted enthusiasm.

"What have you guys been talking about?" Christopher asked, taking a seat next to Pete.

"Homework and a little speculation," Fisk replied.

The students nodded.

"For a moment there, I was afraid you were going to ask him if he was part of that 'vast right-wing conspiracy' that the President likes to go on about." Rolling his eyes, he made it clear he was joking.

Pete looked at Harley, who seemed about to speak.

Chuck eyed Fisk speculatively. "Wouldn't a real conspiracy have to be small? I mean, if a big organization was actually plotting, wouldn't you think they'd be caught? The President's theory can't have any factual basis, can it?"

The question was innocent, and Fisk saw it as a direct attempt by the young man to redeem himself for his earlier silence. *If you only knew.* "No. The very idea that any conspiracy would be 'vast' strikes me as being impossible." He could imagine the arguments that would ensue between these three in the coming days. *You have the idea, guys, but you lack the insight necessary to make the leap.*

Christopher nudged him and cocked a thumb toward the front window. A long, dark limo had just rolled to a stop. Four men were getting out, each taking up station around the car. A fifth man, whom Fisk recognized, entered the coffee bar. He flashed a smile in Fisk's direction and moved to the bar to order coffee.

"Time's up. My ride is here, and it's very much past my bedtime," Fisk told the trio as he stood.

"Thanks for the company," Christopher told Pete, who seemed to be leader.

Fisk nodded to Harley and Chuck. *Nice kids. Dangerous ideas, but nice kids.* "Work on it. You never know, you might have something," he told Harley.

"I could be standing in the middle of a conspiracy right now, and I wouldn't know it," Pete said, shaking his head and smiling weakly. Fatigue and uncertainty had sapped his enthusiasm.

"Take your time, and be patient. You might be surprised what pops up when you least expect it."

Christopher shouldered his satchel. Fisk moved ahead of him, leaving the coffee bar. He didn't look at the bodyguard paying for his coffee at the counter. Stepping into the night, he breathed in the cool air. He slid into the back seat of the limo; Christopher joined him. Knowing that his watchers would be anxious, Fisk reactivated his tooth implant. The rest of the security detail piled in around them.

The limo's driver put the car into gear and merged with traffic.

The bodyguard with the coffee turned to get a good look at Fisk. "Any bruises?"

"None that I care to mention." Fisk relaxed into the plush seat.

Monday
June 2, 2014
South Gate
The White House
Washington, D.C.
1:59 A.M. EDT

Curtis Crain yawned, despite the fact that he'd only been on shift for an hour. Checking the thermostat for the air conditioner, he adjusted the lighting in the armored kiosk for the tenth time in a half hour. As a uniformed Secret Service guard, he rotated through a variety of assignments. Gate duty was his favorite.

He read the memo in his hands one more time. It was short on details and long on protocols. *Increased security measures because of the Treasury Secretary's disappearance.*

"Wouldn't have happened if I'd been there. I would've--"

The instrument board in front of him beeped. A small panel showing the silhouette of a generic automobile blinked. Reacting out of habit, he laid his right hand on the molded pistol-style grip that housed several of the booth's controls. The grip, set into the side of the chair, reminded him of the controls he'd seen in many helicopters.

"Vehicle approaching," the booth's computer-generated unisex voice announced.

"Check exterior lights."

"Exterior lights at 100 percent."

Leaning forward in his chair, he watched the driveway through the armored transpex. He stole a quick glance at the instrument board. *No other indicators. Good.*

A white four-door sedan with a civilian license plate rolled in to his field of view. It came to a stop three feet from a concrete and steel crash barrier. The barrier could be raised or lowered from several different control points around the White House.

"Great," Crain muttered, thinking the car was packed with

tourists. Touching a stud on the pistol grip, he heard his voice sound through speakers on the outside of the booth. Squinting, he was unable to make out the car's occupants through the tinted glass. *Nighttime and tinted glass. Just great.*

"Sorry folks. The White House is closed for the night." Raising his left hand slowly, he rested his index finger over the alert button. *Always ready. The President counts on it.*

The driver's door opened, causing Crain to flinch. The man who got out wore nothing more than bright orange and yellow swim trunks and a pair of sandals. In his right hand, he held up a piece of ID. Careful to keep both hands in easy view of the guard post, he shouted, "Secret Service! Protective Agent Dillon Gibbons. I have a Class Five emergency."

Crain touched the alert key on his instrument board without thinking. "Holy cow! Stay where you are. Everybody's coming."

Secretary Brown huddled on the back seat of the car, still nursing his grief. He sobbed, fists knotted in his lap. The unfairness of Corin's death was more than his rational mind could justify. *Why couldn't it have been me?*

Gibbons poked his head back inside the car. "We're in. Andy, please lie down. We can't let anybody see you." Reaching over the driver's seat, he latched a powerful hand around Brown's neck to guide him. Brown pulled his knees up and rested his bare feet on the back of the passenger's seat.

They waited. Eventually, the car began to move past the guard post. For an instant, the car's interior was bright as day. The light made Andrew blink, breaking his morbid train of thought. "I need clothes."

"Okay, hang on. We'll be going downhill. It's just the ramp to the underground parking area. Just another minute, sir, and we can sort this whole thing out." Doing his best to watch *everything*, Gibbons drove the car slowly down to the White House parking level.

Secretary Brown couldn't know it, but his ordeal had only just begun.

Monday
June 2, 2014
Presidential Quarters
The White House
Washington, D.C.
2:10 A.M. EDT

"Until you can get me stone cold proof of Brown's whereabouts, I'm not going to make any statements. I know we have to go on record, but let's give him some time. I'm sure that, whatever Fisk arranged, he left a trail of evidence that will take the mystery out of the man's disappearance." Madeline set down her coffee cup and regarded her press secretary with thinly veiled agitation. *You have a lot to learn about how I do things.*

"You need to step back and take a fresh look at this. I appreciate your interest, and the fact that you're ready to back me up in regards to Fisk, but this is an altogether different problem. There are things going on that you don't know anything about."

"We can't wait much longer. Did you know that the Communications Director isn't returning my calls? The press is already on to the fact that somebody destroyed the Coast Guard's audio records. If they ever trace it back to Fisk..." Angel fidgeted, lowering her eyes.

"They won't confirm a thing." Madeline smiled patronizingly, smoothing the white silk of her evening dress.

"Let me do my job and confirm that he *is* missing. We need to look sympathetic."

"I've already warned you off. Fine. If you aren't going to take the hint, then I'll just have to be blunt. I don't need your support. Not now. You're being kept out of this for your own good."

Angel went silent, her worst fears confirmed. *I thought it might be something like that.* Looking down at her floral patterned pantsuit, she felt her stomach flutter with a mix of fear and anticipation. Folding her hands in her lap, she considered her options. *I need to slow down.*

I already have her confidence. I don't need her anger.

"Andrew was an unwilling participant in my administration. He'll be missed, if for no other reason than his financial brilliance, but the fact remains that he wasn't a team player. We've come too far. Too many things have been set in motion. I couldn't take the chance that he would fail me." The fire of ambition lit in her eyes as she laid it out. She reclined slightly, gauging Angel's reaction to the new truth of her existence.

Angel mulled it over. *This could be the weakness I've been looking for, Daddy.*

Ever since she could remember, Angel had known what her father did for a living. His patriotism had rubbed off on her. Each time he came back to her, it reinforced her faith in the nation he served.

Now, as she sat in front of her president, she sensed the approach of an opportunity for revenge. In a fondly familiar tone, her father's voice rang out in her mind. *"You might be on to something, kiddo. Let's follow the clues, and see where they lead."* With her father's conviction and her own ambition, Angel straightened, embracing her new opportunity. *I hear you, Daddy. I hear you.* "I understand. Will there be anything else?" she said allowed, bowing her head in a show of defeat.

Both women started as the shadow of a female Secret Service agent fell across the coffee table. "Madame President? There's a situation down on the parking level that requires your attention. We found Andrew Brown." The woman adjusted the earpiece of her secured radio.

Stunned, Angel and Madeline looked at each other, each taking the other's measure.

"Well. I'm not clear on what this means, but I would guess that Fisk has outdone himself. Again." The notion that Brown had somehow come around to her way of thinking sent a chill up the President's spine. *Fisk, you are amazing. What did it take? Bribery?*

In all her years of association with Preston Fisk, very few of her opponents had actually been suborned by threats. A scant number had given in to exquisitely timed blackmail. The majority had been overcome by money. The possibilities intrigued Madeline immensely.

Angel nodded appreciatively, hiding her own thoughts. *If*

you ordered Fisk to kill the man, why is he downstairs in the garage? Unless...

"Come along. You're in this far, you might as well see it through." Madeline stood with fluid grace. Looking down at Angel, she felt infused with the power that springs from chance meeting destiny. *Fortune favors the bold, does it not? I am bold. Whatever this new wrinkle is, I'm sure I can make it work for me.*

Angel collected her papers and put them in her briefcase. Rising to her feet, she followed the President down to the parking level in silence. *Something went wrong. I can feel it. Might be the same kind of thing that went wrong for you, Daddy. Wouldn't it be ironic if the same sort of botched cover-up that got you killed also got us the revenge we wanted?*

Monday
June 2, 2014
Underground Parking Level
The White House
Washington, D.C.
2:30 A.M. EDT

"Right this way." The agent led Madeline and Angel into the secured embarkation point. The protected garage was reserved for the arrival and departure of the President and other dignitaries. The enclosed space was separated from the rest of the underground parking level by a pair of heat-resistant ceramic composite blast doors and was large enough to accommodate either a single one of the military's largest armored vehicles or two presidential limousines.

Madeline halted just inside the door, raised an imperious hand, and peeked out. The blast doors at both ends of the hardened bay were closed. The stark white walls and dull grey floor reminded Madeline of a prison cell. The harsh lighting banished any hint of a shadow, enhancing the feeling of sterility. At the far end of the chamber, near the blast door to her left, a white, four-door sedan was parked at an angle. All four doors hung open. A trio of agents in shirtsleeves and surgical gloves were going over the car's interior with a variety of electronic detection devices. A distraught and dirty Andrew Brown stood in front of the car.

Madeline watched him for a long moment. Running a hand through unkempt hair, the man seemed lost and bewildered. Clad only in dark blue swim trunks and a torn grey sweatshirt, Brown wiggled his bare toes on the cold concrete floor. Lost in his own grief, he seemed oblivious to what was going on around him. Next to him, a well-muscled man with a deep tan and short blond hair stood a full head taller. He was obviously protecting Brown.

Well, Madeline nodded with certainty, *that explains how he survived. Chalk up another one for the Secret Service.* She noted with mild interest that the bodyguard was wearing nothing more than old sandals and a pair of bright yellow and orange swim trunks. *Impressive. The man's practically naked and unarmed, yet he's still confident.*

The muscles on Gibbons' broad chest flexed with his hand movements as he described what had happened to the Browns. Two female agents stood close by, nodding and prompting as the debriefing continued.

Madeline turned away from the partially opened door. "What's going on down here? Who called me down here for this?"

"I did, Madame President, and I'm glad you're so prompt."

Bristling at the man's surly tone, Madeline straightened, turning slowly to face Conroy Horn, director of the White House Secret Service protective unit.

"Do you have any idea what time it is? Why are you even here?" Madeline glanced at her bare wrist, and then looked around for a clock.

"I was in the Old Executive Building, watching the auxiliary status boards. We got another terrorist alert from Homeland, so I was just checking it out. You know how it is for an old bloodhound. I might not be young enough for the chase, but I'm not too old to watch." *And I have, too. Watched, and waited. You've gone too far.*

"I see. Your concern is--"

"My concern is why I'm here. You've gone too far this time. Whatever is going here has crossed the line." He took a challenging step forward.

Angel was no stranger to this kind of confrontation. Careful to remain silent, she assessed her options. *You're too late. Shooting from the hip will do you no good.*

"What are you talking about?" Madeline demanded, locking eyes with Horn.

"Please, let's not make this difficult. We both know why you're here. Come on in, Metz. You need to see this." Horn took another step forward. His dark brown suit matched his eyes, giving him an even more determined expression. *I wish I could say that having you here was a stroke of luck, but I know better. You trust me about as far as I can throw you.*

Madeline flinched as Metz, followed by a pair of junior agents, walked into the room. The duo flanked the inner door, keeping their eyes averted.

Realizing the importance of the moment, Angel willed herself to be invisible.

Metz, dressed in a beige suit and maroon tie, ambled into the room as if he had no cares. He towered over his boss, not even bothering to look down at him as he took his place near the president. Smiling through his mustache, he looked at his president and let his mirth travel to his eyes. He slid his hands into his pockets. "I hope you know what you're doing. Things aren't like they used to be. This'll either make you or break you."

Director Horn eyed his deputy with open contempt. At just 5'6", Conroy Horn was the very embodiment of 'average.' From his taste in simple off-the-rack suits to his ordinary haircut, he had never pushed the style envelope at all. His no-nonsense lifestyle had translated into his work ethic, a fact that both Carl and President Hill knew all too well.

"Madame President. The agent responsible for guarding Secretary Brown tells me that your man Fisk was responsible for the attack on the Brown's sailboat. That, combined with the fact that you've undermined my office at every turn since you've been here, leads me to believe that--"

"I told you he'd go off on you." Metz gave Madeline a sidelong glance.

"Just shut up and listen," she commanded. Looking down at Horn, Madeline made the most of her one-inch height advantage. *I'm going to break you for letting this happen.* "Whatever it is you think you have on me, it's not going to amount to anything. It may have escaped your attention, Mr. Horn, but this is my presidency. It's a whole new world--and it belongs to me and those I favor."

Horn shook his head slowly. The strength of his convictions gave him the willpower he needed to speak his mind. "Not if I have anything to say about it. I've been through four presidents. I know what's what. I can't stop you from bringing shame on your administration, but I sure can have some say about what you do to the institution. Fisk's connection to you is direct and unambiguous. His actions on your behalf have endangered the life of one of my agents and directly resulted in the death of Secretary Brown's wife. You are under arrest."

The power of the director's words forced Madeline to look away for a single heartbeat. The irony of the situation caused her stomach to roil with fury. She watched Angel silently take it all in. *Smart. Very smart.* "How dare you!" she breathed with flared nostrils. "How dare you make such *unreasonable* accusations? You could consider the possibility that I know what I am doing. It's not as if this sort of thing doesn't happen--" *I DON'T need Fisk to fight my battles for me. Nobody can stop me!*

With the certainty of her future crystallizing, Madeline cast a sidelong glance at Metz. The unspoken agreement passed between them. *Don't discredit him. Don't ruin him. Kill him.*

"Not when it involves a member of the Service. Not now, not ever. The law permits us a certain degree of discretion in what we overlook. When you went after Brown, you crossed the line. You involved a protective agent," Horn said angrily, his dusky features darkening.

The two men by the door looked at each other with raised eyebrows. The third agent shook her head and left the room, scowling. Carl touched his well-tanned Adam's apple, narrowly avoiding a cough. Angel looked at her president, taking a small step back toward the nearest wall.

"Very well." Madeline reached behind her to close the door. "Since you're so concerned for the sanctity of your beloved 'Service,' let me spell it out for you. Stop this here and now, and I will--"

Metz took his hands out of his pockets. "Wait just a minute. There's no need for you to get involved in this. Let me handle it." He firmly believed that people like Horn had held him back for too many years. *Hypocrites like you have the nerve to turn a blind eye to something only when it suits you. This is the 21st century. Nobody cares about the "clean hands" policy.*

Madeline turned to face Carl with manic fire in her eyes. "One more word from you, and so help me..." Fists clenched at her sides, she let her words trail off with deliberate menace.

Carl closed his mouth, certain that he'd overextended himself.

"This is all very touching, but I think we can leave the question of 'honor among thieves' for later debate,'" Horn interjected. *I should have gotten to a phone before I came down here. There are a lot of people in the chain of command who need to know about this.*

"Okay. You've made your point. Just what is it you want?" Madeline tugged a wrinkle out of her dress, ready to pounce on the first wrong move that Horn made. *Everybody wants something, even men of principle.* As far as she was concerned, "principle" just meant "higher price."

"I want a full investigation of this incident. I want you to answer for what you've done. I want to see both of you prosecuted to the full extent of the law."

"Are you nuts? I can't believe I'm hearing this," Metz breathed. He ranted, "You want to prosecute me for *this*? I have news for you, old man. It's too late. You had your turn. Times have changed." As far as he knew, there were less than two dozen people left in the upper ranks of the Secret Service who shared Horn's outmoded beliefs.

"Your deputy makes a good point. Arresting me will end a lot of careers--starting with yours." Even as she spoke, Madeline knew that Horn wouldn't give a fig about anybody's career, including his own. *I can see it in your eyes. You'd go down with us, and like it. I don't need Fisk to tell me that.*

"Metz has been cooperating with you ever since you were sworn in. I know about the rogue SWAT cops, too. I have names, dates, account numbers, and dollar amounts. You're not the only one who knows how to fight for what you want." Turning on his heel, Horn addressed the two agents at the door. "Get backup. Take Metz to holding. Escort the President to her quarters." He pivoted to face Madeline and played his last card. "You have until 7 o'clock this morning. If you don't resign, I will have you arrested for the attempted murder of Treasury Secretary Andrew Brown." *If I were a married man, I'd have second thoughts. But I'm not. I love this country, and everything it stands for. Serve and protect, remember?* The fact that his president hadn't bothered to justify her actions, nor explain herself in any way, further convinced Conroy that he'd been right about her all along.

The two agents who had come in with him hesitated. Both looked at Metz for direction.

Sensing their divided loyalties, Horn reached for the comm panel on the wall. "You two are on report." He pushed the alert key.

Putting her hands down at her sides, Madeline felt her anger slowly ebb. The usual reflex to reach for a telephone never surfaced. *I can do it. I know I can. I can feel it.* Waiting for a handful of breaths, she searched her soul. Her need to rely on somebody else to solve this problem was nowhere to be found.

"Wait for the opening, and then come see me," Madeline said softly to Metz as Horn spoke forcefully into the wall comm.

Metz cringed as Horn gave the order for his arrest. "What? I'm not just gong to stand here--"

"Stop and think." Madeline turned her back on Horn as another pair of agents rushed in. "That's what Fisk always tells me. Now I'm telling you. Your people will get you out of holding. When they do, come and see me."

Metz could feel his eyebrows climb up his forehead as her words began to make sense. "You know what I've got to do?" he whispered.

"I do," she assured him with a grim nod.

"Are you nuts? I can't do these people on the premises. Homeland would--"

"Just get out of holding, and then come see me. Let me worry about Homeland Security."

Monday
June 2, 2014
Underground Parking Level
The White House
Washington, D.C.
2:40 A.M. EDT

"She came by in a broadside pass. The throttle was wide open by the sound of it. She was taking on water every time she broached a wave," Gibbons explained to the senior agents. With his adrenaline rush gone, he calmly recounted the events that led up to the sinking of the *Almighty Dollar*. Despite the late hour, he showed no signs of fatigue.

"We'll get you over to repro and see if we can't get a sketch. Ten to one, she's not in Homeland's database," one of the women said.

The two agents had listened to the story twice now. Gibbons' recounting was both impressive and consistent.

"I don't want to rule anything out, Sandy. You and Debbie should take Secretary Brown for a proper debrief. No reason we should all have to stay up through the night. I'll wait for the guys from Central." Gibbons scratched the back of his neck.

The Secret Service headquarters complex, including the offices of the overall director and much of its non-Treasury staff and equipment, was based in Franklin, Virginia. The relatively new facility rivaled the CIA's installation at Langley. Built in 2009, it was nicknamed "Central" for its passing resemblance to New York's Grand Central Station. Grand Central had been remodeled around the same time, giving the huge train station a more modern look.

"What happened next?" Debbie prodded, keeping a careful eye on Brown, who was leaning against the hood of the sedan.

"You said she fired a grenade launcher. What kind?" Following routine procedure, both agents were repeatedly grilling Gibbons about his ordeal. They asked him different questions each time, looking for

457

holes in his story and forcing him to dredge up additional details.

"It reminded me of the old Russian stuff. You know, the kind they used to fit to their assault rifles for special forces duty." Using hand gestures, he mimed the long snout of the launcher.

"And?" Sandy asked as she swiped at a loose strand of hair.

"It took me an hour to find Secretary Brown. He's pretty tough. When the Coast Guard helicopter didn't come, we tried to find the emergency locator beacon. It was just luck that the tide carried us back in fairly close to shore. I memorized the addresses of the homes we hid in."

"Are you sure nobody saw you?" Debbie doubted that the two ragged men, struggling ashore after almost 12 hours in the water, hadn't been seen by *someone*.

"I was careful to stick to the summer cottages. The three that we went through were boarded up, but they weren't hard to get into. The last one had a serviceable phone, but like I said, I wasn't sure if it would be safe to call in, given that Preston Fisk is the President's special friend."

The agents nodded. The story was more than impressive, it was scary. If Gibbons was right--and there was no reason to suspect him of lying--then the attempt on Brown's life had come straight from the President. Each woman was aware of the implications. Shifting loyalties in the protective unit had caused many veteran agents to seek transfers. The majority of those who stayed owed their allegiance to Metz, who was rumored to have very close connections to the President.

Sandy, who had relayed the initial report to Metz via secured phone, felt uneasy. *This is going to get messy.*

Looking first at her partner, and then at Gibbons, Debbie said nothing. *Hard to believe. Nine years on the job and it all comes down to a guy with a tan and sand in his shorts.* She racked her brain for an excuse to leave.

"This car's clean. No trackers, no antitheft, no nothing. Just your plain, old, run-of-the-mill civilian job rocket," a balding man in white shirt and green tie commented as he hauled himself out of the driver's seat. Standing, he stripped off his rubber gloves.

"Leave the car where it is." Metz confidently strode across the parking bay, his smile broad and cordial. "Sandy, Debbie, would you please escort Secretary Brown inside?" "The debrief team from Central is on their way, and we need to give Mr. Brown a chance to get his bearings." *Cutting it awful close. Hope this works.* He was relying on the practice, common to all law enforcement agencies, of conducting question-and-answer sessions immediately after crimes or violent acts.

The two agents sifting the car's interior got out and stood up.

Gibbons shook Brown's hand reassuringly before allowing him to leave. "We did it, Andy. We got through. All you have to do now is go with these ladies. They'll get you some clothes and something to eat."

"Clothes?" Brown looked down at the torn front of his sweatshirt.

"Right. Then food. Then our people would like to ask you a few questions. Nothing too tough; just about the last 24 hours or so. Okay?" Careful to avoid the subject of Corin, Gibbons watched as the grieving man was led out of the secured parking area.

When Brown was gone, Metz turned back to the remaining agents. Taking a long look at Gibbons, he shook his head. "You're going to make agent of the year for this. Hope your sunburn doesn't ruin that pretty-boy face." Stepping around Gibbons, he satisfied himself that the other man wasn't armed. *I'll bet you'd break my neck if you knew what was coming.*

Gibbons laughed with everyone else, running his hands through his hair. His fingers came away gritty. "Sir. Whatever this is all about--"

"Will be explained in short order," Metz interrupted forcefully.

Gibbons watched eyebrows rise as the agents behind Metz registered their own curiosity.

"Sir. I heard their whole conversation. If the order goes out to arrest Fisk, I'd like to be on the team." Gibbons turned to face his superior.

"Listen, trust me. Put a lid on it until you have a chance to be fully debriefed. I promise you that this will all work itself out."

Unable to see the look on Metz's face, the three agents behind him looked at each other uncertainly.

"I see." Gibbons noticed the behavior of the men standing around the car. *I get it. The lid's already coming down on whatever happened to start this whole mess.*

Metz smiled thinly, confirming the understanding that flickered across Gibbons' face. *My, but you're hot on the trail, aren't you? Sure wish I could ask you to stay quiet about all this, but I know you won't.*

"When do I debrief?" Gibbons asked, now conscious of the grit in his shorts. *Change the subject and let Director Horn handle it. I'm sure he'll fill me in when he gets the chance.* He looked up to Horn.

"I'm sure they'll be here in a few. Say, why don't you hit the shower? Use the locker room on this level. I'll pass the word so that they know where to find you." Metz put his hands in his pockets, looking thoughtful. *That should give me enough time to deal with Conroy.*

Protecting his job and serving his president were now the same thing for Carl Metz. His future was now completely dependent upon hers, and he knew it.

"Sounds good. Anybody know if the scavenger closet has anything in it?" The agent made a show of hitching up his shorts. Protective agents often relied on the expedient of stashing spare clothing in the locker rooms they used. Years of accumulation sometimes resulted in the discovery of the most unlikely items. Resorting to the "scavenger closet" was a common joke among those who knew about it.

"Yeah. I saw a couple of dresses in there. Might be a tight squeeze, but..." a bald man replied, letting his words trail off as he waggled a flat hand in an "iffy" gesture.

"After what I've been through, all I ask for is matching pumps and a hat that doesn't hide my ears." Tossing off a mock salute, he headed for the exit.

"Well, I don't think this car's going anywhere," another man huffed, thumping the roof. "Not unless somebody hotwires it again."

Metz waited for Gibbons to get out of earshot. *Okay, I know you guys will work with me, but I want to hear you say it.* He turned his back on the door as Gibbons closed it behind him. Licking his lips, he took a long slow breath before making his play. "Got a minute?" *You help me, and I help you.*

"Sir?" the third agent asked, finally pulling off his rubber gloves.

"I've just come from a meeting with the President. She's got a

460

little problem that she could use some help with."

The fellow with the green tie looked up from a piece of electronic sniffer gear that he held in both hands. "Is what Gibbons said--"

"Yes, but she had a good reason for doing it. That's why I need your help. A lot rides on what we do in the next few hours. It's going to be a real squeaker. If we don't shut this thing off now, it'll hurt everybody. You follow me?"

"What does Director Horn say?" The third agent walked slowly around the white sedan.

Metz looked closely at the man, sizing him up. *You're just looking for something to cover your butt. Fine by me.* He swept his iron gaze over all three men. "Director Horn...is part of the problem." Under the harsh light in the secured parking area, he felt exposed and vulnerable.

"Ah, heck. This sounds like Clinton all over again." Tossing the gloves onto the car roof, the bald man tugged at his belt buckle in agitation. Metz didn't respond to the comparison.

The Clinton administration had been very eventful, behind closed doors. A decade and a half after those turbulent years, the dust was still settling. The social, political, and legal precedents spawned between 1992 and 2000 were still having their effects on White House policy and conduct.

With their wives, children, and careers foremost in their minds, the three men nodded acceptance. Cooperation would be total as long as it spared them from the catastrophic alternatives.

"Stay with me," Madeline said tersely over her shoulder. Angel followed silently.

Flanked by a pair of protective agents loyal to Horn, President Hill walked through a security checkpoint without acknowledging the uniformed guard behind the counter.

"This isn't over. Not by a long shot," she said with cruel certainty.

As she passed the guard, Angel thought of her washed up plans. *If I'm not careful, Metz will upstage me, and I'll lose my chance to gain her confidence.*

"I know what you're thinking. You think I'm going to call him, don't you?" Madeline turned abruptly to face Angel directly.

Angel said nothing as the group piled into the elevator.

"The answer is definitely no. This incident doesn't change anything. If anything, it underscores my need to be rid of him. He's never failed me before, and while I don't pretend to know why this happened, I can't rule out the possibility that it was deliberate." Her blonde curls swayed with the force of her words.

Angel was silent for a long moment as the elevator rose. "We won't know what Fisk had in mind until Brown's been debriefed, but I see your point. Can you count on Metz to handle things on this end?" she asked with a guarded expression that didn't quite reach her eyes.

"He has no choice. The alternative is...well, the alternative just *isn't*," the President replied emphatically as she exited the elevator.

Monday
June 2, 2014
The White House
Washington, D.C.
2:57 A.M. EDT

As the head of the White House protective unit, Conroy Horn held one of the most stressful jobs in the Secret Service. The position had lost a lot of its appeal over the previous few terms, but it was still a necessary tour of duty for those aspiring to bigger and better things. For Horn, it represented the zenith of his career. The fact of the matter was that he had no greater ambitions.

Pausing to gather his thoughts, Horn loitered in the stairwell that would take him back up to the ground level. Two agents waited silently just above him. With the door closed, he leaned against the brass handrail. Grasping it with both hands to keep himself steady, he chewed on his lower lip. *What have I done? Have I really just threatened to arrest the President of the United States?*

Time crept by as he considered his options. He looked at his silent guardians. They didn't return his gaze. *Both of you must be loyal to Metz. Is that it?* Looking directly at them men, he tried to put things in perspective. *For whatever reason, the President sicced Fisk on Secretary Brown. Seems clear enough that she wanted him killed. Fisk meets with Brown while he's out sailing. They have a conversation, details unknown. Brown's angry about whatever Fisk said. Fisk leaves the area and a woman in a speedboat attacks the Browns. Brown lives and Gibbons brings him in.*

"We should go," one of the agents prodded, upset with the way Horn was staring at him.

He looked each agent in the face as he considered dismissing them. *If I blow them off, they'll go straight to Metz or the President.* Straightening, Horn pulled the wrinkles out of his coat and checked his tie. *If I knew what Fisk said to Brown, it might change a few things.*

"All right. Let's go," he replied with a sweep of his hands. Turning, he went back down the stairs and entered the hallway of the underground level. He smirked in satisfaction when his protectors were slow to follow. *Come on, guys. You didn't expect me to give that easily, did you?*

"Sir?" the agent nearest the door asked, starting to reach out.

"Just follow me, okay?" Horn looked him in the eye as he slipped through the door.

Calm. You're still in charge. Make it work.

"Where are we going?" the man asked as they moved back down the corridor.

Horn smiled to himself, grateful that his back was turned. *Wouldn't you like to know?*

As he walked down the silent corridor, passing through two security checkpoints, doubts began to creep in. The uniformed guards at the checkpoints nodded at his passing, apparently unconcerned with whatever prompted their boss to be roaming the White House underground at this late hour.

Passing an empty conference room, Horn suspected he had been out-maneuvered. *I see. Metz isn't going to holding, is he?* His trained ears picked out the sound of a shower. Water hissed and spat with a faraway echo behind the door of a men's locker room. *That has to be Gibbons.*

"Nature calls." Horn motioned towards the locker room door laconically. "Stay out here. As long as you fellows have made up your minds about which side of this thing you're on, how about letting me have a few minutes alone?"

"Sir, please. This is hard enough. There are things that have been going on with Metz and the President for a long time now. We're just looking--"

"Shut up, Tony," the other agent hissed. "Don't say another word. Just let the man go. This'll be over with soon enough, and you don't want to say anything that they might call you on."

Horn held up both hands like a referee. "Easy. I promise not to flush myself." *So, Metz really is making his move.*

Walking into the locker room, he took off his jacket. *I should have seen this coming,* he mused as he headed for the shower area. Peeking around the corner into the communal showers, he saw a man from the chest up surrounded by steaming jets of water. Framed by gleaming white tile, the man rinsed the lather of shampoo from his short blonde hair.

Conroy reversed course and walked back to the locker room door. Placing his coat on a bench, he quietly locked the door. The bolt slid silently into place. *That's Gibbons, all right. I hope he has something to tell me that I can use.* Returning to the shower area, he approached the bathing agent.

Gibbons was just putting down a bar of soap when he registered movement.

"Agent Gibbons, I need to ask you some questions," Horn said, trying to be casual. Resting his shirtsleeved arms on the tile counter, he ignored the water that seeped through the cuffs.

"Yes, sir." Gibbons reached for the faucet. His tanned body, slightly pink under the bronze glow, was beginning to itch.

"No, leave it on. I need to speak to you privately." Horn looked toward the entrance.

Gibbons leaned against the shower wall, oblivious to his own nudity. "What's going on?"

"President Hill is into something. Metz is helping her. I need to know what Fisk said to Brown. It can make a difference in how this whole thing turns out."

Gibbons didn't usually question his superiors. From his point of view, if this incident was to be covered up, then so be it. It was well known that Deputy Director Metz thought very highly of President Hill. The unspoken division in loyalties between Horn and Metz had been going on for nearly two years. Agents and support staff had been forced to choose sides in the silent conflict within six months of President Hill's inauguration.

Conroy Horn was the man Dillon most wanted to be like. Horn's uncompromising nature and attention to detail were refreshing in a government where mediocrity was the order of the day.

"Run that by me again?" Horn wiped a line of sweat from his forehead.

"Believe me, I know how kooky it sounds."

"So, Fisk makes one last play to keep Secretary Brown in line, but it falls on deaf ears. Did Fisk say or do anything else that you can recall? Something that would suggest a threat?" Stepping back, Horn reached for a towel to wipe his face.

"He never threatened him. Just kept going on about some deep dark secret that he was willing to share." Gibbons shook his head.

"Tell me about that secret. What did you get out of it?"

"The usual stuff. You know how those hired guns are. They think they own the people they work for. Fisk was going on about that, and how he had some hidden agenda that Andy would like, but Andy wouldn't hear any of it."

"Fisk leaves and you get attacked," Horn summarized, wadding the towel in both hands.

"In a nutshell, yeah." Gibbons straightened. Watching the

Director's dark skin sparkle from the moisture in the room, it was hard to know what he was really thinking.

"I've already said I wouldn't play along. You need to know that. I gave the President an ultimatum, but it may not pan out. I don't know who I can trust."

Gibbons set the washcloth aside and left the shower, heading for a towel that lay folded on a bench nearby. "What do you want from me?"

"Can you remember anything else?" Horn huffed the steam out of his lungs.

"I keep coming back to that hidden agenda thing. Fisk wanted to explain something. Said he could explain it all if Andy would just give him the chance." Gibbons sat down on the bench, stroking his chin.

"But he didn't?" Horn shuffled his feet, checking his watch. *Have to wind this up.*

"Oh, no. Andy was really cranked. I'm not sure, but I think Fisk and Andy had words before, like within the last couple of days. Fisk kept telling Andy that he wanted him to be around when President Hill crossed the line. He sounded like he was expecting her to do something wrong and wanted Andy to be a witness."

Horn checked his watch again. Wiping a drop of water off his nose, he looked at Gibbons. "What kind of person would you say Andrew Brown is?" *Fisk knows she's going to cross the line. That's why he wants Mr. Brown so close at hand.*

"Type-two personality. Segregated type-A behavior patterns. Real big on saying what he means. Even his wife was up front like that."

Watching Gibbon's face and hearing his words, Horn felt the vibe. *Ah. You respect him. He's a decent guy.* "He's a man of principle?" *I should go. They'll grill you pretty hard when they find out that you talked to me.*

"Sure." Gibbons got to his feet.

"All right." Horn detoured to a toilet stall, reaching in to flush. The water roared loudly as he reached for his jacket. "I appreciate your insight. Just one more thing."

"Yeah?" Gibbons stopped toweling to listen.

"I'm not going to tell anyone we had this conversation, and I strongly suggest that you don't mention it to the people who debrief you. As I said, I'm finished around here. There's no need for you to join me in the unemployment line." He walked over to the locker room door, stopping just long enough to look Gibbons in the eye before he left.

Dillon gave some thought to what Horn had said. Reaching over the counter, he turned off the water. *Better just drop it and pretend as if it never happened.*

Monday
June 2, 2014
Old Executive Office Building
Washington, D.C.
3:19 A.M. EDT

Metz nodded to the trio of men standing around his office. "We're covered." Setting down the telephone, he breathed a sigh of relief. "When the Director gets in this morning, she'll find everything she needs to get rid of Horn on disciplinary grounds."

"You're sure she's going to buy this?" the man with the green tie asked. The others nodded their approval of the question.

"Oh, yeah. Horn's finished. Remember, she had to put up with him during the last administration. She's tired of his old school attitude. Trust me. We're not the only ones who'll be happy to see him go."

The agent nearest the door rubbed the stubble on his chin. "That leaves Gibbons and the uniform at the gate who let him in." The unspoken question hung in the air like a dark cloud.

"Round them up. We'll use the same fake debrief on Gibbons that we're running Brown through right now. I've told you what the President told me. She'll be very grateful to all of us for getting the lid nailed back on this thing." Despite the speed of the last hour's events, Carl felt firmly in control.

"That guard'll want to report to his shift supervisor. You know how they are, so proud of that badge and white shirt that they just got to follow the rule book to the letter." The man with the green tie cocked an eyebrow in mild disgust.

Metz pursed his lips, considering. The fluorescent tubes in the ceiling hummed as he thought. "Write him up. If he likes the rulebook so much, check it out. See how many regs he busted tonight. Check the new Homeland circulars, too. Anything you can gig him on, do it." The man with the green tie left the room.

"You want to wash him out?" the last agent observed, chewing at his lower lip.

Metz nodded, touching the edge of his salt-and-pepper mustache. "Yes. Let the review board do it, nice and legal. That way he's got no chance for an appeal."

As they left the room, the third agent told his cohort, "That's not going to shut him up. People like him usually go to the tabloids. Do you really want that?" The other man shook his head emphatically, rolling up the sleeves of his shirt.

"Let him talk!" Metz called after them. "The conspiracy buffs will run with it and we'll have a built-in smoke screen. Besides, he didn't actually see Brown in the back of that car. He might put the pieces together after the fact, but it won't matter."

Once they were gone, Metz looked around his office. One of many such spartan work holes, it was used on a project-by-project basis. Office supplies littered nearby shelves. The grey metal desk was bare except for the telephone. On the far wall, six battered filing cabinets stood guard. Taking a deep breath, he picked up the phone and dialed. Rubbing his cheeks tiredly, he ignored his own stubble.

The voice on the other end of the line was alert. "Clay."

"Metz," he replied with authority and a smile.

"New instructions. Brown is in isolation. Gibbons' debrief is almost done. He's going to play along."

Carl switched the receiver to his other ear. *He knows what's good for his career.*

"Hey, I just got a note. Horn's left the building."

"He did? Did he sign out?" Metz stopped in mid-scratch. *Giving up already? So much for you, then.*

"Yes. Ledger says he's going home."

"How long ago did he leave?" He felt the surge of suspicion course through his veins.

"Five minutes." Clay paused to confer with somebody.

Metz felt the muscles in his neck tighten. "Did he take his chaperons?"

"Nope. I was kind of thinking you warned them off..."

"I'll get back to you. I need time to think. Make sure Gibbons gets the full treatment. He has to believe that he's being questioned by a real oversight panel. You understand?" He hung up without waiting for a response. Stepping out into the empty hallway, he breathed deeply to get his stomach under control. *So close. So very close.*

Walking down the corridor, Metz stopped in the empty lobby. Hands in pockets, he stood lost in thought. *I'm putting it off.* Moving slowly, he walked over to a padded bench, and sat to think. *I'm putting it off because it's never been done before--and it scares me.*

The knowledge of what he was about to do gave him new respect for President Hill. *How does she do it and make it look so easy?* Pressing the elevator call button, he savored the absence of his regular bodyguards. *Better enjoy it while I can. Something tells me that I won't be going anywhere without them anymore.*

The elevator door opened. Stepping inside the car, Carl pressed the button for the ground floor. As he rode in the elevator, he turned his attention to the only real threat remaining. *Fisk is not out of my reach. I have to remember that. I can see him putting Horn on his payroll just to keep his options open.*

"Like I'm going to let that happen," he snorted. *No wonder she wants Fisk dead and buried.*

As he exited the elevator, he asked the sleepy attendant, "Situation?" He carefully projected confidence as he approached the counter. *Just another day at the office.*

The woman looked up from her terminal, touching a remote telephone earpiece with a delicately manicured hand. She hadn't expected to see anyone at this hour. "My board is clear." She looked down at the compact holographic screen, tapping at the keyboard in her lap.

"Is she still up?" Metz leaned on the counter, watching the display change as the woman called up a classified location monitor.

"Yes, sir." She turned the monitor's projector around so that he could easily read the display. Decades-old security procedures prevented them from speaking more directly about the presidential "situation."

"Sign me out. I'm going home."

"What about your chaperons?" she asked.

"They have...things to do." Metz indicated secrecy with a gesture.

Monday
June 2, 2014
Presidential Quarters
The White House
Washington, D.C.
3:22 A.M. EDT

"Thank you, Jeffrey." Madeline nodded as the Asian man left the sitting room.

Pushing the serving cart ahead of him, Jeffrey's usual white and black livery was clean and crisp. There was no hint of fatigue about him. He had appeared with the serving cart only moments after her request for coffee had been made through the kitchen intercom.

Picking up the exquisitely crafted china cup, she took in the aroma of the Brazilian blend. Seated casually in her favorite chair, the President looked across the coffee table at Angel, who was stirring her coffee with a small silver spoon.

"How does he know when to be here?" Angel asked with admiration. Placing the spoon carefully on the rim of the saucer, she began to relax.

"His quarters are just down the hall. Whenever I'm up here, it registers on the computer workstation in his apartment. He's probably updated by the Service agents or some such. He's awake whenever I am, I do know that much,"

Madeline's approval of Jeffrey, and his exemplary track record as presidential caretaker, were not commonly known among the White House coterie. Angel suspected that Madeline liked keeping the secret of his prowess under wraps.

The telephone on the antique table next to Madeline chimed softly for her attention.

Angel looked at her cup, pondering the need for more sugar. *Metz. Whatever he's doing, he's making sure to touch base with her.*

"Yes?" Madeline answered, holding the receiver delicately.

"Metz. Brown's being put away for safekeeping and the agent who brought him in is cooperating. The files you gave me are on their way to the main office. I've spoken to the Service O.D., and he agrees with your assessment of the situation. Horn will be brought up on charges--insubordination and obstruction."

"You had no trouble reaching him?" Madeline smiled cordially at Angel, indicating the call was bringing good news.

"The OD? He's on call 24/7. I got him at home. He knows Horn. Plays golf with him every now and then. He's of the opinion that Conroy's a nice guy and a good friend, but not very flexible."

"Tell me more," Madeline purred, her confidence rising. *This crisis is over, and Fisk had nothing to do with pulling it off.*

"That's going to depend on what you want to do with Secretary Brown."

Madeline leaned in toward the phone, her senses going on alert as Metz spoke with excessive clarity, his tone thick with urgency. *So, you're willing to go that far, are you?* The unspoken thought made her stop.

Her election had solidified her resolve to be rid of Fisk by any means necessary. The serendipitous way in which her underlings were wrapping up the fiasco surrounding the botched Brown assassination made her wonder. *I've overestimated Fisk's value, haven't I? All those years that I thought he was indispensable to me--was I wrong?*

As far as she knew, Fisk had never hurt her, beyond the obvious emotional strain that resulted from his purposeful distance. His unwillingness to become romantically involved, or be anything more than her tool, now made more sense. The insight chilled her.

All I have ever really needed are people who understand me and what I am trying to do. Fisk understands me. He knows what I'm trying to do. He accepts my attacks against him as part of his job. And my destiny. The cold matrix of the realization blew apart in her mind's eye, each thread flashing by in a fiery arc. Fisk's casual words from three weeks before screamed like a whirlwind through her consciousness. *"Why be satisfied with better debt terms when that same debt, no matter what the terms, can gain you something that nobody since Julius Caesar has had?"*

"Madame President?" Metz prompted, unsure of what to make of her silence. Afraid that she'd misinterpreted his question as an expression of weakness, he decided to hedge his bets by repeating himself. "What do you want to do with Secretary Brown?"

"Let me know when you've finished with Mr. Horn," Madeline grumbled, still mesmerized by the fireworks in her mind. "It's all so clear to me now."

Monday
June 2, 2014
The Fisk Residence
Chesapeake Bay, Maryland
4:30 A.M. EDT

Rolling his shoulders, Fisk enjoyed the shower's hot spray. His skin began to turn a soft pink from overexposure to the heat. Tensing his abdomen, he turned to his left, allowing the shower's steely needles to work their magic on his stress. Breathing in the steam, he resisted the urge to pull away. Images of his late evening spent with Josephine lingered with a wan pleasantness as droplets of water gathered on his closed eyelids.

"Oh, yeah," he finally sighed, using both hands to rub the muscles on the back of his neck.

A loud knock sounded on the bathroom door. Once. Twice. Three times.

Fisk registered the urgency of the coded knock. *What now? If it doesn't involve Madeline, a terrorist attack, or the end of the world, I'm going to have words with somebody about their lousy timing.*

"Come!" he bellowed over the roar of the hot water, reaching out to steady himself with one hand as he turned off the shower. He took one last deep breath to capture the cleansing steam hanging thickly in the air.

The door to the bathroom opened hastily, followed by the sound of shuffling footsteps. The door quickly closed behind the new arrival. Griff's tired, gravelly voice cut through the steam. "Your comm was off. Geez, do you think it's hot enough in here?"

"The only way to go," Fisk replied from behind the shower door.

"The President is on the line. She sounds a little cranky, too. Better grab your jammies and scoot." The steam caused Griff to cough.

"Coming." Fisk ran his fingers through his hair, squeezing out long streamers of water.

"Want me to round up the gang?"

"Why should I be the only one having fun? Wake the cook while you're at it."

Monday
June 2, 2014
Interstate 95
Near Richmond, Virginia
4:44 A.M. EDT

As he drove, a plan formed in Horn's mind. *If I know Metz, he'll go straight to the Director. She won't hesitate to remove me. That witch never did like me.*

As the person in charge of the presidential protective unit, Horn almost never got to drive himself anywhere. Ten-year-old directives from the Department of Homeland Security forbade such important people from going anywhere unescorted.

As he relished the freedom that came from being behind the wheel of his own car, he knew better. *My "freedom" is a sign of my disgrace.* His chaperons had chosen to abandon him. *Is this the part of the movie where I have a bad accident on the way home?* The thought made him shiver.

The six high-speed lanes of Interstate 95 heading out of D.C. were heavy with the usual night-shift traffic. The stream of fast moving cars flowing from the nation's capitol was a torrent compared to the few vehicles entering it on the other side of the median.

Horn decided to further revel in his independence by switching on the car's radio. A late night call-in program was on the air. An angry caller was on the rant.

"Honestly, how can you say that? Do you really think it's a coincidence that the Treasury Secretary goes missing just a few days after having that kind of press conference? I think he was trying to tell us something--"

"Not my department," Horn muttered, reaching for the dial. Surfing, he settled on a station playing light jazz. He turned the volume down, driving onward bathed in the light-hearted sound of the music. The surrounding area was ablaze with the usual neon glow, fluorescent glare, and holographic glitter of mingled commercial and residential enclaves. The jeweled spray passed over the hood of his sedan, adding counterpoint to the music.

Keeping his moves in sync with the jaunty music, he eyed the rearview mirror at regular intervals. His tired features showed none of the worry that he felt. *Are they letting me go because I'm no threat? Metz has probably put his own spin on my confrontation with the President.*

Checking the rearview mirror again, he watched the Alexandria off-ramp flash by. *One phone call from her. That's all it'll take.* Looking down at his speedometer, he eased his foot pressure on the accelerator. The car dropped from 65 miles per hour down to the more legal 55. *I'm sure the press will crucify me.*

Feeling very alone, Horn continued on his way, depressed despite the uplifting beat of the soft-flowing jazz. *I don't know what I did to end up like this.* He switched lanes with a rapid flash of turn signals, and then turned his mind back to his previous inspiration. *I have to know what Fisk said to rattle Andy Brown. If it means talking directly to him, so be it.*

Taking the first off-ramp that led to an anonymous suburb of Richmond, Horn reconsidered going home. Located in the heart of Virginia's state capitol, the small house was nestled deep inside a secured neighborhood. *If Metz is going to plant me, that's where he'll do it.* Knowing that he had a tracking device hidden somewhere in his car, he decided to make it work for him. *Stopping for gas just short of home isn't at all unusual.*

Turning a corner, he slowed to a stop. Waiting at the quiet intersection, he eyed the gas station across the street. *I have to stop thinking like a victim.* Fingers drumming on the steering wheel to match a sudden brass-and-drum crescendo in the music, Horn waited for the light to turn green.

Hearing it from Fisk might not solve my problems, but it'll make me feel better. The idea of working on such flimsy motivation made him chuckle at his own weakness. *I'd have to talk to him anyway, just to be sure that Metz was on the level.*

The traffic light changed, and Horn drove across the intersection into the brightly lit station. Concentrating, he switched off the radio and pulled into the full service lane. *For all I know, this isn't what it looks like.*

Motion sensors detected the approach of his car. A chime sounded to alert the station's attendants. Switching off the engine, he watched the jumpsuited man approach his car. He quickly made a pass around the car, before going for the gas pump.

Horn signaled which fuel grade he wanted and reached for his personal wireless phone. Tugging it out of his coat pocket, he smiled. *Been carrying this thing for years. Glad I kept it paid up.* Flipping it open, he put on his reading glasses so that he could see the old-style number display. Turning on the car's map light, he reached into his coat pocket for a well-used blue notebook. Flipping through the handwritten pages, he found the number he was looking for. Committing it to memory, he put the little notebook away.

The gas station attendant tapped on the driver's side window to get Horn's attention. "Got to swipe your card, dude," he said with a muffled California accent. Holding up a credit card reader, he pressed it up against the window.

Horn set the phone down and opened his wallet. Holding the credit card up to the glass, he carefully lined it up with the scanning port of the machine.

Pressing a button, the attendant scanned the card. A green indicator light showed that the transaction had gone through. "Thanks. Be done in a minute." The attendant flashed Horn an OK gesture, clipping the card reader back on his belt.

Horn went back to his phone. Punching in the number to Fisk's consulting group, he was careful to add the extension that would put him through to Fisk's nighttime troubleshooters. The car began to vibrate with the sound of gasoline going into the tank.

Here goes, Horn told himself with a sour smile. Pressing the dial button, he waited as the phone beeped, chirped, and squealed its way through the unlisted number.

"Cosmopolitan Systems. How may I direct your call?" a woman's wide-awake voice answered on the second ring.

"I'm sorry. I must have the wrong number." Conroy glared at the tiny digital readout on his phone. *My fault. Never trust a number that you haven't dialed in more than a year.*

"Who are you trying to reach, sir?" the operator asked, her cheerful tone undiminished.

Thankful that she was the helpful kind, he thought, *I should have known that it couldn't be that easy.* "That's quite all right. I'll check my number and dial again. I'm sure it's my fault. Thanks anyway." Folding up the phone, he let it slide into his lap. *A man like Fisk must change his phone numbers on a regular basis. Given what he could be involved in, I can't say as I blame him.*

Horn looked up in time to see the attendant give him a double thumbs-up. Turning to scan the area in all directions, he satisfied himself that he wasn't being obviously watched or followed.

The attendant went back to the secured booth. Though Horn couldn't see the Interstate, he could hear the dull roar of the traffic. He started the car and pulled out of the station.

"I'm sorry to be calling at this hour. I don't know what else to do. Director Horn accused me of having Brown killed. There were witnesses. I don't know what to do. He's given me until 7 o'clock this morning to meet his demands, or else," Madeline's voice said through the speakerphone, turning hateful as she spoke of Horn. Fisk and his advisors were seated around the room, listening in total silence.

Fisk took a sip of coffee. "What are his demands?"

"He wants me to confess or resign. Look, unless he can produce a body, he's got nothing. You know it, and I know it. But--"

Fisk cut her off, pointing to a pair of advisors. "Media." They nodded and left to carry out the unspoken orders implied by the command.

"What can we do?" Madeline's tone was now a study in grief.

"I understand. What is Metz doing?"

"Covering his backside, I would imagine." Madeline snorted as the lie came out flawlessly. The assembled advisors exchanged meaningful looks with each other.

"All right. Let me get my people together and brief them. We'll have something cooked up in an hour."

"Could you meet me for breakfast?" Madeline asked pleadingly.

Fisk watched his advisors shake their heads in a collective no. "Can't. I've got an appointment that I just can't shake."

"What can possibly be more important?" Madeline asked incredulously.

Fisk tried not to grin at his president's distress. *This is the perfect moment to drop my resignation on her.* "I have a doctor's appointment.

These guys are very expensive and hard to book. I might be able to make lunch, if that's--"

"Is something wrong?" Madeline interrupted, clearly taken off guard, "You're not dying, are--"

Fisk remained silent as one of his advisors held up a voice stress analyzer and signaled for a dramatic pause to play on Madeline's red-lined emotions.

"Oh, my," she breathed when he didn't immediately answer.

Two of the advisors motioned him to go with it. Griff shook his head, grinning silently because he knew that Fisk was making it up as he went along.

"I was going to tell you. It's just that...there have been... complications. To be honest, I had planned to tell you in the next few days. After this appointment."

"I don't know what to say. I suppose that I could--" Losing her focus, she wasn't able to continue as Metz had instructed.

"Hey, it's not that bad," Fisk interjected as if he were trying to keep his own spirits up.

"I see. Will this affect your professional responsibilities?"

The advisors exchanged hand signals, and then nodded in agreement as it became obvious that Fisk was angling toward his resignation. With the first part of their plan nearly complete, the only thing remaining was to get out alive.

"I will have to resign," he admitted with a steady voice.

"Stop. Please, don't say any more." Madeline snuffled.

The group sat quietly as she struggled to compose herself.

Fisk leaned closer to the phone. His urge to play it up was almost uncontrollable. "I didn't want it to be like this."

"I know. Is your condition terminal?"

"If I stay in this line of work, yes." He resisted the temptation to pick up the handset.

"This isn't my fault, is it?" Madeline was surprised by her own show of grief.

"I did this to myself. You know how it is. The job consumes you." Fisk watched with interest as some of his advisors looked away, obviously uncomfortable.

Madeline forced herself to get back into the game. "Who are you seeing?" *I know you better than you think. You'll live just to spite me.*

"Nobody that you'd know. Look, I need to round up my people and get on this problem. If Metz bothers to show himself, tell him to keep an open phone line. I may need to call him with instructions. One more thing. Get your press secretary out of bed and tell her to be ready for maximum denials."

"Yes," Madeline sighed as she hung up.

Fisk waited to make sure that she had, in fact, cut the connection. When the phone beeped and went silent, everyone breathed a sigh of relief.

"Okay folks. Break it down for me, and let's meet for a working breakfast in ten minutes." He got to his feet, pulling at the lapels of his bathrobe. Waiting for all six of the sleepy advisors to leave, he went back to his room to get dressed.

He slipped into a designer jogging suit and laced up a pair of comfortable athletic shoes. *Might as well dress down to make everyone feel a little more at ease.* Within five minutes, he was on his way back to the den.

Griff shambled out of a nearby guest room, pulling on a blue T-shirt. His hair was still damp from a hurried shower. "I have news. Cosmo got a call that they traced back to a civilian wireless number belonging to Conroy Horn. I had them play back the recording. It sounds like Horn, too."

"Why would Horn call Cosmo?" Fisk wondered as they headed for the stairs.

"Either he got a wrong number or he was looking for you." Dressed in casual cotton slacks and open-toed sandals, Griff looked like he might fall asleep at any moment. "That was genius the way you slipped her the resignation." He fell in next to Fisk.

"Civilian number, you say?" Fisk took the stairs slowly as he thought.

As Doris had predicted, the Founders had taken it upon themselves to schedule the removal of his wetware electronics. Keeping to his vow of secrecy, he pressed on with the topic at hand.

"Yeah, 'bout half an hour ago," Griff replied after a cavernous yawn.

"Call him back. Let's see what the man has to say."

Tuesday
June 3, 2014
The Horn Residence
Richmond, Virginia
5:02 A.M. EDT

Horn ignored the gate guard as he drove into the secured neighborhood. The roaming patrols and security cameras did little to assuage his growing fear. *I should feel safe here, but I don't.*

He stopped at an intersection a block away from his house, thinking. *What am I really afraid of? I've been letting my imagination run away with me.* Tapping the accelerator, he pulled into the driveway. *I'll take a shower and call the Director when she gets in. Between the two of us, I know we can sort this out.* He turned off the radio and hesitated before turning off the car. *Is she going to believe me?*

Opening the door slowly, he listened to the sounds around him. *Of course she will. Once she gets a look at Brown, she'll believe me.* A light mist had fallen, leaving a shine on the pavement. Tiny beads of water reflected the glow of the streetlights. Somewhere, a lonely cricket chirped. *I know she doesn't like me, but not even she can deny that President Hill is out of line.*

Looking up, Horn frowned at the dense clouds that blotted out the stars. *Storm clouds. How appropriate.* He heaved himself out of the car. *Driving myself was nice. Going to have to do that again sometime.*

Looking up at his house, he allowed himself a moment to stretch. *That'll add a nice dollar figure to the retirement fund when it sells.* Thoughts of retirement were suddenly unpleasant. *Please, let her resign. This country doesn't need another scandal.*

His wireless phone beeped, breaking his train of thought. Lying on the front seat of the car, it rang twice. Checking his watch, Horn flipped the phone open. *Maybe it's a wrong number.*

"This is Conroy Horn."

"Mr. Horn, Preston Fisk here. I understand you wanted to speak to me."

Horn looked at the phone as if it had turned into a snake. "How did you get this number?" *As if I had to ask.*

"What did you want?" Fisk replied.

"Yeah. Just tell me one thing."

"Certainly." Fisk seemed genuinely cooperative.

Loosening his tie, Horn tried to focus. "Why did she want him dead?"

"What are you talking about? What's going on?"

"Secretary Brown. I know all about it." He reached out to close the car door.

"I see. Sounds like we need to meet." Fisk put his hand over the phone to talk to somebody.

"No, we don't need to meet. Just answer the question." Horn started walking toward the house. Using a tiny remote, he locked the car doors as he walked. Behind him, a tan four-door sedan rolled up into his driveway at an angle.

"This isn't the sort of thing we should be doing over the phone."

"Hang on a sec."

Horn turned. The driver's side window came down as the car slowed to a stop. Years of training and finely tuned instinct told Horn that he was in trouble. Caught between the house and the car, he had no place to go as the muzzle of a silenced firearm came into view over the side mirror.

Turning his back on the car, he lowered his head and ran for the house. The unseen driver fired three times. Each armor-piercing round found its mark. The customized 9-millimeter bullets tore through the protective fabric of Horn's overcoat, knocking him to the pavement. Antiballistic fabrics in his coat and clothing prevented bullet penetration. The hydrostatic shockwave did its worst. Internal organs thumped inside his chest as they ruptured.

Trapped inside his numb, dying body, Horn knew that someone with intimate knowledge of Service protective measures had shot him. The type of hypervelocity ammunition used on him hadn't been available to the private sector for five years. It was the only known weakness of the protective fabric that safeguarded the lives of so many government personnel.

As his head struck the wet driveway, the car pulled back and away. His body convulsed from the trauma of the attack. Unable to move his arms or legs, Horn panicked as his eyes rolled uncontrollably.

"Horn?" Fisk's voice projected from the phone that lay just out of reach.

Conroy forced his lips to move as blood began to fill his lungs. "Mnah."

"Are you all right? What happened?"

"Din'..." Horn worked to enforce his will over his shattered nervous system as another voice came through the phone.

"I think he's been shot. Background analysis shows an 88 percent chance that a silenced weapon has just been fired."

Horn blinked as he struggled to understand what the unfamiliar voice was saying.

"Stay off this line," Fisk commanded.

"Nn." Horn's vision began to sparkle with floaters as his heart stopped.

"It wasn't me. You understand?" Fisk said, the volume of his voice rising.

"Meth," Horn slurred as blood filled his mouth.

Prompted by his advisors, Fisk hung up.

A roaming security detail found the unconscious man ten minutes later. He was pronounced dead two minutes after the paramedics arrived.

Monday
June 3, 2014
Interstate 95
Near Richmond, Virginia
5:23 A.M. EDT

Metz talked as he drove. "It's done?" He glanced at the hands-free indicator light on the dashboard.

The voice coming back through the wireless phone was scratchy with static. "We got it. Video storage was automated, just as you said. It wasn't hard to get in and short out the system. Anyone who checks it out will think it's been down for at least an hour."

"Did you burn the data stores?" he asked as he aggressively changed lanes.

"All of them. It's a cheap system. Wasn't hard."

"Okay. I'll be home in just six minutes. Be ready with the call. This has to sound good for the boys in Homeland. Don't screw it up." Metz reached out to turn off the phone while he looked for his off-ramp.

His plan was simple. He would be home in just a few minutes to get the call informing him that Director Horn had been killed. Since he had already signed out, nothing would be amiss when the special investigation began. He was counting on the speedy, yet predictable, reaction of the Department of Homeland Security.

He parked the tan sedan in his driveway, careful to resynchronize the active tracker in the glove compartment so that it would give its correct location to the Service monitoring system. A second active tracker had been hidden in a nearby flowerbed to falsely identify the car as having been parked for the last half hour. Switching off the second tracker, he took it inside with him.

Inside his photographic darkroom, Metz submerged the small electronic device in a fluid that rapidly dissolved it. Careful to avoid the rising vapors, he flushed the chemical solution down the drain as the phone rang. He answered the call on the third ring.

"Metz," he grumbled with genuine fatigue.

A woman's voice sounded shaky but in control. "Sir, this is the Joint Operations Center. We've got a situation."

"Who is this?" Metz asked as if he were shaking off slumber.

"Agent Bachman. Sir, Director Horn has been killed."

"What?" He surprised even himself with the shout.

"Twenty minutes ago. The Assistant Deputy Director for Homeland is putting out a terrorist alert. Since you checked out without chaperons, I have to ask you to stay in your home and lock the doors until our people get there."

Metz grinned to himself at the quoted procedure. "I'm in bed, for crying out loud. I'll be dressed when they get here. Okay?" He paced in the crimson glow of his darkroom to feign what he knew should be conflicting emotions. "Round up the department heads on my say-so. No exceptions. I want to be ready for Homeland when they call. You got me?"

Soaking wet, Anne Carroll picked up on the third ring. "Hello?" she said as she wrapped a large towel around her torso.

"Anne Carroll, please." The soft Southern accent of a woman's voice sounded through a stifled yawn.

"Speaking." Anne walked back in to the bathroom to pick up a hairbrush.

"I'm calling for the White House Press Secretary. Ms. Cutter asks that you join her for breakfast and a special session. Can you be here by 8:30?"

"Where is 'here,' exactly?" Anne's investigative mind prompted.

"I'm sorry. My day hasn't started well. Ms. Cutter would like to meet with you at Cyrano's. It's a little bistro in the Congressional Zone. Do you know it?"

"Yeah, I know the place. Just be sure that they have my pass ready at the gate." The small untruth passed her lips easily enough. *Never been inside the Congressional Zone before. Should be fun.*

"Already been e-mailed. Thank you. Have a good day."

Anne turned off the phone and laid it down. As she brushed her hair, she thought about the call. "Sellout," she muttered at the fogged mirror.

Tuesday
June 3, 2014
Office of the Director
Department of Homeland Security
Washington, D.C.
8:05 A.M. EDT

Carl checked his tie before going in. He saw Harry Oswald standing alone, next to the Director's desk. Metz considered the implications. *Harry Oswald. Counterinsurgency. Great.*

"What are you doing here?" Carl asked. *As if I didn't know.*

"Come on in. Have a seat." Harry leaned against the desk.

Metz chose to stand behind a nearby chair, placing his hands on the high, leather back. "I know who you are. I know what you do." *You can't stop me. Not now.*

"Then you know I'm here to clean up your mess. You're playing a very dangerous game, and you're about to lose. That's why I'm here. To make sure that you don't lose." Harry nodded imperceptibly to salute Carl's directness.

"What do you want?" Metz could feel his stomach tighten out of fear.

Harry Oswald, Director of the Counterinsurgency Unit of the Department of Homeland Security, was a living legend. He was a feared legend.

"Calm down. Sit." Harry pointed at the chair Metz was standing behind.

"I'm supposed to meet with the Director. I don't have to talk to you."

"The Director sent me. If you're not smart enough to--"

Carl's nerve slipped. He stepped around the chair to sit. "Okay."

"We're willing to tolerate a lot, Carl. In today's world, we're willing to tolerate more than we should. Ten years of hunting terror groups, both here and abroad, has taught us to be open-minded about how things get done in the service of our nation. When you stop and think about it, we might just be our own worst enemy." Harry rose to look down on Metz.

"I don't know what you're talking about," Carl replied, challenging Oswald with his steely gaze.

"You killed Director Horn. You did it because he got in your way. You did it because it served the interests of your president." Harry reached back to touch a control pad on the desk.

Metz watched in shock as clear video footage appeared on a large monitor on the far wall.

"As you can see, the cameras we hid around Horn's house caught the whole thing. Too bad you didn't have your goons sweep the area before you made your hit."

Carl said nothing as the digital image froze, showing a clear view of himself behind the wheel of the car, silenced pistol in hand.

After a long pause, Harry turned off the monitor.

"What do you want?"

"I don't really care about your politics, but I do care about this country. Nobody, and I do mean nobody, hurts this country on my watch. Period. Not even you."

Carl shut his eyes to give himself a moment to think.

The Director of Homeland Security had never shown his true colors to the media, despite his considerable exposure. Internal gossip and rumor hinted at his hidden patriotic sentiments, despite the politicized image he had gone out of his way to cultivate.

Oswald, who shunned the media, was well known to intelligence and law enforcement insiders for his never-ending quest to remain professionally apolitical. His devotion to duty had deep patriotic roots.

Considering what he knew about the two men, Carl decided that he had nothing to lose. *Everyone has a price. What's yours?* "What do you want?"

"I want you on a short leash. The Director wants you to stop killing people without sanction. And we both want you to be a whole lot more focused on your job." Harry spread his hands magnanimously. When Metz didn't say anything, he continued.

"You and I both know that this president is unique for a variety of reasons. I don't care about your politics, but I do care about hers. Since you started working for her, she's become quite the little schemer."

Again, Metz said nothing.

"See, you're mine now. Your politics are my politics. With that recording, I can have you on a plate with fries any time I have a taste for it. Do you follow me so far?" Harry's expression told Carl that it wasn't an idle threat.

"The President is a different issue. Like I said, her politics matter. She can do more harm to this country than you ever could. Problem is, we can't touch her. Yet."

"What's wrong with her politics?" Metz asked, sensing an opening.

"Preston Fisk," Harry pronounced, watching Metz jerk upright as he spoke the name. "I thought so. He's really got you worked up, hasn't he?" Smiling broadly, he was ready to reel in his catch.

Metz blinked, realizing that he'd given too much away. "I don't know what you're talking about."

"You killed the wrong man. Horn was never a real danger to you, or to her. Fisk, on the other hand...he's a different story. That man has worked very hard to put every crooked politician that he could find into office."

"If you know anything about Fisk, you know that he's not the easiest man to deal with."

Harry nodded. "Considering who he works for, I'm not surprised."

Metz bowed his head at the rebuke.

"Let me spell this out for you. We both know she's playing fast and loose. If she pulls off this debt thing, she's going to be more popular than ever. If she screws up..."

Metz looked up at Oswald. *Ah-ha.* "Is that all you want?"

"No, that's not all I want. You'll roll over on her if, and only if, the time comes, on our say-so. In the meantime, she needs to be deprived of her ability to do any more harm to the country."

"Fisk," Metz pronounced with a sour face.

Harry made a show of being thoughtful. "She wants him dead. We know she's put you on the case. We've been monitoring those old bank accounts you've been using." He gave Metz a glance that conveyed greater knowledge.

Metz got to his feet. "I can do it. As long as you give me--"

"You know how this works, Carl. If you're straight with us, you'll never see the inside of a courtroom. If you're not straight with us, I'll personally make sure you go to prison for the rest of your natural life, however short that may be. If you won't serve this country as a member of a very respected institution, you will serve it as a very public example of what it means to--"

Metz raised a hand in surrender. "Okay, I get it. There's just one more thing."

"What's that?" Harry asked benignly.

"A warrant. A federal warrant for Fisk's arrest."

"On what charge?" Harry seemed intrigued by this new wrinkle.

"The attempted murder of the Treasury Secretary."

"Last I heard, Secretary Brown was still missing. The financial community is having kittens, and the stock market is having a cow. What do you know that we don't?"

"We're the Secret Service. I wouldn't expect a patriot like you to understand what we go through with these politicians." *When will people like you learn that there is no such thing as "the greater good?"*

"Just so you and I understand each other, I want Fisk alive and in court. I want him to answer for all his dirty politics. You give me this, and I let your president keep her job. The Director might even put in a good word for you, so that you get Horn's job. If the President asks, you can tell her that the Fisk conspiracy was taken down to prove to her that she's not above the law. Besides, without his protection, she's got to play nice. If she doesn't do right by this country, people like me will always be here to stop her."

Tuesday
June 3, 2014
Office of the President
The White House
Washington, D.C.
8:25 A.M. EDT

"Josephine. How are you?" Madeline looked up from where she sat.

"Real busy. They'll be ready for you in the Oval in five minutes. This is for your call to Mr. Ramirez. These numbers are accurate as of 6 this morning." Josephine sighed over the stack of notebooks and folders she was carrying. She pulled a thin folder off the bottom of the stack. As she handed it to Madeline, she paused to look at the other items.

"My word. How on earth did you manage that?"

"Called them." Josephine checked her watch as she selected another folder.

"This one is for your 9:45 call to the French President. They have five days left on their term as head of the EU. There's a thing from State. They think the French are going to want some kind of action on their antiterrorism proposal that's up for a vote in the UN."

Madeline rifled the pages in the second folder. "Stanley never did this kind of homework. I've seen your schedule. How on earth do you have time to put this kind of thing together?"

"I have no life," Josephine sighed as she pawed the stack in her hands. *Never mind all the stuff that Fisk's people faxed over to me.* "Here, this is yours, too." She held up a third folder.

"This would be?" Madeline prompted as Josephine checked her watch again.

"Those are the morning meetings. When I got in this morning, your e-mail said you wanted an update. There it is."

"Is something wrong? You seem rushed."

"There's just so much to do. Everything's backlogged. The Congressional requests--"

"Do you see that woman over there?" Madeline pointed to the next room.

Josephine turned to spy Lorraine busy at her desk. "Yes."

"She works for you now. As soon as I see Larry, I'll have him make it official." Madeline smiled broadly.

Josephine blushed.

"She's got six people that work for her, and she's well past her retirement date. I expect you can teach her a thing or two."

"I--" Josephine's blush gave way to fear.

Madeline let the moment hang while the office buzzed with busy staffers. "I want Stanley's mess cleaned up in six weeks. If you can do that, you can keep the job. Understand?"

Josephine nodded, looking at her watch again. "I really have to go."

"Go. Just remember, all I care about are results. Do what I ask, and I don't care how it gets done." Madeline dismissed Josephine with a wave.

A Secret Service agent materialized nearby. "Madame President? The call to Ramirez is ready."

"Where is Metz?" the President asked.

"Still in with the crew from Homeland. The Director for Service choppered in, and she is...cranked."

"I would think so. Mr. Brown?"

"Metz wants to know if you can find out where Fisk is having his medical. We don't have anything on file."

Inside the Oval Office, a pair of technicians was running final checks on the holographic transmission system that President Hill would use to make her scheduled calls for the day. The Oval Office itself was too small for the equipment to be permanently placed there. Instead, it was set up and used as it was needed.

"We're good to go," the lead technician informed the President as she entered.

"Right. The remote is on your desk," the second man said as he shut down his diagnostic laptop.

Madeline signaled her protector to wait until the men had left the room. "Shut the door," she ordered, taking her seat behind the massive black oak desk.

"I'm not surprised that you can't trace Fisk's doctor. The only people who seem to know where he is at any given time are those he chooses to inform." An idea blossomed.

"Half the doctors in this town are unlisted--" the agent started.

"Watch and learn." Madeline picked up her phone, dialing Josephine's extension. When the voice mail recorder activated, she spoke casually.

"There's a little something I need you to do when you get back from your meetings. Fisk is unavailable. He's gone in for a doctor's appointment of some kind. I'm rather picky about the doctors I use. Find out who he's seeing and get back to me. Anyone good enough for him is probably just the kind of doctor that I want." Hanging up the phone, she smiled thinly.

"She's in good with *him*?" the agent asked doubtfully.

"He gets to everyone at some point," Madeline observed bitterly. *Everyone except me.*

Tuesday
June 3, 2014
The Oval Office
The White House
Washington, D.C.
8:31 A.M. EDT

Folding her hands, President Hill looked straight at the video camera. Her short blonde curls framed her steel grey eyes, providing her the usual regal bearing. The camera, perched ten feet in front of her, followed her every move. To the right of the camera, a holographic screen crouched on a small cart. Its emitters hissed in response to the coded bitstream overlap that cluttered the long-distance call.

"The loss of Señor Brown is unfortunate. The financial markets miss his calming presence. It would seem that we might have to move up our timetable. I trust that your people are prepared to broach the subject with mine." Ramirez bowed his head slightly, speaking with the quiet calm that was his trademark.

"Indeed, they are. You have my assurances that our deal remains in effect. The negotiating officers will move forward as instructed. For all intents and purposes, this thing has a life of its own," Madeline replied.

"I am glad that you see it this way. My people will be much reassured. There is also the added benefit that the secret of your currency recall program remains intact."

"I think they already know," she replied, referring to Congress. "What they don't actually know, they suspect. Never under estimate the power of politics. Even if they found out about it, what can they do?" She smiled warmly.

Ramirez bobbed his head. "True. Many of your presidents have worked quietly to put this in place. The time for stopping it has passed. Still, the transfer of raw currency will go a long way toward silencing your critics. It is a shrewd move, even if it has taken decades to prepare."

"We're taking this very seriously. When the time comes, the whole world will see for itself that we can hunt terrorists and balance our economic affairs at the same time."

"We look forward to seeing your courier with the final package."

Ramirez paused to listen to someone off-camera. "Pardon. One of my advisors would like to know if it is acceptable to make contact with your negotiators now." He stopped to get more information from the off-camera source. "We would like to be seen as showing concern for the loss of your Treasury Secretary. It will also allow us to begin making certain inquiries about your banking system that may take some time to complete."

"Certainly. It will look spontaneous. The boost to our approval rating will put many of your bankers and financial advisors at ease. I am glad to be working with such an enlightened and responsible person such as yourself."

Tuesday
June 3, 2014
Secured Site 6
Adkins-Hathaway Clinic
Alexandria, Virginia
9:00 A.M. EDT

"Must have been some kind of happening last night. I figured you to be all bright-eyed and bushy-tailed for this," Christopher observed, careful to keep the limo riding smoothly over the uneven asphalt.

"Something came up. Something that needed my personal attention." Fisk was grateful for the aspirin that was now beginning to work on his tension headache. With less than two hours of sleep, he was finding it hard not to be surly. It had been a few years since he'd been so deprived of rest. *The last night of the general election if memory serves. Madeline was so mad about not winning by a decisive majority that she was up all night ranting to me about it.*

Moving up the driveway of a small and very private clinic, Christopher brought the limo to a stop under the carport near the front door. The sun had yet to peek out from behind scattered clouds. Elongated by the jet stream, the clouds promised rain later in the day.

"We're out front," Christopher said casually.

"Confirmed," Griff's voice rumbled from the car's phone.

An older woman in a white uniform and distinctive red hair opened the carved wooden door that led into the clinic, stepping aside to allow a pair of well-dressed men to pass.

Fisk got out of the car after Christopher triggered the door locks. Fishing around inside his limp mind for some expressive humor, he failed to notice that the red-haired nurse was actually somebody that he knew.

"So, Doctors. We meet again." Frowning at the poor quality of what should have been a snappy remark, Fisk reflected on his last meeting with these two men. *I wonder if they ever thought this day would come?*

Dr. Adkins was tall, thin, and dark-haired. Decked out in a slate grey suit, his receding hairline and grey temples made him look the part of an aging, wealthy physician. Approaching the car, the intense man seemed to be scanning every inch of Fisk with his penetrating green eyes. Further down the ramp, Dr. Hathaway was much older and showed it less diplomatically.

Fisk took note of Hathaway's bare crown. *Not a hair on his head. I'm too tired to remember if he had any last time or not.*

Standing under the marbled arches of the carport, the elderly doctors hesitated. Christopher noticed the way both men, as well as the woman in white, watched Fisk. In the silence of the moment, he had the impression that they knew something he didn't.

Out of the corner of his eye, Fisk watched Christopher. *Great. One more thing you don't know. I'll get somebody else to clue you in later.*

"Sorry to keep you waiting. I was just taking it all in. You two have, well, you've--" Moving slowly, he kept smiling despite a rush of mixed emotions that caused his right hand to stay clasped on the car door.

Adkins stepped forward to offer Fisk his hand along with an intense but crafty smile. "We got old. Turning back the clock is very expensive. Just ask our patients."

Hathaway ambled up to clap Fisk on the shoulder. "My word, you look beat. What are you doing that's putting my best work through such a wringer?"

Fisk smiled sheepishly, averting his eyes for an instant. He realized that the bags under his bloodshot eyes, combined with his drawn complexion, made him look terrible. Touching the knot of his tie, he glanced down at his charcoal grey suit. *A well-dressed mess.* Adkins and Hathaway had been looking after him since his recruitment in to the conspiracy. Despite his fatigue, he wanted to be on his best behavior. "I don't want to bore you--" Fisk started.

Hathaway raised a commanding finger. "Oh, no, you don't. I've waited 15 years for this story, and I'm going to hear it all. You can tell us when we're finished taking out your comm." Taking Fisk by the arm, the old gent started to turn for the door of the clinic.

"Remember, we made you who you are today. We deserve to know all the grisly details."

Adkins made a scissors motion with one hand as he laughed at the inside joke. Behind him, Enola frowned at his flippancy.

Christopher cleared his throat. "Excuse me."

Fisk untangled himself from his physicians. "Christopher. These are Drs. Adkins and Hathaway. Two of the best leading-edge medical and surgical minds on the planet."

"Pleased to meet you." The driver stopped to shake each man's hand before touching his thumb to the trunk's fingerprint-sensitive lock.

"I'm not slated to bring any luggage," Fisk told him.

"Still flawless, after all these years." Hathaway folded his arms.

"Don't start with me. Not until we have him on the table," Adkins retorted.

Fisk pivoted in place at the remark, eyebrows raised.

Adkins smiled benignly. "It's just doctor talk. Trust me."

Christopher opened the trunk, taking out a white garment bag. "I'm going to be counting all his parts before you guys go to work. If I find out that he's missing anything that he might want later, I'll come back so that we can have some more of that doctor talk. Trust *me*." He nodded as he handed the garment bag to Fisk.

"I see," Hathaway grumbled, giving Christopher a mildly disapproving look.

"He's a lot more awake than I am, and he doesn't know either one of you. Let's calm down and take this inside." Fisk shouldered the bag.

Adkins bobbed his head. "Let's do it. By the way, your lady friend is doing well."

"Doris?" Fisk followed the two men up the ramp toward the door.

"She's very resilient. Of course, we've had to do some minor reconstruction." Hathaway paused to hold the door, so that Enola could go on ahead of the group.

"What do you mean?" Fisk latched onto the doctor's last comment. Turning, he caught sight of Christopher standing next to the car. The large man was gesturing at Fisk, indicating the garment bag.

Adkins brutally nudged Hathaway aside as he came inside the clinic. *Good job. Just blurt it out. Why not draw him a picture? We've probably said too much, as it is.* "What he means to say--"

"What?" Fisk looked over his shoulder at the hand that held the white plastic bag.

"What's that for?" Adkins shifted to one side, allowing Fisk to pass.

"I don't know." Fisk stopped as the door to the clinic closed behind them. Holding the bag at arm's length, he unzipped it halfway. Behind the three men, a woman in a blue pantsuit stood next to the door.

Ignoring the presence of what he assumed to be a guardian, Fisk eyed the contents of the bag. "Ah," he said, catching the folds of supple black leather in one hand. "This belongs to Doris. Her favorite coat." Stroking a broad lapel between forefinger and thumb, he could feel a sense of nostalgia growing in his consciousness. *Something about this coat feels familiar.*

Hathaway butted into his field of view. "I can take that to her. I've been meaning to check up on her this morning, anyway."

Looking down into Hathaway's eyes, Fisk was momentarily transfixed by the emotions he saw played out on the old man's face. *What's the matter with you? You're afraid of something.* Looking sidelong at the black leather trenchcoat in his hand, he wondered, *You're afraid of a coat?* "I'll do it," he resolved, swinging the coat limply on its hanger. "She's here because of an order I gave, so it's only fair that I bring this to her." *Another piece of the puzzle? Maybe.* He waited for the unseen presence that lurked in the back of his mind to react. Nothing. *Okay then. Let's just play it out, and see why at least one of you is afraid of this coat.*

"We've really got to get started," Adkins said as he lightly touched Fisk's shoulder. "There's some, ah, rather sensitive proctological work that has to be done, and it'll take us most of the morning. I'm sure that we can have somebody take that to her."

"Proctology?" Fisk used the comment as an excuse to swing the coat out of the man's grasp. *I guess we really do know where they put the tracker, don't we?* Rumbling in sync with his thoughts, Fisk's stomach registered its complaints in advance.

"Yes. Which is why we'll need all the time we can get--" Dr. Adkins stepped around Hathaway, ready to make another attempt.

"That settles that. The least you can do is let me take this to a very good friend before you get down to the business of turning me inside out." Fisk slung the garment bag over his shoulder.

Struggling to keep his smile and mannerism intact, he cursed his fatigue. Sidestepping the two doctors, he crossed the lobby in a handful of easy strides. He flagged the attention of a nurse behind the marble counter. "Excuse me. Which room is Doris in?" Pointing at the garment bag with his free hand, he began to feel a little foolish. *I'm tired, my head hurts, and nobody wants me to handle this trenchcoat. This is about as silly as it gets.*

Hathaway bustled over to the huge marble counter. "Please, let us handle this."

Fisk's ears pricked up at the plaintive tone in the doctor's voice. Watching peripherally, he caught Adkins glancing nervously at the corridor just beyond the receiving counter. *Let me guess. You don't want me going down there.*

"That's quite all right. I'll just find my own way." Following him to the nearest corner, the silent nurse watched in worried fascination as he confidently marched down the main corridor.

Still in the background, Enola watched with a poker face as Fisk spun on his heel, taking the left branch with a nod. She then turned to watch the two doctors argue over who was going to get to make the first in a series of hurried phone calls.

"Proctology, indeed. Anybody with an ounce of sense would have said something more appealing, but no, you had to spur him on by grabbing for that coat," Hathaway scoffed, grabbing for the phone on the nurse's desk. *If Fisk ever realizes that the coat he's carrying belonged to Jason, we're in big trouble.*

Enola finally asserted herself. "Both of you, stop it." Severely thin lips parted in a grin that would have been mischievous on anyone else.

Submitting to her will, Hathaway put down the phone. "It's the coat--" he protested.

"I know all about the coat. His daughter gave it to him. It has great sentimental value to him, and to Doris. And, I know the risk it represents as a memory trigger."

"Well, then, you understand that we've got to--" Adkins interjected.

"Do nothing. If I know Doris, this will all be over within a few hours. After that, it won't matter."

Adkins flinched. "Oh, no."

"Yes, gentlemen. The Founders took the vote. Doris has been given the official termination order. All we can do now is stay out of her way."

Stopping at the intersection of the clinic's four corridors, Fisk glanced to his left. The interior of the posh clinic was decorated in green-dominant earth tones. Cut glass fixtures allowed common fluorescent lighting to blend with the marble ivy-and-vine carvings that adorned the walls.

At the far end of the corridor, a quiet man dressed in casual slacks and pullover sat on a bench beside a closed door.

You must be here on orders from the Founders. Fisk strode towards the man, careful not to close too quickly. Doris had warned him that he would be vulnerable during his visit to the clinic. *The most logical place to get to me. Wonder what she has in mind to get me out of this?*

"I'm Preston Fisk. Do you know who I am?" He was careful to keep the garment bag on his shoulder.

"Yes. Can I help you?" The guard laid one hand on an athletic bag next to him. Getting to his feet, he put down a tattered paperback novel.

Fisk stopped at a polite distance.

The sentry stood, craning his neck to look down the hallway.

"I need to see Doris." The desire to return the coat was overpowering. He didn't question it.

"Is everything all right, sir? I don't think you're supposed to be down here." The man sensed something unusual in Fisk's tired demeanor.

Unslinging the garment bag, he offered it to the guard for inspection. *So, you're here to watch her, not me. Interesting.*

"I'm just doing her a favor. Say, have we met?" *Casual. Calm. Friendly.* His customary charm warmed his tone despite his fatigue.

The man smiled appreciatively as he patted down the empty coat.

"Three years ago. You were just passing through Portland." The man handed the coat back.

Slinging it back over his shoulder, Fisk pressed his advantage. "Who recruited you?" he asked, taking his time. *Calm. Casual. Friendly.*

"She did. I used to work for the IRS. I found one of your floating accounts, and...you know." He shrugged.

Fisk smiled congenially. He straightened to his full height, hefting the garment bag. "Well. This is her favorite coat, you know?"

"Yes, but I have, well, I have instructions."

"Right. I get you. Can't let anybody in." *Can't let me in, or can't let her out?*

"Can't let you in. Sorry, but those are the orders. They said especially you."

Fisk could tell that the guard was uncomfortable with his assignment. *If I wasn't so tired, I'd be scared. Come on, get it together. If I can't get past this guy, I deserve to be shot.*

He flicked his tongue around his mouth to make sure his comm implant was still off. "Look, we're all on the same side, right? I'm going to deliver this coat to that woman. She got hurt because of me and I intend to do this one small thing to make it up to her. What we do, what *you* do, isn't all sit and wait. Am I right?" He pinned the man with his bloodshot eyes.

"Yes, but--"

"But nothing." Fisk advanced half a step, his benevolent mask slipping just a little. "I take care of my *friends.* You're all my *friends.* Understand? Let me do this for my *friend.*" His eyes narrowed as he spoke the last word. *I don't care if you're the guy they sent to kill me. You will let me pass.*

"I have rounds to make. Usually takes me five minutes. Okay?" The lie would have been unconvincing even under normal circumstances.

Fisk ignored the man's discomfort. "Thanks. I owe you one." Pausing to check his tie and smooth out the front of his jacket, he watched the guard sling the athletic bag over his shoulder and walk slowly away. *Calm down. He's just doing his job. Nobody suspects a thing. Just let Doris play her hand. If she can't get us out of this, nobody can.*

Fisk peeled the trenchcoat from the garment bag and pulled it from its hanger. "Let's see what all the fuss is about?" he muttered. He put the retreating guard out of his mind. Dropping the bag on the bench, he held up the coat to examine it. *So why am I so fascinated with you? You're short for me by a good four inches.*

Opening the coat, he wasn't surprised to see an old style, zip-out, antiballistic liner, designed to stop bullets. By the look of it, it had seen more than just a little use over the years. Small patches in several places around the shoulder, chest, and abdomen showed where this coat's owner had taken a number of hits. *I've been shot at, but never hit. This must've hurt. A lot.*

Turning up the collar, he caught a slight whiff of perspiration. The odor sparked a twinge of recognition in the back of his mind. *Something about this coat is familiar.*

Checking the manufacturer's tag just under the collar, he rubbed his fingers over a pair of initials that had been hand-sewn into it. Each letter was thick, almost childlike, in its stitching. Rubbing his thumb over each one, he could feel the specter in the back of his mind come alive. *I know...*

A sudden lance of pain forced him to close his eyes. The world tilted harshly to one side. Blazing through his frontal lobe, the searing heat of the moment drove reality away. An image projected on the inside of his eyelids. Unearthly blue light. Medical instruments. An impression of masked faces looking down at him. The pain was terrible.

Turbulence roiled in black waves at the edge of his consciousness as he stepped into the tastefully decorated room. Fear overlapped shadowy recollections of something unnamed as he finally laid eyes on Doris.

Reclining on her back, long hair splayed on a broad white expanse of pillow, Doris welcomed him with a smile that seemed to speak on more than one level. "I thought so. You never did know when to leave well enough alone." Tucked under the covers, she appeared healthy despite her wounds.

Fisk kept his eyes on her smile as he closed the door behind him, ignoring the thin, white tubes that ran from her chest and shoulder to a pair of medical monitors. Walking around a swinging lamp and table platform, he could feel her measuring every inch of him. *I think she knows who I am--was.*

The revelation made him stop abruptly. Unstable from fatigue, the barriers that separated him from himself fouled his judgment.

"I just...I brought your coat. I thought you might want it," he explained, placing it on the visitor's chair next to her bed. The unnamed thing in the back of his mind writhed in irritation.

Doris watched him for a long moment, her hands clasped over her chest. *You're dead on your feet. Who let you get this tired?* The events of the last few days had obviously caused Fisk to overextend himself. *Just look at you. You don't even know why you brought it to me, do you?* The suspicion that he wasn't fully in control of himself flourished in her alert mind. *As tired as you are, I wonder how much of the "real" you is speaking to me right now.*

The possibility was just too much to resist. Thinking back to Griff's encounter with Jason on the yacht, she was instantly jealous. "Come here. Closer." She licked her lips.

Stepping closer, Fisk pushed the table and lamp array aside. "Yes?" He raised an eyebrow, propping his elbows on the rail of the bed.

"Do you trust me?" Doris asked, searching his face.

"Of course." he replied without hesitation.

"Then trust me now." She raised a hand to his chin, stopping just short of contact. "I've started looking into that matter we discussed, just like I promised. What you're thinking and feeling right now is part of that. I'm close to having it all worked out, but for now I need to ask you to leave it alone."

Fearful anticipation was reflected in the depths of his blue eyes. *She knows. I can ask her, and she'll tell me.*

"You saw the man in the hallway?" *It's him. He's looking right at me.*

"Yes. Very athletic fellow. I have the feeling that he's not a tourist."

"That's right. Look at me."

"What?" Fisk blinked, thinking that he'd missed something.

"It's almost over. I need a few more days. Then you and I can have that conversation."

"I'm not sure I follow." Even as the lie crossed his lips, he knew she wasn't talking to him directly. In some way, she was talking to him indirectly.

Seizing on his moment of fear and confusion, Doris propped herself up on the bed. "Sophie misses you." She held her breath. The mnemonic trigger had never been used before. If it worked properly, the Fisk persona would reassert itself. The effects would be temporary, at best.

Fisk blinked. For an instant, he seemed disoriented. *I am Preston Duquesne Fisk. I couldn't possibly be anybody else.* The duality in his stream of consciousness vanished. The specter in the back of his mind was gone, forgotten.

"What were we just talking about?"

"I was just telling you to be patient. I'll be leaving the clinic before you do. Play along with these guys until I come back. I have it all worked out. I'll get you out of here." Boring into him with her eyes, she hoped he would understand. She also hoped that the part of him that mattered most would also forgive her. *I'll cross that bridge when I get to it. He may not even remember.*

Fisk stepped back from the bed, pulling at the sleeves of his coat. "Sorry about that. Lost my train of thought. Say, what are you going to do about him?" He nodded at the door.

"The guy in the hallway? He's their 'Plan B.' Don't worry about it. I've got this whole thing wired. You just do what I say, when I say, and we'll all live happily ever after."

Fisk turned and walked to the door. "Right. You did tell me it might go down like this. Just one thing. Who is J.C.?" *What on earth made me ask that question?*

Doris brushed at her forehead, looking away with a sigh. "J.C. gave me that coat." *That tears it. If this room is bugged, we're in big trouble.*

"I see." *He must be some kind of guy if you're wearing his coat like a good luck charm.*

Doris looked at him without emotion. "He's a hard man to reach, but he knows the score. It'll go badly for all of us if you let on that you know about him. Do you understand?" Hoping to turn the admission into a binding force, she emphasized the need for caution.

He stopped once more, considering her words. *I missed something, didn't I?* "I'm guessing. The plan requires that I be ignorant of J.C. I don't know how I could screw things up by knowing about him, but I'll steer clear of the topic."

"The Founders are touchy about J.C."

"Really? What kind of person is he? What does he do?" Fisk asked, intrigued.

"Go!" Doris pointed at the door with ice in her voice.

Slipping out of the room, Fisk was surprised at how her sudden anger motivated him. Closing the door, he shook his head. *Lots to think about once I've had some sleep.*

Scooping up the empty garment bag, he walked briskly back down the corridor. Fired up by a sudden rush of adrenaline, he racked his brain for any clues that might shed light on the identity of J.C. Turning the corner, he caught sight of the two doctors and their nurse, crowded around the receiving counter. *Whoever you are, J.C., you must lead an interesting life.*

Hathaway was just looking up, phone in hand, when he caught sight of him.

Fisk held up the empty garment bag. "She was asleep, so I left it for her." Approaching the two doctors, he read them closely. *Nervous. Worried. Well, now. Somebody's got a secret.*

"Asleep?" Hathaway snorted.

On the far side of the desk, Adkins was openly suspicious. "You didn't actually speak to her?" *Incredible.*

"She's got tubes sticking out of her." Fisk waved, as if to erase the unpleasant image.

The nurse looked dubiously at both doctors. "I'll let her know that you stopped by. When she wakes up."

Hathaway wiped a line of perspiration from his forehead "I don't suppose we'll be needing this, then." Hanging up the phone, he moved away from the desk.

Pulling at the cuffs of his shirt, Dr. Adkins smiled woodenly and gestured toward the interior of the clinic. "Shall we?"

He smiled down at the nurse behind the receiving desk as he handed her the garment bag. "I couldn't be more ready. Could you take this?"

"Certainly."

"All right, then. Let's get started. I haven't had anything to eat or drink in the last two hours, but I've got to tell you, I've got enough caffeine in me right now to kill a horse."

Tuesday
June 3, 2014
Secured Site 6
Adkins-Hathaway Clinic
Alexandria, Virginia
9:21 A.M. EDT

The more Doris thought about her encounter with Fisk, the more it bothered her. Dragging her eyes around the small private room, she examined everything in close detail to take her mind off her worries.

Her trained eyes made quick work of the medical equipment, furniture, and various fixtures that around the room. Looking over at the coat, she saw that it had been professionally cleaned and repaired. *I've got so much to do before I'm ready to save him from himself. Have I overextended myself? No, that's not quite right. It's him that I care about. Have I endangered him?*

The telephone on the nightstand next to her bed warbled softly. The unexpected sound jarred her into a sitting position. Her whole body was wracked with pain as the tubes in her shoulder flexed to follow her sudden movements. Catching her breath and gathering her thoughts, she picked up the phone on the third ring. Holding the phone in her right hand, she steadied herself to keep her damaged shoulder from moving.

"Yes?" Though she wasn't angry at the interruption, she sounded like it.

"Hello, darling." Enola's stately tone conveyed her concern. "Are you all right, my dear? You seem to be in some pain."

Holding the phone with a steady hand, she glanced quickly around the room. *I didn't think my people would find your camera.* Her determination to save Fisk from the forces that threatened to consume him had reshaped her acceptance of Founder surveillance.

With this woman's help, she planned to make it work for her instead of against her.

"Relax, dear. I can't see you. I can hear you, though, and you sound like you're in pain. Your people got all our cameras. Have they been treating you well? I'm all too aware that Messieurs Adkins and Hathaway sometimes have divergent points of view about the care they prescribe for our people."

Doris breathed a sigh of obvious relief and lay back on the mattress. She relaxed as unseen computer controls adjusted the mattress to the contours of her body. "I'm fine. It's nothing I can't handle."

"I see. No sedatives. Really, now. I've been shot a time or two, myself. Take the drugs, dear. Trust me."

"What can you tell me about Adkins and Hathaway? What instructions do they have?"

"Let them do their job. Dr. Adkins assures me that, with proper rest and some of his bioregenerative care, you'll be leaving the clinic within the week."

Doris didn't need to be told that she was being scolded for resting "improperly." She held the phone loosely next to her ear. "What can I do for you?"

"Has Fisk been to see you?"

"He has," she admitted, unwilling to volunteer anything more. *You already know too much. I have to either trust you or kill you.*

"I understand that he came to the clinic with only two hours of sleep, and that there was some incident involving your coat." Enola struggled to keep her tone neutral to avoid letting Doris know that she was on-site.

"I was asleep. When I woke up, my coat was on the chair." She faked a yawn. Turning her head, she looked speculatively at the item in question. *I trust you to be watching me, no matter what you say.*

The Founder's voice trailed off with just a hint of mirth. *We're lying to each other. How glorious.* "Very well, then. If that's your story, I see no reason why you shouldn't stick to it."

Eyes narrowed to predatory slits, Doris scanned the room once more. *Okay, so we both know we're lying to each other.* "What do you want?" she repeated.

"This is your official notification, as per the plan. The vote has been taken. The decision has been made to terminate Fisk."

"What made up their minds?"

"Andrew Brown. They feel that his death will result in a criminal investigation. Our analysts are projecting high odds that the investigation will uncover our efforts. In today's climate of mistrust, you can see how this is possible."

"I understand." Doris wiped her eyes, speaking slowly to avoid sounding distressed.

"I'm sorry, dear. There is more."

"Go on." Doris silently reached for a tissue to wipe her eyes and nose.

"They've anticipated you. The guardian assigned to you will see to Fisk in the event that you do not follow through."

"I've seen him already. I know who he is, too. Good choice. He's not going to be a problem as long as I continue to have a free hand." She tossed the used tissue neatly into a nearby wastebasket.

"But of course. It has taken a bit of doing, but everything is in place. I'm not in my prime, but I'm still the best there is."

"Can you cover for me when I leave the clinic? I'll only need a few hours."

"Yes. The brain trust delegated this unpleasant task to me as a punishment for my outspoken behavior in this matter."

Doris got the distinct impression that the old woman was proud of herself. Despite herself, she smiled at the Founder's audacity. *Outfoxing the foxes. "Old school" at it's finest.* "You bad girl, you. Are there any other stumbling blocks that I should know about?"

"Yes. Dr. Hathaway."

"Yes?" Doris had already assumed that she'd have to kill both doctors.

"After I left the room, the old boys got together over some tea and scones. If both you and the alternate fail to dispose of him as planned, the doctors will be ordered to kill him by lethal injection. I'm not supposed to know about this. It is their way of keeping me in check. As if they could."

"I see." Doris thought for a long moment. "Would they do it? I don't intend to give them the chance, but, for the sake of argument, would they?"

"Hathaway would do it, without question. He's in awe of us. That and he likes the whole secrecy thing too much. George Adkins is another matter. He sees Fisk is his progeny. He also knew Jason in his former life. No, I daresay the attachment is too strong for him to cooperate."

"Killing Hathaway will put an end to this clinic. Are you ready for that?" Doris knew how much the Founders relied on the advanced genetic medicine that the two doctors practiced.

"Nobody deserves to live forever, not even we few. Hathaway's research has been closely documented. Someday, somewhere, somebody will master his techniques. If we don't live to see it, that's just too bad."

"All right, then. It's settled. When I leave here, I'll drop off the grid. Plan for five hours. I'll need at least two. After that, just run whatever interference you think you can get away with."

"Good luck, darling. For his sake, and for yours, I hope you make it." Enola hung up.

Lying flat, Doris willed herself to rest. Slowing her breathing, she concentrated on relaxing her body parts one at a time. *They'll let him have a nap, and then give him a physical. I know what I have to do. I know who I have to do it to. I'll make my move before dinner. They'll never know what hit them.*

Within minutes, she was asleep. Lost in a disorienting limbo, she wandered through the frightscape of her own mind. Images of her past mingled with the dark future that she feared the most.

Through sheer willpower, she found herself standing at the door to the programming lab where it had all begun. Seeing it for what it was, she boldly walked in. Wrapped in the comfort of his black leather trenchcoat, she faced the recreation with unshakable determination. *This is a dream. It's not real. It began here, but it won't end here. Not so long as I live.*

Walking boldly into the brightly lit room, she approached a powder blue medical examination chair. Hands buried deep in the coat's pockets, she could feel her mastery of the situation growing. Stopping next to the chair, she ignored the contents of the room. They began to fade.

Within seconds, the walls vanished under the pressure of her will.

Left only with the examination chair, Doris looked down at the padded seat, ready to confront what she knew she'd find there.

Taking her hands out of the warm pockets, she reached down to pick up a pair of glossy black-and-white photos. Each had small flecks of fresh blood spattered on it. Holding them up, she ignored the tiny crimson droplets as they ran down the slick paper. The photos felt brittle to her touch. Forcing herself to go on, she examined each picture closely.

In her left hand, the image of Preston Fisk shook slightly as she studied its carefully planned, precisely executed features, not quite complete. Grease pencil marks on the print showed clinical lines of further surgical alterations. His smile radiated fearless charm with just a hint of dark promise. Tiny black squiggles indicated the changes needed to construct that winning dental work. Meticulously groomed, his eyes shone brightly just below a hairline that hinted at youth and virility. A pair of thick lines indicated the patient's original receded hairline.

Looking at the second photograph was harder than she thought. Somehow, more blood had collected on her closed palm than had run over the photo. Straining with the effort, her neck muscles tightened as the bloodstreaked image came fully into focus.

The face in this frame was also male. A powerful jawline, etched with a single scar from some long ago incident, contrasted with defiant eyes that promised no mercy. Grey hair, with just a touch of white at the temples, cast the lean face in a portrait of harsh commitment.

"I promised," Doris said aloud. She repeated the long-ago vow, feeling her shoulders knot. "I promise that nobody will hurt you. Not so long as I live. I will always be there for you." Forcing the two photos together, her words rang through the surrounding emptiness with the same heartfelt conviction with which she had first spoken them.

Beads of sweat rose on her forehead and neck as she defeated the unseen force that kept the two images from making contact. The act of merging the photos cleansed her of any final doubts.

As she woke, she flinched with a terrible jolt. Hot gnawing pain coursed through her damaged shoulder and down her left arm. The sheets tangled, forcing her to stop thrashing. She was shocked to see the plastic tubes in her clenched hands, covered in a light spray of her own blood.

```
Tuesday
June 3, 2014
Training Camp
Cascade Mountains
Washington State
6:50 A.M. PDT
```

Garrison poked his head inside the Colonel's tent. "You wanted to see me?"

The old man was bent over his field table. "Come on in. Have a seat."

"The Hun said you had good news." Garrison plopped down on a camp stool. Soaking wet from a combination of sweat and morning rain, his BDUs hung limp on his muscular frame. Water puddled at his feet as he wiped moisture from his brow.

The Colonel dropped his pen. "Yeah. Good news. Look, it's truth time. You ready for some of that?"

Garrison nodded.

"Ever since you got here, we've been feeding you sublims. Nothing extreme, mind you. Facts and figures, a few gigs of management principles, and the like. We did this on orders from Them. You follow me?"

Garrison blinked. "Uh, that's good news?"

"It is for you. You finished our program faster than we thought you would. How are those headaches, by the way?"

"That's what was causing them?" He flinched.

"Yep. Shucks, we spiked your food with enough drugs to put down a horse, but it didn't seem to help. Sorry for that."

"Why are you telling me this?" Garrison asked indignantly.

The Colonel sat forward in his chair, hands folded. "I believe in what you're doing. Even if you don't know the full scope of it yet, I do, and I'll be dipped if I'm going to lie to you about it. I have very specific instructions on this matter. Those crusty old farts don't want me to tell you anything that you don't need to know. Well, screw them. To be fair, you need to know a lot more than you're being told."

"I see. I suppose I've been too busy to think about it." Garrison looked down at the damp earth between his muddy boots.

"All part of the plan," the Colonel responded, shaking his head with regret.

"How'd you do it? The subliminal education, I mean."

"The gear was in the cot. Half of it was, anyway. The other half was inside the chemical toilet. Hey, if it makes you feel any better, some folks pay a thousand dollars an hour for this stuff."

"I didn't know the technology was commercial."

"For the right people, it's very available."

"What happens now?" Garrison asked with growing dread.

"Relax. That *is* the good news. No more headaches. You've got three weeks of weapons and tactics left and you're out of here. We'll give you two weeks worth of vacation, and then you'll meet your new management team. After that, it's all up to you."

Tuesday
June 3, 2014
Cyrano's
Congressional Zone
Capitol Hill
Washington, D.C.
9:45 A.M. EDT

Anne didn't know what to say. Sitting across from the Press Secretary, she kept her poker face as mixed emotions roiled inside. Seated in the back of the exclusive bistro, a row of artificial plants hid the two women from view.

Angel put her fork down. "All I'm saying is that you may have been on to something. I had my people get copies of your work from Channel 6. Everyone else gave up trying to crack Fisk's shell a long time ago. You seem to be the only person who saw through him when the rest of us couldn't."

"I started my own look-see last year. I don't want to sound ungrateful. Nobody's forcing me to lay low, but...that wasn't my best work, if you know what I mean." Anne picked at her crepes as she talked.

"Right. It wasn't good for your career."

"Didn't hurt me, but it didn't help me, either," Anne lied.

"Mm. All that's about to change. That's why I asked you here. How would you like to put that past work to good use?"

Anne nodded, trembling inside.

"Okay. Here's the deal. I'm prepared to give you an exclusive. All you have to do is be in the right place and report what you see. Then, follow the President's lead. She may choose to build him up or tear him down. You, as the last person to be critical of him, would be our expert. Somebody we can call on, if it becomes necessary."

"'Him' meaning Fisk."

"Yes."

Anne finally met Angel's steely gaze. "Sounds like you're planning something."

Angel set her napkin aside. "I'm not planning anything. I'm not even here. We never had this conversation. In fact, I have to go. My schedule has me in other places, doing other things. Tell me now, are you in or out?"

Anne laid both hands in her lap to hide their fidgeting. *The moment of truth.* After a decade spent in obscurity, she found herself drawn to this opportunity with a mixture of fear and anticipation. Unable to speak, she nodded silently, aware that her shoulders slumped. *Everyone who's anyone in this business has been somebody's conduit. I should have accepted that years ago. It's true what they say about regional media markets. Sell out to get out.*

Angel pretended not to notice the resignation in Anne's capitulation. "All right. Keep your wireless on and be ready to roll."

Tuesday
June 3, 2014
Joint Operations Center
Old Executive Office Building
Washington, D.C.
12:00 P.M. EDT

"It's coming off the fax now," the aide told Metz as she breezed by. Standing in the middle of the busy room, Carl nodded.

"That'll be the letter of intent," one of the task force commanders told him.

Turning to the man from Homeland Security, Carl pointed at a large overhead display. "When we get that warrant, things will happen pretty fast. The feed will go live to your office. You'll be able to see what we do, when we do it."

"That's hardly necessary..." the liaison protested.

"Humor me. This isn't your average domestic. This guy is pure evil, and he has the security to back it up. Besides, your director is watching everything I do. If I don't give him a front row seat, what's he going to think?"

"Director from Service on line two," a comm tech said, passing Metz a handset.

Metz activated the phone and held it up to his ear. "Yes, ma'am."

"The Attorney General has agreed to our request," the stern female voice said. "We've got until tomorrow morning to reveal to the press that Andrew Brown is alive and well. Which reminds me, why was he so stoned? The man's got enough tranqs in him to put down a herd of elephants."

Metz spoke up over the noise in the ops center. "Have you actually seen him? All he can do is go on about his dead wife. If he wasn't blubbering about a Fisk conspiracy, we'd never know about the connection."

"I've seen him. I just wish you hadn't doped him up so bad. Look, you take him alive. Hear me? The AG isn't willing to file definite charges, so the warrant doesn't specify charges. It's only good for holding to question."

"What's he scared of?" Metz held out a hand to accept the fax.

"Are you kidding? Not even you can be that dense, Carl. Filing charges on this guy without more proof is like--"

"I know."

"No, you don't. You're playing with fire. If this goes wrong, it smears the President. If that happens, Carl...you're mine, and I promise, it'll be slow and painful."

Carl grimaced at the thought of being trapped between the Directors of the Secret Service and the Department of Homeland Security.

"I know my business. We just got your fax. The liaison from Homeland is here and we've got a scrambled feed routed to his boss. When we get the warrant, I'll call you back for a go/no-go confirmation. Okay?"

"You don't even know where the man is, Carl."

"We'll find him."

"You do that. It'll take us a few hours to work out the fine points. With any luck, we can get local law to serve the warrant. I don't suppose you'd have any ideas?"

"The Mayor likes to cozy up to anyone with an office bigger than his. I'm sure he wouldn't mind lending SWAT to serve the warrant. D.C. Metro would love it, and we can always use some good will with them."

"Consider that letter of intent your go sign. I want to be as far away from this as possible. Keep that little weasel from Homeland in the loop as much as you can. I don't care who gets most of the credit for this. I just don't want any negative press."

Tuesday
June 3, 2014
West Wing
The White House
Washington, D.C.
2:40 P.M. EDT

Josephine tried not to panic. The message left by the President on her voice mail recorder was obviously a test. "Come on. You've got all the doctors at Bethesda on speed dial. What do you really want?" she muttered as Lorraine came, unseen, into her office.

"I was going to ask you the same thing. Do you know who I just got off the phone with?" Lorraine, her pose angry, stood in the doorway.

"What?" Josephine plopped down in her chair Lorraine stomped into the small office.

"Don't you dare give me that. I've been reassigned. My whole section has been placed at your beck and call. Do you have any idea how much of an upset this is?"

"It wasn't my idea. There's just so much to do, and Stanley made the most unbelievable mess..." Josephine said, raising a pair of folders in each hand.

"Do you know how long it took me to get this job? You're lucky I don't wring your neck. In case you haven't noticed, you're not the only one cleaning up other people's messes."

Josephine stopped sorting folders. Looking at Lorraine, she composed herself. "I'm really sorry, but I have no idea what you're talking about. I'm just as shocked by all this as you are." In her last briefing, a member of Fisk's group had lectured her heavily on the need to be diplomatic.

Lorraine pulled back. "My word. You really don't, do you? I'm sorry for going off on you. I really didn't mean what I said about wringing your neck. It's just that you got me transferred from the President's--"

"I work for the President, so, technically, you haven't been transferred from anything. In fact, you're actually getting closer to the action, if you know what I mean." She kept her studious gaze focused on the older woman, very conscious that she was using persuasive techniques that learned late at night from a man that she knew very little about. *This is so weird.*

"I doubt that. Until today, I was--"

Josephine swiveled in her chair as she tapped her computer keyboard. "See this? This is the President's complete schedule. They're going to get somebody else to fill my old job. Now, I've got it all on tap: social calendar, Congressional appointments, state functions, and, of course, the national security stuff. If I don't know about it, it's probably so classified that they'd have to kill me if I found out about it."

"Tosh." Lorraine waved a hand.

"Oh, come on." Josephine knew that she had to cement Lorraine's loyalty now, or lose it. "We're here to serve the greater good, aren't we? Working for the President means a lot of things. You and I are both on the same team. Right?"

"When you put it like that, it's very hard to be mad at you." Lorraine paused. "To be honest, I'm glad Stanley is gone. If you think this is a mess, you should see what the rest of us have to deal with." Her brow furrowed in disgust.

"How many departments does this affect?" Josephine asked. "Be honest. I'm not a career hack. I want to make a difference."

Lorraine choked her way past the unintended insult. "Ah-hem. Well, as a career...*professional*...I think it's fair to say that everyone has been affected. You know, I thought we'd be stuck with him all term."

Josephine nodded as she began to shuffle through a stack of disk carriers. "The President is a wise woman. This really wasn't my idea. I'm sorry if it upset you."

"I wouldn't say that it upset me. It's just that a 'reassignment' is usually not a good thing. Here in the White House, you're either on your way up or you're on your way out."

Josephine nodded again. *You've been in limbo for so long. Funny, I never thought of that before.*

Tuesday
June 3, 2014
Joint Operations Center
Old Executive Office Building
Washington, D.C.
2:45 P.M. EDT

Metz sat alone in his office. He cast a glum eye around his surroundings, jumping when the phone rang. He reached out to key the speaker. "Metz."

"It's me." SWAT Commander Lucas didn't sound very happy.

"You got the warrant?"

"This is low, even for you. You know we never make an official move against anyone we've been contracted to deal with. Never."

"It's not my fault that your crew was next up on the rotation," Metz lied. *You'll never know how easy it was to arrange.* "Take it up with the Chief of Police. You know how he likes to cater to Homeland. The way I see it, this can work for both of us. You've got a legit warrant, and we both have official sanction." He steepled his fingers on the desk blotter.

Lucas was clearly galled. "The warrant says 'questioning.' There aren't any charges. Have you got any idea what they'll do to my people if we cap him? Our whole operation'll be ruined. If the City Attorney doesn't rip me a new one, Fisk's lawyers will gut me like a fish. No. Get somebody else. This isn't the kind of retirement I had in mind."

"You're not listening. I told you, we have sanction. Official sanction." Metz tapped the speakerphone petulantly.

"Bull." Lucas was clearly not impressed.

"The deal's being cut now. Secret Service and Homeland will hand off to D.C. Metro. There won't be any aggressive assets from Homeland. They'll have observers and attorneys on site, but you'll have a free hand."

"How far up does this sanction go?"

"You saw the warrant. The Attorney General--"

"The Attorney General can bite me. How far up does the sanction go?"

"Far enough for me to risk using you," Metz admitted sourly.

"What about the FBI?"

"The Bureau has its own problems right now," Carl replied, referring to a series of scandals crippling the once-proud agency. "They've been arresting too many people on terrorism charges who turn out to be innocent. Homeland is not happy with them. Trust me, they don't want to be anywhere near this."

"We'll do it. We can't let him walk, not with what he might know. It would be bad for business."

```
Tuesday
June 3, 2014
West Wing
The White House
Washington, D.C.
2:58 P.M. EDT
```

"Aren't you going to stop for lunch?" Lorraine asked Josephine.

"No time. I've got some snacks, though." Lorraine seemed more at ease after nearly ten minutes of chatting.

Josephine was impressed with what she had heard. Like most career bureaucrats, Lorraine felt that the system had let her down. Her enthusiasm had long since been crushed and replaced with grim pragmatism.

"Listen to me ramble," Lorraine fretted, embarrassed. "All I ever wanted to do was make a difference. When we leave here, nobody will ever know if we did our jobs well or if we totally screwed things up."

Josephine's newfound respect for Lorraine came as a surprise. *I had no clue that you were an idealist.* "It's okay. Your secret is safe with me. Want one?" She opened a desk drawer, took out a small bag, and offered it to the other woman.

"No, thank you. If you don't mind my asking, just how did you get in so well with her?"

Josephine blinked. "The President? I'm not really sure." *They told me this would happen.*

"Wouldn't have anything to do with Preston Fisk, would it?" Lorraine asked casually.

"I think it did," she responded, struggling to speak the half-truth convincingly. "You and he have something in common, you know." Aware that she was intentionally sidestepping the question, she averted her eyes.

"Don't tell me we're related. My family couldn't produce a man like that if we tried."

Josephine looked her in the eye. "You're both complicated. You both made compromises to be where you are today, and you both know what you really want."

"Anyone who looks at the man can see that he hasn't suffered. Whatever compromises you're talking about couldn't have been that bad. Still, he can compromise with me any time he likes." The saucy look she gave Josephine came and went with the blink of an eye.

"That's not what I mean."

"You'd know," Lorraine challenged with a catty grin.

Tuesday
June 3, 2014
Secured Site 6
Adkins-Hathaway Clinic
Alexandria, Virginia
5:30 P.M. EDT

Fisk sat alone in the small dining room. Picking at a small salad, he couldn't recall the last time he'd been here. Most of the time, Adkins and Hathaway came to him. The clinic was something that he'd known about but never been involved with--a line item in the budget.

The clinic provided a wide range of services for the members of Fisk's inner circle, as well as helping to quietly support the less affluent members of the organization. As part of its cover, it also had a few high profile clients who knew nothing of its hidden agenda.

Glancing around the room, Fisk examined the photos on the walls. Famous and near-famous faces from the last ten years smiled back at him. His own picture was noticeably absent.

Dressed in trendy sweats, he felt relaxed and well-rested after his long nap. The events of the last 24 hours no longer troubled him.

"How are you feeling?"

The cultured voice startled Fisk out of his reverie. He turned to see Enola enter the room. Still dressed as a nurse, the tall, alabaster-skinned redhead carried herself with an almost regal bearing.

"I was wondering when you'd show up." He motioned her over to his table.

"I've been here all day. Then again, you were quite spent when they brought you in."

"Enola, you blend in all too well." He got to his feet and pulled out a chair for her.

"It's a skill, one that, I dare say, has gone out of style. How are you feeling?" she said as she sat down.

"Much better." He nodded vigorously. "I didn't expect to sleep so long. I was hoping to be in and out of here by tonight, but Adkins and Hathaway have other appointments until some time after 6. Factor in dinner, and they won't get to me until after 9. After that, three days of general recovery, whether I like it or not."

"Don't blame them. They have to keep up appearances, you know. I have it on good authority that the glitch in their schedule came up while you were sleeping. They had no idea it was coming," she said with a gleam in her eye.

"I see. Anything you'd like to tell me?"

"No." Enola sat primly erect.

"I know that look."

She softened as she reached out to fidget with a teaspoon. "Darling, there's a lot I don't tell you. Trust me, it really is for your own good." She put down the spoon and looked directly at him.

"Well, then, to what do I owe the pleasure of this visit?"

"Doris. How was your visit with her?"

"Different," Fisk admitted slowly. "I don't know what it is about that coat, but I kept getting the impression that Adkins and Hathaway didn't like it. If I didn't know better, I'd swear that they didn't want me coming in contact with it, let alone delivering it." He puffed out his cheeks and sighed.

Enola remained poker-faced. "Mm. What did Doris tell you?"

"That's just it, I can't remember. I know I took the coat in to her, and I know that we talked, but, it's gone." He snapped his fingers.

"Now that you are rested, it might come back. Fatigue has a way of robbing the mind. Besides that, the poor woman is in pain. She probably didn't have that much to say."

"Yeah, I feel badly about that, too. I wish--"

"Shh. It's quite all right. These things happen."

"They've been happening an awful lot lately. Before I came in to eat, I got the update on our tactical units. I had no idea the casualties were so high. I can't get Griff to talk to me about it. I don't know if he blames me--"

"Of course he doesn't blame you. Nobody blames you. Believe me, this whole enterprise could have been much more costly. Your efforts to avoid bloodshed have been admirable. Time and again, the committee has been very impressed with your ability to avoid the taking of life when it was not otherwise necessary."

"Hmm." Fisk bit down on his tongue to avoid responding.

"I know *that* look all too well. You're biting your tongue."

"Hmm."

"Say it," she demanded.

"Say what? What am I supposed to say? You sit there and tell me that the committee is so proud of me, and then--"

Enola held up a hand, palm out. "Please, let me explain."

"What's to explain? I agreed to the termination option. That doesn't mean I have to like it." Fisk was taken back by the ferocity of his own anger.

Enola silenced him with a stern look. "I'm here to help. If the committee were unanimous, you'd be dead by now. We both know it. The fact is that the committee is *not* unanimous. I may be the only dissenter, but I am here with you now. They are determined, but misguided. They are slaves to the plan, slaves to a way of life that has gone out of style. In short, they are wrong."

"I don't know what to say. I've been trying not to think about it. I know it sounds irrational, but I really have been deliberately shutting it out."

Enola gave him an understanding look. "I would have expected nothing less. You don't give up. You never will. It's a special consistency that sets you apart from other men. You may be fearless by design, but you are not without conscience. We sometimes forget that conviction is a double-edged sword. To achieve our goals, we must sometimes resort to that which we despise. You've done your best to put the committee out of your mind because it interferes with your mission."

"So, what now?"

"Doris will come for you after she leaves the clinic. She needs time to make arrangements. I don't know the full scope of her plans, but I can make an educated guess."

"They told me I'd be walking out of here in three days. That means action on her part inside the next 72 hours." As the possibilities whirled through his mind, his tongue began to probe for his implant.

"I wouldn't do that if I were you. The committee has already taken control of your secondary tactical team. Even now, they are in position around this clinic, waiting."

Fisk blanched. "They can't co-opt everyone, can they?" *Doris and I have already had this conversation.*

"Certainly not. The committee assumes that primary tactical, which is in the building right now, will refuse to act against you. It's really quite simple. With all the recent casualties, it wasn't hard to reconstitute a secondary team with people who would follow their orders instead of yours. You were never supposed to know. I'm the leak. Might as well make use of an old job skill. I used to be quite good at it, too."

He nodded calmly. "Haven't lost your touch." Coping with adversity was part of the Fisk persona's reflexive nature. The ability to shrug off fear and self-doubt came at the expense of more natural self-preservation instincts.

"Thank you," Enola preened. "Your ability to inspire and keep loyalty is what scares them. You're an asset like no other, and it scares them. They could lose control of you at any time, and they know it."

"When I agreed to the kill option, I never thought I'd be in any shape to countermand it. I always assumed I'd be incapacitated. I don't know, maybe I just don't like the idea of giving up. I never thought of this as a one-way ride."

"An interesting choice of words." Enola paused. "When you agreed to front our organization, you knew the risks. So did we. I'd be lying if I said we expected you to make it this far. Yet here you are, alive and kicking. Perhaps you never thought of this as a one-way mission, but we did. In this, we were very, very wrong."

"I don't know how to lose," Fisk sneered in a poor attempt at humor.

"There is more truth to that than you know." Enola glanced down at her folded hands for a long moment. "I make no apologies for the committee. They're treating you no differently than they were treated, back in the day. I don't expect you to understand it entirely, nor do I expect you to like it."

"I get it. I don't know why I never thought about it like that, but that's water under the bridge. You're right. I did know the risks. I knew that this job might take my life. But I also knew that it was worth doing."

"There is no need to preach to the choir, darling. Please, accept my presence for what it is. The only thing left to do now is wait for Doris."

"I've never seen her fail. Still, even if she can get me out of here in one piece, where would we go? What would we do? This is the 21st century. I can't hide from somebody of your caliber, and I know it."

Enola looked at Fisk for a long moment. "In time, the committee will be gone. Even with the miracles that doctors like Adkins and Hathaway can offer, we are still only mortal. All she has to do is get you away from here. After that, all you have to do is outlive us."

Tuesday
June 3, 2014
West Wing
Office of the President
The White House
Washington, D.C.
5:59 P.M. EDT

Josephine knocked on the door to the President's office.

"Come!" Madeline responded loudly.

"I'm sorry about the time. The schedule was such a mess, and--"

"Please, you don't have to knock. You have full access. As long as that door isn't locked, you just come right in."

Josephine closed the door behind her and stepped forward. The office was as it had been for the last century, simple and very photogenic. A quick glance allowed one to take in the small touches that personalized the room as being Madeline's office.

In a chair to her right, Chief of Staff Larry Hodgekiss sat with a fistful of papers rolled up in one hand. "Hello. You've turned out to be quite the surprise package. I'm sorry for ever doubting you." He nodded at her.

"Being underestimated has its advantages. Really, I'm just doing what has to be done."

Madeline leaned back. "Don't be so modest. That's an order. You've done more for this office in the last two days than some of my staffers have done in the last week. That folder you prepped on the French situation was brilliant. After I got off the line with the French President, I had it sent over to State with a note to tell them that I want more of that kind of thing from them, and not you."

"That's right," Larry chimed in. "You did it in 15 pages. The preconference reports we get from the State Department are much bigger and a lot less readable. Hey, I've got to go. I'll let you know when Metz is ready. I'm just going to make sure that Angel has all her bases covered."

Madeline looked up. "I've already spoken to her. Just make sure you're available when the press conference starts. If she needs to go good cop/bad cop, I want you waiting in the wings."

"Right," Larry confirmed as he left the room.

Madeline speared Josephine with an inquisitive look. "So, what have you got for me?"

The young woman looked down at the disk in her hands. "These are the updated schedules. With Lorraine's help, we have a clear picture for the next two weeks."

Madeline took the disk and laid it aside without looking at it. "Please, have a seat. It's time you and I got a few things straight."

Josephine sat across from the President and waited.

"Where do you stand with Preston Fisk?"

"I don't stand anywhere with him. Don't get me wrong, he's a nice guy, and all, but he's not really my type." She blinked as she struggled to maintain eye contact.

The answer threw Madeline, as intended. "Really? What's not to like?"

"Now that I've gotten to know him a little, he's a lot too dominant for me. He knows what he wants, and he knows how to get it." The answer came out evenly, despite the roiling of her stomach.

"Right. It's hard to work in his shadow."

"Yeah, that's it," Josephine replied, seizing on Madeline's point to mask her own thoughts. "I don't know how you do it. He makes everything sound like it's the right thing to do. It's no wonder he gets around. With an attitude like that--"

"I think I may have misread you. If what Larry tells me is even half true, you're more than just a diamond in the rough. Fisk certainly has a talent for spotting the best and brightest. It's one of his more redeeming qualities."

Josephine couldn't help the snicker that escaped her lips. *I can't believe I'm doing this.*

"Did you manage to find out who his doctor is?" Madeline asked after composing herself.

"I haven't had a free moment. Your voice mail didn't sound like--"

"Has he ever confided in you? I know you haven't known him very long, but has he ever mentioned any illnesses?" Madeline sat forward intently.

Josephine was stunned. "What? No. What's going on?"

Madeline steepled her fingers as she studied the staff assistant. "It may be nothing, but the last time I spoke with him, he said something about going in to see his doctor. The impression I got wasn't good. Look, I know this might come as a surprise to you, but he and I haven't always gotten along."

Josephine said nothing. *Stay quiet and play my part,* she counseled herself. *Separating what I know from what I'm supposed to know is hard. How does he do it?*

"It's true," Madeline said, waving off the other woman's silence. "We fight. For a long time, I didn't know who was the real President, him or me. He got me here, but the rest has all been on my terms."

Unsure of herself and what she was witnessing, Josephine nodded. *He wasn't kidding when he said you were conflicted. Are you really as dangerous as his people tell me?*

Madeline could sense Josephine's fear. "I'm sorry. I don't mean to ramble. The thought of losing him to a disease just isn't in my worldview. Can you forgive me for lying to you? I suppose I'm a little too possessive, but I really do want to find out what's going on with him." When she looked up at Josephine, she was pleased to see that she had struck the right chord.

"I can make some calls. I don't know if anyone will talk to me, but I'll try. He looked so healthy the last time I saw him--"

"I know." Madeline grinned slyly. "During the election, I swear he didn't sleep for two days straight. He still looked like he jumped off the cover of a magazine. People in his line of work have a lot of stress, as well as a lot of enemies. He doesn't drop out of sight like this very often, and I'm pretty sure that you and I are the only ones in this building who even suspect why." With all her skill, she willed the catch in her throat to come through at the last moment.

"I can't promise anything." *You're pushing my buttons, just like they said you would. Why doesn't the Secret Service know where to find him?*

"I wouldn't ask anyone else. You seem so capable, I just thought that you might be able to help me." Madeline watched the clock on her desk as it registered 6:15 P.M. *Either you're smart or you really can't help me. I hope this doesn't take too much longer. Then again, we are talking about Fisk. I have to remember that.*

"Let me finish up a few things. I have two committee calendars to finalize, and then I'll give it my best shot." In the back of her mind, Josephine thought about the wireless phone that Fisk had given her. The small device, and what it connected her to, made her squeamish. *He's right about you, isn't he?*

"I'd really appreciate it if you could give me an answer tonight. I've got a dinner slated from 7 to 9. After that, I'm free. I expect to hear from you before I turn in."

Tuesday
June 3, 2014
West Wing
The White House
Washington, D.C.
6:50 P.M. EDT

Alone in her office, Josephine stopped to look at the small window. Seated behind her desk, she couldn't see the Rose Garden. The glow cast by the sodium lighting array outside came though her small window as a dull orange glow.

Glancing at her office door, she breathed a sigh of relief. *Door closed. Door locked. Lorraine and company gone.* Satisfied that she was truly alone, she used a remote control to close the blinds on the tiny window. Routine security sweeps prevented her from having any locked drawers. Knowing this, she kept the phone in her purse, as if it had been hers all along. Fisk's people assured her that she now had a wireless account that would stand up to future scrutiny by the Secret Service.

"Wonder if I have to pay the bill on this thing," she muttered to herself as she took the little phone out. Laying it on her desk, she sat back to think.

She had gotten a phone call from one of Fisk's employees the night before. A man with a gravelly voice told her that her office was temporarily free of listening devices. "We arranged an equipment failure. It's temporary. After the first of the month, you won't be able to use that phone while you're on White House property. It does have an autoscrambler, but they'll be watching you, recording everything you say and do. Don't call us unless it's very important or you're in a jam that you can't get out of," he had told her.

Josephine thought about Fisk and her leather-bound scheduler. *He took a risk when he told me about it.*

Looking down at the tiny phone, she felt her stomach flutter. *She could be using me to get to him, couldn't she? She wants him dead, and she can't find him. That would explain--*

The knock on the door made her jump. "Come in!" she squeaked as she scooped up the phone in both hands.

The door's voice-activated lock clicked open. Angel poked her head in. "Have you got a minute?" she asked with practiced congeniality.

"Of course. Come in." Josephine couldn't release her grip on the wireless phone.

Angel closed the door and moved across the room to sit. "So, you're the famous Josephine Harper. My secretary hasn't been this rational in a long time. Thanks." Nodding, she brushed long golden strands of hair from her eyes.

"I'm just doing my job. Thanks for the compliment."

She watched Josephine fidget with the phone. "I don't have a lot of time. The President has a state dinner starting any second now. I just stopped by to ask a favor. Did I come at a bad time?"

"No. I was just going to make a few personal calls," she explained, rocking the little phone back and forth in her hands.

"We may need to block some time tomorrow morning for a press conference. Larry said you were the one to see about that. So, here I am."

"If he gives the go-ahead--" Josephine started to turn.

"He's busy with something just now. We passed each other in the hall and he told me to come find you. You'll probably get the e-mail later."

She managed to pry one hand free of the phone. "Right. Let's see." She reached out to stroke her computer keyboard. She adjusted the monitor so that the hologram was pointed at Angel. "You should be able to see the same thing from your workstation. There's nothing classified slated for tomorrow. We can bump all these." She pointed at the early morning appointments. "Looks to me like a good 30 minutes. All the way up to 11 o'clock. Is that good enough?"

Angel pursed her lips, thinking. "I think so. I can't remember the last time I saw the schedule looking this flexible. You really are good."

"Can I ask what it's all about?"

Angel ignored the query and rose to her feet. "That's great.

Somebody will call you. Can you be here by eight? There's just no telling how soon we might need to get started."

"I'm here by 7."

"Great. That's great. Somebody will call you if it comes up."

Josephine stayed quiet as Angel closed the door on the way out. After readjusting the computer monitor, she glared at the phone in her stubborn hand. *I guess I'd better make that call.*

Tuesday
June 3, 2014
Joint Operations Center
Old Executive Office Building
Washington, D.C.
7:25 P.M. EDT

Carl shook his head in frustration. "Play it for me again."
"We can't clean it up any more. The computer has all the repeaters in a 400-mile radius tagged. We might get something cleaner once we've had a chance to download the digital," the technician replied from in front of a large console.

"Play it, will you?" Metz rubbed his temples in an attempt to stave off a tension headache.

The technician turned and pressed a button.

"Cosmopolitan Systems, can I help you?"

"Hello. My name is Josephine Harper. Do you know who I am?"

"Yes, Ms. Harper, how can I help you?"

"I can't be sure, but I think something is going on that Mr. Fisk should know about."

"Can you be more specific?"

"Not really. Something is going on around here. Earlier today, the President asked me to find out who Fisk's doctor is. Shouldn't she already know that? I mean, the Secret Service would have that on file, wouldn't they?"

"Ms. Harper, are you calling from inside the White House?"

"Yes."

"I'll have to ask you to hang up. We'll get back to you with instructions, okay?"

"Right."

"I told her it wouldn't work." Metz gave up on the headache.

"Sir?" The technician adjusted her glasses.

"It's nothing. She must know that the gear in her office is down. She wouldn't make a call like that if she thought we'd be listening in."

The technician swiveled in her chair to face him. "We still can't explain how our systems went down on Sunday. She doesn't sound like she'd know anything about that. Besides, it was dumb luck that we got this at all. If I hadn't been here, the computer would have logged it as anomalous traffic. My guess is that the two aren't connected."

"Do we have anything at all on a firm called Cosmopolitan Systems?"

"Custom telecom. Small. No Defense or government contracts. Looks like some wireless and broadband hosting for a handful of privately held firms," the tech rattled off from a nearby monitor.

"Great. It's a cutout." Carl closed his eyes in frustration.

"Looks that way to me."

Metz got to his feet with a groan. "I'll be back in an hour. It's going to take me at least that long to get the wiretap cleared. Stay here. If you leave for any reason, make sure that somebody is here to receive confirmation of the tap when it comes in. How long will it take to trap their phone logs?"

"Two minutes. I can do it faster if you let me tap their signal repeaters before the warrant goes out. The computer can tally the initiating numbers and call destinations a whole lot faster that way. We'd know about any calls to or from Cosmopolitan Systems in real time."

"We have too many agencies involved as it is. Isn't there some way we could get around all that FCC trash?"

"Congress doesn't want us to intrude like that. FCC has to be brought in. Sorry."

"Forget Congress. Just tell me who I have to call."

"This number." She offered him a small slip of paper.

He nodded. "That's more like it. Okay. I'll have them fax you the approval. As soon as you start the repeater trace, send the alert to the team leaders. I don't want anyone coming back to me later saying that they didn't get the word." Turning, he left the room.

On the mezzanine outside the communications room, he paused to gather his wits. Down on the floor of the Joint Operations Center, routine activity was keeping the place busy and loud. Taking it all in, Carl felt like a would-be king surveying what might one day be his domain.

Going to his office, he paused along the way to confer with his subordinates. "Throw him a bone. Let what's-his-name from Homeland work with the AG's office to get that warrant on Cosmopolitan Systems served."

"It's not going to matter who does it," the man said, turning in his chair. "The only problem I see is this. This is Fisk's profile. See here?" The man pointed a stubby finger at the text on his monitor.

"Lawyers on speed-dial," Metz snorted as he leaned over to read. "Big deal. All you have to do is tie up that jet and helicopter so that he can't go anywhere. It's bad enough that we've got to deal with the Virginia State Troopers. Let's keep the lawyers out of this, if we can." They both nodded silently over the problem of jurisdiction.

In the previous ten years, state governors had become eager to have terrorism cases tried in their jurisdictions. The public relations windfall from a single high-profile case was impossible to measure. The trend had its roots in the early years of the century, when the nation's legal system had first struggled with terrorism.

"Serving on his cutout will tip our hand. I really hope you're right about this. If he's not guilty of anything, we're going to be making one whopper of a mistake."

Metz stood up to stretch his tortured back. "If he's not guilty of anything, he should come quietly. That reminds me, I need to use your phone."

"Go ahead. I'm going to grab a sandwich. You want anything?"

"Sure, whatever they've got." Metz sat down as the man moved aside. He picked up the phone and dialed.

Seated in a large chair at the middle of the operations center, Griff swiveled to speak to each of his subordinates. "Set condition red. Notify all sections that we are shutting down. Have we got any Category Two personnel in the building?" he asked the night Overwatch commander.

"No," the woman confirmed as she sat down at a workstation. She hooked up her neural interface and said, "Begin masquerade."

Griff waited for her to finish issuing commands. "Time?" he swiveled to ask the man behind him.

"Three minutes and eighteen seconds since we received the warrant. There's a police cruiser rolling up to our front door now," the other man said over his shoulder.

Governments and law enforcement agencies around the country had been using the internet to exchange electronic "paperwork" with the private sector for a decade. Paperless transactions, such as the serving of search warrants, were now daily occurrences in most parts of the nation.

"Acknowledge the warrant. Don't send any text. Just click the accept button and terminate the internet connection."

After much hesitation, legal and commercial institutions were now connected to each other via the internet. Lawsuits in federal courts were still being decided about the ethics of this new form of intrusion.

"Warrant is accepted. It's a minor search warrant. They want to see our phone logs."

As Griff watched the security camera feeds, a man dressed in a dark suit got out of the police car in front of the building. "They wouldn't come back here unless they were looking for a connection to Fisk. It's got to be that call from what's-her-name." He gave the Overwatch commander a grim look.

Overwatch glanced at her screens. "Harper. Josephine Harper. They must have put a trace on the repeater net. Says here that the screener asked where she was calling from. If she made that call from inside the White House, they could have trapped her signal path and traced the call." Turning her projection so that Griff could see it, she shook her head.

Griff sighed in resignation. *It's always the little things.* "Right. They probably couldn't crack the encryption, but they didn't need to. Ah, nuts. She led them right to us." He swore as he stood.

"How do you want to play this?" the commander asked. The security monitors showed black-and-white images of a police-escorted lawyer entering the building.

Griff walked over to the workstation. "No choice. Masquerade. Show them the dummy logs and hope they fall for it. If they trapped the signal paths from our licensed repeaters out of this building before they sent that warrant, we're done for."

"I want to move the helicopter. They have a pad out at the clinic, and I've feel better if it was there for him." Overwatch looked up at Griff as she adjusted the interface jack behind her right ear.

Griff turned to give the order to a waiting subordinate. "Do it. Wind up the jet, too. If we move them, we can see if they're under surveillance. I have a bad feeling that somebody is throwing a net."

"Sims. Enter and run what we have. Crosscheck any parallels and give me an updated threat assessment in ten," Overwatch commanded. Across the room, a group of technicians got busy working up the new computer simulations.

Griff pointed at his watch. "You've got five to make your final preps, and then let's get out of here. We need to be gone when the cops start looking this place over."

"What about Harper?" Overwatch asked.

"Let's finish up here and relocate before we deal with her. She's probably on her way home by now, anyway."

Tuesday
June 3, 2014
Secured Site 6
Adkins-Hathaway Clinic
Alexandria, Virginia
8:50 P.M. EDT

Must have needed the sleep more than I thought. Alone in her room, Doris began to dress. Her clothes had been cleaned and placed in a small closet on the far side of the room. In the back of the closet, her shoulder holster and gun lay wrapped in a towel.

Slipping on her shoes, she leaned on the end of the hospital bed. She released the clip from the gun and examined the bullets in the spring-fed magazine. Satisfied, she put on the holster and slipped the gun in until it was snug.

Reaching for the trenchcoat out of habit, she paused. *He's not that good. He might just fall for it.* She left the coat draped over the end of the room's only chair and turned to look at the door.

Nodding, she walked back over to the bed and sat down. Reaching for the nurse's call button, she made herself comfortable before pressing it. *One way to find out.* Thumbing off the safety, she raised the silenced pistol and took aim at the door.

Five heartbeats went by before the door to her room opened. The guard poked his head into the room. "Is everything okay?" His glance immediately stopped when he saw the coat draped over the chair. It was enough to satisfy his initial concern that Doris might be up and around.

Braced for the shot, she fired. The round penetrated just above the man's left ear, near the temple. The sound of the man's bursting skull drowned out the mechanical cough of her weapon. Viscera sprayed the wall to his right, and he collapsed.

"Everything is just fine," Doris muttered as she slid off the bed.

Rolling her damaged shoulder experimentally, she nodded. *Not going to get much use out of this.* Walking over to the small sink and cabinet, she opened the little cupboard. The prepared syringe was right where she'd left it.

"Let me help you with that."

Doris flinched at Enola's suddenly appearance in the doorway.

"Since you did ring, I might as well make myself useful." Padding into the room, she shut the door while expertly avoiding the blood still draining from the dead man. She took the syringe. "Nicely done. Sit on the edge of the bed,"

Doris complied silently.

"I'm afraid there is no time to do this gently. Turn your head. Don't look at me." She tapped the needle to remove any bubbles.

"What's his reporting interval?" Doris asked.

Enola gave her the shot through the fabric of her blouse into the damaged shoulder. "He didn't have one. He was supposed to stay close to you until he knew that you had done your job. The committee won't know he has been cancelled until after the fact." Stepping back, she pretended not to notice Doris work her way through the pain of the injection.

"What else can you tell me?" Doris reached out to pick up the brass casing from the bullet she had fired. "Here. A souvenir." She handed the still-warm casing to Enola, who took it graciously.

"I will cherish it," she said cordially, dropping it into the apron pocket of her smock. "Don't worry about him, either. I'll find something to do with him. It's been years since I've disposed of a body. Could be fun."

When Doris didn't laugh, she continued, "I'm glad you are so well-rested."

"Where is Fisk now?" Doris was waiting for the medication to kick in.

"Reading, in the library. I called in a few favors to arrange a sudden snag in their schedule. Messieurs Adkins and Hathaway are busy treating one of their more lucrative clients for a sudden back injury."

"So they won't get to him tonight?" She tested her now numbed shoulder.

"I should think not. The client I chose is well known for his cantankerous demeanor. By the time they are done with him, they will want nothing more than a light dinner and sleep."

"Outstanding."

"Appreciated. Although, I must tell you that I was trying for a more substantial injury." Enola bowed her head solemnly.

"What went wrong?" Doris tried her shoulder again.

The older woman scowled. "Antilock brakes,"

"Right. How compliant will they be?" She reached for her coat.

"Adkins told the committee that he would not carry out the order. I wish I could have seen the looks on their faces. We're all so used to getting what we want. Compliance is taken for granted. Hathaway, on the other hand, is a different story. He did not object, so I must assume that he will obey, if it comes down to that."

Doris pointed at the corpse on the floor. "You take care of him. Then disappear. I'll go and talk to the primary team myself. A lot of them have been with us for five and six years. I'm willing to bet that loyalty to Fisk might mean more to them than orders from people they've never met. After that, I'll need those two hours we talked about."

Tuesday
June 3, 2014
Joint Operations Center
Old Executive Office Building
Washington, D.C.
9:02 P.M. EDT

"Okay." Metz hung up the phone and turned to address his staff. "We got him. They fed us a fake phone log, but we got them through the repeater trace. He's at a private clinic."

"How sure are we?" somebody in the crowd asked.

"Comms crosschecked every number dialed to and from Cosmopolitan Systems in the last 72 hours. The clinic comes up 19 times. It's the only number that doesn't correspond to a commercial address."

"The old boy must be in for a physical," somebody snickered.

"I don't care if he's getting his oil changed. We tipped our hand by serving on Cosmo. I want our lawyers ready to go in ten minutes."

He then pointed at a pair of his subordinates. "You two. Round up the troops and let's get on-line with the Virginia Governor's office."

A man in shirtsleeves stood, saying, "We've got an call from Alexandria PD. Their boss is protesting the D.C. SWAT."

Metz pushed his way over to the man. "Use your brain, will you? We're serving a federal warrant. We can use any resource we want. Don't bother me with stuff like this again."

He couldn't remember the name of the next man he singled out. "You. Find the rep from Homeland and get him whatever he wants. Keep him busy until we get this warrant served."

"He's probably going to want dinner."

"I don't care if he wants to get laid. You keep him out of our way until I personally call on your wireless. Got me? If we're lucky, Fisk's lawyers will tell him to come quietly. After all, it is a question-and-answer warrant. We could end up looking real good if we can keep Homeland out of it."

The man nodded as he shouldered his way out of the office.

Carl stopped to gather his thoughts. "Okay, get the Director on the line. I'll brief her while the rest of you coordinate with your sections. Don't let any of the observers jerk you around. This is our operation, and it's going to stay that way. If anyone gets flak from the Alexandria PD, transfer the call to me and I'll chew their ears off." His bravado was rewarded with several nods and chuckles from around the room.

Word of the pending arrest had leaked out to other law enforcement agencies. The high profile of the case had caused many of their chief administrators to jump at the chance for a piece of the action--and the eventual media exposure.

"Which agency found him?" somebody asked.

Carl sneered. "We ran the trap and tap on his cutout. We got him. The most unbelievably complicated thing I've ever seen. Just goes to prove that you can find anybody if you look hard enough."

"Welcome to the 21st century. Routine procedure," another voice chimed in.

"There's nothing 'routine' about this guy. Remember that. We have one thing going for us. He doesn't know that we've got Secretary Brown--"

"Shouldn't he be moved?" a unit chiefs asked.

Metz turned to face the man. "No. We could be wrong about this whole thing. All we have to go on are the words of one extremely screwed up man and a single protective agent. Fisk's lawyers will have a field day with them unless we do this by the numbers. Besides, if he did know we had Brown tucked away some place, I'm sure he would have moved on it by now. We'd have heard from his lawyers. If we're lucky, he'll come quietly."

Tuesday
June 3, 2014
Secured Site 6
Adkins-Hathaway Clinic
Alexandria, Virginia
9:14 P.M. EDT

The primary tactical team leader nodded as he sipped his coffee. "We're in."

Doris leaned in the doorway to the small room. "I thought you might be. How far will you go?"

The man was surrounded on three sides by closed circuit monitors and a control board. He gestured at the screens. "I think we have to go all the way. You saw it for yourself," he said, referring to the serving of the warrant at Cosmopolitan Systems. "We've got to assume that they already know where we are. I think Griff's right. They want to hold him for questioning. The thing I don't get is the timing. It wouldn't be hard for them to stake out his homes or the office and just wait for him."

"She's not being patient any more. She's got something on him, and she wants to use it."

"Griff should be relocated within the hour. The helicopter gets here about then. We have to find out where the secondary team stands. If they're not with us, we could be in trouble."

"What do you want to bet that guys with the warrant will be here before then?" Doris stood, brushing the wrinkles out of her coat. *So much for my plans.*

"Not taking that one. There's just one more thing," the operative replied as he rose to his feet.

"You take care of things on this end, and I'll go and see to the doctors myself."

The tac leader took a hesitant step forward with an outstretched hand. "You're just as quick as they say you are. By the way, my name is Colby. I don't know how this is going to play out, but I'm thinking we should be on a first name basis for the duration."

Tuesday
June 3, 2014
Secured Site 6
Adkins-Hathaway Clinic
Alexandria, Virginia
9:20 P.M. EDT

Doris walked into the small dining room with her coat open.

Adkins and Hathaway sat at the center table. A light dinner was laid out on white linen and fine china. Hathaway was lecturing. "So there you have it. Ah, Doris. Come in. I didn't expect to see you up and about until tomorrow. Please, come and sit."

Smiling casually, Doris took a chair next to him.

"Who took out your tubes?" Adkins asked uneasily as he put his napkin down.

"I did." Doris nodded cordially as she peeled out of her coat. The holster kept her weapon snug and ready below her damaged shoulder.

"You really should let him have a look. Wouldn't do to be pulling stitches, especially as your work is done." Hathaway sipped his tea.

"Later. I've come to discuss orders."

"Right. You'll have to excuse the recalcitrance of my friend. He disagrees with the committee's decision."

"Really?"

"I am not having this discussion," Dr. Adkins said indignantly. "You've all gotten carried away with this deception. You've lost sight of why we did this in the first place. I will not take that man's life. He has come too far. He's given up too much." He pounded his fist on the edge of the table.

Hathaway wrinkled his nose disdainfully. "Pay him no mind. He's the one who is out of touch. For as long as I have known him, the good doctor has always been directed by his idealism. Please, let me reassure you, all is in readiness. We had an emergency to deal with, but that's behind us now. We can be at your disposal first thing in the morning. Providing, of course, that you have not already dealt with the matter yourself."

Adkins tossed his napkin on the table and stood. "I've had enough."

"Sit down," Doris commanded as she drew her gun and tracked it on Adkins with practiced ease.

"There's no need for that. He won't betray us," Hathaway spluttered.

"He won't, but you will." Doris swiveled. Placing the barrel of the silenced pistol in the middle of Hathaway's forehead, she squeezed the trigger. He jerked back in his chair under the impact of the close range shot. Blood and brain matter spattered the table directly behind his fallen chair.

"Yeow! What are you doing?" he screamed, overcome by the sudden death of his longtime colleague.

Holstering her gun, Doris picked up the hot brass from the tabletop. "Sit down, doctor. You and I need to talk."

"Do you know who you just killed? He's the top man in his field." Adkins reached for a handkerchief to wipe his face.

"Not any more. Now sit down, or I'll--"

Adkins raised his hands in a quick show of surrender. He kept his eyes on Doris as he pulled up his chair and plopped into it. "Okay! Sitting. Can I assume that the other guy they sent is dead?"

"Yes. Now let's get down to the matter at hand."

"Wait just a minute. I don't think you understand what you're up against. There's a member of the committee here, in the building." Adkins mopped at his face again.

"Not any more," she smirked.

"You didn't..." Adkins was appalled.

She looked him in the eye. "That's for me to know and you to find out. I know about your refusal to carry out the Founders' directive. How far does that go?"

"Geez. I thought you were going to kill both of us." Adkins slumped in his chair.

"Day's not over yet. I still can."

"I'm with you. Just tell me what you want me to do." He laid his shaky hands on the tablecloth.

"Tell me about deprogramming him."

"What? Now? Are you kidding me?"

"Tell me." She indicated Hathaway with a nod as she toyed with a fork.

Adkins wiped his chin. "Sure. It's a lighting and chemical backstep regimen. Flashing lights and drugs."

"How portable is it?"

"Very. Two large briefcases." Adkins swallowed as his composure returned.

"Where is it?" Doris put down the fork.

"Here. They used to keep it at Secured Site 1. I was afraid they'd destroy it, so I pulled some strings and had it moved out here. Told them that I wanted to update the software. They never asked for it, so I just kind of never sent it back."

"Listen to me very carefully. I will say this only once. Gather up what you need and be ready to leave here when the helicopter arrives."

"Helicopter?" Adkins asked, straightening.

"Don't concern yourself with that. Pack whatever you need for deprogramming and be ready to go when I come for you."

Adkins gave her an earnest look. "You can't run from these people. They spent the best years of their lives doing this kind of thing. The protective teams--"

Doris stood up and began shrugging into her coat. "Is there anyone else in the building that I should know about?"

"We don't keep patients here overnight except for members of the committee. Speaking of which--"

"I told you not to worry about her." Doris tied the belt on her coat.

"Which means that she's gone."

"Out of here, if she knows what's good for her," she replied as she stepped away from her chair.

"She's in on it, isn't she?" He perked up.

"She is."

"What about him?" Adkins pointed at Hathaway's body.

"Leave him. Where is Fisk now?"

"Before the caterer dropped off our dinner, I was talking to him in the library."

Tuesday
June 3, 2014
Presidential Quarters
The White House
Washington, D.C.
9:29 P.M. EDT

"Josephine Harper to see you," the agent informed the President.

"Send her up," Madeline replied as she sat down.

Alone in the sitting room that she liked so much, she allowed herself to relax. The formal dinner had been taxing. Her feet and lower back hurt just enough to put her on edge. Closing her eyes, she savored the silence.

The agent cleared her throat as she entered the room ahead of Josephine. "Ma'am? I'll be in the next room if you need anything,"

"Certainly." Madeline composed herself as Josephine walked in. Madeline smiled. "Well now, what have you got for me?"

Josephine had decided that the direct approach would be best. She stopped next to a chair. "I couldn't find out who his doctor is. I did try. You know how some people are. Maybe he just wants his privacy. I don't think I would tell anyone about my medical problems."

"I see. It was worth a try. I've spent so much of my life being public that I sometimes forget what it's like to be private. To have secrets." *If you only knew.*

"Everyone has secrets. Is there anything else I can do?" *If you only knew.*

"We may have a press event on our hands tomorrow. Has anyone talked to you?"

Josephine nodded. "Angel. The scheduling is done."

"Really? Oh, I didn't mean that the way it sounded. It's just that I'm not used to having things go that smoothly. You really are a miracle worker." *So, now I know. You're good at what you do. You're just not that important to Fisk. His loss, my gain.*

"Do I need to be in early?" Josephine asked out of habit.

"You'll have to ask Larry about that," Madeline replied, waving off the question.

"I'll just come in early." She checked her watch as Madeline stood.

"He's still here someplace. Just ask one of the Service people on your way out. They can tell you."

"I'll do that." Josephine accepted the dismissal and left the room. Stopping in the hallway, she turned to find the female agent sitting in a chair nearby. "The President said that Larry was still here. I need to see him."

Seated, but alert, the woman gave Josephine a quick once-over before responding. "Everybody's in on this, aren't they?" she quipped.

"Excuse me?"

The woman nodded sagely as she got to her feet. "It's okay. I know all about it. He's down there. Second door on the right." When Josephine hesitated, she became impatient. "It's okay, really. Secretary Brown is sleeping like a baby. The way I hear it, they shot enough tranquilizers in him to put down an elephant."

"Wow. He must have been in a real state." Josephine commented.

"He's been here since real early yesterday. I don't know why they're keeping it under wraps. Having him around creeps me out. They say he kept going on and on about his dead wife before they put him down."

"Goodness." Josephine's mind raced with the implications.

"Tell me about it. I am so glad I'm not married." The bored agent rolled her eyes.

"I'll stop by Larry's office and just leave him a message. I don't really want to get involved with this. I'm not good with emotionally disturbed people."

Tuesday
June 3, 2014
Secured Site 6
Adkins-Hathaway Clinic
Alexandria, Virginia
9:30 P.M. EDT

Fisk sat alone in the library. Dressed in trendy but casual sweats, he reclined on a leather couch, watching television. A WNN news bulletin had his full attention.

"The wreckage of the Treasury Secretary's sailboat was picked up by Coast Guard searchers earlier today. Authorities will not speculate on the cause of the disaster, but sources close to the investigation have confirmed that the two-masted sloop was being restored from a state of significant disrepair."

The commentator was replaced by a stock photo of the aging sloop and a voiceover from a man with a New England accent.

"The *Almighty Dollar* was built a long time ago. Andy and his wife bought her as a fixer-upper, if you know what I mean. Done most of the work on their own. The old girl was looking right nice the last time I saw her."

The image faded, bringing the newscaster back into view. "Rumors continue to circulate about a distress call issued from the vessel just minutes before the tragedy. Several amateur radio operators have told federal investigators that they overheard Secretary Brown and another man talking to Coast Guard dispatchers. WNN has been unable to confirm this rumor, and we stress that it is just a rumor. The death of any famous person is often clouded in controversy that can sometimes lead to unwanted misunderstandings."

Fisk nodded in silent agreement as the library door opened. He smiled at Doris as she slipped in. "TV off," he commanded as he sat up. Across the room, the big set went dark.

Doris closed the door.

"Talk to me." Fisk stood and went to the wet bar.

"You've spoken with Enola?" Doris moved to stand across the bar from Fisk as he poured a small glass of orange juice.

"Yes. The docs put me off until tomorrow, too. I don't suppose that was your doing?" he joked as he pushed the glass across the bar.

"Hers. Do I look that bad?" Doris cast a dubious eye on it.

"Worse," Fisk nodded grimly, pouring another glass of juice.

"Fair enough." She took the beverage in her right hand. She raised it in a toast and downed it with one gulp.

"So. What happens next?" Fisk asked, leaning on the bar.

"The feds served a warrant on Cosmo. It's a sure thing they're looking to serve a warrant on you. They probably want to talk to you about Brown."

"We've made a lot of mistakes lately."

"We're overextended," Doris replied, flashing him a weak smile.

"True, but they haven't compromised us. If they knew what we were up to, you can bet--"

"I know." Doris slapped the glass down on the bar, and then looked directly at him. "Look, things are going to get really strange in the next few hours. Griff is relocating. The helicopter's been called and, if I know him, the jet will be on standby somewhere."

"Lawyers. I hope nobody forgot to call the lawyers." Fisk teased as he took a sip of juice.

"Knock it off. I know what you're doing."

He arched an eyebrow over the rim of his glass. "Is it working?"

"Yes. I keep forgetting that you never give up." She finally laughed.

"Never."

Doris said nothing for a long moment, looking at him. *If I leave the clinic, I might lose track of you. With the dragnet closing in, I suppose we're both here for the duration.*

Fisk watched her examine him. *You're upset. I don't know what this does to your plans, but it really screws up mine.*

"Again I ask, what's next?" He laid both hands on the bar.

"Get dressed. When the helicopter comes, we go."

Fisk rounded the bar slowly. "Are the Overwatch teams with us?"

Doris leaned on the bar to rest her bad shoulder. "Primary is with us. I don't know about secondary. Colby's checking on that now."

"Colby?" Fisk's eyebrows went up.

"Primary team leader."

"Any other loose ends?"

"Not any more."

Fisk gestured toward the door. "Shall we?"

Doris allowed him to lead the way into the hall.

As they walked, Fisk continued, "That warrant doesn't scare me. Whatever they think they know can be nitpicked by our attorneys 'til the cows come home. Have we got a sim for this?"

"Several," Doris replied without enthusiasm.

"I want to see them." He made a fist and struck his open palm with it. "We can beat this thing. All we have to do is prevent the plan from being exposed. How hard is that?" He shrugged.

"I think we've already been over this," Doris grumbled as she kept pace.

Fisk stopped at the intersecting corridor. "It's not in me to give up. We've come too far. Done too much. My career as a political strategist is over."

In the low light of the passageway, Doris couldn't see his face directly, but she knew he was giving her one of his pragmatic looks.

"This thing with Brown falls too close to the President. Even if they can't pin anything on me, there will always be some small doubt. All I need to do at this point is stay out of prison. After that, all we have to do is outlive the Founders. You've got my back, right?"

"Always."

Tuesday
June 3, 2014
Secured Site 6
Adkins-Hathaway Clinic
Alexandria, Virginia
9:41 P.M. EDT

Griff's craggy face loomed large on the tiny monitor inside the clinic's security station. "They got the helicopter. FAA inspectors are all over the jet, and the security detail on the yacht is on the line right now. Seems that Homeland filed inspection warrants on all our transport assets." His image bounced as the car he was riding in hit a bump.

"We can still drive him out. Christopher just arrived to drop off some stuff for Fisk. I can catch him before he leaves. Where are you?" Colby stood next to a chair, working the safety tabs on his bullet-resistant vest. Like the rest of his team, he had changed into black BDUs. The costume was intended to confuse law enforcement, as well as to impart a psychological edge to the members of the protective team.

"Have you heard from secondary? We're ten minutes out from Secured Site 9."

"No. It's not time to worry, yet. I know Tucker. He's probably having a serious heart-to-heart with his troops." Colby shook his head as he picked up a compact submachine gun.

"Yeah, he'd better make up his mind. I've got the call in to activate the reserve, but there's just no telling how long it'll take for them to get into play."

"They've got the high ground by now. There are five tall buildings around us. Each one should have a shooter by now. The limo's armored. As long as they don't have antitank, we'll be fine." Colby checked the magazine in his weapon.

Griff scowled. "If the Founders gave the order, there's no telling.

You have to assume that they anticipated everything. It's what they do."

"I've got to go." Colby racked the slide on his weapon.

"Colby? Good luck, man."

Tuesday
June 3, 2014
Secured Site 6
Adkins-Hathaway Clinic
Alexandria, Virginia
9:44 P.M. EDT

Christopher knocked on the door.

"Come!" Fisk shouted from inside.

The driver stuck his head in to the room. "You decent?"

"That depends on who you ask." The consultant stood in front of a mirror, looping his tie into a Windsor knot.

"They told me to bring you this briefcase before I went home. Where do you want it?"

"Over there. So, how are you holding up?" Fisk gestured to a chair next to the bed. Turning sideways, he examined his profile in the mirror.

Christopher placed the briefcase on the chair. "Thanks for asking. I'm not really sure you want to hear the answer."

"Try me."

Christopher shuffled uneasily. "Did your guys really kill the Treasury Secretary?"

"They did," Fisk nodded as he sat on the end of the bed.

The driver took a step back. "Can I ask why?"

Fisk lowered his head, folding both hands in his lap. "Before he was appointed to the job, Andy Brown was a different man."

"I hear that," Christopher muttered. *I'll never be the same again myself.*

"When he talked about banking reform and fiscal planning in front of Congress, we honestly thought he was just telling them what they wanted to hear. When he outlined his concerns over the national debt, we thought that was just his ambition talking. As it turns out, he was a better man than we thought. He saw his chance to step up, put his own greed aside, and do something about a very real problem. Unfortunately, we mislabeled him and kept him out of the loop." He spread his hands in defeat.

"That doesn't sound like a good enough reason to kill the man."

Fisk raised a finger. "Ah, but there's more. Much more."

"I'm not going anywhere." Christopher propped himself up against the doorframe.

"Andy was the right man, in the wrong place, at the wrong time."

"Says you."

"He would have compromised the plan. When he wouldn't play ball with Madeline, we had to neutralize him to make sure that she succeeds with the debt settlement."

"If this plan of yours is so great, why didn't you just bring him in?"

"I tried. I met with him face to face. It just didn't take."

"What did he object to?"

"He objected to *me*." Fisk pointed a finger at himself.

"That bothers you? Isn't it a little late for that?"

"It's a lot too late for that. Walk with me."

"Where are we going?" He stepped back as Fisk reached for the briefcase.

"Security station. I'll explain on the way."

"Look, you started all this. I can appreciate your guilt, but don't you think you're being overly dramatic?" Keeping pace with Fisk, he did a double-take as a man in black BDUs trotted by. "Who in the world was that?"

"Nobody." Fisk rounded a corner and continued walking.

"You're kidding." Christopher lost a step. *No, he's not. Shut up.*

"I set the whole thing in motion. I understand that. If there's any one thing gnawing at me right now, it's the fact that Andy Brown didn't have to die. He's not the only one, either." Fisk paused to open a pair of French doors.

"Would you stop feeling sorry for yourself? How long have you been doing this, anyway? Ten, fifteen years?" He followed Fisk into a long corridor.

"Fourteen." Fisk stopped abruptly.

"That's a long time to carry a guilty conscience. Guilt is something I know about. My last employer? For the longest time, I thought I was the one who got him killed. I kept telling myself, 'If I had only been there.'"

"Mm," Fisk intoned noncommittally, shifting his eyes.

"One of the first things they teach you in my line of work is that you're going to make mistakes. You're committed to this thing. You know it, and I know it. If you had to do it all over again, you would. Suck it up, man. You've put too much on the line to back out now."

Fisk barely hid a smirk. "I think you're the first person bold enough to tell me that."

"These people have been with you a lot longer than I have. They've never seen you fail. They're used to you always being the smart guy. They aren't going to know you're at the end of your rope unless you tell them."

Fisk accepted the chastising with lowered eyes. "You sound pretty sure of yourself."

"I've only ever been sure of one thing--doing for others before you do for yourself is harder than it looks. In your own way, you're a patriot. I haven't quite figured it all out yet, but I know you're not in this for yourself. Someday, I hope I can wrap my brain around it. Until then, I'm just going to have to settle for kicking you in the head."

"Consider me kicked." Fisk checked his tie with exaggerated humility.

Tuesday
June 3, 2014
Secured Site 6
Adkins-Hathaway Clinic
Alexandria, Virginia
9:59 P.M. EDT

"Police cars, here and here." Colby pointed to each of the small monitors as he spoke.

Perched on the edge of the workstation, Doris looked him in the eye. "Which means they have them at all four intersections. We just can't see the other two."

"Mm. These two have no place to hide. If they did, we wouldn't see them, either."

"Wonder what's holding up their lawyers?" Doris mused as she watched one of Colby's team walk past.

Colby snorted as he put down his cup. "Alphabet soup. If the warrant is real, and it didn't start from Homeland, there's got to be half a dozen agencies involved."

Doris looked up as a side monitors came to life.

"Overwatch is online," a stern female voice came through speakers in the ceiling as Griff's tired face blossomed onto the screen.

"We're plugged in. What's your situation?" Griff asked, nodding to someone off-camera.

Doris stepped back from the table edge so that the camera could find her face. "Surrounded. I spoke to the pilots for the jet and the helo. They've got FAA inspectors all over them. Seems that somebody phoned in a hot tip that there might be drugs on the jet and unlicensed guns in the 'copter."

"Yeah, I know. It gets better. We have an update from Cosmo. Their warrant came from Justice at the request of the Secret Service. It was specific about locating only. You know what that means."

"The real bombshell is on its way." Colby sat down in the room's only chair.

Fisk poked his head into the room. "Talking about me again, eh?"

"Where have you been?" Doris checked her watch.

"Getting a civics lesson."

Christopher waited silently outside the security station. Doris looked at him for a long moment.

Colby swiveled around to look up at Fisk. "They have us hemmed in. All four intersections. Police cruisers with two men each." He tapped a key that brought Griff back on line. "Gang's all here. Shoot."

"Heck of a night, eh? I have news. Our sources inside the D.C.P.D. found out that the Secret Service and the mayor's office are burning up the lines to a whole slew of agencies. These guys have a hold-and-question warrant for Fisk relating to, and I quote, 'the disappearance of Andrew Brown.' You know what that means?" Griff lowered the faxed page to stare into the camera.

"He's not dead. Or they have a witness," Colby replied. "They're being slow about serving their warrant. That's the only thing that matters to me. Let's get him out of here. We still have the car. I want Christopher to drive him out of here." He exchanged a meaningful glance with Doris.

"I've already seen the sim on that. The cops have him staked out. They can pull him over and detain him. They don't need a warrant for that. If you try to run him, they can add resisting arrest to their charges. No, this is the part where the lawyers earn their pay."

"You can't be serious," Doris protested.

"We both know better. Odds are on that those cops aren't in the loop. Messing with them will only make things worse. Look, I know how you feel. The whole situation bites. Consider this. They're probably trying to serve a bogus warrant. That tells us that they're either trying to get a shooter in real close, or else they're looking to smear him in the press. We've updated our sims to account for Metz. That guy is some piece of work."

He picked up a small headset radio and waggled it at the monitor. "And let's not forget about secondary tactical. If they're not talking, it means they're not on our side. We have to assume that they've got the perimeter fully covered."

"Yeah," Griff muttered, looking down.

"Where's the reserve?" Doris asked, considering their options.

"They won't be in play for another six hours. You have to remember, these guys are coming in from all over the Eastern seaboard. We beep them, and they come running as fast as they can without blowing their covers. Most of those guys had to finish out the regular work day before they could book a flight."

Christopher added his own thoughts with an embarrassed smile. "Pardon me. I couldn't help but listen in. They want you to move him. You've got guys running around in the lobby dressed like SWAT cops. When I put it all together, you've got some serious trouble on your hands." He stepped forward to point at the small monitors. "I've seen this before. You need to stop thinking like your big secret is going to get you killed. All we have to do is give them what they want. See? Those cars in the parking lot probably belong to the docs, right?" He tapped on two of the monitors.

Enlightened, Doris filled in the blanks. "Use those and the limo. Shell game."

"It gets better. Places like this usually have a linen service--"

"Four vehicles negate four police cruisers. Even if the cops scan them, we can put two warm bodies in each. Once we scatter--" Colby snapped his fingers.

Griff checked an off-camera monitor. "You'll have to hurry. The linen truck gets there early sometimes, between 10:45 and 11. Stop talking to me and make it happen."

Tuesday
June 3, 2014
Union Station
Capitol Hill
Washington, D.C.
11:22 P.M. EDT

Josephine sat by herself, drinking fruit juice. Watching the people come and go around her wasn't helping her nerves. *What do I do?*

The small restaurant was styled to resemble a sidewalk cafe. Despite the late hour, Union Station was still a very busy place. Increases in agency funding, coupled with the creation of new government offices, meant that Capitol Hill was transformed into a computer-enhanced bureaucracy that never slept.

Sitting out in the open, Josephine felt exposed. *Calm down. Think for a minute.*

The shuttle ride from the White House to Union Station had been scary. Speculation about Brown's disappearance was still being widely talked about on the global airwaves. Newspapers toted by some of the riders still had the story on the front page. Conversations she overheard made it clear that the President was getting a lot of sympathy for the loss of such a valued Cabinet officer. *He's not dead. She has him under wraps. Why?*

The idea that President Hill might prefer that Secretary Brown was dead was chilling. Looking down at her purse, she thought about the phone. *What have I gotten myself into?* Time passed and the crowds thinned.

The waiter appeared out of nowhere, making her flinch. "Can I get you anything else? We're getting ready to close," he said as he began rounding up stray chairs.

"No, thanks." Josephine checked her watch and started. *11:30? Oh, no.*

"Whoever you're waiting for didn't show, eh?" he commented over his shoulder.

"I was just trying to gather my thoughts." Josephine finished her drink.

"Got a lot on your mind?" The young man stopped what he was doing to pay attention.

"Yes. I just don't know what to do." Josephine pushed her chair back and stood up.

"Try me. It can't be that bad." He smiled confidently.

"Oh, yes, it can. A few hours ago, I wouldn't have believed it. Now..." She averted her eyes as she slung her purse over one shoulder.

The young man wiped his hands on a small towel as he spoke. "I know that look. My name's Chuck. You have to remember where you are. This is Washington, D.C. You've got your politicians and your patriots. Then you have everyone else. The trick is, you can't always tell them apart. You and me, we're part of the 'everybody else.' We're the ones trying to figure it all out." He pointed in the direction of the Capitol Building. "Those are the politicians. Some of them are patriots, but most of them are simply politicians."

"I see. You figured this out all by yourself?"

"Not me. I'm still in school, trying to make up my mind which one I want to be. Actually, my friends and I were talking about this just the other night." The gleam in his eye told her that he was serious.

"The 'everyone else' doesn't appeal to you, eh?" Josephine wrinkled her nose. *Doesn't appeal to me, either, now that I think about it.*

"Nope," he replied, shaking his head emphatically. "Ninety percent of the people who come through here are part of 'everybody else.' They let stuff happen, and they don't think about what it really means. They don't ask enough questions. They take it as an article of faith that, if the politicians screw up, somebody else will be the patriot, and ride in and save the day. Nah. Being 'everybody else' stinks."

"I see. Thanks. I think it's time for me to go."

"Just figure out which one you want to be. The rest will take care of itself."

Tuesday
June 3, 2014
Secured Site 6
Adkins-Hathaway Clinic
Alexandria, Virginia
11:59 P.M. EDT

"Midnight," Doris read from the clock on the far wall. Christopher checked his watch. "I don't think the linen truck is coming."

Standing inside the lobby, Fisk watched his protectors.

Colby changed channels on his headset radio, and then shook his head. "Nothing at the loading dock. That's Tucker for you. He probably had it stopped before it got here so that we couldn't use it as cover."

Christopher turned. "The limo's armored. Suppose we just load up and take your goon squad along for the ride? I figured it out. You want to get him into Maryland so that they have to waste a few days on getting him transferred, or some other jurisdictional thing."

"Hole in one," Doris nodded.

"I've been thinking about that," Fisk said. "I don't think we should hide anymore. The opposition is just too determined. Therefore, I propose that we go over to the attack."

"It's Madeline. This whole thing is about pinning a murder on you which they may or may not be able to prove," Doris replied, flustered.

"It doesn't matter if they can prove it. I know Madeline better than I know most of you. She gets what she wants, by hook or by crook. No matter how you slice it, I, as the paid advisor to the President, am finished. I can leave D.C. in chains or in a box. At this point, I think she'll settle for either one."

Doris found herself momentarily speechless.

Fisk turned, looking each person in the eye. "I am not the issue here. The issue is whether or not we can keep our secret under wraps."

"What are you talking about?" Colby asked, incredulous at being left out.

Christopher nodded. "You guys have been too smart for your own good. I've said that before. You've all played your parts so well that nobody knows about your dirty little secret. Even if they did, who would believe that *the* Preston Fisk would be mixed up in anything like that? He's right. They can try him, but he'll probably walk. Your secret stays safe."

Doris and Colby looked at Christopher for a long moment.

"Give me a break. You guys need to get out more," the driver said, taking a step back.

"He's right, you know," Fisk said softly.

Doris shook her head. "That still doesn't solve the other half of our problem."

"The Founders won't let that trial happen," Colby said, shaking his own head.

"The Founders are human. I've still got this," Fisk said, gesturing at his mouth to indicate the comm implant. "What's to stop me from issuing a few 'executive orders' of my own?"

His passion made Doris think before she spoke. "There isn't anything stopping you, except the possibility that they have other backups--people loyal to them who are just waiting to finish what hasn't been done here."

"Hey!" Griff shouted, trying to make himself heard.

All heads turned to look at his image on a view screen on the far wall.

"I'm tapped into the clinic's net. Stop whining. We've got more immediate problems. There's an unmarked police car pulling up in front of the clinic. Colby, get back to the security station and coordinate your team. Tell them to stay out of sight. Where's Dr. Adkins?"

"Packing," Doris stated flatly.

"On my way." Colby jogged off.

"We'd better go." Doris took Fisk by the arm.

Fisk hesitated. "No. Christopher's right. We've been too clever for our own good." Checking his tie, he turned to face Griff's image. "You'd better turn that off, but stay on the line so that we can speak later."

Griff nodded and his image winked out, replaced by a video fish tank.

Christopher bobbed his head and went for the front door. "Let me do this. I'll catch them before they get inside. If I don't come back soon, you'll know they held me for questioning."

Doris turned on Fisk as Christopher went out. "I am not going to let them arrest you."

"Hey, come on. This is me you're talking to."

She forced herself to stare into his dominating gaze. "I know. I also know that we're up against two very powerful adversaries. I know what you're thinking. Sacrifice your political identity and avoid compromising the plan. Then play hide and seek with the Founders until they all die from old age."

"Bad plan?" Fisk arched an eyebrow, aware that he was being glib.

"No." Doris broke eye contact.

"He's right," Griff's image said as it came back up. "I don't mean to butt in. Doris, he is right. I've lost contact with nearly ten percent of the network in the last few minutes. The Founders may already know that Fisk isn't dead. It's going to take me a while to sort it all out, but I have to assume that those units are not on our side anymore. If they went dark without being told by me, it means we're going to lose the rest of the organization soon."

"I know. When Christopher gets back with the warrant, we'll go."

Fisk reached out, taking hold of her arm. "You're not hearing me. I'm not going to run. Even if it is a trap, they can't hold me if they can't prove--"

Doris shrank under his touch as his grip hurt her wounded shoulder. "They don't want to hold you. It's just their way of getting close to you."

Griff threw up his hands. "The Founders can wait. I've got our best lawyers on the line right now. They assure me that this kind of warrant involves maximum police protection. Once they take him into custody, he'll be snug as a bug in a rug. If they want him, they'll still have to go through you and the rest of Overwatch to get him."

"Please. You're hurting me." Doris stepped away from Fisk.

"Sorry." He raised his hands when he realized where they had been.

"We're compiling a sim now. The early numbers look good. Even if they do get a conviction, we can get you out in two years or less." Griff watched new data come up.

Composing herself, Doris continued. "Okay, okay. One crisis at a time. We dodge the feds. I know things about the Founders that you don't. These people have been hiding from entire governments for most of their adult lives. If we don't disappear now--right now--they'll find us. We can't afford play out this charade with the lawyers."

"Nobody wants a clean getaway more than I do. If I don't at least pretend to cooperate with whatever Madeline has cooked up, though, we stand no chance of getting away from anyone. Who knows? The Founders might lose track of me in the shuffle. As long as their investigation stops with me, the Phase One organization can vanish. If I give them an excuse to dig, everything we worked for may be undone."

"He's right, Doris. I don't like this any more than you do. Even if, for some strange reason, Brown is still alive and kicking, our attorneys can handle it. Odds are on that he's probably not happy about the President's behind-the-scenes deal with the World Bank. That's good ammo for legal team."

"Which leaves you free to work you miracles," Fisk told Doris.

"Hey." Griff stopped to listen to somebody off camera. "As interesting as this is, I've got a lot on my plate. I need to make some calls and find out where our people stand. I should know inside of two hours if we have enough support to pull this off."

Fisk checked his watch. "Christopher hasn't come back. Did they hold him?"

"He's out in the patient parking lot, chatting up a storm."

Doris gave an appreciative nod. "Stalling."

Fisk snapped his fingers. "Griff, get me a conference line with our attorneys. I want to meet this thing head on. And call the media."

Griff stepped out of camera range for several seconds before flopping back down in his chair. "You are not going to believe this," he grumbled, tapping at his keyboard.

"What?" Doris took a step towards the monitor.

"Josephine Harper. She's on the line right now. Something about Brown being alive and well at the White House."

Wednesday
June 4, 2014
Joint Operations Center
Old Executive Office Building
Washington, D.C.
12:25 A.M. EDT

Metz cleared his throat. "Say that again?" He gripped the handrail that surrounded the central dais in the large room. On all sides, team leaders and specialists watched and waited. SWAT Commander Lucas' voice came through clearly on the speakerphone.

"I'm looking at him right now. The officer of the court is signaling that Fisk will comply with the warrant. She's talking to some big guy in a suit who came out of the clinic. If they keep at it much longer, he might even get her phone number." A small titter made its way around the operations area.

"What's the status on your video?" Carl asked, knowing that Lucas had arranged for a "technical difficulty" so that his snipers could take their shot anonymously.

"All I know is that they are working on it. It's not going to matter much in the next few minutes." Lucas bluffed with a hint of impatience.

Carl looked up at the array of holographic monitors that remained blank. Shaking his head in an obvious show of frustration, he said, "It's not on our end. Don't you people have a remote unit, or something? We'd really like to see this as it goes down."

"On our budget? We're lucky to have bullets." Lucas laughed as if he meant it.

More snickering made the rounds, even causing Carl to smile. He stepped close to the rail and leaned down to whisper at one of his aides. "Homeland?"

The man pointed to a glassed-in booth up on the mezzanine.

"Go make his day. Ask him to do us a favor and get a video remote

575

out to the scene. By the time he gets done screwing around with that, the whole thing'll be over."

The man grinned and went to do it.

Carl straightened and raised his voice to be heard over the pickup. "Lucas. We're going to see if we can't get you some video backup." The prearranged phrase told the SWAT Commander that he had a free hand.

Wednesday
June 4, 2014
Secured Site 6
Adkins-Hathaway Clinic
Alexandria, Virginia
12:28 A.M. EDT

Doris stood in the clinic's drug dispensary. Behind her, the secured door stood open with a smoldering hole in the locking mechanism.

Dr. Adkins stood next to a stainless steel counter, putting on a pair of surgical gloves. "I didn't think to get the key from the pharmacist before he left."

"It's okay. I always try to carry a micro-therm. Old fashioned, but effective." Doris shrugged out of her coat.

Adkins prepped a syringe. "How's the shoulder? Describe it. I need to know if you're pulling stitches."

Doris moved her shoulder experimentally as she sat on a nearby stool. "Hurts to move. I can feel the stitches tug if I shift it too far. It's not bleeding. Feels like it's getting hot and swelling."

Adkins stepped forward with the syringe and a sterilizing swab. "Hazards of a local anesthetic. They wear off too fast for somebody in your line of work."

"Just do it through the fabric," she said as she braced herself.

"Open up," Adkins responded, gesturing impatiently. "You're not going to show me anything I haven't seen before. I want to have a look under the bandage after I inject you."

"Not necessary," Doris told him coldly.

"I don't tell you how to break people. Don't tell me how to fix them." He reached out to undo the top button of her blouse. Chagrined, Doris pushed his had away, finished undoing the buttons, and slid the blouse over her shoulder.

"Here we go." Adkins swabbed an area of exposed skin before injecting the solution. "So, you seem a little off your game." He

577

looked over the rims of his glasses at her as the medication flowed. Tossing the swab into the recycler without looking, he kept both eyes on his work.

"How would you know?"

"Are you kidding?" Adkins smirked as he withdrew the needle. "After all the work we put into you? You're like the daughter I never had. An angry daughter, but mine nonetheless. I know your profile. The real you. You're at your best when you've got a mission." He laid the edge of the bandage back in place. Stepping back, he peeled off his gloves. "That looks good. I should change this dressing in the next couple of hours, though."

Doris said nothing as she refastened her top and reached for her coat.

"This is really getting to you, isn't it?" He tossed the gloves into the recycler.

Stepping over to a small table, Doris picked up her shoulder holster. Laying the coat down, she removed her gun and checked it. The long clip came out of the pistol with a tiny mechanical noise.

"Are you packed?"

"It's in my office, ready to go." Adkins leaned against the counter.

Doris hesitated before putting the clip back into the gun.

"You really think that will solve your problems? You can't kill everybody who threatens him." Adkins stood and took off his suit coat, tossing it to a nearby chair.

"Court of last resort. I wouldn't expect you to understand." Doris sheathed the gun and put in the holster.

Adkins waited for Doris to turn and face him. "Why? Because I'm a doctor? No. Dedication is something that I understand all too well." He softened his tone as he adjusted his glasses. "You'd do anything to protect him. You feel like you're about to fail, and it's driving you nuts."

"It wasn't supposed to turn out like this," she said, pulling the coat closed around her.

"He's my patient, too. He's also my friend. If there's anyone in this building who knows how you feel, it's me." He sighed, stuffing both hands into his pockets.

Doris looked hard at Adkins for a long moment. "I'm sorry if I rubbed you the wrong way. After the way I dealt with Hathaway, you must think I'm a real piece of work."

"I saw the frustration in your eyes when you pulled the trigger. Donnie was a lot of things, but he was also my friend and my business partner. I know why you did it. I don't like it, but I understand it. You're dedicated to what you do. You don't like the way things are turning out, and it's affecting your judgment."

"Mm." Doris felt her stomach lurch as the doctor's words hit home.

"When a doctor loses a patient, it feels like we, personally, failed. We blame ourselves. Intellectually, we know that we did everything we could, but there's always this nagging little doubt that lingers. It doesn't go away, either." He looked at Doris sympathetically.

"How do you live with it?"

"Try harder with the next patient. Accept."

"Accept. That sounds a lot like giving up."

"Acceptance means knowing in your heart and in your mind that you explored every option and used every tool at your disposal. Let's go see what's happening. Nobody's giving up. Not him and not you. Give those drugs a minute to kick in. Once the irritation settles down, you may be able to think more clearly."

Doris followed quietly as he closed the door.

Wednesday
June 4, 2014
Secured Site 6
Adkins-Hathaway Clinic
Alexandria, Virginia
12:40 A.M. EDT

Jasmine's image was displayed on a split screen, alongside Griff's. "Media's on the way. Every lawyer that we write a check to is awake and speed-dialing their paralegals. And I took the liberty of calling our friends in the catering business. Coffee and deli plates are on their way. I have just one question. This isn't in the script, if you know what I mean. What am I supposed to do now?"

"Speaking of lawyers, where is Tothberg? Why isn't he on the line yet?" The clinic's conference room was just large enough for Fisk to feel alone.

"That's my fault," Griff said. "He and his firm had a contingency plan for your arrest. When I called him, I think he set it in motion. I didn't tell him not to, so...I'm sure he'll get back to us when his paper tiger is on its way."

"That's not a bad thing. Should I talk to Josephine? Is she still on the line?"

Griff checked his monitors. "No. She called from home. She's pretty broken up just now. She thinks she let us down. Let's leave her alone."

"Speaking of being left alone--" Jasmine waved a hand at the camera.

Fisk smiled at her. "Right. It's only a matter of time before somebody decides to subpoena my records. Go down to the office yourself and have a look around. If you don't think it should be there when the feds show up, get rid of it. Then run the bases. Make sure everyone who knows about the plan has their story down pat. Leave the rest be. They can't tell what they don't know."

"This is going to ruin a lot of careers, you know that?" Jasmine shook her head. "Yours and mine, included. You can expect a lot of them to be angry when they show up for work in the morning."

The Fisk Group Consultancy was a legitimate business, employing many people. His loss of credibility in the face of a high-profile investigation would professionally taint the people who worked for him. Innocence or guilt wouldn't matter. In the field of high-stakes politician "handling," he and those around him would be shunned.

Fisk nodded. "Tell me something I don't know. Are you sure there isn't any other way?"

Her large brown eyes widened in despair.

Fisk chose his words carefully. "This is the easy part. If, as Josephine says, Andy is alive and well, it's going to be his word against mine about what happened out there. I already know what Tothberg is going to say. He's going to tell me to sit back, shut up, and let his defense team nitpick the prosecution's case until it falls apart."

"What's the hard part?" Jasmine asked, unwilling to accept Fisk's good-natured kidding.

"The Founders. They are so hidebound about their secrecy that they won't stop until they've got me cold on a slab in some quiet little mortuary."

Griff took a piece of paper from somebody off-camera. "Yeah. I'm working on that. I knew it. Jaz, can you handle the media? We're losing more of our network. I can't tell you if they're being liquidated or just not picking up when we call."

"Sure. Count me in." She sat forward.

"What's the probability that the Founders are liquidating our assets?" Fisk asked.

Griff held up the crumpled page. "I don't know yet. It's too early to tell. The plan allows for the loss of all Phase One assets. What? Great. Just great. They have Christopher in custody. Two cops and a suit are headed for the front door. You're going to have company."

"I suppose that's my cue." Fisk got to his feet and checked his tie.

Griff stared back at Doris.

She stood behind the seated Colby, who was busy directing his team. Deft fingers pecked at two different keyboards as he moved his people into protective positions. He sighed and sat back. "That's it. Fisk, the cops, and their lawyers are in the conference room. Legal is tied in. They should be talking up a storm. Want to see it?"

Griff nodded, wiping his face in a gesture of fatigue. "We're tied in here."

"I don't need to see this. Do we have any more options?" Doris laid both hands on the back of Colby's chair.

"No. Are you okay?" Griff looked closer at Doris.

Colby checked a peripheral monitor. "I have two men outside the conference room door."

"I'm okay. Just having a hard time with this." Doris brushed stray hair out of her eyes. "Things are falling apart around here. People are jumping at shadows. Tucker's still not acknowledging our comms, so we have to assume he's going to follow orders."

"I've been thinking about that." Colby rested both hands in his lap. "Can we feed the police an anonymous tip that would get them to search the buildings around us? Tucker's a cautious guy. If it even looks like the cops are sniffing around his positions, he'll bug out."

Griff smiled at him. "I appreciate your dedication. Fisk has the final say on these matters, and he's made up his mind to thread the eye of the needle."

Doris nodded silently at the reference to a time-honored spymaster's gambit. *Evade one pursuer by deliberately allowing yourself to be detained by another.*

"Yeah. How often does that work?" Colby asked.

"It's what they used to call a 'dead man's play.' Take a walk, will you? Give me a few minutes alone with Doris." Griff's expression was compassionate, despite his fatigue.

"Right. I'll check the perimeter. Come on, Doris. Have a seat." Colby swiveled the chair in her direction. "Watch that board. These are your monitor keys. There's the interface jack, if you want it. Call me on this if anything comes up. I'm gone." He pressed a small radio into the palm of her hand and left the room.

"How would I know?" Lucas asked Metz in exasperation.

"All I'm saying is that they've been in there too long." Carl's temper was slipping badly due to a profound lack of sleep.

Lucas stepped in close to Metz and started yelling. "Why don't you just shut up? You didn't have to come down here. We have it under control." In the shadow of his command van, his contempt for the other man was partially hidden.

"I had to come. Somebody called the press. We're about to have uncontrolled video on the scene. On top of that, those jerks from Homeland are getting pushy. The longer this takes, the more questions they have that I can't answer."

"Calm down. We do this all the time. We're gathering up the media and keeping them over there. They can't even see the clinic from where they are." Lucas pointed, his finger moving clockwise around the parking lot, stopping at a group of news vehicles. Looking down at his black uniform, he eyed the shine of his boots. "We have all the intersections tagged. I brought in two teams for this op--one to act like the real deal, the other one to take the shot. If that doesn't thrill you, I've got a little something in here that will drive you wild." He reached out to touch the van's dark metal.

Carl ran tense fingers through his hair as he surveyed the lot. Sodium vapor lighting cast a surreal glow over the proceedings. Uniformed officers were visible near the media pool. Scanning the nearby structures, he glanced at the command van.

"Let's go inside. I don't want to show up on the early morning news." He rapped his knuckles lightly on the cold skin of the vehicle.

"You're joking, right?" Lucas spat out his contempt for the assembled reporters.

"No." Metz fidgeted. *An uncontrolled photo linking me to this is the last thing I need.*

"Well, I guess we really do have a surprise for you." Opening a flap on his vest, Lucas pulled out a sheaf of papers. Shuffling through them, he plucked out a single page with a flourish, and handed it to Metz.

"I don't have time for this."

"Read it," Lucas urged, mischief in his voice.

Metz scanned the document. "This is brilliant. You can do this?"

"You're not the only one who can pull a rabbit out of his hat. Nobody will question another terrorist attack. Especially one that claims the life of such a notable public figure."

Wednesday
June 4, 2014
Secured Site 6
Adkins-Hathaway Clinic
Alexandria, Virginia
1:02 A.M. EDT

"Talk to me," Griff said quietly after a long moment. Around him, the members of his control team sat quietly. With most of their network disbanded or in hiding, they had very little to do. Above them, the Greek restaurant had been closed for several hours. Peripherally, he took note of the status monitors hanging over each workstation, confirming that the people involved in the conspiracy were receiving their final orders or told to disappear. In just a few more hours, Phase One project would be completely dismantled. No trace would remain. "I gave you a free hand. I assume you've got some wild stunt cooked up to whisk him away. Give." To his practiced eye, Doris had mixed feelings about recent events.

Doris' image appeared on the monitor in front of him, looking small in the high-backed chair. She looked over her shoulder at the closed door. Realizing that Griff's earlier show of acceptance had been for Colby's benefit, she bit back the urge to snipe. For once, he had acted like her. Now she was on the verge of acting like him. The irony made her snicker.

"What's so funny?"

"Us. We planned for everything except this."

"Yeah. I don't think he expected to get this far. Remember the early sims?" He wiped at his chin.

Doris nodded at the recollection. "Nine programmers quit. They couldn't take the stress of all that variable tripping. I was about ready to shoot a few of them, myself." *That was a long time ago.*

"When the committee told us they'd be happy if he lasted four years, I was about ready give it up right there." Griff shook his head bitterly.

"When I think back to what we did in the first four years, I have a hard time connecting the dots. How did we get from there to here?"

Griff considered. "Commitment. Dedication. Maybe some luck."

"Loyalty. He believed, and so did we," Doris corrected softly.

"So, where does that leave us?"

"Do I still have a free hand?" she asked as Griff swiveled in his chair to look at a pair of displays.

"That depends on what you intend to do. By 7 a.m., the whole Phase One network will be shut down and gone. When the feds come for his office, they won't find anything they aren't supposed to."

"You didn't answer my question."

"Yes, you've still got a free hand. But there are a few things you should know." He reached for a piece of paper.

Doris stiffened. "You want to remind me that saving him is not your job. You have Phase Two to be worried about. You also want to remind me that losing him was, and still is, an acceptable outcome."

Griff crumpled the page. "That is not fair! Not from you. You've spent the last 14 years orbiting him like some kind of satellite. You're too possessive. That's been your problem all along. 'He' is not *real*. He's a construct -- a 'thing.' We don't think of him like that because we've been around him too long. The Fisk persona was built on top of Jason's courage, conviction, and commitment to our country's future. The Founders brought the project to him after his wife died. Don't you understand what that really means?"

When Doris didn't respond, he continued. "Out of respect for him, and everything he did for them, they gave him a chance to be a hero and do something that might--*might*--save his country from decline and failure. He was never supposed to come back from this one. That was never the point."

The statement hit Doris hard. Griff sat silently, watching her wilt. After a painful, awkward pause, he gathered his wits spoke again. "Fisk was built to be an optimist. He will never give up because he literally doesn't know how. Jason told us both--"

"Stop." Doris raised her head.

Griff raised his voice to speak over her. "They've got you surrounded. Even if you could convince him to go out through the sewers, they'll catch him. You know it, and I know it."

"Are you telling me to kill him?"

"I gave you a free hand. I stayed out of your way, and I pulled a few strings to keep the Founders off your back. If he goes to prison, he might save the plan from being uncovered, but who'll save him?"

Doris closed her eyes in frustrated consideration.

"Come on, Doris. I'm not telling you to kill him. I'm asking you to end the mission. We've spent the last decade on the most outrageous op anybody's ever heard of. We did what Jason wanted. We sped things up--a lot. Not even the Founders can argue about the results he achieved."

"They've got a lousy sense of gratitude," she retorted.

Griff found it hard to look at her as she slumped, defeated, in her chair. "They're just doing what comes naturally to them. We used to be in that line of work, remember? There are politicians, patriots, and spies. Jason once said that if a politician and a patriot had a child, it'd grow up to be a spy."

Doris snorted at the faint memory of the joke.

Griff tried to make eye contact with Doris. "I've got to get off this line. I don't like this any more than you do. If he's still in there, I know he's waiting for you to do the right thing."

Wednesday
June 4, 2014
Secured Site 6
Adkins-Hathaway Clinic
Alexandria, Virginia
1:15 A.M. EDT

The lawyer's image projected his confidence. "I see no reason why we can't proceed. As long as Mr. Fisk is comfortable with everything we've discussed, we can conclude this conversation."

Fisk nodded at the large holograph projected on the far wall.

The representative from the Attorney General's office also nodded. "I agree. How long will it take to get somebody from your office down here?" Looking around the posh conference room, the young man checked his watch.

Tothberg checked his own watch. "No more than an hour. That should give you all the time you like to make preliminary statements to the press. I will personally walk out with my client. We will proceed into custody of the Virginia State Police."

"You do understand that they will remand Mr. Fisk to federal custody almost immediately?"

Fisk and his lawyer nodded without speaking. "After the press conference," Tothberg corrected mildly.

"I'm glad we could work this out." The ambitious young man rose, offering Fisk his hand. He tilted his head at the pair of police officers who had come in with him. "These men will be watching the front and rear exits. Just a formality. You understand?"

Fisk pumped the lawyer's offered hand sincerely. "Certainly. I'm surprised at the number of agencies involved in this."

"You and me both. From the faxes I saw, there are way too many cooks for this soup. I've never seen this much effort used for a warrant to question."

"Don't say anything to that," Tothberg admonished Fisk.

Fisk grinned at the fishing expedition. Behind him, the monitors on the wall went dark as his lawyer and other support staff went off-line. "Down the hall, and to the right, there's a secretary's station with coffee. Keep going past that, and you'll see the bathrooms," he told the uniformed officers as he followed them out of the room.

Expressing their thanks, the officers continued on their way.

The representative from the Attorney General's office walked with Fisk. "Can't blame a guy for trying. They called me in to serve this thing without any sort of an explanation. I'm not on the team that handles this kind of thing. Can you--"

"No, I can't, and you know better than to ask."

Wednesday
June 4, 2014
Secured Site 6
Adkins-Hathaway Clinic
Alexandria, Virginia
1:15 A.M. EDT

Standing alone under the covered driveway, Doris breathed in the night air. Knowing that there was a uniformed officer standing just inside the lobby was more painful than she would have admitted. The sodium lights in the parking lot added cartoonish length to the retreating lawyer's shadow. The police cruiser parked at the intersection stood out under the glare of the street lamps. Wiping a single tear from her face, she tried to ignore the red and blue strobes that danced off the buildings on the other side of the street.

Across the street and down the block. The parking lot's big enough. They probably have a command post and enough cops to keep the media in line. As she assessed the situation, Griff's last words came unbidden to her mind. As long as she had known him, he had never deliberately hurt her. Even now, the idea that he was just being spiteful didn't appeal to her. *He's not that judgmental,* she reminded herself.

Several cars passed the clinic. Somewhere overhead, a jet roared into the night sky. The sirens of emergency vehicles wailed in the distance as the city's millions went about their business.

Doris turned her back to the street as she struggled with a sudden attack of loneliness. *He's not that possessive, either.* Fighting back the rising tide of emotion, she coughed with her hand over her mouth.

Inside the clinic, the officer seemed preoccupied with the lobby's furniture and decorations. Watching him through the window, she leaned her good shoulder up against a column. The indifferent behavior of the man quickly angered her. *He stands there drinking coffee without a care in the world.* The irony made her snort. *Why should he care? He doesn't know.*

Pushing both hands deep into the pockets of her coat, she flinched at the reflexive gesture. In that instant, she knew that Griff had been right. "Jason Cutter had a reputation for knowing what to do under any circumstance. That's how I prefer to remember him." She surprised herself by speaking the thought aloud.

Her right hand closed around something at the bottom of the pocket. Grasping the item, she pulled it out. In the near darkness, her favorite pair of shooting glasses unfolded in the palm of her hand-- glasses that Jason had given her a lifetime ago.

```
Wednesday
June 4, 2014
Secured Site 6
Adkins-Hathaway Clinic
Alexandria, Virginia
1:25 A.M. EDT
```

Fisk met Doris in the lobby and smiled congenially. "There you are. We've got a few things to work out."

"Where's Dr. Adkins?" she asked, still gathering her composure.

"In his office. On the telephone, talking to one of our attorneys."

"I need to see him," she said flatly.

"You don't look so good. Do you need to sit down?" Fisk leaned in close.

"Later. What did you need?" She sniffed, aware that her eyes were red from crying.

Fisk nodded silently at the officer who paced the lobby. "Come with me. We need to go over some things."

As they walked, Doris watched Fisk intently out of the corner of her eye.

They walked into a presentation room. Fisk closed the door and gestured for her to take a chair. "I can see that this is hard on you. Sometimes I forget that you're there. I want to apologize for that. I haven't been myself lately, and it may have affected my judgment."

"You've got a lot on your mind. Anyone else would have snapped under the strain." She found it hard to evade his gaze. The trenchcoat pulled at her damaged shoulder as she sat, causing her to flush with the effort of staying composed.

Fisk looked down at his hands. "Yeah. Look, this is hard for me, too. I'm used to having a lot more help." He gestured at the comm implant in his mouth. "Before we get together with everyone, I need to ask you for a favor."

"Yes?"

"Colby and his men are going to slip out through the sewers when I leave. I've asked him to take Dr. Adkins with him when they go. That leaves just you and me. I need you to hang on to something for me." Opening his jacket, he took out his wallet. Doris watched in silence as he peeled back an inside layer of loose fabric, carefully tugging at the edge of a worn photo fragment. Raising the old-fashioned image to eye level, he examined its many cracks.

"I'm really not sure why I hang on to this. Each time I get a new wallet, I tuck it away. Sometimes, when nobody's around, I find myself looking at it. When they book me, it might get lost in the shuffle. I'm not particularly superstitious, but it really is the closest thing I have to a good luck charm. Would you hold on to it for me?"

Looking down at the black-and-white image, Doris felt her throat constrict. *This shouldn't be possible.*

"Those eyes. He reminds me of somebody. I just can't recall who." Seeing the distress in her eyes, Fisk was not sure how to continue.

"Where did you get this?" Doris whispered. Tentatively, she reached out to pick up the photo fragment. Looking at Fisk with a stunned expression, she recalled the moment all those years ago when Jason had cut up the original photo. *You saved a little piece of yourself, didn't you? Right in front of me, too.*

"I've been wondering the same thing for the last ten years. I have no idea where I got it. All I know is that having it is very important. Will you hold on to it for me?"

"Has anyone else seen this?" Doris forced the words to come out evenly as she turned the fragment over between numb fingers.

"Garrison, and now you. It seemed right at the time. If I did my job right, Bill isn't going to have much to do in the next 20 years. I suppose I showed it to him to ease his fears about what he's getting into. Who knows? Maybe that's me in a past life. Maybe I kept the thing to make my peace with something connected to that life."

"I think I understand. I'll hang on to it." Doris put down the old photo. *Griff was right. You never planned to get out of this alive, did you?*

"Great," Fisk replied. He seemed genuinely relieved. "I have to go." He stood, and then stopped. "I don't blame you for any of this.

I want you to know that. Even if they convict me, I'm out in five years or so. There's enough money in the offshore accounts to make sure I don't starve. Besides, you've got my back, right?" He smiled confidently as he opened the door.

Doris watched helplessly as Fisk left the room. Turning back to the table, she picked up the fragment. *You didn't ask me to come with you; didn't tell me to leave with the others.* "As long as I live, nobody will hurt you."

Thursday
June 4, 2014
Mobile Command Post
Alexandria, Virginia
1:49 A.M. EDT

"Here he comes. All units stand by," Lucas said as he set down his cup.

Standing in the rear of the van, Carl said nothing as he smoked in the open doorway. Because he was technically "not there," he had no pull--nor did he wish to. He had come down to the perimeter of the containment scene to ensure that his handpicked team of agents and administrators could keep a lid on the unexpected media presence.

The meddling of Fisk's legal team had cost precious time. The delay had allowed local and regional media to send reporters and field units to bear witness to the arrest. To make matters worse, Fisk's lawyers had cut a strange deal with the D.C. Attorney's office. Virginia law enforcement would pick him up and later turn him over to federal agents. *What kind of advantage could that possibly give him?*

Lucas adjusted his headset and flipped a switch. "Shooters, take your marks." Technicians seated to either side of him began redundant systems checks to ensure that their video surveillance net was still closed and secure. In the previous five years, several police departments had been savagely embarrassed on national television when rogue media personalities had "arranged" real-time broadcast of poorly executed arrests.

Metz flicked away his spent cigarette and closed the door. His only concern was the successful cover-up of Fisk's murder. As he sat, he reviewed his options.

"All teams report ready. Camera net is secure," a technician announced.

"Subject is crossing the parking lot with his attorney," a hushed voice said, emanating from the tiny speakers around the van's interior.

"Crossing initial point now. Range is 200 meters."

From where he sat, Metz watched the image of Fisk and his attorney on the overhead monitors. "Who are the uniforms?" he asked.

"Alexandria PD. Unimpeachable witnesses," Lucas mumbled.

"How does this go down?" Carl scanned the page in his hand.

Fisk and his lawyer casually strode across the empty parking lot. Metz fumed; Fisk was chatting while he walked. The black-and-white image showed him to be in good spirits.

"We've got two teams in the field," Lucas explained while tapping at his keyboard. "We've also got a dozen uniforms around the perimeter from every agency that had to stick its nose in our action. When the event happens, everyone will see exactly what they expect to see."

"Does 'everyone' include Fisk's security?" Carl asked as Lucas keyed his headset radio.

"Wait for it. Let everyone get a good look at him. Shooters, zero your mark. Team three, move to secondary mark."

On the monitor, Fisk and his lawyer reached the crosswalk. Across the street sat a police car, apparently locked and empty.

Lucas drained his coffee cup and swiveled back to Metz. "See that cruiser? There's a terrorist cell in D.C. that's been making explosives. The feds don't think we know about it. Some bureaucrat in Homeland has had them under surveillance for the last five months. A few hours ago, we ripped off their stockpile and wired it to the bottom of that car. We'll remote detonate it from here. As soon as the bomb goes off, my people will raid what's supposed to be a drug lab."

Carl gave the page back to Lucas and picked up the thread of the plan. "The drug dealers die in a shootout. Somebody in Homeland is chewed out for waiting too long to take down a known terrorist cell. Federal investigators match the chemical signature from their lab to the bomb in that car."

"You *try* to head up the investigation. Homeland will take it away from you. Let them take it, but raise a lot of Cain along the way," Lucas advised. Switching back to the primary net, he turned his chair to face the console.

"Teams One and Two, prepare to dismount cover. Officers, move in to collar. He's coming in quietly." Lucas was now speaking for the official record. Every word he said over the net was being recorded. In the aftermath of what would look like yet another terrorist attack, journalists around the world would have no reason to suspect the truth. Conspiracy theorists would be just as baffled when all agencies involved in this unfortunate event complied fully with information requests.

Metz watched the screens with intense interest. His heart raced as he considered the long-term ramifications.

"Target on mark," one the technicians said quietly.

The light had changed, so Fisk and his lawyer had just crossed the street. A trio of uniformed officers from different agencies went out to the curb to meet them. Standing on the sidewalk, the consultant turned his back to the police car. His lawyer pointed to where the media waited.

Changing channels, Commander Lucas flipped a switch on his console. "Team Three, commence raid," he commanded, reaching for a remote control.

Behind him, Carl watched unflinchingly as Lucas pushed the button.

Wednesday
June 4, 2014
Secured Site 6
Adkins-Hathaway Clinic
Alexandria, Virginia
1:52 A.M. EDT

Doris positioned herself inside the ventilator on the roof of the clinic. Getting the gun and scrambling into the ductwork had taken longer than she had thought it would. Her wounded shoulder had forced her to climb slowly and deliberately. From her vantage point, she had a clear view of both the parking lot and the intersection. She noted several police vehicles in various positions around the lot and a number of news vehicles clustered to one side.

Suddenly, a police car near the entrance exploded. As the shockwave from the blast hit the building, she dropped the partially assembled rifle and screamed.

On her knees within arm's reach of the ventilator grid, she cowered reflexively as pieces of debris ricocheted off the clinic's fancy exterior. Tiny pieces of plastic, metal, and glass found their way past the grating. Doris reached for the leather coat that lay folded close by. Pulling it over her face, she felt the sting from a hundred small wounds as the shrapnel ate into the flesh on the backs of her arms. Lightheaded from the sudden mental and physical trauma, she passed out.

Wednesday
June 4, 2014
Presidential Quarters
The White House
Washington, D.C.
7:29 P.M. EDT

Looking at herself in a full-length mirror, President Hill sighed. Alone in the bedroom, she was still fidgeting with her clothes when a female protective agent stuck her head in.

"We have to go, ma'am."

Glancing at her medium-grey blouse and skirt, Madeline was struck by how closely she resembled a funeral mourner. Black shoes rounded out the effect. Her red-rimmed eyes and the bags under her puffy eyelids had been carefully accented by makeup and a tearing agent commonly used by film actors. The effect was positively morbid. *Perfect.*

That her outward appearance didn't mirror her inner condition gave Madeline some comfort. She had been moved to involuntary tears when Metz called to give her the news of Fisk's demise. Wanting Fisk removed from her life was much different than actually having him gone. The reality of it had hit hard at first.

I should have somebody get a copy of his medical records, she decided as she turned to leave. *It would be terribly ironic if he really were dying of something.*

Entering the main sitting room, she was met by Larry. "How are things?" She glanced around the room.

"Our esteemed Communications Director is working his chops off, and Ms. Cutter is her usual stellar self. Metz called. Brown has left the building. He didn't say any more and I didn't ask."

"Do I assume that we have full containment?"

"Yes. We have nondisclosure agreements from everyone. Some of them needed the usual incentives, but it's nothing we can't hide or lose track of."

"Is the Coast Guard on board?" she asked as she continued to primp.

"They're being difficult. We didn't get to their investigators fast enough. They're still calling it a 'disappearance.' My guess is that somebody high up isn't buying in."

"It's been five days. He's not coming back. They know that. Find the holdout and deal with him."

"All the same, the operative word is 'disappearance.' When the time comes, we can spin it. Smother the Coast Guard brass in sympathy over their dedication. The usual."

"Ms. Cutter's surprise?" the President asked as the female agent prodded her along.

"Crain? He signed. Didn't even ask why. Metz told me that he can have the guy transferred to the Georgia facility once he's confirmed as the new director of the presidential detail."

"Angel said he could be screened out. Why are we making special arrangements for him?"

Hodgekiss rubbed his hands together. "He doesn't know anything. I want to keep it that way. Let somebody else fire him. Crain fancies himself a patriot. With that agreement, he thinks he's keeping the faith. He won't say anything that could be traced back to us. If we need him to wave the flag for us later, we can always--"

"I understand. Besides that, it gives Angel one less card to play."

"She is ambitious," Larry admitted, following as Madeline left the room.

"She works with a purpose. I can see it in her eyes. She has an agenda, just like everyone else in this town."

"Maybe she wants your job," Larry theorized with a tired smile.

"She's not that connected. She does want something from me, though. I just don't know what it is. She has Fisk's eyes."

"Leave her to me. The moment she starts acting like Fisk, I'll let you know."

Wednesday
June 4, 2014
Press Room
The White House
Washington, D.C.
7:55 A.M. EDT

Anne blinked at the seating assignment. *No more standing in the back like the rest of the rookies.* The plastic card that the press aide had given her showed that she had a tenth row seat. *Ten out of twenty. Not bad.*

At the front of the large room, Angel appeared at the podium. She was dressed in neutral colors. Her expression was composed. *I get it. This is my first reward for being your friend. No turning back now. I'm in, so I might as well get used to it.* Anne's trained eye caught the hints of makeup that masked fatigue lines. *Long night, eh? That means there's going to be a real story here.*

Around her, the representatives of the press were gossiping about Fisk's violent death. Struggling to her seat, Anne checked the internet connection to her recorder. *A month ago, it would have mattered to me. Now, I'm not so sure. Like so many other things in my life, I was probably wrong about him.*

Angel's commanding voice cut through the chatter. "Can I have your attention, please? I'd like to get started."

The reporters took their seats. The room became hushed as cameras and microphones were brought to bear. Anne made sure that her recorder was on before she sat back to listen.

"At approximately 1:55 this morning, Preston Fisk was killed by a car bomb planted by terrorists. The attack happened while he was leaving a private clinic in Alexandria, Virginia."

Angel paused for effect as the correspondents reacted to her disclosure. Smiling benignly at the cameras, she embraced the podium with both hands as she continued. "Before the President makes her statement, I want to clear up a few things. Federal authorities did have a warrant to question Mr. Fisk about the disappearance of Treasury Secretary Andrew Brown. Mr. Fisk was never a suspect in the case. They only wanted to pick his brain, in the hopes that some new angle might come up for them to investigate."

Anne's pulse quickened. The Press Secretary didn't shift her pose as she spoke. *Your story is like the man himself--too perfect.*

Angel paused again, looking down with a calculated degree of shame. "After some investigation, we have determined that our friends in the law enforcement community were a little too energetic in their serving of that warrant."

Anne focused her attention on Angel's body language. *You know an awful lot about something that happened just a few hours ago.*

"I want to be completely clear. Federal authorities never considered Mr. Fisk to be a suspect in the disappearance of Treasury Secretary Brown. Mr. Fisk's attorneys may have been misled by several factors which were out of their control." Angel waited another moment, watching the reporters for their reactions. *Like dogs to the hunt,* she snorted inwardly. *To me, he's another victim of an uncaring government. To you, he's just another headline. Just something to talk about until the next commercial break.*

"I wish I could say more. This is a tragedy. President Hill lost a good friend and advisor. In the last ten years, Preston Fisk has helped to shape American politics in so many ways. He will be missed."

As Angel stopped speaking, the audience fell silent in sympathy for her skillful show of grief. *It's going to take me a few months to pull it all together, but I think I've got enough proof of what really happened here to get my revenge.* The certainty of it made her heart leap in her chest. *Too bad Fisk will never know that he was instrumental in avenging my father.*

Wednesday
June 4, 2014
West Wing
The White House
Washington, D.C.
8:01 A.M. EDT

Josephine was beside herself with grief and frustration. Alone in her office, she stared dully at a computer monitor as the various news reports and commentary programs came and went. News of Fisk's spectacular death had been splashed across the airwaves since the event. The loss of her Treasury Secretary to a boating accident was generating a lot of sympathy for President Hill in the American media. The Coast Guard's hesitation to declare Brown and his wife formally lost at sea was playing well with most Western news organizations. Middle Eastern news groups were less kind.

As she watched the President's press briefing unfold, bile rose in the back of her throat. *This is a cover-up.* Fisk's private agenda and her feelings for him combined to create inner turmoil. *What am I supposed to do?* The wireless phone he had given her was snug in her purse, close at hand. Fear and anticipation merged in a nervous flutter as she waited for it to ring. The secret that had seemed so glamorous the day before now felt like a liability.

Political fears battled with patriotic conviction as she considered what to say if Fisk's people should call. *I had to sign the nondisclosure agreement or I would have been out of a job.* Wiping a stray tear, she focused on the source of her fears. Projected in three dimensions, President Hill stood at the podium in the Press Room.

"As you can see, we have brought all our resources to bear. The loss of these two great men affects us all. I will do my very best to carry Andrew Brown's vision of fiscal responsibility into the future. From now on, I will pursue his plan to mediate the nation's debts just as passionately as I pursue our decade-long quest against global terrorism." Pausing, Madeline surveyed the room through blurry eyes.

The image was too much for Josephine. Reaching for a handkerchief, she sniffed softly while dabbing at her tears. *I don't know what hurts more, the truth or the lies.*

"We live in dangerous times," President Hill said, remaining stoic for the cameras. "The stakes for our national survival are getting higher all the time. The challenges we face today would have been unthinkable ten years ago. As long as I knew him, my good friend Preston Fisk never backed down from those challenges. I will always be inspired by his courage."

Wednesday
June 4, 2014
Training Camp
Cascade Mountains
Washington State
4:59 A.M. PDT

"How bad is it?" the Colonel asked Hunziger as the two walked across the camp.

"They blew him up. WNN is calling it a terrorist attack." The big man padded along in the false dawn with surefooted ease.

The Colonel was careful to keep his voice low as they walked between tents and around piles of equipment. "Good night, but I'll bet Griff's fit to be tied."

"Nobody answers on the primary net. I think we have to assume that Phase One is totally shut down."

"Okay. Wake him up, but don't tell him anything. Just get him up and around. I need time to think." The Colonel stopped just short of the communications tent.

"Right." The big man turned away.

"How much time is left on the current training cycle?"

"Two weeks. You want to break camp?" Hunziger zipped his jacket.

"Yeah. I still have to call you-know-who, but that's what I'm thinking. It doesn't look like we're going to get the luxury of a smooth transition. The last thing I want is a helicopter load of trouble dropping in on us."

"I'm with you. Call the plane before you talk to them. The sooner we get Garrison out of here, the better. It'll take that long to get the rest up and fed. After what we put them through, most of them will be happy to leave early."

Wednesday
June 4, 2014
Training Camp
Cascade Mountains
Washington State
7:00 A.M. PDT

Kneeling on the floor of his tent, Garrison struggled with his duffle bag. He tried not to speculate on the significance of what he was hearing. The camp was alive with urgent activity. He worked the big snaps in place, rising to his feet as Hunziger pulled the tent flap aside.

"That was fast."

"Not much to pack."

"No sweat. You won't be taking it with you."

"Why did you tell me to pack it, then?" Garrison reached out to turn off the lamp.

"Just keeping you out of trouble until we had everything figured out. Relax. All the mystery is about to end."

"I see." He pushed his way out of the tent. Dressed in flannel and denim, he looked down at the red laces on his boots. "Something wrong?" He cast his eyes skyward. Rain clouds were moving in. The high peaks were already hidden.

"Couldn't tell you, even if there was." Hunziger pointed and started to walk.

"That bad? I may not be very good on the rifle range, but I do know when you're not shooting straight with me." Garrison rubbed his hands against the morning cold as he followed, leaving the duffle in his tent.

"You're done here. That's all you need to know."

Garrison took note of the direction they were walking and stayed quiet. Overhead, turbo-props roared as a twin-engine airplane screamed in low over the camp. He turned as if he were watching the airplane. *Looks like everyone is packing to leave.* Trucks were being loaded. Large tent frames stood like wooden skeletons as many of the camp's residents packed or said goodbye to each other.

"Something is wrong, isn't it? Tell me." He matched strides with Hunziger.

The big man pointed to the plane as it taxied back from the far end of a nearby field. "It's better if you get the whole thing in one dose. What I know, and I what I think I know, doesn't make up the big picture." The plane's engines drowned the rest of his statement out as it braked to stop and shut down.

Garrison stopped walking. "Don't I get to see the Colonel?"

Hunziger reached out a big hand to start him moving again. "He wanted to be here. There's too much to do and not enough time to do it in. After I put you on the plane, I'll be sure to give him your regards."

Garrison shrugged free. "Is this all there is?"

"No. That plane is going to take you to what comes next. You'll get all the answers we couldn't give you."

"Wait just a minute. You guys put me through the wringer, and you lied to me--"

"I know, and I'm not sorry. You know why you're here. All of these people are here for the same reason. Most of them know even less than you do about the plan."

"I'm fed up with being the last one to know anything. I understand the plan. I understand my place in it. Now, tell me, what's going on?"

Hunziger gritted his teeth. "I have orders. Very specific orders."

Garrison bristled to match the trainer's posture. "We're not in the Army. If I'm supposed to lead this thing--"

"You're not in charge of anything, yet. Get on the plane. They're going to take you someplace where you can get all the answers you want."

"Where?"

"I can't tell you. Somebody might hear."

The two men paused, suddenly realizing they were being watched by a dozen spectators.

"See?" the former soldier growled at Garrison.

Defeated, Garrison lowered his fists and straightened. He offered his right hand to Hunziger. "This isn't happening like I thought it would. I don't know what I expected, but it wasn't this."

Stepping back, Hunziger glared at the crowd before accepting Garrison's handshake. "Come on. For what it's worth," he confided as they walked, "I think you've got what it takes. You can do this." He gestured at the plane, which now sat with its stair-door down.

"The Colonel said that I'd never see him again. Does that go for you, too?"

Inside the aircraft, the pilot and co-pilot went over their checklist.

Hunziger unzipped his coat and reached behind to draw a small pistol. He held the weapon out to Garrison. "Here. Take it."

Garrison accepted the weapon and held it up to eye level as he worked the safety. "What are you trying to tell me?"

"I didn't say a word." He chucked Garrison on the shoulder and walked away.

Monday
June 16, 2014
23,000 Feet Over Pennsylvania
6:55 P.M. EDT

Snug in her seat, Doris nodded as Garrison finished his explanation.

"It's one thing to hear about the Founders. It's another thing entirely to actually meet them. I understand a lot of things now that I didn't get before."

"I'm glad you're adapting. I wish I could have been there for the meeting." Dressed plainly, Doris tried to ignore the bandages that swathed both of her arms. Folded in her lap, Cutter's trenchcoat remained close, despite her feelings about his loss.

The executive jet's soft lighting cast a surreal glow as nearby staffers attended to their own affairs. The dim glow from the monitors gave a sense of purpose to the relaxed atmosphere.

"Adkins does good work," Garrison said, casting a disapproving eye on Doris as she scratched.

Glaring at him, she primly placed both hands in her lap.

"Better. Can I ask you a question?" Shifting in his chair, he rolled his broad shoulders in an attempt to relieve some of the stress from sitting.

"Yes."

"Why are you here? Fisk never talked about you. The way you appear and disappear, I got the idea that you're one of his bodyguards."

"Was," Doris corrected with just a hint of bitterness.

"Sorry. I'm still getting used to it."

"I don't think I'm ever going to get used to it. There are things you don't know about him that are...important to me."

"So I gathered. As much as I thought I knew about the plan, I feel like I know less than I did before the... thing. You know." Garrison felt distinctly uncomfortable about any subject that related to Fisk, and it showed.

"Get used to it. Not even Fisk knew it all." Doris brushed her hair aside.

"That's what I've been afraid of. I've heard some things about you, and I'm just wondering..."

Doris snuck in a quick scratch. "Yes. I know what you've heard. They called me his guardian angel. I wanted that to be true. I believe in what he was doing. I believe in it enough to still be here. I'll protect you. I'll work with Griff to coordinate your other security measures. I'll do for you what I did for him."

"The Founders..." His voice trailed off. He was unsure how to proceed.

"It was his own idea. If he was at risk of compromising the plan, I had standing orders to kill him."

"Answers that question."

"Not entirely. You're wondering if the same rule applies to you."

"I assumed--"

"It does. Not because they said so, but because I say so."

"Fisk meant that much to you?" He could see the spark in her eyes.

"Maybe I'll tell you about it some day. Until then, just do your job."

"You don't like me, do you?" The question slipped out before Garrison could stop it.

Doris appeared affronted at having been caught so easily.

"It's kind of obvious. You stormed onto the plane without any introductions. For the last hour, you've been grilling me. Not chatting-- grilling. I could go on, but you get the idea."

Doris bowed her head in mock surrender. "Would you like to start over?" She pulled back to regard him from a safe distance. *You're not real to me just yet.*

"Please. I'd like to be on the good side of Fisk's guardian angel, if I can."

Doris smiled thinly. *I begin to see why he picked you. You've got the touch.* Seeing him in action, she had to admit that the man was more than he seemed. *You're genuine. Not constructed, like he was.*

"I don't know what I expected." Doris kneaded the soft leather of the coat.

"I get you. You're comparing me to him, and we don't match."

"I..." Doris began.

"It's okay. You're not the first person I've gotten that from. I've had a lot of experience at being compared to other people. Just ask my ex-wife. She knows." He smiled.

When Doris didn't react to the joke, he pushed on. "I didn't know him as long as most of you. I still don't know why he picked me. I can't match his polish. I certainly don't have his confidence. To tell you the truth, I don't think I deserve to be the one doing this."

"That's why he picked you. You have more in common with him than you know. You don't want to be doing this. He told me the same thing, many times."

"Really?" The idea was powerful and inspiring to Garrison, "What else did he--"

Doris could feel her defenses popping up. "You're also pushy. Look, I don't mean to sound unreasonable, but this is all happening so fast. Give me time to get used to you. If you don't give me any reason to hurt you, we might be able to talk sometime."

"I'd like that. I'll try not to give you any reason to whack me so that we can do that some day."

Doris stopped kneading her coat. "Accepted. In the meantime, I'll watch your back."

Jasmine appeared out of the semi-darkness. She looked at Doris, grinning mischievously. "I knew I felt some love going on over here. If you're done with him, the advisors would like some of his time before we land."

Doris acknowledged the comment with a small tilt of her head.

Jasmine continued, "It's my fault, Bill. I told her I'd bug her until she came over to make nice with the new boss. I didn't think she'd actually do it."

Garrison nodded tactfully, opting for silence as he watched Doris get up and move to the front of the cabin. "Can you do me a favor?" He unbuckled his seatbelt and got to his feet.

"Sure." Jasmine produced a small handheld computer.

"I want to hit the restroom and then make a phone call before the vultures get to me. Keep them off me for at least ten minutes, will you?" Straightening, he stretched.

Jasmine nodded. Unlike Fisk, Garrison wasn't very formal with his staff. His demeanor, both personal and professional, was radically different from Fisk's. She wasn't finding it hard to get used to him.

"Personal call?"

"Yeah." He still wasn't comfortable discussing his love life.

Jasmine wagged the palmtop at him. "We've got a lot to do. Ten minutes. No more. If you take any longer, I'll send Doris to get you."

"Slave driver," Garrison kidded as he moved off.

Griff scowled transmitted clearly through the digital connection. "He's calling that reporter."

"It's an approved relationship," Doris countered. "Jasmine's keeping him on a short leash, as it is. I'm ready to give him a chance." Keeping both arms below camera level, she used the edge of the workstation to scratch her bandaged wounds.

"Good. Can I ask what changed your mind?"

Watching Garrison hold a wireless phone in one hand and a cold drink in the other, Doris paused to consider her answer. All of the old certainties were gone. Letting go of Fisk had also meant letting go of Jason. The wounds might never heal. "You did," she admitted with a small, sour pout, checking the volume on her terminal. "You were right about him. I just didn't want to see it. It's been a very busy 14 years, and I got caught up in it. I don't suppose I ever had your objectivity."

Griff nodded in silent appreciation. "My ulcer keeps me in check. Every time I lose my objectivity, it threatens to kill me."

Doris smiled at the joke--after making sure that nobody was looking.

Monday
June 16, 2014
General Aviation Terminal
Ronald Reagan International Airport
Washington, D.C.
7:45 P.M. EDT

"Remember, we're starting from scratch."

"I know, Doris, I know. I just hate going through airport security," Garrison muttered as he shrugged into his suit jacket. Waiting for the rest of his advisors to leave the plane, he stood in the aisle and fidgeted with his tie.

"We're going last for security reasons," she told him for the third time. "It may not matter now, but in the next few years you should have enough clout to make this necessary."

Garrison snapped, "I get the idea. We get off the plane. We go through two security checkpoints on our way out. Piece of cake."

"Give." She held out her hand.

"What?"

"The gun. Give me the gun. You don't have a permit to carry firearms. I do. Give it to me."

Seeing movement at the back of the plane, Garrison looked away, trying to stall.

"You'd better get used to *that*," Jasmine told him as she elbowed her way past him. "She'll nag you until it becomes second nature."

He reached for his briefcase. "I had bodyguards when I worked for the Association. I'm not completely new to this. Did Fisk have to put up with this?"

"Yes," both women replied, in stereo.

Garrison reached into his coat pocket for the gun Hunziger had given him.

"It's okay. I told Hun to give it to you," Doris said, pocketing the weapon.

"You did?" Garrison didn't notice as Jasmine left the plane.

"Powerful people don't carry guns. They pay others to do it for them."

"What was the point?"

"For your meeting with the Founders. I wanted you to have options."

"Options?" He followed Doris off the plane.

"Just in case they didn't like you," she replied.

Monday
June 16, 2014
General Aviation Terminal
Ronald Reagan International Airport
Washington, D.C.
8:05 P.M. EDT

"Welcome back to Washington, Mr. Garrison," the airport screener said, reading his name off an eye-level monitor.

Taking his ID card back from the screener, Garrison moved to join his entourage. Within minutes, they were out on to the passenger loading level.

Doris took him by the elbow and steered him toward a waiting limousine. "The rest of us will catch up to you later," she said softly. "I've arranged for you to have some quiet time. Just remember that you will always be under surveillance." The harsh glare from the overhead lights gave her a more sinister look than she deserved.

"Right. Private. I suppose you'll be watching me?" He stopped to watch the rest of the group get in a large passenger van and leave.

"Something like that."

""Why are you doing this for me? I was ready to--"

She gave him a cold glance. "I know what you were ready to do. It's going to take a few weeks for the advisors to get used to you. Give it a month. Then you can start ordering them around like you own the place."

"I thought you didn't like me." He took a few more steps towards the waiting car.

"I need some time to get used to you, too," Doris replied, echoing her earlier confession. "This is different. If you're going to succeed, you need to have a healthy outlook. That means healthy relationships."

Garrison stopped just short of the limo as Christopher got out. "You make it sound like I need help with my love life." The idea was extremely distasteful.

"Those people are more than just your advisors," she said as the driver reached out to open the passenger door. "They will run your life down to the smallest detail--if you let them."

Garrison's right hand came out and his mouth moved to form a greeting that was drowned out by the thunder of a passing jet. He repeated, "Glad to meet you."

Christopher looked his new employer in the eye.

Doris stepped back as the men shook hands. As they sized each other up, Garrison realized that Christopher was fractionally taller. Christopher was impressed with Garrison's strong grip and easygoing manner.

"Two hours," Doris told Christopher with a knowing glance as she withdrew.

"Two hours?" Garrison protested as she faded into the crowd.

Christopher scanned the area for possible threats. "Relax. Fisk told me all about what's-her-name. Let's go."

Garrison slid into the big car's back seat and closed the door.

Once they were on the highway, Christopher said, "I know how you feel."

"They told me about you, too. We're quite the pair." Garrison rubbed his chin. The darkness around them was kept at bay by a dazzling stream of lights that cast a glow over the fast-moving traffic.

"It's not as bad as it sounds. Once you get over the shock, everything starts to make sense." The driver guided the limo through a lane change.

"How well did you know Fisk?" Garrison asked, feeling more at ease.

"Not very. I only met him a couple of months ago. He opened my eyes to a lot of things. Made me think about what's been happening to this country."

Garrison didn't respond for several minutes. "Pull over."

Christopher found an off-ramp and pulled into the parking lot of a fast food outlet. He unclasped his seatbelt and turned around. "I've seen that look before. I've even seen it in my own eyes when I looked in a mirror. If you have doubts, you can use the phone. Call her."

Garrison laughed aloud. "Is it that obvious?"

"It is obvious to me. You have stuff buzzing around inside your head that you can't let out. It's driving you nuts. You're trying to decide what to tell her. Heck, if I let you, you'd run away." To emphasize the point, he locked the doors.

Garrison reached out to knock on an armored window. "I wouldn't get far. There's a security detail with automatic weapons out there, watching me. After they got done laughing, I'm sure they'd track me down."

"You can't let yourself think like that. You've got people looking out for you, that's all. I've been briefed on her. Anne sounds cool to me. Not my type, but hey, probably just right for you."

Garrison licked his dry lips. "I've been trying to figure out what I'll say to her. She thinks I've been in a hospital, recovering from an accident. I've only seen her a few times, and I don't really know if--"

Christopher shook his head vigorously. "Look at you. You're a mess. Not only does she matter, you know what you've got to do."

"I can't."

"Sure you can. You just have to be prepared for what comes next. If she rejects you, you're just going to have to suck it up and move on," he said emphatically as he scanned the area around the car.

Garrison sat forward. "What makes you think she'd blow me off? See, here's the thing. I'm not like Fisk. Everybody keeps telling me that I've got to be myself."

Christopher puffed out his cheeks in frustration. "Everybody fronts."

"I want to tell her the truth," Garrison blurted, as if it were painful to speak. "I can live with the rest of it. I just need to tell one person the truth. Is that too much to ask?"

Christopher looked away. "I hear you. You don't have to be like Fisk. That man was unreal. He could lie to the devil and make it stick. But I don't think he ever loved anybody. Not that he held back, you know? It's just that getting your oil changed isn't like having attachments."

"Are you seeing anyone?" Garrison asked.

Christopher shrugged. "My life is too screwed up right now. If I was a woman, I wouldn't date me." They shared a laugh over the remark.

Garrison jerked a thumb at the fast food joint. "Does this place have a drive-thru?"

Christopher craned his neck. "Sure. You got a taste for junk?"

"Yeah, I do."

Still grinning, the chauffeur put the car in gear and headed for the drive-thru lane. He glanced at the dashboard clock. "We aren't going to have much time."

Garrison threw off his seatbelt rebelliously. "We can eat on the go. I'll call to cancel dinner. You're right. I should just tell her the truth and hear what she has to say."

Monday
June 16, 2014
Thomas Jefferson Memorial
Washington, D.C.
9:15 P.M. EDT

Anne barely noticed the people around her. *I can't believe I'm really doing this.* Walking from the secured parking lot onto the grounds, she clamped down on her anxiety. Bright lights split the night, casting long shadows that swallowed the few visitors who came at this late hour to see the monument to America's third President.

Despite the limited nature of their relationship, her worst fear seemed to be coming true. *He wouldn't let me come visit him in the hospital. Even if he did call me once a week, he still kept me out. Why else would he cancel dinner and ask me to come here?*

In the distance, she caught sight of him. Leaning on a railing, he appeared to be brooding as he was watched a ferry glide down the quiet waters of the Potomac River. *Looks like he's trying to figure out how to tell me off.*

Dressed formally, his coat lay folded over the rail nearby. The dark wool fluttered in the mild breeze sweeping over the large expanse in front of the memorial dome.

She stopped without realizing it. *Wait. That's not the look of a man who wants to dump somebody.* As she examined him more closely, her instincts picked out a few things. *He's shaved off what was left of his hair. He's not favoring a leg. No casts. He must have recovered.*

A tall, dark-skinned man strolled nearby. To Anne, he appeared to be unusually observant. Dressed inconspicuously in a common grey coat and tie, he seemed to be just a little too casual. His orbit also intrigued her. He never seemed to stray very far away from Garrison at any given moment. *Hmm. Bodyguard. Well, now, what have you been up to?* She started forward. *This isn't about me, is it? That's not why we're here.* Walking faster as her relief increased, she ignored the bodyguard and called out.

Turning at the sound of her voice, Garrison favored her with a broad, genuine smile. "I was starting to think you might not come," he told her as they hugged.

"I almost stood you up," she admitted as they turned back to the rail.

"What, did you think I was going to dump you?"

Looking him straight in the face, She hesitated. "I'll admit, it had crossed my mind."

He put his arm around her. "The thought never occurred to me."

"Really?" Anne smiled and stayed close.

"Not even once." He jostled her good-naturedly.

She let her eyes wander over the waters rolling by beneath them. "I don't know what I was thinking. I've had a lot of my mind lately. I'm having regrets about something I did, and it's getting to me."

"I can relate, though I can't imagine what you could do that would be so bad."

Anne paused for a long moment before answering. "I'm used to uncovering secrets, not keeping them. The White House is like a magnet for secrets, you know?" When Garrison nodded, she continued. "A lot of the rookies that come through the press corps get offered special treatment if they say good things about the President. It's an initiation, a test. If you pass, they leak stuff to you--help make your career."

"Sounds hard. How do you stay out of trouble?"

Anne shrugged. "I don't know yet. I sold out. I've never made that kind of deal with anyone. I suppose it's what keeps getting me in trouble. Why I've never--"

"Hey." He reached out to steady her. "This is me you're talking to."

"Am I wrong to feel this way?" she asked.

"A wise man once told me that advancing your career is like selling your soul and buying it back just before retirement. When you get right down to it, this is a compromise that you don't want to make. What you want to do and what you have to do are two different things."

"That's what I like about you. I can talk to you about anything. Feels like it, anyway."

"Everybody needs somebody. Please, walk with me." He gestured downriver. "We all need friends and confidantes. Sometimes, if we're lucky, we find both in the same person. As long as we have somebody who can hear us and understand what we're afraid of, we can get by."

"You figured this out all by yourself?"

He shoved both hands into his pockets. "The past two months have changed me. I had my own deals to make, and I'm just as unsettled as you are."

"Why is that?" Anne took hold of his arm as they walked.

"Have you ever gotten involved in something because you believed in it, only to find out that it ran deeper than you ever imagined?"

"You just described my career. I wanted to be a journalist because I thought truth led to freedom. Seems like every time I turn around, there's another politician with something to hide. My search for truth and freedom hasn't gotten me very far. But you're right, it does help to have somebody to talk to."

He grinned, gathering his courage. "Yeah, I hear what you're saying. The fact of the matter is that those truth hiding politicians you're going on about have placed me in a very interesting situation."

"Interesting, as in a new job?" Anne surmised.

"You could say that." Garrison's heart began to pound in his chest. "I'm having a hard time accepting it, though. I've been told that I was the right person, in the right place, at the right time."

"Sounds promising. Tell me more."

He shuddered with relief. "I was hoping you'd say that. I've got some things I need to get off my chest. If I don't tell somebody, it's going to eat me alive."

Anne loosened her grip on his arm. "You talk. We'll walk."

Garrison paused, thinking. "The whole thing started nearly six years ago. Actually, it goes back even further than that, but I don't have all the details."

Behind them, Christopher fell back a few paces. "Perimeter check," he said softly into his collar mike.

"Overwatch is on-line," a stout male voice responded through the tiny receiver in his ear. "Primary tactical is deployed. Condition green."

"I'm falling back six meters to give them some privacy," Christopher replied.

"Roger that," Overwatch confirmed as the couple continued their slow walk.

"You can imagine how surprised I was when Fisk told me what his real agenda was. I know it sounds crazy, but it appealed to my sense of patriotism..."

Printed in the United States
41430LVS00003B/1-48